S0-AFN-242

Acclaim for
Some Dance to Remember:
A Memoir-Novel of San Francisco
1970-1982

"With this epic tribute to the first decade of gay liberation, primarily in San Francisco, Jack Fritscher has created a world that's easy to get lost in. Vivid, erotic, and sometimes gut-wrenchingly truthful, *Some Dance to Remember* is also a testament to what went tragically wrong in gay men's lives, and society overall, in those long-gone golden days.

I found plenty of characters to love in these pages. They reminded me of people I knew too well whom I loved and lost, either to the notorious excess of the times, or to the holocaust of AIDS. This book gives us a reason to celebrate all those lives again—even the tragic ones—and with luck, even our own. It garners us a fresh, more compassionate perspective on an era that flooded our lives with both promise and confusion.

A complex story of raw sex and audacity, and above all a story of love, *Some Dance to Remember* will linger in your thoughts for a long, long time."

—Marilyn Jay Lewis
Founder and Executive Director, The Erotic Authors Association

"Jack Fritscher's *Some Dance to Remember* is a novel—and a staggeringly original and completely absorbing piece of work—but as a work of fiction it provides us with much of what we look for in detailed social history. Fritscher is not just a fabulist (although he is a terrific one) but a cultural historian as well. Here is San Francisco's gay male scene in the 1970s and 1980s as never told or documented before. *Some Dance to Remember* thrives with detail, trivia, and the particulars of how life was lived, how men thought, dressed, acted, interacted, and conducted their individual and communal lives. This is a historical document that is both vital and important to how we think about and remember our shared historical past."

—Michael Bronski
Author, *Culture Clash: The Making of Gay Sensibility*;
The Pleasure Principle: Sex, Backlash, and the Struggle for Gay Freedom;
and Editor, *Pulp Friction: Uncovering the Golden Age of Male Pulps*

"The San Francisco of the 1970s, chronicled with cinematic intensity in *Some Dance to Remember,* was still recent history in 1990 when Knights Press first published this brilliant record of gay life before the shattering ground zero of AIDS. Fritscher's mythic panorama of plot and character gazes with a steady eye across an astonishing, astounding spectrum of queer lives. Fifteen years on, this sprawling fictional (but memorably factual) saga, set in and exploding from the heady, headstrong, headlong decade-plus of 1970 to 1982, has lost not a whit of its muscular passion, its punchy immediacy, or its transformative literary impact."

—Richard Labonte
Reviewer, *Books to Watch Out For*

NOTES FOR PROFESSIONAL LIBRARIANS AND LIBRARY USERS

This is an original book title published by Southern Tier Editions™, Harrington Park Press®, an imprint of The Haworth Press, Inc. Unless otherwise noted in specific chapters with attribution, materials in this book have not been previously published elsewhere in any format or language.

CONSERVATION AND PRESERVATION NOTES

All books published by The Haworth Press, Inc., and its imprints are printed on certified pH neutral, acid-free book grade paper. This paper meets the minimum requirements of American National Standard for Information Sciences-Permanence of Paper for Printed Material, ANSI Z39.48-1984.

Some Dance to Remember
A Memoir-Novel of San Francisco
1970-1982

HARRINGTON PARK PRESS®
Southern Tier Editions™
Gay Men's Fiction
Jay Quinn, Executive Editor
Greg Herren, Associate Editor

The Man Pilot by James W. Ridout IV

Shadows of the Night: Queer Tales of the Uncanny and Unusual edited by Greg Herren

Van Allen's Ecstasy by Jim Tushinski

Beyond the Wind by Rob N. Hood

The Handsomest Man in the World by David Leddick

The Song of a Manchild by Durrell Owens

The Ice Sculptures: A Novel of Hollywood by Michael D. Craig

Between the Palms: A Collection of Gay Travel Erotica edited by Michael T. Luongo

Aura by Gary Glickman

Love Under Foot: An Erotic Celebration of Feet edited by Greg Wharton and M. Christian

The Tenth Man by E. William Podojil

Upon a Midnight Clear: Queer Christmas Tales edited by Greg Herren

Dryland's End by Felice Picano

Whose Eye Is on Which Sparrow? by Robert Taylor

Deep Water: A Sailor's Passage by E. M. Kahn

The Boys in the Brownstone by Kevin Scott

The Best of Both Worlds: Bisexual Erotica edited by Sage Vivant and M. Christian

Tales from the Levee by Martha Miller

Some Dance to Remember: A Memoir-Novel of San Francisco 1970-1982 by Jack Fritscher

Confessions of a Male Nurse by Richard S. Ferri

The Millionaire of Love by David Leddick

Transgender Erotica: Trans Figures edited by M. Christian

Skip Macalester by J. E. Robinson

Chemistry by Lewis DeSimone

Friends, Lovers, and Roses by Vernon Clay

Beyond Machu by William Maltese

Virgina Bedfellows by Gavin Morris

Independent Queer Cinema: Reviews and Interviews by Gary M. Kramer

Seventy Times Seven by Salvatore Sapienza

Going Down in La-La Land by Andy Zeffer

Planting Eli by Jeff Black

For Beth Hernandez-Jason

Some Dance to Remember
A Memoir-Novel of San Francisco
1970-1982

OH! HOW WE DANCED!

Jack Fritscher

Jack Fritscher
September 5,
2011

Southern Tier Editions™
Harrington Park Press®
An Imprint of The Haworth Press, Inc.
New York • London • Oxford

For more information on this book or to order, visit
http://www.haworthpress.com/store/product.asp?sku=5430

or call 1-800-HAWORTH (800-429-6784) in the United States and Canada
or (607) 722-5857 outside the United States and Canada

or contact orders@HaworthPress.com

Published by

Southern Tier Editions™, Harrington Park Press®, an imprint of The Haworth Press, Inc., 10 Alice Street, Binghamton, NY 13904-1580.

© 2005 by Jack Fritscher. All rights reserved. No part of this work may be reproduced or utilized in any form or by any means, electronic or mechanical, including photocopying, microfilm, and recording, or by any information storage and retrieval system, without permission in writing from the publisher. Printed in the United States of America. Reprint - 2006

PUBLISHER'S NOTE
This is a work of fiction. Names, characters, places, and incidents either are the products of the author's imagination or are used fictitiously, and any resemblance to actual persons, living or dead, business establishments, events, or locales is entirely coincidental.

First published in 1990 by Knights Press, Inc., of Stamford, Connecticut.

Cover design by Lora Wiggins.
Cover concept by Mark Hemry.

Library of Congress Cataloging-in-Publication Data

Fritscher, Jack.
    Some dance to remember : a memoir-novel of San Francisco, 1970-1982 / Jack Fritscher.
      p. cm.
    ISBN-13: 978-1-56023-327-5 (pbk. : alk. paper)
    ISBN-10: 1-56023-327-3 (pbk. : alk. paper)
    1. San Francisco (Calif.)—Fiction. 2. Bodybuilders—Fiction. 3. Gay men—Fiction. 4. Authors—Fiction. I. Title.

PS3556.R5694S66 2005
813'.54—dc22

                                                                              2005002511

For George and Virginia,
who raised me at the movies,
for Mark Hemry,
for Robert Mapplethorpe,
and for the 14,000 veterans
of the Golden Age of Liberation
who each gave me
a piece of his heart . . .

What think you I take my pen in hand to record?
. . . But merely of two simple men I saw today
on the pier in the midst of the crowd,
parting the parting of dear friends,
The one to remain hung on the other's neck
and passionately kiss'd him,
While the one to depart
tightly prest the one to remain in his arms.

—Walt Whitman, *Leaves of Grass*

CONTENTS

Preface

SAN FRANCISCO
THE GOLDEN AGE
The Titanic '70s
The First Decade of Gay Liberation
(Stonewall to HIV)
1970-1982

"Bliss was it that dawn to be alive,
but to be young was heaven."

—William Wordsworth, *The Prelude*

"Whoever did not live in the years
neighboring the revolution
does not know what the pleasure of living means."

—Charles Maurice de Talleyrand

This memoir-novel is a literary structure akin to independent film. Dialogue rules. Time is folded. Characters drive the plot. A voice-over guides nuance. The chapters are reels. The first sentence outlines the entire story. Scenes are numbered for shooting. Drama collides with humor. Beauty slips on a banana peel. The narrator, Magnus Bishop, is *auteur* directing the *mise en scene*—which is everything that appears on the page to aid the reader willing to time travel to the past.

The narrator's point of view gives camera angles on characters, crowds, streets, cafés, galleries, bars, baths, clothing, furnishings, and rituals of sex and magic. The camera eye tracks through large and small scenes in medium shots and close-ups. The boom mike mixes sounds of music, voices, and flesh. The editing technique is collage, juxtaposition, re-vision, deconstruction, and double-exposure of dozens of texts real within the fictive world of the memoir.

Threading pop culture from John Dos Passos' *USA Trilogy* (newspaper headlines, newsreel films, journals) to Margaret Mitchell's *Gone with the Wind* (the O'Hara clan; Hollywood heroines' man trouble) and Andy Warhol's film *The Chelsea Girls* (twelve stories running four hours simultaneously on two screens), this "screenplay novel" purposely requires twelve hours of reading to reveal twelve years of history. For those who enjoy curling up with a book, such a layered story, such a longer-form novel, going wide and deep can be an absorbing journey out of oneself into otherness.

The content is the essence of queer literature. Honest *eros* is not closeted to protect the reader from psychologically driven acts of human sexuality. This is not pornography. This is a documentary of the glorious mood swings of the first decade of gay liberation. The revolutionary 1970s enlightened sex the way the French Revolution enlightened reason.

This is also a fable of how we invented our lives and pioneered a new lifestyle in that sanctuary window between the invention of penicillin and the viral *Götterdämmerung*. This is the fictive autobiography of a specific group of people in a specific place at a specific time. Real historical people walk through the story, anchoring the plot. Equally grounding, the very important subplot of a straight family going crazy protects the gay lifestyle from being singled out for criticism. All humans are in equal emotional extremis.

In the 1970s salon that surrounded *Drummer* magazine when I was editor in chief, and at 4,380 daily brunches during twelve years on Castro, I listened to men spin stories of their birth siblings from hell, of lovers who wouldn't stay, of lovers who wouldn't leave, and other archetypal tales of our bawdy Chaucerian culture. (The Castro is our Canterbury.) I had to be present to write this history, but I am none of the characters, nor are their politics mine.

I thank the critics from *The Advocate* to *The New Republic* for their reviews, particularly Samuel L. Steward, and Michael Bronski, who wrote in part:

> There are scores of minor characters, hundreds of episodes, thousands of historical details, and a plot that makes *Gone with the Wind* seem like a short story. . . . *Some Dance to Remember* is a great ambitious work and a rarity in modern fiction: a novel of ideas. . . . Fritscher is concerned not only about telling the truth of gay men's lives—how we lived and loved, struggled and survived—but in examining in the psychological and philosophical underpinnings of those lives—the intricate interplay of self-expression and self-destruction, of sexual autonomy and erotic dependency. . . . He has recreated more than a decade of gay his-

tory—its sights, smells, nerves, and guts. If *Some Dance to Remember* both astonishes and bewilders, seduces and frightens us (often at the same time), it is because Fritscher has captured with intelligence and love, the way we live, both then and now." —Michael Bronski, *The Guide,* Boston

Veterans of the liberation wars who survived the Titanic '70s tend to recall that decade with nostalgia and gratitude. They were young, alive, and guests at the twelve-year celebration kicked off at Stonewall. As the 1970s party cruised forward, the innocents on board had no hint of the iceberg of HIV that lay ahead. Some of the survivors write letters asking "how did you read my dreams; how did you read my diary?" They assign the book to their younger lovers, and they lament revisionist Puritans who missed the party and disrespect the decade for decadence, disco, and disease. The 1970s didn't cause AIDS. A virus caused AIDS.

In 1968, I was fortunate to be one of the founding members of the American Popular Culture Association, which helped introduce diversity to American studies. Even before Stonewall, I knew the professional importance of writing about queer culture as it happened. In the gonzo New Journalism fashion of the times, it didn't hurt that the professor was also a participant. This memoir-novel is eyewitness reportage. In bars, baths, coffee shops, and airplanes, I wrote the first bits of this manuscript on scraps of paper in 1970. I finished the final edit in 1984. Various gay magazine editors published excerpts, which test marketed reader feedback. In late 1988, the daring, darling, straight publisher Elizabeth Gershman wrote, "I'd fucking kill to publish *Some Dance,*" which she did on Valentine's Day 1990. The manuscript was ready for publication in autumn 1989, but I hated the 1980s. "So it won't be the last book of the 1980s," Elizabeth said. "It'll be the first book of the 1990s about the 1970s."

This is a story of the way we were coming out *en masse* from the American closet. Because queer history has no more memory than the remembrance we give it, perhaps this book will be of interest to readers who today are thirty-five and who celebrated their twelfth birthday in 1982, the year this story ended. At the post-millennium corner of 18th and Castro, one can feel the ghosts, the haunts, the spirits.

Once upon a time after Stonewall. . . .

The soundtrack of this story is the Eagles' *Hotel California.* It ignites the emotion of "being there." The 1976 album spent 107 weeks on the charts through 1979. Every disco, bar, and bath dropped needles on its vinyl. Each track is a picaresque character study of ecstasy and excess: "New Kid in

Town," "Life in the Fast Lane," "Wasted Time," "Victim of Love," and the title song with its dark, Sartrean no-exit lyrics. For readers open to mixed-media experiences, the opening chords of the song "Hotel California" are my *madeleine.*

Some dance to remember.

Some dance to forget.

Acknowledgments

The author gratefully expresses appreciation to the following people whose assistance and encouragement brought this popular-culture memoir-novel to publication and kept it circulating on shelves, in commentary, and in classrooms: Mark Hemry, David Sparrow, Robert Mapplethorpe, David Van Leer, Edward Lucie-Smith, Elizabeth Gershman of Knights Press, Ruth Miriam Haungs, Leonard J. Fick, Thomas R. Gorman, Stanley Clayes, Tim Barrus, Fred Glynn, Richard Labonte of A Different Light bookstores, and Ray B. Browne with Pat Browne of the Popular Culture Association, Bowling Green State University.

The author was partially funded by a grant from the National Endowment for the Humanities (NEH), as well as by a grant from the State of Michigan.

Michael Bronski's review *"Some Dance to Remember,"* which is quoted in the Preface, was first published in *The Guide,* Boston, July 1990.

All of the characters and narrative in this memoir-novel, including historic names, persons, places, events, products, and businesses as dramatized, are fictitious, or are used fictitiously. Events and characters are not intended to portray actual events or actual persons, living or dead, and any similarity or inference is unintentional and entirely coincidental.

Virtual Movie Poster

SOME DANCE TO REMEMBER

The COSMOS. The SOLAR SYSTEM. The EARTH.
NORTH AMERICA.
CALIFORNIA. SAN FRANCISCO. 18TH & CASTRO.
FOLSOM STREET, SOUTH OF MARKET.

The Golden Age
1970-1982

A Drop-Dead Blond Bodybuilder
A Gay Magazine Editor
An Erotic Video Mogul
A Penthouse Full of Hustlers
A Famous Cabaret "Chanteuse Fatale"
A Hollywood Bitch TV Producer
A Vietnam Veteran
A Trailer Park Wife
An Epic Liberation Movement
A Civil War between Women and Men . . . and Men
A Time of Sex, Drugs, & Rock 'n' Roll
A MURDER
A CITY
A PLAGUE
A LOST CIVILIZATION
A LOVE STORY

REEL ONE
Welcome to the Hotel California

1

In the end he could not deny his human heart. Always he had known, long before he came that drizzling California night, with the gun in his hand, to the gymnasium, that his life, scaled down, of course, would be forever like the newsreel of the Widow standing, alone and in black, with her tiny son, his hand saluting as muffled drums rolled across a dazed and weeping landscape. In the movies one image dissolves into another. The *dissolve* itself is metaphor of change. He, now looking thirty-seven years old, managed a drive-in movie against the screen behind his high forehead. He had Movietone newsreels from his black-and-white childhood of a plane crashing into the Empire State Building, of VE Day and Hiroshima, of Korea, the Papal Holy Year, and the wedding of Elizabeth and Philip. He knew by heart the first campaign footage of Camelot and the final Super-8mm Zapruder strip shot in grainy Technicolor in Dallas. He had images of draft cards burning up in defiant flames; inserts of dogs lunging at black bodies on the Edmund Pettus Bridge in Selma, Alabama, oh yeah, hungry dogs of Alabama; of American cities burning in protest; of the Summer of Love; and of terrified Vietnamese fleeing their American saviors on the evening news.

Chronology was not his style. Feeling was. Sometimes he forgot to breathe. Sometimes he remembered he would have to pay for the good times. Once on fortune's wheel, everything is fixed. Sometimes he had that high-flying feeling of a person who goes starved to bed. Sometimes nothing mattered. Sometimes everything mattered too much.

He was smaller, more real in size, than the huge Widow, who, like him, would forever mourn her love, ended abruptly like his, but who, unlike him, was not approaching the gymnasium stage where his victorious blond bodybuilder lover was posing, handsome, muscular, golden, brilliant, shimmering with sweat, triumphant in the final moments of the Mr. California Physique Contest.

1

Waves of applause washed him closer and closer to the bank of the stage. He felt himself moving in slow motion through air as thick as celluloid.

The gun was in his hand.

His hand was pulling the gun from the holster of his pocket.

The man he loved more than life itself was turning, nearly naked, smiling with intensity in the cone of hot overhead spotlight, into a double-biceps shot . . .

2

Rewind. Back up. Whiz. Whirr. Click. Bang.

"I want to belong," Ryan Steven O'Hara wrote in his *Journal*. "I want to belong to that tiny, terrible elite: men who live their lives beyond the limits and never die in their beds."

His life was a pursuit of manhood. Ryan O'Hara fancied himself Orion, the star-hunter stalking the Constellation of the Bear. Sometimes reality slapped him up against the side of his head.

"You're one kind of man," Julie Andrews said to James Garner in *Victor/Victoria*. "I'm another."

"What kind is that?" the virile Garner asked.

"The kind," Julie Andrews said, "that doesn't have to prove it."

Ryan tried not to protest too much. He knew he was as much a man as Julie Andrews. He adored her ideal purity.

Ryan's masculinity, and in some quarters I run the up-front risk of immediately losing empathy for him, ran exclusively homosexual. He never apologized for it; nor will I for him. You may stereotype him, or dismiss him, or chalk up what happened to him during what the media called gay liberation as the just desserts of a faggot who immigrated to San Francisco, tried everything, risked everything, and maybe lost everything.

But don't. Don't put his story down.

Sometimes outlaw men and defiant women, who dare to stand outside our normal pale, reflect back a bit more of our straightlaced selves than we first imagine. When all's well ends well, we call that comedy. The rest is tragedy. But, sports fans, that's all entertainment. There are more questions here than the simple one: how gay liberation, so happy, outrageous, and political, wound up critically wounded in an intensive care unit. Mainly, what I want to know is, how men and women lose their balance in the high-wire act of love.

This all began, once upon a time, back in the madcap days before real estate boomed in San Francisco; in the days when the first Irish and Italian merchants in the Castro sold out to Tommy's Plants and the Castro Café; in the days when gays bought dumps and everybody on Castro was a carpenter; in the days when gays were more hippies than clones, long before New York faggots arrived to Manhattanize the Castro; long before fisting and coprophagy, when crystal was still something collectible on the sideboard; long before murders, assassinations, disease, and Death, when sex three times a day was still the great adventure. It dissolved. It changed. What first seemed like Mecca shifted on the fault line to someplace east of Eden. They were innocents. For all they did right, for all they did wrong, for all their pursuit of sexual adventure, what they searched for in the bars and baths and cruised on the streets was, heart and soul, for them all, no more and no less than human love.

3

There may be only one sin in life: the ultimate violation of human rights is not the taking of a human life; it is the breaking of a human heart.

4

Music up. Vamp. Step. Step. Step. "Castro! That's where I'm goin'." *Bump. Bump.* "Castro! That's where I'll play." *Slow grind.* "Castro." *Hula Hands.* "Where hot lips're blowin'." *Bump. Grind.* "Castro! Where nights are . . ." *Left bump. Right bump. Heavy grind.* ". . . gay!" *Shake Midler tits. Bump. Grind. Bump.* "Castro!" *Go down on mike. Play Carmen. Flutter. Whisper.* "Where all those handsome gay boys . . ." *Stop. Breathy Mae West double-entendre intonation.* ". . . wind their playboys' windup toys!" *Belt.* "Castro!" *Dirty bump. Dirty grind. Then NYNY-Liza strut, strut, strut. Shout.* "Divine decadence, darlings!" *Big Minnelli finish.* "I'll see youuuu . . . in C-A-S-T-R-O!"

Ryan's baby sister was appearing at the Castro Palms. Margaret Mary O'Hara was the Queen of the Castro. She billed herself as Kweenasheba and lived with a bevy of six gay boys above the Bakery Café three doors from where 18th Street collides with Castro Street. The intersection was the heart of Gay Mecca. It was the place where, when Gray Line tours took them there, Midwestern tourists felt they needed a passport. It was there Ryan kicked up his motorcycle one afternoon when he called unannounced on his little sister. He rang the bell. No one answered. The music was loud Tina

Turner and the door was open. Halfway up the stairs he met a young gay boy. "You live here?" Ryan asked.

The stoned chicken looked deep into Ryan's eyes. "Mister Man," he said, "I don't know who lives here." He moved his hand to grope Ryan's jeans. "But I'll go back upstairs with you."

"Thanks." Ryan pushed the boy's hand away and pointed the kid down the stairs. "Later," he said.

Ryan found his sister lounging in a white Queen Anne ball-and-claw bathtub. Boys tumbled up and down the hallway. "Hi, Ry," she said, and she raised her legs straight up in the air, something like the 1940s' pop art of the bathing beauty with her fanny in a champagne glass and her feet in high heels thrust up higher than the rim.

"Hi, yourself," he said. "How high are you?"

"High enough." She sat up in the tub. Ryan was astonished at the full-blown size of his eighteen-year-old sister's breasts. "Ain't they a pair?" she said. She put her finger coyly to her mouth. "But dare I forget," she said. "You don't have a taste for milk shakes."

"Don't be a bitch. It hardly becomes you."

"Don't be a prig. It's unbelievable in you."

Margaret Mary morphed into Kweenie, rising from the tub elegantly as Venus on the half shell. Rivulets of water streamed down her leggy frame. Ryan reached for her grape-colored chenille robe. "You look good," he said. He was proud of her dancer's body.

"But not good enough for you to do it with me, huh?" When she was four, and he was twenty, she had asked him to kiss her the way he kissed his girlfriends. She hadn't known then what she knew now. "If you ever change your mind," she said. She folded her arms across her breasts and placed her delicate hands on her shoulders. "Who am I?" she asked. Years before, Ryan had taught her how to pose. The game endured between them. Somehow Margaret Mary's talent for becoming Kweenasheba who could become Bette Midler or Mae West or anyone on stage had started way back home in Kansas with this charade.

"Too easy," Ryan said. "Vanessa Redgrave. *Blow-Up*."

Two naked gay boys, both blond, chased each other down the hall. "You like them, Ry?" she asked. "I know your thing for blonds."

"No," he said. "Too young. You live in a chicken coop."

The phone in the hallway rang. Kweenie hopped naked and dripping from the tub and raced for the phone, bumping past Ryan holding her robe. She slid in and snatched the receiver right out from under the grasp of one of her roommates.

"Cunt," the twinkie blond said.

Kweenie held the phone between her wet breasts. "A star," she said to the boy, "is a star especially in her own home. Now bug off, Evan-Eddie!" Then in her sweetest virginal voice she said, "Hello. Backstage. Blue Moon." She paused. Her voice hardened. "I should have hoped it was you. When the fuck are you going to get me something?"

"It's not her agent," Evan-Eddie said to Ryan. "It's her dealer." He scrutinized Ryan. "You are her sister, aren't you?"

"Put in your contacts, dude. I'm her brother." Ryan loathed the gender-fuck mother tongue of Sodom-Oz where *brother* switched with *sister* and *he* came out *she*. "And keep your pronouns straight."

"I have such a hard time keeping anything straight. I'm a poor little fag." He tentatively touched Ryan's leather jacket. "I'm not a heavy-duty Mister Man like you. I mean I prefer to do my mother's act."

"Call your shrink," Ryan said.

"Who do you imitate? Your big, butch dad I've heard so much about?"

"The only one performing an act in our family," Ryan said, "is Margaret Mary."

"Honey," Evan-Eddie said, "we're all acting."

"Except," Ryan said, "when we're reacting."

"I love your act," Evan-Eddie said. "You, a leather queen from Folsom Street. Your sister, the Acid Queen of the Castro. Ain't you a pair of parodies? You write leather filth. She sings dirty on stage. You must come from quite a family."

"Actually," Ryan said, "we're cannibals."

"Margaret Mary said you were Catholic."

"Catholic cannibals." Ryan moved in on the boy, half threatening, half teasing. "We go to mass and communion and eat the body and blood of Jesus Christ. Then we eat little boys like you."

"Oh, stop it, Mister Man. Pinch my tits. Make me cum." Evan-Eddie pushed both hands together in his crotch and ooched over, pursing his lips, shaking his luxurious blond hair, making little squealing sounds.

Margaret Mary caught sight of the pose. She held her hand over the receiver. "Who is he, Ry? Who's he doing?"

"Fuck," Ryan said, but he couldn't resist their little game. He looked at the undulating boy. "Marilyn Monroe. *Seven Year Itch.* Holding down her skirt."

Margaret Mary signed him thumbs-up.

Evan-Eddie blew him a kiss. "Be my daddy?" he said. "You're *très* fun. You'd love to spank me."

"Don't be perverse."

"You sound exactly like my father. He hasn't spoken to me since I was twelve and bleached my hair blond for my coming-out party in the toilet at the local park."

"Bleached?"

"Mister Man, one thing you better learn before you get any older is there is no such animal as a real, honest-to-God, true blond. Well, there's a few natural blonds, but most of us are fakes, frauds, phonies. Disguising the goods. Like you big bad men cinching in your guts with leather corsets—excuse me, belts."

"Look again, dirtbag," Ryan pulled up his tee shirt, revealing his flat belly.

Evan-Eddie cooed. "Meet me tonight. Ten-ish. Backroom. Jaguar Bookstore."

Ryan straightened his fuck-finger. "Wanna play *Chinatown*." He threatened to stick his finger nail-deep up Evan-Eddie's left nostril. "You'd be easy to recognize, sissy boy, with no nose." He pushed the boy away.

Margaret Mary squealed with delight into the phone. "Thanks. *Ciao*. Good-bye." She dropped the receiver into its cradle and paraded her dripping, naked body as imperious as Isadora Duncan toward her brother. "Kelsey got the Palms to extend my run. She's such a good agent."

"Congratulations," Ryan said.

"Kisses on your opening . . . again," Evan-Eddie said. He kissed his fingers, looking hard at Ryan, and planted them in Margaret Mary's crotch.

"Let's get out of here," Ryan said.

"But I'm having," the twinkie blond moved in on Ryan, "such a good time."

"Not you, shit-for-brains. Her!"

"I didn't want to go out with you anyway. You're so tall, dark, and balding."

"Evan-Eddie," Margaret Mary said, commanding as Kweenasheba, "go sit on something long and thick. Leave this man alone."

"Oh, so now he's a man and I'm not?"

"I love you, Evan-Eddie. Don't push me."

"Yes, my sweet dominant mistress."

"Really, E-E. Don't be such an ass." She pecked him on the cheek. "Will you be a dear and clean up the bathroom for me? My big brother's taking me out."

"Dear heart," Eddie said, "what movie will people think you are? But, of course! *Ryan's Daughter*."

"E-E?" she said. "Eat shit and die. Come on, Ry. Let's go."

5

Something there is in love that rules out amnesty. For everyone. For every word and act. For every promise and betrayal. For every reason and passion. For all sins of omission and commission.

Love interests me. Intrigues me. As well it should. If love were easy, everyone would be in-love.

Ryan in his romantic fantasies wanted to be a sexual soldier of fortune. He marched from the Midwest to California in quest of other men, preferably jocks, and precisely in conquest of blond bodybuilders. Ryan, I think, started his search for the perfect body the day he discovered he didn't have one. "I'm no movie star, but I know how to get what I want."

Ryan's face and aerobic build were attractive enough. As a child, he had suffered the embarrassment common to many cherubic curly-haired boys. Women in their 1940s' clothes stopped his mother to say, "He's too pretty to be a boy. He should be a girl." Something in Ryan's baby gut tumbled. He hardly knew what, but he knew he did not ever want to be a little girl. Little girls grew up to have female trouble. Those two words, perhaps because the women ordered him to run out and play when they said them, locked together in his head: *female* and *trouble*. So he endured the women's dismissal gladly and ran out to build his forts in the woods behind the house. Ryan somehow was always building fortifications. I think his passion for real estate took root at the same time the women in his mother's kitchen shooed him to the porch, and he went in search of other boys to share his forts. He liked hunting boys. Something outdoors in the treble heads-up shouts of older boys at play drew him irresistibly. He liked entering into a group of strange boys and picking out the best one for his best friend.

Ryan's curly dark hair slipped slowly up his forehead which he minded at first in his mid-twenties, growing the compensatory beard, and then after thirty not so much at all. Some young gay men, balding themselves, ran from his bravado. Some men read his aggressive balding-bearded Look as style.

"I think of myself," he once told me, "as a sports car with the top down."

He made humor with words. He seduced with his voice. He was *Pillow Talk.* When he tied men up at the baths, he discovered dirty talk enhanced the sex scene. His words could cause a hard-on. Out of the sack, on Castro for brunch, he was smart enough to dish himself harder than anyone could needle him. It was the best defense. It kept tongues sharper than serpents' teeth from calling Ryan O'Hara "Miss Scarlett" to his face. He was not self-deprecating. He was self-accepting, or so he thought, his baldness having forced him to be realistic and stoic about what he could not change.

I think if a gay man can accept his own receding hair as a naturally evolving male Look, he achieves a kind of triumph of acceptance unknown to those who try to imitate twenty-one forever. Long hair was the fashion when Ryan first moved to San Francisco. He loved the Castro Rocks Baths and the muscular hippies with long blond braids who found an opposite attraction in his short black crewcut. He was one of the first balding and bearded gay men on Castro in the days when Castro was young, long before the crewcut and beard turned into the signature of the Castro clone. He felt sorry for men like the massive bodybuilder, Casey Viator, who wore toupees because they couldn't accept certain male truths about themselves. His sex talk in bed led to freelancing erotic writing.

"Baldness," he wrote in a gay magazine where models are always twenty-one and hung, and no hero is bald unless he is shaved, "is a natural secondary male sex characteristic. A totally male Look. Attractive to men. It keeps grown-up men from looking androgynous. It forces self-actualization. Never fight nature in yourself. What's hotter than a young balding blond college jock? Look in the mirror and never look back. Tell anyone who asks that you got bald making U-turns under the sheets."

When he inaugurated his own magazine, *Maneuvers*, he took an editorial policy of glorifying men over thirty. The movie, *In Praise of Older Women*, had sparked the idea. He wrote the word *daddy* and it entered the gay lexicon. *Maneuvers* became a hit.

Suppers at Ryan's Victorian, over the hill from Castro in Noe Valley, revolved around talk of sex and gyms and drugs and real estate and foreign films. Ryan's Irish tenor voice, trained to sing high mass in the seminary, was like Paul Simon's. Not that he was a singer. But he could match Simon note for note on "Bridge over Troubled Water" without any strain. From four years of university teaching during Vietnam, he had learned to project a certain presence with his voice. He was a talker. From the soup to the nuts, Ryan was up. Intense. On. Active. Purposely seductive after the fashion of men who realize if anything good is going to happen to them, they'll have to play their hand with whatever strong suit they have been dealt. Ryan's wild card was a Joker full of sarcastic, punning, maddening, needling, blasphemous wit honed first among his adolescent classmates in a Catholic seminary, then perfected over brunch in restaurants on Castro, and finally merchandised in the pages of *Maneuvers* magazine, whose trademarked cover line each issue was, "What You're Looking for Is Looking for You." His tongue was incisive. He never took a broad ax if a rapier would kill. He could murder with his tongue. He was not a man to leave a scene agonizing over things he wished he had said. He was, with all the pop import of California astrology, a Gemini in a City founded in Gemini. He was elusive, mercurial, always thinking a thousand recombinant thoughts a minute.

"He was a liar," his first lover Teddy said.

Teddy.

Poor sweet Teddy. With a shelf life from 6/9/69 to 1977.

Teddy had dragged his feet when Ryan told him they were moving from Chicago to California. "No!" Teddy freaked. "San Francisco's where you go to lose a lover." But Ryan assured Teddy he wanted no more than to open up their relationship. "Trust me," he said, and Teddy had trusted him. Teddy entertained a strange belief that he had a special sexual hold on Ryan as long as they stayed in the Midwest. He never realized, through all their eight years together, that nobody could ever quite capture Ryan who was Orion, one of those men who is the hunter not the hunted. He was the one who had hit on Teddy during one July Fourth weekend at Chuck Renslow's original Gold Coast bar in Chicago. Ryan had been out less than a year and he wanted to be in-love. Teddy, freckled and red haired, seemed a fair choice. He was the boy next door. He was sexy and Ryan was certain that sex could turn to love. That is perhaps the most romantic of fatal notions. Only fools fall in-love, pledging their infinite love forever in a finite world where all is change and nothing lasts, and still you buy furniture and silverware together. So they made love and a life together, too innocent then to know that love's inevitable failure is the main reason why a person finishes life with a sense of panic at being torn away from the tangled bedclothes of sexuality and self-deception.

For four years Ryan had taught at Loyola University in Chicago and Teddy joked about his status as faculty wife. Ryan had corrected him. "You're no wife. You're a man. You're my partner." Teddy had said, "I was only joking." Ryan was not laughing. California was on his mind. They packed their household into a U-Haul truck and drove westward across the mountains, sleeping naked outdoors at night, servicing truckers at rest stops along Interstate 80. Ryan bought the Noe Valley Victorian at 25th and Douglass the day they arrived in San Francisco. Real estate was rolling like *Monopoly*. Life was a cabaret. During the first three years in the City, Ryan and Teddy clung together, fought, reconciled, entertained the troops, and fought. Loud words gave way to long silences, and Teddy threatening suicide.

Late one night Ryan told the crying Teddy who saw the end coming, "I love you, Teddy. I do no kidding love you." Ryan talked 7-Eleven convenience talk, the kind of bull you know a hungry old lover will swallow like junk food. He said it exactly the way Tony Perkins had said to Tuesday Weld in *Pretty Poison*. "I do no kidding love you."

In San Francisco, Teddy had gotten in the way. He couldn't keep a job for fear of not keeping a constant eye on Ryan. He seethed if Ryan said hello on Castro. Without changing his boyish smile, Teddy could conjure instant Evil Teddy. Men asked Ryan, "Teddy's hot but what's with his vibe?"

"You need," Ryan said, "to live on your own for a few months. You need to have some friends who aren't my friends."

"I don't want anyone else," Teddy said. "I'll never let you go."

"Your meal ticket's punched out. So's your free ride. Get a job."

Suffocating captivity drove Ryan-Orion mad. I think more than anything in his heart of hearts he wanted nothing more than to be captured; but unless it was precisely the right man, it was a bondage he would never allow. Not in a million years. Not until he found the Ideal Man of his dreams.

Not until Kick.

Not until Kick captured Ryan completely.

"Kick? Kick." Ryan was talking long distance to El Lay. "Is that his stage name?" He grilled Dan Dufort who told Ryan he had a friend Ryan must meet. "I'm suspicious of blind dates." But that first night, when Ryan first saw Kick, he dropped the suspicion. Something clicked in his very soul. Ryan stared in awe. At Misericordia Seminary he had learned the words of transubstantiation. *Hoc est enim corpus meum. This is my body.* Muscular blond flesh and blood walked into the Platonic Ideal he had tucked away in the back of his head about the way a man is supposed to be. The sweet treble call of boys' voices at far-off games deepened down into the slow southern drawl of Kick's first Alabama "Hullo."

Kick. With a shelf life from here to eternity.

Kick was a man's man, to hear Ryan tell it, an angel's angel, a god's god. His was the perfect body, the classic face, the supernal blondness that was the object of Ryan's search that something in life could be ideal.

I myself thought Kick a bit slick, but I recognized the type. Everybody can recognize the type: the man who since he was a little boy is popular on the playground, always a captain in sports, the jock who dates the prettiest girls, the muscular guy in the showers who makes boys with high IQs and swimmer's bodies jealous as shit. There is something about handsome, husky, blond jocks that has filled everybody from Hitler to Madison Avenue with lust. Especially if, like Kick, their genes take to bodybuilding, and they groom themselves like impeccable Highway Patrolmen parading their stun-gun good looks with all the Command Presence of a man carrying himself with absolute self-confidence.

Kick could get away with murder.

One night, when Ryan sat with Kick at the Castro Palms, Kweenasheba took a handheld mike, sat down on the edge of the stage, and sang soft country-blues, with a twinge of lust for Kick in her own voice: "His pickup grin's flashin' across the juke joint floor. Redneck an' handsome. Blue-jean eyes lit from above. Chancin' with dancin', flirtin' with love." Ryan and Kick were hardly listening. They were staring into each other's eyes. At least, Ryan was staring into Kick's.

"God," Kweenie told me after she first saw Kick, "He's so drop-dead gorgeous he should carry drool buckets for innocent bystanders."

Kweenie and Ryan were psychic twins born sixteen years apart.

I must warn you. I am a professor of American popular culture at San Francisco State. I am not inexperienced in my observations. I am not gay, but I am a scholar—no, a student—of the gay subculture so important to San Francisco. I like gay men and lesbian women. Gays have always been a wonderful affront to received taste in America. That makes them interesting. They know how to make us react. You do not have bearded men in nuns' habits on network television without offending someone; and in the stylish offense of a man like Sister Boom Boom, quite often, comes the shock of awakening society needs. Gay men and lesbian women have been avant garde gadflies to straight American society. They exist to teach us irony. We are better off because of them. Our interiors are better designed. But that is academic. What is personal to me is that, once, while jogging Venice Beach, I met a woman friend who had run into a Golden Man. The look in her startled eyes was the same wondrous look I saw in Ryan's face when first he told me about Kick.

Recently, lecturer Quentin Crisp, that brilliant British pioneer of world-class queers, warned the yearning world of homosexual lovers that there is no tall, dark man of their dreams. But Ryan, the night that Crisp held my campus lecture hall in queenly thrall, would not have it so. Crisp gayly fielded questions after his lecture. Ryan challenged Crisp's velvet-glove rhetoric with a boxing glove. What a show! Both men respected the other but neither budged an inch. They locked horns at the political heart of the gaystyle matter. Ryan, plucky as Quentin was plucked, was playing Patrick Henry in some movie or another, exposing publicly for the first time his theory about emerging, evolving, masculine homosexuals. Ryan virtually said, "Give me homomasculinism or give me Death!" Quentin, ever the showman, turned an aside to his fans, wryly arched his brow, and brought down the house.

Ryan himself laughed, but his shot, like another shot heard round the world, had been fired. That night the Revolutionary War was not about tea and taxes, but about Sissy-Brit tea and sympathy versus American-Butch coffee and sex. Ryan, still radical from the Sixties, could not help rebutting. He wrote later in his *Journal:* "The internationally received popular stereotype of effeminacy was Crisp enough, and terribly British, but is not hard enough to play ball in America." Ryan's appetites flew directly in the face of Crisp's philosophy the way that passion always will. As much as Crisp denied the dashing, tall, dark man, Ryan truly believed in the existence of the Golden Man. He believed that bodybuilders are half-man and half-god the way centaurs are half-man and half-horse. He also believed in Tinker Bell, the fight for love and glory, and the sweet, sweet promise of blond muscle. Everything for Ryan was metaphor.

Many people feel me ambiguous, and somewhat of a sore thumb; but understanding of my role and my voice, be assured, is part of the mystery here. As a pop scholar, I feel bound to investigate a love affair, especially a love affair of this popular sort that ran for three years at the corner of 18th and Castro, an intersection suitable for the painter Hogarth. The street was their medium as the street has always been for gay men. The street is for cruising. The street is for parading. When gay people liberated themselves at the Stonewall riot, they shouted, "Out of the bars and into the streets." The street is a confirmation of the public side of gay life and politics. Walt Whitman was the good gay poet of the streets. The street is the place where, when you go there, you know you're out of your closet.

Maneuvers magazine made Ryan visible. Kick's body was more than just another streetside attraction. Together they became an instantly Famous Couple on Castro Street. On the big screen over its glitzy bar, the Midnight Sun showed candid telephoto closeup videos of them holding court on Castro in the afternoons, leaning against the window of Donuts & Things, drinking coffee from yellow plastic cups. The camera loved Kick; and Ryan, more famous for his words than his face, was always at his side. More than one queen wished Miss Scarlett dead, because they saw him as all that stood between them and Kick.

"What's that balding faggot have that I don't have?"

"Kick Sorensen," was the answer.

They stood on their tongues trying to figure what the Famous Couple had in common. Kick's contribution was obvious. He had Universal Appeal. Ryan was the ringer.

"I hear they have sixteen inches between them."

"Yeah. Twelve-to-four in favor of Kick."

To me the bigger curiosity concerned more mysterious workings than sex appeal. I wanted to know, in the game of love, how a one-night stand turned unexpectedly for them both into an off-ramp to Alpha Centauri.

Mysterious forces propelled both men toward one another. Ryan, on an enchanted El Lay evening, had indeed met a stranger across a crowded room. So had Kick. But while their blind date that first night seemed the very essence of gay lust, the kind Ryan sold by the column inch in *Maneuvers*, somehow, very quickly, sometime between midnight and the next dawn, this match of writer and body artist, something like a same-sex Arthur Miller and Marilyn Monroe, became much more than trick rock 'n' roll.

Somehow, I think, Ryan and Kick accidentally tapped into a Force Field so basic and so human that it thrilled them narcotically, before it terrified them totally.

That first August night in El Lay something clicked. Kick posed and Ryan talked his sex-rap. Recreational sex became unitive sex became transcendental sex. They pushed out the bounds of the finite, conjuring sexually, riding into dangerous psychic territory where neither was himself, and each passed through the other, until they triangulated a third Entity: a Power, a Force, a supranatural Being neither at first fully recognized, and, once conjured, neither could ever live without again. Something more than love muscled in on them.

Crisp may be right. There may be no tall, dark man; but Ryan had seen at their first meeting, and this I reveal as plainly and without prejudice as I can, the face of the Golden Man. Knowing Ryan's Catholic metaphysics, of one thing I am absolutely certain; and don't misunderstand what I, a confirmed atheist say, when I say it with qualification, not on Ryan's part, but on mine, that Ryan had glimpsed the very face of God.

6

On the title page of his dog-eared *Billy Budd,* Ryan wrote, in the most legible scribble of all his random notes, what must have come to him, suddenly, as a single, illuminating, uninterrupted, crystalline vision of sexual elegance.

That first night when I first saw Kick, I recognized one of life's long shots at the Perfect Affirmation.

He was a man.

He had a man's strength and fragility, a man's grace and intensity, a man's joy, and a man's passion. He seemed my chance to celebrate the changes in me as growth. He was so fully a man, he was an Angel of Light.

To him I could say nothing but *Yes.*

One thing, you see, I know for sure: Nature very rarely puts it all together: looks, bearing, voice, appeal, smile, intelligence, artfulness, accomplishment, strength, kindness. That's what I looked for all my life: the chance to say Yes to a man like that.

I look in men for nothing more than that affirmative something that grabs you and won't let you look away. Maintaining my full self, to have some plenty to offer back in balance, I've looked for some man who fills in the appropriate existential blanks, for some man to be the way a man is supposed to be, for some man to keep on keeping on with, in all the evolving variations of friendship and fraternity, beyond the first night's encounter.

I've looked for that to happen: to be able to say Yes inside myself when a good, clean glow of absolute trust settles over the world.

Honest manliness is never half-revealed. When it's there, it's all right there in front of you. The hardest thing to be in the world today is a man.

Start from the beginning. Start from before that innocent prehistory in those Druidic eons when men consorted with the gods. Consider those ancient fables celebrated by the classical Greeks. Consider the Vatican's magnificently oversized marble Hercules. Consider the naked bruising statue of Vulcan, Forger of Steel, standing astride a hill overlooking Birmingham where Kick was born in Alabama. Then you can better understand Ryan's passion for men's heroically muscular bodies.

When Ryan first saw Kick, I dare say, his fantasy spanned a million years.

7

"You're a strange new mutant," Ryan said to me. "A scholar of American popular culture. You're a vulture feeding on your contemporaries. It used to be, when things were what they used to be, that scholars would wait a decent fifty years at least before daring to dissect people and their behavior. But you? No! You pounce right on us. You formulate us like butterflies on the heads of pins. You dissect us. You poach us. You're a culture vulture. Do you know the difference between a vulture and a pop culture scholar? Of course, you don't. A vulture waits till you're dead to pick on you."

"Fuck you," I said, "and your high horse."

Ryan grinned.

This was my first meeting with him and he was spieling me. "Asshole," I said. I had called to do an interview with the editor of *Maneuvers*. It was a leather and S&M magazine, but I hadn't expected to be abused. "Don't waste my time attacking me. You don't know who I am." I could tell he was testing me. "I'm here to find out who you are."

Ryan unbuttoned his fly and flipped out his penis. "That's who I am," he said. A sizeable chunk of meat, as Ryan would have written in his fiction, lay on the chair between his leather thighs.

"That's of small interest to me," I said. "I know how to play 'Dueling Banjos.'" I bluffed him by patting my own Levi's crotch.

"I'm gay," Ryan said.

"I'm straight," I said.

He broke up. We hit it off. I think I was the first person ever, and probably the last, to tell the flamboyant Mr. Ryan Steven O'Hara to shut up.

I make no apology for my vocation. I make my living as a dispassionate observer. I believe one must study culture quickly before it melts. Memory and memoirs only make the past glow. I love the firsthand immediacy of another of my interviews, Sam Steward, the Father of Gay Erotic Writing. He was a joy telling his merry tales of Gertrude and Alice and Thornton and the rest of the Charmed Circle. Who but the living, breathing Sam, the last survivor, could tell the intimacies of Bilignin, how he, one night, stumbling into the bathroom, caught sight of Gertrude, one hand trying to cover her mastectomy that only Alice had ever seen. No one had even known that Gertrude had cancer. But Sam knew. That's the kind of firsthand reportage that is the essence of pop culture: get it while the source is alive and kicking; poke at it while it's fading; perform an autopsy while it's still warm; keep to the immediate evanescent facts and feelings that will evaporate before they can be recorded; leave the eulogies to historians studying the world through the rearview mirror. I prefer watching the world through the windshield: not where we've been, but where we are and where we're going. An odd approach for an ivory-tower professor, but one that involves a person deeply. Sometimes dangerously. Something like covering El Salvador, or San Francisco, under fire. Writing history is dead and distinctly different from the vicarious adventure of witnessing a whole people being carried away by history.

I admit I'm a fame-and-failure junkie. Not mine. Others. I entertain an almost perverse curiosity about the ironies of American culture. I want to know why the postmodern craze for derivative pastiche, quotation, and appropriation succeeds seamlessly in Spielberg and Lucas and fails in the lurid flash films of De Palma and the post-*Apocalypse* Coppola. I am more interested in the delayed-stress syndrome of Vietnam that affected Ryan's brother, Thomas a'Beckett O'Hara, than I am in that curiously flawed war itself. I am more interested in the generic emotional effects of MTV than I am in any Number One song ever. Beatlemania interests me far more than the Death of Lennon. I am more interested in the American males' sports obsession with muscle and size than I am in knowing which bodybuilder is contractually owned by which publisher of which glossy physique magazine. I want to know how men achieve a certain Look, a certain Attitude, a certain way of Being. I want to know why star-crossed lovers, such as that woman created by John Fowles, wait for the French Lieutenant who, like Godot, never shows. I want to know why Ryan cruised in the fast lane, certain that what he was looking for was looking for him, praying for the first time ever he'd see the like of Kick's face. Kick, you see, was not the French Lieutenant, nor was he Godot. Unlike them, Kick showed up. Saint Theresa, beloved by Saint Truman Capote, was proven right again: "There are more tears shed over answered prayers than unanswered."

On a more mundane level, Ryan's friend, the streetwise porn-video mogul Solly Blue, had warned him: "In California you've got to be careful what you wish for. You might get it." I want to understand sexual politics. I want to understand how Dan White revised gay history one November morning when he crawled through the basement window of San Francisco City Hall, high on junk food, and shot the liberal Italian Mayor, George Moscone, and the gay Jewish Supervisor, Harvey Milk. I want to understand how White brought an outrageously playful community, with little more than sexual freedom on their minds, together in a way that he neither wanted and they could never have foreseen. Especially, I want to know in all their infinite variety about all American women and American men. America, I tell my students, is a wonderful country that has yet to be discovered.

My name is Charles Bishop. I am only peripheral to these events of passion and illusion. I was a bystander taking notes. I thought I was not part of any of this. Yet, I must confess, what happened to them all touched my heart one way or another, a fact that for a very long time my cynical, atheist critic's head hardly believed. Now I am working my way back. This is my only deep, dark secret. I must work my way back. Back from what once was called a nervous breakdown. Not a real nervous breakdown, mind you. I wasn't myself touched that much. But from a tenth-rate nervous breakthrough. The kind you don't see a psychiatrist for. The kind you work out for yourself. By examining all the pieces that push you to the limit. By examining all the bad things that happen to good people. By trying to figure how golden fliers become star-crossed jumpers.

Like Ryan, I left the Midwest to start a new life teaching in California. I like the academic life. It's sheltered. It gives a man time to himself, even with endless papers to grade. My time made me accessible to Ryan. Ah, yes. In some ways we were very much alike: me with the analytical need to listen, and him with the emotional, Catholic need to confess.

My masculinity, and rein in any ambiguous cynicism about *closets,* runs exclusively, when it runs at all, straight toward older women. I am more asexual than consciously celibate. I remain perhaps cooly interested in—forgive my slight pedantry—the existential ramifications of human love. Somehow, Ryan Steven O'Hara seemed to me, if anything, at first proponent then victim of the new romantic, liberated sensuality trying to fit itself into the inexorable mainstream of twentieth-century existential constraints. Translated, that means he was trying to find love in the face of Death, but not the same way *The Advocate* proclaimed the safe-sex of the New Homosexuality in the face of the Acquired Immune Deficiency Syndrome. Ryan and Kick were, long before AIDS, when San Francisco was still Eden, something like Adam and Eve, a couple with something special. In his heart, Ryan carried a priestly purity; in his body, Kick carried a manly nobility. This mutual recognition, achieved through the transcendence of hardballing sex and drugs bonded them together. Actually, both of them were something like Adam before the Fall. And nothing like Eve.

What I must tell you makes me feel like a film editor whose footage has all run off the reel and lies in tangled snarls on the dusty floor. I must make sense of it. Stories in the movies all make sense. Maybe movies—something all these film fans never understood—are a crock. Maybe movies lie. Maybe in assembling the footage of what happened what I too want to know is what the tall dark writer and the short blond bodybuilder had in common. I think I know.

It was body and blood and soul and divinity.

The writer took up bodybuilding and the bodybuilder began writing. Falling through the looking glass, mirrorfucking, each becoming the other, they fathered that third mysterious Entity that lifted them out of space and time and made their world stand still, in a space out of time, for almost three years when for both of them there was no one else.

Ryan, by the way, nicknamed me "Magnus," because, he said, I reminded him of the stern rector of Misericordia Seminary, the Very Reverend Monsignor Magnus Linotti. "Magnus," he said. "Magnus Bishop. A perfectly ironic name for a cynical, atheist critic." Kweenasheba picked up on the name game because of her counterculture taste for changing given names. Solly Blue endorsed it because all his hustlers had street names. Kick and the others simply followed suit. So I, Charles Bishop, from Peoria, Illinois, nicknamed by Ryan O'Hara from Peoria, Illinois, became, in San Francisco, California, Magnus Bishop.

Kick's was a nickname too. "Without a nickname," they say in Chinatown, "a man has no chance to become rich." Kick was born rich, the only child of an athletic, horsey, handsome couple whose roots went back three generations in the American South, and before that, to the icy blond, arctic midnight sun of Norway, and before that, if Ryan was to be believed, to the Planet Krypton.

How the real Billy Ray Sorensen, southern-born and Alabama-bred in Birmingham, became the bodybuilder titled Mr. National Physique, Mr. Golden Bear, and Mr. California, is part and parcel of my pop culture theory that people tend to be like their names, given or assumed.

"Kick" was short for "kickstand," a name dropped on Billy Ray in his high school shower room by a coach who joked in front of the other lathering players: "Hung like that, boy, you ain't got a dick. You got yourself a kickstand." The nickname stuck in the positive upbeat way things always stick to good-looking, well-built, blond athletes. For those on whom the gods smile, they positively grin.

I'd like to say none of this happened to anybody. Yet, with all Ryan's *Journals* and videotapes, Kick's muscle trophies, the pile of their mutually passionate letters, and the hyper-male fetish-clothing belonging to both of them spread around me here in my study, I have good reason to believe, sitting alone here at Rancho Bar Nada, facing westward over the Pacific, that something enormous happened. Something beyond their control. Something one or both of them, and I say this metaphorically, sold their souls for. I want to find the name of that Entity they conjured between them. I want to know where are they now, and why am I alone with my feet and my head tangled in their footage? Remember that. And remember this. If any other mystery hides here, it's who is Magnus Bishop. Pay attention, I tell my students. There's a quiz at the end.

Somehow backtracking the facts of Ryan and Kick as a Famous Couple is irresistible. I often tell my film students that it never offends me that a particular lifestyle is presented on screen as long as it makes dramatic sense and the lighting is good. Despite what Ryan's starstruck mother taught him, life is not always as pat as the movies. So let me continue, hopefully with a compassion for people who once were my friends, the job of the editor. That's all that remains, you see, when you're not as much of an urbane traveler as you think you are, and they leave you behind to pick up after them.

All I know for sure is that no matter what they once were, they'll never ever be the same. That's why, after all, everyone comes to San Francisco. This is how love, or what passes for love on this planet, goes haywire.

8

Movies are made or betrayed by editors sitting alone at their Movieolas viewing and reviewing hours of footage. A sequence is picked here. A close shot inserted there. The editor punctuates the director's hours of linear footage with sometimes no more than the subliminal flash of a single frame. The cinematographer's angles are cut to intensify the perspective on a scene. Actors' timing is re-paced. Character becomes dramatic, comic, romantic, elusive, mysterious, more vulnerable, more vicious. Plot tightens, or jump-cuts to the surreal. Emotions are led, guided, seduced, betrayed. Beauty and terror collide. Scenes juxtapose, repeat, invert. Villains ride unrepentant into the sunset. Beauty takes a fall on a banana peel. Editors, usually women in the film industry, give American movies their final glossy vision. Under a scissors, decisive as the Three Fates, places and people appear and disappear. Faces end up on the cutting room floor.

These days, everyone in America is writing a screenplay. Ryan's was titled *Half of Noah's Ark,* "Because," Ryan said, "San Francisco, especially the Castro, has one of every kind." All of us play the lead in the movie we're living. If that conceit of our times has any truth, Warhol made it quite clear that our movies are at best short subjects. "Everyone," Warhol playing Mephistopheles, had whispered into a hanky over a microphone, "will be famous for fifteen minutes."

Ryan had the good sense to avoid moving to Hollywood when he left the Midwest for California. Instead of El Lay, he took his life on location to San Francisco. "I'd never move to Hollywood," he said. "You can get lost in Hollywood. You end up like Marilyn in a tangle of sheets with the phone on the floor. Besides, as the Castro's greatest party producer, Michael Maletta, always said, 'In San Francisco, everyone is a star.'"

Maletta's was no idle observation. San Francisco, unlike Los Angeles, is small and familiar: hardly more than a simple fishing village with an opera. And a tolerance for colorful characters. In three fast generations, the Beats of North Beach begot the Hippies of the Haight-Ashbury who begot the Gays of the Castro. Because San Francisco is the easiest place in California to do parole, eighty percent of the convicts released in the state go directly from jail to the City's Tenderloin. It's a sleazy, dangerous neighborhood of small hotels, of mattresses burning in gutters, of pub-crawling drag queens and whores and hustlers, of old people waiting to die and new boat people scrounging aluminum cans to live.

The Tenderloin is a war zone.

The Tenderloin was Solly Blue's totally urban place of funky preference. It was his life. Its delinquent tough boys were his business. Their bodies were zoned commercial. He hired them in, and shot artful porn videotapes of them solo on screen as if they were specimens trapped in solitary confinement. They flexed and posed, showing off their tattoos and big dicks and buttholes. They talked dirty to the camera, asking Solly's mail-order customers if they wanted to "slob on bob," stroking their dicks, masturbating to full spasm, spitting cum and saliva at the camera. Personally they were straight. Commercially they were anything a patron wanted them to be. They were the throwaways and the runaways of America, kids born, back in the deep South or the Midwest, to some strange calling to the streets of El Lay and San Francisco.

"And they're all twenty-something," Solly said. "Like us."

He taped them, had hustler sex with them, gave them more money than they earned or asked for, had them sign a model release, and sent them back to the streets. In the Tenderloin, where he lived, Solly Blue was a star the way movie directors are stars. He was as much an *auteur* as Truffaut, but the young men who brought him other young men didn't know that. His money made him famous with the boys and the boys, particularly quite some few of them, had no idea how famous Solly had made them on the home-video porn circuit. Solly Blue was a marketing genius.

Ryan often disguised himself to walk the streets of the Tenderloin. The neighborhood was a perfect match for his frequent bouts of depression.

"Convicts, alcoholics, immigrants," Solly Blue said. "Judy Garland exposed the truth. San Francisco's Golden Gate lets no stranger wait outside its door."

Ryan always ended up at Solly's penthouse. Teddy, ever jealous Teddy, accused him of having a hot affair on the side. Not with Solly, for godsakes, but with somebody! A terrible fight ensued.

"I'll never let you go," Teddy said.

"Alright, already. Okay. I get the message. It's okay. Stop worrying," Ryan said. "I've never balled Solly."

"You have sex with his hustlers," Teddy said.

"I've always liked hustlers."

"What's that mean?" Teddy was pissed. Ryan was expert at saying one thing and meaning another. "I'm not a hustler."

"And Castro isn't paved with yellow bricks."

"I need you," Teddy said.

"Ryan wanted to be needed, but not by the likes of dear sweet Teddy," Solly Blue said. "Teddy was life-size. Ryan wanted someone larger than CinemaScope. He was ripe for Kick's picking."

"If I'm not needed," Ryan said, "I don't know how to relate to the world."

Monsignor Magnus Linotti, the rector of Misericordia, had encouraged Ryan, telling him the essence of a vocation was the world's need for handsome, manly, young priests. His father, sick and dying those twelve long years, had cornered Ryan's ear and whispered how much the family needed him. Teddy had needed him. The priests' pinched souls, his father's illness, and Teddy's whining, exhausted him. He was depressed. He thought not so much of actual suicide as about the idea of suicide. He read Ernest Becker's *Denial of Death.* His curiosity overrode his emotions. He was down, but he wasn't ready to kill himself; he was merely sniffing around the edges, the way a porn writer sniffs around an asshole for a story, to imagine what suicide might be like. He never wrote a *Maneuvers* story ending with the cliché of gay suicide. He was, if anything, intellectually curious only, because he was in his mortal soul afraid of Death.

If Ryan thought of suicide, he was in the right City. He drove regularly across the Golden Gate Bridge to spend weekends near the Russian River in Sonoma County at his small ranch that he called Bar Nada. He felt the Bridge's strange attraction.

"Some nights when I drive back to the City, and the fog is sweeping in over the railings, all orange from the Bridge lights, I see ghosts. The Golden Gate Bridge is the most haunted place in San Francisco," he said.

I was hardly afraid that Ryan would do himself in. At least, not from the Bridge. Ryan was a flier not a jumper. I might explain that the City's notoriously high suicide rate is misleading. Native San Franciscans rarely jump off the Bridge. It is mostly outlanders, anonymous immigrants from the dark interior of the American continent, with only a few months in the City, who are jumpers. No one, no one who is anyone, ever jumps off the industrial-strength Bay Bridge coming in from Oakland. It is the Golden Gate, and only the gracious Golden Gate, that has the singular siren mystique.

You can't really understand San Francisco without understanding the Golden Gate Bridge.

I think California draws high-fliers from all across the country. New beginnings in America have always beckoned westward. California is as far west as you can go. When even that last hope of California's promise becomes, like everything else, betrayal, the Golden Gate's siren height, spanning land's end to land's end, gives those would-be upwardly mobile aspirants who wanted to fly so high, one last ironic chance to dramatize the talent for daring they couldn't even give away: one soaring flight, out and over and down into a deep Pacific sea of surcease.

"Gravity sucks," Ryan wrote. "Gravity holds us bondage on this prison of a planet. Gravity is the bottom line for angels flying too close to the ground."

Ryan had seen enough of love in San Francisco to have learned the country-western wisdom of Aristotle who said, "Love makes a man a romantic; the loss of a lover makes him a philosopher." When you can't beat something, you join it. When you can't find love, you settle for sex. The Bridge is, perhaps, the last chance of the existentially betrayed to flaunt gravity's unbeatable revenge on all the world's high-fliers.

When, I wonder, and how, does a flier become a jumper?

One of my university students, a glowing young freshman girl, asked me why so many books and films are always so depressing. "Why aren't artists content to show happy people having good times?"

I handed her that morning's *Chronicle*. Page two featured a shot of a young man sitting on the rail of the Golden Gate Bridge. He faced the City. Jumpers always face the City; everybody's movie requires a blockbuster audience, especially for the final reel. The athletically built boy was naked. His head was shaved to a Mohawk. He had padlocked his ankles tight together with a heavy chain. He had handcuffed his wrists together behind his back. A blond California Highway Patrolman was leaning, black-gloved hand outstretched, to the bound boy. The patrolman's mirrored sunglasses doubled the image of the perching figure. The photo was an esthetically perfect shot. Seconds later, the boy arched his buttocks and dropped, cutting like a rock through the wind, naked and shaved and bound, into the cold currents below. Tourists on a Bay excursion cruise, the article reported, cheered and applauded.

"Why?" my student asked.

"Because they got what they wanted."

"That's why?"

"Why not?" I said.

She looked stymied.

Explaining the *why* of anything has never been my strong suit. That's one of the reasons I find wrestling through the effects of Ryan's life an exhausting exercise. *Why*, after all, isn't really a whole question. *Why* is only the yin of the yang, *why not?*

The Bridge fascinated Ryan. He once joked about entrepreneuring a small business, printing engraved invitations. Something in quiet good taste for a suicide: "Golden Gate Bridge. 9 PM. Midspan. Cityside. RSVP regrets only." He proposed starting a service to throw off the Golden Gate Bridge the ashes of cowards who had always wanted to jump, but were too chicken, and lived out the natural length of their unnatural lives. He should never have joked about Death.

Solly Blue's first lover had jumped off the Bridge one New Year's Eve. "He was very clever," Solly said. "If he had jumped any other day, I probably would have eventually forgotten the date. He wanted me to remember him every New Year's. And I do. I can't help it. He made me hate New Year's."

The tourists on the excursion cruise got what they wanted: the shocking beauty of the naked boy's fall, the horror of his splattering, splashing Death, and the moral superiority of flying back to Kansas telling tales of lurid California, and how good it feels to be back home.

"Everyone should get what they want," Ryan said. "At least some version of it." Ironic that ultimately Ryan got it, and got it good. "Oh, how you do me when you do me like you do," he wrote to Kick.

9

It happened one night. It started with their first meeting. Ryan had flown PSA from San Francisco to Hollywood/Burbank. Teddy was still living with him, because, Ryan said, "Teddy can't afford to move out. He needs first and last months' rent plus a security deposit." Teddy worked minium-wage jobs in fits and starts that drove Ryan mad. "Every six months, Teddy has some medical problem." Ryan was beside himself. "In the eight years we've lived together, I had to get his teeth fixed. I'm talking every molar and bicuspid. Guess who paid good Doctor Percodan? I mean tooth decay in this day and age? Not tonguing around in my mouth, thank you. I read somewhere tooth decay is contagious." Ryan was a hypochondriac who would go berserk with the onset of AIDS. "After his teeth, Teddy had surgery to repair a torn cartilage in his knee. He claimed I tore it when I tied him up. I told him he shouldn't have struggled so much. Then he had a kidney stone, which was right before his hepatitis. Then came the series of allergy shots. He'd endure anything rather than work."

The downward spiral of gay men, I've found, goes with the territory. A man, straight or gay, can't follow his dick around and not expect to lose ground in the real world.

"And during his allergy shots, he had a tonsillectomy." Ryan rubbed his thumb to his fingertips. "Guess who paid for it all? Teddy was an attractive twenty-four-year-old strawberry blond when I met him. He never got over being a hustler. He'd work New York for awhile. Then Chicago. He said I rescued him from being an alcoholic." Ryan was resolute. "Believe me when I say my Finishing School for Gay boys is closed. From now on, I want full-grown adult men only." His madness those days was the kind of madness one sees in men saddled with bitter loyalties to old lovers they can't seem to dispose of in a gentlemanly fashion.

In those last days, Teddy kept to himself in the Victorian flat that had always been more Ryan's than theirs together. His room was a pile of old clothes, magazines, and boxes of Styrofoam peanuts from the packing cartons of photographic equipment Ryan had bought for him.

"You spoiled him," I said.

"I loved him," Ryan said. "I still love him. But I can't stand him." When finally Ryan ordered Teddy to move out, he refused. It took several of us, including a gay San Francisco cop, to coax him from the house. He did not go gently. There was a fight. Physical blows. He held onto Ryan tighter than I have ever seen anyone cling to anyone else. He was hysterical.

"You made me move with you to California," Teddy said. "Now you're abandoning me." He was terrified of going out into the world alone.

"That's precisely why he has to go," Ryan said. "He's hiding out in me. He has no friends of his own. His only friends are my friends."

When we dragged Teddy screaming from Ryan's apartment, his fingernails tore into the carpet like a cat being pulled on its belly out the door to the vet.

Teddy's forced exit had been shaped sometime before. The last straw had been the Friday evening Ryan flew to Hollywood/Burbank. Teddy had been supposed to drive him to San Francisco International.

"I can't find the car keys," Ryan said.

"You can never find your keys."

Ryan grew frantic about missing his flight. Teddy searched all Ryan's pockets hanging in his clothes closet. Teddy had always taken care of keeping track of things Ryan couldn't be bothered with. The search for the keys escalated into name-calling. "If you don't find them, I'll have to call a taxi," Ryan said. "You asshole!"

"They're your keys, asshole," Teddy said. I admired nothing so much in the boy as his ability to put up with Ryan's stormy temperament. Anything Ryan gave him or paid for, believe me, Teddy had earned.

The taxi arrived. Ryan was in a movie. "The airport. And step on it!" The gay driver, thrilled by the classic line, careened past everything on 101 South. He roared into the airport, wheels squealing around curved ramps. Ryan jumped out at the PSA stop and threw the driver a wad of bills. "Keep the change, pal!" Ryan said.

Everything in his life somehow seemed to depend on making this flight. Six months before, Dan Dufort, a man Ryan had taken into his bed from the CMC Carnival, had promised to fix him up with a good-looking blond bodybuilder he knew in El Lay. Ryan had watched professional musclemen posing in nonsexual commercial videotapes nightly in his bedroom. All the straight, big-muscled names displayed themselves in slow motion on his screen: the brothers, Mike and Ray Mentzer; the blond Mr. America, 1965, Dave Draper; the ultimate manimal, Pete Grymkowski; the moustached blond Scott Wilson; Rod Koontz with his "*Thee* Animal" tattoo; Big Daddy Bill Pearl, and a dozen more, always excluding Schwarzenegger whom Ryan found big but not erotic. "He looks like something Hitler shit." Ryan had grown tired of muscle fantasy. He wanted reality. Quite the opposite of Miss DuBois.

"There are no real bodybuilders in San Francisco," Ryan said. "El Lay. That's where. Venice Beach. That's their Mecca. Like Castro is ours. Maybe I should have moved to El Lay. I moved to California because this is where the bodybuilders come from all across the country. But I couldn't move to La-La Land. It scares me too much. I get set down in the middle of it and I can't comprehend it. In San Francisco, I go stand at the top of any hill, and I know exactly where I am."

At the Hollywood/Burbank airport, Ryan picked Dan Dufort out of the crowd at the arrival gate. Dan was an intermediate bodybuilder. He wore a tight white tee shirt and faded Levi's. His biceps were pumped and tanned against the white cotton. His white teeth smiled. His face was sunburned and oiled with a down of fresh sweat from the humid Los Angeles night. In a couple of years, he was going to win the Gay Games physique contest.

"You look great," Ryan said.

"We've had a change of plans." Dan reached for Ryan's camera case. Ryan's heart sank. The fight with Teddy and the big tip for the taxi driver had been for nothing. Dan read his face. "Kick's not coming over tomorrow night." Ryan suddenly felt his car keys in his jacket pocket. "He called an hour ago, and asked if it was okay if he posed tonight instead of tomorrow night." All Ryan cared about at this moment was the news that would sat-isfy his lust for flesh-and-blood musclemen. "So I told him to come on ahead." Ryan was relieved. He'd have to apologize to Teddy. "I couldn't wait for you to see him. Everything I've told you is true."

"Including," Ryan said, "that you're a master of understatement?"

"You'll see for yourself." Dan smiled like a man with a big surprise. He drove Ryan back to his house off Santa Monica in West Hollywood. The hot August night smelled of jasmine. Dan's apartment was austere, perfect, poised, calculated to the display of extraordinary muscle. A spotlight can on a black track hung in the center of the bedroom ceiling, angled for perfect posing display opposite a floor-to-ceiling mirror.

Ryan wrote in his *Journal:*

We smoked a joint and waited. The radio sounded the way radios sound in a new town: different commercials, different weather forecasts. I was nervous. All my life I had idealized men in a classic sense. I'd fantasized about the thickness, the big-ness of bodybuilders. *Bodybuilders.* The word itself. *Bodybuilder.* A builder of bod-ies, taking meat and sculpting flesh by deliberate sweating design. The building of a body. A man's body. The architectonics of muscle. The taking of flesh to make a man into a muscleman. Another incarnational word: *muscle. Muscleman.* A com-plete investigation, no, celebration of the complete male. Could he be as good as I hoped, as good as Dan said? He was, I had been told, extremely handsome. Had he truly the perfect body and the perfect face for dramatizing whatever athletic clothes or uniforms he carefully chose to wear? Was he really coming to make me cum? Could he really let me worship his muscle the way I have so long wanted?

Ryan had waited his whole life for this night. In long ago summers in the Midwest, riding in the backseat of his family's car, he had watched men not even knowing why he watched how they moved, looked, groomed, and car-ried themselves. His whole boyhood had been an indescribable ache for what he had not then known, other than the sight of some man made him say to himself: "I want to be like him when I grow up." The thought of touching such men never crossed his mind; the thought of making love to such men never entered his head; the possibility of handling an athletes' body, stroking his rock-hard muscles, breathing in the sweet sweat scent of his hair lay in the vague unseen distance for him like a far rainbow's end.

He ached for the roar of the crowd and the smell of the Coppertone.

Flying back from El Lay, Ryan tried to capture something beyond words. He wrote on the only paper available. I transcribe these essential words here from the back, no kidding, of unused PSA airsick bags. I found them stuffed in the back of his *Journal.* There's an innocence here like *Love: Round 1.*

10

Pacific Southwest Airline. Seat 5A. Window
8 PM Sunday, August 21, 1977
PSA Flt 101: HOLLYWOOD/BURBANK TO SFO
Kick's red Corvette pulled into Dan's drive. Dan met him at the door. Kick entered. He was better than any man I had ever seen. And I've seen stunners. His face alone, his body yet unseen, was perfect. Desire filled me. Everything I ever wanted to do with a man, to a man, or have a man do with or to me, flushed through my body. My eyes, and I'm not lying to exaggerate, came, looking at him. Never have I ever seen anyone who looked so noble, handsome, classic. The light in his blue eyes showed something more sensitive than I could ever have hoped for in a man of such physical beauty. He had no vanity. No Attitude. He was what he was. He simply walked into the room and controlled the furniture, the radio, the breeze from the windows, everything, with his Command Presence.

I shook his hand and sat down, knocked out by his beauty, afraid I might turn him off by being taller. He and Dan stood in the center of the room and talked. I sat silent. Speechless. He turned and smiled down at me. He said nothing but he communicated everything. His eyes looked deep into me. Reassuring me. As if I already heard his heart say: "Here I am. Look at me. Look at what I was born with. Look at what I have worked at improving. I like it. You like it. It's all here. A gift to us. Let's share it. Let's enjoy it. Let's let go with no reserve. Let's get off on it together."

I wanted to hump his leg.

He had dressed himself in fantasy gear he thought would please me. He had tucked his blond body into an impeccably tailored California Highway Patrol motorcycle uniform: high-polished, calf-hugging black boots; the tan wool-serge breeches bulging tight around his muscular thighs; the black-leather police jacket, accessory belt with handcuffs, nightstick, and gun in the holster. His gold-framed cop glasses accented his tanned blond face. His hair was cut, groomed, and the kind of translucent blond that runs from black-blond to platinum. His bristle of moustache was authoritatively clipped military style. He was a bulk of a man. No fag in cop drag. He understood perfect police dressage. He presented himself to me uniformed like a sculpture for an unveiling. I could tell he had an immense capacity for man-to-man fantasy play. He was, in fact, teasing me and I was loving the foreplay. Dan had promised me a bodybuilder. Kick himself intensified the promise one step higher. He offered me my first reading of his physique as an ideal man in authority. He was perfect. He walked, flesh and blood and muscle, right into my abstract ideal of what a man should look like. He filled in all the blanks. He was my every fantasy. He was the kind of man I looked up at when I was a boy and thought, "That man. That man. That's the kind of man I want to look like when I grow up."

Kick terrified me. Never in this life did I expect the fulfillment of ultimate fantasy. But, my God, if this sexual wish to dive straight to the heart of pure masculinity can be filled, what other wishes in life can I hope to come true? Most bodybuilders give no indication that their muscle can be used for anything but flexing. Kick, in his CHP uniform, went beyond decorative muscle-for-muscle's sake. He was an enforcer. He was a more real cop than most credentialed cops ever dream of being. He was a CHP recruiting poster.

Kick was the way a man should be.

He finally sat down opposite me. Dan fired up a joint. We talked about the heat and the smog. He said he had never been to San Francisco. He asked me what the city was like. Dan sat back and grinned, listening to us making our way through the small talk with steady gains toward discoveries of everything we had in common.

Kick and I were not strangers.

We almost instantly recognized we were Old Souls.

I masked what I was sensing, afraid he might not recognize what I already knew. I asked him about bodybuilding.

"The summer I was twelve," Kick's voice was an easy Alabama drawl, "I spent three months with my uncle and aunt. They ran a filling station with a diner outside of Muscle Shoals." He grinned. "I didn't quite know then how much I'd learn to love that name. About the second week, I started noticing this young trucker came in every day. He talked to me the way a grown man, who's not much more than a big kid himself, jokes around with a kid. I remember he had cut the sleeves off his flannel shirt. He asked me if I wanted to feel his arm. I reached up. Way up, I remember."

Kick raised his arm, smoothing his moves through the gestures of his story.

"I was such a little guy then, and he was so big. I wrapped both my hands around his bicep. For the first time, I felt how strong and hard and big a man's body could be. I hung on to his arm and he lifted me up. Swung me right up off my bare feet, up out of the dust. Face to face. After that, I guess I pestered the shit out of him. Every day for the rest of the summer, without my asking, he let me swing from his arms, betting me he was strong enough to hold his flexed double-arm pose while I hung, my face to his chest, with both my hands on both his biceps. I could hear his heartbeat and I wanted arms strong as his. He bet me I could chin myself from that position." Kick grinned. "So I pulled myself up, the first time half-climbing his tall body. By the time summer was over, I was hanging from his arms and chinning myself up to his face. All that next winter, back in Birmingham in my own bedroom, I stood in my white cotton underwear and started flexing my arms. Sort of posing the way boys do when they're home alone with a mirror. I studied my arms. I imagined them growing big and hard. Like his. You should have seen me. Squinting my eyes. Concentrating on them to make them grow. Moving to an angle in the old mirror that, when I caught the distortion just right, made my arms look bigger than they were. It gave me an image to grow into. I really worked at it."

He lowered to a manly modesty.

"I guess I have lucky genes. My mom and dad have good bodies. They said I was eating them out of house and home. The next summer I went back to Muscle Shoals. I was about four inches taller and a few pounds heavier. But the trucker wasn't stopping by anymore." He leaned forward, rested his forearms on his thighs, raised his face, and looked me straight in the eye. "So that's how muscle turned me around. Especially on arms. They're Big Guns. That's where a man shines. Ask any guy to show you some muscle and ten-to-one he'll flash you a biceps shot. It's natural. If I ever compete, I don't care if I win or not, as long as I can take home the trophy for the Best Arms. So," he said, "That's it. That's how I got hooked on muscle."

Kick relaxed back into Dan's chair. He was smooth, slow, easy. Natural. The El Lay night was hot. I could smell his body heating up the leather of his police jacket.

Sweet sweat was building up in him. His blond face glistened. He was in no rush to wham-bam. His discipline of slow southern savoring kept him in cool control of his courting foreplay. He was intent on pleasing me. He smiled at me the way a man smiles when he's giving a new friend a gift. "I think I better take this jacket off," he said. He stood up. He reached for the zipper. Everything slipped into slow motion. His blue eyes squinted, sizing me up. Slowly, deliberately, he grazed the back of his hairy blond hand across his strong All-American jaw. His holster and gun and night stick shifted. His shoulders and chest bulked huge under the jacket.

One part of me thought, omigod this is Hollywood! Another part of me thought, Oh, God, this is Heaven! The best gay sex scenes are half of both.

I was hooked to the tits. I couldn't resist him and didn't want to. I picked up his scene. I jumped on in. Words came tumbling from my mouth. Sextalk. Muscletalk. Mantalk. The scene had begun. I wasn't acting; nor was he. We were doing a number on each other, a real number. His hand slowly pulled the zipper down every tooth of the leather jacket.

"When you take it off," I said, "this will be my first look at you."

He smiled and pulled off the CHP jacket. Slowly. So slowly. That was his style to move southern-slow in the El Lay fast lane. First one muscled arm. Then the other. All his moves like the slow-motion muscle movies I watched every night in my bedroom. He wore a tan CHP short-sleeve wool shirt. It bulged like armor over his chest. His gold seven-point star stood out on his left pec. His eighteen-inch upper arms filled the precisely tailored sleeves to bursting.

He was arms. Heroic arms. His thick forearms were downed with soft golden hair. His wrists were squared off in the classic way wrists are presented in men's watchband ads. His hands were perfect, defined, and powerful from gripping iron weights. His fingers and the backs of his hands were downed with sunblond hair. His nails were clipped short. His arms, hands to shoulders, were arms to worship. This was no false god I had before me. In sex, I have few inhibitions. With him, I had none.

"You are," I said, "perfect."

He smiled, and something in the way he smiled assured me there was no vanity in him. Only an honest pride. He was a man who realized the body perfect for himself. He was a body artist, a muscle artist. Bodybuilding is a subjective sport, but he was as objective as any sculptor unveiling his work.

He kept his look straight on me. His fingers reached for the buttons on his police shirt. Again, slowly, deliberately, he opened the shirt: at his neck, down across his hairy blond chest, down the length of his washboard belly. He pulled the shirt tails from under his belt. He dropped his arms down to his sides. He rotated his shoulders. The tan wool shirt pulled open over his chest and tight gut. He smiled at me, and slowly raised his left hand to palm inside the open shirt. I watched his hand run up the ripple of his belly and then smooth and cup his pectoral muscles. Already he had shown me more than I ever expected. He might have stopped and I could have flown back home happy. I've always loved seduction.

He peeled his uniform shirt deliberately off first one shoulder and then the other, revealing how wide side-to-side were his shoulders, how thick front-to-back was his chest, how wide were his lats under his shoulders and alongside his chest until they narrowed down to the tight V of his waist. He handed Dan the shirt, and stood before me, stripped to the waist, with his high-booted legs apart. The tailored lines of his motorcop breeches clung to his thighs, swelled over his butt, and bulged at his zippered fly.

God! Was I getting material for *Maneuvers*! He was the incarnation of every mighty sexual hero I had ever conjured up in my erotic fiction. He was a vision stroked out of my one-handed study of hundreds of videotapes of bodybuilders. He was theology, literature, myth. He was Adam before the Fall, Billy Budd in full bloom, a male god rising tanned from a blue sea with the vine leaves of a satyr wet in his hair. He was what I had always wanted. "You are," I repeated, showing the proper ritual respect owed to an artist generous in sharing his creation, "perfect."

"You told me," he said to Dan, "that your friend liked muscles." Then he shined right on me. "Your friend," he said, "loves muscles."

"Your muscles. I love your muscles," I said. I had been lost and now I was found. "I love your proportion, your bulk, your definition. I love your symmetry. I love your Look." I could not bring myself to say to these men, that suddenly in my always terrified heart I was a little less afraid of dying which I had been born afraid of. Looking at Kick, I knew that if a Being were to meet me on the other side of the squeeze of Death, that if there were a sweet Jesus, then what must eternal heaven be like, if Jesus only looks this good, and this good feeling infusing my body lasts forever?

The night heated up. Kick stripped in the spotlight. His chest and abs glowed with thick blond hair. Long golden fur fleeced his thighs and calves and feet. He sported the body of a bear. His dick was more than most nylon posing trunks could pouch. We played musclesex until the hour before dawn. Kick posed and flexed under my oiled hands. Something more than sex, something like an understanding, was bonded between us. Dan knelt off in the corner stroke-watching the match he had made. He said later that Kick and I both were like beggars at an ecstatic feast, that we were perfect yin-yang, that gods need worshipers as much as worshipers need gods. I only know that I knelt before Kick for hours, rising up, stroking and sniffing and licking his body, eyeing his face close up, breathing his sweet breath, and for hours he posed, tireless, flexing arms and chest and belly and legs. He encouraged my sexual muscle-rap, following my words with his moves, as if I was scripting a scenario he had waited all his life to hear. We were smiles of a summer night, rising together up to that moment before climax, falling back, savoring the pleasure, rising up again, until our final mutual salute to triumphant masculinity.

Honest manliness is never half-revealed. When it's there, It's total. Roman emperors could have tortured me to Death, and with my eyes upon him, and his gladiatorial smile upon me, I could have been, even at his hands, the most joyous of martyrs.

I knelt in front of him, between him and the mirror, sizing up the perspective of his muscle in the posing light. I had never before been ambidextrous; but I found my right hand reserved for myself. My left, as if for all my life I had been saving a virgin hand for stroking his hard-pumped muscle, palmed the contours of his body. I ran my left hand up his magnificent calves and thighs, not daring to touch his long hard rod for fear the muscle-worship would revert to purely genital sex. His dick was veined as thick and heavy as his arms. I ran my hand up his washboard abs and stopped, flat-palmed, where his belly met his hard rounded pecs. We both dripped sweat. He looked down upon me, and for the first time our eyes locked into an affirmative understanding. He raised his magnificent arms wide, never taking his eyes from mine, and rolled his broad shoulders. My hand on his upper belly felt his pecs harden and his abs tighten. He took a deep breath, and with all his might, flushing red, muscles pumped and veins roped around them, he intensified his look deep into my eyes, and pumped down tight and hard into the Most Muscular pose. His body quivered. Veins corded his massive neck. His jaw line set hard. Heavy streams of sweat poured from his blond hair, down his forehead, around his eyes, along his lantern jawline, and dripped, I want to say like sanctifying grace, down on me. I looked deep into his resolute face. We hung in perfect balance: the adoring worshiping the adored. I knelt in high fealty to his presentation of ideal manhood.

Our eyes locked tighter in an unspoken Energy of understanding. Hours before, we had left Dan behind, watching in amazement from the corner. Then we rose from the room, the mirror, the light, the clock. We moved to another dimension. We rose in that frozen moment to where the only clock was the one heart ticking between us. He held his body in the full locked-down power of his muscle armor. He was as graced with spiritual energy as he was with physical muscle. We were beyond words. My eyes looked hungrily into his, feeding back what he was giving out, circulating his energy back to increase his muscularity, to heighten our intensity, look to look, face to face, soul to soul. If there is a Jesus who meets me at Death, and if His face is to reassure me, then let Him look at least this good, and let that good feeling of that frozen moment be the beatific vision that lasts forever. Inside the moment of our intense look that held no secret from each other, I knew this was no false idol I had before me. At this moment, more than any spent kneeling before the Blessed Sacrament, I experienced true adoration.

"I worship you," my voice said, and my voice was not my voice. Something that belonged to both of us was speaking. "I worship your muscles, your bodybuilder face, your muscleman soul, I worship all men in you. I honor all men in you." I fell into a litany of worship, stroking myself, rising slowly up toward his glorious face, shooting my seed over his veined thighs, and without pause continued on pleasing his insatiable satyr hunger. My pleasure in him pleasured him even more. My energy toward him caused him to pump out more male intensity. I hardened again. He displayed his double-arm shot bringing his Big Guns to full flex. My hand ran up his body and held firmly onto his biceps. I began to pull myself up to his chin. His eyes stared straight ahead into the mirror behind me, and, without touching himself, he shot hot rivers of seed and sweat down my face and chest.

Later, he said, "I felt I was taking all your energy. I usually pose alone. No one's ever followed along so well. I don't want to take anything from you."

I held my palms toward him. "Does a man holding his hand out to a fire ever feel he's giving rather than receiving heat and light?"

I wanted Kick. I wanted him soul and body. Through incarnated muscle, he opened his soul to me, for longer than an instant, and I, through my worshiping words, opened mine to him. We knew nothing about each other; we knew all there was to know. I wanted his spirit. My journey at long last ended. We had both shot in salute to what passed between us. It was not private parts, not crotches, not mere ejaculation, not sexual spasm. It was total whole-body orgasm. I wanted his Being. My homosexual searching had been no more than a physical trek across the geography of men's bodies to find this man's homomasculine essence through the medium of his muscle. With Teddy, at the beginning, when he was so young and tender, I thought I had surrendered, in sweet, sweet surrender to love; but Teddy is a petulant manchild. He maneuvered me into fathering him. Teddy is not grown up enough, not adult enough, not man enough to fuck my soul.

I push on my sweet tooth of Death. Sitting on this plane, flying home, I know I will never see Kick again. He will become one of those nights that on my Deathbed I will remember. Sometimes perfect acts are better not repeated.

We lay in each other's arms with the El Lay dawn already coming in the windows. "Sleep well, my fellow worshiper," he said. He kissed me. "I know," he whispered, "that you know what we know." I buried my face in his neck. He closed his eyes and drifted off. His breath, his slow even breath, in sleep was sweet. I can never thank Dan enough. Nor ever forgive him. Lying last night folded in Kick's huge arms, the thick hair of his chest warm under my left palm, I memorized the moment I know will never come again, and ached with the truth of Teddy still to be dealt with on my return: our life together is an escalating craziness like the speeding wild taxi drive to the plane. If I had missed the flight, last night would never have happened. I know I have to stop Teddy from keeping me from meeting other men. Last night was proof of that. I'll never forget lying in the tousled sheets with Kick, him sleeping, me knowing, with my head on his shoulder and my nose in his blond hair, the fact, the godawful fucking fact that in a finite changing world, no ticket is a round-trip fare. Life is a one-way ride through distraction to oblivion. This man with these muscles in whose arms I felt so shielded was a handsome, distracting way station on a journey I know we all must make alone. I slept and tried to dream that I might die before waking.

11

All I, Magnus Bishop, can say about that is: we all remember what we need to remember. I picked Ryan up at SFO. Teddy stayed home with a petulant headache. Just as well. Nothing steps on an ejected lover's last line like the galloping hoofbeats of his fast-approaching replacement.

"So how was Superman?" I asked.

12

"I know I'll never see him again," Ryan said.

13

One springtime a helicopter high in the Austrian Alps swooped down to find a pretty girl singing about the hills being alive with the sound of music. Thus began one of the most popular musical love stories, told like *Cabaret* against a background of fascism. In another season, a late summer, a helicopter, high above the coastal California hills north of San Francisco, buzzed low along the winding banks of the Russian River, turned and traveled three air-minutes south, hovering over a small Sonoma County ranch. The children in the yard at Bar Nada called their uncle Ryan from the house. He looked up in amazement. "Stay where you are," he told the triplets. He headed out to the rolling pasture. The sun behind the blades of the hovering helicopter blinded him. The noise was deafening. The downdraft whipped the tall field grass into a frenzy around his legs. He stood his ground, shielding his eyes, as the chopper slowly descended from the sky, touching down in a whirl of shimmering grass seed. The door popped open and out jumped the golden man of bodybuilding.

"Your ranch is beautiful from the air." Kick shouted over the roar. "I love you!"

I was visiting Bar Nada that weekend, watching the antics of Ryan's brother and his family. Kweenie was with us and so was Teddy. The full catastrophe. We all gathered on the back deck. The rotors stopped. The pilot stayed in his cab. We watched the two men talk in a far-off pantomime in the middle of the sun-swept field.

"What the hell's that chopper doing here," Thom demanded. He was Ryan's and Kweenie's brother, born between them, but he was nothing like them. "Choppers. I hate choppers. I hate anything that reminds me of Nam."

"Maybe they'll give us a ride," Abe said. He was the single boy in Thom's set of triplets. Ryan's brother was a man of untender mercies. He thought it clever to name the boy and two girls, Abraham, Beatrice, and Siena. Beautiful names on their own, but not if you nickname your triplets, Abe, Bea, and Sie.

"You're not riding in that damn thing," Thom said. He ordered his children like a drill sergeant.

"Thom," Kweenie said to no one in particular, "did two tours in Vietnam. Anything to get away from this family. But two tours, my dears, count them, two! I think that exposed him to twice as much Agent Orange."

Ryan and Kweenie, and even Teddy, ran snide commentary on the family's battering ways, as if they were a TV sitcom, hoping they'd respond to the barbed humor. They poured water on ducks' backs. They insulted Sandy and the triplets to their faces, and mother and kids laughed perversely whether they got the joke or not. They thrived on any attention. Nothing really bothered them because, no matter what was said, their critics were all gay or at least bisexual like Kweenie, and the family's self-inflated trump card was that no matter what the fags and lesbos said, they'd always be queers and dykes, and the family was absolutely, triumphantly straight. "And that," Thom once pronounced, "is where it's at!" What style they had was loud, vulgar, and destructive. I knew Ryan must be dying with mixed emotions out in the pasture. The last thing he would want the perfect Kick to see would be his brother's raucous family, especially Thom's wife Sandy who slouched out to the deck in her housecoat and pink scuffies.

"She's the only woman I know," Kweenie said, "who can violate the dress code at the Kmart."

For almost fifteen minutes, Ryan and Kick talked. Ryan's posture told me all I needed to know. He was dumbfounded. Always he had been the pursuer not the pursued, the lover not the beloved. Well, if God, as Ryan once thought, had called him at the age of fourteen to be a priest, then why couldn't this outrageous blond muscle god descending out of the sky on a golden whirlwind, call him to be his lover?

Teddy, awakened from a nap by the noise, stumbled out to the deck.

"I don't think," Kweenie put her arm around Teddy, "that you're going to like this high-tech pastoral scene."

Sleepily Teddy surveyed the situation. "Oh, shit! He can fly!"

"With no visible means of support," Kweenie said.

"Ry says he's independently well off," I said.

"From what? His home-wrecking business?" Teddy said. "What else has he got that I don't have?" From all Ryan had told him about that night in El Lay, he figured the broad-shouldered blond meant trouble. "What kind of high-wire stunt is this helicopter bit?"

Actually, Kick was more comfortable than well off. His father had given him a stake and he had earned a bundle building spec houses back in Birmingham. He told Ryan he had a degree in architecture. He himself had built most of what he had designed. He preferred to be known as a carpenter by trade.

Solly Blue had laughed under an arched eyebrow. "All that and a face and body too? I want to check out his bank account, his diploma, and his references," he said. "Something everybody should do before they take a lover."

"I think it's fabulous," Sandy lit a Lark. "Only Ry would have such exciting friends. It's like *General Hospital*."

"Shut the fuck up, you dumb bitch." Thom turned on his hapless wife. "I want that chopper off my property."

Teddy, always protective of Ryan, said, "Your property? It's Ry's ranch."

"It's all family," Thom said. "Ry said so when we moved in."

"Ha!" Teddy said. "That's what he tells you. That's not what he tells me. He defers to you. God knows why."

"What's *defer* mean?" Sandy asked no one in particular.

"Because we're family."

"The Snopes were a family," Teddy said. "So were the Jukes and the Kallikaks."

"I knew some Jukes," Sandy said.

"Relatives, no doubt," Teddy said.

"Zip it or I'll clip it," Thom said. "You're not even family."

"I'm his lover."

"You're his whore!"

"Either way," Teddy said, "a man can pick his lovers and his whores, but only God can make a family tree."

"Don't talk X-rated in front of the kids," Sandy said.

"Why not?" Bea said. "You talk worse yourself."

"You little bitch," Sandy said. "Go to your room."

"Bea's not a bitch," Sie said to her mother. "You're the bitch."

"Don't you fucking talk to your mother that way," Thom said.

"You're all three bitches," Abe said.

His two sisters and his mother glared at him like the three hags at the opening of *MacBeth*.

"Thommy, stop them. I won't be abused by my children."

"Want to bet?" Thom said. He thrived on helter-skelter.

"Thommy, you bastard," Sandy said. "Make all three of the little sonsabitches go to their rooms."

"You heard your mother." Thom moved threateningly toward the triplets.

"Where's Diane Arbus when you need her?" Teddy whispered to me. "Maybe I should run on out into the field and invite Mr. Muscles in for a free show. You know, *Genetics on Parade*. The war hero and his adoring All-American family. If I have to fight fire with fire, I might as well get serious. Next to these people, the Borgias were a nice Catholic family. Ry coached me for four years so I could stomach them for more than five minutes. Now I'm supposed to find them amusing. When," he huffed, "have I ever done what I'm supposed to?"

Ryan had adroitly moved Kick around so his broad back was to the deck. He had bought this place in the country for quiet romantic weekends. Don't ask how Sgt. and Mrs. Thomas a'Beckett O'Hara and family moved in one foggy night and took up residence. Ryan was always a soft touch. He was the oldest, and his father, as he lay dying had asked him, exactly like the movies, to take care of his younger brother and sister.

"Obviously, we are not," Kweenie said, "the family Von Trapp." She poked me in the ribs. "You're such a silent observer, Magnus. A Quaalude for your thoughts."

"If Ry's as good a talker as I know he is, that helicopter will be taking off very soon," I said.

"But will my sweet brother get what he wants?" Kweenie said. "I don't normally dig muscle types, but that face! Leave it to Ry. Whatever Ryan wants, Ryan usually gets. I only hope he's careful. I'm the voice of experience. All extremely gorgeous people hustle in their own way." She pulled me into her warm bosom. "Including *moi!*"

I held her, looking through her hair, that was henna red that weekend, at the longshot of the two men in the pasture. Kick put his arm around Ryan's shoulder and together they walked to the waiting copter. The pilot revved up the engine. They hugged the way straight men hug: they embraced and their chests touched briefly, but their hips stayed almost shyly apart. Kick stood for a moment on the step. He was the very picture of the noble savage sprung from the dusty backwoods of Alabama, the golden athlete raised on shit-kickin' southern music, coming of age listening to the Allman Brothers while he humped Miss Alabama in the backseat of his red Mustang convertible.

As the copter rose into the bright sky, I watched Ryan stand solitary, looking up, at the glorious, noisy, straight-up ascension that defied the bounds of gravity. In my arms, Kweenie turned to watch the grand exit. "What do you think?" I asked.

"I don't know," she said. "Play it as it lays. I think Ry wants to be swept away. He doesn't even know this is already too good to be true. And neither of us, Magnus, will spoil it for him. Let him enjoy it. For now, what is, is. When I did *Carousel,* there's this song at the beginning: 'What's the Use of Wondrin'?' You know, like wondering if your last reel will be sad, wondering if you should quickly break it off and run away now, before the ending, but you know you can't, because he's your own true love, and that's that."

The helicopter swooped off south toward the City and connected Kick back to LAX. Ryan stood for a long time in the field watching the sun-raked distance into which the man who said he loved him had disappeared.

14

Ryan was captive of a secret promise.

He had fled his family in the Midwest, but first Margaret Mary and then Thom had followed him to California. For twelve years, their father had struggled through a death-defying illness. His agonized lingering terrified Ryan. He recognized his father's decaying body as his own Death threat sent from someone, sent from somewhere. In the tenth year of his sickness, and after his twenty-first major surgery, Ryan's father held onto his eldest son's hand and said, "Take care of them all for me." Charley-Pop meant his wife, Annie Laurie, and he meant his young daughter Margaret Mary. "But especially," and he was very clear, "take care of Thom. No one knows like I do how much help your brother needs." He squeezed Ryan's hand. "A father knows," he said. "Promise me, Ry." He looked directly into Ryan's eyes.

This was it, Ryan knew: his father after this long fight was admitting Death, was letting Death waft like a small breeze in through a door he was slowly opening. If his father died, there would be no male generation left between him and his own Death.

"Ry?" Charley-Pop said, and he held his son's hand tenderly, "you don't have to say anything. I know what you'll do. You're the man in the family now."

Ryan wanted to say, "I'm the faggot in the family, dad." But he knew, whether his father knew or not, that for all that he was no less a man. For ten years, he had taken care of his sister and his mother, and, in a warmly affectionate way, his father. Thom, with his mercenary heart, was always gone, killing time in one military installation after the other. Thom fought the war in Nam. Ryan fought against the war in the streets, always coming back to his father's bedside, sometimes at home, more often in the intensive care unit of Saint Francis Hospital.

Every visit back introduced Ryan to some new horror of modern medicine. This time, the time of the promise, his father lay motionless, gaunt, in the crisp white bed. His blood circulated through clear dialysis tubes. The pleasant nun in attendance walked Ryan out to the hall explaining that dialysis was really like a giant washing machine. "It's my father's blood, not his laundry," Ryan said. "I'm sorry." He apologized quickly, thanked the sister, and walked down to the end of the long terrazzo corridor. He had in this hospital his fill not of the nuns, but of the priest, their chaplain, who one bloody night, when Ryan discovered his father unconscious and hemorrhaging alone in his room, told Ryan, that God must want another Saint Charles in heaven. Ryan had grabbed the startled priest by the lapels of his black suit: "My father is going to live!" It was probably the first time the priest had ever been told to fuck himself. After that the chaplain confined his ministrations to Annie Laurie. Ryan could not mind that. For his mother, priests provided her only consolation. Ryan wondered what she really thought about his leaving Misericordia Seminary the year before his own ordination to the Catholic priesthood.

The hospital was in a continual state of remodeling and reconstruction. The old wing where Thom and Margaret Mary had both been born was, in the last days of that Illinois June, nearly leveled by the wrecker's ball. "For ten years," Annie Laurie said, making conversation in waiting rooms, "they've been rebuilding the hospital around us." Ryan paced the length of a corridor that ended abruptly where the wrecking crew had stopped for the day. The gutted hall glowed with the dark luster that happens before a Midwestern twilight. At its western end, huge swaths of opaque plastic sheets billowed inward from the updraft. The broken lip of the hall floor stopped abruptly six stories from the hard ground. The hospital was suffocating him. He could feel the barometer falling. He knew if he climbed over the lath and plaster debris, and through the plastic, he could stand on the ledge of a hall that had once led to obstetrics. No one was around to stop him. A construction worker's sandwich sat abandoned on an improvised two-by-four of a table. No nurses or nuns hovered around this drafty end of deserted corridor. Far down the hall, behind him, he watched them, kind women, starchy and white, sailing silent through the pools of light at their main station.

He climbed through the dust and plaster shards. He needed to be anywhere no one could find him. A hospital has no privacy. He needed air. He needed to remember to breathe. He needed great gulps of air. The ragged concrete ledge ended with snaggled rebar twisted by the powerful wrecking ball. He stood on the narrow ledge, six stories above the rubble below. He leaned back against the plastic. The rising wind flapped its edges around his legs. From the high ledge in the hospital on the high hill, he could see for miles across the rolling prairies. A heavy June thunderstorm was moving in over the flat skyline of Peoria. The air was violet. Lightning flashed. He knew how to read Midwestern summer storms. He counted the seconds from the lightning until the thick roll of thunder rumbled from the western farmlands and across the city. Every second between lightning and thunder told how far he was from the center of the storm.

At first flash, he counted to nine. Minutes later, between flash and thunder, he counted to six. His breath grew shorter. The rain was moving in a curtain toward him from the west. He counted to three. Lightning and thunder were almost one. The first rush of rain blew up under the overhang of the corridor above him. Mist sprayed his face. The plastic beaded up with moisture. His hands and back pressed flat against the wall. The storm swept up in a rising vortex in front of him. The falling pressure took his breath away. He was crying, for the first time in a long time, really crying. The downpour was soaking his corduroys and madras shirt, and no one was around anymore to tell him to please come in from the rain. For the duration of the storm's passing front, he stood facing whatever wild energy of lightning and thunder the twilight could conjure. "I'll invoke any god," he pleaded.

For the first time with any real clarity, he saw through the rain into the past, into his dying father's past, into the past whose history until this moment had been lifeless as the three paragraphs in the *Jackson County Register* of 1904: the wife of Michael Fitzpatrick O'Hara had been killed in a Minnesota cyclone. But the statistic was far less than the jolting vision he had of his grandfather's first wife standing at the top of the storm-cellar stairs, holding their ten-month-old Aurelia in her arms, her long golden hair fallen loose and flying in the wind, shouting for her two young sons to run to her in the shelter. His grandfather started up the thick wooden stairs. He was knocked flat by the gust of wind that sliced a piece of flying sheet metal clean through his young wife's neck. Her face, shrouded by her flying hair, showed no surprise. Only her arms reacted, pulling her baby in close to her breast, then straightening out rigid. The baby fell and was killed in the bloody tumble with her mother's head down the storm-cellar stairs. The confined shelter roared with the blast of the cyclone. His grandfather, then a young man, struggled up against the wind. The suffocating dust turned to mud as rain blew into the cellar across his wife's headless body at the top of the stairs.

Michael O'Hara had not known where to turn. Near his knees, full within his terrified sight, his wife's head rocked back and forth, her hair alive in the vortex. A thin trickle of blood ran from the baby's mouth. His wife's eyes bulged open and unblinking. The cellar door crashed closed. He was in darkness. He felt for the wooden stairs with his hands. They were wet with rain and blood. His two sons in those few seconds that lasted forever had not yet made the cover of the cellar. Then the cyclone lifted the door open and up off its hinges. The pressure sucked him part way up the bloody steps. As fast as it hit, the storm roared off and away. He pulled himself up through the debris. He found his two sons clinging to the branches of the one tree left standing in the devastated farmyard. He had immigrated all the way from Ireland for this, he thought, and pulled his crying sons to himself.

The young widow from the next farm over, her own husband dead two years from typhoid, helped with the burial of his wife and baby. Within the year, in the grand brick Catholic church in the little town of Fulda, Minnesota, they were married quietly by a German priest in a ceremony attended by her three young children and by his two sons. In another year, they had their own child, a son, Ryan's father.

"Promise me," his father had said. He was a child of storms. He was born out of sudden violence that came from the sky, and he was dying by slow degrees. He frightened Ryan the way a person alone in a house is frightened by his own image caught sudden and distorted in a mirror. Like father, like son. What if he himself should become so ill at so early an age? Fear of illness, fear of Death took up nest in his heart. Death depressed him. Maybe the promise, made and kept, could keep sadness and sickness and Death at far away bay. "I promise, Charley-Pop," he said. "I promise I'll take care of them all."

15

"I love you," Ryan wrote in an affectionate note to Kick. "I love us. I've gone beyond being infatuated in-love with you. Funny, I have to get around the way you look so I can love you despite your looks. I'm the man most wished dead on Castro. Guys think I'm all that stands between them and you in their beds. I don't care who either of us plays with on the side. As long as we remember you and I are the home team. I love you more than I've ever loved anyone." And he meant more than family, lovers, friends, life itself.

"I'd die for you," Ryan said.

"Don't die for me." Kick's smile lightened the heat of Ryan's dark passion. "Live for me."

Ryan loved Kick's powerfully positive suggestions, because they came from strength. Ryan had been born depressed. He had been drilled in the *Baltimore Catechism* of negative guilt, that very Catholic spin on things Annie Laurie had used to raise him the way she wanted. "Kenny Baker," so sweetly she said the boy's name, "stayed out past midnight last night." The tone in his mother's voice inferred that Ryan must never stay out past midnight. Neither she nor his father ever ordered his obedience directly. Ryan often bragged about the way his parents had raised him. "They never told me to do anything," he said. "My parents always arranged things so I'd know what I was supposed to do. I was the best little boy in the whole wide world."

When he announced at the age of fourteen that the next school year he wanted to leave home for Misericordia Seminary, his parents, who wanted nothing more in life than to be the greatest thing a Catholic mom and dad can be, the parents of a priest, sat him down for a talk.

"You're not going to become a priest to please us," Annie Laurie said.

In fact, they had raised him from birth to be nothing but a priest. Girls, at worst, were occasions of sin; at best, untouchable. Especially Ryan's classmate, the daughter of his parents' best friends, the apple-cheeked Madonna Hanratty. If ever a schoolgirl in her plaid-skirt uniform were perfect for Ryan, it was Donna whose budding Roman Catholic breasts, cradled in her white linen summer halter, made him think his curiosity about her was mortally sinful. He placed Donna on a pedestal, with a reverence born of terror. She loved him like a brother, but she teased him, experimenting with her own sexual wiles, virginally vamping him, despite Sister Mary Agnes's warnings to her that she not tempt a young man away from his vocation to the priesthood. Ryan had heard about that sinful breed of Catholic woman whose idea of big game is bagging the parish priest. The more Donna teased him, the more frightened Ryan grew about sex and sin and Death; and the more resolute he became in his priestly vocation which was his safe refuge from the mortal sins the nuns and priests warned him were to be found in the eager flesh of young girls.

Ryan, to save his soul, knew he must sacrifice everything worldly. To save his life, which he long sensed was somehow different, to keep his life from dying in a Midwest cow town, he had no choice but to run away from home, the way fourteen-year-old boys ran away from home in the polite fifties. All the way to Misericordia Seminary.

"It's your life," his father said.

"Whatever you want to do," his mother said, "is alright with us, if you're sure."

"But if you're not sure . . ." Charley-Pop was playing devil's advocate. "We think maybe you should wait until after high school."

"High school?" Ryan said. The word embodied everything they had suggested to him was worldly and tempting and bad. They had themselves, high school sweethearts, talked of high school as the place that had stopped their progress dead.

"If Charley-Pop could have gone on to college after high school," Annie Laurie said, "he would never have worked at the dairy. He wouldn't have driven that awful truck for Mid-American."

"I wouldn't be selling washers and driers now," Charley-Pop said. He was proud of the living he made. He was the department store appliance sales-man with the distinctive bow tie, in fashion or out. Customers might forget his name, but they always came back asking for the man with the bow tie. He wanted more for Ryan and Thom.

It was in high school Kenny Baker learned his first year to smoke and drink. "Kenny's gotten too wild for his own good," Annie Laurie said, and she meant for Ryan's own good. He knew she wanted him to drop his friend. It was in high school that Donna Hanratty had gotten pregnant. Ryan was sorrier than his mother when Donna, his Madonna, proved them all right about sin in the flesh of young girls. It was in high school that Kenny Baker's older brother, a short muscular varsity wrestler, was killed during his senior year. He was drunk and speeding and drove his car at three in the morning over the embankment of the new concrete expressway, rolling end over end, thrown finally from the disintegrating car, impaled through his guts on the steel post of the cyclone-mesh retaining fence. Dying, most likely, in a state of mortal sin, while his screaming girlfriend tried to pull him off the post with both of her broken arms.

High school was pagan sex and Death.

"I might lose my vocation if I go to high school here," Ryan said.

His father took him for a ride the Sunday before he was to leave for Misericordia Seminary. "Ry, I want to tell you something," Charley-Pop said. He stopped the '57 Plymouth Belvedere in a turnaround glade on the dusty country road. They sat parked deep in the forest, shaded from the hot September sky. Leaves waved in the soft breeze and made dappling spears of sun motes come and go on the dusty hood of the dark blue car. "When it first happened to me, I thought I was hurt." His father stared straight over the steering wheel and through the windshield. Ryan had no idea what *it* was exactly, but he sensed Charley-Pop leading him into dangerous terri-tory. "I thought something was wrong with me. When it happens to you, I want you to know it's nothing to worry about."

Ryan felt a first peculiar turn of real sexual panic in his stomach. This was worse than all the spiritual fear Madonna had caused. Why was his father, this man whom he loved so much, talking dirty to him? He wanted to es-cape from the car, but in the stifling heat he could not lift his hand to the door handle. Besides, where would he run? They were miles from home. His father would think he was crazy.

Ryan had to stop him. He had to stop the feeling in his stomach. He had to stop the stirring he felt swelling in his loose Bermuda shorts. His cock was uncoiling and it hurt. He did not want the vague pleasure he knew must be the sin of impurity they all feared so much. "I know all about it," he lied. "You don't have to tell me."

Charley-Pop, relieved, put his hand on Ryan's bare knee. Ryan wanted to pull away, but he did not. His young balls ached. Something in him was betraying the long schooling of his purity. The nameless thing he feared late nights in his bed and in the dark of the confessional was here. It filled him with want. It was scary, this thing. It smelled of hell and felt sweet between his thighs. He wanted his father to hold him, tenderly hold him, closer than he ever had before.

Ryan sat stock still. The shadowy thing he wanted with this man, who had been a three-sports star in high school, was not in his father, but was in him only. Whatever it was, Ryan was smart enough to know that. This one-sided ache was more than wanting to be like-his-father when he grew up. This was the first time in his life that Ryan consciously experienced one thing meaning two things. His father's hand on his knee was his father's hand, but it was something else, something Ryan felt in the pit of his stomach, something vague he had no name for, something he did not know even existed, something he would later call passion.

"You don't have to tell me." He lied to his father for the first and last time in his life. "Sister Mary Agnes instructed us boys about what we need to know."

Later that afternoon, Ryan rode out to the Bar-H Stables with Kenny Baker. They squandered four dollars for two hours on two horses to celebrate Ryan's last weekend before leaving for Misericordia.

That final Sunday afternoon, in the early evening, Ryan's rental horse, at the last bend of the return trail, sensing the comfort of the stables, broke into a startling gallop. Ryan was terrified. The horse's pace was too fast for him. He dropped the tied reins to the horse's neck and hung onto the saddle horn with both hands. The horse, taking its head, rounded the curves of the trails, cutting tight under the sticker branches of the low-hanging trees, trying to knock Ryan off its back.

Ryan had been carried at full gallop, scared and weirdly thrilled, holding on for dear life. He had cum involuntarily in his pants.

Five days later, Ryan left home, afraid his accidental ejaculation might have cut him from the state of grace. Fear made his train ride a blur. He arrived in Ohio at Misericordia Seminary, dragging his army-green foot-locker. The cuts and scratches on his arms and face were nearly healed. He went to confession immediately, trying, not too successfully, to explain what had happened. The priest seemed understanding. Ryan was relieved. He was thrilled those first days by the majestic Catholicism of the seminary. The architecture was inspirational gothic, something Ryan later called Misery's reign-of-terror decor. He was fascinated by the forty-foot-tall, nearly naked, bearded, muscular Jesus hanging crucified over the main altar. He liked the side chapel of Saint Sebastian, tied, suffering, stuck with arrows, "stuck with eros," he later said. But it was the huge, handsome Jesus that immediately caught his interest and for ten years held his attention. This Jesus, though Ryan hardly knew it then, was his first lover, and a hard act to follow, unless you were Kick Sorensen.

At Misericordia, Ryan was one of the prettiest of the new class of minor seminarians. Some of the older boys showered him with attentions he refused to understand. He prayed to the huge Jesus to shut impure thoughts from his mind. Fear of hell and love of God combined to keep him steadfastly free from masturbation. He was the epitome of the perfect Catholic altar boy. Thom, I think, was himself always attracted to that in Ryan. Their parents, the nuns, the priests always prodded Thom to follow the good example of his older brother. Ryan hardly noticed that his younger brother, finding Ryan the favored son, began reacting like the prodigal. To Ryan, Thom was a tagalong whom he resented the way the firstborn son often resents the second born, the potential usurper of their parents' affection. Ryan refused to be Thom's hero; Ryan was himself looking for heroes. At Misericordia, he found them in the older seminarians. His friends were always the best of the seminary jocks.

"The better athlete you are on the playing field," Monsignor Linotti said, "the better the priest you'll be." It was the old jock equation men have always made. It sounded good to Ryan who knew, of course, that Monsignor Linotti was right. If Ryan wasn't really a jock himself, he could make up for it by accepting the older boys', the best of the older boys', invitations to go off to the woods to wrestle. Ryan spent every semester tumbling body over body, hugged and held and fighting back, pulling punches and rolling down the ravines to Misery creek that ran into the Olentangy River.

Ryan was a good sport. He wrestled like Ado Annie in *Oklahoma!*

He could rarely best the older seminarians physically, so he topped them with his imagination and his words. He invented a new game: fighting slow-motion the way brawlers sometimes wrestled in the movies. In slow motion, he figured, with his long, lean build, he had a better shot at giving even the huskies a run for their money.

Not until Ryan was eighteen, four years into the seminary, did he begin to realize fully that the rough-and-tumble brawls seemed more like some kind of sex than sport. He wasn't dense. He was pure. He wrestled with their bodies and with his feelings. He was confused. He liked these muscular, older boys. Besides, sin, they had drilled into him, was in the flesh of young girls.

No one had ever said anything about older boys.

Yet a nameless warning hummed in Ryan's vigilant soul. He had a way with words in English and Latin classes, but he had never heard the word *homosexuality;* or, if he had heard it, the word meant nothing he could fathom exactly. Monsignor Linotti tended to speak in abstraction, except for the time before Christmas vacation when he told them all if anyone asked them what time it was in a bus station toilet to kick them in the crotch and run. It hardly seemed charitable to Ryan, but he was nothing if not obedient.

What worried him most was the return of the nameless feeling he had first felt with Charley-Pop. The boy he had it for was David Fahnhorst.

I remember he said it was on an October afternoon of his senior year in Misericordia Seminary high school. He sat with his best friend, the strapping Dave Fahnhorst, who was the captain of that and the president of this, down on a bench overlooking Misery Lake. The feeling he had for Dave Fahnhorst was lodged in Ryan's heart, not yet in his crotch. He was in-love for the first time in his life and in his confusion he did not know it.

"I can't wrestle with you anymore," Ryan said.

Fahnhorst, a big German farm boy from Ottawa, Ohio, looked puzzled. He palmed his hand through his blond crewcut.

"You . . ." Ryan hesitated. He ached for the full hug of Fahnhorst's husky arms.

"I what, Ry?" Fahnhorst's blue eyes pierced Ryan's resolve. Ryan felt suddenly deferential to the big blond jock. Maybe he should forget it. It was nothing. At least it was nothing he had a name for. Except maybe a vague sense of sin. "This," Ryan later said, "was how I got so twisted." His deference gave way, in his young Gemini heart, to resolve to protect his innocence.

"You press against me too much."

"What do you mean too much?"

"I don't know. I mean too hard." He meant Dave Fahnhorst's big German schlong, stiffening in his black chinos, pressed too hard against his belly. But he could not say that then.

"I can't help it." Fahnhorst was mystified. He knew where he was heading and he had thought Ryan hadn't minded. They were planning on being priests together. "We're buddies. I like you."

"I like you too." Ryan thought of Monsignor Linotti's warning against special friendships.

"You're fun." Fahnhorst interlaced the fingers of his big hands together and dropped his clenched hands like one big fist between his spread knees. He bowed his head down and forward. He was himself in-love with Ryan and Ryan, for no reason, was hurting him. "I mean you're so . . . goddam . . . pretty."

"I don't know what you mean." Ryan was too unsophisticated to know that long before young boys know they're gay, they read some lines like Blanche DuBois.

"You're so pretty," Fahnhorst conjugated Ryan's name like an erotic litany he used as a nightly jerk off mantra. "Ry, Ryan, Ryan Stephen, Ryan Stephen O'Hara, you should be a girl."

There was that dreaded line again. Ryan fled from the bench at the lake. He thought something was wrong with him if he caused those feelings in another boy. When Ryan told me this, years later, he said, "In those days, I didn't want to be an occasion of sin for anyone. Now I write pornography for men to jerk off to. Can you believe I was once that pure?" I could believe it. Ryan of God had a will of iron. When he refused to recognize the first bud of homosexuality in himself, he was honest in his ignorance. He was not feigning like *Agnes of God:* "*What* baby?" When he was committed to something or someone, he went all or nothing. He became what they wanted. I think that's what made Ryan give himself up completely to Kick. Ryan was a chameleon. Most gay boys are. It's survival. He was eager to please. He became whatever people wanted. An astrologer told him that adaptability was characteristic of Geminis: to find what somebody else's trip is and give it to them in spades. That's what he did, if not for Dave Fahnhorst, then for Kick Sorensen. He was fully what he was when he was dedicated to what he was doing. When he was a Catholic seminarian, no boy was more holy.

"Dave Fahnhorst loved me," Ryan said, "and I was too pigheaded pure to let him. I denied myself everything. I never even masturbated until I left Misericordia when I was twenty-four. Stop laughing! I didn't want to go to hell. I really believed all that stuff. Priests never tell you that masturbation is the main way to maintain your center."

When later he began his promiscuous search for the perfect man, the man selected for audition in his bed became for that night the only man in the world. Hoping each next man would be the right one, Ryan gave every man he met the benefit of the doubt.

It was a gift Kick would enjoy to full advantage.

Perhaps, and this is Magnus Bishop talking, the only curse on liberated homosexuality is the all-too-easy access openhearted men give one another to their homes, their bodies, their hearts, and their souls. It's an innocent trust, this belief in the homofraternity among men whose preference is each other. It's an incurable irony, more terminally dangerous than disease, that this gay innocence continues to exist, so frequent and so many are its betrayals.

"Men should make love at the baths," Solly Blue said. "Never take anyone to your lovely home."

16

Kick was clever. On his visits to San Francisco, he purposely moved a heartbeat slower than all of madcap Castro. He drawled when he talked. He moseyed when he walked. His style was an appealing mix of down-home redneck and southern gentleman. His gray Crimson Tide tee shirt with ALABAMA screened in red across his broad chest said it all. He was Bama-Alabama. He was an original: more archetype than stereotype and certainly no cliché. He was no Castronaut. He brought Ryan, who was speeding on fire in the fast lane, to a grinding halt. Kick was virtue on the prowl. The boys on the Castro sidewalks parted like Kick was Charlton Heston and they were the Red Sea. He had no eyes for them. He had come to the City for Ryan. Slowly, deliberately, he began to coach Ryan onward toward a pristine manliness that Ryan feared he had betrayed in himself with too many cheap tricks and cheaper thrills. Before Kick, Ryan had been the Wife of Bath. With Kick, he became Caesar's wife. Or at least the emperor's new, uh, lover.

"Castro's the place where," Kick said, "you can see men do to themselves things you hoped you'd never see men do to themselves."

Kick set off an alarm in Ryan. He pierced the veil of the Castro. He saw things and said things. Ryan thought him a seer and a sayer. He marveled that the bodybuilder and he thought so much the same. "Sometimes I think," Ryan said, "you can read my mind." Kick had an edge. He had known of Ryan O'Hara long before Ryan had ever heard of Kick Sorensen. Kick had read Ryan's writing in *Maneuvers*. He read the lines and he read between the lines. He figured he knew Ryan. Kick had something to say. He wanted Ryan to say it. He was too reserved to blow his own horn. He wanted Ryan to articulate the meaning of his muscular body.

He was more than meat.

He was a sculptor.

He needed an agent.

His plan seemed simple. Until that first El Lay night when the *click* between them turned Kick around to something, well, more personal. He suddenly felt silly as a starlet pursuing a press agent. He suddenly felt like Arnold Schwarzenegger falling for Woody Allen. Never wanting to do the right thing for the wrong reason, Kick had descended by helicopter on Ryan. He had planned to confess, "I set out to use you, but instead, I love you." When he opened his mouth, he said simply, "I love you." If he had said, "I wanted to use you," Ryan would have said, "You can use me till you use me up." But he hadn't and the fast bloom of their relationship surprised them both.

"Nobody," Kick said, "has ever treated me better than you. You surprise me. You understand me. I've never allowed anyone in so close to me."

The ongoing suspense of Kick gradually revealing his magnificent self excited Ryan. One evening before sex, one of the few times in their three years together when they went somewhere other than to bed, they attended *Evita.* Ryan placed his hand on Kick's muscular arm when Patti LuPone, playing the thrill-seeking Eva Peron, sang about the Argentine peasants to her Magnus Bishop, Mandy Patinkin's Che: "They must have excitement, and so must I!" Kick was the hero of a hundred tricks, a thousand faces, a million revelations to hear Ryan tell it.

"Almost every night," Ryan wrote to Kick, "we conjure this thing, this power, the Entity between us, and we never lose ourselves."

Kick wrote back on stationery with the letterhead of *The Daily Planet.* "You're the most fun I've ever had."

Ryan glowed.

Appearing nightly in his bed was the man all of San Francisco wanted in the sack.

Kick equaled Ryan in his twists on musclesex. Kick liked bondage, not so much the constraint as the drama. He liked the mythological feel of his muscle against ropes and chains and leather. He could have been a muscle-bondage centerfold for *Maneuvers,* but Ryan advised him against sex modeling if he wanted to compete without compromise in physique contests.

They played nights of heroic bondage sculpture, starring Kick as Prometheus Bound and Hercules Chained. "I'm bound in muscle," he confessed to Ryan. "You of all people can understand what bodybuilders really say when they talk muscle. *The ropes of muscle coiling around my body. The veins corded around the muscle.* Nothing turns me on more. I like exhibition of muscle sweating and straining against chains and rope and leather straps." Kick peeled back another layer of himself. "But when you look the way I do, there's a curse on the gift. Everybody always wants me to tie them up and treat them like shit. I'm not into degradation sex. I'm into heroic celebration sex."

Ryan understood. Kick needed a man to tie him up. Bondage was one of Ryan's favorite sexsports. A fetish Kick knew from the pages of *Maneuvers.* For their first Christmas, Ryan ordered an industrial-weight latex rubber bodysuit with hood tailor-made for Kick. Complete with hands and feet, the one-piece black suit covered Kick's body and helmeted his head inside the full hood with mouth and nose and eye holes. A heavy zipper ran up Kick's back from the base of his spine to the top of his blond head. Skin-tight layers of black latex encased his sculpted body. His long, thick blond dick pointed erect and hard through the black-rubber cockring in the crotch. His balls hung big and low. Completely encased in rubber, Kick posed intensely: thick black latex pecs, abdominals treaded like tires, biceps big as baseballs, thighs and calves hard as pilings. His bulk was so defined each muscle flexed distinctly. Abstracted by the beautiful sheen of black latex, he was a massive, beautiful chunk of rippling black-rubber sculpture, a blond man transmorphed to a dark angel, posing and flexing his wide-winged lats, sculpted to life by the rubbing, stroking, warming of Ryan's adoring hands.

Watching Ryan's Latex Videotapes, I sense a kind of necrophilia, as if Ryan were courting a muscular, black, inexorable Death. He was almost Bergmanesque finding love and Death and the whole damn thing in the sweating black-sheathed body of a blond Scandinavian.

Solly Blue, who was always a sage, was closer to Ryan. "Of course," he said. "Ryan's always been half in love with easeful Death. It's a writer's romanticism. Writers need to be depressed to write. At least good writers. That's why they all kill themselves one way or another. At least American writers."

When Ryan's friend, Hank Diethelm, the owner of the Brig, the most popular leather bar South of Market on Folsom, was tied spread eagle in his own basement, strangled, bludgeoned, and set afire by a casual trick, I accompanied Ryan to the memorial service at the Neptune Society's classic Columbarium on Loraine Court behind the Coronet Theater on Geary Street. The once-glorious edifice, having survived the 1906 earthquake, had fallen with the ravages of time and neglect and grave robbers to a cold

Wordsworthian ruin during the 1930s until restoration began in the late 1970s.

Men, accustomed to meeting at bars and baths, gathered at the massive bronze door in small groups unsure exactly what to do. Death was new to them. This was the first grand gay funeral. "At least he doesn't have to grow old," they whispered. The majority of the mourners wore full leather gear. They were Folsom Street men, good-looking and gruff, a decade or two older than the boys on Castro. Leather for them was an attractive saving grace. Leather transformed aging bodies. Leather was tighter and smoother than skin. Leather cinched and corseted and disguised bodies which rarely, if ever, darkened the iron-pumping, designer-muscle gyms on Castro. Leather was a fetish that extended a mature man's sex appeal for another dozen years.

"Can you believe it?" Ryan whispered to me during the service. "We're witnessing a whole new gay phenomenon." He pointed to a row of bearded men in full black leather wiping the dark circles under their eyes with red bandanas. Their grief was real. Ryan was not so cynical as to be blind to that. Death was bad enough, but premature Death at the hands of a murderer was almost more than he could bear.

Liberated life in San Francisco had become in too many sorry ways a serial Death sentence indeed. Murderers found gay men easy prey. Their bodies all too frequently turned up stuffed into barrels in Golden Gate Park and in dumpsters South of Market. Drugs took their toll in overdoses. The occasional suicide was inevitable. However it was Death rode into the City, nothing stopped the party. Death in the early days was considered no more than bad taste. It took Dan White's assassination of Harvey Milk to make gay Death seem real, but even Harvey's Death, when everyone was young and healthy, seemed no more than a fluke of politics.

Ryan wrote, in an unpublished manuscript dated Monday, November 27, 1978, the day of the assassination:

Castro could hardly regard Dan White objectively. They knew no more about him than the way he was the November morning he took his gun in hand. Murder is the ultimate passionate act. I saw Dan White box his last Golden Gloves fight, three days before he turned thirty. He was tough, cocky, aggressive. Brooks Hall at the Civic Center was filled with cops and firemen. White had been a fireman before he had been a cop. Once on either force, always on both forces. The traditional rivalry between the police and fire departments jelled into a mutual cheering as their Danny Boy punched the lights out of his opponent. The referee had to pull him off the other fighter several times, sending him to a neutral corner to cool down. Always the beefy young White tore back to ring center, jabbing, punching, pounding. He was determined to win his last fight. He was determined to show his stuff to the cheering crowd of his department buddies. He was tougher than Rocky. He was meaner than an amateur fighter need be. Head bent, advancing, going for the kill, he was determined to crown his Golden Gloves career with a final victory. He had a passion for confrontation, the more public, the better. Sweat and blood flew with his last punch. He flattened his opponent and stood dancing and jabbing over his prostrate body for the count. "He murdered the guy," they all said.

I remember a Dan White no one else seems to remember, his arms raised in victory, with the crowds screaming pleasure at his win, which seemed to me more like a kill. I remember his passion as he danced around the ring, dripping sweat and blood, touching his gloves to the outstretched hands of the cops and firemen who stormed the ropes to touch their champ.

Dan White had passion.

I think Dan White had more real passion in his trigger finger than there is in most of the drug-hard cocks at the baths. Harvey was a victim of whatever White's passion was, and if this is not too simplistic, it was that, besides all his political reasons, he was murdering in Harvey Milk the very homosexuality he needed to murder in himself. Anyone who saw Danny White box could see he was a driven man.

Whatever White's real motive, Harvey Milk was dead, and in Death he became larger than life, something that did not happen to White's other victim, Mayor George Moscone. Suddenly everyone loved Harvey. Suddenly gay liberation had a martyr. Harvey's beatification as a saint drained some of the sorrow. He seemed like the first gay person ever to die and in dying he had transcended spiritually.

Castro was never a street of sorrows. Harvey was not dead a month before a story, recounted with the kind of gay hilarity that laughs even at Death, made the rounds of the bars and br%ncheries: how some of Harvey's mourners snorted coke on the sailing sloop hired to spread his ashes over the Pacific waters outside the Golden Gate. The punch line was that several stoned mourners, as the gossip escalated into a joke and the joke became an urban legend, had gone all the way and snorted carefully laid out lines of Harvey's ashes.

I think you must remember that to gay men everything is a joke.

It has to be.

Otherwise, their lives would be unbearable.

Why else would shops on Castro make small fortunes selling Generic Blues tee shirts saying, "Don't cry for me, San Francisco"?

Death, in Ryan's stories, was erotic, heroic, tempting, beautiful. As much as bodybuilders were the life force, they were angels of Death, escorts of the dying; repeatedly, like Tennessee Williams' Christopher Flanders in *The Milk Train Doesn't Stop Here Anymore,* they hold out their strong arms to guide the cleansed soul directly into the muscular eternal embrace of God's Big Daddy arms.

Stuffed in a torn-out centerfold from *Blueboy Magazine*, February 1977, was a sheet of stationery from the Cabana Sands Motel in Venice Beach dated before Ryan had met Kick. On it, Ryan had written words that seemed to have sprung from the vision he saw in the centerfold pictures of the sexy young model, whose name was Roger, and whose face and body, all muscles and tousled hair, glistened with the kind of sun-sweat young men sweat only on Southern California beaches.

CABANA SANDS MOTEL. Death? I'll know Death. I'll be seated somewhere hot and bright, squinting painfully toward the beach, trying to clear my vision which movielike will have become all blurred about the edges, and I shall want to clear my sight to resume my sweating cool glass of Perrier and I'll look up.

He will be there. Suddenly. Unexpected. Waiting. Turned in upon himself. Leaning back against the white stucco wall. His body tanned, stripped to the waist, wearing those long white nylon beach trousers that will cling wet to his thighs, wet from his healthy sea-sweat, from a plunge in the sea. A white sweatband will coil his dark hair. His face will be turned down toward his white transparent crotch, the drawstring opening a V-shaped area of winter-white skin above his cock which will be hard and held covered in his right hand. His left hand will hold out the drawstrings to slow the slide of his clinging wet pants down his strong cyclist's thighs.

He is very muscular: arms, shoulders, chest, legs. He has a black moustache which, with the curl of hair over the white sweatband, obscures seductively his perfect dark face. But I know him. I know that boy, who in the village is called Roger. I know that when he looks up, finally, from his crotched hand, across the distance to my eyes, that he will be beautiful, that he will lift my heart, sweet savior, right out of me, and carry me up into the brightness and light and heat of the sun, and my eyes will pain no more.

Death is no less than the brightness and heat burning in a young man's body.

Then I'll learn the secret some of them know, those golden ones, running from a Castro bar to a waiting Mercedes or a slick Ford truck, hair styled and washed, jeans or slacks, perfect, and somehow all the same, because they know the secret, and they're not telling, not these perfect golden boys who traffic only among each other, signaling their secret to pick each other up at bars, to ball each other at the baths, to lounge together weekends on the Russian River and months on end in Laguna Beach and Palm Springs.

Solly Blue refuses to go out anymore where the boys with the secret hang out, "Because," he says, "they only make me feel bad." The way someone who thinks he's an insider feels when he discovers he's an outsider, because no matter how far in you make it, there's always a still more intimate, precious, charmed circle. Not all gay men are created equal. Cocks to karma. Maybe I'm not a nice person. Maybe I'm jealous because the boys with the secret always remain twenty-seven, lean and muscular and hairy and hot. I'm now thirty-four. Solly's thirty. Why do we think they've sold their souls for some transitory, skin-deep beauty? Are multiple Polaroids of Dorian Gray stuck aging up in the otherwise empty closets?

The new liberated species seems everywhere. They come and they go, I'm sure, like flowers for a season. They have first names but no last. They have phone numbers, best written in pencil, and no addresses. I see them on Castro Street and think of them; but not seeing them, I do not think of them. Individual boys can move out of town or die, and I'd never know, because it's only in seeing them that they are there. Not seen, individually they do not exist. Not seen, only the general memory of them provokes in me not an aching jealousy, but an aching desire to penetrate to the heart of their secret hyper-gay fraternity.

Will Death reveal the secret? Will Roger, hoisting me to heaven by flap of his muscular wings, whisper to me the secret I know he, behind the muscle of his body armor, conceals? Will the brightness and light become so light and bright that in a flash I will see what, in spite of careful observation of everything in my life, I have somehow missed? I know I am missing something. In all that light will I finally see? Where is the handsome bodybuilder who will coach me, who will take my hand, and, leading me toward the only vocation I want, leading me toward perfect manhood, smile at me, shine on me, and say to me, "Follow me."

Such, in the years before Kick, with Teddy around his neck, was Ryan's idealized, aching desire. Through all his adolescence, he had studied older boys and young men, not knowing what it was he wanted with them anymore than only to be like them when he grew up. Now he was grown, newly moved to San Francisco to pursue the secret, and he felt betrayed. No man, no shaman priest, and no coach, not even his father, had ever taken him in hand and explained to him how it is that an American boy grows to American manhood. He had trusted they would and they had not. They had not confided the secret passage some boys seem to know as naturally as they pull on their virgin jockstraps at thirteen.

In his first two years in the City, Ryan had not yet written anything erotic. He had left university teaching in Chicago to work as a technical writer for a large corporation in the Financial District. He had slept his way into his job at Glass Tower Engineers. He thought it was cute at the time. He had met the man who became his boss at Dave's Baths, and for a time his boss had been a sometime lover. Then Teddy had conjured up Evil Teddy and caused a scene and the man had grown angry and made life at the office miserable for Ryan. He wanted Ryan to quit. But Ryan would not.

At night, exhausted by nine hours' writing of engineering proposals on nuclear-waste repositories, Ryan lay awake moaning in his rooms, not exactly feeling sorry for himself as much as wondering vaguely if all people crawled off alone in the darkness to anguish over reasons outside their control, feeling some big mistake, if not some big joke, lay in his not belonging here, having never been consulted, plunked down on this planet, belonging somewhere else.

He had to defy gravity.

He had to gain altitude.

He had to fly.

He had the Golden Gate blues.

He told Solly on the phone he never meant to cry, but each night as he lay down in his bed the water table of sorrow tilted inside him, his body quaking, life having ticked off another day at the Glass Tower, another day toward his Death, making him, in those long minutes between Valium and sleep, making him a thousand years old. He plodded through the day at his desk editing engineering reports that raped the environment. "This work is unnerving. It's immoral. I'm working on Department of Defense contracts for nuclear-waste repositories on Indian reservations. Sometimes I envy window dressers. You know: faggots who get to do something pretty during the day. I mean creative. Like carpenters."

By night, he began to write pornography. "I'm overheated and under-ventilated. I've got to defuse myself somehow. I write with my dick in my hand."

"You've put in three years," Solly said. "You should get some time off for good behavior."

"My boss thinks good behavior is letting him suck me off."

"Why don't you quit?" Solly asked.

"Who would feed Teddy?"

After sundown his mind picked up speed.

Teddy holed up in another room. Ryan refused to sleep with him until he found a job. Ryan regretted his refusal, but he stuck to it. He missed the fa-miliar cuddle of their night's sleep. "Doesn't anybody ever stay together anymore?" He tried strangers, but found nothing worse than an alien in bed. No one but Teddy knew exactly how to sleep with him, back-to-belly, turning belly-to-back in some perfectly natural horizontal choreography. His bed was empty. He needed Teddy more than he wanted him. He needed excitement. He needed the sunny balance of somebody physically athletic, an upbeat sportfucker who suffered none of the *mondo depresso* soul-searching that plagues writers inspired by anhedonia.

Teddy I thought even more sorrowful than Ryan. Neither of them could enjoy normally pleasurable experiences. How can straight parents, clueless, guide their little children who are not straight?

"Teddy's sadness," Ryan said, "is superficial. Like a cartoon of sadness. Maybe Teddy's my real mirror. Maybe that's why we can't stand each other these days. We're exactly alike. We're both jokes."

Ryan invited Teddy back to his bed. Out of all the quarrels and venom, they still had one thing going for them, the thing that had brought them together at the Gold Coast bar in Chicago: as long as they didn't talk, they were good in bed. "That's the solution," Ryan said, "sex partners should never speak outside the sack." They were mutually convenient.

Teddy was a red-haired boy. He was not a man. "I don't love you," Ryan said to him. They were on their first scouting trip to El Lay. Ryan had insisted on staying at the Cabana Sands near Muscle Beach. They lay side-by-side on a blanket in the sand. The ocean was as blue as the sky. A low surf rolled idly toward their feet. This was the first time they had taken acid together. Teddy had tears in his eyes. "You're so goddam manipulative," Ryan said. "You can cry on cue."

"You're the only one who makes me cry."

"I'm the only one who does anything, everything, for you. Food, lodging, tuition, plane tickets. Your teeth. You've got the price of a new VW in your mouth."

"It was all your idea to make me into something."

"So become something. Anything. Be yourself. Get a job. Stop hiding out in me."

"I can't. I'd be a bum, an alcoholic. I'd be dead if it weren't for you."

"I wanted to love you more than anyone or anything in the world." Ryan could not bear the tears streaming through the Coppertone on Teddy's freckled skin. "Don't cry," he said. There was a long silence between them; they had lived together for three years; they would continue to live together for five more. "You cry too easy." Ryan reached for Teddy's hand, and would not let him pull away. "Listen," he said. "Forget it. Okay? It's not me. It's the drug talking."

Later that afternoon they made furious love.

Many nights of their last year together, Teddy cruised out to trick. Left alone in the Victorian, Ryan could not bear to go out. "My aura's too sad." He tried making solitary love to himself, finding some semblance of God in his cuming, finding the blinding amyl-nitrite vision that God is what you jerk off to, that what you see when you're cuming is God, only God will be more so, because He will last longer, and passing over into Death will be to slip into the vortex of holy orgasm forever. Aching to have a life before dying, Ryan rehearsed his dying nightly, cuming often with tears streaming down his face for the sweet sad joy of understanding nothing at all.

"Orgasm," Kweenie said, "is Ry's cure for the blues. Too bad it's not working."

"All I live for is to cum," Ryan said. "Everything in between is intermission."

Insomniac, Ryan walked from room to room chasing the ghosts he had brought to his old Victorian. At Misery, he had received all the minor holy orders of the Catholic priesthood. He was an ordained exorcist. He pursued phantoms in the night. Men were his only distraction and they weren't good enough. He entered rooms for no reason. He left rooms for no reason. He turned on both televisions to different channels. He switched on the radio, all the lights, the four burners on his small Wedgewood stove, and the oven. He ran the faucets in the kitchen and bathroom sinks. He turned on the shower, and listened for the gas water heater to kick on. He plugged in the blender and the Hoover upright vacuum cleaner and left them roaring in place. He turned on his new electric typewriter. "It's better to light one candle than curse the darkness." His house roared with sound and glowed with light signifying next to nothing. The gas wall-furnace burned blue and orange near an open window. His reel-to-reel tape deck pounded out heavy rhythms. He lit a candle in front of Teddy's picture. The face of the red-haired, moustached boy flickered between a stuffed deer head and a staring fox fur Ryan had rescued from the Saint Vincent de Paul Thrift Shop. Wandering naked through his booming, blazing house, he threw himself on top of his electric blanket and lay, in the days before video, watching slow-motion Super 8 movies of bodybuilders thrown up against his wall in heroic poses, projected the way he preferred his men, three times larger than life. If the house was empty, he would give it the illusion of fullness. He was his own high-tech poltergeist. He haunted himself. His utility meter spun in expensive circles. "Everything in the house is turned on—except me."

He had only himself to exorcize.

Teddy told me once how it had been between them in the last screaming weeks of their relationship.

I think, and this is only my casual observation, that when men go against the norm and love each other, they love each other somehow more intensely, precisely because the world is against them, and when that intense love ends, its passion becomes enormous rage, at each other, and at themselves, for making the straight world seem right and them seem wrong.

Teddy and Ryan pushed and pulled at each other until quarreling and clinging slipped past bickering and bitching into knock-down-drag-out wrestling and fist fights, followed by cold silences and colder apologies.

"I was afraid to leave him," Teddy said. "You don't know how safe I felt with him. He can make you feel like the most wonderful guy in the world. I wish we could have been together forever. Or at least together the way we were back in the Midwest. Back before he insisted we move to San Francisco. He packed up everything. Including me. He told me I could go or stay. He told me he wanted me to go with him. I think he was afraid to move all the way to the west coast by himself. For myself, I figured that time with him was better than time without him. He used to say that to me, back there, that time with me was better than time without me. We weren't in California even a year before the opposite was true. He got along fine without me. As long as he wasn't depressed. As long as it wasn't night and dark. As long as he could get to sleep."

The stoicism of the betrayed had hardened Teddy's face.

"I was good enough for Ry until we moved out here. Then I wasn't good enough. He told me I was keeping him from meeting the people he needed to relate to. I don't know how. He was relating, if you get my meaning, to three guys a day. Like he had a quota. Like he was keeping score. Like he was auditioning guys for some part only he knew about."

I must tell you: when Ryan lived with Teddy in the Midwest, even before they moved to California, they flew the Great Gay Bermuda Triangle of SFO to LAX to NYC. "When you're gay," Ryan explained, "travel is cheap. Someone's always inviting you to stay. You find yourself admitted into circles that otherwise, without money or name, you'd never access." He laughed. "But you have to be hot and good in bed."

On the leather circuit, especially with the attractive, laggard Teddy in tow for three-ways, Ryan was in play. His new face in town, his fast repartee, and his aggressive sexual kinkiness opened doors to him I've only read about in *People.* In the sixties, Ryan had known nearly everyone worth knowing in the big-league designer and pop-art sets in Manhattan. He spent time at Warhol's Factory. He skipped teaching his university summer classes for two days one June, dismayed that Warhol had been shot, standing side-by-side with art critic Mario Amaya. Ryan himself felt wounded, reading the newspaper accounts of bullets entering flesh he knew intimately. Vivid in his mind forever after was the image of the elevator doors of the Factory opening, revealing Valerie Solanas, the proto-feminist founder of SCUM, the Society for Cutting Up Men, gun in hand, shooting down in surprise attack the man she told police had too much power over people. Poor Mario, discussing art, was caught in the fusillade.

Two days later, Sirhan Sirhan put Bobby Kennedy's anguished face on the front page: his head, cradled in his wife's arms, oozed life across the tiled kitchen floor of the Ambassador Hotel in El Lay. Warhol's headlines were bumped in fifteen minutes to a small update and quickly buried.

Both events gave Ryan his first real taste of bicoastal urban terror. Coupled with his father's saga of illness, he felt more mortal than ever.

"Anyway," Teddy continued, "Ryan had all these guys coming and going in and out of him and the house. He was very San Francisco. Tricks fed his ego. But nothing ever satisfied him. He always wanted more; and more was never enough. I figured he had over nine thousand guys during the eight years we were together. He probably came with them all. He only needed me for fill-in sex. You know what I mean, Magnus? The kind of affection old lovers have for each other when the honeymoon's over."

He meant when the passion was gone.

"He'd come home from the Barracks or the Slot wanting still more. Hardly anything satisfied him. He tried everything: whips, chains, fisting. He stuck mostly to grass. And Quaaludes. Late nights, scrubbed clean of Crisco, as if you could ever scrub clean of Crisco, he'd crawl into bed with me, and hold me, and I'd hold him back, half asleep, and silently, as if we'd never had words with each other, he'd start massaging my tits and we'd make love. Ryan was good in bed, but as soon as he climbed out of the sack and his feet hit the floor, he turned into the world's biggest asshole." Teddy shook his head. "But in public on Castro or Folsom, Ryan was always on. Especially after he quit his straight job and became Mr. Wonderful Porn Writer. He was expert at talking guys into bed. He used his writing the way he used his mouth. He knew how to talk a guy to orgasm. Sex-talk scenes were his specialty. Guys fantasized about star-fucking him. They never lived with him."

Teddy clasped his hands together. "Everything was his. His money. His property. His furniture. His decisions. His work. He treated me like scum. He said I didn't care enough about those things. His things. It wasn't enough that I cared about him. He wanted proof that I loved him. I was too naive then to say to him that the proof was that I was there asleep and waiting in his bed when he dragged himself in from a marathon night of sex at the Barracks."

Teddy's face was sad.

"He expected me to take whatever he dished out, and when I took it, he'd twist it, in that special way he could twist everything, and despise me for taking it. What could I do? He had a way with words that was too clever for me. That's why I first hit him."

Teddy shrugged.

"I admit I hit him first. Sometimes I held on to him, because I figured he needed someone to grab ahold of him, and hold him; but he'd fight me off, yelling that I was making him claustrophobic. That I was smothering him. That he couldn't breathe. That I should let go and leave. He only made me hold him tighter because I didn't want to leave him. Life with him was better than any life I had ever known. He rescued me from the streets. When we met, I was—I don't know if you know this—hustling between New York and Chicago. But I wasn't, you know, making ends meet. I was mostly hanging out in bars waiting to score with some john and I was drinking a lot. At first, he liked the idea I was a hustler. He thought that made me exciting. Then after awhile he tried to save me. He wanted to make me more like him. When I couldn't be what he wanted, he accused me of wanting him only for his money."

Teddy looked at me, expecting me to be able to sort out the truth.

"He accused me. 'Once a hustler,' he said, 'always a hustler.' Then came the salt in the wound. He'd tell me I was too old to hustle the streets and the bars anymore. He told me I was too fat to be hot. That's when I busted him in the chops."

"Because it wasn't true?"

"Because it was."

Consider Ryan considering Teddy. Teddy was an outsider like Ryan. He was a tagalong like Ryan's brother Thom. Neither Teddy nor Thom was part of the charmed circle of hot, elite men that Ryan wanted to crash.

Kick was different.

He was not only one of the boys.

He was the leader of the pack.

He was a man's man.

Anyone could see that a hundred yards off.

When Ryan met Kick, he felt if he himself was not fully one of the boys, the boys with the secret, then at least he was in the final stages of learning how to be one of the boys, a mystery whose secrets had both eluded him and turned him on from boyhood. In Ryan's heart of hearts, in his outsider's heart, he had always felt there existed tighter male fraternities within the general fraternity of men. He had foregone the fraternity of heterosexual men to enter the fraternity of celibate men who were priests. He had abandoned the fraternity of straight men to enter the more secret fraternity of homosexual men. Yet even in that narrowed fraternity, he had discovered even tighter circles of kinship. Man hunts what he likes and discriminates against the rest. Ryan cruised through the bars and baths. He was in the parade, but not feeling part of it. The night was too gay and cold. He needed

heat and light. He set his sights on that impenetrable circle of homomuscular men he adored from afar. He went from man to man trying to
fuck his Ideal into existence. Drugs helped. Especially poppers that could
turn Godzilla into God.

That El Lay when Kick walked into that Ideal and filled it with his aura
and his muscle, Ryan found his target. What is love-at-first-sight if not that
moment when someone suddenly matches in the flesh the ideal image that
the seeker has always carried in his heart and head? It's tragic if the feeling
isn't mutual. It's a gift of the gods if the love is requited. Ryan played it cool.
Kick was too good to be true, but was no more, Ryan felt, than he wanted or
deserved. He spun head over heels when Kick pursued him as much as he
wanted to pursue Kick.

Under the roar of the helicopter that Sunday at Bar Nada, Kick had
asked Ryan to fly to El Lay. Three weeks later the blond bodybuilder who
strode out of Ryan's wet dreams drove him in the red Corvette to the top of
the hill above the HOLLYWOOD sign overlooking the smog burning the
topless towers of El Lay.

"If you can find it in your heart to love me," Kick said, "you won't have to
leave anything behind. If you want, I'll show you everything you ever
wanted to know about muscle."

Los Angeles spread out below them like all the kingdoms of the world
that could be Ryan's if only he would take up this calling, this vocation, to a
life as manly and noble and pure as a disciplined bodybuilder.

"You know," Kick's blue eyes looked deep into him, "you can have anything you want."

Kick was offering himself.

"Why me?"

"You are," Kick said, "the richest man I know."

Sirens shrieked through the boulevards below them. An alarm went off
in Ryan: he flashed on his Victorian and the deed to his ranch, his safety deposit box, his bank account with the savings from the tidy days when he had
pulled the salary of an associate professor. He was shocked, wary, that he
should be told this.

After all, Teddy . . .

But then he rationalized, no, realized, that this man, this golden bodybuilder, knew and cared nothing about his assets. Besides he had his own:
the beach condo, the Corvette, the Harley-Davidson Sportster, the extrava-
gance of the helicopter.

Kick must have seen the flush in Ryan's face. "I've known since that first
night," he said, "what you've always known about yourself. You have a rich

soul." He reached out his massive, hairy arm and touched Ryan's beard with his hot hand.

There are people who burst into flames, incredible cases of spontaneous human combustion, people crumbled literally to ashes by searing flames that reach two thousand degrees while their clothes are not even singed. These are bizarre cases baffling to the scientific community; yet they are well documented in tabloids the world over. They are part of the folklore of our popular culture.

Kick rose like a Viking warlord up on the block alongside the nagging Teddy.

"You know in your heart," Kick said, "what you can live with, and what you can't live without."

Teddy went down the toilet.

"You want excellence. I want quality. We want the same thing."

"Yes," Ryan said. "Yes."

"Then it's settled." Kick folded Ryan-Orion into a bear hug. The arrangement began a tale of two cities. Ryan flew back to San Francisco. Kick kept his Venice Beach house. Long distance connected them nightly. Kick drove his red Corvette Stingray up I-5. His visits became more frequent and longer. He could not leave and Ryan could not let him go. They were finding the unfindable in each other. The end of one weekend began to meet midweek with the beginning of the next.

"So," Teddy said, "why doesn't he, like, move in? Why do I always get sent off to Bar Nada? Who do you think you are? Who does he think he is? Who do you think I am?"

"I don't give a fuck," Ryan said.

"I saw you first." Teddy was crying. "Eight years. . . ."

"To you I'm the fastest checkbook in the West. Your account's closed, buddy. You're overdrawn. Flat busted."

"Disgusted. You can't be trusted." Teddy pulled Ryan to him and held him so tight he couldn't fight free. "I love you, you sonuvabitch. I'm your lover."

"You're a tenant renting a room in my house."

"Goddam you." Teddy squeezed Ryan tighter. "I have some rights."

"All you've got, you asshole, is kitchen privileges. Now let go of me!"

"Not until you tell me you love me."

"I don't love you. Let me go. You're making me claustrophobic."

Teddy shook Ryan as hard as he could. "Tell me you love me!"

"I don't love you, you idiot! Let me go. You're hurting me."

"You're hurting me. I want to hurt you. I want you to tell me you love me."

"I want you to move out. I mean it this time. Let go of me, and, goddammit, move out!"

Teddy held Ryan out at arm's length with one hand on his throat. As hard as he could, with his other hand, he slapped Ryan across the face. The blow spun Ryan free. He ran to the front door, escaping from his own house. "Move! Goddammit! Whatever was left between us you finally shattered. Nobody's ever hit me before."

"That's a miracle." Teddy was coming toward him down the long hall, slowly at first.

"I won't be your abused lover." Ryan was backing out the open door. "I don't come from a family that hits each other."

"Your family's a laugh," Teddy shouted. He was approaching faster.

Ryan went for Teddy's jugular. "Your father beats your mother!"

Teddy broke into a run coming for Ryan's throat. Ryan stooped down, and with all his might, pulled a hard yank on the long oriental runner exactly at the moment when Teddy's feet hung in midair gallop. His next step came down on the fast-sliding rug and he sprawled screaming across the waxed hardwood of the hallway. Ryan dashed down the porch steps to the safety of his VW Rabbit. He fumbled for the door key, but Teddy was not chasing him. He had crawled to the front door and was lying across the threshold broken like Stanley calling for Stella. "Ryan! Don't go." He was crying. "Don't go. Ryan! Ryan! Ryan! Don't leave me."

Ryan looked across the street to see if the gay-boy clone couple they rarely spoke to was looking out from behind their Levolor blinds. They weren't. He shouted over the car roof back at Teddy. "I hate this. I hate you."

"I love you. I love you."

"Move out!"

"Please. Please. Please. Please."

"Omigod." Ryan closed his eyes, but he could not close his ears. He climbed into his pea-green Rabbit with the MANUVRS license plates and peeled out from the curb. "Omigod," he said, and he was crying. "What have I done?"

He drove west to the beach, to the ocean. Waves of guilt washed over him. "A man's got to do, oh, chow yuk, what a man's got to do." The late afternoon turned to a brilliant twilight. The sun disappeared out beyond the far horizon. In the evening mix of dying sun and rising moon, two ships, lit brilliantly, passed in the soft light, one heading safely into shore, one heading steadfastly out into the dark ocean.

Ryan found a phone booth outside the Cliff House. He called Kick long distance. "Don't come up this weekend," he said. "Those are hard words to say to you."

"What's the matter?"

"Nothing. Nothing's the matter. In fact, everything's probably perfect. Teddy's moving out this weekend."

"Why don't you fly down here? There's a Mr. Western States contest Saturday."

"I want to, but I can't. I better stay here and make sure he really moves out." Ryan hesitated. "It's okay if I don't fly down? I mean this isn't a test, is it?"

"Would I test you?" Kick's voice was warm. "I love you. You're a madman. Whatever's going on up there, I understand. I love you."

"I love you too. I want to see you, but I can't."

"Then you should stay. I'm being selfish wanting you to come. My friends down here think I've met a miracle man. I want to show you off."

If my witness serves any purpose in all this, it is balance. Despite my protests of noninvolvement, remember, I, Magnus Bishop, became somehow the father confessor. I heard the several sides of various collisions. I think they all told me the truth. But what is truth? And who am I? *Rashomon?*

That night of the big fight, Ryan could not sleep. At 4:30 he heard Teddy come into the house. He waited long minutes in his big bed to see if Teddy would go to his own room or come climb comfortably in with him. He heard Teddy drop one boot and then the other. He heard the toilet flush. He heard the soft pad of Teddy's gray wool boot socks walk off to his own room. He heard the sound of the bed creak under Teddy's exhausted weight.

Ryan called Teddy's name. He announced in a voice too loud for the late hour that he was ill. He hated himself calling Teddy. He hated that he had to lie about his perfectly good health, but he needed attention, and if Teddy's was the only attention available, then he was shameless. Besides, Teddy owed him.

Teddy climbed wearily out of his own bed and stood at the door of Ryan's room. "Are you physically sick?" Teddy asked. He was wary. "Did you take something? Or are you just insomniac. Again."

"I need," Ryan said. He could not find the word. "I need . . ."

"If you don't know what you need, I can't help you."

"Come in here. Lie down with me."

"What's the matter with you. You said you wanted me to leave you alone. You told me to move out. I don't like it here anymore. I won't be able to sleep in here. This used to be my bedroom too, you know. Why can't you say what's the matter?"

Ryan, the writer, grasped for a word to explain. Over Teddy's shoulder, the digital clock read 4:40. Dawn was already gray outside the windows.

"If you can't say what it is, it can't be too important," Teddy said. "You always have a word for everything."

"For some things, words fail," Ryan said. "Some things cannot be spoken." What he meant was, some things cannot be asked. Some things, if they have to be spelled out to someone who should know, are not worth saying. If Teddy could not see what Ryan needed, or would not give it to him, then asking for what was not given betrayed the integrity of the sharing.

All Ryan needed was to be held. Just held. Just for a moment. To fold his body into the warmth of another man's body. To imagine how warm his father's body might have felt that hot afternoon in the car in the woods. To warm himself with the familiar shared warmth of Teddy's body against the cold dawn. "This is your chance," he wanted to say to Teddy, "to regain your ground. Love me because you love me, not because you're desperate." But he said nothing. If he had to ask to be held, then the holding could never be the same as an embrace freely given. He could not ask Teddy for it. This was the test, the supreme test, for them both: the one could not ask, and the other could not figure out what was to be given. They stared at each other impassed, like two men trying to go opposite directions through the same door at the same time: neither one moving to the right or left, both waiting for the other to step aside, or step forward, to solve the squeeze.

Hindsight tempts me to think that if one or the other or both had reached out, they might have changed the course of their personal history. They might have salvaged what had been a genuinely innocent, boyish love between them. They might have averted slammed doors and loud voices. But at that moment, when their future history could have been born or aborted by a simple embrace of human love, neither man reached out, and events began to collide the way people on foggy freeways crash into each other. No matter now. What's done is done. The truth is that Ryan alone could have stopped all of this if he had wanted; but not knowing what he wanted more than adventure, he knew he at least did not want to stop the madness around him, because deep down Ryan liked hysteria. It distracted him from his anxiety blues. The crazier the world the less crazy he felt. The faster the track the less time to be depressed. Ryan was my friend, but I won't fail to admit that if Ryan wasn't exactly the cause of all this, at least he was to the maelstrom what the eye is to the hurricane.

Ryan was the center. None of these people would ever have crossed purposes if somehow or other they had not wanted something that Ryan had. That cutting edge, that way he had of pushing reality with words, of course, is the point of my working through this wreckage of fools who spoke the word *love* more than any word they knew.

Ryan, lying in his bed, with Teddy sitting on the edge, ready to bolt for refuge in his own room, could not say the words. He was slightly amused. Teddy proved his suspicion correct that if people knew what he was really like they would flee for their lives. He planned to be very careful with Kick.

Teddy knew, but Teddy was more scared of the world than he was of Ryan. Teddy knew men existed who would gladly do to him the unspeakable acts he wanted and feared they would do. In the gay world, where there are no limits, Ryan was his protector.

"If you're what having a lover is all about," Ryan said. "You're my first, last, and only lover. I'll never speak the word again!"

Ryan was always in a rage about love. He thought love could change people. He knew he would be changed by Kick's love. He was planning on it. He had wanted to change Teddy, but Teddy had not changed. Ryan burned a slow smoulder because Teddy had somehow failed. He could not forgive him. He went into a rage that someone he had chosen, someone he had trusted, poor Teddy, had failed to understand, by design or defect, what intensity and depth of feeling Ryan had attempted to share with him.

"I understood him," Teddy said.

But I knew he hadn't, not always, especially not that crucial night when Ryan had called him to his bed, and he would not lie down. Teddy hadn't understood at all that cold gray hour before dawn. If he had chosen to climb between the bed covers and hold Ryan that night, he could have held him forever. Kick or no Kick, he could have salvaged everything between them. Ryan was offering him a truce. He was offering peace terms. If Teddy had climbed into Ryan's bed that night, he would have so emplaced himself in Ryan's heart that Kick would have been no more than a long-distance affairette. But Teddy was too gun-shy to stand his ground. Ryan never pulled punches with him. He could not figure what snare Ryan was laying to capture him. He grew nervous sitting on the edge of the bed.

"I have to go to my own room," Teddy said. "Don't involve me in whatever it is you're trying to talk about. I'm tired. Don't give me your insomnia."

"It's not contagious," Ryan said.

"With you, everything is a plague. I've got to get some sleep. I'm sorry I'm not up to your late late show. I didn't know I was going to have a few beers and some grass and meet a big, bearded Canadian with an uncut dick and a hairy chest and belly."

"I'm glad you did. I'm glad you enjoyed it." Ryan meant it. But he needed the accustomed comfort of Teddy's body sleeping next to him. It was as close to proof as he could come that he was not in solitary confinement inside his own skin. But if he had to ask for it, the proof would not be there. Teddy had to give it, someone had to give it, without being asked.

"So one last time. What's eating you?" Teddy asked.

"I can't say it."

"Coming from a big mouth like you that's something. I thought you had a spiel for everything." Teddy stood up from the edge of Ryan's bed. "If you can't say it, Ry, it doesn't exist." He turned his back on Ryan and walked toward the door.

"If there is one sin in life," Ryan sat up shouting in the bedcovers, "you just committed it."

Teddy retreated through the door, turned and said, "I'm sorry, Ry."

"Here! Tonight! Committed here in this bed tonight!"

Teddy pushed the door to Ryan's bedroom closed and padded softly down the hall. Behind him, he heard one of the last things Ryan ever said to him.

"You Judas!"

17

Within two months, Kick was living in Ryan's Victorian. "I haven't moved here," Kick had an indirect way of taking to Ryan, "because you're here; but I wouldn't have moved here if you weren't."

Kick knew how to hold Ryan. His big arms made Ryan feel safe. Ryan's house made Kick comfortable. They were a pair.

The Entity took up residence with them.

Kick was an exhibitionist pleasantly surprised that Ryan could equal him in exhibition. On Castro, Ryan delivered a gentle Attitude that declared to the hunks who gravitated around Kick that Kick was as built in his head as he was in his body. Kick, in his soft spoken way, matched Ryan subtlety for subtlety, handling adroitly every queen and musclehead who doubted they could really be a couple.

"Most bodybuilders," Kick said, "are more competitive than communicative." He winked at Ryan. "For me, men have to be more than competitive."

"What do they have to be?" Ryan asked.

"Like you," Kick said.

"Whatever that is," Ryan said.

Both were performance artists. Kick knew how to handle men beguiled by his handsome Look. Ryan knew how to manipulate men with his words.

"Even if you have become a Famous Couple overnight," Solly Blue told Ryan, "you're still somewhat of an odd couple."

"This isn't the first time," Ryan said, "that I've been laid because of my mouth."

"Spoken like a true cocksucker."

"Like seeks like except when opposites attract."

Ryan was purposely vague. Solly knew about the musclesex. He didn't know about the bondage. He would never have approved. He hated bondage. He had to. He could not have sex with hustlers who might tie him up. That would be a Death sentence. He had canceled bondage trips out for everyone.

"So, beyond his looks, what do you have in common?" Solly asked.

"I never kiss and tell."

"That's all you do. Your magazine is all kiss and tell."

Very late one night, tumbling in the covers, Kick sat up and straddled Ryan's chest. They were laughing at their offbeat affair. "We could be dangerous," Kick said. "We could take on the whole world." He stretched his huge arms up, flexed, and slowly lowered his hands flat down on Ryan's turned-on tits. "You and me, man. We're on a roll." Kick lowered his muscle-packed body, grinding the full heft of his power slowly and sensually into Ryan. Their hard cocks rolled sweaty between them. Ryan pushed up hard and confident into the dream man whose shoulders and arms held him in tight embrace. Their tongues intertwined, and pumping and hugging, they came to the good old bellybucking Princeton Rub.

Kick had Universal Appeal. He was everybody's type. On Castro, guys rubbernecked. Cars rear-ended each other. Queens fell up the stairs at Paperback Traffic. The Norse Cove Deli grew silent when they entered. Even Nureyev, out touring the Castro for an afternoon, snipped off a fast double take. "I guess," Ryan said, "Rudy knows a body when he sees one."

Kick grinned. Straight men, and gay, pumping iron at Gold's Gym on Valencia Street broke their silent Attitude to say hello to Kick who trained only with Ryan.

"You're my coach, Ry," he said. "I've always wanted to compete. I can't do it alone. We'll win together."

Kick promised Ryan they would always go for the best in life. *Quality* was Kick's code word. His expectations of life, and he had the gifts that proved his expectations were correct, meant nothing less than the best of everything. He had built his body more with visualizations than he had with weights. Ryan saw it happen the nights of their musclesex before the mirror. Kick was living proof of the power of positive thinking.

"Ry," Kick said, "I really meant what I said. You can have anything you want, you know."

"I want a body like yours." Ryan teased him.

"I want a head like yours." Kick played back.

"I'll settle for your body."

"I'll settle for your head."

"You don't care if I'm not a bodybuilder."

"You don't care if I'm not as smart as you."

"I'm not smart. I'm only clever."

"Whatever you say, coach. But I wouldn't have chased you if you weren't the damndest package I ever did see."

"I'd never have been caught if you weren't on top of all those goddam muscles. Nothing's worse than beef with more pump than soul."

"God!" Kick laughed. "How'd we get so perfect!"

"Funny, how in a way," Ryan said, "we both had to get around each other's bodies in order to get inside our heads."

"Funny, isn't it," Kick said. "Funny and fine."

Their first New Year's Eve together was private. They skipped the big disco party at Trocadero Transfer and bowed out of the private party tossed by the best of the A-gay muscle crowd. Instead, they had driven, three blocks from the corner of Market and Castro, halfway up the mountain path of Corona Heights. Kick parked the Vette and they hiked the steep trail to the craggy top. The City was alive below them. They stood holding each other, watching the fireworks flash and boom through the soft gauze of fog hanging motionless over the City.

"You're the best man I ever met," Kick said.

Ryan was held tight by the man he was sure had fallen to Earth. If ever Ryan were to be rescued from the thick air of this strange planet, if ever they were to be beamed back up to wherever Kick had come from, Ryan knew that the rocky outcropping of Corona Heights was the pickup place. The red lights of Sutro Tower blinked like terrestrial signals west against the moon. Kick's arms embraced him. His warm breath through his blond moustache touched Ryan's mouth making one breath between them. The moment was so right, so pagan, on the rock-slab steps of the raw mountain only three circuitous blocks from the hyper-civilization of Castro, that Ryan's old Catholic heart pounded with superstitious fear. "We'll have to pay for all this." He recovered with a small laugh. He remembered the line from *The Boys in the Band* about every one of them willing to trade their immortal souls for a half hour of skin-deep beauty. But Kick's beauty was more than skin deep and Ryan hardly cared if for all this mortal joy he should burn forever in hell. He was head over heels.

The intensity between them that first New Year's Eve was the same as the night they had won Kick's first physique contest. They had driven back to the motel with four trophies. Kick never said, "I won." He always said, "We won. You and I, coach. We won." Kick took the Most Muscular trophy to a jewelers and had it engraved with both their names, "From the Champ to the Coach." He gave the golden trophy topped with a victorious bodybuilder to Ryan for his own.

Ryan certainly had helped Kick with his posing. Their muscle movies and videotapes exhibit the talent of both men: one before the lens, one behind. Ryan once said when he visited my apartment that he watched his tapes of Kick when Kick had to return to El Lay on whatever business he had there.

"I think," he said, "that the ultimate ritual act of worship in the twentieth century is a grown man, stripped, naked, stoned on grass, with poppers by his side and clamps on his tits, greasing up his dick, kneeling on the floor with his face four inches from the video screen, masturbating to glorious closeups of bodybuilders flexing and posing."

He gazed somewhat idly into one of those designer mirrors that looks like a chrome hubcap surrounded by seashells. "My face will probably fall off from terminal video burn." He palmed his hand up his high forehead. "Maybe that's why I'm balding." He turned to me. "Do I look hot?" He didn't wait for an answer. "For my type, and I am a type, I look hot."

Life and lust, as much as Death, led Ryan to the discipline of bodybuilding. And to the worship of bodybuilders. He was little different from straight males turning rowdy when they see athletes they adore exhibiting their flesh and muscle in arenas and rings, on stages and playing fields; but he, more than they, understood how homomuscularity was different from homosexuality. The attraction men, even straight men, have for other men who are athletes proves that men can love and admire other men as long as the other man is more ruggedly handsome, more muscular, more a cocksman, with more earning power. American men idolize other males who are top dog. American women go for men who are the underdog. American homosexuals love top dogs with big dicks. Ah, yes, I know, all generalizations limp.

Ryan, having quit his technical writing job at the Glass Tower, began to write even more torrid fiction of man-to-man musclesex.

In his *Journal,* he reasoned that a man's body, ideally developed and then tensed into the graceful flow of a posing presentation, skin bronzed, sweat running, and veins popping, was the ultimate existential act of physical defiance shouting I AM HERE into the cadaverous face of Death. Ryan needed, really needed, Kick's body, the cuming strength of his good seed, his good genes, to hold back his fear of his own body that he felt too closely linked to the body of his father who had died so young so slowly.

Ryan was so concerned about Charley-Pop that he once said, "My one outside hope, as much as I love that man, is that my mother will finally confess to me that I'm her love child, her little bastard. Fat chance. She was a true Catholic bride. She was always totally in-love with him, and he with her. Besides, God help me, I look exactly like he used to look before his pancreas exploded inside him and started eating his guts like lunch meat."

The weight of the world was in Ryan's face.

"The poor man's suffering was a disaster. It destroyed our family. Everybody in Peoria thinks we held together so bravely. Matter of fact, we've all become mad as hatters in a textbook example of a dysfunctional family. At least, Thom and Kweenie and I have. My mother grows more translucently saintlike every day. She lived to make her man fight to live. I don't think she understands that all three of her children, unlike her, are terrified that what happened to him might be passed along to us. She only married him. She's not descended from him."

He found the antidote.

Muscles were all.

Sport.

Art.

Ritual.

Sex.

Bodybuilding pulled an adult man together. Whether a muscleman was displayed in full glorious competition pose in a double-biceps shot, lats spread, legs thrust forward, or was standing in noble repose, the bodybuilder was simply the way a man should look in his full body armor, if he was to protect himself from the onslaught of everything that adds up to Death. Bodies, healthy, well-developed bodies, spit, if ever so briefly, in the face of Death.

Kick and Ryan agreed that the death of El Lay's most famous professional bodybuilder, this side of Arnold Schwarzenegger, had been an avoidable disaster. The former Mr. America was the talk of the gyms. He had taken so many steroids to beef up his mass over the course of his professional career that his liver had grown terminally hepatic, his hair fell out, his muscle collapsed, and he died less than six months after diagnosis of cancer of the bone marrow.

"Steroids kill," Kick said. "It's a shame. Bodybuilding is supposed to be a health sport."

"It's as far," Ryan said, "as a man can get from Death."

"We'll stick with coke and MDA," Kick said.

"And poppers," Ryan said.

"Definitely poppers."

You needn't be a student in my American pop culture class to see that Ryan and the general public had some differences of opinion about bodybuilders. Straight folklore knocks bodybuilders as the dumbest of big dumb jocks. Gay folklore insists that bodybuilders are hung like stud mice. Kick suffered neither debility. Ryan's sex videos of Kick, in competition condition, jerking off in front of a mirror visualizing the Look he was perfecting, show both a Zen master sculptor at work and a male animal "with," as Ryan wrote in his *Journal,* "probably the largest piece of dirty-blond meat in captivity." Kick outstripped even the legendary blond muscleman, Frank Vickers, in the Colt Studio classic, *Pumping Oil.*

Living with Kick, Ryan learned to read the person living inside Kick's muscles. If gay boys on Castro recognized Kick's appearance, Ryan went them one farther, penetrating the difference between Kick's appearance and Kick's reality. Kick was an itinerant apostle of manhood. He was not a clown cruising Castro like an orangutang in a spray-painted tee shirt.

Most massively big bodybuilders, gay or not gay, up from El Lay for a visit, hunkered down Castro, to see and be seen, all their muscles competitively flexed, parading in pose-downs of two or three, each outcrunching the other, exaggerating every movement, pulling at their crotches, walking shoulder to shoulder, clearing the sidewalk. In front of them like offensive linemen, *Muscle Fucks from Outer Space,* shoulders and lats and arms spread wide like a squadron of vampire bats.

Kick was a champ not a chump.

"You develop muscle," he said, "to show it. But you want the Look to read right. You want Command Presence, but you don't want gay bar Attitude."

He stood relaxed next to Ryan in the sun in the tiny garden park in front of the Hibernia Bank, which the Castronauts dubbed Hibernia Beach. Kick, in cutoffs among the gay boys, slowly stripped off his gray ALABAMA tee shirt. His fetish for his own golden body hair was erotic contradiction to the strip-shaved Look bodybuilders affect for competition. Upholstered under a thick layer of his perfectly patterned blond hair, Kick's pecs and belly and legs dazzled in the afternoon sun. He was unusual. He was a natural man, a natural bodybuilder. He was a ripe candidate for the Mr. Golden Bear contest at the California State Fair.

If any physique competition should have been open to unshaven, hairy bodybuilders, with body hair counting for extra points, it should have been the Golden Bear. When Kick began competing, Ryan spent hours shaving his grand body smooth. Kick watched the revelation of his bare muscle as Ryan razored off the inch-long blond hair from his shoulders, back, chest, belly, arms, hands, butt, legs, and feet.

"There are some sacrifices," Kick said, "a man has to make."

His relaxed Look, off the contest stage, because of his symmetry and polish and finish, was more a casual muscular All-American jock Look rather than a bulked, beefed, steroid bodybuilder. People could relate to him. He had the gift of Universal Appeal, something more than mere muscle can give, and something muscle alone can often destroy. He was Ryan's BMOC on Castro. He was the embodiment of every sex hero Ryan had ever written about in all his erotic stories.

Kick had a body.

He had a face.

He had a soul.

"Sometimes," Ryan said to Kweenie, "I think he sprang from my head, through my dick to my fingertips, into the keyboard of my computer, and appeared fully developed on my monitor. I only had to tap the screen and take his hand and pull him out of the video screen into reality. Like Michelangelo striking the statue of his Moses and commanding him to speak. How's that for conceit?" He pulled at her arm. "What movie are we?" he asked.

"*Butch and Sundance?*" Kweenie said halfheartedly.

"Try *West Side Story*." Ryan said. "I love him."

"You're his!" Kweenie hissed. "And every little thing he is . . ."

"I am too," Ryan said.

"Don't you just wish," Kweenie said. But she knew what her brother meant. Kweenie herself in her young life had seen a dream or two walking. And Kick was one of them.

Only a fool lacks desire to become, really become, his fantasy.

Kick projected a manly balance that was his main appeal. He never betrayed the gift: on the street he was good example; in the bedroom he was heroic lover; even on the physique contest posing platform where animal aggression is expected, he charmed audiences and judges and Ryan's heart all over again with the virile intensity of his muscular, handsome, blond charisma.

18

Indulge the pop culture professor if you please. As I said, there will be a question to solve the puzzle—theirs, mine, and ours—at the end.

American sports tend to be objective and subjective. In objective sports, the basketball drops or does not drop through the hoop. The tight end either catches the football or he doesn't. The tennis pro makes his serve or he misses. Objective sports may have referees and umpires, but they are mostly yes-or-no athletics. Everyone basically sees the same results.

Subjective sports like gymnastics, skating, fencing, and bodybuilding determine winners or losers not by definitive touchdowns, but by judges' opinions. Of all sports, bodybuilding is the least understood because it is the most subjective. If gymnastics has a right way to move on the flying rings, bodybuilding has several right ways to execute the mandatory poses that display the bodybuilder's various muscle groups separately and together.

Who wins a physique contest is often as much a trick question as which is the best art form: literature, painting, or music. The results depend on subjective values and enthusiasms. Most Americans like their sports cut and dried. For that reason, bodybuilding has been slow in coming to national acceptance as more than a cult sport. Someday it will, when Calvinism dies, and when it does, bodybuilding will finally become an Olympic event.

Physique presentation is a sporting objectification of self that is art and science, logic and feeling. A bodybuilder needs to know his body. He is dancer, actor, salesman. He is a contradiction in terms: a romantic existentialist. He strides barefooted across the stage with a dozen other bodybuilders. He takes his place in the lineup. He stands pumped and oiled and nearly naked, his two hundred and thirty pounds tucked into his tiny four-ounce posing briefs. He poses without movement. A perfectly sculpted statue. He radiates victory. He asserts his Command Presence under the hot lights. He calls the eyes of judges and audience to the quality edge of his muscle. Size. Symmetry. Power. Proportion. Bulk. Definition. Striation.

Vascularity. Grooming. Look. His superior Command Attitude reduces the other highly competitive muscle to beefcake. His posture states HERE I AM.

Winners know how to peak for the contest day. Three weeks before competition they cut carbohydrates from their high-protein diet to remove the last micro-pinch of body fat that might obscure muscle display. Workouts intensify to carve out the lean definition of each separate muscle in the bulked muscle groups. A week before, the entire body is strip-shaved for the first time to allow any cuts or shaving rash to heal. In the last forty-eight hours, diuretics drain the minute layer of water between the muscle and the skin. The skin, paper thin, form fits the striae of each muscle, showing the minutest furrow like tiny grooves on granite. The vascularity of the veins snakes around the muscle almost on top of nearly invisible skin. The tan, by contest day, must be perfect and the body smoothed to a final shave before it is oiled backstage.

Contests are grueling twelve-hour affairs. The Pre-Judging, where the contest is actually won or lost, begins at ten in the morning, and, depending on the classes, Teenage, Men, and Weight and Age Divisions, can last until the early afternoon. By the evening show at eight, the judges, of whom there must be at least five, have tallied their votes. The Pre-Judging audience, smaller and hard core, can only have guessed at the winner. The audience for the evening show is larger, fans and friends and family, hot to party and cheer the parade of muscle bodies and wait eagerly for the names of the four finalists and the winner.

In the morning, the contestants arrive early. They saunter into the green room. They check in disguised under thick jogging suits and bulky nylon athletic jackets. They carry enormous gym bags. Some arrive alone. Some have the company of their training partners or their coaches.

The room is silent. Brows furrow with concentration. They psych each other out. One by one they begin the slow strip of their jackets and gym shoes and sweatshirts and tee shirts and sweatpants. Each reveals his stuff slowly. The offstage competition posing has begun.

Arms, big guns, appear. Broad shoulders. Huge pecs. Washboard abs. Thunder thighs. Big, naked bubble butts. In unshaven groins, penises sprout tight with tension or hang long and thick with languorous confidence.

Attentive buddies fold the contestants' clothes into the gym bags. They wet their hands with baby oil and begin the even slather of the huge muscle bodies. The bodybuilders slide into their nylon posing briefs. Most pull their penises straight up toward their navels and let their balls hang low in the pouch. They pin the small white paper with their contest number over the front left hip of their briefs.

This is ritual.

Some play tug-of-war with their partners, pulling white towels back and forth to bring up the day's glossy pump on their years of hard muscle building. Others move to the ton of iron delivered to the theater for the day to polish their muscle, most often their arms, one last time before marching out on stage for the real competition of group comparison, flexing in unison mandatory poses, then individually, each one mounting the dais alone to pose for sixty seconds to music of his own selection.

Ryan, driving the Corvette to San Diego, could only guess what lay in store. That first morning of their first contest, when he and Kick entered the greenroom, Ryan thought he had died and gone to heaven. He was surrounded by more than twenty naked bodybuilders. He tried to keep custody of his eyes. He folded Kick's clothes and knelt at his feet, oiling up his legs to his shoulders. Ryan, during a scene of musclesex, had convinced Kick to replace baby oil with olive oil, because its sheen was more lustrous and its essence more classic.

"Whatever you say, coach."

Kick was up. He thought it was a good omen that his assigned contest number was *One*.

The morning Pre-Judging ran nearly three hours. Ryan was beaming. Kick glowed. They met during a break backstage.

"You look great out there," Ryan said.

"I feel great out there," Kick said. He motioned for Ryan to move in closer. "Spread some more oil on my chest." He pointed toward the watch pocket in Ryan's Levi's. "Give me a hit," he said. He reached into Ryan's pocket for a small snifter of coke. He blew two lines. "Now you," he said.

"I'm already wired," Ryan said.

"Come on." Kick put his arm on Ryan's shoulder. The heady smell of contest sweat and olive oil made Ryan's tits ache. "We're here to have a good time."

Ryan swacked off the snifter.

"Again," Kick said.

Ryan snorted another line.

"It's good for the vascularity," Kick said. He thrust his arms, fists down, alongside his thighs, flexed, and popped his veins. "Nice, huh?"

"Sexy."

"I want you to know," Kick said, "how much fun it is to be inside this body." He chucked Ryan under the chin.

"Every man on that stage would like to be in your body. They might as well go home. You're going to win."

"I know."

After the Pre-Judging, Ryan drove Kick in the Corvette to a coffee shop. Kick ordered an orange juice with four raw eggs. Ryan ordered, but was too hyped to eat.

"Keep your strength up," Kick said. "You want to shoot a terrific video tonight." He stroked his high-top gym shoe up and down Ryan's leg. "Muscle TV."

Kick was triumphant in his evening posing routine. Through his video monitor, Ryan caught every graceful nuance. He knew the choreography he had coached by heart. He had even selected Kick's music. He was bored with uninspired muscleheads posing one after the other to the clichéd themes from *Exodus, Rocky, Star Wars,* and *Superman.* Ryan chose Tchaikovsky's "Marche Slav." Its thunderous power matched Kick's smooth and commanding posing routine.

He flexed. He shined. He was pure, hard, blond muscle. His hair and face and jaw accentuated the blond brush of his moustache, groomed trooper sharp. His physique flowed from his head. He hit each pose hard. He had appeal. There was no quiver from the muscle exertion or the coke. He displayed every body part alternating always with the dozen ways he powered out his arms.

The crowd called out for more.

He hit the Most Muscular pose three times and threw his arms up over his head in victorious salute. The muscle crowd rose cheering to their feet.

Here was a man.

"Alright, gentlemen," the head judge said over the loudspeaker. "We're calling the five finalists out on stage for a pose down. This is the final comparison, man for man, to determine the winner. Ladies and gentlemen, these are our five finalists. Number One, Kick Sorensen. . . ."

Ryan heard no other names.

The five finalists strolled out on stage. Each picked a spot and hit a pose, playing the cheering audience. Kick owned stage center. He threw a double-biceps shot and then crunched down into the popular Most Muscular. The crowd went wild.

"Give yourselves some room, fellas. Spread out. Make sure you're in the light."

The finalists sought their places. Kick held center stage with two musclemen moving to each side. They all stood heels close together, toes pointed out, elbows extended, arms hanging down.

"Alright. Let's do a double-biceps pose on three. I want you all to hit exactly the same pose at the same time. On three. One-two-three. Hit your pose."

Kick raised both arms. His biceps peaked under the hot light. He was arms and more than arms. He worked his pecs. He tightened his abs. Always he was working his legs. Contests are won or lost on legs.

"Okay. A lat spread from the front. On three. One-two-three."

Kick positioned his thumbs behind his waist with his fingers front pointing down his hips. He swung his elbows out, lifted his chest, spread his shoulders, and opened wide his lats, holding the pose, then twisting slightly from the waist, left to right, catching the best play of the light.

"Now a side-chest pose. Your favorite side. Take your positions. Quiet, please. We want a side-chest shot. Rotate the sides. One-two-three."

Kick stood on his left foot and the ball of his right with his right knee bent to display his right calf development. He turned his head to face the judges straight on. He clasped his hands above his right hip and pulled his left shoulder toward the audience. His arms read like an awesome frame around his massive pecs.

"Now a side-tricep. Your favorite side. Take your positions. On three. One-two-three. Hit it."

Again, standing sideways, yet facing the judges, Kick rested on his left foot. He placed the ball of his right foot behind him, flexing his calf. He shot his right arm down his outside thigh, displaying the horseshoe definition of his triceps. Then reaching his left hand behind his butt, he shifted the pose, taking hold of the hand facing the crowd to pop his tricep even more. He instinctively knew the extra flourish needed to show off the fine detail of each muscle to its best advantage.

"And relax. Turn toward the curtain, please. Give yourselves room, fellas. Spread out. Okay. Double-bicep from the rear. On three. One-two-three. Hit it."

Kick was born to show arms. From the backside, his biceps mounded like twin baseballs on the girth of his huge arms. He powered into the biceps shot, spread his shoulders, and kicked in a rearview of his left calf.

"Gentlemen, let's have a back lat spread. On three. One-two-three. Hit it."

Kick thrust his butt out. His perfect glutes caught the light. A woman behind Ryan screamed. Kick tucked his thumbs behind his waist and opened his elbows, wide, spread his back, slightly at first, and then opening the left side to its full plane, and then the right, both wings from his waist to his shoulders in perfect symmetry. The back of his blond head glowed atop the column of his thick neck.

"Relax. Face front, please."

The crowd had settled on a favorite. Someone set up a chant of "Number One! Number One!" The number Ryan had pinned on Kick's brown nylon briefs.

"May we have some quiet, please. Face front, please. May I remind you, Number Three, that these are mandatory poses. If you're not sure which way to turn, look at the men next to you."

The crowd cheered and hooted.

"Alright now, fellas. Flexing the legs, display the thighs. One-two-three."

Kick locked his hands behind his head, elbows wide, armpits rampant. He flashed his washboard abs and thrust one leg and then the other out for judgment. The thickness of his thighs broke up into distinctly displayed muscle groups. The contestant on his right moved his own leg toward Kick's, daring closer comparison. The crowd went wild. Kick lowered his hands to his waist, thrust his leg toward his competitor, flexed it, looked at the other bodybuilder, then pointed, grinning, to his own thigh, bulked, carved, cut, vascular, and tanned. He looked up from his leg and threw the crowd a devastating so-what-do-you-think grin.

"And relax. Fellas, we're going for your favorite ab shot on three. One-two-three. Hit it."

Again Kick locked his hands behind his head. The crowd was with him. He kicked out his right leg, resting his foot on the heel, working his leg length, giving more than required, locking his abs into the sculpted ridges Ryan's tongue knew by heart. He carved his abs tight, then sharpened them tighter. The crowd chanted "Number One!" Kick's whole posture, arms up, leg extended, belly displayed, seemed to focus the light on the full pouch of his posing briefs. Ryan, at the last minute in the greenroom, had slipped Kick's balls and cock through a brass cock ring to accentuate the big package. "I want them to see everything you've got," he had said. He wondered how much a big cock and balls registered with the judges, many of whom were older, closeted gay men. On stage, Kick radiated pure sex. Women in the crowd were shouting, "We want Number One!"

Ryan shouted into the din. "Dream on!"

"And relax. Catch your breath, fellas. We're going to do the Most Muscular now. Your favorite Most Muscular. On three. One-two-three. Hit it."

Kick raised his arms wide, elbows above his shoulders, then slowly, hunched, leaned over, and powered down into the Most Muscular crab pose. His right leg led his left. His arms were Most Muscular. His chest pumped like a barrel. His head was up. His face back. His chin out. The cords in his neck spoke power. The crowd loved him. He broke the pose and hit it again. Then again. This last time in full lockdown, revolving his fists one around the other to play the brute force of his upper body and massive arms.

"And relax. Now there will be sixty seconds of free posing. Remember, fellas, this is a pose down. This is your final chance to show why you should be Mr. Western Pacific Coast. Take your sixty seconds. Use it, please."

The disco music came up over the cheers of the crowd. Each contestant tried to outpose the other. They moved, freestyle, pose against pose, topping each other: arms, chests, backs, abs, and legs. They moved sideways. They turned front and back. Kick stayed confidently in place in the melee. He had found the best light. He was center to the group. They were good. But he was power. They were competitors, but he was brooking no competition. He ignored them jockeying into him, following his poses, trying to lure him into following their competitive moves. Instead, he grinned, thrust out his chin. His blond hair and his moustache glowed. He played straight to the audience, straight to the judges, straight to Ryan behind his video camera in the first row. Kick was surrounded by bodybuilders, but he was more than a bodybuilder. He was a Lord of Light.

The crowd turned to near riot. Fans with cameras rushed the lip of the stage. Applause. Whistles. "Number One!"

The minute of blasting music stopped. The crowd rose cheering louder. The head judge called for quiet. The auditorium soothed down expectantly. Finally, he named the fifth and fourth and third runners-up. The three men took their trophies, kissed the girl who presented them, and moved off to the side. Kick flexed his pecs and ran his hand down his rippled belly. The hall grew tense. Expectant. Kick stood next to Number Nine. He reached out to shake Nine's hand. Calls for "Number One!" flared here and there from the orchestra and balcony. "Number One!" Time stood still.

Ryan knew there was no God if they came this close and lost. In the pause, Number Nine hit his best Most Muscular. Kick raised both fists into his best double-biceps shot of the night and killed the guy with his arms.

"Number One! Number One! Number One!"

"Quiet, please." The judge was a sadist. "We have three trophies to award before we announce the winner of the Mr. Western Pacific Coast Contest." Ryan knew. He knew that he knew the verdict. "The trophy for Best Legs goes to Number One, Kick Sorensen!"

Kick hit a severe leg pose then threw his arms up in salute. Number Nine reached to shake his hand. The young blonde woman carried the Best Legs trophy to Kick. She leaned forward to give the winner his customary kiss. Ryan watched Kick deftly turn his mouth away. The blonde bussed his cheek. Kick set the trophy down at his feet.

"The trophy for Best Arms," the trophy Kick coveted most, "Number One, Kick Sorensen."

Kick hit a single side-biceps pose. The crowd cheered. He was sweeping the competition. Number Nine realized he was going to place second. Kick received the second trophy from the blonde girl and placed it near the first.

"Number One! Number One!"

Kick was a generous poser. He obliged the cheers, roiling a double-bicep shot down into one last Most Muscular pose. Number Nine, a sport to the end, followed suit. The audience screamed as Kick took the trophy for Best Posing.

Under the roar, the judge's words were lost as he named the second runner-up. Number Nine heard. He raised his arms in valedictory and turned to shake Kick's hand.

The audience rose screaming to their feet.

"The winner of the Mr. Western Pacific Coast title is . . . Number One! Kick Sorensen!"

Ryan nearly died. "Omigod! I love you, Kick!"

Kick pumped off a succession of killer poses. He raised his prizewinning arms high over his head. The cheering rose as he accepted his First Place trophy and headed toward the posing platform. He mounted the dais and placed the four trophies at his feet. The four finalists grouped themselves on the platform's lower levels with Kick in top place. Photographers crowded to the foot of the stage to shoot the winners with cameras and flash guns.

Ryan toyed with his own anonymity. "Wasn't that Number One somethin'?" he said to a small group of three huge powerlifters.

"Yeah," they said.

"I hear this is his first contest." Ryan cast bread on the water.

"You're shittin' me." The guy curled his twenty-inch bicep up to stroke his thick moustache.

"Not me," Ryan said.

"Then the guy's even more of a dude." He turned to his partner. "Hey, Doyle. This is Blondie's first contest." Then he saluted Ryan with his big meat hook. "Yeah, buddy."

That night Ryan drove the red Corvette, crammed with the four big trophies, back to the Motel San Diego. Laughing and exhausted, Ryan stripped and lay back on the bed.

"Lie still, coach." Kick arranged the muscle trophies carefully on the sheets around him.

"Now I know," Ryan was hot with anticipation, "what Oscar winners do when they get home."

Kick, smiling, moved back from the bed. Slowly, sensually, he stripped himself out of his green Adidas warm-up suit. His tanned body still glistened with the olive oil and sweat of the competition. With his thumbs, he pulled his tailored brown posing briefs down from his waist, down past the brass cock ring circling the root of his big blond dick and balls, down his official Best Legs in Ten Western States.

He had become very serious. For a moment, he stood and studied Ryan who was awestruck at this intimacy following so quickly the public physique presentation. The applause was nothing compared to what they saw in each other's eyes. In all their private nights of making love, no night had begun with such wide-open celebration of Kick's exquisite manliness. The world for the first time had acknowledged what they had privately known and pursued so intensely for so long together. The victory belonged to them both. They were united. They had gone public in their quest for manly excellence, and the crowds were eating it up.

Naked, in his All-American prizewinning glory, Kick moved toward the bed. He lowered himself slowly down on Ryan's naked body.

"I've wanted all my life to do this," Kick said. "This way. This time. On a night like this. Tonight's a special one."

He meant make muscle-love man-to-man, lover-to-lover, bodybuilder-to-coach, in those triumphant first hours after the winning of his first physique contest. Their separate boyhood dreams of manhood had conjoined.

"It's you, Ry. This is my personal best. From me to you. There's no other man."

At the start, the only promise they had made was never to become ordinary to each other.

"I want to lay it all on you, coach."

The Energy between them was stronger than ever.

Hours later, exhausted in each other's arms, in the quiet before the San Diego dawn, Kick whispered to Ryan.

"You won't laugh," he said. He rubbed Ryan's belly frosted with dried glaze. "I mean it seriously."

He moved his golden face in close to Ryan's and announced it like a mandate to the writer whose cheek rested in the fragrant under-cove where Kick's arm and shoulder joined his chest.

"Someday," Kick said, "I want us to be a story told at night in beds around the world."

Ryan's hungry heart came running.

Send in the Clones

1

Clarinet intro. Then bass and soft piano. "Maybe next time, I'll be Kander." Kweenie parodied the blues, doing Liza doing Judy. "Maybe next time, he'll be Ebb." In the baby pinpoint spot, she was all bowler hat, big eyelashes, red lipstick, and spit curls pasted on each cheek. "Maybe next time for the best time . . ." Her red-sequined Judy-jacket reflected darts of spotlight around the supper club. ". . . he'll be totally gay." She blew a kiss to her drummer brushing her beat. "He will do me? Fast! I'll be homo? At last!" Outing her lust for gay men, she teased the lyrics. "Not a 'lady' anymore like the last hag and the hag before." She picked up the chorus. "Everybody loves a lover." She expanded. "So everybody loves me." Her green fingernails clawed the air above her head. "Lady Castro. Lady Folsom. Take a big look at me!" She hit all the right poses to make them love her. "When all you boys are in my corner, I'll blow you all away!" Channeling Judy's invincible voice, she became Liza the Conqueror. "Call me Kweenie! Call me Kweenie!" She thrust jazz hands up framing her face. As the audience rose to their feet, she exploded. "Maybe next time, maybe next time, you'll love me!"

The supper crowd at Fanny's loved Kweenasheba. She was as good as Ryan at being other people, but she, singing torch usually best sung by divas one scotch-and-soda past their prime, knew when to quit. She finished her set and came to my table. "What movie am I?" she asked.

Before I could say, *"Cabaret,"* she said, *"Imitation of Life."* She affected a certain world-weariness.

"Seen much of Ry?" I asked.

"Not since Kick moved in." She had an envious look in her eye. "Do you blame either of them?"

"Solly says Ry's writing some top-secret project."

"You sound like a reporter for the *National Intruder,*" she said. "Are you keeping notes?"

"The unexamined lifestyle is not worth living."

"Magnus, dear Magnus." She took my hand. "You're such a bag of horseshit. All I know is Ryan is holed up with Kick. Solly Blue is pissed. He has—how do you say in English?—no love for Kick."

"Why not?"

"Don't ask," Kweenie said. "Solly says he has reasons."

"Such as?"

"He won't say. At least, he won't tell me." She signaled for an orange juice. "I think he's jealous. Ryan told him that Kick's the Most Original Thinker he knows."

"That used to be Solly's title."

"Precisely," Kweenie said. "But these days nobody's as good as Kick." She threw her hands up. "Ryan says they discuss stuff. He calls it *stuff*."

"Stuff? What kind of stuff?"

"Mantalk," Kweenie said. "Ry told me it was mantalk."

"He means it's none of your business."

"And none of yours." She disliked her brother excluding her with a word like *mantalk*. She knew if she had been born Ryan's brother, their relationship would be quite different. They would have made love, which he denied her and himself, not because she was his sibling, but because she was female.

"They're in-love," I said.

"They're two gifted boys playing grown-ups and getting away with it."

Because of Kick, Ryan's life, like his erotic writing, had assumed a creamy, dreamy, soft-core porno look: everything slightly more real than real. Kick was one of his fictional superheroes incarnated like Pygmalion's Galatea and Henry Higgins' Eliza. Their life together was an enameled dreamtime: clothes by *Gentlemen's Quarterly*, sets by *Architectural Digest*, bodies by Colt Studios out of *Iron Man*, script by Ryan out of Lewis Carroll by de Sade.

"Living off center is a necessity," Ryan said.

What neither Kweenie nor I knew then was that Ryan was in the last throes of his final draft of his *Masculinist Manifesto*, which he subtitled *A Man's Man*. I think he had some idea of the sensation, but had no idea of the controversy, the long essay would cause when printed with erotic photos and distributed in tabloid format on San Francisco street corners. Not that Kick and Ryan invented everything in the *Manifesto*. More that Ryan pulled together something growing and mobilizing toward a confrontation in San Francisco: the singular popular front of freshly uncloseted male homosexuals was breaking up into subgroups of politics and attitude fueled by lesbian feminist separatist women.

Ryan intended the *Manifesto* as the very off-center voice of the most invisible queer of them all: the manly homosexual.

The *Manifesto's* opening line read: "The hardest thing to be in America today is a man."

"They're probably holed up," Kweenie said, "writing dirty stories and taking dirty pictures."

"*Maneuvers* keeps them off the streets," I said. "That's the function of gay porn."

"Without it what would little boys do?"

"Forget it," I said. "They're in-love"

"I know they're in-love," Kweenie said. Her orange juice arrived. "Just like the movies. There's the smell of popcorn in the air."

2

Solomon Bluestein was a movie mogul. He was the Sam Goldwyn of the Tenderloin. He started out in 1969 shooting little porno films on Super 8 and evolved into erotic videotapes he sold mail order. Solid Blue Video, Inc., was a money machine paying quarterly taxes. Solly never hired the expensive, interchangeable blond twits or the coltish modelles who populated gay films. His stars were real trash: runaways, throwaways, street hustlers, ex-cons. He was a grand cross between Fagin and Father Flanagan.

"I'd rather smell the sweat from a straight young wrestler's dripping armpit than have sex with a gay boy."

His *cinema verite* videotapes were legendary on the pudbuster circuit. His technique was high-toned. His material was low-down. His gross was boffo. For thirty bucks, he outhustled his hustlers. He coached from his tough guys the hard-assed Attitude that attracted and frightened people in the street. He understood beauty and terror.

Ignoring his own advice, he warned his customers in his brochures: "Never take these boys to your lovely home."

His stars were dangerous graduates of the best Youth Authorities from east coast to west and points south. To a trick, they were, so they said, personally straight, professionally mercenary, living in cheap rooms in sleazebag hotels, drinking beer and Jack Daniel's when they could cadge it, smoking cigarettes and dope, shooting up, screwing with tough little teen hookers, proud of their hustling, bragging, "Shit! The old lady's a working girl. So I work the streets too."

One after the other the boys stripped for his color-sound camera, posing solo, oiling up naked, running their mouths, flexing, spitting, grinning, flipping the bird, showing their muscles, delighting in abusing fags for money, flipping their dicks, bending over and spreading their assholes, spouting clichés like "Eat it, queer," finally lying back, pounding their pud, jerking off watching straight porn on video, cuming for the camera, inviting dirty fags, oh yeah, to lick up their big loads from their tight bellies and big balls.

"Ah yes," Solly Blue said. "I give them a chance to spill their guts. How novel. They've always been told to shut up. Nobody ever asked them what they think about anything. I do. I let them be. No censorship, no direction, no nothing. It's sex. It's always sex. Does anyone realize I make Andy Warhol movies? All I tell them is their performance is supposed to be jack-off material. They don't need a government grant for the arts. They've hustled enough faggots. They know what faggots want. I know what faggots buy. Faggots don't buy love and kisses. Faggots buy verbal abuse and physical domination. So that's what I sell. Supply and demand. They can never get enough. Thank God. I'm the only one selling rough trade."

Once plugged into the network of San Francisco hustlers, Solly never had to leave his apartment. Word got around about his ten dollar finder's fee. Every model had a homeboy. "Hey, bro, it's cool." The buddy made a video-tape and introduced the next guy.

"My boys are not gay," Solly said, "and they're not straight. They prefer easy women, but they love easier money. They don't like to work, so they hustle. As long as they've got the bodies for it."

He poured himself another in his chain-glasses of real Coca-Cola. With sugar. With caffeine.

"My boys may not know much, but they know sex and violence. My only control over them in this penthouse is to get the violence out of them on videotape, and the sex out of them in bed."

Solly Blue's position was no pose. "I'm an existentialist, minimalist realist." He was bottom-line honest. He hadn't darkened the door of a synagogue in years, but he was a major patron of the ACLU, which, he said, was the same thing. He had taken his kinky personal obsessions and ingeniously turned them into a commercially successful business. "Terror is my only hard-on," Solly said. "I'm only happy when a bully roughs me up in the sack. I've never liked sex with gay men. I like the danger of these street boys who strip and strut and show me their muscles and tattoos. I like the way they sit on my chest, twist my tits, and spit in my face. I like to see their hard dicks bobbing while they've got their hands around my throat tight enough to convince me to cum."

Ryan called Solly at least twice a day. If he failed to answer, Ryan immediately feared the worst. Guns. Knives. Blood on the mirror. Brains on the carpet. Terminal choke holds. The swollen tongue protruding black from the mouth. Roaches feasting on the undiscovered corpse. The traffic in Solly Blue's Tenderloin penthouse, where every room was painted the same dark blue, was dangerous.

"Everybody who comes through my door," Solly said, "is either buying or selling something: bodies, drugs, you name it."

Solly had been robbed at gunpoint, knifepoint, and fistpoint. He had been roughed up and tied up. He had been burglarized even though he rarely left his apartment. His boys watched his comings and goings from the street. They spied on him. So he stayed put on his couch, connected to his friends over the telephone, and wired to his boys through the network of the streets. In a way, his boys held him hostage for his art.

"I have the only penthouse in the City furnished in early Salvation Army." He gestured at oddments of recycled blond end tables, pole lamps, and faded chairs and sofas. "The movie set of the damned," he said. As low-class props, the junk furniture fit the hustlers videotaped upon them. "I can't have anything here that anybody would want," he said. "The tape recorder, the tape duplicator, the color TV. They're temptation enough. To say nothing of all my blank tapes and my master videotapes these boys would erase to record wrestling." Solly always expected the bottom line of abuse from his boys. "One day one of them will kill me," he said. "I've already lived too long anyway. There's only one thing to be in life and that's twenty-one and tough." Solomon Bluestein saw his boys the way he saw his life: in finite terms. "What is, is."

Ryan saw his own life as the launchpad to infinity, to transcendence, to spirituality, to purity, to idealism, to life everlasting. Classic, clean, athletic manliness turned Ryan's head, but he appreciated Solly's Sartrean pursuit of mean street hustlers whose tattoos, lean hard bodies, and redneck attitudes took no shit. Their penchant for boxing, wrestling, and karate led Solly to a deep-seated respect for their knives, guns, and deadly nunchuks. He courted their danger. He found honest excitement in victimization.

"I pay them money to spit on me," Solly said.

Ryan understood his friend's sexual preference, but for his own part he had no intention of being a victim. His sexual preference was not victimization; it was celebration. Solly warned him that the difference between them was semantics.

"What kind of fool am I?" Solly Blue asked. He paused and pointed at Ryan. "A kind no different than you."

"Then we're both fools," Ryan said.

Ryan loved Solly because Solly dared to please himself living out a dimension of sex that Ryan understood but found foreign. "The sex games Kick and I play," he said, "are different from you and your boys. We may play similar games, but we do it with mutuality, with regard for one another."

"My boys regard me," Solly said, "as the source of the cash. How does Kick regard you?"

"He regards me as the person he's let in closer to him than he's ever let anyone."

"How genteel! How aristocratic! How southern-fried!"

"How unlike the low-rent ingenues that sit on your face!"

Tiger was a case in point.

Tiger was a fresh seventeen when he zoomed on his skateboard past Solly on that block of Market Street in front of the hustler bar called the Old Crow, the oldest operating gay bar in town. Solly's head turned. This boy was special. He had potential. Solly pulled two twenties from his pocket and rubbed them under his nose across his moustache. His eyes locked straight into Tiger who glided back to a fancy stop.

"Follow me," Solly said. He was intense. Tiger could not resist. Solly knew immediately what it would take Tiger five years to learn: this boy was the hustler he would take on as his son.

Solly grew more firm in his dick and in his fatherly resolve when he learned that three years before, Tiger had pleaded guilty of attempted murder after he smashed his mother's skull with a hammer and stabbed her in the chest with a screwdriver as she slept on the sofa in their Daly City home. Then he masturbated, cut his wrists, and drove, bleeding, to the police station. In the hospital he managed to get off a karate kick that broke a policeman's jaw. His mother survived the attack and visited him twice in the two years he was sentenced to the California Youth Authority. She scolded him for the several prison tattoos etched on his arms. When he was released, he called her from a phone booth. All she said was, "Hello?" And he hung up. He headed for the Tenderloin. In the Youth Authority he had learned the street value of a healthy, muscular, suckable young body. He had the mean good looks. Solomon Bluestein had the bucks.

"He calls me 'Dear Old Dad,'" Solly said. "We're made for each other. Maybe more than you and Kick."

3

Ryan's paradigmatic scene with his father in the woods captured the essence of his male self in relation to all other men. To Ryan, writing retrospectively in his *Journal* when his father had driven him to the woods to instruct him in sex before he left for Misericordia Seminary, it was the primordial ritual of the older man initiating the younger man into the fraternity of men.

Ryan's father, trying to reveal the secrets of sex had simply touched his son's knee, but he set off in Ryan the first realization, the first startling realization, of what Ryan wanted: men, and the company of men. Exclusively.

The last weekend in Peoria confirmed Ryan's spiritual resolve to go off to Misericordia to live with other males. Ryan knew that as a priest he could not, would not be expected to, associate with women. The priesthood was the perfect closet, the idealized, spiritualized, socially acceptable way of stating a preference for men's company over women's.

As a boy, Ryan had wandered equally between the porch where the men talked and the kitchen where the women talked, until the women dismissed him. The men never dismissed him. They acted as if he weren't around them enough. They included him. They teased him, poked at him, picked him up and played with him, told him jokes—even dirty ones, which they laughed at doubly hard when he did not understand. They wrestled him about, tousled his curly hair. They picked him up in their arms and tossed him sky high.

"When I was a child," Ry said, "I rarely touched the ground. I thought I could fly. I was always being thrown up in the air."

Between flights, the women brushed the smudges off his clothes, combed his hair, made him wash his face and hands. The women tried to ground and tame him. The men circled about him with an air of wildness.

"Are you your mama's boy," his uncle Leslie asked him, "or are you your daddy's son?"

Leslie O'Hara was Ryan's youngest uncle, himself hardly more than a grown boy. He leaned on the porch rail waiting Ryan's answer. Leslie O'Hara, the uncle he adored most, was a Catholic seminarian, husky for his age, smaller than his older brother, Charley-Pop, and almost ready for ordination to the priesthood. He was twenty-four but he had not given up liking to tease his oldest nephew.

Ryan was seven years old. He was puzzled. He thought he was the child of both his parents, and yet his seminarian uncle broke down that balance in his riddle and made Ryan choose. The circle of men watched him, Charley-Pop especially. His uncle Leslie grinned at him. "Speak up, Ry."

Ryan thought hard about it: he was his mama's boy, and he was his daddy's boy. "I am," Ryan answered, staring straight at his father's boots resting on the wood porch floor, "my daddy's boy."

His father picked him up and threw him into the air, twirling him around, and landing him in his lap. "Hey, Les," Charley-Pop said. "How's that for an answer!"

"You'll be a man's man," his uncle Les said, "more than you'll be a ladies' man. I can tell."

Years later, when Ryan had left Misericordia at the age of twenty-four, his uncle Leslie, who had been an ordained priest for nearly fifteen years, asked him again the same question in a different way.

They stood alone in the privacy of the locked sacristy room off the main altar of Saint Patrick's Church. Ryan had served as altar boy at Leslie's mass and was helping him remove and fold his vestments.

"So now you're out in the world," Leslie said. "Do you like teaching boys or girls better?"

Ryan was puzzled again. He suspected another trick question. A student was a student, but there was a look in his uncle Leslie's eye that made him say, "I like teaching boys better."

His uncle moved toward him, put his anointed hand on the back of Ryan's neck, and kissed him on the mouth. "I love you, Ryan," Leslie said.

His uncle, a year past forty, was handsome in his roman collar. They stared eye to eye. Leslie smiled. He knew Ryan better than Ryan knew himself. He moved his strong hand to the back of Ryan's head and pulled his nephew into a close hug. He pressed his hard cock through his black cassock against Ryan's virginal groin. Ryan felt his own cock hardening. He did not resist what he knew he wanted. He stood passive, feeling his dick straining in his corduroys to be freed, released, liberated by a priest, by his uncle.

"It's okay," Leslie said.

His hand unzipped Ryan's pants and pulled his nephew's stiffening cock from his white cotton undershorts. His own erect penis stood out at hard attention from his black cassock. He was a grown man, the best kind of man, a priest. He was handsome with the mature athletic look of the jock he had been in the seminary. He checked the locked door to the sacristy and pulled off his cassock. In his black pants and white tee shirt, he was the image of his brother, Charley-Pop.

"It's a . . . mortal sin of impurity," Ryan said. The head of his cock glistened with a dear pearl of anticipation. "Isn't it?"

"Not," Leslie said, "when it's done with love."

Ryan regretted more than ever the lost moment with Dave Fahnhorst, but the muscles of Leslie's arms and chest felt good to Ryan's tentative touch. "Hold me," Ryan said.

"Trust me," Leslie said. He fell to his knees and put both his big hands on Ryan's butt. His warm, wet mouth descended slowly down the length of Ryan's hard shaft.

For the first time, the time he realized he had been waiting for all his life, Ryan was made love to by a man, and more than a man, his uncle, a priest.

4

From the first, in those early liberated days after Stonewall, as the sixties became the seventies, men slid easily from nights on Folsom to afternoons on Castro looking for ways to kill time till another night South of the Slot. Castro was a street awakening with a certain post-Beat and post-hippie style. Like time-lapse photography, the Castro Café, Tommy's Plants, and Paperback Traffic kick-started the funky revival of the lazy old neighborhood.

The Castro merchants who weren't charmed were alarmed. They remembered how fast Haight Street had declined to a hippie skid row in the three years after the famous Summer of Love in '67. Some jumped at the chance to escape. Homosexuals in a changing Catholic neighborhood frightened them more than blacks. Gay sex reared its head. The shopkeepers sold cheap and doubled their money. They fled from brisk new businesses like the Jaguar Bookstore. The Jaguar, with its twenty-five cent admission to its backroom rendezvous, made turnstile sex, with In-and-Out privileges, a convenient trysting place for strangers cruising the streets for tricks with no place to go.

Bars blossomed on Castro with trippy acid names like the Midnight Sun, Toad Hall, and Bear Hollow. A gay man could buy a used book at Paperback Traffic to read over eggs and coffee in the Castro Café before having sex at the Jaguar, drinking a beer at the Midnight Sun, getting some steam and some more head at the Castro Rocks bath, and heading home with flowers from Tommy's Plants.

Communes and salons sprang up. The artist Cirby, Robert Kirk, the star bartender at the Midnight Sun, lived above the Owl Cleaners at 19th and Castro with nine roommates. They called their Victorian flat the Hula Palace, so dedicated was its decor to thirties' and forties' Deco. From windows draped with flowered fabric, they surveyed the growing phenomenon of the Castro. Once a month, they opened their doors: a poet reading in one room; a photographer exhibiting in another; a dancer pirouetting among the palms in an archway while a scene from a two-character play was read. Sylvester, young, black, and not yet a star, sang for the elite. The infamous performing group, the Cockettes, sat about on white-wicker chairs dreaming up their stage names: Pristine Condition, Filthy Ritz, and Goldie Glitters. Mink Stole and the two-ton actperson, Divine, both East Coast crossovers from filmmaker John Waters' Baltimore entourage often sat in state, holding the A-Group in hilarious thrall.

In 1973, the Hula Palace combined with two other flats full of neighbors to throw a tasteful, gargantuan garage sale. Their corner, that Sunday, was so spontaneously mobbed, Sylvester couldn't keep himself from singing for pure joy in the middle of the intersection with his two backup singers, the Weather Girls. The Hula Palace's extempore garage sale blossomed exactly one year later into the first Castro Street Fair.

Everybody was an excited, uncloseted refugee, come from somewhere under the rainbow to Oz aspiring to accomplish something openly gay and grand. Whitman's all-gender barbaric Yawp was howled in the streets round the clock. The Castro Café changed from greasy spoon to a sort of Algonquin Club for writers. Claude Duvall established the Noh Oratorio Society in his communal apartment. Harvey Milk, clerking his own camera shop, developed, besides film, a neighborly interest in politics which early earned him the sobriquet, "The Mayor of Castro Street." Liberation, as a pop culture movement, was more than sex; it was tea and art, rights and outrage, parties and bars, costume and creativity, the fun and celebration of inventing one's new self, free, within the group identity.

The good times rolled. Word was out. Cross-country long-distance lines lit up like the telephone scene in *Bye Bye Birdie*. San Francisco called like Bali Hai. The crowds on the sidewalks doubled. A man was a tourist one summer and a resident by the next. Robert Kirk, walking a block to work from the Hula Palace to the Midnight Sun, purposely, one afternoon, spoke to everyone he knew, stopped and talked, not just waving a passing *hello*. Ninety minutes and 118 men later, he arrived at the Sun where everyone knew everyone else. The parade of immigrants was wonderful, and the melting pot was hot, but the population explosion meant there were no degrees of separation. Everyone knew everything about everybody. The next day, Robert Kirk, overwhelmed by all the sex refugees, moved to El Lay.

Meanwhile, on Castro, *Attitude,* the ultimate gay posing routine, was born and found a welcome place to hang out. Attitude was the style. Attitude leaned against lampposts and lounged in doorways on Castro. Attitude was the invited guest at brunch and the meat pursued at the baths. Attitude determined who was hot and who was not. Attitude was an aggressive statement of gay identity and fraternity. Attitude found strength in numbers; and there were more numbers on Castro than any of the immigrants had ever imagined hiding out in their closets in Keokuk, Kokomo, and Kalamazoo. Attitude gave the finger to everything that was past. Attitude was calculated to scare the horses. Attitude saluted the free new lifestyle that each day invented itself at the ground zero of 18th and Castro.

The fragile alliance of gays began to build to a strong sense of community on the Castro strip. When the closet doors opened all across America, the gay men walked out with their bags packed and headed to the Mecca of Sodom-Oz.

Who were all these strange young men and what did they want?

How exactly did Castro happen? I want to know what it was that suddenly summoned such a vast variety of homosexuals to San Francisco. What was the mysterious call they heeded during the very early Seventies, congregating from all across America into the freewheeling spin of the most permissive City in the nation's most progressive state? What jungle drums called so many living so singularly to come at the same time to the same place?

"It's a divine call," Ryan said. "Gay people have a vocation."

"A vocation?" Solly said. "To what?"

"To finally show the world, once and for all, what homosexuality is really all about."

"Call Anita Bryant," Solly said. "Call Jerry Falwell."

"I came to San Francisco following the same voice that called me to Misericordia and the priesthood."

"Nu-nu nu-nu," Solly hummed the "Theme from *The Twilight Zone*."

"What movie are you?" I asked.

"I'm not any movie," Ryan said.

"You're *Close Encounters*. You're Richard Dreyfus piling dirt in his living room. You're all those characters in the movie trying to get to that mountain where Truffaut played a musical light show for the aliens."

"Aliens?" Ryan said. "I think we homosexuals are the aliens. The outsiders. The outlaws. The refugees."

"Give me your tired, your poor, your wrinkled," Solly said.

"The greatest treason," Ryan said, "is to do the right thing for the wrong reason."

"What's that mean?" Solly said.

"Ask T. S. Eliot," I said.

"Some have come to Mecca for the wrong reasons," Ryan said.

"Give me a wrong reason." I was making mental notes.

"A professor at Loyola told me that a priest had to be more than a priest to get invited into his house."

"Can't say that I blame him," Solly said.

"I mean a man has to be more than a homosexual to justify his existence."

Solly smirked. "This sounds like Kick talking."

"I want to know," Ryan said. "Who are all these immigrants and sexual refugees and what are they besides homosexual?"

"They're meat." Solly was direct. "Like you and me. And Kick. Meat. That's what. That's what they are. Meat."

"So why are they all here?" I asked.

"Many are called," Ryan said, "but few are chosen."

"Are you chosen?" Solomon Bluestein pointed his finger directly at Ryan.

"Kick chose me," he said. "That makes me one kind of chosen."

"Personally, I've never been chosen," Solly said. "Never. Not even for a pickup game when I was a kid. Those boys on the playground ignored me. Except when they beat me up. That's why I came here. Now I do the choosing. I take my money and I hit the Tenderloin and I point at a hustler and he comes home and does what I choose him to do. That's why we all came here. To choose what we want to get and what we need."

Cliff's Variety and the Star Pharmacy at 18th and Castro understood. The sexual refugees wanted everything. They wanted more. They wanted it now. Cliff's and the Star gave good Attitude. Money was money and discretionary gay cash was fine U.S. tender. Both businesses catered to the new neighborhood and survived. The pharmacy across 18th street didn't, and died, and became the upscale Elephant Walk bar. One straight storefront after another fell before the trendy onslaught of gay money.

Bored with renting, the new immigrants started a real estate boom. The tired Victorian flats surrounding Castro changed from straight hands to gay and then changed looks. The gay restoration was in full swing with hammers and paint brushes. Off with the asbestos siding! On with the colorful post-hippie paint jobs! In with the track lights! In with the plants in woven baskets! Up with the Levolor blinds! Fairy dusting, buying a dump and making it pretty, changed the look of the Castro. The *Chronicle* and *Examiner* took notice. Remodeling the bourgeois Victorians created homes and laid-back jobs for gay entrepreneurs otherwise unemployed back in those tie-dyed, Day-Glo days when, as Solly said, "Every faggot on Castro claims he's a carpenter."

The early gay renaissance saved the classic Castro Theatre from demolition to make way for condos at the crossroads of Market and Castro. At the eleventh hour, the Castro Theatre, long since a second-run grind house, was restored to its movie-palace glory and declared a historic landmark, running repertory cinema, and featuring between the nightly double features a live organ recital that always ended with Jeanette MacDonald's "San Francisco" to remind the audience that they had arrived where they had always wanted to be: in a City risen from rubble while a dizzy soprano warbled.

The Castro crowds grew. Hippies worked the street shaking donation boxes for the Haight-Ashbury Free Clinic. An artist with colored chalk drew huge Sistine Chapel heroic figures of muscular naked men on the sidewalk; his transitory street artistry was erased by thousands of pairs of cowboy boots, combat boots, hiking boots, high-heeled sneakers, and toe shoes. Male belly dancers took up Sunday afternoon residence in front of the Hibernia Bank filling the air with drums and tiny finger cymbals. Street traffic gridlocked at 18th and Castro. Cars and pickup trucks and motorcycles ate up the parking.

Things happened.

A gay man who had a bit part in *Chinatown* went berserk inside his giant-tired Ford F150 in the middle of the intersection of 18th and Castro, rubbing Oil of Olay all over his face, screaming in three languages how moist he was. At the same corner, a woman, early one morning, aided only by gay bartenders with white towels, gave birth to a baby on an 8 Market/Ferry Muni bus. A robber was shot to death by a cop in front of the Hibernia Bank, right in the street in the middle of the crowd, during the first Castro Street Fair. The *Chronicle* the next morning printed a photo of the street scene with Ryan caught standing near the dead body. A runaway roofing truck aflame with hot tar slammed into a car on 19th Street and burned two young women to Death.

Castro was a cruising ground. Everyone was young and in heat. Castronauts jammed the sidewalks. Dopers and drinkers weaved in and out of the bars. Small-time dealers, loitering in the doorways up and down Castro, brazenly hawked joints and speed and Quaaludes. Men hung out to see and be seen. They congregated around the Harleys, Kawasakis, and Mopeds parked side by side in front of the All American Boy clothiers and the Nothing Special bar.

"Vehicles are an extension of gay sexlife," *Maneuvers* said. "You are what you drive."

Burnt out on Castro? Cruise over to Polk. Bored by Polk? Head down to Folsom. Tired of Folsom? Try Land's End. There's always a blow job wait-

ing out on the wooded trails winding down to the ocean rocks. The best gay
sex is always public sex. With the sex, especially on the rocky outcroppings
of Land's End, there's always danger, the kind delivered by the fag-bashing
hoods up from Daly City driving the parking lot at Land's End and cruising
the dark back streets of the Castro. The gay community united against violence. Referee whistles became *de rigueur* first for safety then for dancing.

Castro characters emerged. On Sundays, when the Star Pharmacy was
closed and aspirin was most needed, where was the lacquered Jackie, the
bouffanted white-wigged cashier and sweetheart of the Castro?

Every morning, at the kiosk in front of the Star, an ancient peg-legged
newsboy cackled out the single, grating, raw word, *"Chronicle,"* until one
morning, he didn't, and no one asked his whereabouts.

On Castro, most people existed only when you saw them; not seeing
them, you did not even think of them. On Castro, most people existed only
when you cruised them; once you had them they were rarely thought of
again. So many men. So little time.

Kweenie was quick to study the eccentricities around her. San Francisco
had a tradition for tolerating the odd. Castro was pushing the City's limits.
Gay women became feminists parsing themselves as radical lesbians, growing hair in their armpits and letting their bodies bloat and sag in parodies of
male truck drivers gone to pot and seed. Leather jackets and feathered boas
came out of men's closets. Both sexes took advantage of San Francisco's tolerance and Castro's encouragement to find new ways to express themselves
so long repressed by the folks back home.

"This planet in its variety," *Maneuvers* said, "suggests so many others."

The street became a district. Castro Street became "The Castro." Things
divided, mixed, changed, grew, and blossomed with the new gay pride
grown heady with its strength in numbers. Evidence was everywhere.
Canny straights went along for the ride.

Mena's Norse Cove Deli was the town pump.

The only thing Swedish about the Norse Cove was the name on the blue
awning. The inimitable Mena was, so legend had it, an Egyptian Jew who
had lost everything when her husband and family were run by anti-Semites
out of Cairo. They fled to Paris where they took refuge before landing finally
on Castro with all the other immigrants.

Maybe that common immigrant experience gave Mena her empathy for
homosexuals. Mena was a legend herself on a street of legends. She was, in
fact, practically the only woman many gay men encountered almost daily.
She saw to it that they were well fed. She was a businesswoman. The value
of the volume of foot traffic on Castro was not lost on her. She had an un-

canny head for figures. No Norse Cove customer ever received a written check. Mena knew, absolutely to the penny, what each one owed.

For two years, Ryan ordered various breakfasts: cheese omelet, French toast, corned beef hash and eggs. For two years, when he approached Mena leaning on her cash register, she said, "$2.82" or "$3.12" or "$2.16." Always perfect, correct, exact.

One morning Ryan walked in and reversed the ritual. He said to her, reversing her code, "$2.82."

Mena gave the slightest sliver of a smile, as much as she ever gave anyone, and within minutes that particular breakfast was brought to him.

Every morning Mena's Norse Cove Deli roared with as much chatter as any dining hall on any campus. On Annie Laurie's first visit to San Francisco, she looked around the Norse Cove, saying in all innocence, "Is there a boys' school nearby?"

Small fraternities emerged. Lions and tigers and bears. Some were organized like the California Motor Club with its annual CMC carnival, and the Pacific Drill Patrol with its members strutting about town in police and military uniforms. Others were looser, sicker, and more elite like the hyper-exclusive Rainbow Motorcycle Club whose members were chosen because they were sex maniacs with public style.

Acid, and poppers particularly, caused more serious gay mutations. Some gays, overdosed on Brut cologne, turned into twinkies. After assassin Dan White's "Twinkie Defense," they mutated further into clones living on Crisco and disco in San Francisco.

"Twinkies and clones live in the Castro," *Maneuvers* said. "They are always twenty-four and always no taller than five-foot-six. They sport clipped black moustaches and short black hair, often with a gratuitous bleached-blond lock left at the nape of the neck. Who can figure the source of the breed? They are born to be gay waiters. They walk too fast from here to there. They smoke Kents. They snort poppers while they dance shirtless at discos. They wear size-small Lacoste crocodile shirts and size 28-28 pressed jeans from All American Boy. They tuck red hankies in their rear pockets. They prefer cleat-soled black logging boots to gain an inch or two in height. They are so petite they can run under tables in restaurants and scrape gum without bending over, because the only time they bend over is for Mr. Fist."

If the Castro was Oz, everyone—man, woman, or in between—could be any fantasy desired. Anything could happen. And often did. In those early days, Ryan ran with the circus. If he was analytical, he wanted only to find the answer to San Francisco's most asked question, "How do I get over the rainbow?"

He sent up the Castro in the Bicentennial issue of *Maneuvers*. Within six weeks, the satire became a best-selling poster.

DESIDERATA OF
GAY DETERIORATA

Go placidly amid the boys and taste, and remember what Southern Comfort there may be in grabbing a piece thereof. Avoid quiet and passive men unless you are in need of Quaaludes. Keep your act together. Speak glowingly of those hotter than yourself, and heed well their color-coded hankies. Know what to suck and when. Consider that two lovers do not a three-way make. Wherever possible, write your number on toilet walls. Be comforted that in the jaded face of all serial fucking and despite the changing fortunes of time, somewhere in Iowa a chicken is coming out. Remember to clip your nails. Strive at all times to fist, suck, fuck, snort, and stand erect. Douche yourself. If you need help, call the fire department. Exercise caution in your affairettes, especially with those closest to you: that dildo you live with, for instance. Be assured that a walk through a backroom bar will wet your feet. Fall not in the urinal therefore; you will chip your caps. Gracefully surrender the things of youth: constant hard-ons, size 28 Levi's, tight ass, new tattoos, boot-camp fantasies, and wet dreams. Let not your popper spill down your nose. Hire models from ads. For a good time, sit on your own face. Take heart amid the deepening gloom that your stretch marks do not show in the red lights at the baths. Reflect that whatever misfortune is your lot, it could only be worse in Dade County. You are a jerk off of the Universe. You have no right to be here, especially in full leather on a bus at 3 AM. Remember that behind the cosmos, there is no great mystery—only a couple of joke books. Therefore, make peace with your master, whatever you consider him to be: Hell's Angel biker or Sugar Plum fairy. With all its talk of gyms, real estate, and rising consciousness, the world continues to fuck up. You may as well fiddle as Rome burns. Be happy. Do what you must and call it by the best name possible. Fist yourself, jack off, and try not to drool. And, above all, remember that if wrinkles hurt, you'd be screaming. Be thankful you were ever laid in the first place. (This inscription was found in the 8th century carved on the wall of the first gay bar at Stonehenge.)

5

Once upon a time, when Kick was graduating college in 1967, he broke off his engagement to Catharine Holly, the Third Runner-Up in the Miss Alabama contest. He was straight arrow. He leveled with her about his preference for men.

"But we make love," Catharine Holly said. "We've made love since we were juniors in high school." She stared at him incredulously. "How could you do that? How could you do that if it were true?"

"Yes," Ryan said. "How could you?"

"She liked my body. I got off because she dug my body. The same as I get off because you like my body."

Miss Third Runner-Up had been riding in Kick's red Mustang convertible when he told her his secret truth.

"How could you?" Catharine had repeated. She had been in no mood to understand that his truth was no personal rejection of her as a woman. Hysterical, she had opened the door of his car and thrown herself into the road. She had skidded on her beautiful face across the gravel on the shoulder of the highway.

When Kick's parents, to whom she had long been the daughter they never had, came to visit her, Catharine had wasted no time, crying her truth from behind her bandages that it wasn't Kick's fault, it was her fault and she was so sorry.

At first Kick's parents had thought Catharine Holly meant the accident. Then, finally, through the girl's sobs, they heard what parents hope they will never hear.

Kick's mother confronted him in the hospital corridor. His father hung back, sheepish, as if he had heard nothing, but had heard too much to even find his voice. His mother's only visions of homosexuality were the prancing sisterboys she had seen in downtown Birmingham.

"You're not one of them," she declared, as only southern women can declare. "You're not one of them, are you?"

"No," Kick said, and he said it truthfully. He knew even then he was the stuff of a different breed. "I'm not one of those . . . people . . . you see downtown."

"I'd rather be dead," his mother drawled, "then evah, evAH, EVAH to think you were like them."

Kick met his mother's searching gaze. "Me too," he said. "I'd rather be dead than ever be like that."

Holding her in his muscular arms, he hugged the accusation from her eyes. His father smiled in relief. He was their golden boy. He was their big, handsome, athletic son, and his hug around his mother's small body answered all their questions.

"Too bad, too bad," his father said, "about young Miss Catharine."

"I can understand," his mother said, "if you never see her again. I pity mean-spirited girls who lie with a vengeance when they lose their gentleman caller."

6

The mind of a writer is a wild country. Anything can happen there. Maybe that's what made Ryan an aggressive success with his *Maneuvers* readers. They wrote him obscene fan mail. They sent him sweaty, piss-soaked jockstraps, used rubbers, and cigars they asked him to shove up his ass and return to them. Ryan never wrote back.

"I don't want fans," he said. "You gotta have friends." He was a magazine writer, not a letter writer.

"My writing to readers is my published stuff. Anything personal I have to say I say in print. My private self is not much different from my public self, but never try to read anything I write as actual autobiography. I always twist the slant on anything that might be true. You have to juice it up to give them what they want, or at least what they think they want."

Over Ryan's desk Kick hung a handlettered sign: "You have to live it up to write it down."

Ryan's stories and articles, and his Masculinist Movement tract, are a matter of public record. The *Masculinist Manifesto* was startling because it was not his usual erotic fiction. It was an essay, a broadside, that upset what the *Chronicle* and *Examiner* both called "the gay community."

"Whatever that is," Ryan said. "Bars and baths and bedrooms and brunch do not a community make." He held out for something, something cohesive, with a larger sense of purpose.

Something indefinable was happening on Castro. Everything changes. In the years after the first flush of gay liberation, more than one voice was asking where do we go from here.

Ryan, more than ever, wanted that over-the-rainbow answer.

Kick was the key to their future.

Kick was not gay. He was beyond gay. He was post-gay. He was a masculine man who preferred masculine men.

Kick had first said to Ryan, "The hardest thing to be in the world today is a man."

Ryan cut from whole cloth the distinction between radical manly homosexuality and gay popular culture. Looking at Kick, he knew one thing for sure: not all gay men are sissies. He wanted young men coming out into the gay world to know they had more options than screaming effeminacy.

Ryan, the former seminarian and almost priest, played devil's advocate. The *Manifesto* questioned gay style: why pronouns like *he* changed to *she* in gaytalk; why gay men carried their cigarette packs in their hands instead of their shirt pockets; why gay smokers gestured dramatically with their cigarettes like a bar filled with a thousand Bette Davises in a trash compacter; why gay clothes fit tighter than straight clothes; why gay men had their hair styled like mommy instead of getting their hair cut like daddy, all the while looking for older men, but not too much older, for godsake, to play dominant daddy in bed; and where did those gay boys learn those mincing, sibilant *S* sounds that betrayed them faster than wearing a sweater while walking a poodle?

Seventy percent of Castro was doing "Their Mother's Act." The *Manifesto* suggested that some entrepreneur could make a fortune by opening the Castro Village Academy of Movement and Speech, with beginning and advanced seminars titled "Your Father's Act." It would be a Butch Academy where students could dance in and walk out. But, of course, the Divine Androgynes would bitch. The queens would say, "But, my dear! Who needs it?" Probably the only takers with any sense would be dykes.

Ryan shook out a grain of salt, placed it on his tongue, and put his tongue firmly in his cheek. He aimed the outraging barbs of the *Manifesto* to catch the hearts and minds of those wondering if being terminally outrageous was their only way to be. After all, outrageous exaggeration was the Castro vernacular and the Castro style. To meet and match it, Ryan wrote the immodest proposal of the *Manifesto* with a large brush on a large page.

Reaction he wanted. Reaction he got. Not everyone caught the joke. He wanted to give manly homosexuals some space on Castro. He wanted masculinism to balance the feminism that had overly converted many gay men into fellow travelers siding with women at the expense of abandoning their own masculine gender to labels of absolute chauvinism. Masculinism threatened the sacred cows of militant feminism and radical separatist lesbianism. Some women thought he wanted masculine gay men to be like macho redneck straight men. He never pushed macho. He suggested that masculine gay men, if it was true to their nature, be like the best of masculine straight men. He never said straight was better than gay. A good man is a good man. He said only that straight and gay were different, and that masculine homosexuality was closer to the decent attitudes of straight men, who were humane, than to the Attitude of effeminate gay men who were sissies out of reaction and not choice. "The person who reacts is not free. The person who acts is truly liberated. If straights can categorize us as women, they know they can oppress us the way they oppress women."

In Chapter One, "Our Fathers, Our Selves," he sounded to some like he was siding with the enemy.

In fact, he was attempting a delicate balancing act that defied sexual gravity.

The *Manifesto* was, in many ways, a useful examination of gay conscience. Ryan never said one species of homosexuality was better than another. He simply articulated the quiet voice of manly queers wanting to come finally out of the last homosexual closet. For the rest, he hoped they all could be the best they could be according to whatever lights were right for them.

He could not divine the effeminate homosexual prejudice against masculine homosexuals.

He had his *sui generis* rationale.

If homosexuals were called to be the best, they should be the best. Much of the *Manifesto* was tongue-in-chic. It was a joke. A send-up. It was a broadside of seventies' Attitude. Ryan wanted to sharpen the cutting edge of homosexuality. "Who are we all really? What are we besides gay?" Putting on Attitude, he questioned Attitude. It figured. Kick made Ryan question everything in his life. But not everyone who bought a copy of the *Manifesto* thought it was food for thought, much less funny.

I hardly agreed with everything Ryan wrote in the *Manifesto;* but agreement was not the point. Satire was. The *Manifesto* was Ryan in outrageous masculinist drag. Kick encouraged him. The *Manifesto* was a *reductio ad absurdum* argument against the excesses of the effeminate gay and feminist lesbian sexual revolution.

Not everyone saw the joke.

The moustached men who wrapped wimples tight around their heads, and called themselves "The Little Sisters of the Pinched Face of Jesus," were all atwitter. At the Women's Abuse Building on 19th Street, above Castro, lesbians planned poetry readings to expose persecution of women by, of all people, a gay man who should know better than to assert his caveman prerogative against feminism. They hated the author's guts. Hearing-impaired lesbians, demanding sign at women's music concerts, shook their fists at the mention of his name.

Kweenasheba sent him a dead bouquet of a dozen wilted red roses. "We'll not be pretty maids sitting in a row."

"This is not what I meant," Ryan said to Solly. "Joke 'em if they can't take a fuck."

"The last thing any movement has," Solly said, "is a sense of humor." He shook his finger at Ryan. "Try and keep yours."

Ryan, truth be known, did not exactly invent the *Manifesto*. Its street-smart guts came from the cafés, the bars, and the baths. He interviewed men. He harvested, then gave voice to, their varied opinions, jacked up with his and Kick's, caring less than a Russian dissident how unpopular his opinions were with what politically correct gay and lesbian liberation dictated. There was more than one way to be nonheterosexual and Ryan spoke up for the strong silent minority of manly homosexuals. The *Manifesto* warned the rising homomasculinist movement to avoid the mistakes of the established feminist movement. His warning to men seemed to defensive feminists to be a criticism of women. He had intended no slight to organized women when he repeated Kick's line, "The hardest thing to be in America today is a man."

He had cracked that small pun long before he had thought of the *Manifesto*. The remark slipped out when Kweenie had wangled him an invitation as a men's erotic writer to facilitate a lesbian women's erotic writing workshop. The women had laughed politely, but during the discussion they chided his erotic writing. They searched to create a more meaningful erotic literature for themselves. They challenged him to write something to socially redeem what they called his pornography. They thought to enlist him in their feminist cause.

Feminists recruit in ways homosexuals never dream of.

If Ryan refused to join forces with them, he had at least heard their message. Those well-intentioned women had ironically inspired the writing of the *Masculinist Manifesto* itself.

"You're not," Kweenie kicked him in the shins, "politically correct."

"I'm not a separatist," Ryan said. "I'm not a chauvinist."

"You're an intellectual bully the way Thom is a physical bully."

"I'm a sexual pluralist. Don't knock a manly idea and masculinist ideal whose time has come."

"You're a fascist."

"And you're a fag hag," Ryan said. "My own sister." He took her hand. He was sixteen the summer she was born. "You're too young . . ."

"I hate it when you say ageist things like that!"

". . . to remember how things were before Stonewall."

"Don't condescend to me, Ry."

"We were all better off when all queers were outlaws," Ryan said. "Now we've all got Attitude. At the top, there's the very-A-Group of millionaire gays, the Delta Nu guys, with their *mondo exclusive* fly-ins they plan once a month strategically around the country. Kick told me. They hire body-builders for weekend bondage and muscle worship. When in Rome," Ryan shrugged, "hustle a gladiator and watch the empire fall. There's rich gays and poor gays and political gays and rainbow lesbians. Folsom gays think Castro gays are twits and clones. Castro gays can't stand Polk Street gays who are of no use to Pacific Heights gays except as cheap hustlers. There are designer gays born under the sign of Lacoste. I kid you not. There's even a gay cemetery in New York state. The designer caskets have little crocodiles on the lids. There's landlord gays and tenant gays and gay Jews for Jesus. There's chubby gays and chubby chasers and gays who hate fat guys. There's even hot, hairy old gays! If Castro were a neighborhood, people would speak to one another. But no! *Hello* on Castro means 'Wanna fuck?' Even Randy Shilts says so. The fact is, you can have a wonderful time at the baths with a guy on Saturday night, and by Sunday brunch, neither of you acknowledges the other's existence. How gay can men get?"

How gay can men get?

There's the ironic thousand-dollar rainbow question.

One of Solly's street hustlers watched some drag queens' bitch fight, and commented: "How gay!"

Out of the mouths of babes.

How gay!

Ryan flashed on the straight boy's razor-sharp slam. "What's the difference," he wrote, "between straight people and gays? Straights don't stand you up for supper." He wondered why the Castro Theatre featured festivals called "Great Women of the Silver Screen." It was three years before "Great Men" hit the marquee of the Castro. He wondered why gay men loved movie mad scenes written for ageing actresses. He questioned the camp fascination with *Mildred Pierce* and *Baby Jane*. What strange gay twist caused good-looking men to dress up in outrageous drag that no tasteful woman would be caught dead in? He wondered why boys like Kweenie's twit-blond roommate, Evan-Eddie, preferred doing their Mother's Act rather than their father's.

He was positive the essence of homosexuality was not a man's wanting to be a woman. Men, who wanted to be women, might bed men, but they were something other than purely homosexual. He meant simply to undo the popular stereotype that when two men are in bed, one of them plays the woman; that when two women make love, one of them plays the man.

He wrote: "When a man and a woman are in bed, among other things they're doing, they're celebrating their sexual otherness. When two men make love, among other things they are doing, they celebrate their common masculinity in a union and bonding that only a same-sex couple can do. Neither thinks of women or of women's roles. That's a straight myth. The same goes for two women getting off together by celebrating everything between them that is essentially female. Same-sex unitive sexuality is as important as mixed-sex procreational sexuality. Besides that, there's more. Everyone should be able to have recreational sex without personal involvement and without the purpose of conception. How outlaw can we get?"

In a City with annual coronations of emperors and empresses, he asked lesbians why they as women never ran for Empress leaving gay men to run for Emperor. Royalty never likes revolution. The question seemed like a stake driven in the heart of gay and lesbian sexual poses.

"You think," Kweenie said, "you're Tom Paine. But you're not, Blanche. You're not. I know what movie you are."

"I'm not playing our game. And don't call me Blanche."

"You think you're a romantic radical like Streisand in *The Way We Were*."

"I suppose Kick is the golden Redford."

"Ta-*DA!*" Kweenie spread her hands. "Be careful," she warned. "There's always a last reel."

Ryan, I think, genuinely empathized with the upward aspirations of the oppressed. The priest in him genuinely tried to respect everyone. He wanted them all to keep carefully their trips' equality. He mistrusted superficial coalitions of alienated movements that muddied one another's causes.

Ryan loved to ruffle feathers.

In San Francisco, it was never individual people seeking their individual rights who dismayed him. It was more the crazy-quilt mix of too many politically correct movements all stampeding together down Market Street to City Hall every time there was a left-field anniversary of Harvey Milk's birth, Harvey Milk's Death, Harvey Milk's circumcision, Harvey Milk's bar mitzvah, Harvey Milk's coming out, Harvey Milk's election, Harvey Milk's last brunch, Harvey Milk's last zit, Harvey Milk's last orgasm.

How many indignant parades could attach themselves to Harvey Milk without trivializing the assassinated supervisor? Every politically correct group in town dragged Harvey out as its champion. "Harvey Marches" from Castro to City Hall became a ritual act of public necrophilia. Ryan thought the marchers' signs would be more accurate if, instead of "Harvey

Milk," they read, "Milk Harvey." Harvey, politicized in Death, was more of a media star than he had been in life. Women idolized Harvey; he was a safe man; he could not betray them and fuck them over; he was dead. Gay men pumped their pecs behind Harvey's face silk screened on tee shirts sold in the Castro. When gay shops sell your image, you know you're dead, you're a saint, and you're commercial.

Ryan would have objected to none of the hoopla if only the blind hadn't tried to consolidate the blind under one unified banner. Finding Harvey had become as trendy as born-again politicians and convicted murderers finding Jesus. The milk train, that Tennessee Williams said doesn't stop here anymore, was parked on a rail siding at 18th and Castro.

"Whatever happened to George Moscone?" Ryan asked. No one marched in the name of the mayor who was gunned down at the same time as Harvey Milk. Was Moscone too much of a straight white male to be reverenced by gay men and lesbian women?

The *Manifesto* proclaimed it was time for men to be interested in men's masculine rights. "God knows, no one else champions men anymore. We're out of fashion. One imbalance has replaced the other."

He questioned the wisdom of outrageous drag queens, transpersons, El Salvadoran refugees, and feminists hitching their causes to the bandwagon of male homosexuality, which they disrespected. They could have their empress coronations, their expensive gender operations, their Sandinista banners, and their Constitutional amendment, but they couldn't sully the purity of homosexual masculinity that the priest in him, encouraged by the bodybuilder at his side, had begun, right or wrong, to champion in words in the press, the way Kick was its model in the flesh on Castro.

Even so, he was more satirist than misogynist, but Kweenie called him an asshole when he blamed the women he dubbed "The Auntie Porn and Violence Battalion" for pouring glue into the coin slots on the street racks selling *Maneuvers* that had nothing to do with his *Masculinist Manifesto*, that had nothing to do, really, with women, violence, or pornography.

"How dare you," Kweenie said, "write about women!"

"I don't write about women. I write about men."

"I'm an offended feminist," Kweenie said.

"Don't be redundant," Ryan said.

"Don't be a prick"

"Don't be a cunt."

"I'm a woman."

"I'm a man."

"I'm a feminist."

"I'm a masculinist," Ryan said. "Your rampant feminism makes me a masculinist. Isn't that reactionary? I'm heading toward the new homosexuality: homomasculinity!"

"Yuck!"

"Until you chauvinist sows stop bushwhacking every man in the world as a chauvinist pig, a masculinist I'll remain, until we can all become what we should be: humanists."

Kweenie threw her autographed copy of the *Masculinist Manifesto* in her brother's face. His inscription to her read: "From the bastard to the bitch."

Ryan felt as hurt as Jonathan Swift would have felt if the Irish had not understood his *Modest Proposal*.

Which they didn't.

7

During Thom's two divorces from Sandy, Ryan more than once had taken care of his brother's sexual needs. "Thom always comes to live with me when he can't take Sandy and the triplets anymore. He comes to me for custodial care. She gets his head all twisted up in his underwear. He acts crazy. Not insane. Just crazy. Patsy Cline crazy. Having sex with him is the one way, really the only way I know, to get him down off the wall. For a few days after, he's not so hyper. We don't make love. We have sex, but we never mention it. Like it never happened. Between brothers, what's to talk about?" Ryan hesitated. "Funny, isn't it. Except for Thom, I don't do mercy-fucks. Do you think my father thought I'd have to do this when he asked me to take care of Thom? Jeez!"

Thom was not the head of his family; he was the victim of it. Sandy and the triplets held him hostage. With all the leadership the Marines had drilled into him, Thom was never able to hold his family in control. I had heard Ryan's jokes about Sandy's Annual Christmas Tree Toss. In one of their monumental fights, she had picked up the tree and thrown it, lights and ornaments and all, across the heads of her playing children, at her husband sitting behind dark glasses and wearing stereo headphones. Three times Thom had convinced her to commit herself to a sanitarium. Three times she talked her way out. I think she was not truly mad or cruel. I think she was desperate, dim in most things, but sly in her whining way of negotiating her life with Thom. She knew if she bore his children, she could have him forever.

"I think Sandy got a little too intense," Ryan said. "She had three kids at once. Clever girl. Once is maybe all he plugged her. Thom swears he prefers sex in the dark. Maybe he means with Sandy. Maybe he lies. When I have him in my bed, I leave the lights on low. He never shuts his eyes. Not even when he cums. He stares like a killer directly into my face."

To make a long story short, let me put it this way, in sort of a flashback to the early sixties when Jack and Jackie's romantic comedy was not yet a tragedy, when there was no war, back before Monroe and Clift and Gable all made their last movie together and died, long before Kerouac and Cassady and Ginsberg in North Beach had ever heard of Grace Slick, when women wore gloves and hats and men wore suits, the summer Merman played *Gypsy* in San Francisco near the movie theater premiering *La Dolce Vita,* one of those last innocent summers before things fell apart.

At seventeen, Thom joined the Marine Corps Reserves.

"That's stupid," Ryan said.

"It's no more stupid than you going off to the seminary when you were fourteen."

"I have a vocation."

"So do I."

"To get yourself killed?"

"We're not at war."

"To kill people?"

"What people?"

"We'll think of someone. Enemies are easy to find."

"Get off my case."

"You're only seventeen. Wait till you graduate. Maybe you'll have more sense."

"If I join the Reserves first, I can take basic where I want when I go regular. This way I get Pendleton instead of Lejeune. This way I don't have to stay in the Midwest. This way I get to go to California."

"This way you get to kill the dirty Gerries, or the dirty Commies, or whoever's dirty the next time."

Thom's face flushed. "In basic, asshole, they'll teach me thirteen ways to kill a man above the neck." Thom reached out and twisted Ryan into a wrestling hold. "Thirteen ways," Thom said, "and I'll start with you."

"Guess again, asshole!" Ryan reached out and grasped, barely at first with his fingers, and then with his whole hand their father's heavy wooden ashtray stand.

"Seminarians shouldn't talk dirty," Thom said. He was trying to drop Ryan to the wall-to-wall carpeting.

"When I'm with dirt, I talk dirt." Ryan spun free. He swung the ashtray stand up into a high arc. He slammed it down onto Thom's neck, whacking his trapezius muscle as hard as he could. Thom hit the family-room floor. "I always," Ryan said, "fight dirty." Thom lay sprawled out on the rug, holding his upper shoulder, boo-hooing the way teenagers cry. "You never learn, do you?" Ryan said. "Catch on, stupid! I've never started a fight with you; but every fight you've started with me, I've won. And I always will! So screw you, asshole. The only reason you're joining the Marines is so you think you can come back and beat the shit out of me." Ryan kicked Thom in the rump. "Try again, Cain, when you're able—which you and the Marines'll never be."

"You're about as funny," Thom said, standing up and dusting himself off, "as a wicker bedpan in a diarrhea ward."

"You're so original I could puke."

"You're a phony, a fake! There's something wrong with you," Thom screamed. "You're some kind of freak! Like uncle Les! You holy-holy types! You're all freaks!"

Ryan was three years from knowing about uncle Les, but Thom knew a freak when he saw one. The month after he finished boot camp at Pendleton, he married, much against his parents' wishes, a fifteen-year-old San Fernando Valley girl named Sandy.

"She wasn't even baptized with a saint's name," Ryan said.

"I have to marry her." Thom telephoned his parents long distance. He was almost eighteen and he needed their permission as much as he wanted their approval.

"Don't give it," Ryan said.

Ryan and Annie Laurie hovered near the receiver in Charley-Pop's big hand.

"Have to?" Charley-Pop demanded. "What do you mean have to marry her."

"It's not what you think," Thom said. "Her father beats her. She had to quit high school. But she's got almost two years and she's real smart."

"Tell them," Ryan coached his father, "they're both too young."

"They haven't known each other long enough," Annie Laurie said.

"If you don't give me your permission so I can marry her in the Church, we'll drive to Las Vegas." Thom at an early age exhibited a distinct talent for emotional blackmail. "Besides," Thom added the kicker, putting his fiancée behind him in his dealing, "Sandy doesn't care whether we get married by a priest or not."

"Oh, my God!" Annie Laurie put her hand over the telephone receiver in her husband's hand.

"Don't give in," Ryan warned. "If they get married in a non-Catholic ceremony, it'll make it all that easier to get it annulled when it falls apart."

"But they might have children," Annie Laurie whispered. "What about children?"

"No child of mine who gets married outside the Church will ever be welcome here again," Charley-Pop said.

"Don't say that." Annie Laurie was intense. "Never say anything like *no child of mine.*"

Charley-Pop put his hand over the phone. "Then we'll have to give them permission."

Ryan threw up his hands and walked away from the huddle. "I'll never be the one to say I told you so," he said. "After all, this is 1961," and something in him rose up, "and people can do what they want."

The whole family took the California Zephyr to the West Coast. For the first time, Ryan was to see California.

"We might as well make a vacation out of it," Charley-Pop said.

Ryan spent most of the trip in the observation car writing in his *Journal.* He was nineteen. He held his three-year-old sister on his lap. During the evening, with the constant roar of the train far beneath them, they lay awake together in a reclining lounge chair, watching the desert, lit only by the light of the stars and the full moon. Ryan pointed out shadows of cactus whizzing by. Margaret Mary was delighted with the scary thrills of Ryan's imagination. That night they slept in the dome car tucked together in one reclining seat. In the morning, with his baby sister's warm body curled into his side under his arm, Ryan watched the mountains ahead of him turn red with the sunrise behind him. A dust devil, spinning wild and harmless, pulled sand and sagebrush up into its spout. Ryan woke Margaret Mary. She looked at the little tornado curiously.

"I'm afraid," she said.

"No, you're not," Ryan said. "There's nothing to be afraid of. This is how things are out West."

At the train station in Los Angeles they all threw their arms around Thom, hugging him, stealing glances at the silent stranger standing shy and withdrawn ten feet behind him. Ryan took a hard gander. He wasn't at all sure at first that the young girl he suspected was the bride-to-be was the real Sandy.

But she was.

"I thought a California girl named *Sandy* would look like Sandra Dee," Ryan said. "I love her chartreuse pedal pushers."

Thom blanched. He hated Ryan's sharp tongue. He pivoted like a snappy new Marine and called the awkward girl hanging back from the family group. "This is my girl," he said. He looked straight at Ryan. "This is Sandy Gully."

Ryan could hardly keep a straight face. She was as much a washout as her name. All she needed was toilet tissue on her heel.

"I hope you'll like her and learn to love her as much as I do," Thom said.

Annie Laurie generously kissed Sandy on the cheek. Their father shook her hand. Margaret Mary climbed up into Ryan's arms. "Don't let her kiss me," Margaret Mary whispered to Ryan. "She's awfully ugly."

Ryan pulled Margaret Mary's face close into the crook of his neck. "I'd kiss you *hello*," he said, astounded by the size of Sandy Gully's nose coming out from between her deep-set eyes, "but my little sister has my hands full."

"You can't kiss girls anyway," Sandy Gully said. "Thom told me all about you being in the seminary and all that. I think it's, like, wonderful to have a brother-in-law who's going to be a priest."

In the rental car, heading for the motel, Annie Laurie asked Sandy. "You've such a lovely, dark complexion. What nationality are you, dear?"

"Protestant," she said.

"We're all in big trouble," Ryan said.

"Shut up, Ry," Thom said. "She's nervous. You're the one making her nervous." He turned to his fiancée. "Tell him you're just nervous."

"I'm nervous really. Just nervous. Thom told me how smart you are and everything, and that kind of makes me nervous. You've got so much school and you read books and everything. I only made it into the beginning of my sophomore year. Then there was all the trouble with the pictures in the shower. I mean there was nothing wrong. I tried to explain what was going on, but I've never been good at explanations, so they expelled me and the boy who had the camera. Thom wants to help me study for the GED."

Their parents exchanged glances. "You didn't tell us Sandy was non-Catholic," Annie Laurie said.

"I told you," Thom said. "When I told you Sandy didn't care whether a priest married us or not."

"That didn't mean she was non-Catholic," Ryan said. "Just that she wasn't a very good Catholic. To us, I mean." He was learning how one thing can mean two things.

"That's what we presumed," Annie Laurie said. She turned a hard stare at her younger son. Thom, like their father, had nothing to say, and Ryan knew better than to say anything. He knew he shouldn't ask questions like how many years in a row Sandy Gully had won hands down the World's Ugliest Woman Contest. The poor girl wasn't a worthy opponent. His brother was. Ryan couldn't hold back. His brother in three insistent weeks had turned their dedicated model of a Catholic family into a situation comedy. This was not the way it was supposed to be. The family that prays together stays together. Until in-laws appear on the horizon.

Their life inside that car on that freeway on their first night in California had become very Ricky and Lucy and Fred and Ethel. Ryan looked directly into his mother's face and repeated her very own words to her: "Just think. They might have children. Isn't that wonderful?" He looked down into Margaret Mary's face.

"Isn't that wonderful," he said to her. "You and I are going to have little nieces and nephews. Little itsy-bitsy, teeny-weenie, little polka-dot nieces and nephews . . ."

". . . with," Margaret Mary blurted out, "great big noses and skinny legs."

Sandy Gully turned on Margaret Mary. "You might be an aunt before you're five years old." She pronounced *aunt* as *ant*.

"I don't want to be an ant!" Margaret Mary screamed.

"We plan to start a family right away." Sandy pulled both guns from her holster. She was not going to back down from the fray. She had ovaries.

"You're good," Ryan said. "You're real good."

"So are you," Sandy said.

"Wrong," Ryan said. "I'm better than real good."

"Sandy doesn't believe in birth control," Thom said.

"Too bad," Ryan said. "I'm beginning to. Also mercy killing."

"And I don't believe," Sandy planted her hooks in forever, "in divorce."

"But divorce believes in you," Ryan said. *I'm sorry. God,* he prayed, *but I can't at this moment help myself. I promise to confess at least ten venial sins of speaking uncharitably.* Then he burst out laughing.

The joke of this marriage had begun.

Thom gave Ryan the look of Death. He had scores to settle, not the least of which was that Ryan had the audacity to be born first. Ryan, and Thom hated himself for it, had been Thom's hero from childhood. "If your grades are as good as Ry's," their parents had promised, "we'll buy you a transistor radio too." They sincerely tried to treat both their boys the same; but their boys were not the same. Ryan was the curly headed altar boy who walked in an aura of goodness. Everyone loved Ryan. Even Thom. But Thom was the only one who suspected Ryan was a shit and maybe a fag. Falling asleep together in their big double bed, they were parochial schoolboys cuddling close, their two voices whispering their night prayers in unison: "God bless mommy and daddy, nannies and grandpas, aunts, uncles, and cousins. Make us good boys and keep us healthy and safe." But Ryan always added a last line: "And make Thommy be better."

He said it for Thom's ears only because Thom was his brother and of your brother you always expect more. Thom knew from the start he'd never be good enough for Ryan. Nobody would ever be good enough for Ryan. But goodness was the only game in town. Thom hated himself for even wanting to be like Ryan. He could only try to compete with the best little boy in the whole wide world. If Ryan would be a priest, Thom would be a soldier. One son for the church, one son for the state. His high-school revenge was to smoke early, drive fast, and marry young.

"Maybe we should say the rosary on the way to the motel," Annie Laurie said.

"I hate the rosary," Margaret Mary said.

"I think we should talk," Ryan said. "Conversation's fun, isn't it?" He turned his attention to Thom. "Congratulations."

"For what?"

"Graduating from boot camp. That makes you a man, doesn't it?"

"I'm so proud of him," Sandy Gully said. "I'm going to convert to be a Catholic."

"That's nice, dear." Annie Laurie sounded relieved.

"I'm going to throw up!" Ryan said.

"Watch it!" Thom's voice imitated the authority of a drill instructor.

"I can hardly look at it!" Ryan said.

"I really mean watch it, Ry. Shut your trap or I'll shut it for you."

"Now boys," Charley-Pop said.

"You and what army?"

"The United States Marine Corps."

"I'm wetting my pants."

"Now boys," their father said for the benefit of Sandy Gully, "let's not let a little friendly rivalry between brothers embarrass the ladies in the car. Let's not spoil our vacation."

"Especially one we hadn't planned on." Annie Laurie held her purse tight in her lap.

"I'll beat the shit out of you," Thom said.

"Thom," their mother said, "you've never used profanity before."

"Profanity becomes him," Ryan said. "Think of it as enlarging his vocabulary. I'm committed to the sacred. He's committed to the profane."

"I'll wale your shit," Thom said.

Ryan looked Thom straight in the eye. "My shit?" he said. Then he began singing: "From the curse of Montezu-oo-ma," and he shocked them all by putting his pure seminarian's hand on Sandy Gully's knee, "to the whores of Tripoli." He stopped singing. "Isn't the Tripoli a B-girl bar in the San Fernando Valley?"

"I'm from the Valley," Sandy said. "I like singing like with *Hootenanny* on TV."

"That'll be enough," Charley-Pop ordered.

"Wait a minute," Ryan said. "Who's being phony here? Neither you or mom is acting normal. What is this? A road show for Thom's benefit?"

"You're all so much fun," Sandy Gully said. "Just like Thom told me."

"Thom's a great judge of character," Ryan said.

"And you're so pretty," Sandy Gully said to Margaret Mary. "Just think. You and I are going to be sister-in-laws."

"Sisters-in-law," Ryan corrected her.

"And you'll be my brother-in-law," Sandy said. She slyly pressed her thigh against Ryan's leg.

"I'm going to be sick," Ryan said.

"Have you ever noticed," Sandy Gully said, tucking Margaret Mary under her pert little chin, "how really pretty little girls hardly ever grow up to be beautiful?"

Margaret Mary burst into tears. War was declared. From that day she hated the girl who was to become her brother's wife.

"My daughter," Annie Laurie said, "will always be lovely."

"You," Ryan said to Sandy Gully, "must have been gorgeous when you were hatched." He pulled his leg away from her. "When's your birthday? Halloween?"

Margaret Mary's tears turned to laughter.

"I wasn't hatched," Sandy Gully said. She hadn't appreciated Ryan pulling his leg away from her. "I can tell right off, Thommy, that Ry's a real kidder."

"The way Thom's a real killer," Ryan said.

"You were hatched!" Margaret Mary screamed. "You were hatched!"

"I wasn't hatched, honey," Sandy Gully said.

Ryan could no longer contain himself. Sandy had not yet even married his brother, and already she had pressed her thigh against his leg. If women's temptations to impurity were so thin, Ryan could hardly understand the fuss about their sinfulness.

"Yes, you were hatched!" Margaret Mary was jumping up and down in the crowded back seat.

"I wasn't hatched!"

"You look like," Margaret Mary said, "the flying purple people eater!"

"Oh, my God," Charley-Pop said, "not her too."

"That's my girl!" Ryan tickled Margaret Mary's ribs till she screamed. He whispered in her ear.

"If you weren't hatched . . . ," Margaret Mary repeated Ryan's whisper. "What else?" she asked.

He whispered again.

". . . why do you look like someone sat on your face?"

"If I ever talked that way in front of my parents," Annie Laurie said.

"You better bag it, Ry," Thom said. "And you too, Margaret Mary. Enough is enough."

"We're going to say the rosary." Annie Laurie pulled her beads from her purse.

"You better double bag it." Ryan was daring to see how far he could push the new Marine Corps grunt. "One bag for her head and one bag for yourself in case hers comes off."

Annie Laurie screamed as Thom tried to climb from the crowded front seat to the back. She grabbed Charley-Pop's arm. As fast as the rental car careened out of the freeway lane, it swerved back knocking Thom down into his seat. Ryan had been ready to sock his brother in the jaw.

"Everybody settle down." Charley-Pop was furious.

"Asshole," Thom said over his shoulder. "I know thirteen ways to kill you above the neck."

"Aw, jeez," Ryan said. "Like, kill me already; but, please, not the face. We've just arrived in Hollywood, California, and I've got to be ready for my close-up."

"I don't understand what's between you boys," their father said.

"In the name of the Father," Annie Laurie said, crossing herself with the rosary beads blessed during the 1950 Holy Year by Pope Pius XXII, "and the Son and of the Holy Ghost. Amen." She intoned the Apostles' Creed, and they all, everyone but Sandy, who sat dumbfound by the way their unison recitation had stopped their conversation dead, began to pray. "I believe in God, the Father Almighty, and in Jesus Christ, His only Son, Our Lord, who was born of the Blessed Virgin Mary, was crucified, died, and was buried. . . ."

"Can you believe," Ryan asked me, "what growing up Catholic in the fifties, early sixties was like?"

I could and I couldn't.

"I was different then," Ryan said. "We were all different then. Those were the last days before Jack Kennedy was shot and the world changed forever."

Sandy's was not the first knee, female or male, pushed into Ryan's; but her knee was, faster than all the others, pushed away. Ryan's sins in those days were all the sins of a tongue sharpened by the stress of enforced Catholic purity. I believed him when he told me I should call the Guinness Brothers because he had kept himself from masturbating until he was twenty-four years old. Physically and spiritually. Ryan fought to cling to the modesty and sexual purity Monsignor Linotti taught him were absolutely necessary for a boy to become a priest.

"My sins of speaking uncharitably were venial enough," Ryan said, "not to worry me. In those days, I lived in terror of only one sin. Impurity. All I ever wanted, because that's all the ideal I ever heard, was to be pure. I felt pure behind the walls of Misericordia. Later, here in San Francisco, I lost it. I purposely tried to lose it. I didn't care anymore about sexual purity. I wanted to be sexy. But when I met Kick, I realized that purity isn't only sexual.

"Kick made me realize a grander manly purity, far more important than the narrow sexual purity the priests taught. That's why I love him. He brought me through his body and his ideals to a purity far greater than the slender sexual purity I agonized over and tried to protect every day and every tempting night of my adolescence. Sometimes I was physically sick I was so afraid of committing a mortal sin of impurity. I was terrified of spending an eternity in the fires of hell.

"The priests made me crazy.

"You try not jerking off for twenty-four years and see if you're not weird. I feel like filing a class-action suit against the Catholic Church for every boy who was terrorized into a seminary in the fifties."

8

In the early days when hippies were in flower, Ryan and Teddy joined the soldiers grouping in the South of Market arena. Three years after the 1967 Summer of Love, the smell of incense and pot drifted quietly from the Haight-Ashbury, through the Castro, and down to the light industrial area of Folsom and Harrison streets, south of the Market Street Cable Car Slot.

Peace, love, and granola gave way to leather, drugs, and performance-art sex.

Already seeded at the corner of 4th and Harrison, the embryonic Tool Box, the leather-bar archetype, forecast the SRO high times blowing in the wind. *LIFE* magazine, always fast at sniffing something new and kinky, splashed the Tool Box across its pages almost exactly five years to the day before the 1969 Stonewall riots in Greenwich Village pitted angry gays who were mad as hell at the NYPD's fag-bashing helter-skelter bar raids. "The 'Gay' World Takes to the City Streets" *LIFE* warned, June 26, 1964: "A secret world grows open and bolder. Society is forced to look at it—and try to understand it."

"My dear," Solly Blue said. "An engraved invitation to every faggot in America couldn't have caused more of a sensation. Reading *LIFE*'s expose in Iowa was like discovering a travel agent's dream brochure. Destiny called me bag and baggage. Garland should have gotten a commission. For years she'd been warbling how San Francisco lets no stranger wait outside its Golden Gate. And who in America is stranger than we?"

Not since word from Sutter's Mill told the miner '49ers there was gold in them thar hills had any proclamation started such a stampede west. Gay liberation was announced, not unsympathetically, like a social pregnancy in *LIFE*. It was born, slapped and screaming, at Stonewall. But what diamond worth its B-movie weight doesn't carry some mummy's curse? Liberation's first angry unity quickly fragmented. Gay lib, birthed as a seemingly homogenous group demanding civil rights, turned fast to factions. Put the blame on Mame, boys. Once a gay man or lesbian woman goes over the rainbow, long-closeted rage turns fast to individualized outrageousness. Stonewall's choral chant, "Out of the bars and into the streets," turned into a zillion soloists singing "I've Got to Be Me," "I Did it My Way," and everybody's favorite tune in the key of *Me*. "Fuck You, Girl."

Unity in numbers, which brought media and political strength to the group, surprised everyone with a slow reverse-English spin that bred intranecine discrimination. Suddenly it wasn't enough to be gay to get into a gay bar. Generic gay became specific gay. Dress codes were enforced. The Tool Box, all leather and Levi's and boots, nailed a pair of tennis shoes to its ceiling with a sign reading "Stamp out Sneakers." Put the blame on Brando, who, a few years earlier, unlike the straight arrow John Wayne, thrust an alternative, skewed, inner perversatility on American masculinity, pulling on a leather jacket and cap, thrusting a thousand pounds of combustion power between his legs, creating a new off-center aggressive way to be male.

That's pop culture. A movie today; a lifestyle tomorrow.

The first men wearing the first leather in the Tool Box were in the throes of their mid-teens' sexual-identity crisis when Marlon in *The Wild One* rode across drive-in screens. Stereotyped by society as sissy boys, they could not fit into that slot anymore than they could square peg into heterosexuality. Sometimes men, forced to ride sidesaddle as the token high-school queer, suddenly, defiantly, straddle saddle, coming of age, encouraged by the silver screen, seeing ways they can be, seeing the way they have to be, because in their secret hearts they already are that way, and the hell with everyone else.

San Francisco's first masculine visionary was Chuck Arnett. He arrived in the City as the lead dancer in the road company of *Bye Bye Birdie*. and never left. Adept at set design, Arnett adapted the movie images of *The Wild One* to the wall of the Tool Box. He painted the gigantic mural that first focused national attention in *LIFE* that something to do with a special breed of men was happening in San Francisco. He changed Brando and James Dean into archetypal black-paint silhouettes, new images of bikers and musclemen and construction workers, against which men measured themselves and their tricks. Arnett's clarion mural, spread across two *LIFE* pages, signaled across America a new image of homosexuals. Men read it, burned their sweaters, packed their bags, and headed west. That Tool Box issue of *LIFE* started the migration to San Francisco that caused both South of Market and Castro to happen. The floodgates were open.

Ryan's *Journal:*

South of Market. May 14, 1970. The Tool Box bar is jammed with men in Levi's and black leather. The music is loud rock.

There are two rooms. In the first, the bar itself runs the length of the room. Men sit on bar stools, congregate at pinball machines, mill around.

In the second room is a pool table covered with a piece of plywood. This is sort of a back room. Men crowd shoulder to shoulder. It's a gently swaying crush. You could lift both your feet and not fall. You could pass out and not hit the floor. The air is heavy with smoke and body heat. Everyone is in some stage of having sex. The room is half lit. Someone has unscrewed one of the two naked red light bulbs. The press of men feels good against my body. So many men crammed together in so small a place.

Tony Tavarossi told me most of them haven't been in San Francisco more than a year or two. Fresh meat. This is my first night in town. Teddy says he likes the back room. I say dive back in. He does.

I walk around. At the bar a blond in full leather, muscular, tattooed, catches me by the shoulder. He says welcome to San Francisco. I say thanks. He says you're new in town. I say I hoped it didn't show. He says my name's Jack Woods; let's go home and fuck. The fast invitation didn't surprise me. What surprised me was he felt free enough to use his whole name. Something nobody does in Chicago.

A couple of years later, when the Tool Box was torn down "To Make Room For Progress," the wall with Arnett's mural stood its ground, towering above the rubble, facing the sunlight and the street, no longer concealed, upfront, thrusting those dark images of men at passersby and at the hundreds, then thousands of men who were filling up the flats, lofts, and single rooms at the old SRO hotels of Folsom and the Victorians of Castro.

After the bars came the baths. The best baths were South of Market renovations of rundown blue-collar hotels: separate rooms with the toilet and shower down the hall. The best if not the first of the early baths was the Barracks. On Folsom at Hallam Mews, the Barracks was behind and upstairs over the Red Star Saloon. The Barracks perfected sportfucking. Everyone went there, stopping in first at the Red Star for a twenty-five-cent beer, smoking a joint, kicking back to the sounds of "It's a Beautiful Day" and Creedence and Janis and the Doors. On Buddy Night at the Barracks, when two were admitted for the price of one, any man out stag made a point to pick up a trick in the Red Star, both sauntering like long-lost fuck buddies out through the door in the back wall of the Red Star that led to the Barracks.

The Barracks was a four-story maze of fantasy sex. In its long narrow corridors, men stripped down to combat boots and jockstraps. Most carried a white towel over one shoulder and a bottle of poppers tucked in their gray wool socks topped with red and green stripes. They paraded the halls and stairwells bumping into newer and newer flesh arriving in those early days. They cruised the open doors of the hundred rooms.

It was a golden time, those first post-Stonewall years with their Haight-Ashbury glow. Everyone seemed young, because everyone was young, born mostly during World War II. Drugs were for going up; there was no coming down. No one had yet overdosed or burnt out. There wasn't the cannibalistic hunger one reads about in stereotyped accounts of gay baths that always end up seeming like the scenario for *Suddenly Last Summer.* The only diseases were euphemized as social and they were few considering the shenanigans. Banners of LOVE, PEACE, JOY hung over the City. John and George and Paul and Ringo sang about me being he and him being me and us being all together.

At the Barracks, each room was a fantasy. Men lay back on sheeted bunks, arms across their pecs, teasing their own tits, surrounded by huge latex dildos of monumental cocks and gut-wrenching fists. In four-poster beds made of heavy lumber, men with chinstrap beards and crew cuts hung cradled in black leather slings, their booted feet spread high in stirrups clipped to the suspension chains, sniffing poppers, waiting for the right man propelled by the right drug to shove his fist up their exhibition assholes.

In other rooms, men, more top than bottom, straddled chairs under the acid-red glow of the naked light bulbs. They thrilled the hall cruisers with their dark threat of bondage and humiliation and real pain. They projected the right Look: their thighs strong in tight black leather chaps, their big chests hairy under tailored leather vests, ropes and chains and metal clamps spread seductively around them, waiting, turning on and turning down most of the hungry, horny men stopping at their door, waiting for the right man to come along to be tied up spreadeagled, whipped, tortured, and fucked.

The Barracks excelled at fuck-music. Over its loudspeakers, Chuck Mangione lifted everyone to the "Land of Make Believe," and singer Tim Buckley, who too soon died of an overdose in an El Lay elevator, wailed "Sweet Surrender."

In other rooms, men uniformed like California Highway Patrolman leaned against the black wall smoking huge cigars, their feet booted in black leather knee-high boots, enticing many, picking and choosing and admitting one, maybe, a bearded lumberjack leaning against the doorjamb of the patrolman's room, both men rubbing their cocks, until the patrolman nodded the lumberjack on in, the door closed, and they did the deeds a big-biceped patrolman does to a hefty woodsman in a flannel shirt and logger boots laced knee high.

Men turned over mileage in the Barracks halls the way they cruised streets as teenagers in their hot cars. They passed from room to room, from scene to scene, climbing up the carpeted stairs, then climbing down again, searching for adventure.

Under overhead lights, on a raised platform in a hallway niche, a hero-ically buffed exhibitionist bodybuilder posed. He stroked his penis. He rubbed his hands over his well-greased muscles. He teased the nipples of his huge pecs. He played to the kneeling, adoring crowd of men. They jerked off to his muscular build with one hand. With their other hand, like Israel-ites kneeling before the golden idol in *The Ten Commandments*, they reached toward him like a god. He shot his load across the rolling field of their open mouths.

In darkened toilets, men lay back in long urinal troughs, jerking off, wet by hot streams from a hundred cut and uncut cocks. In darker stalls, men, late arrivals without reserved rooms, sat squat on cold porcelain, Rodin-esque, living statues waiting William Burroughs' *Naked Lunch*. In the orgy rooms, men stood four deep around the central bed, and pressed up against bunks, sucking dicks and assholes, fucking butts and faces, swapping deep-tongued spit, kneeling to lick feet and thighs, rising to hard washboard abdomens, bending to bite on turgid tits, knowing whom they tongued, not knowing who in the pig pile below them sucked on their dick and balls, reaching out to fold in a new handsome hunk standing fresh and aloof and watching the action, pushing away the hands of insistent ugly trolls, cuming, shooting, collapsing in the swaying surround of tight-packed bodies, trying to inch their way back to the door of the steaming orgy room to escape to the coolness of the halls, sidestepping the naked bodies writhing on the carpeted stairs, descending delicately over fellatio and sodomy down to the juice bar in the lobby, to catch a second wind, to smoke a joint, to check in with friends and fuckbuddies, to watch the newly arriving meat being buzzed in at the door.

"It's better," Ryan said, "if straight people don't know places like this exist. If they knew what went on here, they'd be more jealous of us than they already are."

Much of San Francisco sex in those early first days was sanctuary sex. The war was on. Students protested in the streets. Nixon was president. The baths were safe haven from the world. There was no tomorrow. There was only the night. The music never stopped and there was no piper to pay.

Ryan was ecstatic. The intensity of male Energy, he was convinced, was religious. They were men, as bonded as ancient priests, assisting in the reincarnational birth of a kind of homosexual religion that predated Christianity. There was the night and the music and the drugs and the men. It was ritual. It was sex. It was raw male bonding.

"Eons have passed," Ryan wrote, "waiting for this specific convergence of so many old souls to worship the Old God who predates Christianity. Our spirits have been harvested from time older than time, collected here and now out of all the uncounted ages of men for this reincarnation in unison. I have no father, no brother, no son more than these men gathered here in this time, in this flesh, in this space more auspiciously than any of us realized at first. Never on this planet have so many men of such similar mind gathered together to fuck in the concelebration of pure, raw, priapic manhood. If the mythic Saint Priapus has never been canonized by the Catholic Church, then he has been made a saint in San Francisco in these halls, in the temples of our conjoined bodies, tangled in passion, slick with sweat, and glazed with seed."

In the Barracks on those nights, dragging Teddy in tow, Ryan, always the outsider, experienced his first great sense of fraternity, of belonging, of being one of the boys. He knew then, those first years after Stonewall and the Tool Box, despite the nightly body count from Vietnam and the first mumblings of Watergate, that it was their Golden Time. He wanted to remember how it was. Life was so fragile. Everything changed. As spontaneously as their lifestyle had combusted, he knew it could burn them down.

Stoned, on his hands and knees at 5 a.m. on the sidewalk outside the Barracks, he watched the sun rise over his car.

"Nothing this good can last forever."

9

"Ry has a number of opinions on a wide variety of topics," Kweenie said, "and all of them subject to change."

Ryan's was a wild presence. Kick was intent and enigmatic with the smiling Command Presence common to strong, silent men. At first it was hard to get a take on him. Ryan kept him all to himself. But some notes rang clear. Kick and Ryan were light and dark, sun and moon, as necessary to each other as brawn and brain. They were good for each other. Kick made a clean impact on Ryan who forgot the depressions and anxieties he had brought with him to California from his childhood, his family, his schooling, and his church.

"Kick doesn't like anyone to be down." Ryan was learning as fast as he could from the golden man of bodybuilding. "He says we're all responsible for our own happiness."

Ryan's big secret was that he had not made himself happy. Kick was the only real and continuing joy he had known.

"They're an improbably grand couple," Solly said. "I hope Ry can keep up. Kick will give him a run for his money."

Somewhere in his youth or childhood, Ryan felt he must have done something good. With Kick, he finally penetrated the A-group fraternity of handsome bodybuilders.

"They're not gay," Kick said. "They're not even homosexual. They're homomuscular."

For a kid once on the outside of everything, Ryan had pulled off what he had always wanted to be: one of the boys. He wrote in his *Journal:*

Le bonheur, Wednesday, June 20, 1979. I am happy. This is happiness. This happiness is high flight. I'm giddy, raucous, uproarious. Walt Whitman would be proud of me. I laugh in bed, at dinner, outside in the sun, on mountaintops at night. I'm dizzy with the spin of happiness. The sheer vertigo of delight scares me as much as it thrills me. I have as much happiness as I can stand, and then Kick shines on me, and I am more happy. Life is a constant up, a spiraling scale of incandescent fragile joy. The higher I go, the rarer the feeling. The higher Kick and I go, the more fragile I feel. The more fragile I feel, the more trusting I become. He could hurt me. He could hurt me worse than anyone, because I have let down all my defenses against him. He requires none. My love for him, if defined, is trust. We are safe people to each other.

In the same *Journal*, dated two days later, June 22, 1979, Ryan scrawled a related fast entry:

Kick is a vacation, an adventure, a religious experience. We dally for hours in bed. He is the most personal sex I have ever experienced, and God knows, armies have marched over me. Ours is not physical calisthenics only. He is so giving as a person, as a man, that I can but try to give back to him something of what he gives so specially to me. He introduces me as "my lover Ry." More than lovers, we are best manfriends. We are adults. Our attitude takes my breath away sometimes. I feel myself shaking, quivering with joy. I expect nothing. I get everything. I find myself, for once, for once in my life, planning nothing. I find myself . . . what? Accommodating? No. Generous. Generous with him. Giving to him. My God, no one has ever loved me by teaching me so much, showing me so much, guiding me so non-directively at this point in my life. . . . Ah. At this point in my life to have a man who knows more than I, in a world that all too long has known less, is true unbridled happiness. He loves me. I love him. We love each other.

Ryan radiated moonglow. He was truly in-love. Kick had given his life ultimate masculine dimension. He wanted to enjoy it world without end. Amen. The genuine passion between them was from the first a sweating, grinding sexual tumble as much as it was the nuclear fusion of two souls. They fucked on psilocybin and floated up together, two melting down into one, on a mushroom cloud. Brightness. Flash. Explosion. Firestorm. Windstorm.

"There is as much beauty," Ryan wrote, "in a nuclear blast as there is in the birth of a whale."

They conjured an Energy together that lifted them outside themselves. There was about them an aura of completeness. Ryan, coached by Kick, was writing better than ever. Kick, coached by Ryan, entered a series of physique contests and won them all.

"Pretty women smile at me," Ryan confided to Kick.

Kick himself smiled. "So do good-looking men."

I, Magnus Bishop, want to know what Energy it was they conjured. What Energy it was they tapped into. What Energy it was that I once saw in their faces and see now in all the snapshots and video cassettes I have spread out around me. I look for clues. I flip through the photographs looking for something Kirlian in the ghost images of the ecstatic Energy they said they conjured between them.

"I'm going to say it," Kick said.

He put his big arms reassuringly around Ryan. Outwardly, his full hug was the kind of hug Teddy had used to turn Ryan into a screaming claustrophobic.

"I'm your lover," Kick said. "You're my lover. We're lovers. We'll always want other men; but you and me, Ryan, we're the home team."

"If you mean it," Ryan said, "and you're not just saying it because you know that's what I want to hear, then say it again."

"We're lovers," Kick said. "I love you."

"I love you," Ryan said. "You're my best friend."

Kick's big arms squeezed Ryan tight into his pumped chest and tight belly. Their hips ground together. Kick leaned back and looked Ryan square in the face. "You are," the most beautiful man in the world said to Ryan, "so beautiful to me."

10

Charley-Pop's long illness went into countdown. Annie Laurie called Ryan. "Your dad's very sick," she said.

For twelve years, with Charley-Pop in and out of major surgery, she had kept her grown boys updated, but she never alarmed them. Margaret Mary from the age of eight had grown up with her father's illness. Thom kept in close touch from wherever he was stationed, except for his two tours of Vietnam. Ryan, before he and Teddy had moved from Chicago to San Francisco, had flown down to Peoria every third month. Mostly, the telephone linked them together.

"I think you should come," Annie Laurie said. "Bring Margaret Mary back with you."

Kick drove Ryan and Kweenie to the airport in Ryan's VW Rabbit. "Your dad will be okay," Kick said. "He's always pulled through before. He's a strong man."

"How can he keep going," Kweenie was bitter, "after all those operations?"

"He's a fighter to have lasted this long. You've got good genes." Kick said. "You come from strong stock."

"What about you?" Ryan held onto Kick's arm in the car.

"What about me?"

"You've got two weeks until the Mr. Golden Gate contest."

Kick smiled confidently. "You'll be back by then. Charley will do okay. Like all the times before. You'll see."

In the intensive care unit of Saint Francis Hospital, Ryan stood next to Charley-Pop's bed. His father looked gaunt. His face was slack. His body was thin as bone wrapped in a skin of pale yellow tissue paper. Ryan stood helpless.

Annie Laurie, her hand fingering her mother-of-pearl rosary beads, was her brave, independent self. She was so calm that Ryan wondered if, at home alone at night, kneeling up in their bed, she screamed at the crucifix hanging over the headboard and fell, crying, facedown pounding her fists into the pillows. She gave no hints. She was what she was. Her children had come home to her and their father, and she was strong for them. She knew it was not easy for them to be together. She prayed to God to know why they really didn't much like each other.

Twice a day each one entered the ICU alone to stand watch over Charley-Pop for the twenty minutes allowed. Between visits, Thom sat chain-smoking Marlboros in the waiting room. Kweenie tried to reach old high school friends by phone and met them in the hospital cafeteria, hoping to get laid if they hadn't turned born-again or gay. Ryan had left Peoria for Misericordia when he was fourteen. He had lost track of his parochial school friends. He feigned interest when Annie Laurie told him that Kenny Baker had finally married Donna Hanratty after she had carried not one, but three of his children. He spent his hours writing in his *Journal.* Once a day he called Kick back home alone in the Victorian. The family hung in a limbo of waiting.

They had hope. Charley-Pop had frightened them before, weakening, falling into coma, vital signs failing, hands cold as ice, then finally rallying, coming back, going home for another six months.

His episodes terrified Ryan. "If I were my dad, I would have killed myself," he wrote in his *Journal.* "at the first onset of this illness, and if not then, at the second stage, when I saw how horrible it was going to be."

Did Charley-Pop know something? Had he chosen to suffer to submit to God's reckless will? Or was Death so fearsome that he chose instead of rational suicide, this endless, mindless suffering?

Thom, after nearly a week of flipping through hospital magazines and biting his fingernails to the quick, announced he had to leave. "I'm flying back to Bar Nada," he said. "I talked to Sandy. She's got me a lead on a job working construction."

"You're such a bastard," Kweenie said, "to believe that lying bitch. Who'd tell her about a job? She just wants you back. She doesn't trust you. She thinks you're sleeping with someone."

"She thinks," Thom said, "I'm sleeping with you." Annie Laurie was at the hospital. Her three children were home alone. The house seemed smaller to them than it had when they were kids. They sat in separate chairs on the summer porch of the big white house on Saint Louis Street.

"It's the same old story," Ryan said. "You're always the last to arrive and the first to leave."

"The doc," Thom said, "told me and mom that he could go on like this for an hour or a year."

"We all know that," Kweenie said. "Every episode he's had has been like that."

"I have a wife and kids," Thom said. "I have to live my life."

"So do I," Kweenie said, "but I don't make up excuses to cover my selfishness. You've always hated it here. You've always hated us. You even hate yourself."

There was no stopping Thom. He said good-bye to Charley-Pop and kissed Annie Laurie and headed for the airport.

Ryan was pleased. With Thom gone, he had their old room with the big bed to himself. In the darkness of the Midwest night he sprawled across his faded Roy Rogers bedspread with his cock in his hand and visions of Kick in his head. Masturbation seemed unholy with his father unconscious and his mother asleep down the hall in her room. But cuming felt like being alive.

He wrote November 1, 1979, in his *Journal:*

Some Halloween yesterday in this horror show of a hospital. I'm a pervert, not because I'm sexual, but because I'm a writer. I want to be here when he dies, not only because I am his son, but because I want to watch his face, his breathing, the twisting of his body. I want to remember the look on his face and the look on my mother's face. I don't want him to die, but if he has to die, I want to watch. I want to know the sights, sounds, and smell of his Death. A father's Death is always a sneak preview of the son's. I want to comfort him. I want to know what I will feel in those last moments watching the man whose seed I am slip away forever. I make no apology. I am what I am. I got that from Walt Whitman, not Popeye or Harvey Fierstein.

Ryan waited another four days. Charley-Pop remained unconscious but stable.

"It's for you," Kweenie said. She handed him the phone.

"Kick!" Ryan was surprised. "Of course, I can come."

Kweenie looked astonished. Kick couldn't possibly be pressuring Ryan into returning to San Francisco.

"I need you, coach," Kick said. "You don't have to do this, but I'm asking you this. I'll never ask you for anything again."

"Let me check one more time with the doctor and with my mom. I'm sure it'll be alright. He's gone through episodes like this before. Every time when he gets better, he always says he wants us to keep on keeping on with our lives. Mom agrees. Let me call you back."

"You're such a shit," Kweenie said.

"Kick needs me."

"Your father needs you."

"My father's unconscious."

"So you'll run off like Thom. His wife and kids need him the way Mr. Steroid needs you."

"Kick doesn't do steroids."

"You're an asshole shit."

"Fuck you! I'm three hours away by plane," Ryan said. "I've been dealing with his illness, crisis by crisis, for twelve years. If I hadn't left when I thought I should, I'd still be living in fucking Peoria."

"So then what does Kick need you for?" Kweenie asked. "Some of those perverse things you do together?"

"He's entering the Mr. Golden Gate Contest this Saturday."

"I forgot." She was testy. "You're his coach."

"He can't compete without me."

"Oh! Really! Truly! I'm sure," Kweenie said. "Just you remember, Ryan O'Hara, there are sins of commission and sins of omission."

"I've nothing to be guilty about," Ryan said.

"You'll get yours."

Annie Laurie made Ryan's exit easy. He stayed by Charley-Pop's bed for an hour saying things he needed to say, hoping his father could hear him, glad that he couldn't, saying them anyway, all those things a homosexual son needs to tell a father sooner or later. "I have to go back, dad. Just for the weekend. I'll come back on Monday. You keep fighting. You hang in there. We're all close by." He leaned over the bed rails and pressed his lips against his father's forehead. Charley-Pop was so cold he felt he was kissing the bone of his skull. "I'll be seeing you, dad."

His mother drove him to the airport. "Your dad will be okay," she said.

"Are you okay?" Ryan asked.

"I'm okay," Annie Laurie said. "I have to be okay."

"I love you, mom."

On the following Saturday, Ryan was cheated. Kick won the Mr. Golden Gate title with his usual ease, but sometime between the morning Pre-Judging and the evening contest, when Ryan was unreachable by phone, Charley-Pop died.

"I'm sorry," Kick said.

"He's better off dead," Ryan said.

"I mean I'm sorry I asked you to come back."

Ryan, with tears misting his vision, looked at his golden man. "You can have anything you want."

"Then I owe you," Kick said. "For this one, I really owe you."

11

After Charley-Pop's Death, Ryan needed something he knew he couldn't have. Kick would not approve. Ryan had it before Kick and he needed it again. He had a need for physical discipline learned in the classrooms and chapel of Misericordia. Monsignor Linotti had drilled into the young seminarians their need to identify with the scourged and crucified young Christ. That discipline, he explained to them, was the discipline of joy. Whatever it was, Ryan needed it with Charley-Pop dead and buried, even more than he needed it before when he had lived with Teddy.

"Are you alright?" Kick asked.

"I'm fine," Ryan said. He deflected Kick from one truth to another. "I was so used to Charley being sick, I can't believe he's dead." He was becoming expert at prevaricating, at denying himself to fit Kick's notion of how the two of them should be bonded together in the world. Ryan took his self-denial as the discipline he needed. It would have to do. Kick's will was his will. It was his new way of being. He told himself he didn't need the old ways of anonymous S&M anymore.

But he was wrong.

"I have to drive to El Lay for a week," Kick said. "Want to come along?"

Ryan saw his chance and took it. "I have some things I have to do," he said. "Christmas shopping."

"A man's got to do what a man's got to do," Kick said. "I've always admired your discipline."

"Actually, I need to be even more disciplined," Ryan said.

"Go for it," Kick said.

Ryan wondered if Kick knew what he meant. He didn't want to betray their relationship, but he needed something more strange than familiar. He could do what he had to do and still remember the home team. Kick's departure was his opportunity.

Ryan left the Victorian and drove to the Barracks on Folsom. At the side door, on Hallam Street, he waited in the Saturday-night line of men inching their way up the two steps into the lobby. The bath was crowded. The sign on the thick glass of the Check-In window read "No rooms. Lockers only." In another hour, the place would be SRO. "No rooms. No lockers." Latecomers would store their clothes for the night in marked grocery bags kept behind the counter.

Tony Tavarossi was manning the lobby window. He was a short, swarthy Italian who had worked nearly every bath and bar South of Market, but never on Castro. He had a chinstrap beard, a Dionysian mind, and a small apartment equipped for S&M play. He had at their first meeting frightened Ryan with his sexual intensity. During Ryan's first year in San Francisco, he had cruised warily around Tony, closer and closer, until contact. Tony was preferentially a bottom, a masochist, but he styled himself as a top's top, a sadist's sadist, a sensualist's sensualist guide.

"When you get tired of working guys over," he had told Ryan, "you let me take care of you." Every three months or so, before Kick, Ryan had needed Tony Tavarossi's care.

At the Check-In window, Ryan nodded *hello* over the loud music. Tony tried to speak through the round steel vent in the center of the glass separating them. Ryan pointed at his own ear and shook his head. He slipped his three bucks through the opening under the glass and signed his check-in card. Tony buzzed the inner door and Ryan walked into the Barracks.

Tony signaled one of the five guys behind the ledge. "Work the window for a second." He walked up to Ryan. They kissed each other. Tony eyed him knowingly. "You look hungry," Tony said. "Do you have anything to check?"

Ryan gave him his wallet.

Tony shoved it into a long narrow safety deposit drawer and locked it. He leaned over the ledge. "If a room becomes available, I'll call your locker number over the loudspeaker." He handed Ryan his locker key and a fresh white towel. "You really need it tonight," Tony said. "I can tell."

"I'm not sure what I need."

Tony grinned like a friend with a secret. "Check out the room to the right at the top of the stairs."

Ryan went to his locker to strip and cruise in the slow ritual of entering the bath.

Tony took a quick break and bounded up the stairs to the third floor. The door to the room was closed. Tony knocked. It opened. He went in. Five minutes later he came out and returned to the front desk. The door to the room stayed open. Three men in black leather chaps and vests sat waiting on the bed. Next to them a large suitcase lay open, displaying leather restraints, chains, and whips. A large can of Crisco sat on the floor. Votive candles burned on the window sill. In that flickering light, clad in leather, the men looked exactly like Arnett's silhouette murals.

Near his locker, Ryan snorted a hit of MDA and sat listening to the music, smoking a joint, until the first rush hit him. He tucked his poppers into his jeans and slowly cruised each floor until he reached the top.

He did not know what he was looking for.

He did not know that the men in the room at the top of the stairs were looking for him.

He was feeling his drug cocktail. He reached the top of the stairs. The hallway of the ancient hotel looked a mile long. He leaned against the wall almost opposite the open door.

One of the men stood in the doorway. His big cock hung greasy with Crisco. He had rings through both nipples. He smiled and motioned to Ryan. "C'mere," he said.

Curious, and turned on, Ryan walked to the man in the door.

"These are my buddies," the man said.

One of the two other men wore a leather codpiece and black leather bands around both his biceps. The third was tattooed and wore a jockstrap and leather gloves.

"We've got something you'd like," the man said, "and you've got something we'd like."

Ryan looked at the men, none of whom he'd kick out of bed. Then he looked up and down the busy hallway. "Why me?" he asked.

"Why not you?" the man said.

The man in the codpiece came to the door. "Besides," he said. He reached for both Ryan's arms. "Tonight's your night. Tony said so."

Their hands on his body felt good. He walked into their room. They closed the door. The three of them paced around his body touching him, putting a gloved finger into his mouth, groping his dick through his jeans, twisting his tits. Slowly, easily they laid him back on the bed and pulled off his boots and 501's. They dressed him in black-leather chaps with the crotch cut out. Black leather framed his naked cock, balls, and butt. His cheeks stood out, round and full, molded by the tight leather. They pulled his boots on and zipped the chaps down tight. They cinched heavy leather restraints around first one booted ankle and then the other. They tightened thick padded leather restraints around both his wrists. He stood in the middle of the room. His cock saluted at full attention. He wanted the pain that was not pain. He wanted their Energy. He wanted to give them his.

The four men contemplated each other. There was no pretense among them. There were no barriers. The stripping had been more than clothes. Ryan was naked in the want they observed and coached out of him. They were not executioners. He was not one of the *penitentes.* This was not Misericordia. There was no real guilt to be expiated, no real humiliation, no real pain in all this ritual.

Ryan, this night, was the chosen. The baths were the opposite of high school where teams picked the gay boys last.

He was honored down to the root of his hard dick.

Torture, like sacrifice, is a relative pleasure. Whatever in the corridors of the Barracks this scene might seem, it was for Ryan a warp more than Saturday night at the baths. The drugs gave Ryan that familiar old feeling.

His head clicked.

He was high, and certain these strangers knew they were, all four of them, concelebrating priests of a man-to-man ritual in the old discipline. They were shamans, more ancient than Druids, invoking priapic gods, congregating among profane men, who themselves, remembering or forgetting, it mattered not, tripped the corridors of the Barracks with motives as ancient as lust. The four were a quartet in perfect alignment. Under a hit of popper, Ryan fell down the violet-colored amyl tunnel with the black spot at the end. He was sure the spot was the moon in full eclipse viewed through a sacred passage of rune-covered stones.

The three men led him to the padded black-leather exercise bench they had moved in for the night. Together they quickly fastened his ankles and wrists to rings welded to the legs. His bare butt rose like a target. The man with the gloves stroked his ass. A heavy powerlifter's belt was laid across the small of his back and cinched under the bench. He was tied in place. They knew their moves. He knew the choreography. He thought to resist, to call a halt, but thought again about this chance to receive.

What they gave Ryan, as much bonding as bondage, as much touching as torture, sent him reeling. They gifted his head, all twisted up in his shorts since Charley-Pop died, with the tender S&M mercies that launch men into sensual out-of-body experiences much like athletes say, when pushing their bodies to the limits, their endorphins kick in, and physical limitations disappear. In the Olympics, records are this way broken and new ones made. In the baths, particularly that night for Ryan, transcendence occurred. The men worked him thoroughly, prepped him, launched him. He entered that pure floating feeling people have when they're starving. He forgot who he was, where he was in time and space. He was in a stage of rising transcendence, the baggage of personality and civilization joyously abandoned to the mystic state of saints.

He was free.

He was outside himself.

Beside himself.

One with them.

Grateful to them.

His body was quivering. They were untying him, bringing him down, laying him flat on his face on the floor, standing him up to see their whipwork, walking him to the bed, sitting in close fraternity with him, stroking him. He was with them and they were brothers, men, all together.

Accepted and full of acceptance, he was in deep relaxed peace, sensually entranced and fully aware, when the most muscular of the three men greased his fist with Crisco and, giving Ryan unutterable pleasure, worked his way effortlessly into him, into the very guts of life. The man's hand touched his heart. Literally. Ryan flew high on the beatific fullness of the ultimate act of male intimacy.

Ryan had found what he needed.

He could not deny that S&M, not the old clichés of sadism and masochism, but S&M sophisticated, redefined in his *Maneuvers* as "sensuality and mutuality," was one of a homomasculinist man's greatest options. To ride, like a primitive young brave, the way a boy called "Pony" becomes a man called "Horse," through sensual, esoteric, tribal rites of passage, that make overbearing reason pale against the body's intuitive resources, is to rejoice in feeling one's male body enter adult sensuality.

Coming down in the three men's arms, Ryan remembered the home team.

Kick would be proud of him, but Kick would never know. Some things were better left unsaid. The bruises and cuts would heal and Kick would ask no questions anymore than Ryan would question what business it was that took Kick once a month to El Lay. Everyone has a secret life.

The night at the Barracks reminded Ryan that long before he had met Kick, he had made himself ready, using anonymous sex to prepare his head and his body, for the moment when the sexually correct man walked through the door. Ryan was erotically ready to do anything anytime anywhere. He once wrote:

Sex and transcendent ecstasy with anonymous men is a rehearsal for the main event with the main man of one's central dreams. I feel a need to practice every nuance from kissing to fisting to become sexually expert, so that the perfect man of my fantasy, when he shows up, will find me ready, willing and able to do whatever trip he prefers. I'll never say *no* to him.

How sad to find, then lose, the love of your life, because you can't do whatever is his prime pleasure. If I ever find him, and I will find him, I never want to have to say to him, no matter what it is, "I'm not into that."

Perversatility is the ultimate homomasculinist talent.

12

Solly Blue telephoned Ryan who clicked on his recording machine. He could tell by Solly's voice he was 'luded out and in the mood for one of his monologs. Ryan had only to listen.

AUDIO CASSETTE #26. Saturday Night. September 4, 1977. "Tiger's just one of my problems. My boys are ganging up on me. The one thing they learn in the joint is that a homo is an easy score. They've manipulated me, because I let them. I've violated one of my own rules: Never fall in-love with a hustler. Always remember that, Ry. Never fall in-love with a hustler. They're all so charming, but the charm is wearing off. They want money, drugs, attention, beer, sex. I can't cut them off cold the way you can tell a reasonable friend *no*. Friends just go off and pout. When I tell a kid who's done hard time *no*, he takes it real personally. He gets vicious.

"Last night, Tiger's buddy Ray who made that great video last week, sat here drinking a couple quarts of beer because his parole officer doesn't see him for another two weeks. So he's drinking and smoking grass. He'll quit three or four days before he has to take his next urinalysis. Why am I in this business? I work twelve hours a day seven days a week.

"Have you ever noticed there are no old pornographers. Did you ever notice that? I started out as a model when I was eighteen. By twenty I was on the other side of the camera. By twenty-seven I had this video business going. Now it's got me going. I've been institutionalized by my own business. My business was once my pleasure. Sex with hustlers isn't even pleasurable anymore. My hand works better. And cheaper. If I'd go out and have sex with gay men and it was bad, at least I'd still have the money.

"Ray was so drunk last night he got vicious. He got into acting the way ex-cons act. It's a good thing Tiger was there. You have to treat ex-cons different. Ray's a murderer. He's done time for murder. He stood there while his buddy cut the poor yuppie's throat. He didn't do it directly, but he did it. He was there, and he's got the murder all twisted around.

"Listen to this. I'm not talking reason like you and I know it. I'm talking meanness. I could hardly believe it when Ray said to me. 'It was shit for us when we cut that dude. I mean, look what happened to me and my buddy. Both of us locked up because of that dead asshole. The fucker deserved to die. He only had thirty dollars, and that wasn't enough for us to pay the two girls we had waiting in the parking lot, and besides he didn't want to give it up.'

"Can you believe anyone reasons like that? These guys will kill you for thirty bucks. Thirty bucks may not be much to you, but when they don't have thirty bucks, it's everything to them. If you understand that, you understand why there's revolution in our world.

"It's no wonder I think about suicide seven days a week. I'm not depressed the way you used to be. The way I think you still are, but won't admit to, because Kick doesn't like it. Suicide just seems like a rational ending, a final taking control of our irrational lives.

"How much longer can I put up with this stuff before Ray comes over with Tiger and they put their little plan together to rob and kill me? I may be suicidal but I don't want to die.

"What I mean is the fun never stops. Do you know all the things I put up with? These punks are as stupid as they are smart. Sometimes I'm more stupid than I'm smart.

"Three nights ago, four of them brought this blonde Swedish girl back to my apartment. They asked to go to the guest bedroom to smoke some dope. The girl couldn't speak any English. She was maybe only fifteen or sixteen. They ran a train on her. All four of them. Tiger included. A couple of them more than once. She wasn't all that unwilling, because she never screamed; but she was fucking menstruating and couldn't even ask for napkins in English. Then I heard them talking they were going to take her out to McDonald's on Market, order her a Big Mac, and run out on her. Leave her standing right in the middle of McDonald's, without a dime, and not a word of English.

"I went into the bedroom. She was sitting up in the middle of the bed. It was a mess. They dirtied my sheets. Punks. She was crying. I sent Tiger out and made him buy Kotex. With my money. Kotex. I don't even like women. I called the Swedish consulate. They couldn't do anything that evening. They asked me if I could keep her overnight. The Swedes are very liberal with their common sense. The next day a black limousine pulled up and took her away. I wish limousines would take them all away.

"You know, don't you, the reason for all this introspection? I'm almost old enough to be a dirty old man—which I've always been anyway. My birthday's coming soon. Call me for my sizes." *End of tape.*

13

Ryan always pumped up his life with intensity. He thrived on the tension of living with Kick. To Solly Blue and me, life seemed risky enough. I avoid risk. But Solly, like Ryan, courted it. It was their common bond. Solly's risks were physical; Ryan's were emotional. Intensity for both was their main hard-on. Solly couldn't really enjoy sex unless some tough young hustler gripped his neck in a threatening stranglehold.

Theirs was not a strange kink. A best-selling tee shirt on Castro was silk-screened: "Beat me. Bite me. Whip me. Fuck me. Hurt me. Make me write bad checks. Cum in my face. Tell me that you love me. Then throw me out like the scum that I am."

Ryan, for his part, burned with a passionate intensity for experiencing as much as he could and survive. I thought he was making up for time lost in Misericordia; he always staunchly denied that. He admitted to no more than that he had moved to California because the Midwest lacks intensity.

Ironically, as a writer chronicling those wild nights, he became an agent provocateur. He had founded *Maneuvers* magazine on a shoestring. He glorified the nightlife of the wild, liberated masculine male. In some ways, *Maneuvers* was Walt Whitman on speed.

In the early notes for the *Manifesto,* Ryan wrote:

The baths teach homomasculinism. In their mazes, men cruise to find reflections of their preferences. More than one Telemachus searches for his daddy, and finds him. More than one Narcissus seeks himself and gladly, madly, drowns in all his reflections. More than one Odysseus looks from cave door to cave door for his young sailing companions. David puts his arms around his Jonathan. Walt Whitman finally sees the night that men of his prediction embrace one another with muscular arms, unembarrassed, in public places. Butch fucks Sundance. Recruits stiffen before the hard-jawed commands of their ultimate Drill Instructor. Nasty bikers kneel to suck off the greasy Wild One. Jocks wrestle with golden champions. Leathermen submit to the rope-tying midnight cowboy who smokes like the Marlboro Man and sits his sweet dingleberry pucker down smack on their faces. Tennessee Williams was right: "Sometimes there's God so quickly," so . . . suddenly . . . so last summer.

Homomasculinists have little, if any, Jungian Anima. On a 10 scale, homomasculinists rate a nine for almost pure Animus. Straight and bisexual and campy gay men are closer to rating what militant feminists would rate as the Perfect One of Total Anima. They are closer to the feminine principle. They are sons of the Matrix. To a masculinist they are that contradiction in terms, a feminist male. They are drawn toward the feminine Anima as naturally as homomasculinists are drawn toward pure masculine Animus. Masculinists are sons of the Patrix.

Neither is better.

Both are different.

Gravity draws all people toward what they like.

Each is to be not only tolerated but respected.

What males feel by nature they are most like they strive out of admiration to imitate. For that reason, homomasculinists think and fantasize principally about men. For that same reason, heterosexual men can be totally straight, and yet cross-dress in private to become like the women of their dreams. Gay men tend to be gender-benders more for the love of feathers and social outrageousness than because they prefer real women. Drag queens rarely dress up as real women. Drag queens, worshiping at the Vamp-Mother Shrines of movie queens, would rather camp out with Frederick's of Hollywood than dress down with Anne Klein. For their part, gay men as a subspecies have evolved only since Stonewall. Gay boys and gay men did not exist in the days before liberation when everyone was a generic queen. Almost as objective correlative proof of like seeking like, more than sexual opposites attracting, gays prefer to ball with other gays who match their degree of Animus or Anima.

Like seeks like.

For the first time, Ryan came back to his basic conclusion.

What you're looking for is looking for you. What you're looking for is like you. So you'd best be careful, both for what you wish for, and what you allow yourself to become, as you create your own best creation: yourself. Tell me the company you keep, and I'll tell you who and what you are.

Ryan one night had stumbled onto something basic about love. Tripping on blotter acid at the Barracks, through a tangle of bodies, he had accidentally cruised an orgy-room mirror. He was turned on by the guy before he recognized his own reflection. The next day he was embarrassed at what he thought was narcissism. Later, he figured from the surprise encounter with his own physical Look, that he really deep down must like himself. He was an accomplished masturbator. "If I don't make good love to myself," he said, "how dare I make love to someone else?"

If Ryan had stuck to masturbation, or at least settled into the uncomplicated calisthenics of California sex, and if in his private life and published writing he had never mentioned the word *love*, no one would have freaked out. Certainly, without love, he was a sportfucker-well-met having the time of his life at the baths.

"Impersonal sex?" he wrote. "I'll tell you about the necessity and beauty of impersonal sex. When you're up to your ass in interpersonal relationships and want some temporary relief from the ongoing demands, the only balance is the glory of impersonal sex. Try it."

Ryan knew his pleasure. He invented gay vocabulary by sandwiching between the polarized classifications, *dominant* top and *submissive* bottom, the more realistic middle ground of *mutualist*.

In *Maneuvers* he wrote: "Some say keys hanging on the left side of a belt signify a *top man.* Keys hanging on the right, a *bottom.* One wise observer has clarified that keys on the right do, in fact, always signify a *bottom.* Keys on the left, he insists, mean no more than *negotiable.* For that reason, a man should save the keys on the left until he's in a true top mood.

"Mutualists are men who give as good as they get. A mutualist does not take another man's sex Energy and leave him feeling as if he'd spent the night playing dildo to a vampire. Mutualists, who are negotiable, who that night can switch both top or bottom, might best clip their keys close to their belt buckles and let the keys hang down to rest along their flies."

Mutualist ads began appearing in *Maneuvers.* Kick composed one of the earliest which was, I'm sure, the essence of all the kinds of games they played. He handed it to Ryan.

ARMSTRONG! MALE ARMS! BIG GUNS! Feel them: thick, big arms, muscle-bulked heavily from sweaty workouts; their huge girth sported in a tee shirt, or subtly concealed by shirtsleeves of well-washed flannel stretched across their mass, now stripped to reveal mounds of baseball biceps cabled with vascularity, and thick horse-shoe triceps, growing bigger before your eyes, the pump of each successive flex further expressing the disciplined power of the life force that built them. With those BIG GUNS lifted high in full frontal display of arm muscle, feel them again. Feel the density of each striation as it's gathered down into the depths of muscle armpits rich with the heavy male scent of bodybuilder muscle sweat. After a bit of smoke and a hit of popper, if you find your nose exploring the depths of those pits, if you can take that big muscular arm in one hand and your dick in the other and discover that between the stroking of the two you're cuming then we're both gonna have fun! I'm on my way to the gym now. If BIG-GUNS rap-n-jackoff make you break into a sweat you can't cool off by yourself, drop a line to me, ARMSTRONG. c/o *Maneuvers.*

"How do you like my ad?" Kick asked Ryan.
"I like it fine. I think I've answered it every night."

14

Solly Blue once dubbed the *Manifesto* as *The Gospel according to Saint Ryan*. "You want to live and die as the patron saint of faggots."

"Can't I be the Gay Pope?"

"Don't be redundant," Solly said. "The problem in any movement is that one tries to stamp out in others what one most fears in oneself. Do you, Ryan Steven O'Hara, maybe harbor secret thoughts of becoming a mustachioed drag queen?"

"Piss off." Ryan considered the options. "I lack the talents to be a drag queen or a saint."

"What if there's no difference?" Solly asked.

"I'll just have to go fuck myself."

Ryan was, I think, as he went about writing for others, wrestling within himself about the deeper, unspoken feelings men in our society are afraid to speak about themselves, especially when they need real affection and sometimes sexual soothing that the world of women cannot give them.

Ryan wrote:

Heterosexuality is older than homosexuality but only by one couple. Heterosexual unions are mixed marriages. And all religions believe mixed marriages don't work.

He punned and played his way through concepts: what was real and what was a put-on?

The Women's Movement has insisted that men can't give women everything they need. Ah-ha! Just so! Neither can women handle all of a man's needs. What's true of the goose is true of the gander. After a year or two of procreational fucking, and a couple of kids, the husband starts going out with the guys, and the wife with the gals. That's when extramarital affairs pick up: when one or both of the couple starts needing the solace and relief of a little recreational, as opposed to procreational, sex.

Up in Sonoma County, more than one married man knew enough to pull his pickup into the discreetly shaded lane leading up to the barn set far back behind Ryan's ranch house. Ryan had a room set up in one of the old granaries off the main barn. Thom knew it was private and he kept Sandy and the triplets away.

Ryan hunted straight men in the county the way gays hunted gays on Castro. He frequently met blue-collar daddies, working construction or driving truck, who, somehow or other with him, shit kicking in the dirt parking lot outside a county bar, let go, and let him take them to him and hold them the way they needed, the way only a man can hold another man.

They loved their wives and children, but their families looked to them to hold everything together, and times were hard with recession. Exhausted by the demands of women and children, they took to other men for the kind of comfort that through the affection of physical release enabled them to go back home relieved.

"I don't need no other woman but my wife," a backhoe operator told Ryan. "What she can't give me, she can't help. What I need, I guess I get from you."

Don't mistake Ryan for the Mother Teresa of Redneck Sex. "And I get what I want," Ryan said, "from you." Ryan had a taste for, and a way with, blue-collar men with gold wedding rings.

"Even if I have to sneak out once in awhile," the backhoe operator said, "I figure my old lady's better off for me being with you. Ain't no man ever gonna break her and me up. If you was a woman, she might have something to be worried about."

"You talk so country-western," Ryan said. "In a good way. Like a country song."

"Whatever . . . You sure as hell ain't no woman . . ." The guy finger-combed his hand through his collar-length hair and grinned. ". . . but you're my bitch."

Between Sonoma County and the City, Kick tutored Ryan to an understanding of real fraternity among adult males.

"Some call it male bonding," Kick said.

Ryan called it Homomasculine Fraternity.

Solly Blue, the wise Solomon, dubbed them "The Gentlemen."

"I'm not so sure," Solly said, "about the crusading journalism. At least if they're hard on others, they're harder on themselves. How can I object? Even if they both protest a bit too much, at least they have style. They've discovered an alternative to queenly elegance. We faggots are nothing if we're not elegant. I'm cash-elegant. Ryan's porn-elegant. Kick is muscle-elegant."

He turned on me.

"You," he said, "are not elegant. You're straight. Straights are rarely elegant." Then he made his point. "Leave it to Ryan's—how do you say?—quiet good taste, to start telling the whole world how they've discovered a new . . . butch elegance."

Solly poured himself another in his endless glasses of Coca-Cola.

"I'm glad Ry's found someone to believe in, even if he is a hustler, and something to crusade for, even if it's mere jousting at windmills. At least I get some sleep. Kick cured Ry's insomnia by wearing him out in bed. That I know for a fact. I get fewer anguished late-night calls."

"Whatever works," I said, "if it works for a while, then let's hear it for the boy."

"Personally," Solly said, "I indulge none of Ry's impulses to make everyone stand at moral attention forever. He's being a bit of a bitch. What do I care if the Castro never cleans up its act? Ryan wants to improve gay boys. Fuck 'em. I hate gay boys. I love straight young hoods. Do I care if my muscular, tattooed teenagers can't discuss Kerouac? Does it matter that they're criminals in their hearts and that one day one of them will kill me? I'm having a great time. I'm a contradiction in terms. I'm an artist. I'm making a fortune making erotic art. Does it matter? Nothing matters."

After reading the first draft of the *Masculinist Manifesto*, Solly, believing in nothing, said to Ryan, "Interesting. Perhaps provocative. But, no offense, a tempest in search of a teapot. What does it mean? What is the agonizing worth? Nothing is worth anything. You think things mean something. Nothing means anything. What is, means nothing. What is, is. Plain. Pure. Simple. You question things. Once a priest always a priest. But I warn you. Do not ask for whom the nothing nothings. You'll be disappointed. It nothings for no one. Not even you. You keep printing this stuff, you better leave town."

"I think I hate you," Ryan said to his best friend. "I think I really hate you."

15

Late one night, at the corner of 10th and Harrison, South of Market, near the Ambush bar, Ryan watched a man in full leather spray paint the white wall of the abandoned Falstaff brewery with the slogan QUEERS AGAINST GAYS. Ryan clapped his hands in joy. He was right. It was true. Something new was quietly afoot South of Market. The *Manifesto* had started as a put-on, a send-up, a satire, but a weird irony, quiet and populist, was slowly turning it true in the streets and the bars and the baths.

Men were reading it, laughing at it and its slam-dunking of gay politics. A reviewer in *A Different Drum* magazine wrote: "Ryan O'Hara's *Masculinist Manifesto* is a quirky twist of insult, humor, and a grain of truth. One begins reading it not believing in masculinism; one finishes it, if not believing, at least not disbelieving that some truth relevant to us as men runs as serious subtext beneath the piquant humor. In the *Manifesto's* every joke and jape and jibe lies a kernel of recognizable truth. It's as if O'Hara, maybe more than he knows, has assimilated by osmosis from the bars and baths and bistros something coming, but not yet fully realized, in what he would call 'man-to-man homomasculinity' as practiced by men who have gone beyond their initial gayness to a vision of their own maleness that must be defined in terms wider than generic homosexuality and specific gayety.

"O'Hara's erotic prose in *Maneuvers* is often experimental. Sometimes succeeding. Sometimes not. At least for this reviewer. If the reader can get around his constant coining of new terms—some are chic; some are cheeky; some fall flat on their butts—then *homomasculinism,* which is his key conceptual coinage, can, for queer identity's sake, work nicely to define for homosexual men a new way to be, as O'Hara would say, 'beyond gay,' into 'post-gay.'

"Ironically, the minute the straight media finally feel at ease with the popular euphemism *gay,* a newer, second-wave corps of homosexual men has been rejecting the word as a trivializing label. Perhaps, for all his bumptious arguments, O'Hara's on to something. Gayness seems these days defined by bars and baths. There's more to homosexuality than that. While this reviewer finds much of the *Manifesto* a bit bizarre and very much too aggressive, I would have to agree that gay liberation's commercialized, politicized Castroid lifestyle has forgotten what pure, radical homosexuality is essentially about: men preferring other men sexually and socially. As O'Hara says, 'Gay men have lifestyles. (In fact, the word *lifestyle* has become the new euphemism for *homosexuality.*) Straight men don't have lifestyles. Straight men have lives. Homomasculine men have lives.' "

"Co-opting the old slurs against us," Ryan wrote, "some of us take perverse pride in calling ourselves *queers, faggots,* and *homos*—anything but *gay.* We are not gay. We are men. The essence of men. A homomasculine man and a heteromasculine man have more in common, in all areas, except the one of their sexual preference, than homomasculine men have with the new cloned species of gays."

The Market Street Gay Men's Glee Club was insulted and went flat singing their most-requested medley of "I Feel Pretty," "I Enjoy Being a Girl," and "I'm Just a Woman in Love." The Gay Men's Twirling Battalion sat themselves down in formation, smack-dab on their batons, and wrote him petulant hate mail on perfumed stationery.

"Darling," one majorette, who signed his name *Mavis,* wrote, "You're too much! Call me!!!"

Ryan had not consciously meant to outrage the already outrageous; but when people are bruised, they find hurt easily everywhere. He should have known better.

One summer night, a gaggle of dykes kicked their motorcycles up along the curb in front of Ryan's Victorian. They gunned their engines, aping Marlon Brando in *The Wild One*, hooting, and throwing their empty beer cans at his front door, shouting, "Is this butch enough for you, asshole?"

Ryan peered outside and stroked his beard. "They're wearing so much studded leather they must have raided a pit-bull accessory shop."

"San Francisco," Kick said, "is full of male impersonators of both sexes."

They watched through the blinds as the women burned copies of the *Manifesto* in the street. The sweet little gay couple across the way slowly twirled their Levolors closed.

"I hope," Kick said, "they're having as much fun as we are."

"I hope they paid for the copies they're burning."

"I doubt that."

Ryan turned up the tape on the stereo, and Kraftwerk's *Trans-Europe Express* drowned out the muffled noise in the street. He pulled his muscleman into him.

"You gonna give your buddy your butt?" In bed with Kick, Ryan affected a slight southern drawl. He lowered his buffed lover to the bed and lifted the trophy-winning Best Legs in California. He loved fucking Kick's splendid glutes. "Gimme that tight dirty-blond muscle butt."

Kick reached his hands up between his raised legs and played with Ryan's tits.

"Oh, how you do me when you do me like you do," Ryan said.

His cock stood erect. He pressed it between the twin scoops of Kick's butt. This was the kind of coaching Kick liked.

"Come on, man. Give your buddy your butt."

He drove his dick home, slow-pumping the man he loved more than anyone he had ever loved before.

16

Ryan had his hand on the pulse of Oz. He was also fighting in others a battle he was fighting in himself. He wrote:

Gays have betrayed essential masculinity by assuming at first, and then wearing too long, the reactionary mask of outrageous freaks. Gay lib's mistake lies in emphasizing our differences from the mainstream of American masculinity, even with all its macho and feminist flaws.

Isn't there an irony in gay activists marching to mainstream the handicapped while refusing to enter and leaven the American sexual mainstream themselves? Separatist gay heterophobes are as dangerous to us as straight homophobes who want to isolate us in camps. Perhaps we'd gain more ground with straight men and women by demonstrating the many overlapping areas of sameness, without betraying our human right to live out the one thing, same-sex orientation, that makes us different.

Give people a chance to relate. How can straights relate to gay rage except with their own anger?

A gay bodybuilder accosted Ryan between sets in the basement gym at the Golden Gate YMCA. "You're dangerous. You want us to come on as good little fags. You're no more than a gay Uncle Tom."

"So," Ryan said, "who and what's eating you?"

The bodybuilder pointed to Kick pumping out his heavy squats. "You're perverting him."

Ryan laughed. "Kick doesn't need any help."

"He doesn't think anyone's good enough for him."

"He's right," Ryan said.

"So what does he see," the bodybuilder ran his hand over his skimpy tanktop displaying his big pecs, "in a pencil-necked geek like you?"

"He sees I'm not a gym bum," Ryan pointed toward the bodybuilder's neck, "with red boils on my shoulders from steroids."

The bodybuilder hissed a harsh, sibilant whisper. "I don't use steroids!"

"I've never met a bodybuilder yet," Ryan said, "who used steroids. It's the sport's best-kept secret."

The bodybuilder moved in close to Ryan's face. "I bet your boyfriend uses steroids."

"Nope. Never."

"That can't all be natural."

"It's totally unnatural. But not the way you think," Ryan said. "It comes from a special Energy. Kick works for his muscle. What sort of work do you do?"

"Hey," Kick said. He wiped his hairy blond arms with his white towel. "How you guys doin'?"

"Hey, man!" The bodybuilder butched up his voice. He reached out to shake Kick's hand. Sweaty lifting glove met sweaty lifting glove. "I was wondering if you'd like to join me for brunch?"

"I'm busy," Ryan said. "I have a deadline for *Maneuvers.*"

The bodybuilder stared daggers at Ryan. "I meant Kick," he said.

"Not now," Kick said.

"You mean *no*."

"I mean *not now*. I don't mean *not ever*. I mean *not now*."

"If it's *not now*," the bodybuilder blossomed into full queen, "then it's *never* as far as I'm concerned."

"I'm sorry you feel that way," Kick said. "Come on, Ry. Let's finish our workout."

"Everybody on Castro knows you two are cunts."

"Take it easy." Kick's voice was even.

"Why you never go out with anyone?" the bodybuilder asked.

"He goes out with me," Ryan said.

The bodybuilder sneered. "What you got I don't got?"

"Everything," Kick said. "He has everything."

"I don't have everything," Ryan said. "My pencil neck isn't pumped up with steroids."

"I'll forget I heard that." The bodybuilder watched them walk away. "But I won't forget it soon."

"Pop a few more 'roids," Ryan said. "When you're big as an elephant, you'll never forget."

"Come on," Kick said. "I don't like men acting like this."

"He said stuff about you."

"Everybody yells stuff at bodybuilders. Like we're public property. They want to fight you. They want to fuck you. Before I walk into a restaurant, I say to myself, they don't know I'm going to be there, but I know they're going to be there. I have to be prepared for them to be surprised and stare and blurt out stuff."

Ryan was pissed, but he lay down on a padded bench to finish his heavy presses. Kick stood behind his head, his crotch almost astraddle his face, to spot him. His cotton gym shorts thrust his firm basket forward through his jockstrap. He reached down his big blond arms to help Ryan lift the barbell into place. His pecs bulged and his armpits bloomed. The smell of his warm sweat filled Ryan's lungs as he inhaled and began the set.

Sometimes life was perfect.

Other times it wasn't.

"You think," the snitty bodybuilder breezed by, "that you're some kind of sex cop? Well, you're not, Blanche. You're not."

Later in the Corvette, Ryan said, "Maybe Mr. Steroid is right. I'm bored with the *Manifesto* controversy. I should have listened to my father. He always said never to talk about sex, religion, or politics. But that seems all any of us ever talk about. We should have listened to our dads."

"What's worth having," Kick said, "is worth fighting for."

Political correctness, like beauty, is in the eye of the beholder. One man's Uncle Tom is another man's Tom Paine.

From drag-queen transsexuals, from leather clones to cowboys, Ryan wanted everything possible for consenting adults, every kind of consenting adult, who kept their outraging kinks—but not their homosexuality—in the privacy of their own homes.

"So much," Solly said, "for the best of gay sex being public sex."

Ryan and Kick maintained privacy. They kept secret their nights of musclesex and bondage. They saved their public exhibitions appropriately for *Maneuvers* and for the stages of Kick's physique contests.

That night in his *Journal,* Ryan wrote:

Kick's presentation of muscle and manliness communicates with people; he doesn't alienate them. (Even though I do.) Straight boys and young men want to be like him. Nobody wants to be like an outrageous drag queen spinning through the Civic Center Plaza except another drag queen. What is the need so many gay men have to outrage the citizens and then wonder why the citizens fag-bash them? The public street may be theater of assault for some and theater of absurd for others, but you don't need Julian Beck and Judith Malina to tell you where theater stops and re-ality begins. I can't buy the notion of gays and clones and drag queens as street ac-tors busily raising the political consciousness of the American middle class taking Gray Line Tours through the Castro. Why should they bother? The secret of the American bourgeoisie is that they will tolerate everything as long as you don't alarm them. These boys have about as much to do with real politics as Richard Nixon. They're not patriots of the movement. They're traitors to essential manliness.

"The Castro they want," Kick said, "is like the Indians who meet the trains in Albuquerque. They want us to dress up in cute little leather hats and Lacoste shirts and have our pictures taken with the tourists."

17

It was Solly's birthday. Ryan was insistent on the phone that Solly forget his agoraphobia long enough to dine out.

"As long as you come alone," Solly said. "I can do without your sidekick. I can't bear a crowd watching me age."

"I'll take you some place decent," Ryan promised.

"Don't threaten me," Solly said. "You know I like to eat with my hands."

Solly preferred fast-food joints sleazy enough to need their own rent-a-cop. He liked places like that. Places where anything can happen. Those plastique places whose hose-down decor, vibrating in late-night fluorescence, made him realize how things can go wrong on a minute's notice.

"Tomorrow night then?" Ryan asked.

"Make it early. I don't like to be out after dark."

The next afternoon, Ryan carried a boxed cake on the 8 Market/Ferry bus down to Solly Blue's Tenderloin apartment. If Solly insisted on junk food, at least the cake could be good. Ryan bumped his way through the doors of the Saint Anne's Apartment Tower. The name was the last reminder that, before the neighborhood was dubbed "The Tenderloin," it was known as "Saint Anne's Valley." The inner lobby clung to its grandeur against all the noise and sirens and dirt and screams and traffic that since its construction in the graceful twenties had ravaged its first-floor storefronts. The main entrance was a haven behind wrought iron. Cupid-faced fountains spit water into deep shells. Spanish tile and curling arabesque columns echoed with the sound of an FM radio playing music reserved for waiting rooms.

Solomon Bluestein was a Libra growing older. Ryan hoped the birthday cake had survived the rush-hour crush. He balanced the pink cardboard box from the Court of the Two Sisters in one hand while he pressed the elevator button to Penthouse 1603. Ryan watched the elevator descend past the small window in the door, its cage like a squadron of metal Xs. Behind the Xs, feet also descended, followed by legs, crotch, belly, shoulders, and surly face. The door split open. The manager of the building stepped out into the lobby like he owned the place. He was followed by a well-built plumber whose tools hung like sex toys around his waist. The manager scrutinized Ryan the way managers are born to sniff. Ryan scrutinized the young plumber who fended off Ryan's cruise by stroking his left hand across his eyes and down his nose to his strong chin in a display of the gold band on his ring ringer. His butch modesty only made Ryan like him more.

Riding slowly up the long tall shaft of the old building, Ryan could not help but think how his life had diverged from Solly's since Kick had moved into the Victorian. At least Solly was kinder to the idea of Kick than Kick was to the idea of Solly. Kick thought any man who messed with hustlers was a sad case. He made a point of avoiding Solly. He hadn't minded when Ryan told him Solly wanted to have dinner alone. Ryan could not figure out the tension between his lover and his best friend.

The elevator lurched to a stop. Solly opened the elevator door.

"You made it," he said.

Ryan was always amazed at Solly's perennially pink and cherubic face. They smiled at each other. They did not kiss. They did not hug. It was unwritten that physical touch between them rarely happened. Deep down both of them liked a certain type of man and neither of them was that type to the other. Still, friends hug; but not Solly. What can I tell you? What could he tell you? Through a glass darkly, they had long before converged: Ryan was Castro afternoons and Folsom nights. Solly was Polk Street and the Tenderloin. They were Uptown Man and Downtown Man in search of sex with the Neanderthal Man.

"Happy birthday," Ryan said.

"At thirty-five, I'm fourteen years past birthdays that are happy."

"Nice mood. I brought you a cake."

"What mood? I'm a middle-aged pornographer. I'm probably going to be evicted from my penthouse because the manager thinks the elevator was defaced by my boys. Tiger has found an honest-to-god girl to ball instead of me. I don't have any money." He was lying. "The beat goes on."

"What is," Ryan said, "is."

Solly stared at the boxed cake. "This is one truly weird irony. Tiger traded his food stamps for some money so he could buy me a cake. He never buys me anything." He lifted the pink pastry box from Ryan's hands so deftly by the string he looked like an Israeli soldier about to defuse a bomb. "So now I have two cakes for one birthday I don't even want. Can I get you a glass of Coke?"

"Yeah. Sure."

"I bought two TV dinners in case we decided not to go out."

"You're busted. Get your jacket."

They walked slowly through the heat of the Tenderloin evening. Solly refused to walk farther than the corner. He stopped in front of a Hofbrau. "I want to eat here."

"Third Reich fast food? Bunker burgers? The Eva Braun fish sandwich? If we eat here, in half an hour, we'll be hungry for power. Whoever heard of a Jew liking German food?"

"German Jews," Solly said.

"Oy and vay!"

"You'll like it," Solly said. "All fascists like it."

"I'm no fascist."

"Reread your *Muscular Manifesto*."

They sat in a booth by the door where Solly could watch the street. The plastic Bierstube's appeal was its location around the corner from the Saint Anne's Apartment Tower. Solly knew, whenever he left his penthouse, everything he owned was in danger. His phone rang frequently with no one at the other end of the line. He was always on guard.

"My boys check me out to see if I'm home. If I'm home, they can borrow money. If I'm not, they can burgle me. Actually, Tiger pointed out the other day that I'm much more a part of their side. I was delivering him a lecture on criminals, and he pointed out that I am one."

"What's one little arrest for pornography? You're an erotic artist whose work is misunderstood."

The waitress took their order.

"My police record says pornographer. I am not Saint Genet nor was I meant to be, but I do understand how the world perceives and defines me. I've always been an outlaw. All artists by their vision are outlaws. All faggots are outlaws. But only an arrest can make you a criminal."

"You always wanted to be bad."

"I'm succeeding. I figure I'm in a downward spiral toward some great crime. Did you know that sixty percent of all American males are arrested at some time in their lives? That's one of Solly Blue's little known facts. The toughest of them all come down here to the Tenderloin. There's probably more guns in this neighborhood than the whole rest of the City."

Their beer arrived.

"A toast to the toughies," Ryan said. He tried to change Solly's mood. He talked of Bar Nada and the City Victorian. He talked of Kick. "I've gathered evidence of the secret signals men use to acknowledge each other."

"Like gaydar—except straight?" Solly picked at the food steaming on his plate. "My boys recognize each other instantly. A hustler always knows another hustler. Like a fag can always spot another fag."

"I'm not talking about like recognizing like," Ryan said. "I'm talking about penetrating fraternities where you don't belong."

"You mean you," Solly said, "and the muscle crowd. You know what movie you are? You're *Planet of the Apes*."

"I'm not a B movie," Ryan said. "I'm a major motion picture. I've shot footage. I'm making a documentary. As a non-blond, I've penetrated as far into blondness as a non-blond can go. I've seen the way blonds look at each other on the street. Blonds acknowledge their fraternity even more subtly than bodybuilders acknowledge theirs. As much as you've penetrated the outlaw circle of hustlers, I've been researching big blond bodybuilders. I work out with them. I'm getting bigger."

Ryan raised his arm the way Kick would have and made a muscle.

Solly laughed.

"What's so funny?"

"You. You are. You only want big arms and shoulders," Solly said, "so you can carry your cross. You only workout so you'll look terrific crucified. Noble. Godlike."

"Come off it." Ryan was amused.

"Beyond Kick," Solly said, "beyond all of it, that's the single, central image hanging in the back of your head. I know you, Ryan. You have visions of redemption."

"Stop accusing me of Catholicism. It's not fair."

"You have visions of a magnificently anguished muscle god whose suffering is for you, who will come down from the cross, or down from the posing platform, rising again, just like Kick's lil-ol'-South'll-rahse agin, to be with you, resurrected along with him, saved, triumphant, ascending to high heaven held in his big strong arms."

"Right. Sure," Ryan said. "That's me all over."

"It is you all over," Solly said. "You've mixed yourself and Kick and that nice Jewish boy Jesus all up in some weird, physical, sexual . . ."

"Don't forget drug-ridden."

". . . pseudo-spiritual idealism."

"Attack me, but not Kick," Ryan said. "What happens between us alone at night when we're conjuring together is hyper-real Energy."

"For somebody so smart . . ." Solly sipped his beer. "There is no savior. There is no safety. Your conjuring is garden-variety Castro lust." He sliced across his sauerbraten. "No. I stand corrected. It's not garden variety, but it is lust. High-toned lust. Blinding lust. Dangerous lust." He waved the meat on his fork. "Kick's no savior."

"You only say that because I told you we've promised always to be safe harbor to each other. Kick told me himself we're safe persons."

"There are no safe persons. There are only murderers and lovers. Serial murderers and serial lovers who are probably one and the same thing."

"You're too paranoid."

"You can never be too paranoid."

"You've got to trust other people."

Solly clucked. "Don't be naive."

"Don't be cynical."

"*Cynical* keeps me alive." Solly drank down the last of his beer. His face, under his thatch of brown-blond hair, folded into a purse of his lips which he wiped studiously with his napkin. The Look was not his usual Look. The Look did not become him.

"What's the matter?" Ryan asked.

"You're my friend. I don't know whether it's the heat or this Deutsch-land marching music. I'm interested, up to a point, in all the antics of your family at Bar Nada. I'm interested in how *Maneuvers* is selling. But the thing I really can't handle any more of—and you're not going to like this—is Kick."

"I'd have never guessed."

"He shapes every word that comes out of your mouth. He's possessed you. You're Linda Blair in *The Exorcist*."

"That's not true."

"Without him drilling his muscle catechism into you, there'd be no *Masculinist Manifesto*."

"You said you liked it."

Solly looked heavenward. "Sometimes, Ryan, you're such an ass."

"You kid me about it. But you said you liked it."

"It's a silly document you should be ashamed of."

"Why?"

"Because it's as fascist as the sauerbraten you're eating."

"Food can't be fascist."

"Sex can."

"Friends don't talk like this."

"Wrong," Solly said. "This is exactly how real friends talk."

"With friends like you, who needs enemas?"

Solly grimaced and hit a rim shot on his glass with a fork. "You're still the innocent little seminarian. Maybe we should wait to talk when you've grown up."

"Talk about what?"

"The way of the world."

"Which way is that?"

"If you have to ask, I can't tell you."

"I'm not innocent."

"You protest too much."

"About what?"

Solly hesitated, "About what it takes to be a man."

"Masculinity is the truly important issue facing homosexual males today."

"Spare me the sounds of your cowboy philosophy. Nobody knows what a real man is. Nobody's seen one in years."

"I have to work through what I have to work through."

"You're sounding more California than ever."

"What are you talking about?"

Solly pushed his plate aside. "I'm talking about Kick."

"You mean the love of my life."

"Frankly, my dear, I don't give a damn."

"About what?"

"About the Great God Kick. I don't mean to be bitchy, but I've had it. I fail to see his charms. Whoever said that everyone should be blond. Who cares if you've found the greatest fuck of your life. You're not the only ones in San Francisco taking nightly trips on gossamer wings. You're not the only ones taking drugs. You two didn't invent sex." Solly stared at Ryan. "I invented sex."

Ryan was amazed. This man, his closest confidant, closer for longer than Kick himself, was not understanding the muscleman or the affair or the changes of the last thirteen months.

"I think," Solly said, "you're still too starry-eyed."

"But you've said nothing before."

"I thought you two would burn out. I thought you'd come to your senses."

"I am in my senses. I'm more sensual than ever before in my life. Jesus! You make me sound like one of those people who've found Jesus!"

"Scratch a Catholic," Solly said, "and get guilt."

"I'm angry, not guilty." No one had ever dared question his relationship to Kick this way. This was more than some jealous bodybuilder's carping in the gym.

"I knew you wouldn't like this conversation," Solly said. "That's why I waited till we were in a public place. I warned you not to take me out. I've been a long time bringing this up, and I promise I'll never mention it again."

Ryan called for the check "Do you want me to come back to your apartment or do you just want me to fuck off?"

"Come back. That's all I had to say. I wanted you to know that as an expert, I can tell you for certain that Kick's a bum. He's a hustler."

"Bull."

"He's a hustler."

"He's never asked for a thing."

"He will. Hustlers always do. I'll bet you pay for all the drugs."

"Fuck you."

"You'll give gladly until finally you can give no more. You're a checkbook and he knows it."

"I'm not one of those guys!"

"Who went to the seminary because he was afraid to go to a regular high school? You forgot America is one big high school. Gay life is everything you ever feared about high school. Only worse. You're scared of bullies. That's why you keep writing that gay life is dangerous. All life is dangerous."

"I'm not in high school anymore."

"But you live and die on Castro," Solly said. "That's one fraternity you better beware of, because those boys' pecking order is size, looks, and cold, hard cash. You want to play in that league? You pays your money and you takes your chances. You are right about one thing: gay boys can eat you alive. So can hustlers. I know. And you've got one living in your house."

Solly reached across the table and almost touched Ryan's forearm.

Ryan wanted to stab Solly with his fork.

"Ry," he said, "Kick is the high school bully all us effeminate little gay boys feared would stroll out of the locker room and beat us up. They were blond, athletic, handsome. They were everything we were not. That's why we secretly loved them. That's what muscles and S&M are all about. Bully worship."

"I'm out of here!"

"I've been afraid of bullies all my life. That's why I love my boys so much. They're bullies I can control. They're bullies I can get even with. Every bully will take a tumble for cash. I make straight bullies have gay sex for money. I make them sell their precious heterosexuality for thirty bucks. That's how cheap the price is on their straightness. That's my revenge on all butch bullies I've ever known. You and I are the same." Solly's face was tender. "We're both into bully worship."

"Kick's no bully." Ryan lied. "We don't have an S&M relationship."

"Maybe not whips and chains," Solly said, "but you've made him your master and he's made you his slave." He raised his hands in surrender. "End of sermonette." Solly grinned. "Actually, the restaurant has proved worthwhile. It's safer to tell people difficult things in public. They control themselves better. There's less chance of a scene."

"I'll never say anything again. I thought you of all people . . ."

"I understand what I understand." Solly rose up from the booth. "I liked you better when you were depressed."

"I thought you'd like me happy."

"I want you really happy."

"I am happy."

"You're porn happy."

"Porn happy?"

"You've left reality behind. You're living one of your porn fantasies."

Ryan deflected Solly. "Ain't it grand? Kick is the reason I came to California."

"You want your cake and to eat it too? Come on back. I've got two cakes, you know."

Ryan placed the tip on the table. "I'm not,'" he said, "starry-eyed."

"What you're doing," Solly said, "is the Vulcan Mind Meld. You're so starstruck you're the movie *Star Trek,* and there's no talking to you."

They rode up the small elevator in silence. The manager of the building, angered by the obscenities scratched in the paint, had carpeted the walls with a busy green print of indestructible indoor/outdoor nylon frizz. Ryan felt claustrophobic.

"What kind of person," he asked, "would glue carpet to the walls?"

"An old queen," Solly said. "See what we have to look forward to?"

"No." Ryan flatly denied his friend.

"Yes." Solly was adamant. "You can pump iron every day; but one morning, just as sure as you woke up gay one morning, you'll wake up as somebody's auntie."

"Screw your birthday blues."

"Only if you're lucky will you turn into somebody's Auntie Mame."

"I love you," Ryan said, "when you're crazy."

"Then you'll love me forever," Solly said.

Ryan stared at his friend in the small elevator. He wondered if Solly was still a safe person. Kick had always let Ryan know that he disapproved of Solly's sleazy lifestyle. It was odd how much his two best friends disliked each other. For years Solly had been Ryan's steady haven. Ryan wondered if, with Kick, he had in fact become starry-eyed or if he simply had outgrown Solly Blue.

People can be chronologically correct for each other, right for a time, until time changes, and they change and grow away from each other. Teddy and he had been that way. He had no desire to leave Solly behind. He needed him almost as much as he needed Kick. He could not let either of them deny the other.

Ryan's cake from the Court of the Two Sisters was three layers of air creamed over with three kinds of chocolate. The sugar rush hit him instantly. For more than a year he and Kick had eaten only omelets, tuna, cottage cheese, raw vegetables, chicken breasts, and black coffee sweetened with pink packs of Sweet'N Low. His system raced. Maybe Solly was no longer a safe person. Sometimes a man has to choose one friend over another. That was a choice Solly could never win.

"Can I use your phone?" Ryan asked. "I have to call him who has no name."

"Don't, Ry." Solly tried to soothe him. "You know what I mean . . . what I meant. Try toning him down some. Unlike you and all the Castronauts who worship him, I don't believe he's a god. If he were a god, I'd be thankful for the evidence of him; but divinity is more than good looks and muscles. He's a man. He's just a man." Solly bit his lip. "He may not even be that."

Ryan dialed Kick. "Hi. It's me," Ryan said. "Yeah. . . . Sure. I'll take a taxi from down here so you don't have to drive the Vette to this part of town. . . . Right. . . . Of course, I'm horny. . . . OK . . . 18th and Castro . . . in half an hour."

Outside the open penthouse windows, the City lights came on all around Saint Anne's Apartment Tower. The rim of Twin Peaks glowed with the falling sun. Ships floated high at easy anchor in the East Bay. The very height of the penthouse gave Ryan vertigo.

Before Kick, in those long years of his depressions, he had feared the easy way Solly's windows opened out and over nothing. He feared maybe deep down he was a flier, if not ready for the Bridge, then ready for a high dive from the window into a wet hanky in the street. But now, with Kick in his bed, he knew he loved the risky business of being in-love.

He turned to say it to Solly, but he could not speak. His new truth was something he had to keep to himself now that he could no longer share it with Solly Blue.

He couldn't tell Kick that, more than loving him, he was in-love with him. They had exchanged promises. He had asked Kick that they never become ordinary to each other. Kick had asked him that they love each other, but never fall in-love.

Never fall in-love.

It was a strange caution, like one of those weird rules in a fairy tale where someone can have anything he wants so long as he doesn't do the one forbidden thing.

"We love each other," Kick had explained. "And we love each other perfectly. Let's not cheapen it like the gay boys do. They fall in-love and can't think straight."

"That's what makes them gay," Ryan had said. "That's why they don't understand homomasculine love."

"Guys say they're in-love with me all the time. I hardly know who they are. They think I'm responsible for their happiness." Kick had shaken his head. "No way. I'm not responsible for other people's happiness. You know that, Ry."

"I'm perfectly in charge of my own happiness."

"That's why I love you," Kick had said. "That's why I know I don't need to tell you never to fall in-love with me. In-love? What does *in-love* mean?"

Ryan groped toward the answer Kick sought. "Being in-love means singing somebody-done-somebody-wrong songs."

"You said it, coach." Kick had put his big arm around Ryan's shoulders. "I want us to have what we have forever." He had brushed his thick blond moustache across Ryan's cheek. "I love you. You love me. The only way I know for us to ruin our love for each other is to fall in-love with each other. That's indulgence. Love is not indulgence. Love is discipline."

Solly was off fussing in the kitchen, and flossing in the bathroom.

Ryan stared out at the City around and below him. Maybe, he mused, Kick and I are too rarified in our values. In what we appreciate, celebrate, create, want. Intensity keeps us together. We are not overextended into principles that are too high. We are, rather, fully extended. We are as fully extended as Kick is fully developed. His body is the measure of our intense push toward the best of everything. In a world that settles for half measures that it reviews as excellent, truly full extension of self-into-quality poses a definite threat to a world that has adjusted downward in praise of mediocrity.

Maybe San Francisco was the wrong place for high-flying love. It once called itself "The City That Knows How." But the City that knew how, forgot how quality was accomplished. Somewhere along the way San Franciscans, always tolerant of the eccentric, had gone too far and given away the store, the way Safeway supermarkets gave away their groceries at gunpoint when the Symbionese Liberation Army held Patty Hearst and the whole Bay Area hostage.

Old San Francisco, with its cable cars running halfway to the stars, had eroded under wave after wave of special-interest groups until there was nothing left for those who remembered old San Francisco but Dan White's gun. The City had opened itself to everyone. No stranger waited outside its door. Finally, overextended, the City began to collapse back inward on itself, beginning that symbolic day when Dan White crawled through the basement window of City Hall and held his own private election. It took him only minutes to assassinate the liberal Italian mayor and the gay Jewish supervisor from the East Coast. That morning San Francisco changed forever, the way America changed the day Kennedy was shot.

Not everyone hated what Dan White did in committing himself fully to what he believed in; but they were little noticed in the media coverage of thousands of gay men and lesbian women marching down Market Street.

After that morning, San Francisco moved under the shadow of the gun that by a single bullet had made a woman its mayor.

Solly would always be his best friend, but Solly was wrong.

The world had begun with Kick.

18

Ryan felt queasy leaving Solly's apartment. The rich cake hit him with sugar blues. For a moment, in the deep Tenderloin canyons of theaters and old hotels, he felt a pang for the narrow fast streets of Manhattan. He hailed a taxi. Traffic swirled around him. The cabbie drove him from the Tenderloin, jockeying through the Market Street cars and pickups and motorcycles cruising through the unusually hot September night. They sped past the Castro Street Station and the gyrating line standing outside Alfie's disco. A few doors west, shirtless men, with red bandanas in their back pockets, hung out the upstairs windows of the Balcony bar. Someone had torn the letter C from the awning. The party continued under the sign "THE BAL ONY."

Ryan waited at 18th and Castro for at least twenty minutes. Kick's red Corvette was nowhere to be seen in the steady stream of cruising traffic. Ryan called the Victorian from a phone booth outside the Star Pharmacy. There was no answer. Twice in the next forty minutes, he dialed again. He felt a surge of panic. Nothing unaccountable had ever happened to them before.

He stepped from the curb in front of the Elephant Walk bar to study the traffic. He calmed himself with a thought from the sixties: whenever you get separated at a demonstration or a rock concert, the best thing is to stay where you are. When he could no longer stand the tension, Ryan jumped into a taxi idling at the curb. Back at the Victorian, the Vette was gone from the garage. Kick's favorite jacket was no longer hanging inside the front door. Ryan came to the only logical conclusion about his lover's sudden disappearance.

He knew what had happened.

A woman in a new pink 1979 Cadillac Eldorado sat screaming in the middle of the Castro and Alvarado intersection. She had been edging her mammoth car out onto Castro at a corner made almost blind by the steep angle of the hill when she rammed the bullet-nosed front end of the red Corvette gunning its way up the climb in the fast lane on Castro.

The impact bounced her twice precisely between her seat and her steering wheel. All around her a thick shower of red fiberglass rained down on her windshield. She reached instinctively for her wipers, and through the falling debris she saw for the first time in her life the most beautiful blond man she had ever seen sitting in the cockpit of the car that seemed to freeze forever into this moment of terminal shatter.

The noise and the red shards of the exploding car body made her clench the wheel with both her thick bejeweled hands. She cried out and thrashed while the blond man sat motionless and cool and invulnerable waiting for the pieces to land and the tangle of auto frames to finish their incredible wrap.

The accident was almost as Solly had predicted hours earlier at his birthday supper.

"One thing I know for sure," Solly Blue had said. "Indulge me on this occasion of my birthday to be philosophical. By thirty-five a man knows in his heart of hearts that everything good that can happen to him has already happened. Then comes a time when you finally sense that everything else you have coming to you will be bad."

I Know I'll Never Love This Way Again

1

Everyone showed at the openings of the Fey Way Gallery South of Market.

"Not *Fay Wray*," Robert Opel said, *"Fey Way."* Ryan had interviewed Opel for a freelance spread on the opening of the gallery March 1978 in *California Art Currents*. He called the tall, thin gallery owner "the most naked man in the world."

Before Opel had moved to the City from El Lay, he had stripped buck-naked and hid himself inside the scenery of the 1974 Oscar ceremony. At the very instant when David Niven was introducing Elizabeth Taylor, Opel broke free of the scenery and streaked past Niven and Taylor. Millions of startled satellite viewers saw Robert Opel naked for an instant. No one remembers what stars won the Academy Award that year; but everyone remembers the man who mooned the whole wide world.

The opening of Opel's Fey Way Gallery at 1287 Howard Street, South of Market, lit the light industrial area with strobes and music and San Francisco stars. Ryan and Kick attended by special invitation.

Kick had not been hurt in the accident that nearly destroyed the Corvette. With his car undergoing full restoration, he was happier than ever to be alive. In a note dated a week after the collision, Kick wrote another in the series of letters each took delight in posting on their refrigerator for the other.

Ry! My mind continues to overflow with thoughts of you. Never before have I experienced feelings that I have experienced since knowing you. Never before have I known total absorbency without consumption. I think we have something more going on here than even we first believed. The world sees us, but is the world ready for us the way we know ourselves to be separately and together?

Daily we learn love. My own definition of love has certainly changed in the last two years. Never has it been so exercised. Never has it been so strong and healthy. I've never known love by such purely masculine definition. Have I told you lately that I love you? Well, fucker, I'm telling you now.

What I want to be is what I am: a man.

What I want to do is love you.

Amid all our being and doing, I'm finding my want fulfilled. Please don't let me take advantage of you in any way. You've been nothing but supportive of me, of us, in every way. I want only to return that support to you. Never, not ever, did I once expect to find the reality that is you, Ry. A man couldn't ask for better than the totally unselfish love you've given me. I love your ass! If repetition can drive home a point, then let me say over and over: I love you, Ryan Steven O'Hara!

"All I hear," Robert Opel said, "is Ryan and Kick, Kick and Ryan. Rickety rack. Down the track." Opel wanted them for his opening. "I want to show you off together." Opel sat in Ryan's kitchen. "You've both spent a great deal of time creating your relationship." He spoke close to Ryan's ear. "I know what you're doing."

Ryan was amused. "What are we doing?"

"He's your greatest creation. You may be Pygmalion. You may be Frankenstein. You may be the Black Lagoon."

"He's my lover," Ryan said.

"He's a bodybuilder."

"He's a man."

"He is art." Opel was intense. "He's a performance artist."

"Who isn't? This is San Francisco," Ryan said. "Everybody's a star."

"He's an ideal." Opel grasped Ryan's hand. "I have a theory that some men bloom early, some men late, some never bloom at all, and some lucky few go in and out of bloom."

"So what do you want?"

"I must show you both off in my performance art gallery."

"Both?" Ryan asked. "Kick? And me?" He spread his forefinger and thumb from the bridge of his nose outward across his closed eyelids. He looked up at Opel. "You want *bloom?* Kick's in bloom. I'm only the gardener."

"Don't shit me," Opel was relentless. "Love's in bloom. *Maneuvers* is in bloom. Even your silly *Manifesto* is in bloom. What a send-up! What a perfect joke! It makes people crazy! Selling it in tabloid on street corners is the perfect trashy touch. It's so *Enquirer!*"

"Inquiring minds want to know," Ryan said.

Opel projected a crazy charm. He was planning to start a new-wave erotic magazine called *Cocksucker.* The week before, he had bought from Ryan for the upcoming first issue a piece called "Muscleman Sex." Something clicked.

"I want you to read from your story while Kick poses on the platform next to you. Sort of a 'Physique Reading.' Our crowd will love it."

The crowd that night, in fact, called out for more. Kick posed and Ryan read. Actually Ryan's lips moved while the crowd cheered Kick's display, bulk-posing first in flannel shirt and jeans, then slow-motion stripping away the heavy cotton shirt, posing in white tee shirt, flexing his arms, finally pulling off his tee shirt, displaying his tanned upper body front and back, then dropping his jeans, stepping out of them without missing a beat, looking huge in his posing briefs, moving through a slower, more sensual version of his posing exhibition than he dared on a contest stage. Never once as he stripped from his shirts and jeans did he cross over the bump-and-grind line with which male dancers make a burlesque of themselves. He was not a stripper. He was a bodybuilder revealing the layers of his Look. Kick got the whole room off.

Kweenie appreciated the commotion. Kick was a star. She knew exactly what Ryan saw in him: Kick was larger than life. She was grateful to him. He had cured Ryan's blues. Before Kick, the only thing Ryan had recognized as larger than life was Death.

Kweenie flushed with the heat of lust she had felt since first she had laid eyes on Kick. She wanted him for herself alone. Who didn't?

"Keep sweating that old, boring depression out of him," she told Kick. "You're his exorcist." In her heart of hearts, she felt so like her brother that she had grown up anguishing that his ups and downs were bad sneak previews of her own emotional life when she got to be his age. But not to worry. Ryan would always be there. Besides, she had made a certain name for herself. After Sharon McKnight she was the crisp toast of gay cabaret society. She was a genuine San Francisco star.

"At least," Ryan told me, "Kweenie didn't grow up to be one of those dykes who wear Bella Abzug hats and smoke long brown cigarettes."

Ryan and Kweenie were quite a show that night at Opel's. Not everyone knew they were brother and sister. They seemed more like loving rivals: each a mirror of the other, and both taking one step toward, then two steps back, in the tangled tango of the hardly restrained feeling they always shared. Even though fear of guilt kept them from coupling, I sometimes thought them the same being, divided by age and sex, and wondered if the sexual tension of their feeling was more narcissistic than incestuous. They were often exactly alike. They had the same taste in men. Kweenie, after her own fashion, was Ryan in drag.

For her brother's sake Kweenie tried to regard Kick without sexual jealousy. She cupped her hands under her breasts, pushed them up into place, and worked her way through the Fey Way crowd toward Kick, standing resplendent in his posing briefs next to Ryan who held his clothes. She swept up to the two men. She became very grand.

"You were wonderful," she said. "Both of you."

She leaned in and kissed Kick on the cheek. The sweet smell of his body was too much. She affected a thick southern drawl. "Southern men," she said. "Ah want you-all to know, Cap'n Butler, that this Miss O'Hara simply adores southern men."

She turned to kiss Ryan. "A girl," she whispered, "just doesn't take away her brother's boyfriend. No matter how much she might want to sing 'Stars Fell on Alabama.'"

Ryan laughed. He failed to notice she was lying through her teeth.

"I liked your act," she said to Kick. "I've always wanted to see you pose. When Ryan reads, you move so well to his rhythms. Or is it the other way around?"

Kick took her hand in his. "Ryan has the rhythms," he said. "I have the moves."

"A perfect relationship," Kweenie said. "Mr. Yin and Mr. Yang."

"More than you know." He kept hold of her hand. He turned his blue eyes long and hard on Kweenie's face. He recognized something in the eyes of the sister that he loved in the brother.

In the long silence between them, Kweenie's nipples hardened.

"So," Kweenie said, "I'm really glad you weren't hurt in the accident." She pulled her hand from his. "And your car's all fixed."

The stereo speakers in the gallery moved into the violin pickup of "Over the Rainbow." Something immediately expanded in the room. A quick silence. A short burst of laughter. The conversation resumed. For an instant, everyone in the gallery had perked up like a patriot recognizing the gay national anthem.

Opel whispered over my shoulder. "Did you catch that?" he asked. "Come over here with me, please."

"Catch what?"

"That moment of silent homage to Judy? Ah, Judy! Judy! Judy! What Marilyn is to the silver screen and the silkscreen, Judy is to our ears." He moved around and confronted me. "Magnus Bishop, isn't it? You're here as a critic," he said.

"I'm here as a friend," I said.

"Whatever," he said. "You're welcome. We're both in the same business."

"How's that?" I asked.

"Icons. I make them. I merchandise them. I enjoy them. You, one step behind, like Inspector Hound baying at the arts, critique them. And me. And the people like Kweenie and Ry and Kick who make things happen."

"I suppose you're right." I could hardly deny my interest in this man about whom the quick-witted David Niven, laying his finger aside his nose said, "Isn't it amazing that this man has gotten the biggest laugh he'll ever get in his life by exposing his short-comings?" Opel's performance that memorable Oscar night was the one breath of real life that year in what everyone agrees the morning after is the longest, most boring tribal ritual that one billion people consent to endure every spring.

Even naked, Opel wore a fine edge of gay rage. He had a talent for gaining media attention for his politics. My clearest image of him, five years after the Academy Awards, was the front-page photo of him standing in the sun outside San Francisco City Hall. He was costumed like "Gay Justice." Nothing overturns a verdict like a gun. Opel pointed his pistol loaded with blanks at a fellow actor dressed as the assassin, "Dan White." In a ritual skit, Opel shot "Dan White" down in the very Civic Center plaza where, forty-eight hours before, the White Night Riot had erupted when thousands of gays, protesting the court's verdict, began a candlelight protest march from Castro Street, down Market, to City Hall. Almost ten years exactly after Stonewall, the crowd, growing outraged at the light sentence given to Dan White, turned angry. The mob roared up, conjuring the birth of aggressive gay power, and attacked City Hall, setting fire to police cars that burned with huge flames that lit up the dark evening thick with smoke.

The riotous 1979 night began on a *MAY DAY! MAY DAY!* May Day afternoon, the 21st, when at 5:30 the jury found Supervisor White guilty of two counts of manslaughter (one could hear the man's laughter) in the shooting of Mayor Moscone and Supervisor Harvey Milk. Rush-hour radio news mixed with Happy Hour outrage. Runners, alerted by activist leader, Cleve Jones, crisscrossed the Castro calling lesbian women and gay men from their apartments. "Out of the bars and into the streets!" Dan White had gotten away with murder. "No Justice! No Peace!" His ultimate fag bashing merited only a slap on the wrist. "MURDER! Not manslaughter!"

What began that twilight as a peaceful march from Castro Street to City Hall escalated to a determined walk to a fast trot to a running righteousness when the angry citizens reached City Hall to find hundreds of police in full riot gear cordoning off the Civic Center Plaza. It isn't very pretty what a City without pity can do. Very quickly the situation became primitive. The seventies resurrected the radical sixties. By midnight the protest turned into a hard-fought, running street fight between gays and baton-wielding cops.

The screaming crowd chanted "Avenge Harvey Milk!" On the steps of the same City Hall where, six months earlier, mourners, on the night of the murders, had held gently flickering candles, this night they stormed the doors of City Hall, rushing up the stairs, tearing the wrought iron from the doors and smashing it through the glass, throwing uprooted burning bushes into the marble halls. They lit copies of the evening *Examiner* with its bold headlines of the verdict and ran down the sidewalk torching nine of the police cars parked at the curb. The black-and-whites sat in a long blazing line, flames and smoke circling their revolving red lights, their sirens moaning like dying beasts.

Dianne Feinstein, throughout the siege, held her ground in the very office where a bullet had killed Moscone and made her mayor. Supervisor Carol Ruth Silver appeared on a second floor balcony holding a single candle. She was a vision. She tried to speak, but was struck in the mouth by a flying rock. Her voice was lost in the roar. She withdrew. Demonstrators kicked over the row of a dozen newspaper vending machines, including Ryan's rack selling *Maneuvers.* They tossed the heavy stands across the concrete moat surrounding the basement level of windows through which White had crawled to enter the building to shoot Moscone and Milk.

Even as the City Hall battle raged, other cop droids, goon squads, anonymous, with badges removed, headed for 18th and Castro. The cops launched a baton-wielding assault on the Elephant Walk bar, wreaking revenge, randomly bludgeoning employees and beating customers. San Francisco went into meltdown. Human blood ran in the gutters.

It was dawn before the police regained City Hall.

Rubble, strewn from Turk Street to Market Street, let the City know that hell hath no fury like faggots scorned. If the legendary Stonewall Riot had let New York and the world know that gay liberation was born, the White Night Riot let the City and the world know that gay liberation had come of age equal to any in a world of violence and terrorism.

"Gays," a wounded demonstrator, doing Peter Finch in *Network,* screamed into a Live Eye TV camera, "are mad as hell. And we're not going to take it anymore!"

The next morning, Milk's successor, gay Supervisor Harry Britt, declared to the press with calm dignity: "Harvey Milk's people do not have anything to apologize for."

Opel took my arm and happily surveyed his crowded gallery. "We are," Opel said, "a charmed circle." He led me toward Ry standing next to Kick.

"Vettes are muscle cars," Kick was saying. "Men look good in a Vette."

"Let me tell you," Ryan was still *on*. "You have to understand the emotional importance of bodybuilders' affection for Corvettes. They're meat wagons." Wine. Cheese. Gallery small talk. "They're designed to show off the hulk climbing out of the cockpit. There's a whole Corvette mystique."

"I never knew that," a man in pressed jeans and a designer sweater said. "How, really, thank you, interesting."

"Bullshit," I whispered through my smile into Ryan's ear.

He was determined to finish. "When two guys in Vettes pass each other, they wave forearm up and fist rampant. 'Yo!'"

Kick made the motion that Ryan described. Anyone could see how they played bravura off each other. Ryan's words gave Kick easy reason to display his arms to the surrounding crowd. Kick's moves made Ryan's cocktail pontificating all the more enjoyable. It was easy to figure the mutual rap-and-flex sex they enjoyed. Ryan talked the scene while Kick powered it out.

"Aren't they a pair," I said to Opel. "One on the ground. One in midair."

"A pair," Opel said, "in the Great Tradition of Pairs: Mickey and Judy, Tracy and Hepburn, Jack and Jackie, Liz and Dick, Sid and Nancy, Daedalus and Icarus." He gestured across the gallery. "When I set up the lighting for their performance tonight," Opel said, "I thought if I was ever going to hit a man with 'Old Master' lighting, Kick is certainly a subject to soak up the watts!"

Kweenie swooped by us. She pulled us tighter into the circle around Ryan and Kick. On her arm she escorted a short gay clone with a black moustache. He was her old roommate, Evan-Eddie, who had cruised Ryan on the steps up to his sister's apartment. He wore a tux. He looked like a singing waiter in a Cole Porter musical. He couldn't take his eyes off Kick. Ryan stood amused, watching the muscle-lust rise in the slender gay boy's face.

"Those arms of yours!" Evan-Eddie unabashedly reached out to touch Kick's biceps. "I'd do anything to have arms like that."

"Even work out?" Ryan shot the line across the circle.

Undaunted, Evan-Eddie said, "But can he talk?"

"He doesn't have to," Ryan said.

Kick smiled his silent smile, a gentleman down to his perfect white teeth.

"At least," Evan-Eddie said to Kick, "when you lose your mind you've got a great body to fall back on."

"Thanks," Kick said. His southern drawl was low and gracious.

"Oh, my dear," Evan-Eddie said. "You have a nutcracking voice. So many of you great big delicious bodybuilders open your mouths and out fly six yards of lavender chiffon!"

"How would you like a mouthful of bloody Chicklets?" Ryan was irritated. Gay wit was too often sleazy putdown rather than satiric send-up. Dish queens filled him with distaste. They seemed part of a rude conspiracy to hack virility from other men's bodies, to destroy pure masculine idealism. They bought latex goods shaped and molded to the heroic size and quality of potent men and inserted them for their unreachable fantasies.

Ryan repeated his offer in clearer terms. "How would you like your teeth rearranged?"

Undaunted as a queen can be, Evan-Eddie flashed his caps and turned to Kick. "What do you see in this bozo?" He pointed to Ryan.

"I'm very rich," Ryan said. "I drive a fast car. I have a ten-inch dick."

"And I have an eye," Kick drawled, "for the proper stranger."

"You won't find anyone stranger than him." Evan-Eddie was on speed. "Let's make a deal." He poked at Kick's pecs and biceps like Hansel and Gretel's hungry witch. "I have a hundred and eighty dollars on me. Enough to rent a piece of meat like you for an hour. A buck a pound."

"Who's working security?" Ryan asked. "I told Robert Opel this gallery needs security. Why aren't Hell's Angels working security?"

"Secure this." Evan-Eddie tapped Kick's crotch.

"That's it," Kick said. He extended his hand to fend off the insults. "Back off. We're nice guys. You're maybe a nice guy. Let's all take two steps back."

"And, doh-see-doh." Evan-Eddie twirled in a circle.

"Come on, E-E." Kweenie tugged at Evan-Eddie's arm. "Let's go." She looked at Kick. "I'm sorry," she said. "Ignore him. His idea of exercise is swimming laps through cheap cologne."

"I'm not leaving," Evan-Eddie said. "I've watched this prick-tease for too long. All those afternoons, darling. Your languor! Standing in front of Donuts & Things on Castro, holding court with the special few who are hot enough for you. Let me tell you something for sure, darlings, for sure. You're living up to your press releases. I know exactly what kind of macho fascists you musclerama fags are."

"Forgive me," Ryan said. "I was beginning to think we knew you too. As it happens, we only recognize your type."

"Why, thank you, Miss Scarlett."

"Shut up," Kick said. "No one calls him that."

"Not to his face." Evan-Eddie stood firm. Kweenie held his arm. He was fuming in the steam of his own lust and rejection, like a train in a 1940s movie standing in its own steam while lovers kiss.

Ryan always loved that bittersweet cliché: one lover with hand pressed against the train window; the other lover standing alone on the boarding platform, both receding into the distance of time and space.

How often had he left Annie Laurie and Charley-Pop that way when they put him on the train at the end of each summer to return to Misericordia. Somehow somebody's always saying good-bye. Funny. It was always his father's face, not his mother's, that he last glimpsed dissolving in the steam.

Evan-Eddie took one last shot at Kick. "I'll dance," he said, "a gay fandango on your grave. You . . . You . . . steroid meatball! Let your hack write about that!"

"I'm going to kill him!" Ryan said.

"Passion! Wonderful!" Opel said. "Art happens NOW!"

"I guarantee," Evan-Eddie said to Kick, "that you won't live long."

"*Wunderbar!*" Opel shouted. "The evil eye!"

"And you," Evan-Eddie said to Ryan, "will live too long."

"Thank you, Vampira," Kweenie said.

Opel led the applause. "Isn't Evan-Eddie's act buffo?" His punch line dissolved the tension to guffaws.

"It isn't an act," Kweenie said. "It's his way of being!"

Opel turned from his little happening, then charged back into the ring of laughter pulling a woman dressed in black jersey. The energy changed directions. "Everyone," he said. "This is January Guggenheim."

"And the answer," January said, "is *no.*"

"No what?" Kweenie asked.

"No, she's not," Opel said, "one of *those* Guggenheims."

"I'm one of *these* Guggenheims," she said. She planted her hand firmly in Kick's crotch.

Just as firmly, Kick removed her hand. "Thank you, Ma'am," he drawled, "for the compliment."

"Darling," she said. "Darling Kick. I've heard so much about you and Ryan. Now we meet." She offered her hand to Ryan. "Your performance was divine."

Opel put his arm around the woman. "January has the green light for a network documentary on the New Homosexuals."

"You are the new ones, aren't you?" January asked. "God knows, I'm bored with the old ones."

"Without fags," Evan-Eddie snapped a look at January up and down, "how could you ever be the rich fag hag you so obviously are?"

January, dripping syrup, put her hand on Kick's arm. "Kick, darling, could you use your great big muscles and punch the lights out of this tidbit boy before I bite off what's left of his balls?"

"Punching and biting! Oh my!" Evan-Eddie imitated Dorothy's terror on the road to Oz. He wrapped both hands around Kweenie's arm. "Punching and biting! Oh my!" Then he switched movies. This boy felt clever only through quotes. "Stella, my sister!" He looked deep into Kweenie's eyes. "There has been some progress made since the days of punching and biting." His schtick was on a roll. He gestured around the gallery. "Such things as art, as poetry and music. Such kinds of new light have come into the world since then." He tugged on Kweenie's arm. "Don't hang back with the beasts!"

"Applause for the clowns," January said.

"Evan-Eddie," Kweenie said. "Get lost."

"I've heard about your new homosexual *Manifesto*," January said. "I've wanted to interview you ever since my Robert Opel told me about you." She turned to Kick, bumping and grinding her words like Mae West. "Now . . . that I see . . . you, I want to . . . use you . . . as my main . . . image."

"You mean . . . mmmh . . . ." Kweenie hated January's bad imitation of what she herself did so much better. "As the . . . mmmh . . . main attraction, don't you, dearie?"

Kick felt surrounded. Women unnerved him. The night was not what Ryan had said it would be. "Ladies," Kick said. "I don't know." He took a refuge in Ryan he really didn't need. "Ry's my only photographer."

"I've never seen a body like yours," January said. "I've never seen a face like yours."

Kick put his arm around Ryan's shoulder. "And you've never seen a mind like his."

"I want you both," she said. "Of course, both of you." She grinned. "I simply adore package deals."

"You're beautiful," Opel said to January, "when you're fawning."

"But I do, I do, I do want them both."

"Who doesn't?" Kweenie said. "Like they're a collectably Famous Couple."

"Thank you, dear," January tried to push Kweenie back. "I understand fame. I'm from El Lay."

"That's no credential in San Francisco." Kweenie held her own.

January sized her up. "Who are you?" she asked. "Who do you pretend to be?"

"I'm the Queen of Sheba," she said. "I'm Kweenasheba. I am who I am. I also happen to be Ry's sister."

"We're all his sisters," Evan-Eddie said. "Like it or not."

"I'm his blood sister. His real sister."

"You sing, or something, don't you?" January said, adjusting her Attitude. "Perhaps I can use you."

"Be my guest," Kweenie said.

"I love your spunk," January said. "We'll have a super time working together." She improvised. The *Manifesto* had caught her attention; but Kick held her interest. She thought him spectacular. "I'm surprised Bruce Weber or Robert Mapplethorpe haven't shot you."

"I'm surprised," Evan-Eddie said, "that I haven't shot them both."

"Ryan," January said, "if you can write a two-minute narrative, we can feature you reading it. You know: a voice-over as we show a long, lingering close-up study of Kick's face and then! MUSIC UP. The camera pulls back revealing all that . . . muscle . . . and power . . . and virility!"

January paused, overcome with the possibilities. "My God! With that face alone we'll destroy the myth of the effeminate homosexual!" She knifed her steely gaze at Evan-Eddie. "One look at Kick's face, his body! The world at large will know! Nielsen families will race to their sets! Fathers will accept their sons! Straight brothers will embrace their gay siblings!"

She pointed one stern scarlet-nailed finger at Evan-Eddie. "You!" she announced. "Evolution has passed you sissy boys bye-bye!"

She began to unfold with expansive gestures. She was like a rose blooming in time-lapse cinematography. She opened her showy self to play the group the way she figured they needed to be played. She knew she needed them. She needed their angle. She needed them to need her.

"Kick will pose for me?" she asked Ryan.

"Don't ask me," Ryan said.

"Ask the blond bubblebutt himself." Evan-Eddie tried for the jugular. "You know the truth about steroids. If he paws the ground once with his foot, it's *yes*. Twice is *no*."

"Goodbye, E-E." Kweenie pushed him away.

"Beasts!" Evan-Eddie shoved off to the perimeter of talk. "They have a name for guys like you," he shouted back over his shoulder to Kick. "You . . . you . . . you . . . Sports Homo!"

Kweenie rolled her eyes back in her head. "I hate his retro-fits."

"Don't ask me," Ryan repeated. "Ask Kick. I'm not his keeper."

Opel relished the melee.

"Have you done any modeling? Any TV?"

"Once, back in Alabama," Kick said, "I posed for a little six-o'clock news show. A double-biceps shot filmed with lasers."

"A double-biceps shot? Show me," January insisted. "I'm a show-me kind of girl."

"Like this." Kick leaned smiling into the pose. "It really wasn't much. Only a quick five-second clip edited in with other sports shots. Kind of a high-energy promo to introduce the evening news, weather, and sports."

"Kick turned down a print ad for Winston cigarettes," Ryan said. "He won't promote something he doesn't believe in."

"Of course," January said. "You don't smoke. I'm sure neither of you does, or ever has, or ever will. On the other hand, I . . ."

Her words faded under to a low voice-over. Ryan's eyes turned from her face. In that instant he had spotted Teddy's entrance through the gallery door. He stopped to sign the guest register. He looked up, feeling, I think, Ry's strong stare. Then Teddy caught a full shot of Kick's luminous blond presence. Before Ryan tossed off half a wave, Teddy turned tail, dragging behind him a leatherman who looked more than a bit the same type as Ryan. Teddy wanted a second chance to love Ryan all over again, but a muscleman he couldn't compete with had taken his place. He didn't need Mr. Universe rubbed in his face. San Francisco was, as he had predicted, the place where you go to lose a lover.

The instamatic moment stopped January dead in her tracks. Something like sorrow glazed Ryan's face. January raised her tweezed eyebrows. She was about to ask paparazzi questions.

The naked needed cover.

"Not to change the subject," I said, "Solly Blue should be here."

"Who's Solly Blue?" January asked. "Is he important?"

"If you're filming the New Homosexuality, he is," Ry said.

"Solly's radical," Kweenie said. "He takes these faggots back to the roots of what they came out for."

"What's that?" January asked.

"Straight men," Kweenie said.

"No," Ryan said. "Not necessarily straight men. But always, gay or straight, masculine men."

"Last week," Kweenie said, "a queen I know asked me to help him go straight. He wanted to know if I knew any straight guys he could date."

Ryan reached out and grabbed Kweenie's hand. "Some women are educable," he said. "We're still working on this one."

"Bastard!"

"Bitch!"

"Boys and girls!" Opel said.

"You mean," January asked, "that gay men don't want to fuck with gay men?" She looked puzzled. "How utterly droll!"

"Not if they can help it," Kick said.

"They?" January said.

"All gay men are homosexuals," Opel said, "but not all homosexuals are gay."

"We're men who prefer other men who are men," Ryan said. "I don't think any of us know where the subspecies of gay men came from exactly. Probably from the city of Lacoste on the planet Faberge."

"Homomasculine men," Kweenie singsonged the line, "have more in common with heteromasculine men than they do with gay men."

"Wait just a minute," January said. "You're confusing me. I don't like to be confused by rhetoric."

"This isn't rhetoric," Ryan said. "It's a concept lesson."

"What you see here before you," Robert Opel said, "are homomasculine men."

"Except for me." Evan-Eddie inserted himself back into the circle. "This is such unmitigated semantic bullshit."

"Does that mean," January said, looking hopefully to Kick, "that you sometimes fuck women?"

"I'd sooner fuck a woman," Kick said, "than fuck an effeminate gay man."

January got the vapors. She reached into her clutch and pulled out a small snifter. She took a hit up both nostrils and handed the coke to Kweenie.

"Help yourself, darlings." Her intensity deepened. "Don't bullshit me," she said. "I didn't come all the way up here from El Lay to eat your San Francisco Attitude. If you're onto something, I want to hear it. But don't bullshit me. I'm serious, boys and girls! I've got the budget for this TV thing. My prediction? If we do it right? Big. BIG! Kick's face and physique! Appealing not repelling! Showing up the sexiness of you . . . what is the term? . . . homomasculine men. I love it! Socko! High Concept! I think I've got it. Premise: conflict of homomasculine men and gay men! The uncivil war! The revelation of a new way to be male! Poignant! Political! Esthetic! Sexy!"

Kweenie stepped into January's face. "Don't forget the Ryanites," she said.

"Kweenie!" Ryan tried to silence her. "Don't!"

"What are Ryanites?" January looked entranced. "I'll believe anything tonight."

"Ryanites are guys who worship the one published picture of Kick and take every word of the *Masculinist Manifesto* to be gospel. They hate militant feminist separatists." She decided to toy with January's push-and-shove. "They keep white sheets in their closets with little eye holes."

January's face turned quizzical.

Kweenie put her finger to her own lips. "Don't ask!"

Kweenie had hit upon the arm's length they all found necessary to deal with January Guggenheim. Ryan recognized almost immediately that January's network deal could afford the *Manifesto* a wider forum. It was time for post-gay masculinism to come out of the erotic underground press. It was time for masculinism to cross over to the straight media. Masculinism deserved as wide a media coverage as feminism. Ryan prepared himself to put up with whatever Attitude January put out.

"I know!" Kweenie said. "We'll all put on a show and save the town."

"My dear," January said, "you're getting the idea."

"Come with me, January," Opel said. "You must meet everybody!"

"Kiss-Kiss," January said. "Let's do lunch. Soon."

"Later," Ryan said. "Whatever." He waved her off. "I intend to use her," he said, "as much as she intends to use us to make her documentary. You don't mind, do you, Kick? You're the way we're going to turn her preconceived notions upside down."

"Whatever you say, coach."

"I'm leaving," Kweenie said. "Are you leaving?"

"We'll walk you to the door," Kick said.

"Actually," Kweenie took Kick's big blond hand into hers, "I have to talk to Ry. Okay?"

"Come on, Kweenie," Ryan said. "Kick's in on everything."

"No offense," she said. "But this is private. You know. Family stuff."

"That's my cue to get lost," Evan-Eddie said.

"It's okay," Kick said. "Go ahead."

Ryan and Kweenie walked out to the sidewalk lit by the bright lights of the gallery. The leather crowd milled around them.

"Okay," Ryan said, "what is it?"

"I'm pregnant."

"You're pregnant?"

"I'm pregnant."

"For God's sake why?"

"For the usual reason."

"You're in-love."

"No. I fucked."

He could not believe that his precious little sister for all her wildness could have betrayed the feeling they had always recognized between them. Kweenie knew that if Ryan were ever to make love to any woman it would be her. She wanted him. Sometimes. Other times she wanted what she wanted.

"Who's the father?"

"Wouldn't you just like to know."

"As a matter of fact, I would."

"I can't tell you. Not now. Maybe never."

"Are you trying to make me jealous?" Ryan asked.

"Yes," she said. "And no. I know we'll never do it. Because you won't do it. But I had my reasons."

"I suppose you want to experience motherhood."

"I thought about it. At first. Now what I really want to experience is abortion."

"Aw, jeez!"

2

"It's time," Kick said, "to make a certain commitment."

"To each other," Ryan said.

"And to muscle." Kick held Ryan in his arms. This happened their second Christmas together. They lay naked on the ancient iron bed Ryan had set up in his studio in the barn at Rancho Bar Nada. The fire in the wood stove was the only light.

"I've got to know," Kick said, "everything about muscle. I want you and me, coach, to take muscle and push it as far as it will go."

"I want to push us as far as we can go," Ryan said. He meant to push the Energy sired by sex between them. He was cautious. He was jealous of their privacy. Going public could be dangerous. The physique contests were one thing. January's TV special was another. Ryan feared agents and contracts and cameras that stole souls away. "I don't want to lose you. I don't want to lose what happens at night between us. I don't want us to lose track of each other."

Kick pulled Ryan into the hard mounds of his pecs. "This is me," he said. "This is you. No matter what happens." He repeated Ryan's own words back to him. "Remember the home team."

"That's you and me, kid," Ryan said.

"It ain't nobody else."

"I want you to have everything," Ryan said.

"All I want is muscle. Big. Huge. Massive. Muscle," Kick said. "I want more guys to learn about muscle. I want guys to hear what you write. That January? She's using us. She can't play a good old southern boy. We'll turn her special into a display of male power that'll blow the old TV tubes right out."

"We want to do the right thing," Ryan said, "for the right reason."

"I understand," Kick said, "what we're doing in the short and long run." He was expert at protecting himself in public. "Trust me. I'm your blond . . . bodybuilder . . . musclebeast."

Later that warm Christmas night, they carried a down-filled sleeping bag out to the drained bed made by the empty cement saucer of an old goose pond. The dark sky over the empty valley around Ryan's ranch glowed with squadrons of stars never seen in the City. Orion hung low and steady amid the shower of shooting stars.

"Orion is my constellation," Ryan said.

"I only know the North Star," Kick said.

"Then you'll never be lost," Ryan said. He pointed at Ursa Major. "You know that one?" he asked.

"The Big Dipper," Kick said.

"See. You know more than you thought."

"Everyone knows it."

"But not everyone knows it as Ursa Major." One thing was meaning two things again. "The Big Dipper is also the Big Bear." Ryan pointed to the sky. "See, how if you look at it differently . . ." He nuzzled his face close into Kick's neck. "You are the Bear," Ryan said. "The Big Bear."

Kick laughed. "And you're Ryan-Orion. Tell me about you, Ryan-Orion. Read me the sky."

Ryan lay down with his head in Kick's lap. "I was Orion, a great giant and hunter. I chased the silly Pleiades."

"What are the Pleiades?"

"They're stars now, too. Back then they were the seven daughters of Atlas."

"So you chased women."

"With a sword. Look! Make a wish! I hounded them until I was killed by Artemis."

"No wonder you're a writer. This sounds like the plot of a Steve Reeves movie."

"Artemis was a woman. A virgin huntress."

"A lady with a gun?"

"She was the sister of Apollo, the god of light and poetry and manly beauty."

"Apollo couldn't save you?"

"He never tried."

"Why not?"

"I might ask you."

"Why me?"

"Because, if I'm Ryan-Orion, you are Kick-Apollo."

"You're joking," Kick said. He paused. "You're not joking."

"I'm on to you," Ryan said. "I know you've come here from another star."

Kick thrust his thick blond hands into Ryan's ribs, tickling him, making him scream in the tangle of the sleeping bag. "You must stop saying that," Kick said. "It's embarrassing."

"It's true!"

Kick rolled full-body on top of Ryan and placed the palm of his hand over Ryan's mouth. He looked directly down into Ryan's eyes. "It's not true," he whispered. He repeated the phrase staring down into Ryan's eyes. "It's not true. I'm going to take my hand away and I want you to say it's not true."

Ryan gasped for air. Kick's serious muscle weighed heavy on him. He looked directly up into Kick's eyes, his face, his halo of blond hair, the sky full of stars behind him.

"Say it," Kick said.

"It's . . . not . . . true," Ryan said.

"I'll kiss you to prove it." Kick lowered his face, grazing noses, brushing moustaches, touching lips, tangling tongues.

Omigod, Ryan thought. *He's lying. I'm lying. We're both lying.*

They wrestled and necked and stopped short of cuming, finally burrowing in together, cuddling and laughing and wishing on every falling star. With their arms wrapped tight around each other, Ryan wondered why they didn't, couldn't, break the bounds of gravity. They were in bondage together, trapped here on this mundane planet, like two visitors unsure they wanted to stay. Ryan had fought his way from the burbscape of Peoria to Misericordia to Chicago to the Castro to the country. He had fought his way over thousands of men's bodies to the safe harbor of Kick's body. He wanted nothing more in life but more of the same.

"Let's take it," Ryan whispered, and he meant muscle, and he meant love, "to the limit."

In answer, Kick pulled Ryan's face to his own.

Through their moustaches their lips met and parted. Their tongues found lodging. Kick's hand on the back of Ryan's head pulled them closer.

"As far as we can take it," Kick said.

He held the kiss so long his sweet breath became Ryan's life-giving oxygen. Ryan was no longer kissing Kick. Kick was kissing Ryan.

Ryan knew, under those shooting Christmas stars up in the country, that this was the kiss against which he'd measure every other kiss in his life.

Later, in bed with Kick, Ryan no longer minded his sleeplessness. That night, back in the iron bed in the barn, with Thom and Sandy's wild family asleep up in the main house, a gay sense of well-being filled Ryan's soul. They had made love again. Kick had fallen into an easy sleep. The bedside lantern dropped soft light across their spent and naked bodies. Nothing this good, Ryan thought, can last forever. He pushed on the moment the way a small boy's tongue plays a loose baby tooth that hurts so good.

"Be here now," he cautioned himself. He thought of Francie in *A Tree Grows in Brooklyn;* she looked at everything as if it were the last time she'd see it. He had never forgotten the line he had read twenty years before in a seminary English class.

He studied Kick's sleeping guileless face, and realized that he trusted this man more totally than he had ever trusted anyone, and his wonder was that he had not surrendered any of himself. The light rhythms of his best friend's breathing soothed him. Even if they continued on forever, every moment of all of it he wanted to remember. Ryan felt he had everything in the world a man could ask for. He smiled about his health and his writing and his ranch and the love he received and gave. He had, he knew, miles to go before he would ever really sleep. He could brave that kind of existential insomnia. He knew in life he already had more than most people ever know is available if only you're attentive enough. He had everything. He was certain that the only thing he now wanted was truly more of the same.

Kick had said everything that Ryan ever wanted to hear from him: "You're the only man I want to keep on keeping on with." Then Kick had said those words that Christmas night, "I love you, Ry."

Ryan pulled his arm from beneath Kick's sleeping blond head. His face was even more handsome in sleep. His naked body, all his fine muscles in repose, looked sculpted by angels. Ryan knelt up in their bed. His left hand moved slowly, lightly over the hairy bodybuilder's shoulders and chest and washboard belly. His right hand took hold of himself, and with the palm of his left hand resting lightly on the sleeping man's gently rising pecs, with the feel of Christmas all around them, awake for them both, solitary no more, Ryan made love a third time that night to the perfect sleeping man.

"I know," he whispered, "you've come from another star."

3

Ryan would not apologize for being a masculinist anymore than for being a homosexual. Kick fortified him. "We're not really homosexual," Kick said. "We're sexually sophisticated." Ryan's writing became more resolute. No longer wrestling alone against the tag team of depression and despair, Ryan changed when Kick came to his rescue. Kick climbed through the ropes into the ring. The crowds cheered. The golden man of bodybuilding tackled Ryan's dark depression and deep despair the way an All-American champion pins two fat and ugly wrestlers to the sweaty mat. Kick's mighty arms held open the ropes and Ryan escaped from the ring of sadness.

Suddenly life seemed more possible than Death.

The angel Ryan had prayed for to beat his dark anxiety had arrived on golden wings. Ryan became a daredevil. He liked wising off in print. He liked the largeness, the exaggeration, the metaphor that is the essence of all writing.

Maneuvers remained erotic entertainment without a breath of controversy. Each cover promised: "What you're looking for is looking for you." The magazine gave good head. Solid smut. Sleazy pix. All nasty leather S&M. A new network of personal ads written by readers and answered by phone or mail. Circulation grew. *Maneuvers'* only competition broke into a sweat.

The rival mag, *Leather Man,* ran middle-of-the-road S&M stories, not-too-dirty photos, and campy copy. Silly cartoon balloons of queenly dialog deflated *Leather Man*'s hardly hot pix of clonish young gay boys wearing leather chaps and chrome armbands available through the mag's 800-number shop. Slender pages of fiction and drawings were a fat-cat publisher's thin come-on to get readers to subscribe to a monthly magazine that was a glorified mail-order catalog to sell leather toys and poppers and his lover's disco records. In the first rise of gay magazines, it was fast-buck publishing. For guys not knowing the difference, *Leather Man* passed as the real thing.

"Lips that touch Naugahyde," Ryan said, shaking his head at his competition's latest issue, "shall never touch mine."

The *Manifesto* made masculinism a theory. *Maneuvers* made it a fashion. *A Different Drum* reviewed the tempest with sympathetic amusement. *Leather*

Man didn't get it at all. Ryan was prick-teasing everyone, even his own kind, and having a wonderful time doing it.

"Homomasculinism," he said to January Guggenheim, "is homosexuality theorized, idealized, and applied man-to-man." He showed her the collection of his incoming mail. She aimed her video camera at the envelopes. Men from all across the country had begun to write to him in ways less salacious than before. One of them was straight. They joined him in their resistance against, "not women and feminism per se," he said, "but against the predatory version of radical separatist feminism."

Solly Blue sat bemused across Ryan's living room, listening to the bullshit roll, and rather enjoying one of his excursions from his penthouse.

Ryan found himself in an ironic situation.

"So," January said. "At first your tongue was planted in your cheek." She had set up her Panasonic video camera on wide angle to record the interview. The big cameras and crew would come later. Little did any of them realize the video would end up in my piles of research. "Where is your tongue planted now?" She fanned the stack of mail Ryan had given her to read. "I mean now that quite a few men, judging by these letters, have responded to your masculinist position?" She wanted him to hang himself. "Queer theory? What is it, darling? Really . . ."

Solly turned to Ryan. "She wants your talking head on a plate."

"We're in the second phase of sexual liberation," Ryan said. "These aren't the good old days on Folsom or the early days on Castro."

"It was simpler then," Solly said. "You blew your mind with drugs and fucked your brains out. Hardly a period for intellectuals. But there they all were, all these college professors on sabbatical, snorkeling at the bottom of a pig pile at the Barracks researching gay pop culture."

"First we had to prove we were strong in numbers."

"Because," Solly tweaked, "we had all been in solitary confinement in our own little closets."

"Then we had to prove we could do anything we wanted sexually."

"The only really good gay sex is public sex."

"What's that mean?" January asked.

"Do it in the street," Solly gestured grandly, "and scare the horses."

"There's more," Ryan said, "to homosexuality than fucking. There is, and I believe this with all my heart, a code."

"Something," January said, "like the Code of the West?"

"That's what he called it in the *Manifesto*. Miss January."

"Thank you, Mr. Bluestein."

Solly raised his Coke glass with his index finger pointing at January. "Ryan didn't bed down with nine thousand guys and not crawl out without some kind of insight into human nature."

"You've had nine thousand sex partners?" January's jaw dropped.

"I didn't cum with them all," Ryan said.

Solly gulped.

"Nine thousand. Give or take a few," Ryan said. "It's only a lifetime estimate."

January looked shocked. "I thought I was a whore," she said. "No offense."

"Steinbeck said," Ryan deflected the conversation from himself, "that with a three-day drunk and a night in a whorehouse he could write anything."

"How very literary," January said. "You've used your sex experiences. You think about them."

"He obsesses," Solly said. "He makes his living writing about them. He makes his lovers sign releases. He makes me listen to him on the phone."

"*Porno, ergo sum.* I live it up to write it down," Ryan said.

"I like that," January said.

"It's Kick's."

"I thought it was Descartes'," Solly said.

"It's cute," she said.

"Ryan's nothing if not cute," Solly said.

An alarm rang in Ryan's head. Kick had warned him that TV people like January trivialized everything. He pulled her back on track. "What we're talking here is a new concept in male bonding."

"That's not cute," Solly said.

"That's grand," she said.

"Don't use the word *grand*," Solly said. "Ryan hates the thought of being grand. Only queens are grand."

"It seems to me," January had an edge of acid on her tongue, "I must be very careful of my semantics with you fellows."

"Don't call us *fellows*." Solly sounded like Bert Lahr playing the Cowardly Lion. "On the outside we look the same as men, but on the inside . . ."

"Proust," January said. "*Remembrances.* Badly quoted."

"Actually," Solly said, "nicely misquoted."

"This is more than semantics," Ryan said. "Different species of gays exist within generic homosexuality."

"I could make a fortune," Solly said, "selling designer videos of a Generic Gay Man. He'd sell like the Neanderthal Man or the Cro-Magnon Man. He could be the 'I. Magnin Man.'"

"Get serious," Ryan said.

"You're too serious," Solly said. "In ancient Rome, when somebody started taking himself too seriously, a slave stood behind him and whispered, 'Remember thou art only a man.'"

"You've brought," January looked at her notes, "something more than abstract masculinism out of the closet. You write about rimming, fisting, water sports, and even scatology as political acts. Do you think your writing has given men permission to do some rather sleazy things they'd never dare do if you hadn't glamorized them?"

"You mean," Solly said, "can a reader sue Ryan if the reader goes out one night and ends up with clap and a colostomy?"

"Solly!" Ryan said. He had wanted Solly present for more than a send-up of January Guggenheim. "There is no blame," Ryan turned up his intensity, "for what goes on in the baths and bedrooms of San Francisco. I learn far more from other men than I dream up myself. My friend here," and he shot Solly a glance meant to corral his mouth, "says that the ultimate political act is being able to do ultimate things with your own personal body."

"Am I on? Is the video running? I'm never on this side of the camera." Solly sat up and pontificated. "Good sex is a combination of mutually exclusive things all performed at the same time . . ."

"Omigod." Ryan said.

". . . each one progressively more disgusting than the last."

"He's on a roll," Ryan said.

"Take notes, lady," Solly Blue said. Leaving his apartment made Solly aggressive out of self-defense. "I'm the queen *du jour!*"

"Your friend Solly is a veritable sage. He should write fortune cookies."

"Lady," Solly said, "if you want *Tales of the City,* go interview Armi Maupin. He's perfectly commercial at what he peddles. He gives you people, and I mean *you people,* like the straight public, the comfortable image they expect of faggots. We're not talking musical comedy here."

"Forgive me." January, who had never in her life asked for forgiveness and meant it, turned to her purse. Archly conciliatory, she reached for her small snifter. "Would you care for," she spoke directly to Solly, "some real coke?"

Ryan jumped back in. "Men need wildness," he said. "In these permissive, feminist times, men need to be radically tough with each other. We need to be warriors. We need to get our balls back."

"Whatever for?" January said between toots.

"I'll tell you what for," Solly said. "Men can't get much physical intensity from women who expect them to be gentle. You women have only yourselves to blame. If women were more wild and adventurous in bed, men, some men, some basically straight men, wouldn't turn to other men."

"Oh?" January said. "You mean women are the cause of homosexuality?"

"I mean," Solly said, "if all a man wants is kids, women suffice as breeders."

"Breeders!" The word shocked January.

Solly was relentless. "Breeders." He repeated it with emphasis. "For when men want procreation sex. When a man wants recreation sex, if his wife can't be levitated out of the passive missionary position, he turns to other women, or to hookers, and when he can't afford hookers, he turns to other guys."

Ryan, the ringmaster, grinned.

"If most dutiful wives," Solly said, "could tune into the fantasies in their fucking husbands' fucking heads they'd run straight out the bedroom door. Women think sex is all candlelight and fireplaces. Men think it's fourth down and inches to go."

"You certainly have strong opinions," January said. "For a pornographer."

"And all of them," Solly said, "subject to whim."

Ryan liked the intensity of their disdain for one another. He had always wanted his Victorian to be a sort of intellectual salon, but one more butch than the Hula Palace. He enjoyed reading biographies with lines like: "In certain Right Bank Beaux-Arts buildings in Paris, the experience of sitting in a drawing room in late afternoon is enhanced by the quality of fading pinkish daylight." He admired the talented ensemble that Robert Opel entertained in his gallery salon: singers like Sylvester and Camille O'Grady, artists like Rex and Tom of Finland, photographers like Robert Mapplethorpe, and writers like Pat Califia, who, ever the macho slut, waltzed through Opel's openings. Califia, raised a Mormon, had, to save her family from the shaming of her possible public excommunication, *aka*-ed herself for the independent Bear Goddess who gave California its name. Ryan, himself identified with Orion, the Bear constellation, respected women, truly talented women like Califia and O'Grady as much as Kweenasheba. They held an almost enshrined place in his old Catholic heart. They seemed all the more fully women for having transcended radical feminism with the feminist humanism of their art. They were women who had performed the impossible the way Mary became a Madonna through virgin birth. Now that was the first truly, and maybe world's only, feminist act. About January Guggenheim, Ryan was still reserving his judgment.

"Love," Ryan said, "has an element of worship."

"Worship?" January repeated.

"The only problem with worship," Ryan said, "is that so few people are willing to let you do it." A smile flashed across his face.

In an instant, he remembered the first night he had parted Kick's hairy cheeks and dug his tongue down to lick his sweet blond butthole in the ultimate act of worship. Other men could cheer and worship Kick's public display of muscle in physique contests, but only Ryan could lay him out flat and kiss and tongue the privacy of Kick's inviolate pucker. Their private rituals were secret. They flaunted each other on Castro. Ryan handled their public relations. Kick remained aloof, mysterious, above it all. They were a pair, all right, hanging out in the afternoon sun.

Ryan was studstruck.

Writing cabaret material for Kweenie, Ryan jotted paraphrase lyrics to "The Girl from Ipanema."

"Muscled and bulked and tanned and handsome, the man from Alabama goes walking, and when he passes, each one he passes, he just doesn't see. Massive arms and blond and smiling, the man from Alabama goes walking, and when he passes each one he passes, goes, 'Ah.'"

Kick was an object of worship.

He was the lord of the Castro.

He was men's most secret dreams.

He was Desire.

"Worship," January said, "sounds so, well, Catholic." She jotted a note. "Of course, that's the priest in you coming through."

"Kick is a case in point," Ryan said.

"Ah," January said.

"Ah," Solly said, "the meat of the matter."

"He's a perfect drop-dead blond," January said. "Worship of him, I can understand. I'd certainly get down on my knees. I mean, I'm an expert on men. I'd never suspect he was, uh, homosexual." She ran the tip of her small finger around her lips. "So tell me about him, darling. I mean I'm really interested. Does he hold up? Sir Larry Olivier, you know him, don't you, Ryan? He was Scarlett's husband in real life. I remember Larry saying he'd dallied with one male and found it not loathsome."

"I do," Solly said, "so love British understatement."

"Cut to the chase," Ryan said.

"The point, dear heart," January said, "is Larry's observation that every athletic champion proves a big disappointment once you pull down his jockstrap."

"Kick holds up," Ryan said. "I'll bet Sir Larry never removed the posing trunks of a physique champion."

"Then it's not true," January went straight to the question, "that body-building is overcompensation for being, well, undercompensated in the meat department?"

Ryan laid it on. "Kick's posing trunks have to be specially tailored. His waist is a medium." He didn't lie. "His pouch is an extra large."

"Of course," January said. "He's complete. What else? Do you have any idea how much we straight women envy you men? Anymore, every good-looking hunk is gay. And I suppose some of them are homomasculine." She smiled. "You see, I am learning your lingo."

"It's not lingo," Ryan said. "It's not semantics."

"It's not even Catholicism," Solly said, "that makes Ryan write. He's driven more to lead the literary life than the religious. It has," Solly looked straight at Ryan, "its ups and downs. Living around a writer is like sharing a house with an alcoholic. I've watched him suffer in total despair over his writing. And for his writing. Isn't despair a wonderful cliché? God knows, the Muse is a bitch."

Solly was not far from wrong. Ryan was bent on the literary life. I saw his liaison with Kick, with this unfathomable perfect stranger, as the same sort of grand passion D. H. shared with Frieda Weekly, around whom Lawrence spun his peculiar, feverish theories about eroticism.

Ryan's rooms expressed and explained, perhaps even better than he knew, what he himself was all about. To understand a man's space is to understand him. Ryan's life, even as a writer, was a visual art. That's why Kick fit in so well. He was the ultimate art object collected in Ryan's gallery. Ryan's Victorian was a kind of movie set providing not only comfort but inspiration to the erotic writer and, well, yes, somewhat theatrical lover that he was with his sex playroom filled with mirrors, track lights, chains, and sling.

When Kick moved in, the tracklight spots were already in place. He was not the first bodybuilder Ryan had met, but he was the best. Ryan was ready for him. His life had been lived in a way to prepare him to meet Kick, the way John the Baptist, who lost his head finally, was born to prepare the way for his cousin.

Ryan's house was something an anti-vivisectionist would torch. The walls were hung with the heads of deer and mountain goats hunted at flea markets. A lady's shoulder-fox hung from its lower lip. Edward Parente sculptures of animal skulls adorned with leather and feathers shared book-shelves with volumes by Emerson and Mishima and Didion. Pictures of Kick and Teddy and other less-involving lovers hung everywhere. Orion, the hunter, liked his trophies. They were his remembrances of things past.

"You're obviously a totemist," January said. She gestured at the array about her. "Your collecting is like your writing. It's a very male way of pre-serving something. Collectors are like hunters. You kill something and then preserve it, and the whole process is your ritual of self-preservation."

"Oh, Dr. Freud," Solly said, "how I wish you were otherwise employed."

"Don't take my zoo too seriously," Ryan said. "It's a collection."

January rose up from the couch. "This is a beautiful picture of Kick," she said. "Did you shoot him?"

"Yes."

She put her index finger on the glass directly touching Kick's crotch. She could see herself reflected over his body like a double exposure. "Some tribes," she said in a matter-of-fact voice, "sacrifice blonds to the sun." Her eyes focused on some far-off moment in her own past. "We eat the gods that first we worship." She turned back to Ryan. "Ironic, isn't it?"

"Frankly, I thought it was more El Lay," Solly said. "Today's star is to-morrow's Kleenex."

January turned to Solly, "First thing tomorrow, darling, do go see your therapist."

"My therapist—I should say my once-and-former therapist—told me," Solly said, "that sometimes we think we're in the throes of some deep spiri-tual yearning, but actually we're just horny." He paused a beat. "I think that's why he killed himself."

"Kick is a wizard," Ryan said. "All us faggots are wizards, you know."

"No, I don't know." January rearranged herself on the couch, folding calf under thigh.

"I mean we're all wizards, descendants of the Druid priests of the old phallic religions that predate the goddess religions of virgin-mothers."

"I've read that chapter," January said. She meant the *Manifesto,* Chapter Three, "Magic: Homomasculinity as the Old Religion."

"I raised you," Annie Laurie told Ryan, "to be independent." She had taught him to cook and to sew and to clean, so that he would not marry some poor girl to have someone take care of him. "No one should marry for the wrong reasons. Besides," she said, "if you grow up to be poor, you'll know how to do all these things for yourself, and if you grow up to be rich, you'll know how to manage the servants."

Her infusion of radical Irish independence knocked Ryan's worldview off the straight and literal and gave him a parallax, metaphorical vision. As much as Misericordia had been his upwardly mobile way out of the cornfields of Peoria, his acquired independence lacquered his inborn homosexuality and gave him fast and rebellious exit from the Midwest standard of a nine-to-five life, a split-level wife, and 2.3 children stuffed in a two-car garage.

His homomasculinity was his declaration of independence from the norm. He wrote in a letter to me, dated Friday, August 26, 1977:

I despise what is normal. It's too expected. I choose to be homomasculine. I could have shut my eyes, bitten my tongue, denied my preference, and managed a wife and children; but I chose the harder path: to make love to men. I need certain men the way certain men need me. Some men need to be loved more than women can love them. Few people ever realize that men can dry up and die for lack of love from other men.

No one knows what causes homosexuality anymore than they know what causes a boy to answer to a religious vocation to the priesthood. No one ever asks what causes heterosexuality. Both are their own special calling. Neither is better than the other. Merely different. Some people are called sexually to procreate. Some are called to recreate. If I had children, I could not truly live the creative, intellectual life. If Fundamentalists are having personal relationships with Jesus whispering in their ears, then they have to accept that Jesus, or whatever the Primal Force is named this time, can call me too. When a muscular, sweaty, young carpenter blows in my ear, I'll follow him anywhere.

If I could choose, and I did not choose, I would choose to be exactly as I am. Homosexuals are forced to choose—not what they already are by birth—but how they are to stand four-square with some dignity against the national religious standard of what is sexually "correct." That is our perversity. We reject the very essence so dear to the hearts of the residents of Straight Street who require everyone to be like they are. "Like seeks like" is okay for them; why is "like seeks like" not okay for us? When we choose to reject the way they are, we call their own standards for themselves in doubt. We make them think about the way they are. When spouses are angry and children are unruly, we are their visions of otherness. They envy us for our freedom from their trap. Their envy turns to hate. They know nothing about our trap while we ironically know everything about theirs.

I have chosen to celebrate manhood, not fatherhood, not husbandry, not anything defined in relation to women and children. My vocation is not to the Church. It is not to homosexual politics. It is only to the fraternity of men.

I suck dick because it smells, tastes, feels, sounds, and looks good.

I suck dick to scare people.

So fuck 'em if they can't take a joke.

Ryan had that edge of inborn gay rage to live up to his identity. That intensity was his virtue. Against all odds, maybe his vice. Teddy could not withstand Ryan's passion. Kick was reveling in it. That was the difference between lover Number One and lover Number Two. Ryan's fervor lay in his pagan nature, rebelling against his Catholicism. Even so, he sought Gemini balance. His strict self-discipline, drilled into him by Monsignor Linotti at Misericordia, led to the peculiar rarefication of his soul that only ordained priests, totally committed to their faith, pagan or not, can understand.

"For some comic relief," Solly said to January, "why don't you ask me about my Brand-X homosexuality. I'm very content with my boys. Plural. Ry wants only one extraordinary bodybuilder god."

"What's so great about your street hustlers," Ryan said. "Twenty-five cents a pound."

January sprang to attention. She moved closer to Solly.

"My boys earn their money because they're men." He was determined to be grand with January to get even with Ryan shoveling his hip-deep bull. "In America, money is the only way of keeping score. My boys are hustlers the way everybody is a hustler. They're entrepreneurs. They're meat on the hoof, and they have the confidence that comes from getting paid for what they are." He shot a look around the room. "When was the last time either of you ever got paid for being what you are?"

"I live quite handsomely, thank you," January said.

"Listen, lady," Solly said, "A Jew knows a Jew. You've got *princess* engraved all over you."

"Ignore him," Ryan said. "He's on a sugar rush."

Solly took a pot shot at Kick. "Gay muscle queens kill me."

Ryan hoped Solly might tip his hand to January about the real cause of his dislike for Kick. More than anything, it was the secret Ryan wanted to know.

"I like blue-collar, working-class muscle," Solly said. "I despise these mondo steroid freaks. You want some facts and figures for your documentary? Five gyms compete for business in the Castro. All filled to capacity. All gay as shit. The boys can't even keep the names of the gyms straight."

"Tell every negative thing you know," Ryan said. He wanted January to focus on the upside of the emerging new Castro.

Solly sipped his Coca-Cola. "Miss January here should see both sides of this gay muscle, forgive me, homomuscular, trip."

"Body maintenance has become important. The new gays are into health. The gyms give balance to drugs and bars." Ryan tried to correct Solly's direction, but Solly was one person he could never control.

"I'm fascinated," January said. "I love antagonism."

"For instance," Solly said, "there's the gym called *The Muscle System*. The pump-and-pearl girls call that *The Muscle Sisters*. *The City Athletic Club* is *The Sissy Athletic Club*. *The Pump Room* satirizes its own name. Not everyone who is homosexual, you see, is as taken with muscle as is Ryan. But then he sees a twenty-inch bicep not only for what it is, but for what it symbolizes."

"You're such a fundamentalist," Ryan said.

"No pain, no gain," Solly shot back.

"Please, go on," January said.

"I shall," Solly said. "That interior design shop on Castro, next to Cliff's Variety, called *Work Wonders*? That's the perfect name for a gay gym. All you guys who all failed gym class, huffing and puffing like the straight guys you desired. Trying to keep your pecs pumped up for Saturday night. If it wasn't so tiring, you'd be funny. Gays could be national heroes. We could solve the energy crisis if we hooked your Nautilus machines to a generator."

He threw a wink at Ryan. He wanted in his own way to play devil's advocate with January. "Is it true that ninety percent of all gay boys mount their Nautilus machines sidesaddle?"

"I love it," January said. "Who was Nautilus anyway?"

"He's the ancient Greek god of expensive spas," Solly said.

"Darling," January said.

"I think," Solly said, "we're beginning to understand each other."

"Don't forget," Ryan said. "All us bodybuilders . . ."

"Oh," Solly said. "Himself is now one of *all us bodybuilders*."

Ryan cocked a bicep bigger than he'd ever had before. "All us bodybuilders trade recipes and decorating ideas and hot tips on real estate."

"That Attitude," Solly pronounced, "is precisely why I don't go out anymore. In restaurants, if you faggots were forbidden to talk about sex, drugs, gyms, and real estate, you'd be mute."

"Sometimes some of us like to spend a couple of hours on a weekend afternoon . . ."

"What a waste of precious time," Solly said.

". . . soaking up the sun standing around the neighborhood."

"Castro isn't a neighborhood. It's a happy hunting ground."

"At least it's happy."

"In neighborhoods, people say *hello* and mean it for what it is."

"A good *hello* on Castro is what it is."

"A *hello* on Castro . . ." Solly looked at January. "Are you sure your video is running? A *hello* on Castro only means you're sexually interested and available. Most of the guys who've slept together the night before pretend they don't recognize each other on the street the next day. It's always: 'On to New Meat!' That's the Code of the West!"

"So that's what a *hello* on Castro is," Ryan said. "It fits perfectly your definition of anything and everything: what is, is. Besides, you lifted my line for your last mail-order brochure. 'What you're looking for is looking for you.' If that's so, then Castro, with all its faults, is still the only place where you'll find it."

"What I'm looking for," Solly said, "isn't looking for me on Castro. What's looking for me is going to have to work hard to try and find me."

"I must use you," January said to Solly. "I think you're terribly fascinating. You'll make a great bit in the special."

"Only if I wear a mask." Solly played Groucho. "On second thought, only if you wear a mask."

"Darling," January said, "whatever turns you on."

"Okay," Solly said. "You can tape me, but let me give you the scenario. Here's something," he aimed at Ryan, "for you and Kick and all your homomuscular buddies to think about. For Jan's TV special—I can call you *Jan,* can't I? Good! For Jan's special, catch this, I walk into that gym where you and Kick workout and shout: 'What insecurity brings you here?' I could shrivel those muscleheads down so far to their real size the camera would need a macro-lens to find them."

"That's a specious argument," Ryan said.

"Is it?"

"You could walk in any place where people are trying to improve themselves and shout that. Compensation isn't the only motivation guys have for working out."

"Compensation is what the world is all about," January said.

"So, tell me, Jan, what are you compensating for?" Solly said.

She turned to Solly. "I like you," she said "I like you a lot."

"Terrific," Ryan said.

"Robert Opel promised me," January said, "that I'd find strange bedfellows on this assignment."

Ryan looked at Solly who looked back at Ryan. They burst out laughing.

"Oh, poo," January said. As she walked up to the lens of her camera, she actually put her pinkie into her mouth and bit its nail with her front teeth. "I'm running out of tape."

4

That night, searching for the right muscle Look, Kick's dick hardened. He picked around in his closet in Ryan's bedroom. All his shirts, even the tee shirts, hung on hangers.

"I love my shirts," he said. He wrapped one of his king-sized, baby-blue plaid Pendletons around Ryan and squeezed him tight.

"They're such beautiful shirts," Ryan said.

"Check this out." Kick held up a soft gray cotton tee shirt. He stood stripped to the waist. He was between contests and his torso was unshaven. His hair pattern was classic: thick across his shoulders, coming down his big pecs, spilling spun-golden over them and on down his washboard abs. ALABAMA was stenciled in crimson block letters across the gray tee shirt's chest. He shot each arm through the tight sleeves and pulled the neck on over his carefully groomed blond hair. He palmed ALA first on one bulging pec and then BAMA on the other.

"The old Crimson Tide," he said. He adjusted the tight band of the short sleeves around his baseball biceps. He ran his hand down the cotton over his tight belly. The shirt fit like a second skin. "This is the right one tonight," he said. Kick had formfitting cotton tee shirts, not all in one size, but in all the several sizes of his arms and chest to accommodate precisely his heft: in contest shape, bulked, or trimmed down between competitions.

"In anyone else," Ryan wrote in his *Journal*, "this could be vanity; but I understand what is in his heart and my heart, and our heart, when it comes to the fetish of his shirts."

Kick turned and hit a pose for no more reason than to delight Ryan. The athletic gray tee shirt transformed his Look from bodybuilder to more of a husky college jock. That was one of the wonders of Billy Ray Sorensen. Most bodybuilders always looked like bodybuilders. Kick defied categorization. Almost more than a bodybuilder, he was an artist, maybe even in the sacred sense of a priest, who could transform himself with mind control, transubstantiate himself with body control.

Ryan, more than once in their bedroom, had seen Kick metamorphose from Kick into almost anything a body artist could conjure on his basic handsome and husky Look. Kick was as believable a college jock as he was a bodybuilder, or, one of their favorite impersonations, a blond, moustached California Highway Patrolman uniformed in blue-and-gold-striped motor breeches and boots, black-leather gloves and jacket, golden helmet, and tan military shirt with short sleeves almost ripped apart from the straining pressure of his huge biceps.

Ryan ran his hand down the belly of the tee shirt. He felt the soft gray cotton over the mat of dirty-blond belly fur. He felt Kick crunch his washboard muscle to ultimate definition for his pleasure. In the palm of his left hand, Ryan was memorizing Kick's body.

"You have," Ryan said, sounding for all the world like Daisy Buchanan adoring the golden Jay Gatsby, "such beautiful . . . beautiful . . . beautiful . . . shirts."

Kick put his hands on his tight waist, arms akimbo, the way football jocks stand around between scrimmages, "Tonight," he said, "we're gonna get into pud. Pecs and pud. Varsity football pecs and pud."

Kick was too good to be true.

Ryan wondered sometimes if he were hallucinating. Was he losing his mind, imagining this phantasm of masculinity who filled in all the blanks of everything he thought a man should be? For twenty-three months they had gone at each other nonstop. They were lovers, and more than lovers, they were friends together. He had made up his mind to ride along with this man whatever way mutuality took them. Even if they should eventually decide to go different ways, no one, not even the beautifully handsome physique champion, could take away from him the wonder of their time together.

Kick was a good lover. He clarified Ryan's life. Kick had pared down his own life to an almost Thoreauvian simplicity. He had pared his body down to transparent skin, hairy and tanned, with no subcutaneous layer of fat, revealing only the cordage of vascularity, of veins wrapped like cables around the defined bulk of his muscle.

Their nighttime lust matched their daytime discipline.

Kick had always called Ryan *coach.* "I know what else you want," Kick said. "You want muscle. Not only mine. Yours." He handed Ryan a training schedule. "I want you to be my official workout partner."

"You'll give me muscle?"

"You can have anything you want."

"Can you make me blond?"

Six days a week, with Kick on split routines, they pumped through their workouts. Kick popped caffeine pills to up his energy. Ryan followed suit. "Whatever works," he said. They ate omelets and broiled skinless chicken. They drank eggs whipped with bananas in the blender. When guys asked Kick about his diet, he described their basic drink. "Put a can of tuna packed in spring water in your blender. Add another can of water. Whip it and drink it."

"The first one," Ryan said, "is the worst one. It tastes like whipped baby shit."

Guys stood gagging on the corner of 18th and Castro.

"You really drink that?"

Kick flashed a single-biceps shot. "You betcha," he said.

The fans looked somewhat dismayed, but the *do-fer*, as Kick called the questions guys asked when they'd say, "What do you do for your arms," they took totally to heart.

There is no lore as esoteric as bodybuilding lore. If a big, impressive bodybuilder said he got his build from drinking blenderized baby shit, in ten minutes every aspiring bodybuilder within earshot would be out trying to score used Pampers from the nearest child care facility.

Bodybuilding is a sport where genes will out. Bodybuilding is also the sport where every aspirant plays three-card draw to improve on the hand dealt him by his genetic code. When the muscle-genes are there, a man pumping iron cannot help but push on out to the limit of his potential. When the genes, as Ryan's were, are more ectomorph than mesomorph, hope springs eternal. And snake oil reigns supreme.

If gossip gets around a gym that Mr. Physique over there, benching 450, with twenty-inch arms, drinks whipped tuna from a blender once a day and swallows 30 mg of anabolic steroids, every muscle-crazed man in the place will figure if one can of tuna and 30 mg of Dianabol does that for him, then they'll catch up and even pass him by drinking three cans of tuna and popping 90 mg of steroids.

"That's why half of them are crazy," Kick said. "They believe anything. They think bodybuilding is witchcraft. If they could only find the right ingredient, the right pill, the right coach, they'd be Mr. America."

With the gay gyms came the steroids. Dianabol was as popular on Castro as cocaine and MDA. Ryan wanted nineteen-inch arms like the two husky dealers who drove up from El Lay to peddle their little blue pills on Castro. He wanted to beef up for Kick. He fantasized they could lock together in mutual musclesex. His heart pounded in fascination of the potential.

Steroids were Eden's apple.

"They're poison," Ryan said. He spoke out against his own temptation.

"These days for a competition bodybuilder," Kick said, "there's no other way."

Kick was telling him something.

"You mean you have to start?" Ryan asked.

"There's no other way," Kick said.

"You've done okay so far without them."

"We want to take muscle as far as it will go."

Ryan tried to adjust his Attitude. He read too much. Steroids lower the immune system, cause cancer, turn the liver to pudding. "You're sure," he said.

"We can visualize every night, but there's only so much muscle mass we can conjure." Kick was confident. "I know this doctor in El Lay. He's into sports medicine. Steroids are okay under medical supervision. He'll monitor me. I'll drive down there once a month. He works with professional bodybuilders. He knows what he's doing. I know what I'm doing. I want you to know everything that's going on."

"I'm not sure," Ryan said.

"You want us to win, don't you?"

"Of course."

"Then it's muscle as far as it goes."

"I don't want anything to happen to you."

"Trust me," Kick said.

"I've always trusted you," Ryan said.

Ryan wondered about his own motives. If he held Kick back, then all the nights they had played sexually with muscle fantasies, about Kick's championship physique, would be a lie. He had to keep on keeping on.

"I'm not saying it's right because everyone takes steroids," Kick said. "I'm saying that because everyone does take them, I have to take them to be competitive."

"You always said you liked communication more than competition."

"I do. But to communicate on an even more impressive level, I first have to compete to win that credibility."

"I want," Ryan said, and he dissembled a bit, torn between his love for Kick and his love for Kick's muscles, "whatever you want. I can't say *no* to you. You've said only *yes* to me. All along. I want . . ."

"Yes?" Kick pulled Ryan on into his sweat-sweet armpit, hugging his head into the deep valley where his massive arm tied into his broad shoulder, his deep back, and his full pecs.

Ryan was lost and found in this contradiction of a man. Who was he to stop Kick from going all the way with his lifelong dream which was so like his own?

"Let's," Ryan said, his voice muffled against Kick's hairy chest, "take it to the limit."

Ryan wrote in his *Journal.*

Super Bowl Sunday, January 21, 1979: I know him now, but very soon everyone will know him. This thing with January is turning into a big deal. Television turns everything into Something. She'll be taping Kick training for his next contest. Attention is being paid to him. I wasn't wrong when I knew from the start what he could do. What we could do together.

Kick's at the beginning of some great recognition. I like that. I like the verification from expert physique judges that I've been really correct in encouraging him on to competition. Not competition really. Comparison. Communication through muscle. I want to watch other men enjoy what I have enjoyed so intimately. No jealousy in that.

The looks and lust of other men are validation that once in my life, we two have met equally and are creating what we want more than anything. Energy comes from both sides. He calls me his coach. He flatters me. I love him for it. I think he could do alone what we do; but if he could, why has he stayed so long and pleasured me so much?

He has the genes I wish I had. I eat his sperm. I drink his saliva. I swallow his sweat. I feast on his sweet butt. I want to become him. I want to be him. What sane man doesn't want to become his fantasy?

He says I have a great soul. (Would that my soul had biceps and pecs.) He says I do him better than anyone. Does he know how much at night I am him? When we swing out on our muscle and bondage trips, does he know that I stop existing because my anxiety stops existing and I fly free. I become him.

A note from two nights ago: Kick was in El Lay for his pre-steroid liver-panel workup. So I watched a TV movie, *The Jericho Mile* about a track coach and a runner who was a convict in Folsom Prison. When the runner-con asked the coach what he was getting out of his coaching, the coach said: "I could run fast. I know how to run fast. But I can't run fast and float free like you. But I know how to teach it. I've waited all my life for someone like you to come along."

For godsake, who cries at TV movies? But tears filled my eyes, because all my life I've been in pursuit of the perfect man in the perfect body, because all my life I've wanted to have a body built to match on the outside the soulbuilder I've been raised, for good or ill, to be inside. I want more than anything in the world to have muscles, and if I can only be realized through Kick, then I'll be satisfied.

Isn't that what love is?

Even settling for his muscles rather than mine is hardly half a loaf. He's complete. All my life, ever since I sat on my daddy's lap, I've waited to match up with a man who was enough his own man to be able to be a part of my life. I've always been the sun in all my relationships. For once I want to feel like the moon. I want my cold aerobic body to be warmed by his muscular heat. I want to lose myself in his light. He can do no wrong. I trust him. He can lead me where he wants. He can do with me what he wants.

Coaching Kick kept Ryan clean. The days were serious training. The nights, serious sex. Ryan stayed three issues ahead on *Maneuvers*. Then two. He was overjoyed. Play was more fun than work. He left the saving of the world to priests, who, unlike him, were not spoiled priests. His vocation was not the world. His vocation was Kick. Other than the *Manifesto*, Kick eighty-sixed Ryan's old social concerns about civil rights and the homeless and Central America.

"They only depress you," Kick said. "I never want you to be depressed."

If the golden man of bodybuilding could train the depression out of him, then for all the Energy Ryan put into him, they would be more than even.

"If you don't think about certain things," Kick said, "They don't exist."

"That's the vice of the versa?" Ryan said.

"Exactly," Kick said. "The more we think about muscle when we play together at night, the more muscle we cause to exist."

"What kind of rebels are you southern boys?"

"The kind that tells you northern boys you think too much." Kick's every intention was good. To be a bodybuilder takes incredibly dedicated single-mindedness. "If you're depressed, Ry, we can't get on with all the Energy we need to do what we can only do if we do it together. Your depression over Vietnam didn't save Saigon. It won't save El Salvador. You can't help anyone but us. Your depression is a no-win situation. We're winners! I want us to win!"

"Kick was so sisboombah," Solly said much later. "He was always up. Like a one-man pep rally for a school that never existed."

"Let's hear it for the home team," Ryan said.

Kick's southern aloofness from all social concerns only made Ryan love him more. Kick's view was consciously simple and he was happy. Ryan was more complicated and he had always been unhappy. He wanted to learn Kick's upbeat lesson. He reached for Kick's hand. "You're every inch a man," Ryan said.

Kick was Ryan's shelter from the rain. Their night games held back Ryan's priestly pain. That was not enough for Kick. He wanted more. He wanted to stop Ryan's acquired pain.

"You don't have to save the world," Kick said. "Save yourself."

"I have so much to learn from you."

"Wrong," Kick said. His steely blue eyes were intense. "You're the coach."

The Look in Kick's face was silent command never to be down. Ryan locked the Look away and denied his sadness. "I'll be happy," he said to himself. "I'll make myself happy. Molly Brown hated the word *down*. She loved the word *up*. *Up* means *hope*."

"Why do we want everything all the time?" Ryan asked.

"Because," Kick said, "we're worth it."

"Then I'll do whatever it takes."

Ryan as a child had believed by clapping his hands he had made Tinker Bell live. Then he grew up to be Tinker Bell, and he had to keep lovers loving, readers reading, people clapping. Or he knew he'd die.

He turned all his attention to keep Kick kicking.

Solly was skeptical. "I think differently from Kick. No matter how massive his muscle, he'll die. You'll die. We'll all die. The universe will die. Eventually the expanding universe will reach, how can I put it so you'll understand, its muscular extreme, and then collapse in on itself not at the same rate it expanded, but faster, cataclysmically faster."

"Stop playing *When Worlds Collide*." Ryan felt a certain triangular tension.

Kick.

Himself.

Solly.

He'd think about it later.

The Dianabol worked. Their visualizations worked. Kick grew. His arms pumped bigger. His veins read like road maps around his muscle. His penis hung thicker and longer. His sexual appetite was insatiable. He was wearing even Ryan out.

"I wanted more," Ryan told Solly, "and now I'm getting it."

"Spare me," Solly said.

Bodybuilding is the sport of evolving gods. That is the romance of bodybuilding. That is its hubris. Ask Yukio Mishima. Mortal men lift weights against gravity's downward pull, using earth's gravity to build muscle that will make them like the immortal gods themselves. Bodybuilding is a rebellious, Faustian, Luciferian act. To achieve the golden bridge to immortality, anything is permitted.

"How you use your body," Solly repeated, "is the ultimate political act. I may not be fond of Kick, but I can appreciate, maybe more than he can, what he is doing."

"What's he doing?" Ryan asked. "I'm supposed to be the activist. Not him."

"Believe it or not," Solly said, "I've always loved bodybuilders in general, if not Kick in particular. There comes a point in size and power and Look when they transcend themselves. They go over the edge. They become gods of their kind. They achieve Universal Appeal. Kick, consciously or subconsciously, has become the man you idealized in your *Manifesto*. Maybe I was wrong. Maybe you should get down on your knees to him."

"I do," Ryan said.

"I know."

"You make me sound like Hitler lusting after a blond Aryan hunk."

"Without the edge of homosexuality, there would never have been a Third Reich, *mein smallische Fuehrer.*"

"Fuck you!"

"Gays and fascists. Both consider themselves the ultimate elite. Don't ever forget that."

Ryan left Solly's penthouse knowing the inevitable.

The ultimate elite.

He understood what Solly was saying.

He must finally, totally, fall down on his knees before Kick.

To do what Kick wanted.

To truly take muscle as far as it goes.

Some people choose longevity.

Some people choose quality of life.

What was it Sandahl Bergman said to Arnold Schwarzenegger in *Conan the Barbarian?*

"Do you want to live forever?"

What an ambiguous question.

One thing was meaning two things again.

Ryan said *yes* when Kick told him it was time.

"Give me," Kick said, "your arms and pecs and shoulders."

As Ryan had done at his First Communion, when he was seven years old, he opened his mouth.

Kick's fingers smelled sweet. He placed the blue pill on Ryan's tongue.

Ryan looked into Kick's blue eyes and hoped for more than he had hoped for all his life.

He hoped for his own muscle.

He closed his lips and kissed the tips of Kick's fingers.

If Death must be embraced, then let me be in Kick's strong blond arms.

He swallowed the Dianabol.

Another bite from the apple of paradise.

Kick led him to the bedroom. "I feel sorry," Kick said, "for anyone who isn't us tonight."

5

Up in Sonoma County the Bar Nada ranch house smelled of Velveeta panfried in margarine on enriched white Wonder Bread. It was a February weekend in the country. Kick, who had driven the Corvette only the week before to El Lay for his checkup with Doctor Steroid, had received a phone call from someone, not the doctor, who, Kick inferred, owed him a chunk of change. He seemed slightly upset. Ryan was not one to pry; but not without some eagerness Kick told Ryan El Lay called him back for the next weekend as well. "Urgent business," Kick said.

Ryan was disconsolate. "Not two weekends in a row!"

As usual, when Kick was away, Ryan invited me along to watch the family circus. "Not," I said, "two weekends in a row!"

"You can't leave me defenseless," he said.

"You? Defenseless?" I said. "Don't be moronically oxymoronic."

The triplets were on the warpath. Sandy was beside herself. "It's all from your side of the family, Thom. All of it."

Abe had discovered masturbation. He emerged from his room only to fry cheese sandwiches and fight with his sisters. Sie was working on her porno vocabulary and Bea had taken to wetting the bed. Thom had forced Beatrice to sleep in Pampers. He had wrestled her to the floor of her bedroom and fastened the diapers on her himself. She howled at the indignity. She told anyone who came in the front door what they were doing to her, and what she planned to do to them. "I'm going to be a lesbian," she shouted. "I'll show them."

Sandy was impassive to the commotion. She sat on the edge of the bench-like brick hearth, chain-smoking, feeding a week's accumulation of wet plastic diapers into the fireplace. She threw them one by one into the fire. They landed white and wet on the burning logs, sat for a moment, turned brown around the edges, and curled up like huge marshmallows, going up finally in a roar over the high hissing sound of her teenage daughter's urine evaporating to steam. One after the other she rationed the diapers into the fire, watching the burning, with the sudden plastic blaze lighting her thin boned face, accenting her hawk-nose and chopped black hair. She was the witch of Endor reading the runes of burning diapers. She was the wreck of a woman whom marriage had made. When Ryan ushered me around the corner and into the room, Sandy did not really look up. She sat on the hearth, smoking and drinking coffee, while hypnotically she burned the wet diapers. Finally, she looked up and said, "What's so funny?"

"Welcome to the Big Top," Ryan said.

"What?" Sandy Gully said. Finally, she laughed, almost seeing what a ridiculous figure she cut. "So, somebody has to do it."

Thom, for his part, cornered Sie at the end of the long green hallway. They were at each other's throats.

"Can we discreetly withdraw?" I asked.

"Are you kidding?" Ryan said. "I promised you a reserved seat at the main event."

The worst storm to hit the coast in a century had blown in from the Pacific. California was under siege. El Lay was sliding away. The Russian River was at flood stage. The small bridge leading up to the ranch from the road was underwater. Horses stood on the hillside with their withers turned into the wind. We were trapped like Brad and Janet in *The Rocky Horror Picture Show*.

Thom was outraged by his insolent daughter. Rain pelted the Plexiglas dome over their heads. Sie had been fifteen when she had first spit in her father's face. The week before, she had run to a neighboring ranch and cried that her father and her mother had beaten her. She had driven Thom and Sandy to their wit's end. Thom went to the neighbors' door and shouted through the screen, "Either you come home now or I call the sheriff."

"Call the sheriff," she said. "You and Mom hit us. You hit us all. You beat us. We're abused children."

"Get your ass out here," Thom said in a low voice, "or I'll have you taken away not as a runaway but as an uncontrollable little brat."

"I want to go to a foster home."

"You're going to end up in a juvenile facility in about five minutes flat."

Thom had no choice. He had to play his trump card. He stormed home and called the sheriff. When the two deputies arrived, they listened while Thom spun out the history. The three men drove down the road in the squad car to the neighbor's ranch.

The bigger of the two deputies crossed his thick forearms. He was blond, muscular, and imposing. Ryan knew the big man used his Look to straighten people out.

Me next! he wished.

"Little girl," the deputy said, "we've got all the details—not only from your father, but from your brother and your sister. You have a choice. Either you go home with your dad, or my partner here and I take you for a ride in the back of our squad car. If we take you in, you might be in juvenile hall for anywhere up to six or eight weeks."

"I don't care," Sie said. "Take me away from them."

"That means," the deputy leaned in close to her face, "six to eight weeks of greasy jailhouse food, no makeup, and no telephone."

Sullen, Sie touched her zits and came home.

Within an hour the three of them were fighting again. Ryan was embarrassed that the law had been called, but to the killer triplets, deputies in real life were no more startling than they were on a TV series.

Thom had commanded platoons in Nam, but his family was beyond his control. The storm trapped them all together in the ranch house. Thom cornered Ryan. "Please," Thom said, "you've got a way with kids. Do something. Maybe they'll listen to you."

"A fine mess this is," Ryan said. "What can I do?" Ryan could hardly keep up, weekend to weekend, with their antics. The information was too garbled. Their program changed too fast. They spoke no English. They spoke *sitcom*. They lived television. Video had penetrated their brains. Cathode rays had driven them to believe that life was a continuing series with a new situation dragged out, built to a climax, and resolved in half-hour segments. They lived on twelve acres of land and at any given moment they all crowded together fighting for territory to keep warm in the five square feet in front of the television.

They were a family of idolaters punished for their idolatry by the very idol they worshiped.

"The three of them," Thom said, "trapped Sandy in our bedroom last Wednesday morning. She wouldn't come out until I came home from work. Our own son and daughters! They said they were tired of child abuse. They told Sandy they wanted to abuse her so she'd know what it felt like. Their own mother!"

"The little darlings," Ryan said. "Have you thought of rolling Valium into their meatballs?"

"This isn't funny," Thom said.

"Maybe we could think up some game to distract them."

Ryan winked at me. "Something like you played last weekend."

"That only worked for a while," Thom said.

The Sunday before, Thom had dressed in his green camo fatigues and taken up a position on the living-room couch. He had thrown open the window and aimed his rifle out into the yard.

"You people," he shouted out to the triplets, "when I say *go,* I want you girls to throw that cracked corn around on the grass. Abe," he commanded, "while Bea and Sie spread the corn, your orders are to open up the chicken coop and chase the old biddies out onto the lawn."

Thom, sailing on double Percodans and black coffee, was oblivious to us watching him from the kitchen.

"Aren't you going to stop him?" I asked Ryan.

"How do you stop a man who has a foxhole dug next to the back deck?"

"This is turning into *Apocalypse Now.*"

"This has always been *Apocalypse Now.*"

"Don't you care?"

"Of course, I care. I actually want to see how far he'll go."

I think one of Ryan's character faults was that he always wanted the intensity of life *in extremis.*

Thom watched the chickens, curious at their liberation, slowly spread out from each other, hunting and pecking across the lawn. The girls each had a supply of brown Safeway bags under their arms. Thom lit a Camel and cupped it in his hand, waiting in ambush. He smoked slowly, relishing the maneuvers.

"Come on, Dad," Sie yelled. "This is boring."

"Shut up," Thom said. "Keep back up against the house. I don't want you in range when the shooting starts."

"I don't believe this," I said.

"Believe it," Ryan said. "Should I be the only witness to all this madness?"

Thom raised his rifle, aimed it through the window, sighted a Rhode Island Red, hunched his shoulder, resighted the target, squeezed the trigger, and dropped the chicken in its tracks.

"Is that supper?" I asked.

The other chickens wandered mindlessly on the lawn.

"Okay, people. Get on it!" Thom said. "Bea, you pick it up and put it in Sie's bag. Abe, I want you to place the bag with the chicken in it exactly where it dropped."

The children followed the orders.

"I like this," Abe shouted back.

"It's gross," Bea said.

Thom took a slow, careful hour, gunning down chicken after chicken. The kids no longer needed orders. After each kill, they bagged the body and set its memorial sack where it had fallen. The lawn was dotted with a random disarray of brown grocery bags leaking chicken blood.

Thom called out to the triplets. "You go play now."

"We are playing," Abe said.

Thom walked toward us in the kitchen. "That takes care of that," he said.

"Of what?" I was incredulous.

"Those fuckers haven't laid an egg in three weeks."

"It's winter," Ryan said. "They don't lay in winter."

Thom turned to Sandy. "Make me some more coffee."

Later, Sandy cooked supper. "We're having SpaghettiOs," she said. "I'm not touching those chickens."

"I told you," Thom said, "there's nothing to plucking and gutting a chicken."

"Yuck," Sie said.

"Then why don't you do it?" Sandy said.

"Because," Thom said, "I'm the hunter. You're the cook."

"Oh, really," Ryan said.

"Fuckin' A," Thom said. "Anyone who doesn't carry their own weight around here can clear out." He stared hard at Sandy who tried for an instant to stare him down, but then retreated.

Abe and Bea, with their mouths full, spent the meal tormenting Sie who had come late to the table from somewhere outside with straw in her hair. "I'm not hungry," she said.

"You've been out," Abe said, "putting cocks in your mouth."

"Sie's a cocksucker," Bea said.

"You're the cocksucker, Bea!" Sie said.

"Yuck!" Bea said. "I don't even eat hotdogs."

"Lesbo," Abe said.

"Boy!" Ryan said, "You guys really know how to make conversation."

"I've told the three of them," Thom said, "that this weekend you're in charge of them."

"Big deal," Bea said.

"I refuse to be in charge of them," Ryan said.

"I told you," Thom addressed all three triplets, "to eat with knives and forks and spoons."

"If you don't," Sandy said, "you won't know how to act when you start dating."

"You don't need forks," Abe said, "to eat at McDonald's."

"Sie doesn't need a knife and fork to eat dick," Bea said.

Bea picked up a handful of SpaghettiOs and threw them at Sie. The nuclear family went into meltdown. Sandy started screaming: "Stop it! Stop it!" Thom pushed his chair back from the table. A mess of salad, dripping with Kraft French dressing, hit him in the face. He roared up at the end of the table. He looked directly at Abe who sat defiantly in his chair. Abe had meant the salad to hit Bea, but he hardly looked as if he cared he had hit his father.

"Do something," Sandy screamed. "Now you see what they're like!"

Thom rose from his chair. He stared down across the table at his son. "You son of a bitch," he said to Abe, "you're going to make my day." He pulled his belt from his jeans and wrapped it around his thick hand. "I've had enough, squatface! This is the end of it!"

Ryan quickly rose from the table. Deep down he hated the triplets, but he was afraid that Thom might hurt them physically as much as he and

Sandy had hurt them emotionally. Ryan turned to Abe. "Get up, Abe," Ryan said in a low voice, "and head for your room."

Abe looked at his uncle in contempt. "Why don't you fuck off," he said. "I don't need your help. You're nothing but a faggot queer anyway." He reached into his plate of SpaghettiOs and threw a sloppy handful into Ryan's crotch. "We don't need you here to help us anymore," Abe said. "I don't like queers in our house."

I had never seen Ryan get truly angry before; but truly enraged he became. "Your house! Your house?" he said. "You ungrateful little bastard. This is my house. I own this house."

The entire kitchen drew to a startled halt. No one had ever seen Ryan so furious.

"You'll never eat another bite in my house," Ryan said.

"Oh, yeah?" Abe took a tablespoon, dug it into the food on his plate, and hauled it to his open mouth.

"Drop it," Ryan said.

"Fuck you," Abe said.

Ryan's anger descended. He scooped Abe's plate up off the table in the flat of his hand and shoved the dripping salad and SpaghettiOs into Abe's face.

"Get him!" Thom shouted. "Get the little bastard!"

The plate in the face knocked Abe to the floor. He lay in an instant garbage heap of food. He rolled over on his belly, his chin on the linoleum, and with both hands he shoveled the mess into his mouth. Ryan sprang from his chair. He dropped to the floor, straddling his nephew who was almost as big as he was, and squeezed the boy's cheeks to force his mouth open.

"Spit it out!" Ryan commanded. Even in his rage, I noticed a cool deliberateness, as if he anticipated every move. He was like Annie Sullivan taming Helen Keller. "Spit it out!"

Thom stood over the two of them. "Listen to your uncle," he shouted.

Ryan shouted up at Thom. "Don't call me their uncle."

Abe grit his teeth together. Ryan squeezed hard on his cheeks with one hand and with the other forced his nephew's lips open. He dug two fingers into the thrashing boy's mouth. He pulled the food spewing out of the boy's face.

"Hit him!" Sandy shouted to Ryan. "Hit him!"

Ryan pulled back still squeezing his nephew's cheeks. "I won't hit him," he said.

Sandy shouted to him again, as if finally he had come as reinforcement to her side in this marriage. "Hit him! Some kids deserve child abuse."

Ryan pulled Abe up by the neck of his shirt. Food covered them both.

Abe was defiant. "Straight," he shouted into Ryan's face, "is better than gay."

"Not," Ryan said, "when a faggot has you by the throat, you little sonuvabitch!"

Abe spit in Ryan's face.

"You ever do that again, and you'll go through life, little boy, explaining what a violent fairy did to your face. Sheriff or no sheriff. No court in the land would convict me of putting all three of you piece by piece through the blender."

Bea and Sie were laughing and slapping each other.

"Stop it, you two," Thom said, "or you'll get the same treatment."

Sie looked at her father contemptuously. "Don't you touch me," she said. "I want you to take me to a foster home."

Ryan, holding tight onto Abe's shirt, turned to Sie, and said, "Get your shit together, little girl. You're sixteen. You don't need a foster home. Kids your age run away."

Bea turned to Sie. "So run away, you little cocksucker," she said.

Ryan pushed Abe toward the hall. "Go take a shower," he said, "and stay in your bedroom until you can come out and act like a civilized human being. Go on!"

Abe gave him the finger, then shuffled off down the long hall.

"Sie," Ryan said, "you get your butt off to your room. You started all this."

Bea looked at her uncle. "No she didn't," she said. "Us kids didn't start this. They started it."

Thom moved toward her.

"It's true," Sie said. "They started it." She pointed at her father and then at her mother. "That bitch gave Abe forty dollars to get her some speed on the playground. He didn't want to, but she made him do it."

From down the hall, Abe called back, "It's true. What kind of mother would make you do that?"

Sandy flushed. "They're all such liars," she said. She stood up from the table and pulled on her coat. "Where's the car keys?" she asked Thom. "I'm going for a drive. I can't take this." She turned to Ryan and me and said, "Now you know why both times Thom went to Vietnam I ended up in a mental hospital." She fled out the door.

Sie marched off to her room.

"I'll clean up the mess," Bea said.

"No," Ryan said. "Why should you? You weren't involved in this fight."

She smiled at him. "Well, I've been in others, Uncle Ry."

"Don't call me that."

"I'm glad you stopped this before it got too bad."

Ryan looked at her in amazement. "You mean sometimes you're worse?"

Bea laughed. "When we're alone, we're horrid. We're good around you. Dad forces us to be. He says we owe you because you let us stay here in your house. Mom says because you're never going to have kids that we're supposed to be like your substitute children."

"I'm going to puke." Ryan actually blushed. "You're kidding," he said.

Thom moved close to Ryan. "She's not kidding," Thom said. "Thank you for handling this."

Ryan resented them all making him play the daddy since Charley-Pop had died. "Wait a minute," he said, "you're the father."

"And you're my older brother, Ry." Thom put his arms around Ryan and hugged him. He was bigger than Ryan and his forearms were covered with tattoos.

Ryan caught my eye over Thom's shoulder. His face turned quizzical. "I don't understand," Ryan said into Thom's ear, "why all this is happening. I don't understand why you let it ever get so far out of control."

Thom buried his head in Ryan's shoulder. He was crying. "I don't know what's happening. I can't take it anymore. I want them all to leave. I want to leave myself. Just get in the car and drive off. I just want to be left alone."

Ryan held his brother for a full two minutes. I could tell Ryan found the hug a strain. He was used to giving sexual hugs to men. He once told me that you could tell if a guy was homosexual or not by the way he hugged. When straight guys hug, they hug chests and shoulders and hold their hips carefully away from each other. When men, who prefer men, hug, it's a whole body press. It had long been a running joke on Castro that guys had to be careful when they went home to visit their families, because they get so used to Frenching everyone they meet that it's hard to remember not to put their tongues down their mothers' throats. Funny, but by the end of the two-minute hug, Thom, not Ryan, had pushed his hips, not hard, but tentatively, into Ryan's.

"I'm tense," Thom whispered. "I'm so fucking tensed out. They're all driving me crazy."

Later that night, something happened. The triplets had settled down and Sandy had gone to bed after her long drive.

"If you want drugs," she had said, not at all in apology, "you tell me a better place than a school playground."

I had wanted, despite the storm and flooding, to head back to San Francisco. This family was better off without witnesses. Facing the raw elements seemed easier than facing our raw hosts. Ryan would not hear of it. "You must stay," he said.

"Must?"

"I hid the car keys." He handed me his first-edition hardback of Norman Mailer's *The Naked and the Dead* and set me down in what they called the "Family Room" on the couch opposite the television. He handed me a bottle of Christian Brothers Brandy and a large snifter. "Read," he said. "Stick around for the jokes."

"Fuck you and the high horse you rode in on," I said. I settled back, watching him, around the covers of Mailer's epic, walk dead ahead in a straight sight line from me, through the small kitchen, into the living room to his brother.

The storm howled around the ranch house the way storms always show up as special effects in horror movies underscoring the dramatic human moments with nature's chill. Slightly pissed at being held captive, I poured two fingers of Brandy, swirled the amber, took a warming sip, and, lowering the curved snifter to my eye, studied how the rich liquor toned the view through the glass distortions. I could spy into the living room most discreetly, a fact, not lost on me, that Ryan, ever the exhibitionist, had removed me from the orchestra to the balcony. He was shameless, setting me up, setting Thom up, but no more shameless than I who opened the shameless-macho Mailer somewhere in the middle, not for reading, but for shield, held at nose level, watching the two brothers flickering like an old-time movie in the firelight. Clever Ryan! He had situated me far enough away that Thom, in his sobbing jag, forgot about me who could see and hear everything. What a bastard!

"What's the longest you've ever had sex?" Thom asked.

"What?"

"You heard me." Thom actually laughed a small laugh.

"Sometimes Kick and I go eight or nine hours at a time."

"On drugs?"

"Sex and drugs."

"The longest sex I ever had," Thom said, "was fifteen minutes with Sandy—until I went to Nam. In Saigon, once, I lasted for almost two hours with a Mama-San."

Thom's revealing intimacy hardly surprised Ryan. They, all of them, his whole family, he guessed, felt they could tell him anything. They could confess all their secrets and sins. In their minds he had come so close to being a priest that in their minds he had become one. The fact he had never married shored up that idea of priestly character. He had become the Father O'Hara they had dreamed in their Catholic dreams. Deep down they all thought he was, living without wife and children, more priestly than queer.

Out of his blues, or maybe more out of the Rorer 714 Quaalude, Thom said, "You may be older than me, but my cock's bigger."

Ryan appeared unsure which challenging remark ticked him off more. "Older," Ryan said. "But with less mileage."

"Older and wiser, I meant," Thom said.

"So wise up yourself," Ryan said. "Stop competing."

"Who's competing?"

"You. About everything."

"What *everything?*"

"All the *everything* you always reduce down to cock size. Like size means something. Stop deluding yourself."

"About what? My cock?"

"About your cock. About *everything.* Forgodsake, who cares about cock? You're a worse size-queen than any faggot I know. You just don't get it, do you?"

"Get what?"

"Life. Living. Forget about our cocks. Jeez. Stop competing. That's not what this is all about. It's never been what it's all about. Not when we slept in the same bed as kids. Not the hundred times you've gotten off with me."

"What hundred times?"

"Stop being so literal. You're so goddam John Wayne you can't see the forest for the trees."

"What's . . . that . . . mean?" Thom's belligerence was succumbing to the Quaalude.

"Must you think foreplay is always a fight? Is that what gets you up with Sandy? Is violence the secret of your sex life?"

"Leave Sandy out of this."

"Gladly."

"I like fighting. I'm a soldier."

"Aren't we all," Ryan said.

"I want to shoot," Thom said. He lay on the couch, facing away from Ryan, staring into the fire, seeing, God knows, some burning in-country Viet village.

Both brothers sat quiet.

The storm.

The firelight.

The hard day.

The late night.

Ryan lounged in the chair behind Thom's head, looking down the length of his brother's familiar, rugged body. Like a shrink with a patient on a couch. Both of them stayed put.

I dropped *The Naked* along with *The Dead* to the floor. I'd read it anyway. Mailer, never my favorite author, had, bowing to the censors of his time, written *Fug you* throughout his novel. He deserved what he got, when, at the height of his first celebrity, he was introduced at a cocktail party to Tallulah Bankhead who said to him, "Ah, yes! You're the young man who can't spell *fuck*." Whereupon Miss Bankhead turned her heels cold on Mr. Mailer.

The Brothers O'Hara remained in a horn-locked *de deux* without much *pas*.

Perhaps it was the unusual clap of thunder, perhaps it was some explosion Thom visualized in the popping fire, but the static tension between them broke. Thom unbuttoned his fatigues and yanked out a strictly government-issue, Army-circumcised, short arm. So it began. Ryan freed himself, and, more studied than a dinner-theater actor who has sung "Sunrise, Sunset" twenty thousand times, stroked his rising shaft. As he did with Kick, so Ryan did with Thom. He began a hypnotic ritual chant designed for each man's head. He started slowly, carefully, feeling his way through Thom's fantasies, talking of exotic women, and more exotic sex. He moved into straight sex slang, spieling a scenario of dominant women dropping their pussies on Thom's mouth. The more intense the scene became the more Thom's dick grew in the firelight.

Ryan was thrilled. Sex would alleviate Thom's violence the way Solly calmed down his bad boys. His own cock hardened. His brother had fallen to his verbal seduction. No matter they were not touching. No matter Thom could not see him the way he could watch Thom. What mattered was Thom's stroking his rod to the rhythms of his brother's voice. Ryan knew all the right words. He kept his place in the chair, and built the story to a pitch that caused Thom's hips to rise and his hand to pull wildly on his cock until, grinding his teeth, and moaning like a dying soldier, Thom's load shot straight up into the air. At full tilt, Thom sported the usual six inches. Thom kept his hand on his dick and fell back into the space where a man is asleep but not asleep with his hand wrapped wet and sticky around his shrinking hard-on.

Ryan did not disturb him. He simply took three final, lackluster strokes, looking at his brother, then shot off into his own hand, sad he had not cum with Kick, but happy that he had, no matter how *pro forma* the mercy-fuck, calmed his brother down to a post-ejaculation doze. Talk about the naked and the dead! Ryan's only solace was that every time he got Thom off was one more reason Thom, unlike Abe, could never have any Attitude toward him about his homosexuality.

Their little scene, staged partly for me, dramatized, as Ryan intended— always pulling me in as reluctant witness to his confidences, a special hybrid of homomasculine sex: two brothers, one gay and one straight, jerking off together. Ryan could have won Thom's inchworm contest, but the gentle- man in him allowed his brother his myopic fantasy. Ryan bit his lip and slapped the face of the sassy size-queen who lives inside every gay man. He sat in sticky silence, connecting disconsolate Energy over the miles with Kick, eschewing competition with Thom for Kick's ideal of communica- tion. Ryan wanted no more than an exorcism, a sexual healing, a sensual crack in his brother's macho armor. I tippled off the brandy. The scene was not without success. Ryan had calmed Thom down to an earlier sleep than he had experienced since before the Tet Offensive or his marriage to Sandy—two not dissimilar traumatic events.

Kweenie with her own taste for sibling passion had a few choice words for Ryan. "You're a bastard," she said. "You do it with Thom but you don't do it with me. It's not incest that bothers you, is it? You'd have done it with me long ago if I had been your brother and not your sister. That's the bottom line, Ry. You've always wished I was your little brother and not your little sister. You reject me for something I can't help. What am I supposed to think about that, when I love you like I do?"

"Revenge," Ryan said.

6

One of Ryan's most poignant *Journal* entries was about Solly: Thanks- giving 1975.

Solly is good at adapting to any situation. His halfway house for ex-cons and hustlers is his professional practice. It's made him cynical, but not jaded. Jaded is when you do it but don't enjoy whatever it is. He is frank. You adapt or you get out. You adapt or you die. He adapts continually. He handles alternate realities well. All the time, I think.

Especially one night, late, a bit drunk and a lot ripped, he told me, confessed ac- tually, embarrassed the way a woman is embarrassed after a rape. No fault of hers, nor in this case his, but the embarrassment acute all the same.

Solly at thirty-five for all his wanting to be a dirty old man, is boyishly attractive.

Some years before this drunken confessional, he was vacationing out of sheer perversity in Beirut, pushing the edge of danger that so thrilled him. The Hilton was under fire. The city was an armed camp of swarthy young soldiers. In two months, the American ambassador would be murdered. But this night, Solly was traveling through the Muslim section in the early evening to ball the son of a gold merchant. The winter before, in a Tenderloin bar, Solly had met the young foreign student who had come on to him as perfect Arabian trade.

"Then he became a terrorist in the sheets. These people are not of the twentieth century," Solly said. "We were very primitive together. Having never fucked above the lower classes in America, you can imagine my surprise afterwards. I found out he was a son of the wealthy bourgeoisie. He was every rugged eastern Mediterranean I had ever seen on CBS. From now on, you can call me the Ayatollah Bluestein."

In a way it was logical he should go to Beirut. Ten years before, he would have gone to Saigon.

"Terror," he wrote in one of his Solid Blue Video brochures, "is my only hard-on."

The Muslim section of Beirut was awash with people. Dark faces pressed against the glass windows of his slow-moving car. What he had been looking for seemed to be looking for him. The driver of his car cursed their luck as the car immediately ahead rear-ended the auto closest to the intersection. The trunk of the car in front of Solly popped open. "Omigod," he said. Bulging from inside the sprung trunk of the small car was a fully clothed, bullet-riddled body. Within seconds a mob careened around all three cars. Veiled women ululated a high-pitched wail from windows above the street. The driver of the middle car was dragged into the street. Solly heard him shout: "It's only the body of a Christian."

Two dozen or more Muslim men inspected, milled about, pushed, conferred, peered into Solly's car, turned away, talked, shouted, then completely surrounded his car stalled in the traffic in their section. What went wrong went wrong very quickly. They smashed the glass of the locked doors. His driver shouted, "American! American!" A gun butt to the mouth silenced him. He fell unconscious, bleeding across the steering wheel. The crowd had no patience with a foreigner who might be a Christian, or worse, a Jew. They punched at Solly without question. They lifted him bodily from the car and carried him into a small shop whose corrugated steel storefront a dark moustached man pulled down from its roll in the ceiling and locked to a ring in the floor.

In the semidarkness, Solly could see very little. Hands held him, pushed him, punched him. A thick-veined fist tore the sleeve off his jacket. A frenzy of ripping and shredding followed. Buttons popped as his shirt tore away. His zipper-fly split apart at the bottom as his slacks were dropped like shackles around his ankles. For a moment, the men held him, fair-skinned in the olive darkness, stripped to his white undershorts. No one moved. The silence was absolute. Then a short thick man punched him hard in the stomach, and his shorts were ripped away. For two hours they beat him with their fists and, holding him firmly with many hands in the stifling room, took an electric prod to his eyelids, gums, penis, testicles, and anus.

It wasn't sex.

It was politics.

He expected to be raped. He was. He at first thought they wanted information. They didn't and besides he knew nothing. He thought at first there was some purpose to his torture, but his suffering had no meaning more than to vent some release for them through his pain. At last, allowed to fall to the floor, he lay flat on his back. He heard a rifle bolt click. He lay motionless. Three streams, he remembered, three streams, exactly three, of piss rained down from the darkness on his face and genitals.

Then they lifted him, pulled up his torn slacks, rolled up the corrugated steel door, and shoved him into the street alone. The door roared down closed behind him. He tried to pull what was left of his piss-soaked clothes together around him to avoid attention, to pretend nothing had happened so that no more would happen, but no one on the street seemed to notice.

In the distance, the shelling of the hotels continued. Gunfire crackled through the night. They had hurt him anonymously, for no reason, for nothing he had done. They had turned on him for some kicks and he felt angry and dirty enough to be sick in the street, next to the burnt-out body, dirty and sick and embarrassed enough to mention nothing to me of the incident until this one night of confidences. And even at that, he seemed to hold something back.

People who are tortured, no matter how or for whatever reason, seem always to gain a reserve, a mistrust, a modesty, born of an astonished, well-grounded fear of their own kind.

"It was a wonderful vacation," he said. He always made a joke of everything. "I love foreign travel."

7

Kick had become Ryan's father. He had replaced the father whom Ryan could forgive neither for dying so young nor living so long so tortured by illness. The exchange of one man for the other was a simple equation. The Long Good Friday, the 13th of April, 1979, Ryan had told Kick on top of the parking deck overlooking the corner of Market and Castro: "I love you more than anyone. More than my father. More than my mother. My brother. My sister. Anyone." He meant, "You are my father. You are my family."

He gave it all to Kick.

Ryan always knew that one thing could mean two things. Ryan had always loved wordplay. It was Charley-Pop's fault. Back in Ryan's Technicolor childhood, his rugged and dashing father had amused and amazed him. He taught him how a riddle means more than the guesser thinks. Leaving a restaurant, Charley-Pop had handed Ryan a book of matches from a fish bowl near the cash register. It read on the cover: "For our matchless friends." Ryan thought Charley-Pop a wonder as he explained the little joke. He saw suddenly the possibilities of the duplicity of words, and maybe the ambiguity of life itself when one thing between two people can mean two different things to them both, but he was too innocent then to let himself be frightened by the prospect.

He would not learn real fright until he was in his mid-thirties.

Late on a spring night, after watching Schwarzenegger as *Conan* nailed up naked to the Tree of Woe, Kick was inspired to play an exotic sex scene. At first they joked about it, but the joshing fell away and the night grew serious. It was typical of the way they had sex. Kick poured them each a hit of the ecstatic drug their dealer nicknamed *Kryptonite.*

"I only want half a hit," Ryan said.

"Name your poison," Kick said.

They toasted one another with the wine glasses. "To Arnold," Kick said. "And to us."

They had both liked the scene in which the muscle-warrior Conan, captured by the evil priest James Earl Jones, was crucified to the mammoth stump of a huge tree on a barren primeval plain. Ryan grew excited as the image of Kick crucified grew between them. They began their preparations. Kick slowly stripped. Ryan anointed his body with olive oil to a high glaze.

In the basement room of the Victorian where they played before three full-length mirrors under the tracklight spots, huge horizontal beams crossed over the heavy upright wooden foundation posts. They stood, both naked, before the crossed beams in the center of the room. Ryan fashioned a small linen loin cloth that he wrapped around Kick's muscular waist, then dropped down to create a pouch for his dick and balls. He pulled the long, twisted length of linen up the crack of his ass and knotted the cloth to the waistband in the small of his back.

"I want to look stronger than Conan," Kick said. "I want us to get more intense than the movie. Let's see what a real musclebeast restrained by steel looks like."

Ryan cinched Kick's wrists into heavy leather cuffs. Ryan's dick grew hard at the prospect of a new worshipful view of the man who relied on him to create the most private of the fantasies he could not perform alone.

Kick smiled at him. "Now you know why I love you," he said. "Now you know when I heard about you and read your stories, I had to meet you."

Ryan, the acolyte, led Kick to the beams. He placed a short wooden barrel at the foot of the cross. He gave Kick a hit of popper.

"I love you," Kick said, "for this, and more than this." He looked deep into Ryan's eyes. "You know, don't you! You *know!* You understand the

Gift. It's not always in a man's body the way it is in mine. But more than my body, it's in my head. You're one of the few men who know I have a head."

"I love you," Ryan said.

The Kryptonite ecstasy was coming on. Ryan raised Kick's huge arm and dug his tongue into the sweat steaming in his armpit. His mind swirled with images of ideal men, men without whom the world would be an intolerable place.

Kick mounted the barrel. His calves, sculpted to the perfection of inverted hearts, bulged as he rose up to position himself. He turned, as he always turned on the posing platform, arms held loosely akimbo from his massive shoulders, his hands hanging down, thumbs in, eight inches out from his thighs, and looked down at Ryan. He flexed his pecs: the muscles striated and defined and rolled, up, then down his chest. His dick tented the soft linen loincloth. His smile at Ryan was triumphant. There was no shame in this crucifixion.

Ryan administered them both a hit of popper. Kick's face, in the low tracklight, began to morph into the face of the idealized young Christ, stripped and crucified, whom Ryan had worshiped since boyhood. He had been trained at Misericordia to be an *alter Christus,* another Christ, but he knew he'd never be another Christ.

He realized a special revelation.

It was not himself; it had never been himself; it was Kick who was the *alter Christus.*

"I'm stoned. I'm stoned. I'm stoned," Ryan repeated to himself. "This is so crazy. . . ." But the vision would not vanish.

"Tight," Kick said. "Tie me tight. I want to feel this." He nodded toward the three body-length mirrors. "I want to see this. I want to show you a show I've never shown anyone before."

Ryan tied Kick's ankles together and then wrapped the rope around the rough-hewn post.

"I want to take it as long as I can," Kick said. "I want to feel the full glory of muscular restraint."

Ryan tied Kick's huge arms wide open on the cross. Kick raised his head and breathed. His chest expanded. Sweat rolled down his face and dripped on his pecs. His cock writhed in the small linen loincloth.

Ryan offered him, the way Christ on the cross had been offered vinegar mixed with opium on a sponge, a double hit of coke. Kick snorted, then relaxed. He twisted one hand to a more comfortable angle on the cross.

"I'm ready," Kick said. "I want you to see a musclebeast more glorious than you've ever imagined."

Ryan pulled the barrel out from under his lover's feet. Kick's muscles tensed. His whole body, hanging under the strain, and triggered by the rush of the coke, took on a pump and vascularity so supernal that Ryan fell to his knees at the foot of the cross. He watched his lover strain and flex like a muscular Olympic gymnast performing the crucifix on the double rings. *I always thought*, Ryan's head swirled, *that it was to be me who was to be crucified.*

He serviced them both with popper.

Kick locked into a massive bodyflex. His loincloth, heavy with sweat, fell away under the strain of his muscle. His dirty-blond cock jutted straight forward over his massive thighs. He took a huge breath and let go. He hung, by his massive arms, crucified, head back and haloed by the shine of the tracklight. Ryan knelt before the sweating muscleman, cruciform above him. He took himself in his right hand and began to stroke his own hardening flesh. The moment grew mystical as Kick struggled, flexed, relaxed, flexed, and endured against the hard wooden cross.

It started as night games: heroic sculpture from drawings and movies. It became some ritual else. Their separate fantasies meshed in the flesh, then separated in their minds, coming back together, each traveling separately, traveling together, finding the Ecstasy, the Energy, the Entity, the boundaries, the limits. Kick was a bodybuilder, crucified, displayed in all his muscular glory, straining against the bondage, flying with the bondage. Ryan was his coach, his lover, his priest. He worshiped Kick's body from the foot of the cross. Coke sweat poured down Kick's naked flanks. The hard rod of his manhood arched over Ryan. The blond man glowed in the spotlight. He began to moan under the weight of his own big body. He saw his own face in the mirrors, handsome over his hanging musclebody. He moaned the moan Ryan always knew meant he was entering the Energy. Ryan followed with his own cock. He clamped the clips on his own tits. He hit them both with popper and tongued his way down Kick's body to his feet.

This was no Imitation of Christ.

This was real.

Kick was more than an *alter Christus*.

He was the incarnation of the real Christ Himself.

Ryan rose from his knees. He licked the sacred sweat from the blond fur of the thighs. He touched his Savior's massive meat. He massaged it, stroked it, while he stroked himself, until Kick's huge prick, throbbing with the tension of the muscle bondage, glistened. His whole body tightened down into a cruciform Most-Muscular position. Ryan's greased hand stroked Kick up to the edge of cuming. Ryan readied himself, stroking faster, his face looking up lovingly at his crucified Savior. He could feel the power rising in the crucified's body. Then suddenly, the white clotted rain shot like saving grace from Kick's lordly rod. Ryan's mouth opened hungrily. In his own hand, his own flesh throbbed to a simultaneous climax.

"Oh, my God," he said. "Oh, my beautiful God."

8

"What you gay boys," Solly said on the phone, "won't do to have fun."

9

Ryan was spending the weekend after the Fourth of July in the country. Kick had flown back to Birmingham. His own father had suddenly died. Solly made a crack about gay boys and karma.

"What do you mean *gay boys?*" Ryan said. He had been dozing, passing in and out of consciousness, watching the veils of ocean fog pass across the moon. He had asked Kick, because Annie Laurie had once asked Charley-Pop the same thing, to look to the moon. "I'll look at the moon," he had said, "and I'll be seeing you."

"You can just listen." Solly's voice sounded soothing on the phone.

Ryan clicked on his recorder. "I'm too stoned to remember anything you say."

"I'm up here in this lovely penthouse apartment. The moon is beautiful over the whole City. There are two fires burning in the Mission. There's smoke and flames. This is the side of the City that burns. Tiger brought me two new Quaaludes. I took one an hour ago. It's quite wonderful. It's Lemmon. It's remarkable. I think, by the way, that I've decided to try heroin. You'll think bad of me for that. But life is what it is. I know that. Everything is what it is. If it kills me, then if that's all there is, I'll keep on dancing. Miss Peggy Lee is the only philosopher I know.

"Actually, the videotapes I've been shooting are better than ever. I always understate my ads for them in my brochures. I must read you a letter that came with my latest orders. 'Your tapes are better than you describe them.' Nobody does what I am doing. Maybe you're right. Maybe I am an artist. Nobody's touching this part of America. Can I take credit for discovering that straight street hustlers are exhibition artists? Opel and I and maybe just me.

"Six years in this risky business. Running it all on the up and up with the IRS. But consorting with murderers. Do you know how many murderers there are wandering loose in this country? Very few get caught. Fewer get convicted. Hardly anyone gets capital punishment. So at any given moment, all these murderers are wandering around the country as if nothing has happened. They killed once. They'll do it again. They're serial murderers. They kill one person after another. It's like the song by the Police: 'Murder by Numbers—one, two, three.' They prey on women and homosexuals and kids. What it is, you know, is the danger. The thrill of danger. Most of the guys I hire for my videos are murderers, or could be murderers.

"I've noticed that petty criminals have lots of tattoos. Murderers have hardly any. Somehow, as much as I like men with tattoos on their arms, I keep remembering that murderers don't have tattoos. There are thousands of murderers loose in this country now. I've been to bed with lots of them. The one who robbed me last year: the nineteen-year-old ex-con from San Quentin. Great thighs. Wonderful sex. Got up out of the bed and pulled out a twenty-two. Lobo came over the other night with a twenty-five. A twenty-two is much more deadly. A bigger gun spends its energy passing right through you. In one side and out the other. A twenty-two has enough force to enter your head and ricochet around making sushi out of your brain.

"Did I tell you I'm going to try heroin? I figure why not. I remember that book title, *It's So Good, Don't Try It Even Once.* I'll wait till after my mother's visit next week. I've booked her on every Gray Line charter tour there is. My mother thinks visiting me is me taking her down to Union Square and putting her on a bus with all the other senior tourists. These new Lemmon Quaaludes are wonderful. My television reception has never been better. I've finally gotten to the point where I can enjoy at least the illusion of success. When my mother sees my apartment, she'll think I have it made. Of course, she's bringing my niece. Some brat I've never seen. The kid's been warned no doubt by my sister that her uncle is, well, odd, and to watch out.

"You know, there's a noose hanging down on a post on a roof way below my windows. This view is really interesting. I'm in a penthouse on the top of the Tenderloin. I feel almost biblical: like I could have been taken to the top of the mount and am being shown all the things that could be mine.

"And all I want, all I really get off on, is the danger from the young street trash I pay nightly. The other day one of them was strangling me just right and spitting in my face and telling me about all the guys he had killed. While I was cuming, I thought how close I was. How close we all are all the time, even if we don't go out and cruise it, recruit it, and pay for it, because what is, is. None of us, you're always saying, is going to get out of this alive. I think, too, our mothers are right. We shouldn't all be going home with strangers the way we do.

"I feel so wonderful. I really like living alone. But I miss Tiger living here. I liked educating him, giving him advice. He was learning. He calls me *Dear Old Dad.* They all call me *Dear Old Dad.* He turned nineteen last week. I really love him. But I really like being alone. My view. My TV. My Presto-log burning in the fireplace. I'm boring you, I know. But I guess I really do love you. I never said that before. And I will come up to Bar Nada to see what you've done. I am interested. I did tell you, didn't I, that I may take some heroin. I figure why not? I want to see the rancho. It all seems like a good idea. Sometimes everything seems like a good idea. Other times, nothing does. Just what is, is. Murderers.

"One of the several reasons I called you . . . Are you sitting down? . . . is Robert Opel is dead."

"What?" Ryan's voice rose loud and clear into the taping on the phone.

"I tried to tell you that murderers are all around us. Someone shot him in his gallery."

"When?"

"Last night, I think. Yeah. I have the article right here. Last night."

"Read it to me."

"I'm too stoned to read. I'm not too stoned to talk."

"Then talk to me."

"It's like this reporter, Maitland Zane, writes. 'July 9, 1979. THIEVES KILL GALLERY OWNER, GET $5.' What the hell kind of name is 'Maitland Zane?' It's so gender-hidden San Francisco. Anyway, *Mr., Miss,* or *Ms.* Zane, as the case may be, reminds us all that Robert streaked the 1974 Oscars and then got shot in his art gallery."

"Robert would be happy."

"Why?"

"The straight press finally called it art."

"Anyway, these two white guys came in with a sawed-off shotgun and an automatic. I love murders. Don't you love murders?"

"I'll murder you if you don't tell me exactly what happened."

"Who knows? Whoever knows exactly what happens? Does Maitland Zane know? I mean, Maitland says Robert was thirty-nine. I thought he was younger. Even if he wasn't younger, he should have been smarter like I'm smarter when it comes to guys like these who came into the gallery demanding money and drugs."

"Was Robert alone?"

"No. Somebody named Anthony Rogers was there. And, I think, some other guy. So was Camille."

"I interviewed her last week for an article. Robert played the clown all around us."

"You forced me to listen to the tape, remember. You show me, write me, tell me every goddam thing."

"You said you like that."

"I lie a lot."

"Fuck you. Is Camille okay?"

"Camille O'Grady was not killed, Ryan, if that's what you mean. I never know if anybody's okay."

"Poor Camille."

"Poor Robert. He argued with these guys. Maitland says Robert begged them to leave. I always beg them to stay. If we have sex, they can have every cent I've got. I change them from robbers to whores."

"I'm glad I know all the identifying marks on your body."

"That's my revenge on you for making me read your *Journal* and watch your tapes: staring at my Mansonized corpse," Solly said.

"I promise to gasp and faint, just like in the movies."

"Stop! Don't talk to stoned people about Death."

"What is, is, whether you're stoned or not."

"I'll ignore that."

"Try to."

"Anyway, the guy with the shotgun pointed it at Camille's head and said, 'Give us the money or I'll kill her.'"

"Robert never had any money."

"Apparently he gave a fine farewell performance. He told the robbers to kill them all. Sort of like playing I-Double-Dare-You, don't you think?"

"Don't be cute."

"So the guy fired a shot into a painting and Opel yells, 'Get out of my space!' Which, of course, they didn't. They dragged Robert to his apartment behind the gallery. Camille and the other two witnesses heard shouting."

"Robert argued with them?"

"His first and last mistake. They said stuff like, 'We're gonna blow your head off,' and Robert says, 'You're gonna have to, because there's no money here.' Am I stoned, or was he stupid?"

"Maybe brave."

"Brave or stupid, he's dead. I'm stoned."

"They shot him?" Ryan asked.

"Maitland assures us that the witnesses heard, and I quote, 'the thump of Opel falling to the floor.' The *thump* of Opel? Bring me the head of Maitland Zane."

"You're really upsetting me."

"Think how upset Robert Opel was. He didn't die at the gallery. The robbery started about 9 p.m. and he was pronounced curtains at San Francisco General at 10:40."

"His final performance art."

"Sweet Maitland talks about that too. It says here that Robert pranced. . . ."

"Robert never pranced."

"Maitland thinks so. Stop interrupting me. Stoned people have a hard enough time remembering what they're saying. It says here in print that Robert, five years ago, pranced across the 1974 Oscar stage as David Niven was introducing Liz Taylor."

"That description, *prancing,* is fag-bashing rhetoric."

"So write Maitland."

"I might. Robert was a legend."

"That's all he is now."

"Maitland gets very *National Enquirer.* Does your inquiring mind want to know?"

"What's worse than to know he's dead and fag-bashed?"

"Nothing, really. Just how Robert stripped in front of Police Chief Davis, that well-known fascist pig, at an El Lay City Council meeting to protest the banning of nudity at city beaches. He was acquitted of indecent exposure."

"I know that."

"But he was convicted of disrupting a public meeting."

"Nothing like a naked cock to disrupt a meeting."

"Remember that. It may come in handy," Solly instructed.

"God! You're bitchy when you're stoned."

"Getting stoned only makes anyone more of what they already are."

"So how's Camille?"

"I only know what Maitland knows."

"Such as?"

"Survivors include Opel's mother and a sister."

"Poor Robert."

"So . . . how's that grab you? You try and tell me about good and evil, and I can't hear you because what is shouts very loud."

"You and your egocentric existentialism!"

"Stop bitching. And stop crying."

"Why should I? Death hardly ever lets anyone say good-bye."

"Stop blathering pseudo-country-western song titles, or I'm going to hang up."

"Don't hang up."

"I wonder what they'll write about me. I can see the headlines now. 'PORNOGRAPHER FOUND POISONED, SHOT, STRANGLED, DROWNED, AND ELECTROCUTED IN TUB WITH MULTIPLE KNIFE WOUNDS by Maitland Zane.'"

In his *Journal* entry for July 9, 1979, Ryan wrote:

At my Death, let gather bodybuilders. One by one in my life these muscular brother-men have placed their arms around me. Now, bonded, let them gather. In the perfect face and body and look of each is all the study of all the universe a man ever needs. I look at one face. I look at all the faces. I see finally the only face that counts. Death is a murderer. Oh, please, my Lord, let Death be not mean. Let Death look like these men. Let Death be a golden muscle angel. Oh, please, my God, when I come to you, let Death be as beautiful as a golden man-angel in flight, welcoming me with open arms. I could have died the morning after the night I first met Kick. Every minute I've lived since then has been an excess of luxury. Take me. . . . But don't take me now.

10

Ryan was as much photojournalist as writer. By the beginning of his third year with Kick, he had shot thousands of black-and-white stills and color transparencies and nearly fifty hours of videotape.

Kick was always *on*.

I remember one particularly poignant videotape: an intense, silent study of Kick's face. "Video portraiture," Ryan said, "captures the subject's essence far better in its multiple frames than any single-frame still shot."

When Kick flew back to Birmingham to visit his widowed mother, Ryan ran the tapes in slow motion and freeze-frame. He studied expressions and movements that in real time occur too fast for the eye to appreciate. He pored into Kick's soul held captive on his video. He masturbated. He remembered, then ignored, Monsignor Linotti's quaint rule of Catholic moral theology.

"During war, for instance," the good Monsignor had said, "when a man and wife are separated, neither spouse, during the separation, may stare at a photograph of the other and masturbate. No matter if they're thinking of their love far away. Masturbation, no matter the circumstances, is always a mortal sin. A man's seed must be deposited in the receptacle of the woman. Masturbation, without question, condemns the masturbator, male or female, to the eternal fires of hell."

Kick himself enjoyed the videos of his body and face. Often they viewed the tapes side by side in bed, stroking each other: buddies in-love with the ideal they watched moving on the bright screen.

"Kick," Ryan said, and I had no reason to doubt this, especially at the pure beginning of their affair, "has a wonderful ability to distance himself objectively from the image on the screen. He understands the concept of Emerson's world view of the *Me* and the *Not-Me*. He understands my position in this whole matter. It's like he becomes me and I become him and we both become the ideal on the screen. We transcend space and time and ego. We conjure together, and as sure as a child may be created between a man and a woman, an Energy is created between us."

Actually, Kick was very like a sculptor, who, after he sculpts, sits back and studies his own creation. In Ryan's bed he could lie back from the Energy he put into bodybuilding and enjoy the beauty of the art object he and Ryan had created in his flesh. "You and me, coach," he said. "We did it. You helped me do it. No one has ever treated me like you treat me."

Ryan knew in his heart it was true. He had never treated anyone the way he took care of Kick. He knew from the first instant he saw Kick what Kick needed and what he himself wanted.

It was the same thing.

"I always believed this was possible," Ryan said. "I just never thought it would happen."

There was that night, straight out of a romance magazine, that stuck in Ryan's head. He remembered it a thousand different ways. Heading for supper at Without Reservation, they had driven the Corvette to Market and Castro and parked on the roof of the Fireman's Fund Building. Instead of turning off the engine, Kick touched the dashboard to push a cassette into the tape deck. "You ain't heard nothin' yet," he said. "Don't get out. Let's do a doobie." He fired up a joint. "Listen to this cut."

They sat knee to knee in the tiny cockpit of the car, laughing as the windows misted up inside and out. Their breath, their words, circled around their heads in a blue haze swirling around the music of a gentle *bossa nova*.

"Who's playing?" Ryan asked.

"This dude, this guy, this amazing guy I know from El Lay."

"Others come. Others go. Me to you, soul to soul."

"This guy is a bodybuilder." Kick held the joint to Ryan's lips. "He poses and sings in Vegas."

"The dream of me and you becomes the dream of us."

"Poses?" Ryan hit, and hit again. "And sings?"

Guitars lifted the man's gentle voice.

"When a man loves a man . . . he trades the world for what he trusts."

"Poses and sings in gay clubs in Vegas." Kick kissed Ryan's fingers. "He writes for Liberace."

"Now you're scaring me."

"Have another hit."

". . . that you love me still the same."

"I should be," Ryan said, "singing this to you."

"Angel, breathing your breath I breathe. Oh, how lovely. In the arms of love . . ."

Ryan touched Kick's beautiful wrist.

"Never treat each other bad. I would give you all I had . . . for one more day with you."

He pulled Kick's forearm to his mouth and exhaled, licking his tongue across the blond hair.

"Soaring to the end of time. Get it right, no end this time."

Kick smiled.

"The magic of our love will win. I'll be guiding you."

Ryan's heart leapt up.

"Soul to soul, man to man. The power of love . . . that you love me still."

"I do love you still, now, and forever," Kick said. Smoke wreathed his face. His thick blond moustache bloomed over his white teeth. "This shit is primo."

"Thrilling till the end of time. . . . We keep on keepin' on."

The lyrics sounded penned by Kick's hand. He was so strong, so silent, so southern, maybe this was a surprise.

"You wrote this. You had him write this. You told him what to write."

"No. No way. Other guys . . . other guys are like us."

"No one's like us."

The song flowed into the chorus. *". . . Soul to soul, man to man . . . that you love me still."*

Ryan took one hit over the line: Sweet Jesus, he understands the Energy we conjure is magic.

"The dream becomes the dream of us."

Kick's hand in his proved the words meant more than the muscle contests.

"Keep on keepin' on."

He could have anything if only he remained true to Kick whose ideals altered his consciousness.

"I'll lift you bright in dark of night."

Ryan began to speak, but Kick put his finger to his lips.

"Others come. Others go. We are home free."

The home team.

"Under stars in dark of night."

Ryan-Orion.

"Ever will I be your guide."

Ryan's heart, ruptured by Charley-Pop's death, was set to burst. Kick had found Ryan brokenhearted in a way Teddy could not fix. Kick could save him.

"Guiding you at your side."

Ryan sensed Kick realized he, not Ryan, was the coach. With Charley-Pop dead, Ryan needed Kick to be in charge. For a while. With all his Command Presence. To be held in trust. Kick, leveling eye-to-eye with Ryan, let the lyric make his pledge.

"Breathing your breath, I breathe."

Nights inhaling Kick's breath; Kick inhaling him back; falling together, high, down into the bed.

"Please," Ryan said, "if this should not be you, don't ever tell me."

"Believing in you, I believe in me."

"I believe in you," Kick said. "You must believe in me."

Together forever.

". . . When a man loves a man, soul to soul . . ."

My lover, my coach.

"I'll wake all your dreams alive."

Kick hit the joint deep, pulled Ryan's face to his, and exhaled into his mouth. He pulled the palm of Ryan's hand to the mound of his left pec, holding it over his beating heart.

"Ever will I be your guide."

They sat stoned, savoring, enchanted with each other.

Finally, Ryan stumbled from the car, laughing, very loaded, exhaling the Technicolor Benday Dots of romance comic books. His hot breath in the cold night blew stoned circles around the million lights of Castro Street reflecting wet below. More Benday Dots bubbled up the pink-champagne neon outlining the tall marquee of the Castro Theatre. Roy Lichtenstein panels pop-pop-popped on the three huge billboards stilted high above the traffic on Market Street with cartoon balloons exclaiming: *What movie am I now? I'm every movie I've ever seen. When do we move to Vegas?*

Kick walked him closer to the railing of the rooftop parking lot. A light mist fell through the glow hovering over the intersection of Market and Castro. Below them, tires sang on the glistening blacktop. They huddled together. Ryan ached with his discipline of self-denial. He wanted to shout

out the truth. He was in-love with Kick. What difference did it make any-more after all that had passed between them?

"I love you," Kick said.

He put his arms around Ryan in the blowing mist. Ryan was crying. Ryan knew he could not say, was not allowed to say, because every fairy tale had one unbreakable caveat, "I'm in-love with you." Instead, he said what he always said, "I love you." And he meant this too, and meant it the more because of the hurt of holding his tongue in check, disciplined against what Kick cautioned might pass for cheap love on Castro. "I love you more than anyone I've ever loved."

"I love you too," Kick said.

They both laughed.

"This is the balcony scene," Ryan said. "Admission twenty-five cents. We're both nuts. *I love you* sounds like *please love me.* and *I love you too* sounds wrung out by torture."

"But I do love you," Kick said. "I do no kidding love you."

"*Pretty Poison,*" Ryan said. "Tony Perkins said that to Tuesday Weld."

Again they laughed.

"I really love you, Kick," Ryan insisted. "You are the greatest love of my life."

Tears and laughter made him, on this rooftop in this foggy night with this golden man, feel absolutely larger than life. His soul careened out-of-body up higher than the glow from the towering marquee of the Castro Theatre.

"Do you understand, Billy Ray Sorensen? It's you I love. Not your face. Not your muscles. I love you the way maybe no one in this whole gay inter-section loves anyone else. The way I know no one loves you. I love you in a way that has nothing to do with sex. I love your soul. I would die for you."

"I want you to live for me."

"I do live for you. You have no idea how much I live for you."

Kick pulled Ryan close to him. He kissed Ryan's cheeks. He put his moustache against Ryan's moustache. Their lips touched. Ryan held tight. He felt Kick's baseball biceps knot around him and pull him into his mas-sive chest. He knew this was the way it was supposed to be. His very breath was squeezed from him. Kick's tongue darted through Ryan's moustache, parted his lips, passed through his teeth, and slid down Ryan's throat.

"Oh, God!" Ryan breathed.

This was no joke. Lichtenstein's cartoon balloons, filled with Benday Dots, appeared above their heads.

"We'll be together forever," Kick said. "I promise. However life takes us, we'll always be together." He held Ryan's jawline in both his iron-calloused hands. "I'll never leave you but once," he said. His blue eyes pierced Ryan's soul. "And that will be when I die."

"Oh, God! I love you!"

If ever Ryan were ordained a priest, his ordination was that night in the swirling mist, anointed not by some Roman cardinal, but by the southern bodybuilder who held his face in his hairy blond hands and breathed immortality into his soul.

"You are," Kick said, "my lover forever."

"And you are mine."

That night on that rooftop something happened.

It was bonding.

It was marriage.

"It was just another cheap balcony scene," Solly said.

I harbor a suspicion that the truth is cornier than we think until the moment when we find ourselves inside some truth that is stranger than fiction. Ryan was a child of the movies. He lived cinema. The way he described the rooftop scenario moved me profoundly.

Imagining that scene, I genuinely wanted to have been seated behind a Panaflex camera in a helicopter that would lift off from the two of them on that roof, holding on them in each other's arms in slow motion in the mist, while the camera rose and they grew smaller and smaller, shrinking against the night, as the rooftop took reference from the intersection and the intersection from the Castro and the Castro from the City and the bright City from the darkness of land and sea until the Earth itself stood majestic against the full moon.

11

January Guggenheim finished shooting her television special in a glorious late October, days before Halloween 1979. Her last three days of shooting featured Kick posing, pumped and oiled, on the rocky outcroppings of Corona Heights with the Castro spread out below his feet. She flew to El Lay to complete her editing.

"You must come down," she said to Ryan over the phone. "I need a rewrite concerning the Opel matter. I mean Death can change things substantially. Of course, Kick can come. You can stay with me. Oh, yes, and, darling, if she's free, bring Kweenie. We'll have such fun."

Late the following March, *The New Homosexuals* scored an okay 11 share of the viewing audience. That was more than enough to make January come off a difficult subject smelling like a rose.

The critics liked it.

The public liked it.

One too many viewers liked it.

In San Diego, lying on his couch, a tall, dark-haired bodybuilder, who by that time had run through all the cash-and-drug pals he ever had, sat bolt upright when January's camera first closed in for a two-shot of Ryan and Kick.

"I recognize you two," he said. "So that's what you're up to."

At Kick's first contest, Ryan had sat next to what looked to be three powerlifters.

The dark bodybuilder recognized Ryan on his TV screen. "Fuck! I thought the geek was lying when he said he knew Blondie."

Then he saw Kick take his arm from around Ryan's shoulder and glide into his posing routine.

All alone, the dark bodybuilder, hardening with the intensity of muscle lust, stared in wonder at the golden man of bodybuilding on his TV screen, and announced, "Whoa! I'm gonna get me some of you!"

As simple as that, the serpent once again entered Eden.

This time his name was Logan Doyle.

REEL FOUR
Trouble in Paradise

1

What they were looking for was looking for them.

Logan Doyle arrived on cue. He emerged from the crowds at the Gay Pride Parade. He was handsome, dark, and tall. He parted his thick black hair down the middle. His trim moustache roofed a smile of white teeth. He had a strong, predatory American chin, and the build of a powerlifter with none of the gut. He had Attitude. He had the Look Ryan and Kick had often visualized in their nightly conjuring of a man masculine enough to come close to a match for Kick. At six two and two-thirty, Logan looked like the answer to Ryan's prayer to find a man, good-looking and muscular enough, to fill Kick's need for a living, breathing fantasy, the way Kick was for Ryan.

Logan was Ryan's chance to prove they were homomasculine gentlemen and not gay lovers jealous of every trick who came along. Ryan knew instantly he would never have sex with Logan. The rule was unspoken. He knew his place, because Kick liked Logan in a way different from the way he liked other athletic guys. Logan reminded Kick of the trucker who, years before, had lifted him upon his big arm out of the hot Alabama dust of his aunt and uncle's gas station and diner.

Ryan forgot Solly Blue's warning to be careful what you wish for in California, because you usually get it. He also forgot Saint Theresa who warned there are more tears shed over answered prayers than unanswered.

Are people strong enough to live with the truth?

Kick had a way of making dark thoughts flee from Ryan's head.

Six weeks after Logan showed up on Castro, Kick sent Ryan home alone to the Victorian. "Wait for me," he said. "I have a surprise for you."

Ryan asked no questions.

An hour later, Kick showed up with Logan. He opened Ryan's shirt and put his fingers on his nipples. "Yes?" he asked. He nodded toward Logan.

Ryan was stunned. No one played Chopin on his tits like Kick. He sucked in breath for the word *Yes*.

"I like surprising him," Kick said to Logan. "I like that Cheshire look he gets on his face."

"Maybe I'll wipe it off." Logan winked and slow-pounded his crotch with alternating fists. "One potato. Two potato."

How old is this guy?

Kick assured Ryan. "One thing you have to understand about Logan is he's a kid. He's a kidder."

"We're all kids," Ryan said. His very soul grinned. The proof stood in front of him. He was, finally, one of the boys.

All three men stripped off their shirts, jeans, and boots. Both body-builders stood naked in front of Ryan. Kick was already hard. Logan was on the rise. Ryan was ready to cum. Kick hit an easy pose. Logan moved in and ran his big hands over Kick's arms.

Kick grinned at Ryan. "I told you," he said, "we can have anything we want." He motioned for Ryan to lie down on the floor.

Both bodybuilders stood over him, flexing for each other, hands stroking muscles, pumping their dicks. The view up from between the pairs of their calves was the best camera angle in the cosmos. Ryan took hold of himself and followed the oldest posing routine in the world. Move for move. Kneeling between the two bodybuilders, one dark, one light, he realized his definitive place in the universe. In the tricky tumble that three-ways always are, someone inevitably feeling odd-man-out, Kick directed the reluctant Logan back, and again back, to Ryan. Kick wanted Ryan and Logan both to discover and get off on what he saw in them. Fat chance.

Logan regarded Ryan as a pencil-neck geek, more obstacle than competition. Ryan tolerated Logan only because Kick, ever the gentleman-lover, was trying to share with him this man he had harvested as an attractive add-on to their dual private pleasures. Ryan knew instantly that Logan was a sexual opportunist, and probably a hustler. He looked familiar, but Ryan dismissed him as no more than a type, the recognizable type that hangs around gyms and bodybuilding contests, and cruises out at night with the express purpose of breaking up somebody's happy home. He knew Logan's competitive superfix-lust for Kick was no way like his own real love.

Ryan hardly needed to be hit with a pig bladder to remember three's a crowd. In *Cabaret,* "Twosies" may have beat "Onesies" and nothing may have beat "Threes," but Ryan, pressed like the ham in a sandwich between the two musclemen, had the distinct feeling he didn't like the movie they were caught in.

An extra was on the set.

He thought it was Logan.

Logan thought it was Ryan.

Kick, more caught up than he knew, was obviously intense on Logan.

Ryan felt like Woody Allen trying to dance with Rogers and Astaire.

Kick tried to keep balance, and Ryan, loving him all the more for his sharing, decided to relieve the tension and eased down. Stroking himself, he lay back on the floor beneath the two bodybuilders kneeling astride him. They pounded on each other's hard pecs, grappling, big hands feeling up the muscle on big arms, leaning in over Ryan, face to face, each to kiss the other. The triangulation was at least nine points short on one leg of a Perfect-10 Scale. So much for having anything he wanted! This was sex, not love. Still the view wasn't bad. Most of San Francisco would have traded places with him.

Witnessing Kick's lust for Logan's physique pleasured Ryan who wanted to give Kick everything, including muscle, even if it wasn't his own aerobic pump. He winked at Kick, sort of a *hoo-ha* high sign, the kind that close buddies on the home team exchange in the presence of a stranger. Kick thought Ryan meant he liked Logan.

One goddam thing was meaning two things again. Fuck ambiguity.

Ryan had only one polite fast way out. He worked himself up to a physical ejaculation that was some light years short of a psychic orgasm. Not that it was esthetically difficult, not with the two handsome bodybuilders rocking in heat across him, not when, wrapped in a beefy tangle of arms and chests and shoulders, both musclemen came, raining white-hot seed across the flat field of Ryan's belly, clotted wet with his own halfhearted load.

The next day Ryan, sorting love from sportfucking, wrote a new chapter for the *Manifesto.* He called it "Homomasculine Fraternity."

Ryan was happy that Kick found in the flesh of Logan's body the same passion Kick had found in Ryan's words. It made no difference that their three-way had been one time only. What mattered was that Kick had shared Logan with him so he'd know firsthand what Kick saw in Logan. Kick remembered the home team.

The taste of Logan's butt lingered in Ryan's mouth.

Bittersweet.

2

"A Night in the Entropics!" Kweenie was appearing in "New Review 1980" at the Mabuhay Gardens on Broadway near Polkstrasse. "Zola! Z-O-L-A. Emile Zola. Girls will be boys and boys will be toys." She tipped the top hat crowning her Dietrich tuxedo drag. "Marlene was a man . . . and so was Zola. Z-O-L-A. Zola." She was triumphant returning from Hollywood after a small part January had cadged for her in Allan Carr's ill-fated *Can't Stop the Music!*

As fast as they had come together, things in San Francisco began to fall apart. Camelot had blown up in John Kennedy's face. The little expanding universe of the Castro imperceptibly reached its farthest limit and began to collapse back on itself in motion so slow no one felt gravity change or the Earth quake. The Old Man's boys grew older. Faces that looked so inviting under the red lights of bars and baths looked vampire white at high noon on Castro. The first generation of free gays was no longer the newest generation. There were new kids in town. Fresher faces showed up the old faces the way dewy milkmaids new to the palace grounds always anger old queens in fairy tales. The first generation had an acid Look etched into their high thin cheekbones.

"Never, my dear, lean over a mirror and look at your face," Robert Opel had said, "not even for a line of coke. Sagging is gravity's revenge."

Opel's fame fused with another Robert: the fetish-face-and-flower New York society photographer, Robert Mapplethorpe. Some even thought both men were one and the same. Both artists hated the third Entity many believed existed: a man named Robert Opelthorpe.

"Beware of third Entities," both Roberts said to Ryan.

The gallery owner Opel had showcased the photographer Mapplethorpe's chronicle of the new Drug Look in his leather fetish shots. Dark circles under the eyes became a trademark of faces marked by drugs the way an even older generation of gays, who had grown up oppressed in the fifties, were marked in the face by the puffy dead-giveaway Look of alcoholics.

A kind of un–Civil War broke to a smoulder.

"Just because he's gay, Mary, doesn't mean he's your sister."

Or your brother.

Power trips abounded. Slaves needed masters. Empresses needed courtiers. Women needed villains. Old queens needed fresh meat. Politicians needed voters. Hustlers needed johns. Everybody needed a lover. Only their dealers needed nobody. The gay community broke into factions.

At an A-Group Pacific Heights party, a blond, big-shouldered swimming captain, three months graduated from Stanford, sat with the elder gentle-queens sipping their aperitifs while the younger gay men rose eagerly from the table to wash the dishes, run the Hoover, and empty the ashtrays from the grand piano.

The piss-elegant host walked over to the stunning blond swimmer and said, "We have a custom here for all new boys. Part of your initiation into our little group. You, my boy, must needs help tidy up the place."

The swimmer remained seated. "What in me makes something in you think I'm your boy?" he said. "I'm from Stanford. I don't clean up after anybody."

The host touched his gold-ringed pinky to his Liberace eyebrow and said something like you'll never eat lunch in this town again.

The swimmer rose up from his chair to his full six foot three and ten inches, and groped himself. "You silly old queen!"

The Hoover died like a soul being sucked into a dirtbag. A cryogenic silence froze the room.

"You . . . you . . . you . . ."

It was a queer kind of civil war. Males turned against males. Gay love turned to drugged sex. Sex turned to competition. You were hot or you were dead. The Castronauts didn't need straight bullies anymore. They bullied each other. Gay style fragmented. Nelly queens were out, but didn't go away. Butch behavior was in. There were a dozen ways to the new "manstyle." One way or another each faction identified and segregated itself.

Ryan had pages of notes detailing a Montage of Rank: rich gays and poor gays, homomasculine men and sissies, carpenters, hair burners, and church fairies who attended Temple and Dignity with organ fairies who thought worship was a Bach recital. Everyone was rated on a Double-10 Scale. Dance? 10. Looks? 3. Total 13 out of a possible 20. Some guys, who in the "dance" department—which meant "sexual prowess"—were 10s, but who in their "Looks" were only 3, Ryan explained to me, you boffed on the sly in private because you didn't want your hot friends to know you were balling a semi-dog who was a pro sex-*artiste* in the sack. Other guys, who were a drop-dead 10 "Looks" in everybody's book, you made certain to ball in public at the baths and in the back rooms, "Because," Ryan said, "when you fuck with a 'Looks: 10' your own sex number goes up, even though you don't tell your brunch buddies at the Norse Cove that Mr. 10's dance performance was *zip*." On Castro the pecking order was maybe more sophisticated than the old high school pecking order, but it was also more deceitfully vicious, and everybody kept track of the gossip.

It was Castro versus Folsom in a Costumerie of Drag: leathers, feathers, construction, cowboy, pec-pumper jock, gender-benders, piss-elegants, imitation white trash, paramilitary, all sporting keys on the right and keys on the left, and back pocket bandanas coded in the perverse-rainbow colors of the gay rebel semaphore: red, yellow, black, brown, and purple for fisters, pissers, sadomasochists, coprophages, and devotees of piercing of nipples and balls and cocks. Bars, flaunting discrimination, invented and enforced drag-specific dress codes. Gay style diversified, then divided, like a rampaging body cell hell-bent on acting out, with total perversity and joy, its every formerly closeted gene and desire that straight society had denounced as recessive, bestial, and sinful. Solly Blue understood. He was like a Greek chorus repeating, "What you do with your body . . ."

Political gay liberation had meant to mainstream everyone inclusively. Social gay style thrived on exclusivity of fetish, fun, fantasy, and a fraternity of favoritism. Certain crowds patronized certain bars and baths. Clubs formed. Chubbies met Chubby-Chasers. Uniform-fetishists founded the Pacific Drill Patrol. Country-Western types two-stepped the night away at the Devil's Herd bar wearing cowboy clothes from Ed Wixson's second-hand store, Worn Out West. Rollerskaters, every Tuesday night, chartered a bus from the Castro to a rink in South San Francisco where they skated in circles through streaming fumes of poppers. Loggers in plaid shirts, and the Bears, older, hairy men with beards, bellied up to the Ambush bar. Disco Queens fought their way into Alfie's, the End Up, Trocadero Transfer, the Stud, and the I-Beam. Biker Leather roamed the Miracle Mile bars on Folsom Street from Febe's to the Black-and-Blue, to Folsom Prison, to the Leatherneck, to the Arena, to the Ramrod, to the orgy-sleaze of the No Name Bar which became the Bolt which became the Brig, to the after-hours pig piles of the Covered Wagon and the Boot Camp *pissoir*, starting over again at the butch Balcony bar on Market. Sweaters and Top-Siders bent elbows at the Lion Pub; the older Suits at "Happy Hour" swam like ageing tropical fish in the huge aquarium windows of the Twin Peaks bar, perched like an open casket for viewing at the corner of Castro and Market.

The Castronauts first cruised Dick's-on-Castro which became Toad Hall, then, evolving into clones, they hit the Pendulum, the Badlands, the Midnight Sun, the Elephant Walk, Bear Hollow, and, when desperate, the Nothing Special. Polk Street was its own special walk through purgatory on the *doo-ta-doo* wild side of cologne queens mixing with the Clearasil smell of chicken rentboys suffering from terminal acne. Hustlers of all kinds stood at the southeast corner of Sutter and Polk under an electrical merchant's sign declaring "Any Object Made into a Lamp." The Tenderloin was rough trade and drag queens. Something for everyone.

It was a Ton of Attitude. The immigrant Manhattanite A-Group crashed San Francisco, intent on Manhattanizing "The City That Knows How." They hosted huge, super-produced bashes, draping their first three-story *Night Flight* party with Christo's Curtain, and hiring, for their second extravaganza, a full San Francisco pier for the jammed "Cecil B. deMillions" Ultimate '70s Party, *Stars*. Attitude pressured everybody who was anybody to dance and fuck till dawn. Reaction to the Manhattanization of San Francisco's public sex style inspired Steve McEachern to redesign his Victorian basement for private fisting parties; he dubbed his exclusive, Invitation-Only *boite* "The Catacombs," and vied with the commercial baths, the Slot Hotel, the Handball Express, the Barracks, and the Hothouse for rough-and-tumble midnight athletes who were Olympic jocks long before the International Olympic Committee ever thought of highjacking the 4,000-year-old classic word, *Olympics,* to their trademarked, corporate hearts. "Fuck them," Ryan wrote. "The real Gay Olympics never happened in any sunlit stadium."

Attitude dictated who was hot and who was not, who swallowed what expensive drugs, who snorted, and who shot up at what right or wrong address. Attitude crept on little cat feet, seeping fast, like the nightly gray fog, through the streets and consciousness of the oldest hands and the newest refugees escaping from the latest Anita Bryants and Jerry Falwells. If without pecs, you were dead, without Attitude you could not succeed or survive.

It was SFO gays versus El Lay gays versus Manhattan gays. The Great Gay Triangle of three cities turned positively Bermuda. Attitude was psychic territory. With men, ultimately, it's always territory, all of them ranked, dragged up, giving Attitude, pissing on their San Francisco patch like Latino gangs fighting for their turf in the Mission. Each kind saw need to take refuge in fraternity with its own kind. If the Castro in San Francisco had a sibling city, it was Berlin with its wall.

Attitude assassinated characters, reputations, and motives with more venom than Dan White ever knew. Dishing was second only to fucking. Only orgasm was more pleasurable than a good gay Attitude put-down. The Attitude Game was great sport, and great hurt. It would take years, and, finally, political and medical terror, before the perverse-rainbow bandana flag of intragay separatism even began to surrender to the Rainbow Flag of Gay and Lesbian unity pulling the fussing, feuding dissidents together in some semblance of community.

Males, during the Golden Time, all but abandoned politics to righteous lesbians. Ryan paid his dues among those rogue males, cruising hard mileage through the beds, bars, and baths. They all paid their dues. They were all in-laws, all sexually related, and easy to trace if the City Health Department files charted out their coital genealogy. It was a smooth coup for the women to take charge. Gay liberation politics became a network and media base for San Francisco's radical feminism to come to strength during the

reign of the City's only female mayor who tried her liberal damnedest publicly not to be what she was in private—a conservative Catholic schoolgirl
who had married a Jewish businessman. When he died, she became a rich
society matron owning blocks of Tenderloin property. "Ultimately," Ryan
said, "the womanist coup was okay. While the men fucked, someone had to
mind the store."

No one thought the party would ever stop. No one was prepared for
trouble in paradise.

Signs and omens were everywhere.

A string of serial murders began South of Market. The streets were dangerous. For the first time, they began to suspect that the murders were not
committed by straight marauders. They began to suspect each other. The
bars were themselves no longer safe haven. Murderers cruised among the
customers. Young men began disappearing at closing time only to reappear
dead in dumpsters in alleys behind Folsom and Harrison streets.

"The danger itself," Solly said, "is a hard-on."

A half-block behind Folsom Street, leathermen stealthily cruised Ringold
Alley. Men lounging in the dark doorways stuck their stiff pricks out from
the shadows into the light of the full moon. Beery from the bars. Fucking after closing time. The dirty back street: more dangerous, more sexy than the
baths. Faceless sex, anonymous black-leather bodies, naked butts, faces
fucked hard, slap of leather glove on tender flesh, clamp and twist of bleeding nipples, hot red glow of cigar tip in the dark, the night cries of pain and
pleasure and cuming, the hiding, the running from the police car cruising
slowly down Ringold Alley past men flattened against walls, men crouching
behind dumpsters, men lying flat behind a car, behind a wall. One man, the
Next One, the next Chosen One, lying between the huge boots of a man
fully masked by a leather hood, drinking his piss, licking his ass, following
him to his van, to his ropes and gag, to the gun hidden under his seat.

A young gay man could go out cruising and end up with his "MISSING"
picture on a milk carton. More than once Ryan had joined search parties
dragnetting the City's baths, playrooms, and dungeons for one of the disappeared. Most often the missing playboy turned up with a big smile on his
face after forgetting to call his lover while spending a wild weekend of
drugged sex tied up in some leatherman's basement orgy room.

Ryan's second brush with violent Death made bigger headlines than
Robert Opel. "BOUND, NUDE BODIES DISCOVERED AFTER SOUTH OF MAR-
KET PICKUPS."

"Have you seen this morning's *Chronicle?*" Solly Blue telephoned. "Kids, women, and gay men are every killer's favorite victims. At least the article's not written by Maitland Zane."

Ryan was already upset. "I'll call you back." Thirty minutes earlier, tears in his coffee, he had clipped the news article with the smiling photo of his friend Tom Gloster. Murder gave Ryan the visions of an empath. Reading the newspaper's cold facts, he shivered with feeling. He could see the ABC-TV movie between the lines. Gloster, a school comptroller, and a guy visiting from Burbank, Richard Niemeier, had both disappeared within a two-week period. Their nude bodies had been dumped in counties, one near, and one far north of Bar Nada. Both had been shot muzzle to the body. Both had been bound hand and foot. The only difference was that Gloster was wearing a black tee shirt when found thirty-three miles west of Red Bluff in Tehama County, a hundred miles from the Oregon border on Highway 36-West. Niemeier was left naked in Napa County with only a turquoise earring.

Jim Morrison echoed in Ryan's head singing "Killer on the Road." Ryan envisioned the long rides in bondage, the terror when each man separately realized the game was real. He ached for Tom Gloster. He imagined all the human details the cold news article left out, all the panic and suffering before Gloster was shot five times in the head. His body was discovered twenty-four hours after he was killed, but he was slabbed away, an unidentifiable John Doe, for six days in a coroner's cold cabinet, the ultimate closet, until Niemeier was discovered by a jogger. Niemeier had been shot once in the back, once in the back of his head, and twice in the face. The counties' sheriffs put the similarities together, and came up with nothing more than the victims' identities. Both men had been last seen at the Brig bar, South of Market. The killer, Ryan intuited, was one of their own. Solly agreed. "It's no straight fag-killer. That's one more reason I never go out. You gay boys are getting way too serious."

Ryan wrote an enraged eulogy in *Maneuvers* titled "Bring Out Your Dead." Harvey Milk had achieved romantic stardom in Death, as if he were the first faggot ever to die, well, fashionably. Gay Death, before him, kept to a whisper, had always been considered, for no reason anyone could articulate, bad taste. CUAV, the Community United Against Violence, might have said that any subgroup, surviving constantly against threat of bashing and Death, goes into a dangerous sense of denial. With the serial gay Death toll rising, the whispers rose to a nervous rash of "dead" jokes. Whenever some man in the burgeoning gay population died unexpectedly, naturally, or from an overdose, or from murder, someone somewhere sometime always said, with an oily laugh, "At least he didn't have to grow old." That, of course, in a City jammed with Dorians and Peter Pans, was a fate worse than Death.

3

It was a fire out of control. Solly Blue heard the first explosion and looked up from the small light tray where his color transparencies of his latest boys were spread out for review. The front curtains glowed orange. He was not at home. He was spending the evening at a photographer's apartment studio on Hallam Street, a tiny mews of ancient wooden apartments off Folsom that catered to the leather crowd. He pulled back the curtains and saw the ball of flame rise up the back corner of the four-story Barracks Baths. It had closed the year before and was under remodel. He opened the door and ran down to the grille of the wrought iron safety gate. Another explosion knocked him back on the terrazzo steps. He ran back into the apartment and called the fire department.

"It's bad," he reported.

He hadn't realized how bad. Hallam Street, with its ancient warren of old wooden buildings, had only one entrance/exit. It was just his luck. He rarely went out. This night was an exception, and to make matters worse, he was alone. The calendar-clock read July 10, 1980, 10:37 p.m. His friend, the art photographer known only as Dane, who had invited him to his studio, was off on a quick errand to the Boot Camp bar to deliver proofs he was completing for an ad campaign.

Solly looked around the unfamiliar apartment. He had nothing of his own with him but two trays of slides to show Dane. On the walls surrounding him hung the work of a lifetime. After Robert Mapplethorpe, Dane was the most famous, and undoubtedly the most talented, of all gay erotic photographers. He had immigrated from New York, taken the Hallam Street studio, and remodeled it into a living space behind a two-room gallery. He was one of the first artists to stake out the light industrial area of South of Market, dubbing it SOMA, the way South of Houston in Manhattan had become the *avant* SOHO. What original work was not on loan or in the hands of private collectors hung on the gray felt walls or lay stored flat in huge drawers.

Solly started to take the framed black-and-white photographs down from the walls. They grew too heavy too fast in his arms. He could save more by grabbing as many negatives as he could from as many drawers as he could open. Another explosion rocked the apartment.

Solly watched the wooden casements around the front windows break into flames. The heat cracked the glass and sucked the curtains out into the fire. Smoke billowed into the apartment. Solly was not one to panic, but a wave of fear crashed across his face. There was no way out but the back door that led to a small fenced yard dead-ended against a three-story brick wall.

There was no back alley.

He carried a rolled manila envelope, stuffed with negs, under his arm and ran out the back door. People escaping the other apartments clambered over the fences, from backyard to backyard, running and climbing in frenzied slow motion through the red glow of the fire and the rain of falling ash. He hated Ryan's movie game. He hardly had time to make up his mind. He was running through a montage of *The Last Days of Pompeii, Sodom and Gomorrah*, and the "Burning of Atlanta" all rolled into one. *Oh, Rhett!*

"I'm going to die."

Solly stood a moment on the landing. He sized up the situation and climbed up to the second-floor porch. It was a chancy leap from there to the porch next door, but it would get him over the fences and then to the roof of a one story brick garage that he guessed by the number of people running toward it was the only way out. He tucked the envelope of negatives into the back of his jeans. He couldn't help if his belt creased them. Bent was better than burnt. Something was better than nothing. He stood on the rail of the porch, wished he'd been more athletic in high school, and jumped the five feet to the next porch. He collided with a man in full leather leading out a naked man wearing handcuffs. The three of them fell in a tangle on the hot boards.

"Sorry," Solly said.

"What?" The leatherman shouted over the firestorm. "What?"

Solly shook his head.

The leatherman lifted the wrists of the man in handcuffs and said, "We can't find the key."

Solly pointed toward the roof of the brick garage already crowded with men shouting to be saved, "We've got to jump for it. You go first."

The man in the handcuffs hesitated. "I can't. I won't."

"We don't have time to convince you," Solly shouted. "You jump or you die."

Straight below was a thirty-foot drop, but it was only six feet out and eight feet down to the garage roof. Two men stood on the edge facing Solly. Firelight played on their faces. They were shouting. The whole block of

wooden apartments was in flames. The men on the roof, their voices lost in
the roar of the fire, made motions to jump.

"They're ready to catch us," Solly said. "If we make it."

Behind and above them searing heat and flames roared through the tar-
paper rooftops and blew out the back windows. Glass rained down into the
backyards. Outside the mews of their entrapment they could hear fire sirens. The clock in the burning kitchen behind the handcuffed man read
10:43.

"I don't want to die in the nude!" The handcuffed man began to cry.

"I don't want to die *period!*" Solly said. He motioned to the leatherman.
"We'll stand him up on the railing and push him."

"No!" the naked man screamed.

They picked him up bodily and stood him on the railing. For a moment
Solly had a boom-shot flash of the absurdity of hanging onto a naked man's
thighs and arms knowing he had every intention of pushing the man waver-
ing on the railing off into the darkness below. *This is why I never leave home!*
"On three," he said, "when we push you, you jump."

"Oh, God!" the man cried "Tell my mother I love her."

"I don't even know your mother," Solly said. He nodded to the leatherman. "Okay," he shouted, "it's getting too hot. We're going to burn out
here. I'm gonna count to three and you jump, asshole. Jump for your
mother!"

"I can't!"

"You can! You're a fairy! Fairies can do anything! Fairies can fly!" Solly
made the count to three mercifully short. They pushed the man who, in the
final moment, jumped from the railing with all the grace he could remember from one dream-week watching the high divers fly off the cliffs at Aca-
pulco. He landed in the arms of the two men on the garage roof. One of his
legs splayed out broken as other dark figures pulled him through the shadows to the other edge of the roof. Solly could see them looking down over
the far edge, hoping for rescuers.

"There's an alley there," the leatherman said. "But I don't see a ladder
coming up."

Down on the roof, every face, red like flat burning pies, gaped up at them
with the flames licking out at their butts.

"Jump!" Solly said. "I don't have much more time to be heroic."

The leatherman, squealing an unearthly soprano, jumped down like a
falling Wallenda into the arms of the waiting men. Solly saw the cheering
mouths open in the middle of the red pie-faces, but he could not hear their
cries over the roar of the flames. The heat was getting to him. He suddenly

began to beat the envelope of negatives tucked into his back. The tip of the envelope had caught fire. He could not swat it out. He felt the porch begin to buckle under his feet. "Fuck it," he said, and he climbed up on the railing, and leapt out into the glowing red darkness with the negatives flaming out of his jeans. He rocketed up and out, soaring like a roman candle, for a moment feeling weightless, without gravity, feeling a joy in life that surprised him, until gravity's real revenge—what is, is—pulled him down, faster and faster down, into the smoke-filled darkness.

* * *

"Needless to say, I missed the roof." Solly sat up in his bed at San Francisco General. "Under this turban, I have a concussion. But can you tell? All I remember is I jumped and then I started flying, and then the next thing I knew I was in the arms of a handsome young fireman with a black moustache and coal-dark eyes. I'll never forget the feel of his mouth on mine. Now I know why they call it the 'kiss of life.' Call him up. Dial nine-one-one. I may have a relapse. I may be in-love. Actually, I'll be out of here in a few days and I'm very philosophical. Somewhat in the manner of the immortal words of one of my favorite philosophers, Miss Peggy Lee. 'Is that all there is to a fire?'"

4

On the second day after the fire, Ryan walked through the front door of San Francisco General Hospital. The *Chronicle* kept the story on page one. The Barracks had burned to a shell. The fire had leveled all the wooden flats around it, leaving a hundred people homeless. Rumors of charred bodies left bound in chains charged through the City. "What gays are to straights, S&M guys are to vanilla gays," Solly had mused. "Outcasts."

In the hospital hall, Ryan heard a familiar voice.

"Ryan O'Hara!"

"If it isn't Jack Woods."

"Miss Scarlett!"

Ryan ignored the barb. They hugged. Ryan felt a coldness. Not like the warmth on that night long before, his first night in San Francisco, when Jack Woods in the Tool Box had picked him up. That hug had led to an intermittent three-year affairette with the muscular blond who had been his first bodybuilder.

"You're looking good as ever," Ryan said. He squeezed Jack's biceps.

"You noticed." Jack's voice had a hard edge. People don't like to be dropped. He was one of the many acquaintances Ryan hadn't seen too often during his two years with Kick.

"What are you doing here?" Ryan said.

"I guess you haven't heard. Tony Tavarossi is in intensive care."

"I didn't know he was sick. What happened? He wasn't caught in the fire, was he?"

"Not the fire. No. It's more like he's disintegrated the last three months. He's had a recurrence of hepatitis. He's had shingles. He's had amebiasis. He's had a cough. He's had one thing after another. Now they say he's got pneumonia. He's bad off. He's on a respirator."

"Can he have visitors?"

"He has a tracheotomy. He can't talk."

"Does he recognize people or what?" Ryan asked.

"I go. I see him. Maybe he wakes up. Maybe he doesn't."

"I'd like to see him."

"What the fuck for?"

"There was a time when Tony and I were close."

"Then you dumped him the way you dumped everybody."

"I've been on an extended honeymoon."

"Bull! That cheap blond has made you too big for your britches, bitch."

"Ah," Ryan said. "So it's Kick."

"I could tell you things about him," Jack said.

"I think our conversation is over," Ryan said.

"Eat shit and die!"

"Yes, we must lunch sometime," Ryan said. "Have your girl call my girl."

"We're talking Tony here."

"We're talking nonsense here." Ryan looked at his watch and glanced at the elevators.

"Hypocrite! You haven't seen Tony in months."

"Then I'll see him now."

"Sure. Make yourself feel better. He's dying."

"How'd you like some open-heart brain surgery," Ryan said.

"How'd you like to step outside." Jack Woods flexed his bulk.

"Not now." Ryan lifted up the flat palm of his hand against Jack Woods. "Later." He split. He turned and walked deeper down the hospital corridor, leaving the blond man, famous for his cigars and his chopped Harley, standing in hulking, sulking, black silhouette against the bright backlight of sun streaming in the glass entrance. Rising alone in the elevator up to the intensive care unit, he felt all the panic his father had caused in him.

He knew the ice-cold rooms of ICU. He knew the Look of dying, of slow Death, of gaunt bodies pumped and flushed through machines, of eyes staring blank from faces collapsed with pain, the wild thin hair of the terminal, the sexless faces of the dying, the gasping for air through dry lips, the twitching of thin arms taped to boards with needles inserted through the paper-thin skin into sunken blue veins, the silent drip of fluids, the thin white hospital gowns crawling up restless thighs exposing pockets of dead sex, all passion gone, Death's passage begun, the suffering, the submission, the end calibrated on beeping machines that with a decision from the doctors and a lover's signature can be turned off, the kiss good-bye, the flipping of the switch, the pulling of the plug, the countdown, the Death watch, fast sometimes, more often slow agony, the sighing of the limp body sinking down into cold white sheets, the whimpering, the crying, the sobbing, the screaming of the survivors clutching one another, trembling fingers clawing in for one last touch, feeling something so warm grow so cold so quickly in the refrigerated white air, when even Death is taken from the dead one, his Death becoming their Death, seeing them realize that one less person lies between them and their own Deaths, pulling themselves finally together, helped by doctors and nurses, crisp angels of mercy, walking them with backward glances out the double doors to small rooms where sobs change to quiet murmurs, where life becomes Death becomes "the arrangements," the body of the dead one wrapped and lifted even as they whisper thirty feet away, wrapped and lifted and placed on a gurney, taken by strangers down the back elevator, to the cold storage of the hospital morgue, where coal-black eyes, bruised with rupture, stare up at white acoustical ceilings that muffle noises they can no longer hear.

"Tony Tavarossi?" Ryan asked.

"Are you friend or family?" The woman's face was pleasant. A stethoscope hung from her neck. Her hands were plunged deep into the big pockets of her jacket. Her badge read "Dr. Mary Ketterer."

"A friend." Ryan knew she knew what kind of friend. At least in San Francisco that didn't matter especially at times like this. He knew in the Midwest, even through the dying, as they always had in life, homosexual men were forced to prevaricate their love. Prevarication, not lying exactly, but not exposing the truth exactly, had for ages been the code and curse of conduct laid on male lovers from the first of their experimental affairs to their last parting from the life partner they finally found they had long and truly loved.

Tony was conscious. He beamed on seeing Ryan. His thin fingers that had guided Ryan through so many nights of pleasure wrapped weakly around Ryan's hand.

"I didn't know," Ryan said.

Tony shook his head. It didn't matter.

"I'm here," Ryan said. He had to twist himself around. He knew Tony knew exactly where he was. "Well, so, you certainly have yourself plugged in."

Tony raised his eyebrows and smiled a yeah-what-can-you-do expression. Then he pointed to his mouth, shook his head, and pointed to the tracheotomy.

"I know. You can't talk. Finally I can get a word in edgewise."

Tony searched with his fingers for a small pad of paper and a pencil. He could not locate it an inch away from his grasp. Ryan guided it into his hand.

"You don't have to write." Ryan made one-sided conversation so Tony could nod *yes* or *no*. He knew from so many hours with his father that those who lay long sick found some strength from outside news. He knew Tony. He considered discussing the Folsom Street fire. He didn't want to upset him, but Tony had lived most of his life on Folsom. He had worked at one time or another in almost every bar and had played in every bath. He was a fixture South of Market. He had been a star.

"Have you heard any news from Folsom?" Ryan tested the waters. Tony shook his head. "The Barracks burned down three nights ago. No one was hurt. The place was empty. They were remodeling the building." He had Tony's interest; the subject was okay. "The whole place was burned out. And all the houses around it. Everybody escaped. About a hundred people have to find new apartments. I guess the arson inspectors found a lot of chains and fried leather. I always knew the Barracks was so hot, sometimes when I'd crawl out of there on all fours at sunrise, I'd think this place has to finally go up in flames. You could see the fire from all over town. Solly Blue says it was like the burning of Atlanta."

Tony smiled.

"Actually, with the way downtown is growing, I suspect they'll build some high-rise on the spot. I think this is the end of Folsom as we know it."

Tony struggled in the bed. Staring at the ceiling, he grappled with the pencil on the paper and wrote the word, "Good."

"Good?" Ryan asked. "Good?"

Tony nodded.

"Ah, I see. You've had it with Folsom?"

Tony raised his hand, cupped his thumb under his four fingers, and flat out chopped three times at his throat.

"So. You've had it up to there?"

Tony nodded *yes*.

Later, in the corridor, Ryan asked Dr. Mary Ketterer, "What's the matter with him? I mean, what's the diagnosis?"

"Your friend is a very sick man."

"What's wrong with him?"

"Right now? Pneumonia," she said. "Did he smoke much?"

"Yes. Did that cause it?"

"No."

"He used poppers. We all use poppers. Did poppers cause it?"

"I can't say poppers caused it. I can say poppers are an insult to the lungs."

"He's not going to live, is he?"

"He's going to die."

"What caused this?"

"Diagnosis? No. Prognosis? Yes." She shrugged sincerely. "Frankly, we don't know what it is."

"How long does he have?"

"That's hard to say. To be truthful, we've never really experienced a patient so distressed. According to his vital signs, a week, maybe more, maybe less."

Ryan sent Kick up to the barn at Rancho Bar Nada. "I've got injured and sick people here," he explained. "Solly and Tony. Take Logan with you. Besides, you need some rest between contests. But don't take Logan near the house and the killer triplets. I think he'll like staying out in our barn. I'll call Thom and tell him you're driving up and to leave you alone."

Ryan planned to see Tony every day, but Solly required more attention at home.

"You are a regular Florence Nightingale," Kick said on the phone. "Make that Lawrence Nightingale."

But Ryan had not seen Tony every day. He knew that Tony's longtime lover, a bisexual married man, was always with him. He knew that Solly wouldn't and couldn't go out of his penthouse where he lay divine invalid on a couch playing Camille. It was easier to visit Solly, who only pretended to be dying, than it was to watch Tony slip away.

Ryan made all the excuses people make when they can't face visits to the hospital. The excuses made him guilty. The guilt finally drove him to Tony's bedside. They were alone together. Tony lay quietly, more in a trance than asleep. Ryan sensed it was the last time. He leaned in over the aluminum bed rail, his face lowering slowly over Tony's face, feeling no heat rise from his friend's cold body, finding surprise at the moist sweat on the dying man's forehead when he kissed him lightly.

"I love you," he said.

He rose up and walked backward, slowly, away from the bed, like a camera at the end of a movie dollying away from some final freeze-frame image that recedes deeper and deeper into the dark screen, like the last shot of *Long Day's Journey into Night*.

"Listen to us in our darkness, we beseech thee, Oh, Lord; and by thy great mercy defend us from all perils and dangers of this night."

None of them knew yet the coming peril that would stalk them all.

5

Things beyond Ryan's ken began to happen. Only later, after Tony Tavarossi died, did pieces fall together. For instance, the evening the Louise M. Davies Symphony Hall opened its doors for the first time, Kick had two tickets comped to him by January Guggenheim who had been in the City for the premiere.

"I must fly back to El Lay, darling," she said to Kick. She was all autographs and sunglasses. "I'm producing a miniseries and my director is in trouble." She handed Kick the tickets. "I haven't seen Ry," she said. She arched a very suspicious tweezed eyebrow.

Kick smiled at her.

"Ah," she said. "Got to fly!"

Kick drove her to San Francisco International in his red Corvette.

"You guys enjoy," she said.

But it wasn't Ryan who sat next to Kick in the Grand Tier of the gala opening.

It was Logan Doyle.

"I figured you were so busy with Solly and Tony and the next issue of *Maneuvers*," Kick explained. "Besides, Logan's never been to an opening."

Opening? Opening? Never been to an opening?

"Don't feed me lines like that." Ryan added the lightness Kick expected in his voice. "Or I may not be able to remain a gentleman."

"We all need some variety," Kick said. He had every reason to drag Logan Doyle out in public. Together they were a physically striking pair of men. The kind of sexy, handsome men who make women in evening gowns hate homosexuality.

At the airport stop for PSA, Kick had pulled the Corvette to the curb. A porter opened January's door and took her ticket and bag, but she had not been in any hurry to leave.

"By the way," January had said to Kick, "I know that you and Ryan know what you're doing. The way you keep your relationship open is super, especially the way Ryan wrote me that you both take special care of the home team."

"Ryan's real special," Kick said.

"But one thing," January said. "Keep that other gorgeous hunk around."

"You like Logan, huh?"

"Remember, I have a photographer's eye for looks."

"Logan's big in that department."

"And one last thing. Can I say it?"

"You can say anything you want." Kick grinned his stunning grin.

"Ryan loves you."

"I know. I love him too."

"No. I mean Ryan is in-love with you."

"He's got that under control."

"What I mean is: Don't hurt Ryan."

"No one's ever treated me better."

"Handsome is as handsome does," January said.

"I'd never hurt Ry."

"What I mean is: Be careful with Logan."

Kick reached to touch the key in the ignition. January stroked his muscular forearm. Tender gold stubble grew soft on his tanned skin where Ryan had shaved away his thick fleece for the Mr. San Francisco contest.

"God! You're hot!" she said.

Kick smiled. "We all know what we're doing." He turned the key. The Corvette roared into life at the curb. "We're big boys."

"Quoth Kweenie," January said. "You're all big boys playing big boys' games." She leaned over, pulled Kick's hand from the steering wheel to her mouth and kissed his palm. "Thanks for the lift."

"Thanks, sailor," Kick said. "Call me next time you're in town."

January laughed.

"Thanks for the advice," Kick said. "Have a good flight."

"*Ciao.* baby, *ciao.*"

When Solly heard that Kick had taken Logan to the Davies Hall premiere, he called me. He was pissed.

"Magnus," Solly said, "there's some things in life these boys don't understand. Some people you take some places. Other people you take other places. If you ask me, and no one did, there's some places you don't take your whore. Ryan tries to make light of this entire thing. He wants that crazy sense of fraternity he's always writing about to work in real life. Reality isn't like his fiction where he can control his characters. He fails to see that Kick isn't clever enough to know there's a difference between lovers, partners, friends, roommates, fuck-buddies, and whores."

"Kick may have a southern drawl," I said, "but he didn't just fall off the turnip truck."

"Precisely," Solly said. "He knows exactly what he's doing."

"And Ry doesn't."

"He doesn't know what Kick is really doing. Ry doesn't know reality like I do."

"We'll have to wait around and pick up the pieces."

"Yeah," Solly said. "Wake me up when the killing starts."

6

Ryan and Thom were both refugees from the America of the sixties, a decade of social concern Kick seemed to have missed altogether, despite what happened at the lunch counters in Birmingham, Alabama. Kweenie, who was ten years old during the Summer of Love, never forgave fate for making her too young to come to San Francisco wearing flowers in her hair. Ryan had tuned her in, as they said back then, to incense and Super 8 movie making, playing sitar soundtracks to their homemade underground films, always starring Margaret Mary, who was starting on her way to becoming Kweenasheba.

"It's my fault she's turned out so crazy," Ryan said.

Kweenie would have been the last one to blame him. Charley-Pop and Annie Laurie had their own ideas, but they trusted Ryan to give Margaret Mary, born in their forties, things they felt their own golden boy could give her. She had loved Ryan bringing home the *Sgt. Pepper* album and *Surrealistic Pillow.* "Go ask Alice." And she was Alice by the time she was nine. She had loved her brother showering rose petals on her face while they listened to Ravi Shankar. Her view, as much as both her older brothers', was from the sixties.

"What movie are they playing?" Kweenie asked me.

I was tired of her game. "What movie is who playing?"

"Kick and Ry. What movie?"

"*Casablanca?*"

"Not yet," she said. "Right now, Kick is the golden, aloof Redford and Ry is the activist Streisand in *The Way We Were.*" She turned up her pert little nose. "Then there's Thom who's playing John Wayne in *The Green Berets.*"

I could have wished my pop culture students were as astute as Kweenie. She was right about them all. As for Ryan and Thom, Vietnam had disturbed them both the way wars always seem to pit brother against brother. Blue against Gray. One a hawk. One a dove. Ryan feared the violence he saw in Thom's face, almost as if Thom were the angry, bestial incarnation of the gay rage Ryan had repressed—no, civilized—within himself. Catholicism had made them both miserable with the threats of eternal torture that coexist in the Church's theology of Death and fugitive lusts. If anything more than sex and drugs and life in the fast lane conspired to destroy Ryan's sense of self, it was the Church and its penitential discipline of self-abnegation. The intense Catholic obsessions with sex and sin had taught him the thrill, the joy, that the intensity of pure obsession adds to life.

The same was true for Thom in a way. He transferred his Catholic obsession to a lockstep militarism. Ryan transferred his Catholic obsession for worship to Kick, who, even when Ryan was not locked in passionate sex with him, was his Christ, was his Adam before the Fall, was his male Muse, was the apple of his eye, the sunshine of his life, his roman candle of Energy and imagination. As the seminary had been Ryan's way out of Peoria, Kick was Ryan's ticket to ride.

Poor Thom. The Marines had been his way out of Peoria, but all Thom had was a worse case of depression than Ryan, a twenty-percent disability from the VA, three monsters, and the ultimate dipsy doodle, Sandy Gully.

Thom drove from his monthly checkup at the Veteran's Hospital in San Francisco to the Victorian and picked Ryan up in his truck. They drove north from the City across the Golden Gate Bridge, through the Rainbow Tunnel, and up the Redwood Highway through Marin, past the X-Rated Drive-In movie ten feet inside the Sonoma County line, on past Petaluma and Cotati to the Sebastopol exit to 116 West. Thom had come into the City on the last of a series of visits to the VA.

Ryan had his suspicions.

Thom said everything was cool. Ryan wondered how many times Thom had reassured him, himself, and Sandy Gully. Everything was not cool.

Sandy had left Thom.

Thom did not know why.

But Ryan knew.

Sandy had fled under cover of darkness with all that she had left of her-self, of any sense of herself, into the night more than a week before.

Sandy was an innocent. Life had confused her and she had confused her life. She had lost all sense of her own coming and going. She found every-thing went by too fast. She had left the Rancho when she realized that Thom had told her in no uncertain terms that she was not his wife.

"I married you!" she said.

"You're another child," he said.

She retreated to the bathroom and locked the door. She looked in the mir-ror. She scrubbed her face. The Mary Kay cosmetics washed down the drain. She saw lines she had not seen before. She pulled at her skin. She brushed her hair back straight from her face. She was not young anymore. Thom had taken to turning out the lights as soon as he came to bed. She had done her duty in the dark. She resented him. "He lays back and I do all the fucking work." Then, remembering the pleasure she still found in his body, no mat-ter how passive to her, she smiled, dried her face, packed on the makeup, feathered her blonde hair back at the temples until the black roots showed, and announced to her face in the mirror, "Thommy, baby, you ain't so hot neither."

In the truck, Thom told Ryan how it had been the night Sandy left. She had packed her overnight case and a brown paper Safeway sack and had driven to Cotati. She parked on the green in front of the Meander Inn. For half an hour, she sat in the car crying. Then she walked into the Meander. Gentleman Tim, an old friend from Ryan's first days in the county, was working the bar. The place was empty. She ignored him and walked to the bulletin board. She read two notices and pulled the third one off the wall and headed toward the pay phone. She glared at Tim. "I've had it," she said. "I've been had and I've had it."

"Tell me about it," Tim said. He knew the story of Ryan's brother's fam-ily.

"Life is shit," she said. She dialed the number from the notice and waited for an answer. She lit a Lark and held it in her smoking-fingers while she pressed the palm of her hand against her ear. Willie Nelson was singing "Mamas, Don't Let Your Babies Grow Up to Be Cowboys."

The woman who answered the phone was interested. She drove over to the Meander to meet Sandy. "You can't be too careful these days. You know?" They hit it off. She was a regular. Tim plied them with drinks and chat. The woman was younger than Sandy. She did not work. She covered her expenses in a South Santa Rosa trailer court by renting out her extra bedroom. "I hope you won't mind," she told Sandy, "sometimes I have men friends over. Well, not friends exactly. You know. Times being as hard as they are."

Sandy had found a rental to share.

Three days passed before Sandy called back to the ranch. Abe answered the phone. "Abie, honey," she said, "it's your mom."

"I know who you are. I don't want to talk to you."

"Let me talk to Bea then."

"Tell her I don't want to talk to her," Bea said.

"She doesn't want to talk to you either," Abe said.

"You two shits," Sie said "I'll talk to her." Sie took the avocado green receiver. "Hi, Mom."

Abe turned away from his sisters. "You're both sluts," he said.

Looking out the speeding truck window at the hills passing by, Ryan wondered why he needed these people. Thom slowly unfolded himself. Always, they all told Ryan too much. The triplets spun out their versions separately and together. Sandy every once in a while confided her hard times locked in her bedroom because they all, even Thom, hit out at her. Thom rarely expressed anything, except when he was stoned. A couple pipefuls brought out a side of him that even he never knew existed. With every passing confidence Ryan pieced together more than he wanted to know about his brother's family.

Straight people made him glad he was gay.

"We're almost there," Ryan said.

The valley looked dry and golden. In front of the ranch they saw Abe standing in the road. He was hulked over, gangly, and wet.

"Jesus H. Christ," Thom said. He pulled his truck up to his son. "What the hell happened to you?"

Abe said nothing. He turned like he was a hundred years old and pointed at nothing in particular. Sie stood on the front deck toweling her hands dry like the Miss Cindypriss they called her. She was the image of Sandy. Every Mary Kay cosmetic that her mother had abandoned was spackled like drywall mud across her zits.

"When I grow up," she said it to make them all scream at her how stupid she was, because she would do anything to get attention, and because her sins, which Ryan was sure were multiple, would not be forgiven by the mere fact that she washed up all the dishes and wiped down the stove, "all I want is to be a housewife."

Ryan had slept around enough to know the predatory look of lust in another person's face. Sie was hot to trot. "I know what you do," he had once told her. "I know what you do and I know what you will do. You can fool all these other people because they hardly bother to look at you. But I look at you. God! Look at you. You're sixteen and strictly ten-cents-a-dance."

Sie glared at him. "You sleep with everybody."

"I'm trashy," Ryan said, "when I want to be because I want to be. I can trash-fuck to enjoy it and then back out of it again. You're trashy all the time. And that," he pointed at her, "is a very real and basic difference."

"Abe! What the hell happened to you?" Thom repeated from the truck window.

Abe pointed toward the back hills lined with huge fir trees.

Sie shouted from the porch, "My bitch sister tried to stab my bitch brother in the leg."

"All that money you spent on charm school for those girls," Ryan said.

"I'll handle it," Thom said. He drove the truck on up into the yard.

Abe came limping in behind them. Sie moved to the edge of the porch. From behind the row of trees, Bea stepped into view. She had a long screwdriver in her hand.

"What happened?" Thom walked exasperated up the steps to the deck. "Beatrice!" He shouted at the girl hanging back under the trees. "You march your ass down here double time!"

Bea walked sullenly out from the tree shadows and began her spiteful slow drag down the hill. She refused to double-time for anyone. They all watched her ill-tempered procession. When she finally reached the deck, she said, "I didn't mean to stab him much." She was expert at dividing guilt. She grabbed Sie by the neck. "Sie poured boiling water on him."

"I did not!" Sie said. "Let go. You're always grabbing me. Are you gay? Are you, Bea?"

"Nice the way they say *hello* when you come home," Ryan said.

"Tell the whole story," Sie said. "I dare you, Bea. B for *bitch!*"

"It was okay until they came into the house," Abe said.

"Who came into the house?" Thom said. "No one comes into my house when I'm gone."

"It's uncle Ry's house," Bea said. She tapped the screwdriver in the palm of her hand.

"Who came into the house?" Thom repeated.

"Two guys I know from school," Abe said. "I was walking down the road."

"You were hitchhiking," Sie said.

"I told you never to hitchhike." Thom slapped Abe on the shoulder.

"Quit it!" Abe said. "I wasn't hitchhiking. They made me to get in."

"So who came into the house?" Thom demanded.

"No," Ryan said. "Who's on first. Abe's on the deck. Bea's at the door. And Sie's in the house."

Thom glared at Ryan. "Stop it," he said.

"When they pulled in the driveway," Bea said, "they both got out and followed . . ."

"They followed me into the house, Dad," Abe said.

"Why didn't you stop them?" Thom said. "I've taught you how to defend yourself."

"I tried to," Abe said.

"You did not," Bea said.

"I did too." He grabbed the screwdriver from Bea's hand. "Get away from me," he said.

"They came right on into the house," Bea said, "and opened the refrigerator and took out a six-pack."

Thom looked from Bea to Sie. Sie had not been too ready with details. "And you," he said, "What about you, Sie?"

Bea stepped between Sie and her father. Bea was expert imitating her sister's whining feminine moves. She moonwalked in place oozing a hootchy kootchy. "Sie," she said, and she delivered the imitation as broadly as her aunt Kweenie could have done. "Sie," she repeated, "walked right up to the guys and grabbed a beer can and said, 'If anybody's going to party around here, it's gonna be me!'"

"You liar!" Sie yelled, but she knew she was caught and a guilty grin exposed her uneven teeth.

"I ought to slap you silly," Thom said to Sie.

"Slap her, Dad," Bea said.

"Thom," Ryan said, "you're too good to these monsters. They're killers." He turned to the three of them. "No wonder your mother left home. In normal families, the kids run away. Not the parents."

"I think we better tell dad everything," Abe said.

"What else is there?" Thom said.

"BB holes," Abe said. "They shot BB holes in the windows."

Thom looked at Ryan who shrugged. "What's a window in all of this?"

"Where'd they get the gun?" Thom asked.

"It was mine. I had it out."

"They asked where the BBs were," Sie said. "So I told you them you kept them in your storage room."

"You're a real good-time girl," Ryan said. "So they loaded the gun?"

"Yeah," Abe said. He snorted his laugh up his left nostril. He had broken his nose in a fall several years before. No one had bothered to fix it. The

Army doctor said they could repair it when he was older and could pick out his own nose. "They loaded it and pointed it at Sie and . . ."

"Go on!" Sie jumped in. "Tell the whole thing, you motherfucker!"

"Stop," Ryan said.

"Keep talking," Thom said to Abe.

"They pointed the gun at Sie and told her to drop her panties because they wanted to see . . ."

Bea could not hold back. "They wanted to see her twat!"

"What happened?" Thom expected the worst.

"I only let one of them stick his finger in me," Sie said. "I didn't want to get shot."

"No Death before dishonor here," Ryan said.

"I wasn't going to take down my panties for those cocksuckers," Bea said. "I told the motherfuckers to get the fuck out of the house. I told them they wouldn't dare shoot me."

Ryan heard the rage of a young dyke rising in her voice.

"And then," Abe said, "Bea punched out the asshole with the gun and took it away from him."

"I told him I was going to shoot his balls off," Bea said. She was proud of herself.

"Jeez," Ryan said.

"You know Bea," Abe said. "She really made those suckers run."

"There's more," Bea said.

"Oh, God, no!" Ryan said in mock horror.

"There was this fight in the yard," Bea said. "That's when they pulled down Abe's pants and tried to shove the hose up his ass. That's how he got all wet."

"What else," Ryan asked, "do the simple folk do?" He had left the City for the county to get away from all this and here it was. The rest unfolded quickly. Ryan could see it all. Abe had chased after the older boys who had pantsed him in the yard. Two-fisted Bea was after them with the BB gun and the screwdriver.

The boys knocked Abe to the ground and pantsed him again. Bea stabbed at them. They kicked at her and tried to feel her up. She fought and clawed and bit back at them. All the while, Sie stood on the deck, waving her beer can, cheering everybody on, keeping the action hot, while her pans of water on the electric stove reached the boiling point.

Bea kicked one of the boys in the crotch. Then she turned on Abe and tried to stab his leg. "You're no help fighting these bastards," she screamed.

Sie threw a skillet of boiling water off the deck. Hot spray splashed through the air. The iron pan skidded hissing across the dry grass. The boys retreated into their car.

Abe jumped in with them to escape both his sisters wielding the screwdriver and the pan of boiling water.

"Crazy bitches!" The boys drove off, screeching down the road, stopping at the corner, and throwing Abe out into the ditch.

"That's where we came in," Ryan said. "I'm certainly glad Kick didn't come up this weekend. What he doesn't know can't hurt me. If he ever saw this, he'd never let me have his baby."

Thom marched the triplets into the house. "I'm calling your mother," he said.

He called her, but she would not come.

7

Ryan wrote on napkins. He sat on the garden deck behind the Patio Café near 18th and Castro waiting for Kick. The ambience was as perfect as a television soap-opera set. *T-a-d-z-i-o.* He wrote the name in large letters. He was Dirk Bogarde in *Death in Venice.* Kweenie might have said he was playing Citizen Kane writing "Rosebud." The napkin blotted the red ink of his felt-tip pen: "No one has ever written about Tadzio's point of view." He hadn't seen Kick in a week. Twice a day they were on the phone. "I'm glad," Ryan had said, "that we're apart these days as much as we're together." Being apart kept them from letting things get ordinary. Ryan had asked Kick the night of their first contest to promise that they'd never become ordinary to each other.

"Ordinary?" Kick had said. "How could we be? We're extraordinary people."

Geography quaked between them.

Kick was on the move, relaxing, hanging out, alternating Castro with the ranch now that the Mr. San Francisco contest was over. Ryan called Kick at the studio up at Bar Nada. Kick called him from the gym or from Logan's flat asking Ryan to join them for supper—not like the beginning when they had asked Logan to join them.

"One thing," Ryan had long before told Kick, "when you're dealing with a writer, sometimes the writer has to decline what he might prefer doing. Deadlines wait for no man."

Ryan had a new project. He had *Universal Appeal* on his mind.

He disliked his own writer's discipline. It was a tyranny he could not escape. He much preferred his fancy of running around with Kick, sunbathing at the ranch, tooling around in the Corvette, hitting the gym, having a stoned good time. Somehow Kick always juggled life right. He had his personal motives, showing up often enough unannounced in the evenings, most often without Logan, dragging Ryan away from his manuscripts, thrilling him in the bedroom.

"You really know," Ryan said, "how to keep a man hanging on."

"You really know how to keep a man coming back for more," Kick said. "I have no intention of losing you to the typewriter."

The early evening air on the Patio Café deck was warm. The crowd was happy. Ryan scanned every clutch of patrons waiting to be seated. Kick was not late. Ryan was early. Next to his coffee cup sat a novel from Paperback Traffic and a folder with the final draft of the text for his book, their photo book, *Universal Appeal*. For nearly three years, Ryan had managed to keep up with Kick and with his own writing deadlines, but *Universal Appeal* had impacted Ryan's normal schedule. Solly's concussion and Tony's Death had kept him away from his typewriter. The editors of *A Different Drum, In Touch,* and *Just Men* sent nervous letters inquiring where were his overdue manuscripts. His own *Maneuvers,* which he wrote cover to cover, was about to publish its first late issue.

His own professional commitments were not as important as his personal project with Kick.

Separated from Kick, Ryan let the writing of *Universal Appeal* take the place of what had been their constant time together. He hardly cared whom he pleased as long as he pleased Kick. This evening meeting at the Patio was his first night out in the month since the Folsom Street fire. Ryan was radiant. Kick would be thrilled that the manuscript was complete. No matter what he ordered from the Patio menu, Ryan knew that Kick was his dessert.

On the phone, Kick had drawled his slow drawl: "Later on, do you want to fuck? Or whu-u-a-t?"

The waiter asked Ryan if he wanted more coffee. Ryan waved him away. He was already wired with stage fright: the kind of fear actors, and lovers, have of not living up to an audience's expectations. For nearly three years, Ryan had managed to be every inch the man Kick expected. Love was a speed trip.

The maître d' appeared on the garden porch and switched on the overhead heating units. The summer evening had turned cool. A family, escorting an ancient woman, entered and sat near Ryan, talking in soft German-

Jewish voices. Their happy entrance and the taped classical music pleasured Ryan. He felt cosmopolitan.

His heart leapt up. He spied Kick. His broad shoulders and grinning face filled the open French doorway with his Command Presence. Ryan smiled one of those smiles of a summer night that come so easily to the faces of lovers. Kick moseyed through the crowd. Diners stopped in midbite. Ryan heard the young woman with the German-Jewish couple say, *"Ausgezeichnet!"* They looked, nodded among themselves, and smiled first at Kick then at her.

Kick looked at no one but Ryan. He wore a large Pendleton shirt patterned with the soft beige and blue that looks dynamite on blonds. The sleeves were turned halfway up his forearms revealing the regrowth of the thick blond hair that matched the hair Ryan had shaved from Kick's body before the Mr. San Francisco and had saved in fetish-Baggies at home in a drawer.

"I missed you like shit." Kick sat down. "Did you miss me?"

"Miss you? Last night I turned on the oven. I lit the gas. I was either going to kill myself or bake a cake. Obviously, I baked the cake. Your favorite." Ryan raised his eyebrows three times in the butch-flirt he had learned from Tom Selleck on *Magnum P.I.* "Later tonight I figured we could have our cake and eat it too."

"Jeez," Kick said. "You look good."

"Aw, go on. You'll look better three days dead than I look now."

"You've got more muscle," Kick said.

"I've kept my workouts up," Ryan said. "Even by myself, you're always there coaching me, squeezing out one more rep."

"I knew you could make great gains." He leaned across the table. "I told you not to be afraid of steroids. You're taking only enough to do you good, not harm."

Ryan knew the bodybuilder rationale. It was the same fatalism as Solly's. What is, is. They took steroids, as if, given all in life that is disappointing and destructive, they, as elite bodybuilders, felt they themselves had a right, even an imperative, to inflict a little of life's possible damage on themselves. Besides, Solly, who had tried heroin, reassured Ryan that a round of steroids could hardly hurt him.

But something, some little voice in Ryan had made him quit. He stopped opening the bottle. He stopped shaking the 5 mg of Dianabol into his hand. He stopped popping the little blue pills into his mouth. With Kick away so much, the steroids turned his vague anxiety into a well-defined stress. His

skin seemed dry. Small lines appeared around his eyes. He was feeling insecure enough without taking the Dianabol. The drug made him feel guilty.

When he was insecure and guilty, anxiety depressed him. It was a small
thing, but in small things often great things are at stake. He decided not to
tell Kick that he was off the stuff. He was still ready to keep their promise to
take muscle as far as it would go, but he was content to let it be Kick's muscle. After all, Kick had said he preferred communicative men to competitive
men, and too many musclemen were competitive on stage and off.

One bodybuilder in the house was enough. Two were too many. Logan
was proof of that. He had that competitive edge. Kick seemed not to notice
it. Ryan didn't need crystal balls to realize that the only way to beat Logan
Doyle was to be more supportive and communicative with Kick than competitive. He put his sharpened fangs away. Words were the only competition he could win. The *Universal Appeal* project was his way to victory.

He hated Logan not because he was with Kick but because he was an
asshole. He was not unaware from Logan's sidelong glances and his pointed
comments about skinny-necked geeks that Logan thought he was a wimp.
In Logan's book, if you didn't have muscle, you weren't shit.

Ryan wondered if Kick knew that Logan had Attitude about Ryan that
Kick couldn't see and Ryan ignored. It was all too complicated.

Maybe Kick knew Ryan's writing schedule, like his time with Solly, wasn't
all that demanding. Maybe Kick knew that Ryan pretended to be busy to
cover his sense of abandonment, haunting at night the empty Victorian.
Maybe Kick thought Ryan had taken a boyfriend on the side to give Kick
time for his affairette with Logan.

Ryan was never sure what to think. He was one half of that other Famous
Couple, Lou Costello trying to find out from Bud Abbott, "Who's on first?"
Hadn't Kick confided during a night of intimate pillow talk: "Logan I like.
You I love."

What a match! Ryan's temperament and Kick's personality. Ryan was
Ryan, dark and brooding, and Kick was southern sun, free as the breeze.
Kick was Ryan's main exercise. Their affair was more of a workout than
pumping iron. Ryan was game. No matter how long. No matter the cost.
He figured he had much to learn from Kick's coaching. His carefree south-
ern sensuality was the strongest arm-wrestle Ryan had ever found to beat
his own urban existential angst. He and Kick had never had a single cross
word. He wanted to keep it that way at all costs. His relationship with
Teddy had been stormy enough to be charted by the National Weather
Service.

Kick leaned in across the white tablecloth and took Ryan's fingers and wrist in both his big hands.

"I love you," Ryan said.

Kick beamed him a smile. Instantly, always, no matter how short or long separated, they had a way of immediately regaining their intimacy.

"What's the book?" Kick asked.

"Nothing, actually. Agee. *A Death in the Family*." He had thought of giving it to Kick who had seemed to survive the Death of his father with hardly a mention.

"You're incorrigible. Sounds like a downer."

"I haven't read it." Ryan prevaricated. "I only bought it as a prop. You know. A single person sitting alone in a restaurant at a table for two. Strangers react differently if you carry a book. The way everyone treats me different when I'm with you."

Kick drew his warm hand casually, quickly, discreetly over Ryan's.

"Oh how you do me," Ryan said.

Kick handed Ryan a small package. "Open it."

"Here?" Ryan said. The young woman with the family next to them ate with one eye on her entrée and one eye on Kick.

"At least peek," Kick said.

Ryan carefully opened the package. Folded inside, were the specially tailored brown nylon posing trunks Kick had worn in the Mr. San Francisco.

"I want," Kick said, "to give a very special man something more than my company."

Your company's all I want.

Ryan lifted the tiny box to his face and sniffed the musty sweat and olive oil. Kick's posing trunks were the next thing to his nakedness. All of that victorious night's contest came back to Ryan. Kick had posed with passion. He had displayed a grand manliness. His face had radiated a celebratory, voracious love of life. In the intense light of the posing platform, he had been more than Mr. San Francisco. He had been Ra, God of the Sun.

A photograph exists from that night. An essential photograph. Ryan, through his telephoto lens, had his eye focused precisely on Kick. Kick's eye in the photo pierces directly into Ryan's lens. They both had clicked at precisely the same instant. Ryan had submitted the black-and-white shot, blown up poster size, to a Financial District commercial art exhibit. He had won the same first place for his intense shot as Kick had won for his muscle. Ryan had refused to sell the picture. He intended it for use on the cover of *Universal Appeal*.

"I hope you'll add my trunks to your collection of fetish items," Kick said. "Never forget you're my coach, Ry. You're my trainer. You're my main man. You're the one who keeps my machinery oiled. What you and I have is special and not like what we have with anyone else." Kick winked. "Trust me. We've both got to do what we've both got to do."

Ryan wanted to hug him, because Kick seemed to know the reassurance he needed without asking for it.

"Sometimes I get all tangled up in my underwear," Ryan said. "I trust you. I know you." He meant that he understood that they were not losing time together. Each needed some alone-time as much as they needed time with other men.

Kick was not always with Logan. "More often than not," he said, "I'm up at Bar Nada alone. Most guys think I'm just a body. They think I can make them happy. Logan's that way sometimes. I have to teach him stuff you've always known."

"Then I don't have to sue him for alienation of affection?"

"Haven't we always tested ourselves against our best and then reached for something more besides?"

Ryan leaned in across the table. "I know," he said. "I'm not losing you. I'm not losing track of you. You're losing nothing of me."

"I know what we're doing in the long and short run."

"Whatever pace happens between us is okay." Ryan, saying the lyrics from "The Love Theme" from *Superman,* spit in the wind. "When you need someone to fly to, here I am."

"I've flown to you tonight," Kick said. "I want us to be alone. I want to air and vent some of our special physical stuff tonight."

The waiter brought Kick coffee and refilled Ryan's cup. Staring at Kick, he ran it over. "I'm sorry," he said.

Kick ordered half a broiled chicken with the skin removed. Ryan ate chicken paprika, but he could hardly swallow. Kick was perfect. What had he done to deserve such a man? Somewhere in his youth or childhood he must have done something good.

He wrote in his *Journal:*

Tears well up in me sometimes when I look at him, when I look through his surface and see the fineness inside. He has a rich interior life. Once I said to him, "You are so fine, so good, so together."And he said, "Like the company I keep." He knows I love him. He knows I am in-love with him, with his body, his head, his whole being.

He is a particular man I love because he gives me so much access to the universal goodness and beauty I worship. He knows I have done the forbidden thing and have fallen in-love with him; but he knows I'll handle it properly, keep it in check, and never hurt him with it.

"So," Kick said, "what's in the folder?"

"The final draft of *Universal Appeal*. All it needs is your *imprimatur* and your signature on the model release."

"Whatever you write is okay by me," Kick said. "I release me in your life to you."

"I really think you should read it. It's bottom-line stuff. It's about you."

"It's about us. It's about this time in our lives."

"Remember this." Ryan raised a warning finger in jest. "Years from now, when they finally catch us and ask us exactly what we were up to, your story and my story may be wildly different and yet totally the same."

Kick shook his finger back. "But there won't be any villains in either version."

"How could there be?"

A mist, strange for summer, drifted down on the flowers and ferns of the Patio garden. At the next table, the old woman said she was cold. One of the men called for the check. Her family rose to leave. The young woman took one last look at Kick, then helped her mother from the chair. They made a slow procession toward the French doors when suddenly the old woman slipped and fell. Kick turned his head at the commotion. Ryan stood up. Gay men at the nearest tables sprang to their feet to help her. She said she was alright. Her family was full of apologies.

"It must be terrible," Ryan said, "when you're old to know your eyesight is failing and your bones are brittle and you are vulnerable to falling."

"It's the old story," Kick said, "of quality of life versus quantity of life. What is our book about if not that?"

"Just a thought," Ryan said. "I read the other day that Lillian Gish spends forty minutes every day on her upside-down board. She says, 'Time is a friend, but gravity is the enemy.' Sometimes old people grow to a wisdom."

"Ry," Kick said "I've got a brain, but you've got a mind. What are you saying?"

"I'm saying that the point of *Universal Appeal* is the taking of strength training beyond strength to achieve power. Power is the ability to apply strength. That's basically what I've written. That's what I think you've done with bodybuilding. I think that's how far muscle can go. Your physical training has brought you a certain power. You're more than a bodybuilder on Castro. You're more than Mr. San Francisco. You're a symbol."

Ryan unsheathed the manuscript. He told Kick about Emerson's theory of representative men and how a strong presentation of self could aid others in defining their own selves. "The way," Ryan said, "you made me more me."

Kick shook his head. "How could I not love a man who not only teaches me about the Oversoul, but plugs me into it!"

"Take your tongue out of your cheeky cheek."

"Someday I'll figure out how I'm me and more than me," Kick said.

"One thing always means two things." Ryan frowned inside, thinking about the Davies Hall fiasco, but he smiled at Kick the way lovers smile across a small table in a public restaurant, thinking more about the evening sport ahead.

Universal Appeal.

Danger lurked in their project. They had always known it. But they had agreed, that for all their keeping the secrets of their relationship a mystery on the streets of the Castro, the time had come to represent Kick in a way more public than even his physique presentations on stage.

"Privacy," Ryan had once warned, "is the last luxury. That's why I never write autobiography."

Both remembered the night when they had first conceived the book. Kick had shown Ryan pictures taken of him when he was nineteen by a photographer in Florida. Kick, in those teenage snapshots, showed all the potential he later actualized in the medium of his body.

"I've always had so many looks to play with," Kick had said. "So many people think there's something vain about looking good. I was embarrassed in my teens and twenties, because I was overwhelmed. I saw what I looked like, but I wasn't ready on the inside to deal with the physical gifts on the outside. It was a struggle for me to go to my first gym. I knew what might happen. I thought I had potential. My dick in my hand in front of my mirror told me that. I had to get over thinking it was wrong to groom and work with gifts you've been given. I held back from going for it. Finally, I had to. I knew I could be as good as, even better, than guys who were making it with their bodies. I had to work out. I had to go to the gym. A lot of guys train hard because they hate their bodies. Not me. I wanted the challenge, the discipline, the Look of a man with muscle."

He turned the pages in the photo manuscript of *Universal Appeal,* watching his images alternate with Ryan's prose.

"Being a man is the most important thing in the world to me. I wanted to see if I could perfect manhood in myself, for myself, and if other men appreciated it, well and good. I thought maybe there were guys like you. I wanted to see what I was really made of. No one was more surprised than I was the way my body took to training."

He handed the manuscript to Ryan.

"Look at those old snapshots. There's no compromise in those eyes; and there's no compromise in my eyes now.

"I never entered the physique contests until you made me psychologically ready, and I judged my body and Look backed it all up. It's the same way with *Universal Appeal*. I don't think it's wrong to cash in on my Look and your talent for words. I don't think it's wrong to present us properly."

The mist grew heavier in the Patio garden.

"We've gone public with the contests," Kick said. "So what if we make a little money going more up close and personal into this book? I could use it. You could use it. Money could free you up from writing the stuff you write that's too good for those gay rags that pay you next to nothing. You could write novels. You could write screenplays."

"You could play the hero."

"I'm sure January would take a film option on anything you write."

"Kind sir," Ryan said. "My only fear with this manuscript is that it will ruin our privacy. I want you out there, riding the public edge. Everyone on Castro wants to be a star, but you're the only one with real potential." Ryan lowered his voice to a whisper. "I'm selfish. I'm afraid if millions love you, I'll see you even less."

"No matter what happens because of this," Kick said, "I give you my solemn promise. You'll go everywhere with me. We're fellow travelers. We're a high-test blend."

"Promise?"

"Promise." Kick positively grinned over the dishes.

"I never want to walk up to you in some strange restaurant someday and have you introduce me as someone you used to know."

"I need you one hundred percent," Kick said, "and I want you more than need you. That's double-edged quality!"

That's a two-edged sword.

Ryan signaled for the check.

Kick reached for it.

"Let me," Ryan said.

He followed Kick out to the sidewalk. The mist had thickened. All around them umbrellas snapped to bloom in the rain. Kick raised his huge arms to the wet sky.

"This is not rain," he said. "It never rains in San Francisco in the summer." The rain soaked his shirt to a second skin across his shoulders, pecs, and belly. "This is no more than a heavy fog." He hit his famous double-biceps pose. He knew it was Ryan's favorite. "It's never raining rain," he held his powerful stance, "unless you let it." He lowered his arms and pulled Ryan to him in the middle of the sidewalk for all the world to see. "I love you," he said. "Be sure of that."

"I am sure of it," Ryan said.

"I want you to be up. I want you to be happy. I want you to keep on keeping on with me. Trust me. I'm having as much fun as I can possibly stand. I want that for you too."

"Then, I guess, we're ready to publish the book," Ryan said.

They climbed into the cockpit of the Corvette. Kick ran his fingers through his damp hair. It was the gesture Ryan loved best. He put his hand on the nape of Kick's neck. Kick turned full face to Ryan and squinted his sexy grin. He pulled the Corvette out from the curb into a wide U-turn in the middle of Castro and headed back to the Victorian.

Ryan, riding with Kick, never looked out the windows. He twisted almost sideways always watching every powerful movement of the man behind the wheel. Kick handled the car the way a man should drive a car. Ryan watched his perfect profile. His pecs bulged when his hairy arm reached to shift, biceps peaked working the stick, hand square on the wheel, his massive legs, rippling under Ryan's hand through his tight jeans, working the clutch and brake, his head set high on his square neck rising out of his broad shoulders, his blue eyes steely and straight forward, a wet curl of blond hair falling down his forehead, the aquiline straightness of his nose over his luxuriantly groomed moustache, the trace of an intense smile on his lips, the jut of his chin covered with two-days' dark-blond stubble.

Ryan's dick hardened. "Omigod," he said, "do I love you."

Kick reached over and tweaked Ryan's left nipple. Wordless, he drove them through the rain-slick streets, turned the corner and headed up the last hill to the Victorian. He pulled slowly to the curb. For a moment they sat quietly. The City lights shimmering wet below them received dimension from a pair of tennis shoes, tied together with their own long laces, hanging over the middle of the street from a utility wire running to Ryan's house.

"I've always wondered why kids do that," Ryan said.

"What?"

"Tie their gym shoes together and throw them up on the wires. You see it all over town. It must be some sort of teenage ritual." He turned to Kick.

Kick looked straight ahead. "Speaking of rituals . . ."

"What?" Ryan said expectantly.

"Nothing," Kick said. "It's silly. But you're the only one I can tell."

"So tell me."

"Logan . . ."

Ryan had known the sentence would start with *Logan.*

"Logan has his problems."

"So do we all." Ryan was intent on being the generous confidant.

"Sometimes his problems are a problem. Nothing I can't handle. But I don't want him to get out of control."

"What exactly?"

"Sometimes he abuses me."

"Abuses you! Who could abuse you? How?"

"He gets on my case. He says I'm short."

"You're not short. You're perfectly proportioned."

"He means for winning any major physique titles."

"Bullshit."

"I want to go for the Mr. Golden Bear next summer at the State Fair. After that for the Mr. California. I don't need his negativity. That's something I never get from you. You always said I could do anything."

Ryan scored a silent two points for himself.

Kick bucked up. "Don't worry about it," he said. "I'll handle it. Logan has a lot to learn from you." He turned toward Ryan. "I know I have a lot to thank you for."

Ryan reached for the door handle. "So why don't you come on in. You're soaking wet. It's time for us to get down to some serious stuff. Like me scratching behind your ears."

"I wanted to," Kick said "I really wanted us to vent some stuff tonight, some really tough stuff, but it's late."

Ryan's heart dropped. "Forget the stuff," he said ad-libbing, desperately trying to keep Kick from driving into the night. "We'll just go to sleep." Ryan couldn't bear for Kick to be lonely or hurt.

"I think I should head back to the ranch," Kick said. "I can be alone there."

"It's an hour's drive," Ryan said. "Besides, I can't bear a half-empty mattress."

"What can I say?"

"Sometimes the thing to say is don't say anything at all." .

"Believe me," Kick said, "I want to play with you. I want you to play with me. But this is as good. This is fine. This talk has been satisfaction." He put his hand on Ryan's thigh. "I'm not saying *no*. I'm saying not right now."

Ryan so feared the translation of that line, he blurted: "I love you."

"I love you."

"You know," Ryan said, "I sold my soul for you."

"I bought it back for you."

"Then let me pay you back tonight."

Kick smiled and shook his head. "I love you, madman!" Kick leaned into Ryan and kissed him.

Ryan's *Journal* entry for that night read:

His blond moustache met my black one. I turn to jelly, but I don't fall apart. "You're so together," I said to him. "It's okay for you to feel down sometimes. Okay for you to come and go." We held onto each other in his car in the rain. "Someday," I said, "I'm going to hug the shit out of you."

"I sure hope so," he said.

I handed him the manuscript of *Universal Appeal*. I got out of the car and walked to the house. He waited till I opened the door, then he started up the Corvette, saluted from the window, and pulled slowly away from the curb. I stood in the door the way I always do when he drives off, the way I learned from the movies, watching him cruise down the hill until he is out of sight, watching after him as long as I can. I came into the house and put on a video I had shot of his face and paid physical honor to him and me and to us with my cock alone in my hand.

Out of my cuming came my mantra for the evening: "Please, know. Please, know! Please, know!" And I spoke through my tears to his videotaped face. And I meant, please know how much I adore you. You are so valuable to me. You are living proof that all I thought in life that was worthy and noble and classic and ideal is possible. I thought it would never happen, but with you it has. If it takes years of keeping on and keeping up with whatever you need to do, I'll do it, because in relating to you, my relationship to myself becomes better and better and better.

It was a lie. Ryan, in fact, was falling apart.

He was losing his last sense of self.

If he fancied himself a victim of love, he wasn't.

Not really.

He was a victim of entropy.

Of Nights in the Entropics.

Things fall apart.

8

Thom's suicide was as unexpected as all suicides are.

SONOMA COUNTY SHERIFF
INVESTIGATION REPORT

Investigating Officer: Det. Sgt. Mike Flagerman
Complaint: Thomas a'Beckett O'Hara
Address: 3207 Rancho Bar Nada Road
City: Sebastopol, California
Report: Death Investigation

DETAILS OF INVESTIGATION

At approximately 0915 hours, I was informed by Sgt. Gaines that Detectives were needed at the above address to investigate the death of the above who was found hanging in the barn at the residence above called Rancho Bar Nada. I requested that the officer on the scene, Sgt. Bill Harter, Santa Rosa Township Police, contact me telephonically. I later met with Sgt. Harter, via Police Radio and found that there were no working telephones in the residence. Det. Nicholas Darcangelo and myself responded to the location after first notifying Capt. Gil Scott of the Criminal Investigation Section.

Upon our arrival at the residence, at approximately 0935 hours, we were met by P/O S. R. Chase and Sgt. Harter. We observed the interior of the single story main residence and noted the deplorable housekeeping conditions. This condition was found to include not only the living room, dining room, and kitchen area, but the bedrooms and baths. Animal excrement was in evidence throughout the house, and much combustible material was found thrown throughout the entire residence.

Sgt. Harter and P/O Chase then took us to the barn about 100 yards from the house. Part of the barn had been remodeled into living space. Here everything was noticeably clean in contrast to the house. The quarters were dominated by weightlifting equipment of the kind found in a gym. The walls were covered with what are called physique posters. This is where we found the body of the deceased. The deceased, who had been discovered by his sixteen-year-old son, Abraham, had been positively identified as one Thomas a'Beckett O'Hara, male/white, age 36. P/O Chase advised us that the victim's wife, Sandra, and three teenage children had left the main residence and were currently in the mobile home of Ms. Bonnie Holiday. This mobile home, where the estranged Mrs. O'Hara had lived for the last two months, is located in Palm Drive Court, #11, on South Santa Rosa Avenue near the Winners Circle Bar where both Ms. Holiday and Mrs. O'Hara are employed as barmaids.

Inasmuch as Grace Life Squad personnel were still present at the scene, I informed them that the Coroner's Office would make the transportation of the body to the morgue and dismissed them from the area.

Det. Darcangelo took eight black-and-white photographs using a 35 mm camera. All but two of these photographs are close-ups and show knots that were tied in the rope, at the ceiling cross members, and toward the rear of the victim's neck.

The victim was found suspended from a nylon rope (white with blue stripe) of an approximate size of ¼ inch and having a length of approximately 12 feet. The position of the body was found to be as follows: Victim's buttocks were approximately 3 feet from the barn floor. The legs were extended out in front of the body at an angle of approximately 50 degrees with both feet still resting on a black leather covered weightlifting bench. His arms were limp on either side, and his head was pulled upward by the body weight against the rope.

As has previously been mentioned, the rope was knotted behind the victim's skull, and there was a dirt mark at the back of the neck approximately 4 inches below the knot. This appeared to be consistent with the rope being pulled up the back of the neck and onto the head.

Approximately 6 feet of rope trailed loose down the victim's back, off the right shoulder blade. Another 4 and ½ feet was observed going from the knot to the barn's cross members. The rope had been wrapped once across both cross members, and a second knot was observed at the bottom of the wooden cross members.

I examined the body and observed the following. Lividity was observed in both hands from right above the wrists and also in the lower legs and feet. The victim was wearing a Medana brand digital wristwatch on his left wrist. The watch had been programmed to display a timing watch in seconds and did not display hours, minutes, or month, as is customarily used. It would appear that the victim either inadvertently pushed the timer button on the watch or was timing his own death. A gold coin of some religious type was worn on a gold-colored chain around the victim's neck, and the chain had not been disturbed by the rope. The victim was clad in black leather military type combat boots, green fatigue pants, military belt, and was stripped from the waist up.

Although I did not notice any signs of a struggle, I did observe a fresh, bluish scar on the top of the victim's right forearm. A USMC bulldog type tattoo was observed on the left upper arm; two other tattoos were on both lower forearms.

I did not feel any evidence of rigor mortis in the wrist or finger joints. The victim's tongue was partially bloated and extended and appeared to be getting black in color. A search of the barn and the main residence was conducted, but no note was found. We did have pointed out to us by Sgt. Harter as a possible clue to motive, or state of mind, that a stereo phonograph in the barn living space was left playing on repeat, and the record on the turntable was an Eagles' album called *Hotel California*.

Following our examination and photographing of the body, and our unsuccessful search for a note, I contacted Mr. Harris Ragsdale of the Sonoma County Coroner's Office. I supplied the above information to him and requested he dispatch Redwood Ambulance Service to transport the body. We left P/O Chase to protect the scene, and Det. Darcangelo and myself went to the Holiday mobile home to interview family members.

Upon our arrival at the Holiday mobile home, we found several neighbors had already arrived to console the widow. As stated above, Mrs. O'Hara had lived at the mobile home for two months. Three days ago she returned to live at the residence where the incident occurred. Both Det. Darcangelo and I attempted to interview Sandra O'Hara, but every attempt was met with hysterics. I began to gather information from Abraham O'Hara, age 16. I was impressed with his ability to relate information, but I am concerned about his mental state and the trauma connected with finding his father's body. His sisters, Beatrice and Siena, who form a set of triplets with Abraham, seem less affected than does Abraham, and they refused to talk with either Det. Darcangelo or myself.

Abraham explained to me that his mother and father had been arguing at approximately 0530 hours this date and that the argument had been loud enough to awaken all three children. At approximately this time, his father had stopped the argument and told everyone to go back to bed. He stated that he intended to go out to the barn and sit up and listen to the stereo, and at this time everyone did go back to bed. Abraham explained that the ranch belonged to his uncle, his father's older brother, a Ryan Steven O'Hara, who, according to Abraham's account, lives in San Francisco and is homosexual. (This would tend to explain the bodybuilding posters.) R. S. O'Hara uses this living space in the barn only on weekends.

At approximately 0815 hours, Abraham woke up and went to the barn to work out with weights as his father and uncle had often encouraged him to. When he entered the barn, he noticed that the stereo was on so that the automatic turntable arm could play repeatedly, but no music was coming from it. His view of the rest of the room was occluded by a bookcase. When he continued farther on into the room, he found his father hanging by the neck from the overhead beams. He ran back to the main house and woke his mother. She came back to the barn with Abraham and the two daughters. When she saw the body, she screamed. She then hit the deceased repeatedly in the face in an attempt to revive him. From the way the deceased's face was beginning to bruise, she must have hit him more than thirty times. In my experience, the bruises are coincident with blows struck after death and are not evidence in themselves of foul play. When she got no reaction, she brought the children back to the main house and tried to phone for an ambulance. Our investigation showed that the telephone lines outside the main house had been ripped out, most likely by the deceased on his way to the barn. Finding she could not telephone for help, she drove the three children all the way to Santa Rosa and Ms. Holiday's mobile home. She was too hysterical to tell Ms. Holiday what had happened, so Abraham was the one to give her the details.

While Abraham was giving me this information, Sandra would interject comments that corroborated his story. All she would say about the argument was that it had to do with one of the other girls at the Winners Circle. It is safe to say then that the deceased was normal and that homosexuality was not an aggravating cause of death, despite the paraphernalia (bodybuilding pictures, gay videotapes, and homosexual pornographic writing) found in drawers and bookshelves in the barn. These materials, according to Abraham, belong to his uncle in San Francisco.

By way of background, we learned that the deceased had not worked steadily since leaving the military. He and his wife had divorced and remarried twice and had been separated on other numerous occasions. The deceased was a Vietnam-era veteran and had recently been under treatment at the VA Hospital in San Francisco. His brother, the above-mentioned R. S. O'Hara, had permitted the deceased and his family to live rent free in the main house for the last 16 months in return for work on the property. At one point, the deceased had taken a number of his wife's sleeping pills. He was treated for a drug overdose at an unknown area hospital. According to Sgt. Harter, area sheriff's deputies had made several domestic runs to the ranch residence. Sgt. Harter was acquainted with the deceased and, on at least one occasion, had referred him to a friend for a job. He did not like his estranged wife working at the Winners Circle Bar, but she, even while estranged, was basically the source of family income which was also augmented by the deceased's homosexual brother. The deceased rarely drank or used nonprescription drugs. His use of prescribed drugs, however, seems excessive. The drugs collected, issued by the Veteran's Administration Hospital in San Francisco, include Percocet, Valium, Ativan, Darvocet, and Lithobid. This might bear further investigation, but again this is also speculation.

Based upon our investigation, we can find no evidence that would lead to any other conclusion but suicide. It is possible that the deceased had stood on the weightlifting bench and leaned back against the rope until he passed out. This would better explain his feet still being on the weightlifting bench. It does not appear that he jumped off the weightlifting bench. I believe that if the heavy iron bench could have been kicked over or could have slid from under the victim, his feet would not have remained on the weightlifting bench.

Upon the arrival of Redwood Ambulance Service, I cut down the body in the prescribed manner, preserving both knots, leaving the rope attached to the victim, and sent it to the Coroner's Office. Det. Darcangelo and I secured the barn and the main residence at 1105 hours.

Investigation complete pending Coroner's ruling.

Signed: Det. Sgt. Mike Flagerman
lcm

9

Ryan threw Thom's Death Report on the floor. "What the hell does that tell me?" Thom was not yet in the ground. "My brother betrayed me." He harbored that thought accompanying Thom's body all the way back to Peoria. By the time the plane landed on the bone-hot runway, Thom had died of natural causes.

"Remember that." Ryan towered over Sandy and the triplets in their seats.

"Who decided that?" Sandy was indignant.

"Kweenie and I decided that," he said. "Only Annie Laurie knows what really happened."

Sandy Gully smirked. "Except for me," she said. "I'm the one who knows what really happened."

"Shut up," Ryan said. "Just shut up!"

"He killed himself because you made him think he was a fag!"

"He killed himself," Ryan said, "because you never made him feel like a man."

They deplaned in silent détente. Annie Laurie greeted them all with hugs and kisses. Holding her arm was their own priest, her brother-in-law, Ryan's uncle, the Reverend Leslie O'Hara. Father Les had held his good looks, but he was older. They all were suddenly older. From Les's smile and warm handshake, Ryan was sure his uncle remembered their summer mornings of sex in the sacristy.

"I'd like to talk," Ryan told his uncle. He wanted to ask how he could remain a priest in a Church that despised homosexuals, but the chance never came, because neither took it. What was to say? Was the priesthood no more than a good living and a better cover? Ryan guessed that Father Les was the same kind of priest he would have become himself. *We do what we must and call it by the best name possible.* Ryan could not have known then that Death's long slow march would claim the Reverend Leslie Michael O'Hara two weeks after his fifty-first birthday. He was Ryan's uncle and godfather, and when he died, Ryan said, "The men in my family don't seem to be survivors. They may be lucky." He looked distressed. "As God is my witness, I predict I'll probably live too long."

The mortuary drove Thom's body from the Peoria airport to the funeral home where he lay in an open coffin for two days. Sandy bitched he was rouged and powdered all wrong. She wanted to touch him up with Mary Kay. Ryan threatened to break her fingers. The family pasted smiles on their faces. They all stayed with Thom, standing on aching feet, greeting relatives and old friends arriving with their condolences. One, if not all of them, said, "Thank God, Charley didn't live to see his own son die."

His own son!

Ryan suddenly felt a surge of jealousy, something he really never felt around Kick—even since Logan. It was a strange mutant, green emotion. Ryan, firstborn, had always felt like Charley-Pop's real and only son. He didn't think of Thom as Charley-Pop's son. Thom was no more than Ryan's little brother, a tagalong, an afterthought. He could not bear to think that people thought of Thom and him as equals, as a pair, as Charley and Annie's two sons.

Thom had finally upstaged him.

"*De profundis,*" Uncle Leslie intoned. "From the depths, we cry unto you, O Lord." He looked magnificent standing at the head of Thom's coffin. He wore the ironic white and gold vestments of hope. Ryan squinted in the bright summer sun and saw a soft-focus vision of the priest he might have become if he could have worked the accord of conscience his uncle must have found in his closeted service to the narrow tenets of his faith.

The month after good old Uncle Leslie died, Solly Blue received back in the mail the last video brochure he had sent him advertising his tough young hustlers. It was marked *deceased*.

"The Reverend Leslie O'Hara wasn't my best customer," Solly said to me and not to Ryan, "but I like doing business with the clergy. Their checks don't bounce."

The funeral was all too complex; but some things were clear. Ryan saw little need to put his arm around his mother. This wasn't *Imitation of Life*. She wasn't Susan Kohner throwing herself on the coffin. She was Annie Laurie, self-possessed, strong in her own presence. She stood by herself, sad and indestructible, glancing only once at Charley-Pop's grave next to Thom's.

Kweenie was another story. She was swathed in a plastic Myoko dress sprayed with Japanese graffiti. On the plane she had wrapped herself in three antique shoulder-foxes and a long feathered boa. Behind her Yoko Ono shades, her eyes looked permanently bruised. She could not stop crying. Suicide, not abortion, moved her to Drama-Queen tears.

Sandy stood with the triplets directly opposite Ryan and Kweenie and Annie Laurie. She had already run up her charge cards against Thom's life insurance settlement. Abe and Bea and Sie looked for the first time in their lives as if they had stepped out of a bandbox. Sandy had rehearsed the role of military widow often enough to pull it off. If she wasn't exactly Jackie Kennedy receiving the folded flag at the end of the ceremony, at least she remembered the TV-version of national widowhood and didn't embarrass them. If she truly hated Thom's family, the feeling was mutual. Ryan hoped her appearance with them was her last.

Uncle Les wrapped the graveside ceremony. Ryan watched everyone trail down the hill after him. Annie Laurie walked Kweenie to the long stretch limos that waited for the family. Ryan turned to Charley-Pop's gravestone.

"So," he said, "what do you think now about Thom?"

He felt a presence cutting into his back. He turned. It was Sandy Gully. Her face was flushed with more than tears.

"I hate you," she said. "I hate him." She threw a single rose hard into Thom's still-open grave. "I know what you did to him. I know what you did with him. I know what you two did together. He loved you and you treated him like an animal. He said you called him nothing but a breeder. He said you called me a cow. You called my children no-neck monsters right to his face. It's all your fault. He's dead because of you. You killed him. You . . .

You . . ." She searched for the word that Ryan feared she would shout for all Peoria to hear. "You . . . You . . . Intellectual!"

Ryan grabbed her arm and fiercely said, "That's homosexual! That's what you mean. That's what you hate. All you bitches hate it."

"I mean I hate you. I've hated you from the moment we met in the train station. I hate you for being what you are. I hate your whole family. I hate Kweenie. I hate Annie. I hate Charley."

Ryan slapped Sandy hard across the face. She fell backwards on her butt across the mound of dirt covered with green plastic grass. From down at the cortege, no one seemed to notice. The grave diggers, waiting to fill in the hole, turned away and continued their smoke as if nothing had happened. They had seen everything graveside anyway.

"I'll sue you," Sandy Gully hissed.

"You don't have a leg to stand on."

"Help me up!" She eeked a small scream.

"Gladly." Ryan bent over her. He put one hand behind her neck and one behind her waist. "Play it as you lay, my dear," he said. "By now they're all watching us. You look every inch the bereaved widow throwing herself down on her husband's grave." He pulled her to her feet. "Stand up, bitch."

"You fag bastard," she said.

They stood on the edge of the grave holding each other as if they were dancing. Their separate grieving became for a brief moment one. In spite of everything. It wasn't a dislike of women that made Ryan gay. It was, beyond his sexual choice, his claustrophobic fear of the meanness of family life. He pitied men who sacrificed their very selves to be husbands and fathers and ended up, if not dead like Charley-Pop and Thom at an early age, then old and gray and outnumbered, the solitary male chauffeuring a station wagon filled with pinched widows with serious hair.

"I know you loved him," Ryan said.

"I know you loved him too," Sandy Gully said. "I'm sorry."

"I'm sorry too," he said.

She pulled herself loose from Ryan and ran down the hill toward the waiting cars.

Ryan stood alone on the top of the hill at the edge of the grave. Behind him, glorious with Indian Summer, the vast expanse of the Illinois River wound lazily through green trees bordering cultivated fields. Peoria was a river town. Thom was born there. Thom was buried there. Ryan vowed he would not finish his life the same. He shook his head at the irony: it was the straight brother, not the homosexual, who had committed the cliché of suicide. Thom had finally upstaged him in the only way he knew. That was his motive. Ryan didn't need to find any suicide note. They all said it was Nam and Sandy and his kids that caused him to do it. They were right, but they weren't completely right. They didn't know everything. They didn't know about the night Thom, loaded with Kick's primo grass, had stood up from the kitchen table in the Victorian and addressed Ryan and Kick as if he were making a formal speech.

"You two are like a couple of . . . ," Thom was too straight to think of calling them anything else, "kings."

"Kings?" Ryan said. "Thank God, he said *kings*."

Sometimes Ryan talked in front of Thom in the third person.

"You have everything," Thom said. "You do everything."

"We go to all the right parties," Ryan said.

Kick played along. "We take all the right pills."

"See! See!" Thom had said. "That air of superiority. I can't stand it. I can't crack it. I can't quote stuff. I can't make everything a joke." He had slumped back down into the kitchen chair. "What I want to know is this. How can two brothers who start out the same end up so different? One living with the . . . well, uh, it's obvious . . . most handsome man in the world. The other well, that's obvious too. . . ."

Mercifully Thom had left the comparison incomplete.

Ryan looked across the horizon toward downtown. He studied the gothic towers of the hospital where they had all been born and where Charley-Pop had died. Delete one father. Delete one brother. He knew he would not come back to this spot until, sometime in the far-off future, Annie Laurie died. Or he himself died. He heard the grave diggers clear their throats. He took one last look down into Thom's grave and said his last good-bye.

"So long, stupid."

10

By the time Ryan returned from the funeral to San Francisco, he knew he had been too long gone from Kick. He missed the man. If life was short, he wanted sunny California days and endless nights. He had long before given up the bleary life of baths and sex with men who could be anybody.

"But I still defend anonymous sex," he said. "When you're up to here with interpersonal relationships, there's no better balance than making love with a nameless stranger who carries no burden of history."

For almost three years, he had touched hardly anyone but Kick. Their start continued ascendant. Even with Logan fucking around, the more they had of each other the more they wanted.

The night of Ryan's return, Kick pumped out a top-notch musclesex posing scene. He knew Ryan was exhausted. "You strip and lie back on the bed," Kick said. He handed Ryan the can of Crisco. "You don't have to do anything but beat your meat."

Kick grinned and opened a surprise package. He stripped and slowly suited himself up in a professional football uniform complete with pads and cleats and black grease under his eyes. He was a dream of a quarterback. He called out plays and numbers, hiking back, faking a pass. His cleats struck the wood floor. He pounded on his pads. He jumped up on the bed and took a lineman's squat over Ryan's body. The helmet framed his face. The chin strap jutted aggressively forward. Ryan ran his hand over the helmet, the face guard, and out across the pads exaggerating Kick's big shoulders.

Ryan wanted to cum, but Kick backed off and hopped to the floor. He slowed the scene down. He shuffled around the bedroom like it was a locker room. He pulled off his helmet, stripped off his jersey, and unlaced the fly of his tight pants. He reached inside, around his jockstrap, and pulled out his cock. His powerful erection defied gravity. Half-stripped, the bodybuilder jock worked through an Attitude Fantasy, posing, flexing, spitting, pumping his dick, laying strategic pieces of his football gear on the bed around Ryan. His routine made him seem the most generous man in the world. Ryan needed generosity. He needed the Energy Kick put out in their cuming together.

He wrote in his *Journal:*

I didn't want to cum, I wanted my hard-on to last forever. I wanted my own pro quarterback to last forever. A hard dick freezes time solid in a man's hand. There is no before and no after. There is only now. The hard-on is "to be." A man's being is his becoming. He becomes the quarterback. His costume is his reality. His posing is his function. Erection is being. Orgasm is becoming. The act is what it is. In the ritual multiples of male sex bonding, we act out the search for the perfect state of being through the perfect act of becoming ourselves through the other. I became Kick. I became as much a quarterback as he was.

The world is divided into the juicy and the nonjuicy. A man has only so many cumings in him to achieve the perfect state of becoming more himself by becoming for the length of orgasm like the man with whom he is cuming. In other men, a man finds alternatives of his self. Other ways of being. There are so many varieties of masculinity that the search for self through otherness is ongoing and never ending. This is the infinity of men, no two the same, each one ideally more perfect than the last, each one a step on the way toward realizing, toward becoming, toward being the transcendent essence of manliness that men worshiping men require.

The romance of ejaculation is the finite limit of cumings a man has in him to achieve union with the infinite. A man has only so many orgasms. When he spends them, he dies. Each cuming must transcend the last. It's not the quantity of the sex circuit—so many men, so little time—it's more the qualitative ascending spiral of circling and rising to bond with men each more perfect than the last. A man remains juicy as long as his orgasms progress toward this end.

Albertus Magnus, the teacher of Saint Thomas Aquinas, wrote, "Too much ejaculation dries out the body, because the sperm has the power of humidifying and heating. But when warmth and moisture are drawn out of the body, the system is weakened and death follows. This is why men who copulate too much, and too often, do not live long; for bodies drained of their natural humidity dry out and the dryness causes death."

Homomasculinity is a calling to this progressive upgrading of the quality of orgasm. Sin is probably the settling for debit orgasms, orgasms that are not transcendent quality cumings but are only sexual spasms, spasms that do not lift the human spirit, but rather only dry the man out.

Homomasculinity is a vocation as much as any call to the priesthood. Homomasculinists descend from the ancient Druid priests whose ritual predates even the Old Christianity. In the seminary, ninety percent more boys left the twelve-year study for the priesthood than were finally ordained. Over those triumphant ten percent on their ordination day, the bishop intoned: "Many are called, but few are chosen." Profane gay men are men who fall short of the purity of the priestly homomasculinist vocation. They turn from the essential act of worship and communion and degrade the sacred sexual exchange of Energy into no more than a numbers game, a kind of serial fucking as dangerous in its own way as serial murder.

This is why I feel a special responsibility to gay men. We were called to something noble and we allowed it to become trivial. I know the *Manifesto* is pious piffle to these day-trippers. I was once one of them. Kick changed me. He converted me. I know the *Manifesto* is read by men who understand the purity of priapic existentialism. What is, is; and what is, is the hard-on that lasts forever.

I know I've sounded elitist, but no more so than the bishop announcing that few are chosen. I fully realize that in my slamming of gay men, of those many who were called but were not chosen, that I'm actually rejecting in them what I long ago rejected in myself: too much no-count sex, too many drugs, sniffing too many poppers to turn Godzilla into God. No more than Quentin Crisp wants everyone to be an effeminate homosexual do I want everyone to be a masculine homosexual; but like Quentin, I want the boys out there in the streets to know the Way of the Bull, the Alternative of the Animus. I want them to know they don't have to do their Mother's Act, when it's their fathers who are so important. Self-actualization is the only game in town.

The day after Ryan's return from Thom's funeral, Solly called him on the phone. "Remember," he asked, "when we used to laugh at men who walked around with signboards saying 'The End Is at Hand'?" He didn't wait for Ryan's answer. "You've missed the real news while you were back in Central

America. I always call the Midwest 'Central America.' Wait until you hear the latest."

Ryan had heard the rumors of gay cancer, but this was the first mention of GRID. Solly read him the grim facts. Ryan thought of Tony Tavarossi dying in the ICU of San Francisco General. He thought of kissing Tony dying in the ICU of San Francisco General. He thought of Dr. Mary Ketterer saying she had never seen a patient so distressed.

He panicked.

"Don't get your bowels in an uproar," Solly said. "Gay-Related Immune Deficiency is not your fate. It attacks gay men. You've always said you're not gay."

Kick was philosophical. "What men I've had," he said, "are body-builders. They're healthy enough."

Ryan tried to match Kick's power of positive thinking. Kick had not seen the dying face of Tony Tavarossi. Ryan did not want Kick to see his speeding depression. He had to get control both of Thom's suicide and the horrifying news, if it was true, of the plague that stood hungry on their threshold. Ryan left Kick in the Victorian and drove alone up to Bar Nada. He had to escape the City and he knew he certainly had to clean up the mess Thom had made of the ranch. He needed time to think about all that the media was saying about the awkwardly named Gay-Related Immune Deficiency syndrome.

"Be thankful, at least," Solly said, "the press is no longer calling it 'gay cancer.'"

"'Gay-related' sounds so 'cause and effect.'"

"They think only our kind gets it. They're sure our kind started it. Don't you absolutely love the politics of medicine?"

Ryan had agonized through his childhood over polio. Every summer, during the polio season, he woke next to Thom in their bed, and both of them, every morning, immediately touched their chins to their chests and their knees to their chins. As long as they could do that, they knew they hadn't awakened with polio, which struck like a thief in the night. Annie Laurie had been careful. During polio season, she followed all the precautions. Ryan and Thom were not allowed to swim in public pools, which were all closed anyway. Their dental work was never done in the heat of summer. They never ate the ends of bananas even when not exposed through the skin. No one knew from what dark place polio had come. Everything was suspect. Everyone knew someone who was in an iron lung, or worse, dead from polio. Parents were in a panic for themselves and their children. They all believed anything and everything they heard about the dread disease.

Every day the radio and the papers listed the number of polio cases reported in the city, the state, and the nation. The news was clear. People died.

Ryan's heart felt faint. Death, despite Kick, seeped like San Francisco fog all around him. He hid at the ranch for two weeks. He could not tell Kick how depressed the facts on the evening news made him. He was thankful he had holed up so long a time with Kick. He felt consolation that Kick had rescued him from the serial promiscuity he had so eagerly pursued upon his arrival with Teddy from the Midwest. A Channel 9 PBS live special fingered multiple sex partners as the primary cause of contagion.

Serial tricking was exposed instantly as dangerous as serial murder.

Ryan resented the plague. If a man couldn't have the sex he wanted in San Francisco, then everyone should go back home where they came from and pursue the careers they all gave up to follow their dicks around.

Every day the news little by little astounded the City. No one knew what caused GRID. No one knew how to cure it. The one grim fact of agreement was that once a man got it, he died.

On the six-o'clock news, Wendy Tokuda read the day's lead story. "GRID is now AIDS. Acquired Immune Deficiency Syndrome. Doctors at San Francisco General announced today that the City's latest AIDS victim died this afternoon. The patient, whose name was not disclosed, died, the hospital spokesperson said, with more than a thousand diseases in his immune-deficient body. He was the second person to die of AIDS this week in San Francisco where more than 200 AIDS cases have been reported. Nationwide, deaths from AIDS now stand at 22."

"Not counting Tony, and how many others," Ryan said, "who checked out before anyone knew what was happening."

For half a month Ryan stayed at the ranch, cleaning up after Thom and breaking out in crying jags for fear that he might already harbor in his body whatever it was that was attacking them all. He resented cleaning up the broken glass in the main house. He resented the closets with peanut-butter sandwiches stuck to the walls and the blood on the bedroom carpet and the filth in the bathrooms and the animal shit in the living-room shag and the holes pounded in the walls and the French door to the bathroom ripped off its hinges and the torn mesh of the screens where the cats had gained entrance from their nightly prowls.

He resented Thom's dying. He resented his father's dying. No one stood between him and Death but Annie Laurie, and now the news was telling him nothing so much as that he might die before her. He was humiliated thinking that he might die of a gay disease. For one whole day, he actually felt he wouldn't mind dying of anything but a gay disease. He didn't want anybody to be able to say: "He'd be alive today if only he hadn't been gay."

Kick sensed something more was wrong than one of Ryan's famous depressions. He loved Ryan enough to drive up to Bar Nada. Alone.

"Come back to the City," Kick said. He was a knight on a white horse. "You're not writing. You're not around enough for my liking. The Victorian's empty without us both." He followed Ryan from room to room. "If it's this disease thing, you can't hide out. We're safe people. We haven't done anything. You don't have to be afraid of it. That's the worst you could do."

Ryan refused, politely, but refused all the same. "I need some more time up here," he said. "God! I love you!"

"I'll never force you to anything," Kick said. "But I want you to think about me driving you back. I'm going out to the barn and pump up a little on the weights."

"Please, don't," Ryan said.

"Why not? If I get a good pump, maybe we could play a little."

"Nobody's been out to the barn since Thom died."

"Somebody's got to go out there sooner or later. Death's nothing," Kick said. "Somebody's got to bring life back to the space."

"If anybody's got the life force," Ryan said, "you have."

Kick walked out to the barn. He had hoped Ryan would follow. After an hour, he came back. "Where were you?"

"I couldn't," Ryan said. "I promised I'd never say *no* to you, but I couldn't."

What he meant was that he was desexed by fear.

"I'm a safe person," Kick said. He moved in close to Ryan and held him in his big arms. "Let me hold you," he said. "Just hold you."

"I love you," Ryan said. "I love you so much. These are the best years of our lives. I don't want either of us to die."

"We're safe, Ryan. Listen to me. We're not going to die. I won't let you. I need you too much."

"Give me a couple of days," Ryan said, "to get hold of myself."

Ryan stood on the deck and watched Kick drive away until the red Corvette disappeared over the crest of the hill. "I will get a hold of myself," he said.

That night on television, there was a clip of Henry Fonda reading lines from William Faulkner's novel, *Sartoris*. "Ever' now and then," Henry drawled, "a feller has to walk up and spit in deestruction's face, sort of, for his own good. He has to kind of put an aidge on hisself, like he'd hold his ax to the grindstone. . . . If a feller'll show his face to deestruction ever' now and then, deestruction'll leave 'im be twil his time come. Deestruction like to take a feller in the back."

"I'm safe," Ryan said. "Death comes like a thief in the night. As long as you expect it, you're safe. As long as I expect to die, I won't." He started to cry. "Why is there a reverse spin on everything?"

The next day, on impulse, he drove back to the City. He wanted to surprise Kick.

The surprise was on him.

Logan sat shirtless in the living room of the Victorian. "I've been staying here while you've been gone," he said.

"I told Logan you wouldn't mind," Kick said. "I'm glad you're back." He hugged Ryan.

"It's alright," Ryan said. *Why didn't you tell me?* He felt safe in Kick's embrace. "Everything's going to be alright."

"Check it out, man," Logan said, "I have to go back to like, you know, San Diego for awhile."

Thank God and Greyhound! You're gone!

Ryan and Kick were together again. Only Kick stood between Ryan and the blues. Everyone knew someone who knew someone who was sick. The news was alarming. In the weeks that followed, those who became sick died quickly. A momentary pall fell across the bars and baths. Some men stopped going out. Some stopped having sex altogether. Some suddenly found a new spark in an old lover's safe eyes. Some tried having what came to be called safe sex where partners were careful not to exchange fluids.

"How," Solly screamed, "can it possibly be sex if you don't for godsake exchange fluids!"

A sizable group simply denied the syndrome's existence.

"It's their civil right," Solly said, "to suck and fuck in dark back rooms."

"This plague," Ryan said to Solly, "has made you a sage."

"I've always been a sage," Solly said, "and a legend in my own mind."

"They're calling this a gay disease."

"They're calling it everything, because they don't know anything. As usual, they emphasize our differences from them. They've always been jealous we have more sex than them. I find it all amusing."

"Amusing? People are dying."

"Considering the crowd you used to run with, I'm sure your Rolodex reads like *The Book of the Dead*," Solly said. "I'm not changing anything. I've never fucked with faggots anyway. I much prefer my straight boys sitting on my face."

"Funny," Ryan said. "Faggots used to feel immortal."

"Except when they feel like Camille."

"How times change."

"Blame Harvey Milk. He died."

"Blame Harvey? My God, he was murdered."

"Aren't most homosexuals murdered? One way or another? Harvey made dying fashionable. At least in San Francisco. No faggot has yet written a book or a play about Mayor Moscone. How soon we forget. We only dramatize the kind of Death that interests us. Death is so romantic. Byron, Shelley, Keats. All the rock stars who die at an early age. Faggots only want one thing in life. . . ."

"Stop it."

"They want to die before their faces fall. Do you know what comes after Oil of Olay? Surgery of Olay. Then Embalming of Olay."

"Maybe Kick's right about you."

"That would be a point in his favor."

"He says you care too much about gay politics."

"Me? Not me. He means you. He talks that way. I've noticed. By indirection. That's how he controls you."

"Stop sniping at him."

"He means you care too much about gay politics. I don't even recognize gay politics. Whatever that is. I moved to San Francisco long before gay liberation. Whatever that is. I've watched what's happened to the City."

"Guys are dying. That's what's happening."

"Remind me to update my mailing list."

"Go ahead play tough guy. You'd feel different if you ever left this penthouse."

"I refuse to go out. It's one of my more wonderful affectations. It's no surprise to me that Kick hates me. I don't trek out daily to a gym."

"Kick doesn't hate anyone."

"Sorry, I forgot. Saint Kick doesn't hate anyone. He only preens himself shirtless on Castro for the passing faggots'—excuse me, homomasculinists'—edification." Solly laughed. "Lighten up, Ry," he said. "I know you're his high priest." Solly insinuated himself. "By the way, I was wondering, where's the other altar boy? The tall, dark, handsome, muscular one?"

"Logan's in San Diego. Kick's been staying up at the ranch, helping get the place back together. He's been up there three weeks."

"You mean he's been missing his personal appearances on Castro?" Solly said.

"God, you're a bitch."

"Don't be gay."

"Kick is a picture of health on Castro. He's what we need now."

"The world hardly needs another hustling prick-tease."

"I'll let that go by."

"So when did he last lay you?"

"He drove in three nights ago. We had a seance. He drove back up the next morning."

"Absence makes the heart grow fonder." Solly flipped the coin. "Out-of-sight out-of-mind." He took a long drink of Coca-Cola. "I'm feeling biblical."

"That empty aphorism isn't biblical."

"This great gay plague is positively biblical. Where's C. B. DeMille now that we need him?" Solly relentlessly tongued his cheek. Ryan fell for the game. "It's all predicted in *Revelations*."

"You don't read the Bible."

"I certainly do. Like the great W. C. Fields, I look for loopholes."

"Asshole."

"Are these Castro boys stupid? It's all in the Bible. Don't they read the Bible? Jerry Falwell reads the Bible. I'm waiting for a gay boutique to silk-screen some tee shirts with the slogan: 'I Kissed A Kaposi's Victim and Lived.' Your gay boys will merchandise anything."

"Don't make light of this. Castro has become the set for a remake of *The Andromeda Strain*."

"If you want to know the real politics behind the plague, I'll tell you how faggots acquire their immune deficiencies."

"Six people I know have died. And one good friend. I kissed him good-bye in the ICU at San Francisco General."

"I'm touched," Solly said, "by your cheap emotion. Disease has made you significant. I bet you boys score body counts over brunch at the Norse Cove."

"Score?"

"About how many victims you've kissed good-bye. Exactly the way you've always kept score at Sunday brunch about how many nameless numbers you'd balled at the baths the night before."

"Why do I listen to this?"

"Because," Solly said, "you have all the superstition of a baptized Catholic. Because you love fire-and-brimstone scenarios. Because suffering and dying from gay cancer, or GRID, or AIDS sounds like a call to gay martyrdom. Because the vision of being tortured naked in hell forever by Lucifer, the most beautiful of all archangels, gives you a hard-on. That's why gay men need S&M."

"Can you lay off me for all the sins of Catholicism? I'm no Catholic!"

"Deny it thrice before the cock crows."

"Where did all this bitterness come from? It's not like you."

"If you're not a Catholic, then you've only exchanged religion for politics. Didn't all our parents warn us never to discuss religion or politics? They knew sooner or later both would come down to a third subject they never discussed: sex."

"Don't scare me," Ryan said.

"I'll scare you if I think it's good for you, Ry. Do you want to know what I think is the truth?"

"I'm not sure."

"I think the Moral Majority's Final Solution is blowing germs, developed by the CIA, into the ventilating systems at the bars and baths."

"You're hysterical."

"First they tried a strain of something nasty out in Philadelphia on a bunch of old farts at a Legionnaire's Convention. That was the control group. The first stage. The media handled it okay. Don't tell me you're so naive politically to think that if there is an undesirable group in American society that certain powers-that-be wouldn't wipe them out if they could? Don't tell me that the CIA wouldn't create a chemical, viral Auschwitz. Faggots own too much property and are politically too threatening. We're the new Jews. Reagan hates us. AIDS will always be Reagan's disease."

"You have no proof."

"Precisely. There is no proof. They're committing the perfect crime. They're tricky. I mean everyone knows that Reagan's son is gay. . . ."

"That's conjecture."

"Look how they've handled him. They hired him a wife. They keep her on retainer. Everything you read about him, and how he gave up dancing with the Joffrey Ballet, only needs to have the word *homosexuality* inserted for *dance*. Oh my, yes! As in, 'From the graceful movements of his early youth, anyone looking at Ronnie Reagan could see his propensity toward . . . *dance!*'"

"Get me a shovel!"

"You know what this Christian country really feels about us."

"I don't believe you."

"You'd better believe me. Everyone believes Jews."

"Now who's the bigot?"

"We're all Jews, Ry. Don't you see? We gays have become a problem the way we Jews in Germany became a problem, but we won't shut up, and they can't kill us outright in camps. We're related to too many straight people who'd object. Besides, the human rights front is too strong in this hemisphere. So they've instigated a medical problem to decimate homosexuals."

"It's a good thing you stay home. You'd create hysteria in the streets."

"There's always hysteria in the streets." Solly was severe. "Let me paraphrase you to you. I may not agree with all you've said and written, but I remember it all." He stood up and stood over Ryan. "What about all your radical politics? Your politically correct lesbians? Your feminists? Even your corny masculinists? You, my friend, are right up there with the lunatic fringe of sex politics that has ruined gay liberation. You will bring down the house on the rest of us little queers who just want to suck cock." Solomon Bluestein was genuinely dismayed. "*Politically correct.* I love that knee-jerk jerk off phrase. You want to know what's politically correct? I'll tell you. What's politically correct is what the government thinks is politically expedient. That and nothing else."

"You should move to Berkeley."

"Ah, to be in Berserkely now that plague is here." Solly was relentless. "Do you remember Reagan when he was governor in the sixties? When he was confronted with all the student protests at Berkeley, he said, 'If there's going to be a bloodbath, then it might as well begin now. Let's get it over with.'"

"You are so amusing," Ryan said. "So very amusing. I love it. But you're wrong."

"I'm wrong?"

"The plague is not a government plot. Homosexuals are all much too delicate for this planet. We have no immunity to its ills and woes."

"You're too New Age in an age that is not new. It's prehistoric."

"Bullshit."

"You're much too cosmic about everything."

"That's why I came to California," Ryan said.

Solly despaired, pacing the room, straightening lamps and ash trays. "Actually," Solly said, "I alone know what AIDS really is."

"What is it?" Ryan said.

"Identity. Acquired *Identity* Deficiency Syndrome."

Ryan pulled a bottle from his leather jacket. "Here's two Valium."

"Thank you. I love downers." Solly swallowed the blue pills with a slug of Coca-Cola. "Don't go. Not quite yet. I have a favor to ask. I want you to take something home with you. One of my boys left it here. I don't want it around." Solly reached into a drawer. "Too much can happen when hustlers come in and out of my penthouse night and day."

He handed Ryan a .22.

With just so easy a gesture, a gun entered Ryan's house.

Blind Parents Raise Invisible Child

1

On 18th Street, Kweenie took over the small stage at Fanny's, a petite supper club catering to gay men with a penchant for *chanteuses*. For six weekends she had played to capacity crowds at the tables, and standing-room only at the bar. She was no longer playing somebody else. She was playing herself, well, almost herself, sounding breathily expansive as her current idol, Bette Midler.

"I've seen," she said in her low stage voice, "the ambiguity of feeling in lovers' eyes." Her long-nailed fingers fanned past her face. *Piano soft.* "I dreamed in a dream I saw a city of lovers invincible. Oh, yes, I have. Where simple men can kiss good-bye on a pier—you know about piers—and never say good-bye. Why? Because one lover is the moon and the other is the sun." She looked down at Kick and Ryan. "This next song—my little art song—is for a special pair of manfriends, and for all you lovers out there who disappear into your lover."

Her voice became hypnotic and dreamy. "You live to make your lover shine, because you really love him, because he really loves you. You look at each other and wonder who is the lover and who is the beloved."

She locked eyes with Ryan. "You wonder what your lover thinks." *Piano up. Soft intro.* "You wonder who will be the worshiper and who will be the hero, who will be the high-flying adored. I hear you ask, oh, I hear you ask at close of day, are you the new person drawn to me? Are you the gentleman I was expecting? Travelers together. You don't ask who will go and who will stay. You just keep on keeping on."

Over the soft tinkle of silver service on china plates, she sang the plaintive lyrics. "We two boys together cling. Arms around each other's necks."

She held the mike close to her bosom with one hand and gestured to Kick with the other. "One the other never leaves. The man who loves me whom I love."

She was beseeching Kick to say to Ryan those words she knew he needed to hear before it was too late.

"Never parting the parting of dear friends." She moved to the edge of the stage. "Ascending to the atmosphere of lovers." Her voice rose, glorious, engaging the lyric with true emotion. "Whoever you are. . . ." She loved the ambiguity. "Whoever you are. . . ." She was singing as much to the brother she idealized as she was singing for him to Kick, whom she loved, and for Kick to Ryan.

". . . holding me now in hand, carry me . . ."

A heartfelt passion came into her husky voice. ". . . when you fly up over land and sea." A silence washed across the room. "We two boys together cling." Waiters stopped at their stations. Dessert spoons rested on plates. Kweenie could not hold back real tears.

"Touching you would I sleep. Not touching you would I die."

She thought of herself, and what Ryan had made her to be. She thought of the successes Kick always said were Ryan's too.

"Carried away eternally."

Something deep within her feared for her brother's very life. She saw Ryan's hand resting on the white tablecloth. "Whoever you are holding me now in hand. . . ." She saw Kick catch her drift. He took Ryan's fingers into his own.

"Whoever you are holding me now in hand, carry me, in your arms tightly pressed, into the splendor of night."

Kick became the splendor. He became a god, rising up on Kweenie's voice, sailing over the heads at the tables, soaring up through the dissolving ceiling, flying through the opening roof toward the moonlit night, defying gravity, defying space, circling ever upward magnificently, almost asleep on the wind, with Ryan, himself light as thin air, following, rising in updraft, invisible almost, lovely as a rising wisp of cloud riding ever upward beneath the moon.

Kweenie held the house in the palm of her hand.

Noel Coward once said, and he included songs as wry as his own, "It's extraordinary how potent cheap music can be."

2

American masculinity makes life very difficult for two men trying to love one another. American women who have trouble with American men might gain some insight from seeing man-woman problems compounded man-to-man, particularly with Ryan and Kick. For my part in all of this, my intent is not to ridicule all desire, but to examine its effect on the human heart.

Love, you see, ambushed them.

They knew they had come to the end of something the Sunday afternoon they lay in the warm grass of the Eureka School Playground outfield. Over the rooftops the noisy roar of the Castro Street Fair wafted on the late summer breeze. Kick had come down from a two-month stay at Bar Nada. Ryan noticed immediately the change in his face. He was drawn. He looked tired.

Tired? Evita tired?

Kick's fatigue broke the brilliant display of his self-defense. His perfect body armor of muscle could not hold back his depression. Logan was wearing him down. Ryan felt sadly triumphant. Kick was experiencing from the inside out the sadness he had always told Ryan was too gay.

They lay on their bellies at right angles facing each other, their heads nearly touching. Kick pillowed his chin on his crossed arm. Ryan matched his move. The Gay Marching Band struck up "If They Could See Me Now."

Kick managed a half smile. "Boy," he said, "if they could see me now. I'm sorry, Ry. We're used to ethyl, and I'm only pumping out regular."

"I can run on regular," Ryan said.

"I can't always be the bodybuilder."

Ryan saw his chance to score one for the home team against Logan. "You don't have to always be the bodybuilder. Not with me. I long ago got around all that." This was his chance to drive home his value to Kick in more ways than in bed. "I love our fantasies, but I love the real you more." Through the chink in Kick's armor, he hoped the truth he had told him so many times would finally, really register. "You're a person, not a monument."

"I love you." Kick was floundering. "I really do."

"What's wrong?"

"Do you know what it's like to have everyone wanting to touch you, and for there to be hardly anyone you want to touch?" He touched Ryan's high forehead. "Of course you do," he said. "I see people touch you when we're out."

"Hardly because I look like you."

"Not on the outside," Kick said. Fine tears welled up in his blue eyes. Ryan had never seen Kick cry. Not even when his father died. Ryan sank his chin deeper into the lawn. He made the blades of outfield grass taller than his eye level. Kick's pain was almost too much for him to watch.

Kick had not accepted his father's sudden Death. It weighed on him almost as heavy as Charley-Pop's lingering Death on Ryan. But it was more than his father.

The bank in Birmingham had tied up his trust fund.

And then there was Logan; some vague trouble that Ryan knew had long been brewing.

But Ryan, and this was part of the secret of his successful intimacy with men, never asked questions. He disciplined himself to a priestly patience and waited until the information, he in truth out of curiosity was dying for, was simply confessed.

"I love you." Ryan primed the pump.

"I love you."

"I love you, Billy Ray, more than anyone."

Kick looked a bit shocked hearing his own real Southern Baptist name.

"Life isn't always up," Ryan said. "God! You know I know that. It's okay for you to come down off the posing platform. It's okay for you to be tired."

"I shouldn't have come down from Bar Nada this weekend." He hesitated. "But sometimes things get a little out of control up there."

"Things have always gotten out of control up there. I think there's a curse on the place."

"No," Kick said. "Bar Nada is a wonderful place. It's me, I guess."

Ryan felt a competitive surge. He could beat Logan's big muscles if only he could be equally somehow larger than life. He had only words, but words were his strong suit.

"I may not have eighteen-inch biceps," he said, "but my arms are big enough to hold you." He caught himself. He remembered his own claustrophobia from Teddy's holding onto him. "I mean big enough to embrace you."

"You're the biggest man I know," Kick said. "Honestly."

"Honesty is all we've got going." Ryan ached to tell Kick how hurt he was by his long absences. He ached to tell him how foolish he was to waste precious time on Logan. He ached to tell Kick that he was in-love with him and that it was time for Kick to respect that and not deny it. But he did not. He did not lie exactly; rather, he dissembled: that quality of saying the almost-whole truth, and nothing but the almost-whole truth, that the other party wants to hear as the whole truth.

"I wouldn't trade this moment," Ryan said, "for six of our usual nights, wonderful as they are. We're beginning to touch each other." He grasped for straws. "We're not even stoned."

"Maybe we should be."

"No," Ryan said. "We don't need drug energy. We need our Energy. Sometimes emotional exhaustion, exactly like muscle failure at the gym when your muscles get so tired you can't grind out another rep, is necessary. Without that final exhaustion rep, the muscles won't grow."

The heart won't grow.

"But I hurt," Kick said.

I hurt too.

Ryan felt something pass over the playground, something like the shadow of a hawk, something like the Nameless Dread he had felt all his life in his own heart, something now stalking Kick himself.

"Trust me," Ryan said. *Logan.* "Through all this. Trust me. You always said we were safe people for each other. I won't hurt you. Why would anybody ever hurt anyone else like that? Don't retreat from me." *Don't go back to Bar Nada.* "Don't retreat from anyone." And he meant Logan. "Especially not ever from me. I'll never crowd you. You know that." He flicked an ant, lost in the blond fur on Kick's arm, into the grass. "You and I both worship the same concept of manliness. You happen to have it incarnate in your body. That's a hard gift. I worship that in you the way you worship it. But beyond that, leaving go of that, I know the difference. I love you, the private real you, wherever you are inside that face and body."

"You can't know what it's like," Kick said.

"I'm finding out. Someday I'm going to write a book called *The Other Side of Death in Venice.* It'll be Tadzio's story. No one has ever considered the psychology of blonds beloved by dark men." Ryan ran his hand through Kick's thick blond hair.

"After all this time," Kick asked, "am I still so blond to you?"

"Fair is fair," Ryan said.

For all his fatigue, Kick lay splendid in the grass. His current sadness detracted little from his Look. If he was not a god come perfectly incarnate to Earth, he looked at least as if some advanced interstellar scanner had computed the ideal male form from all of Earth's sculpture and painting and then filled out that form with shining golden protoplasm from some pleasant alien star.

"I wish this pain would pass," Kick said. "This never happens to me."

How can you let Logan call the shots?

"It's happening now," Ryan said. "Maybe it's good it's happening now." *God knows I'm an expert when it comes to depression.* He never felt more like a father-confessor than at this moment lying in the grass.

Ryan later wrote:

Maybe this is one of the few honest-to-god human things I can do for him, something no one else has done: simply be, be there, be present, when these moments knock him flat. There's no denying them. People flicker through life's flashes all the time refusing to acknowledge the darkness between the frames of intense light. The darkness, too, is intense. Sometimes people make it to midlife without saying, "Okay, this is what is." They think they're never going to have to face some pretty unpretty stuff, and then, when they least expect it, some evening after supper when they're carrying out the garbage, between the third and second step from the bottom, the full dark Nameless Dread of what they've so long refused to admit existed hits them. They break down. They go to pieces. The light that shone so brightly while they were very, very, very young begins to dim as the clock ticks the dimmer down, and even the most golden see how ultimate is the darkness.

"Somehow," Kick said, "so many guys think I'm responsible for their happiness."

Ryan knew he meant Logan, but the guilty flee when no one pursues. "I'm responsible for my own happiness. We're all responsible for our own happiness."

"Exactly," Kick said. "No one needs the burden of keeping someone else happy." He meant even more than Logan; he meant half of Castro. He was a popular man. Guys imitated his Look. They tried to dress like him, to walk like him, to workout like him. They cut their hair like him. They wanted to be him. Ryan recognized the adulation other men gave Kick. He himself, at least every other day, wanted to be, if not Kick, then like Kick. All their time together had made Ryan's starving want a hunger, an endless, aching need; but he kept it under control. "And all this gossip," Kick said, "that I may be from another planet."

"How California!"

"I can't believe guys are walking around thinking that may be true."

"Where could they have gotten that?" Ryan feigned Ah-do-declare innocence. "Those clever Castronauts will believe anything."

"They better get over it," Kick said.

Ryan looked hard at Kick, the way Star Children dropped down from some other galaxy might almost recognize in each other the echoes of their disremembered home star.

"Is it true?" Ryan dared finally blurt the question directly. "Is it true? Maybe you can't tell me. Maybe you don't quite remember." He was awash in a wave of vague homesickness. "You know I recognized you the moment I met you. I know you're you. We both know you're something else besides." Ryan was deadly serious but he covered himself by tickling Kick in the ribs. "You must tell me. I need to know. I need to know if you've come from some other star to make me one of the boys?"

"Please don't try to humor me," Kick said. "I'm not up to teasing."

"Me tease you?" Ryan said. He backed off to the fixed dissembling distance and pulled out the kid gloves Kick required.

Kick was who he was, and that was his attraction. He was himself. He never tried to be someone else on the street where Attitude, being something other than real self, was all the vogue.

"I sometimes wish I was ugly." He choked. He recovered quickly. "I wouldn't know how to live life if I was ugly. But what am I supposed to do," Kick said, "when my Look seduces men without me even trying to seduce them?"

"Enjoy it."

"How can I enjoy it when they say I make them unhappy because I never go with any of them?"

You've gone with a few. With one too many.

"I don't know," Ryan said. Who could have figured there was a curse on the diamond of sex appeal? "I can only wonder what it must feel like to be able to walk up to anyone and have them."

"I don't want anyone. I hardly want anybody."

Ryan felt him slip a notch away.

"Too few men hold up in intimate contact." Kick smiled. "You hold up. You don't ask questions."

"I have a caution," Ryan said, pulling Kick back towards him, "about our book. I think we better put *Universal Appeal* on the back burner. At least for a while."

"I think you're right," Kick said. "I'm not all that ready to go that public at the moment. I can't function that way. I'm tired of being everybody's good example. I don't want it backfiring on me."

January's special caused enough trouble, huh? "When the time is right," Ryan said, "we'll do it."

Kick rubbed the back of his hairy forearm across Ryan's lips. "We have all the time in the world," he said.

Three blocks away, under the ticking clock on the Hibernia Bank, a cheer welled up from the Castro Street Fair where the crowds, shoulder to shoulder in the streets, pushed and shoved and cruised, laughing, shouting, stoned, and dancing to the music from the bandstand set up in the street near the marquee of the Castro Theatre. The party went on without them.

"I guess we're missing all the fun," Kick said. "I want to keep on having as much fun as we can possibly stand."

"Are we having fun yet?" Ryan asked.

"We've always had fun. The best fun."

They both sensed their relationship had clicked another notch toward something unknown.

"We don't see each other as much," Kick said, "but when we do, we pick up where we left off. We're good together. The best."

He stood up against the western sun. His shadow dropped Ryan into cool eclipse. He reached out his hand and pulled Ryan to his feet.

"The next time," he said, "I promise not to be so down."

Ryan hugged him.

"One other thing," Kick said. "Logan came back from San Diego last Monday. He closed out his apartment here before he left. I knew you wouldn't mind if I let him come up and stay with me at the ranch."

Ryan's heart sank. He knew he could not say what he wanted to say, so he said, "Of course, I don't mind. You and I both know what we're doing in the long and short run."

"Trust me," Kick said. "Trust me to do right by you always."

"I love you," Ryan said. "How could I not trust you?"

3

The late California autumn came down upon them in a fall of colors. Everywhere the talk was of AIDS. Monday morning in the offices of San Francisco the phones rang from company to company as gay men called each other to tally up who they had heard in the weekend bar gossip had come down with the plague. Private sex had become dangerous enough. Public sex had become a scandal. Disease brought more controversy. Politics entered the bedroom. Gay sex had finally scared the horses.

The baths became a civic issue. The Mayor's office had a tiff with the director of public health. Madame Mayor wanted the baths closed, but the director was against it. The woman was pitted against the man, and the man resigned. Gay activists rallied around constitutional rights, fearing if the baths were closed that a new era of repression would next close the bars and eventually the gay press.

Auschwitz was around the corner from 18th and Castro.

The real breach in the civil war between gays was between those who favored civil rights and those hysterics who chose a medical quarantine for health. Who was right? Who was wrong? Who could say in the disfiguring face of the A-Word? The truth was, straight San Francisco grew frightened of the gays in their midst. They feared for the purity of the City blood supply in the local banks. They sounded like Nazis worrying about the purity of Aryan blood. But the gays would be nobody's Jews. They marched against bath closure in Harvey's name. The baths shut temporarily, then reopened with safe-sex guards patrolling the halls to prevent exchanges of bodily fluids. The Marx Brothers could have starred in an impossible new comedy: *A Night at the Baths.* Attendance dipped, then rose slightly, and leveled. Sex became even more than ever an ironic denial of Death. The late-night back rooms, never ready to say die, invented Safe-Sex Jerk Off Nights. Free condoms. The bars stayed busy as ever.

Kick, two days after the Castro Street Fair, had fled the Castro for Bar Nada. The City and the plague were too much for him. Every two weeks or so he drove to the Victorian to let himself go, to vent the kind of sex he could have only with Ryan.

Between times, Ryan pined away, his depression deepening, keeping himself sane by beating himself to orgasm with Kick's image before him, posing in slow motion on the video screen.

Half a loaf was better than none.

Ryan was preparing the Christmas issue of *Maneuvers* when the doorbell rang. It was late on the Wednesday night before Thanksgiving and he was expecting no one. He was doubly surprised when it turned out to be Kick standing on the doorstep of the Victorian with his suitcase in his hand.

"I've come back from the ranch," Kick said. The implication which Ryan could neither acknowledge nor question was that Kick's affairette with Logan was over.

"Where will you stay?" Ryan asked. He knew the answer.

"Birmingham," Kick said. It sounded like a major threat. "Unless you let me stay here with you."

Ryan could not help but think he had won. He was like the long-suffering wife in so many Warner Brothers movies, bearing up courageously while her husband took a ridiculous header with some bimbo showgirl.

"It worked off and on for a couple of months or so," Kick said.

"Where is he now?" Funny that neither one mentioned Logan's name.

"He's still at the ranch. He has no place to go. I told him you wouldn't mind if he stayed there till after New Year's."

Ryan had avoided the ranch since the first days after Thom's Death. He hardly wanted to spend the holidays at the scene of the suicide.

"I knew you wouldn't want to go up there now."

"It's okay," Ryan said. He would have agreed to anything to have Kick back in his bed for Christmas.

"I need to come back to hit the gym. I want to get into top shape again. There's the Mr. California contest in the spring."

"Mr. California," Ryan said. "I like the sound of that."

"I need you to help psych me up for it," Kick said.

"I need you," Ryan said. "This AIDS thing is killing me. But why should it? I'm not interested in anyone but you."

"We're not exposed," Kick said. "For the last three years, who've we had sex with? Hardly anyone."

"When you're not here, I want you. When I can't have you, I think about cruising the bars, but I don't because I don't want anyone but you and even if I did, I wouldn't, because for the first time in my life strangers scare me."

"It'll be like old times," Kick said.

He hoped that Kick's revolving relationship with Logan was over for good. He was no fool. He was determined to be gentlemanly. If Logan had been good for Kick for a while, then he deserved at least to have a place to stay until after Christmas. Besides, Ryan had long before learned never to say anything about the absent party when a couple was breaking up, because if they kissed and made up, as often happened, they'd both hate you for anything you said. So Ryan stayed silent, even though he wished Logan dead: first for taking Kick away from him so often, and then for treating Kick badly.

"My New Year's resolution is to take possession of the ranch again." Ryan made his intention clear. "He can stay there for a while."

"It's better to have someone there than to have the place stand empty," Kick said. "Besides, he has some business to finish. When that's done, he'll leave."

"What business could he possibly have?" Ryan asked.

Kick beamed a surprise. "He's been growing pot in that old greenhouse behind the barn."

Ryan was shocked. "We could all get arrested!"

"It was my idea too." Kick softened the news. "I figured we could make a little money on the side. He knows all about cultivation. I told him we'd divide the profit three ways."

"Three ways? Why three ways? I'm not involved No way!" *I hate three-ways.*

"I helped him remodel the greenhouse. He's been tending the crop since late summer. Besides, the place is yours. You have a right to get what's coming to you as the owner."

"We're all going to end up in jail."

"Don't worry about it," Kick said. "We got a late start in the season, so we'll have a late harvest. But I guarantee you it will be ready right after New Year's. He's rigged up a high-tech grow-light system. You could use the money, right? He knows how to unload it. He has connections to sell it in San Diego. He figures a late crop will bring more because the earlier crops all had to compete with each other. There's always scarcity after the holidays." Kick smiled his killer smile. "It's okay, isn't it?"

Ryan could refuse him nothing.

4

He wrote in his *Journal:*

I wonder why I can't say *no*. I wonder why I don't say what I really want to say. I know why. I love him. I want to live for him. I want to give myself up to him in sweet, sweet surrender. I want to be everything he wants me to be. I know that's sick in a way, but, God knows, I'm bent, sick, and twisted.

The nuns wanted me to be pure.

The priests wanted me to be holy.

My father wanted me to be athletic.

My mother wanted me to be myself.

All these people knew about sin, but only my mother knew about real sin. As a girl she had learned that she had best live for her husband. Luckily, Charley-Pop was the man of her dreams. Even so, she always said she wouldn't jump off a bridge because everyone else was, and the arch of her finely plucked eyebrow intimated that "everyone else" also included Charley-Pop. She always did as she pleased, and that pleased Charley who felt it was his husbandly right to encourage his wife. Annie Laurie was headstrong but not willful. She was independent but not mean. She was religious but not superstitious.

She thought most women were silly, dishonest things who lied and connived their way through their husband's suit pockets looking for spare change. She had many women friends, but she also had ideas about the way women should ideally be. Something in her style taught me early on that the worst thing anyone could do was not be themselves, and that the worst offenders of this commandment, which was my mother's commandment, were women.

The nuns, women themselves, made her seem correct. They taught me that young Catholic girls were a source of temptation to sins of sexual impurity. Maybe they were lesbian nuns. Anyway, I never really understood that, because wait as I might for it to happen, girls, Catholic or otherwise, never materialized as objects of desire.

Then, from my mother, I discovered that she found the worst kind of female trouble to be women's sin of self-denial. Naturally, I came to think of most women as examples no man should imitate.

Charley-Pop, on the other hand, reinforced the nuns and the priests. They all talked about my becoming a man, but their talk was all abstractions and mortal sins. They couldn't make it clear to me what a man was. I lacked something. Perhaps the kind of understanding that happens not in the head but in the flesh. I wanted naked men to break through the doors of my dormitory at Misericordia and march me out in front of all the other boys and war-paint me purple and wrestle me around in the grass in a circle of roaring firelight and make me wear a tight loincloth.

I could not even imagine sex between people then. I knew men and women did something, but I didn't know what, and when I finally asked at eighteen what it was I knew I could never have imagined anything as bizarre as the sex in heterosexuality, and I wondered however did anyone ever think up something that disgusting? No wonder straights never want to talk about sex. No wonder gays can't shut up.

In addition, naive simp that I was, I had no idea men could have sex with other men, but I knew of a vague longing I had to be with and be like other guys. I lacked something more than factual and emotional sex education. I lacked a dramatic—even Hollywood—rite of passage to manhood.

My life might have taken a totally different turn if my father on my sixteenth birthday had, more than driving me to daily mass, given me some ritual icons of passage like a razor, aftershave, a jockstrap, and condoms. But Catholic boys never receive such gifts.

Somehow I misunderstood all the signals from my childhood. The nuns hardly meant that I should never touch girls. The priests saw my "holiness," born of fear of hell, to be a calling to their priesthood and I in terror followed.

Charley-Pop wanted me to be what I knew I could never be: a jock like he was. So, instead, I became the perennial buddy of jocks, the way I was a buddy to him. My mother meant for me to be me. Instead I tried to be what she wanted me to be, that is, what I thought she wanted me to be. I branched out from my family to Misericordia, always being, instead of me, what I thought the priests wanted me to be. A priest must be all things to all men.

I'm a chameleon.

That's why I've been good in bed on Castro and Folsom, and especially with Kick. I'm so eager to please I'll do anything to pleasure anybody especially when they've got what I want. That's the bottom line: I'll be anything anybody wants. I've traded self-realization into self-abnegation.

That's my mortal sin.

I should have listened to what my mother really said when she told me, "Don't become a priest for me. Do it for yourself and for God if you think that's what God wants you to be." All she wanted for me was the Ryan-ness of being Ryan. All she wanted was for me to be me. She would never approve of me trying to be not-me to please Kick or anyone else. She could have hung out happily with Emerson at Concord. Jeez! Why do I always understand everything intellectually but fail to understand it emotionally?

She would never object to my loving Kick because he was the same gender. "I know what goes on in the world," she said. "I'm not dumb. I don't care. As long as no one forces anything on me or on you." She would have only one objection to Kick: that I have given up another chance to be to my own self true in order to keep

Kick happy and coming back for more.
   So what am I going to do about it? And when?
   Don't ask me. Ask my dick.

5

"Oh, Magnus," Ryan sat with me in a Castro restaurant, "identity is like AIDS. We should have listened to our mothers. Our mothers were right. Be yourself. Don't do what others do. Always wash your hands after you go to the bathroom. Don't eat after other people. Don't take rides and candy from strangers."

"At least with the plague on," I said, "you've more time to spend with me."

"I need to talk to someone sometimes," Ryan said. "I've always liked you, Magnus. I've made you executor of my will. I hope you don't mind."

"I'd mind if anything happened to you," I said.

I truly feared for him, for Kick, for Teddy, for all of them. The news from the Centers for Disease Control in Atlanta was not good. Two cases of AIDS were diagnosed every day and the diagnosis was a Death sentence.

"I'm leaving everything to Kick and Kweenie and my mother and Solly, but I'm leaving you enough," Ryan said, "to handle all my papers, writings, photographs, and videotapes."

"You're being overdramatic."

"These are dramatic times." He looked at me and raised my water glass. "This very tumbler may be infected," he said. "Remember the tea scene in *Cabaret* when Liza told Marisa Berenson they could get VD from teacups."

I remembered.

"I know it sounds alarmist," Ryan said, "but what are we doing eating in a gay restaurant?"

A certain paranoia rode a pale horse down Castro. I watched things change in San Francisco. The six-o'clock news was a nightly dirge. AIDS was a surefire pull for viewers. The terrifying news was not good. AIDS was associated with four groups, three of whom were people who weren't all that socially acceptable to the real Mr. America and his Mrs. From the start, hemophiliacs, dependent on the public blood supply, had the public sympathy. The rest were third world Haitians, intravenous drug users, and the group most widely infected—gay males.

"The worst thing to be in the world today," Solly said, "is a gay Haitian hemophiliac junkie trying to maintain his job as a waiter."

AIDS was a medical mugging. The disease hurt the image of gay men worse than any fag-bashing had ever hurt any gay men kicked to the sidewalk by young toughs in from the burbs of Orinda and Moraga to bag themselves some queers. The gay press called for candlelight marches from Castro to City Hall to focus attention on the government's lack of funding for immediate AIDS research. The gay view was that Legionnaires' Disease, and the toxic shock syndrome that afflicted young middle-class girls, had both been funded immediately to find a fast cure. The news said nothing so well as the fact that AIDS was untreatable. It had no prevention. It had no cure. And the people with the money hardly seemed to care.

The initial medical opinion warned that nearly all gay men had come into contact with the immunity-suppressing virus. After fighting through to the grudging acceptance of gay liberation, which was only a dozen years old, gay men found they were suddenly social pariahs once again. Straight San Francisco treated the Castro like a leper colony as subtly as some had tacitly approved the gun in Dan White's hand. Almost overnight, fewer and fewer straights dared to come to the Castro for a chic supper and a movie at the Castro Theatre. In downtown offices, straight people gathered around Xerox machines and wondered if they could still go to lunch with the amusing gay men with whom they worked.

The uncivil tension between Pacific Heights gays and Castro gays and Folsom gays widened momentarily. Cocksuckers blamed the fuckers who blamed the piss drinkers who blamed the fist fuckers who blamed the scatmen; and everyone blamed the shooters with their needles. Finally, even while the panic—and it was real panic—rose in those first months, they all knew they had no choice but to band together to save themselves, because no one else would save them. Their history taught them that.

Not everyone who was gay had come out to their parents and family, and suddenly some of the dying had to make long-distance phone calls to announce the double punch of news that they were gay and they were going to die of AIDS.

From San Francisco and Los Angeles and New York the phone calls and letters reached out across the whole country. Parents who knew their sons were gay, and parents who suspected their sons were gay, feared for the lives of their boys. Some could talk of it and some could not, anymore than they could overtly acknowledge what they knew to be their son's sexual essence. Annie Laurie, I'm sure, was praying her rosary for Ryan and all the friends of his she had ever met, Kick included.

Kick was unmoved. He had the antidote: a sound mind in a sound body. Positive Attitude was everything. For him, bodybuilding was the key to health. He quoted to Ryan from *Sun and Steel*, the Yukio Mishima book about bodybuilding that Ryan had given him for his thirty-fourth birthday.

Mishima, complaining that men are weighted down by the same sagging pull of gravity Ryan had long before recognized, advised that the sweating and pumping of bodybuilding flushed gray existential gravity from athletic males, much the same as Melville saw his perfect blond seaman, like Terence Stamp, in *Billy Budd*, his young muscle facing existential Death, being hanged at sunrise, take on in his firm flesh the full rose of the dawn.

After the one weekend of his depression, Kick regained his indefatigable upbeat ways. Pumping iron could defeat AIDS. He insisted he was at the new dawn of his own muscle. He refused to discuss AIDS. For him, the epidemic did not exist.

Ryan knew better. He knew that the Dread he had always feared was roaring like a fire out of control across the horizon of San Francisco rooftops. He knew that finally the Nameless Dread had a name.

But Kick would not allow him to speak it. Whatever Kick wanted, Kick got. He was the only relief Ryan could find. He embraced Kick as his refuge, his safe harbor from AIDS; but deep in his heart, deep in that part of his heart that he always kept from Kick, he secretly feared that Kick and he were clapping as hard as they could to make Tinker Bell live, and this time they might not be able to clap long and hard enough.

Their nightplay was as good as it had always been. They roamed naked together through candlelit rooms full of flowers. Kick produced endless small packets of Kryptonite.

"Okay, Superman, mix me half of what you take," Ryan said. He trusted Kick. He never looked at the mixture he drank in the wine glass Kick handed him. Whatever Kryptonite was, it worked quickly and gently. It rose and peaked during three hours of sexplay. By the fourth hour, its rush was spent so completely by the greater rush of orgasm that even Ryan was able to drift off to sleep without his usual Valium.

"We've found the drug that's right for us," Kick said.

Nightly he mixed the cocktails and brought them to Ryan in the mirrored playroom. They conjured a new Energy transcendence on the old. Ryan worked his invocations on Kick's hard new muscle. His training for the Mr. California was zipping along. Kick had been big before, but now he was growing larger, massive, with an even more precise symmetry than he had displayed in the Mr. San Francisco.

So close those nights were the two of them that they pushed out farther the bounds of the finite, moving from the flesh, through the worship of the extravagant muscle they both loved, to some ecstatic plane outside space and time where for a few brief shining moments they hung suspended together beyond words, blended finally and totally, the one into the other, so that no longer were there two of them. There was only one. Two hearts, two minds, two bodies melded together into one Edenic being. They checked out from Earth on high flight to paradise. More even than before they defied gravity and rose the way lovers always rise, transcending even *le petite morte* of the body with the soaring aspirations of two souls become one.

I knew of those dangerous nights. Ryan could not but tell Solly and me. We both knew that whatever happened between them in the mirrored playroom in the basement of the Victorian checked out in both the look on Ryan's face and the undeniable change in Kick's Look.

Something even in Kick's face shifted. The man himself metamorphosed, during those autumn days at the gym and during those nights of Ryan's imaging chants, into a blond Viking warlord, heroic: huge thighs, exquisite washboard abs, thickening pecs and back and shoulders, and a pair of arms without peer. He stopped shaving his body. A golden layer of Nordic blond hair upholstered all his muscle. He was, by anyone's tally, a sight to see.

Solly mused that he thought that both Ryan and Kick, and Ryan more than Kick, were in a dangerous psychological situation. "I don't have to be a Jungian analyst to wonder how they can get that high without an air traffic controller. Freud might approve. Jung wouldn't."

I abstained. I am, after all, a critic. I can only judge something after it happens. One thing I knew for sure. Ryan, during these nights of Kick's return in the month before Christmas, was more turned on than ever, and Kick played so lovingly with him that Ryan could forgive him anything and everything that had ever happened with Logan. Ryan hardly cared that Logan was tending marijuana up at Bar Nada. Kick made him forget, at least for the hours when they worked their sexual magic, that AIDS stalked the City.

On the December anniversary of Pearl Harbor, Kick made one startling comment. "I love Logan," he said.

Finally there rang out that crystal-clear moment of truth, when a sound like the far-off peal of a bell on an ice-cold day can be heard nearly around the world.

"I love Logan." Kick said it again. "And I love you. But I love you both differently. I want you to understand that. I know you do. You always have. I need you to." Kick had thought a great deal about his situation. He hardly wanted to be torn between two lovers. "I want to come out of all this with two friends."

He loves me and he loves Logan? Ryan for an instant hated his own body—not for the spiritual reasons the priests at Misericordia had taught him—but for a different reason. *But he wouldn't have to love him at all if I could put my head inside Logan's body.*

If Ryan had learned anything in dealing with a Southern man like Kick, it was patience. He would wait to say what he would not say now. Instead, he said, "I know you need a man to fit your fantasies the way you fit mine. I want you to have everything. Only, don't lose contact with me. What we have is too good to lose."

"I know," Kick said. "Neither of us can conjure alone as well as we can when we're together. We have special times, you and I, but there's other kinds of special times I need to have with Logan. I don't want either of you to be jealous."

"I'm not jealous." Ryan spoke what he thought was the absolute truth of a generous heart. "Really I'm not. I never have been. You can have anything you want. But I've seen him hurt you."

"Sometimes he hurts me," Kick said.

"I hope I've never hurt you." Ryan fished.

"You've never hurt me. You and he are nothing like each other, but . . ."

"But you more than love him. I can tell." Ryan remembered Kick's commandment to him. "You're in-love with him."

Kick looked Ryan directly in the eyes. "Yes. I'm in-love with him."

"Are you in-love with me?" Ryan knew the answer and did not fear it.

"We always said we'd never fall in-love with each other."

"Other lovers do. Why do we have to be different?" Ryan said.

"Because what we have is different from anything else in the world. We have spectacular sex. I love you for that. I love you for your head. If I fell in-love with you, it would ruin everything."

"How would it ruin anything?" Ryan asked.

"It would trivialize the grand passion we both have for muscle." Kick was a good student of a better coach. He had learned from Ryan to speak words Ryan's way. "What we have is what you're always talking about."

"What's that?"

"Something existential. It affects our very existence."

"Logan doesn't affect your existence?"

"No." Kick drawled softly. He wished Ryan no hurt. "What I have with Logan is something, well, romantic." He took Ryan's hand. "You're a necessity to me. He's a luxury."

Ryan found it strange that he liked the concept. Love was a necessity. Romance was a luxury. He was beginning to hate semantics.

"I don't love him the way I love you, but I've been in-love with him for some time now."

"I've always known it," Ryan said. He damned January Guggenheim's documentary. If only they hadn't been so bold as to go public, spreading Kick's image across ten billion cathode ray tubes, showing him up on the TV screen in Logan's apartment in San Diego.

He knew for certain they'd never publish the words and pictures of *Universal Appeal*.

Ryan was no doubt a fool for love, but he wasn't that much of a fool. He had known from the moment of Logan's sudden arrival on Castro that Kick had fallen immediately in-love with him. He had hoped that Logan would wear thin. But he had not. He had hoped Logan would be a casual fling. But he was not. He knew it for certain the first time Kick had come back to him bruised by a tiff with Logan. He knew that the fights that drove Kick down from Bar Nada were lovers' quarrels.

"You and I have always talked of our gentlemen's agreement," Ryan said. "I've always been gentlemanly with you and I always will be."

"Don't you see?" Kick asked. "This is my chance, your chance, our chance to live the total concept of homomasculine fraternity."

"But you're in-love with him," Ryan said.

"No more than you're in-love with me."

"You've always known that?"

"From the very first night," Kick said. "I've always admired the way you kept it under control. You have more self-discipline than any dedicated bodybuilder. I love your control. If there can be a purity to being in-love, you've got it, Ry. In that way, I want to be exactly like you."

God damn the irony! "I always thought it was the other way around."

"You're the only man I know big enough to handle this. We've never crowded each other. Why should we start now? We can have anything we want."

"I thought being in-love was something you had declared out-of-bounds."

"I thought so too. At first." Kick was all style. Good-looking people can get away with murder. He kept himself ingratiated to Ryan. "But you handle being in-love with me so well that I figured I could learn that from you too. You're my coach, Ry. You teach me things. You seem so happy in-love with me. I wanted to feel that kind of happiness too."

I should yell. I should scream. I should fight. "Then I want you to have it." Ryan made up his mind to mean it.

"There's enough of me to go around," Kick said. "Big muscles. Big heart. Big soul."

6

I knew only later what Ryan did not know then. Kick had moved up from oral steroids to injectable Decadurobolin. He was on the needle. He was on the juice. Ryan should have suspected that Kick's great increase in muscle growth was due less to mind control and imaging than it was to chemicals, but he wanted to believe in the power of Kick's head and heart to create naturally the new physique that was on a par with professional bodybuilders.

A man has only so much soul to fill up his flesh. If he takes steroids, his body grows so unnaturally big his natural soul cannot expand to fill it up. The soul stretches, dilutes, thins, weakens. All the former natural Force and Energy pales even as the false Frankenstein flesh grows bigger. Magnanimity, largeness of the soul, is a relative gift. A lucky man is born with enough soul to fill his body. He is gracious, kind, loving.

Steroids undo a man's natural luck. His body, in a kind of retro anorexia nervosa, outstrips his soul. His flesh thickens the way one's hands thicken after applauding a great performance; the hands still move, articulate, around the bones and sinews, but they are bigger, harder, less sensitive than before. They don't feel like the same hands. Once so thickened by steroids, the bodybuilder becomes duplicitous, like the alcoholic who is a surreptitious drinker, trying to work both ends against the middle, the way Kick worked Ryan, to pump up the soul he knows has become nervous, anxious, too small for his pumped-up flesh. His soul becomes lost in his huge new physical proportions. He falls from grace.

Once, Ryan had recognized Kick as Adam before the Fall. He could hardly recognize this new Kick who had come back to him speaking of love for Logan.

The steroids had made his body bigger. He wanted Ryan to make his soul grow to fill it. All along, Ryan thought that Kick's magnanimity had been larger than his natural body. Within that big-souled limit, he had rationalized Kick's careful use of the unnatural oral growth hormones.

Musclemania has no conscience.

Ryan would allow almost anything that could make Kick's physical being grow to match the Energy of his soul which he touched so intimately in their night-games. What he should not have allowed was Kick's body growing too massive for his soul. But Ryan did not know that Kick told only the half-truth. He masked the source of his muscle growth. He talked of harder workouts with Logan. He never mentioned the real intensified motives for his monthly trips to Dr. Steroid's castle laboratory in El Lay. He never mentioned the tiny Deca bottles and the hypodermic syringes the doctor gave him in trade for sex. Only ugly bodybuilders pay cash for steroids.

Kick masked the truth.

Ryan dissembled.

They both lied.

They both wanted more.

Kick bent over, his butt in the air, and took the needle from Logan. Logan wanted to take muscle farther than even Kick had imaged. Logan persuaded Kick to up the dosage. Sticking Kick gave him a sense of power. Kick did not say *no*. He watched Logan shoot himself up. He was the handsome, dark, muscle-beast of Kick's own private dreams. He knew how to play "Hot Cop," and Kick liked to get arrested. They were on a fantasy trip of their own.

"Steroids are great," Logan said. "They're like injecting coke."

"The side effects of steroids," Solly said, "is Attitude."

Without Ryan's knowledge, and without his coaching, which might have saved him, Kick passed the point of no return. His body grew too big for his soul. His Energy dissipated, thinned, spread out through his new bigness. He was shot full of steroids and more ruggedly handsome than ever. He was what Ryan would later biblically call "a whitened sepulcher."

Ryan had been mistaken. He had thought Logan to be the source of Kick's depression that day of the Castro Street Fair when they had lain in the grass of the Eureka Playground. He never suspected that Kick's anxiety was a side effect of the steroids.

Ryan had truly believed in Kick's magnanimity, because he truly believed in his own. He knew his own soul, his own Energy was bigger than his long, lean body. More than one trick had told him, "When I first met you, I thought you were much smaller than you are." The truth was, Ryan's magnanimity projected a certain power. Kick had seen that their first night together. That was, in fact, the very reason Kick had taken up with Ryan. "You are the richest man I know," he had said. He meant not in property, not in money, the way a cheap hustler might have worked the angle, but richness of soul.

"The way," Solly said later, "an expensive hustler works his even more expensive angle."

Ironically, finally, when Kick's own muscle became larger than his own soul, Ryan's magnanimity became a reproach to Kick. What is reproachful becomes something to exploit. Kick went over the edge so subtly I think he hardly realized his fall. He was essentially a good man. It was more that he knew he needed from Ryan some way to regain the very Energy he knew he was losing in himself as his soul thinned and weakened and he fell in-love with someone he knew in his heart of hearts was not evolved enough for him. He had taken a step not up, but down, the old evolutionary ladder.

Kick's legitimate pride in himself, once his soul grew thin and wasted by the systemic plague of the steroids, was replaced with a certain vanity, the sin of the thin-souled. He lost proportion. How ironic. Proportion was the very thing he had sought to achieve in bodybuilding.

"Contests," he had said, "are won on proportion of legs and arms to torso and head."

In Ryan's videos of his first physique contests, Kick had radiated a finessed proportion of body and soul and manly energy. In later videos, he showed only brute physical proportion of arms and legs and pecs and shoulders. He moved from the idealized sport of bodybuilding to the hard-core business of the muscle game. His new heavy-iron muscle Look at first masked the fact that he had lost the essential proportion of body and soul.

He had become meat.

His face, which Ryan thought had changed when he came back that night before Thanksgiving, was a dead giveaway. Among bodybuilders on steroids, there is at first a slight change in the shape of their faces. I've never seen a professional bodybuilder who didn't have more chin than seems humanly possible. Initially this change is aggressively attractive. Every man wants more chin. But then this acromegaly, this slow rearrangement of the face, after a number of years, can produce prominent, often uplifting, enlargement of the facial bone structure. Is Schwarzenegger's newly refined movie star face a plastic surgeon's reduction of his bodybuilder acromegaly? I wonder. Ryan had thought the slight change in the forward thrust of Kick's strong chin was simply another notch in the intensity of his manly Look. He had loved him for his face as much as for his muscle and his soul. Ryan had no objectivity at all. The lover never really knows the beloved.

7

On that night before Thanksgiving, neither knew that they were on a trajectory of ruin. Sometimes it is better not to know the future. What I tell here, I tell from the rearview mirror. I know now what Ryan was too innocent to know then. What is, is, Solly constantly, irritatingly, repeated. And what was, was that Kick was about to break Ryan's heart as he himself lost the heart Ryan had first immediately loved that El Lay enchanted evening when Kick came through the door and walked, more than he walked into the room, into the fulfillment of a magnanimous image Ryan had always carried in his heart of what the perfect man should be.

"Of course I'm in-love with you," Ryan said. "And you're worth falling-in-love with. No offense to Logan, but is he worthy enough for a man like you?"

"Logan has his faults. He's learning. Maybe he'll learn some worth from me. The way I learned true worth from you."

Worthiness was not Logan's long suit. He had arrived from San Diego where he had survived dealing grass and working some not-so-vague body-building scam. He had been hustling musclesex and he had worked his way through every buyer in town. He found no problem in splitting for San Francisco. When he first played his hand at the corner of 18th and Castro, he epitomized what the street was about, and he dragged Kick down into the thick of it. The two of them became showboats.

"Showgirls," Solly said. "A gay man with a lust for bodybuilders is like a straight man with a thing for Vegas showgirls."

Castro had been Ryan's stomping ground long before it became Logan's and Kick's. Solly had given up on the Castro completely, and like many men no longer went near the neighborhood. But Ryan had found at the intersection of 18th and Castro a certain vitality that, for all its faults, he wished to chronicle in his writing. He wanted to capture it. He may have knocked it, but down deep he liked it. The gay emergence was the only shell game in town. Castro, after all, was what was happening in San Francisco, the way that, years before, the Haight-Ashbury had produced the flower children, and before that, the North Beach of Kerouac and Cassady and Ginsberg and Ferlinghetti had produced the Beat Generation.

I understood Ryan's analytical genealogy. It matched mine as a pop culturist. The Castro was the latest manifestation of the libertine dream of Kerouac and Cassady who both finally gave up on the travesty that media attention had made of the Beats. Like them, and the Kesey hippies after them, Ryan saw the gay dream desaturated, gutted, by people who lost the essence of what it all meant, and went instead for the glitz, exchanging life for lifestyle, encouraged by types like January Guggenheim who had their own reasons of gain to exploit gay liberation. Nothing ruins a popular grass-roots movement more than making the cover of *TIME* magazine. Ask Leonard Matlovich. His face on that pioneering 1975 cover with the declaration, "I am a homosexual," ruined his life.

Sex, more than love, was the Castro style, but *lover* was the word most used. For every real lover, ten imposters lurked. Vampire tricks cruised the night. Anne Rice, who lived in the Castro, knew. Ryan knew. He tried to drive a stake through such love's heart.

Ryan understood the intersection. Both its joys and its dangers. He knew how to move counter to its beat. "What movie are we?" he asked Kweenie. They had stood, her first weekend in the City, when she was still Margaret Mary, at 18th and Castro. "We're *Blow-Up*."

He had warned his sister to be careful to maintain herself against the Castro beat. He had told her how David Hemmings had coached Vanessa Redgrave. "Hemmings," he had said, "takes Redgrave home and puts a jazz record on the stereo. She begins to snap her fingers to the insistent beat and she is very uncool trying to get with it. Hemmings stops her, tells her *no*, teaches her how to snap her fingers off the beat, shows her how to move to her own rhythms against the rhythms of the record. He shows her how to remain herself and still enjoy the music. He teaches her how to be cool."

Kweenie built her meteoric singing career on that advice alone.

Ryan at first maintained his own beat. It's not the drinking that makes a person an alcoholic; it's the inability to function. A man following his cock around can't be too careful. One morning he might wake up caring about nothing but sex, and call into work dead. The Castro style spit in the face of function. Something in the Castro afternoons and the Folsom nights drowned out the pure message of the siren call that had brought them all to San Francisco. The downward mobility of gay men became a street virtue on Castro where SSI checks were waved as victory flags against the straight system.

Did the quality of orgasm suffer? In the *Manifesto* Ryan theorized:

As there are women who have never cum, so are there men who have often ejaculated, who have often spasmed, but have never really cum. Perhaps a man can't truly know his own masculinity until he has transcended simple ejaculation and truly cum in his head and his heart and his body with another man. The coming together of gay liberation in San Francisco is a chance for the great rebirth of masculinity Whitman predicted. Where else can one see so many males, many highly talented, most educated to the nines, the majority of them from middle-class families who had spent a fortune on orthodontia?

The potential was staggering. He saw their mass vocation as a call to productive grace which, if applied correctly, could lead to a rebirth of the male prerogative which had so suddenly lost out to the bitchy rantings of a toothy, ravenous feminism. It wasn't masculinist separatism he wanted. That was merely temporary antidote to separatist feminism. What he wanted for women and men was a renaissance of humanism.

His was a call for men to function in their own way. Kick became his su-preme symbol of a man who creates himself, whose self then becomes meta-phor of communication to others to allow them to realize that as one man can create the magnificent Entity of himself, so his example can encourage each one to create his own self in his own way.

Bodybuilding was his main metaphor for self-creation in all its infinite varieties.

Truth belied wishful thinking. Philosophy means little to men following their dicks around. Hardballing sex leaves little time for contemplation, for courting, for romance, for all the little niceties of interpersonal relation-ships. The more depersonalized the sex, the less reason there was for anyone developing himself as a person. Was it tongue-in-cheek when Boyd Mac-Donald, who published the very popular underground magazine *Straight to Hell*, wrote, "I'm not a person. I'm a piece of meat."

The Meat Mentality pervaded Castro. Most of the men on the street did nothing but cruise and fuck. It was understandable in the first flush of com-ing out of long-repressed closets. Ryan had lived that way for his first five or six years in the City. He had loved his life in the fast lane, but after awhile, quantity wasn't enough. He set out to find quality and he found Kick. He found a joy well beyond the fun of anonymous balling. Kick turned him around. He no longer spent all his Energy late nights in dark baths. With Kick, he hoped to make up for lost time precisely as he had hoped to make up for lost time after he had left Misericordia and gone into the world. He was glad his sexual panic was ended. He wanted to share that idea.

"What movie are we?" Ryan asked.

"*The Prodigal* with Lana Turner?" I said.

"No," he said. "The main Castro movie is *The Rocky Horror Picture Show*."

"That's you all over," Solly said to Ryan.

"Why?" I asked.

"Because of the song," Solly said. "It should be Ryan's main theme."

"What song?" Ryan asked.

"'In just seven days,'" Solly said, "'I'll make you a man!'"

"I was thinking more," Ryan said, "about *Rocky*'s line that fits life on Cas-tro. 'Madness takes its toll.'"

It had hurt Ryan to see Kick grow more and more gay. He had wanted Kick to maintain, to be as big as the heroic Hercules he had seen on the screen when he was a child. He needed Kick to remain archetypal with an aura, because an archetype fallen was no more than a stereotype.

"Actually," Solly mused, "all archetypes are stereotypes, and vice versa."

Ryan squeezed his eyes shut and held his ears. He clapped his hands to make Tinker Bell live. He stopped going down to Castro altogether.

Acquaintances kept him posted, more than he wanted, on Kick's frequent street appearances with Logan through those lonely two months of Indian summer. Ryan was frightened for Kick. He thought of him as an innocent abroad. He was a southern boy swept up in a Northern California whirlwind. He did not know what Ryan knew from his years in the City. The downward mobility of homosexual men as they exit from straight middle-class values and come out into the gay lifestyle is legendary. Kick had once been a carpenter. He hadn't touched a hammer in over a year. He and Ryan had spent many an afternoon hanging out on Castro, but they had stayed above it, on top of it. Ryan had told him about Vanessa Redgrave in *Blow-Up.*

Identity meant nothing to Kick in the company of Logan. Kick was giving up himself to become what Logan wanted. At Misericordia, Ryan had been warned against falling in, as Monsignor Linotti said, with bad companions and special friendships.

In his long absences from Ryan, Kick suffered a shift in Attitude, which he tried to conceal from Ryan whenever he returned, like a lost little boy, to Ryan's doorstep. Ryan grew fearful for him, hearing some of the antics Logan had involved Kick in on Castro.

One Sunday afternoon on the corner, a shouting match had erupted between them. Actually, Logan had done the shouting, but Kick had not discreetly withdrawn. The story had sounded very gay to Ryan, but he dismissed it as gossip. He knew the story must be garbled. He knew that any fighting, much less a public squabble, was not Kick's style. He knew that Kick could maintain. But he was wrong. Something he did not know had happened. Something he could not acknowledge had occurred.

He denied that the intersection of 18th and Castro was crowded with gaping witnesses.

The steroids had a deeper, aggressive side effect.

Kick had become in those two months with Logan a street-corner bodybuilder posing and prick-teasing in the thin-sliced afternoon sun in front of Donuts & Things. Vanity had overtaken his pride. He had picked up Street Attitude. He was slouching against storefronts like the people his mother had warned him not "evah" to become.

Kick had gone Logan's way. He had been seduced by Logan. He had become a fool for love. He had fallen in-love. He had committed the very sin he had warned Ryan never to commit. But where Ryan had fallen in-love with what once had been a noble man, Kick had fallen in-love with a gay muscle hustler and the consequences were as different as rising and falling.

Ryan should have recognized Kick's slip from the moment he fell. He was an expert in deciphering when one thing meant two things. But Ryan saw nothing, refused to see anything, blinded as he was by love; and what he did see, he denied.

Kick with Logan was a very different man from Kick with Ryan.

In those two months, Kick threw himself into massive, split-routine workouts. He was growing. His neck disappeared into his huge shoulders. He telephoned Ryan to mail him checks to tide him over until his trust fund was busted. Gossip abounded. Kick and Logan were an item. The Castro-Folsom crowd's society columnist, Mr. Marcus, who was the envy of the *Chronicle*'s famous Herb Caen, squibbed almost weekly about "those two outrageous muscle-hunks about town" in *The Bay Area Reporter*. Logan introduced Kick to the freebasing cocaine crowd. He and Ryan were not strangers to drugs, but this outrageously elite Double-A-Group was something else. They were good-looking. They were rich. They threw outrageous parties. They danced the night away. They were perfect for Kick. They denied AIDS existed. The usual pair of muscle hustlers, up from El Lay for Labor Day, joined their party, and boldly peddled steroids, both pills and juice, to the hundreds of gay guys pumping their pecs up at the gyms.

Rarely has a bodybuilder really ever admitted to taking steroids himself; but, when pressed, he always admits knowing someone who has.

"Steroids?" Kick said to anyone who asked. "Don't be ridiculous." Smile. Wink. Grin.

Fiat lux.

Dianabol became the most abused drug on Castro.

Ryan refused to hear anything about Kick's new taste for the fast crowd of hot men. He had never been able to get Kick to go anywhere but to bed. But I believed what Kweenie and Teddy told me. Ryan would not hear that, fueled by drugs, his muscle-beast had become a party animal.

"It's only a lark," Ryan said.

"Thou fool," Kweenie said. She knew all about Kick. She protected Ryan. She kept a secret she could never tell him. It had been raining one afternoon. Ryan was at work. She had let herself into the Victorian. Kick, fresh from the gym, and stripped naked for the shower, had shouted, "Who's there? Is that you, Ry?"

"It's me," she said.

Kick, pumped sweaty to the max, had made no move to cover himself. She had moved in on him, talking to him, admiring his muscle, doing

Ryan's act. She had known about the Third Runner-Up in the Miss Alabama contest. If she couldn't have Ryan, she'd have Kick. He was a sucker for muscle flattery. It had been fast and easy. Kick gathered worship where he found it. Brother and sister were so alike it was all the same to him. Neither Kweenie or Kick had even promised never to tell Ryan. That was implicit. Had Kweenie not had the abortion, Ryan, who was the ultimate fetishist, would have kept the baby, especially if blond and only if a boy. Had he known, he would have killed them both. Not for their fucking. Not for her conceiving. But for her aborting, with money he had lent to Kick, the only thing he couldn't have: Kick's child.

"Let him have his fun," Ryan said to Kweenie. "I want him to have everything he wants. He knows what he's doing. And most of all, I know what he's doing. This won't last long."

Ryan committed the last sin a person can commit against his own soul. He lied to himself.

His lie covered his anxiety.

He could not sleep, insomniac again, sleeping single in a double bed.

Kick failed to heed the plea his mother had made in the hospital corridor after the Runner-Up for Miss Alabama had thrown herself from his car. He failed to recognize that in certain, distinct ways the downtown Birmingham faggotry that his mother had despised had been carried cross country from all the little downtowns of America to the great big downtown of 18th and Castro. Ryan would one day tell Kick that he had become what his mother had loathed back in Birmingham when she had asked him directly, "You're not like those people downtown, are you?"

Kick, living high, with his paternal inheritance still frozen in Birmingham, had joined the gay, Gay, GAY ranks of all those photographers, writers, artists, and performers on Castro who never photograph because their cameras don't work; who never write because they've got this, you know, block; who never paint because the light in the apartment isn't right since the roommate made them move their bedroom to the back of the flat; who don't perform because, well, San Francisco is not New York, New York, you know.

I knew. I spent time on Castro. I watched what Ryan no longer came down to see, and I remembered.

Kick had become a gym bum in the Castro zoo.

He rented by the hour.

Ryan knew none of this. He shut it all out. He didn't want to believe it of Kick. He never asked questions when he knew the answer; so he saved face. He kept up appearances. He was more angry at Logan than jealous. Sharing a lover with a man is one thing. Sharing him with a needle is another. He was lonesome for Kick. He wanted him back.

And come back Kick did.

Rebounding.

So often that Ryan felt like a basketball backboard.

Each time Ryan met him with open arms.

"I feel like I'm using you," Kick said.

"If you're using me," Ryan said, "you can use me till you use me up."

"How could this happen to me?" Kick said. "I'm in-love with him, but it's not working. We argue. He puts me down. He tells me I'm too short to win the Mr. California. He's jealous of my muscle. He says I'll never be big enough. He doesn't understand my kind of muscle the way you do. I know it won't last with him. I know it will last with us. I only want to enjoy him for as long as I can make it good."

"Are you still flying to Birmingham for Christmas?"

"Yes."

"Good. You two need time apart." Ryan ran his hands over Kick's huge arms. "I think we need more time together."

"I hear what you're saying," Kick said. "I know you'll understand."

"I understand anything."

"Then you'll understand how much I want to go back up to Bar Nada to see him one more time before I leave."

You fuck! Ryan was speechless.

"You've been a good sport," Kick said, "for so long."

Kick played Ryan like a tuning fork. He hit upon the identical psychol-ogy that Ryan's parents had used to raise him as an obedient son. "Kenny Baker," Annie Laurie had mentioned in her gentle offhand way, "stayed out past midnight." Ryan had learned early on that she meant that he, as well as Kenny, should not stay out past midnight. She never ordered his obedience directly.

Charley-Pop, in more ways than one, was exactly like Kick. They both shared the quiet jock heart that Ryan worshiped. But Kick was a trickster. Once he learned how to play and exploit these indirect ways of reaching deep into the heart of Ryan's compliance, he had the control he needed to take advantage of a man who loved him more than life itself.

"This is a chance for us," Kick drummed the lesson home, "truly to show that homomasculine fraternity works." He repeated Ryan's line from the *Manifesto* as a perfect device to have his way.

Love is blind, deaf, and dumb, but still takes you in, lends you money, and eats your shit.

You can have anything you want.

"Go up to the ranch. I want you to," Ryan said. "I only ask one thing."

"Name it."

"Remember the home team." The cheer was weakening to an echo. It was his only lifeline in a sinking situation.

"I love you too much to forget."

"I'll never ask you for more than that," Ryan said.

"I promise I'll keep it short. Not like the two months this Fall."

"I don't mind being put on hold once in awhile," Ryan said. "But don't put me on hold too long."

"I won't," Kick said. "But, please, never hang up."

"Me hang up on you?"

"A man's got to do what a man's got to do."

"Then do it," Ryan said.

"I'll only be gone for the weekend. Logan sold some of the grass. I need to pick up my split of the cash to pay for my plane ticket home. I'll bring you back a lid. It's really good shit."

Kick headed for the ranch.

Ryan headed for the big depression.

8

Ryan tried to be stronger than the onslaught of Christmas on Castro. Kick had flown back to Birmingham. Logan, the weekend that Kick had spent with him at Bar Nada, insisted the deal for the grass had fallen through. There was no cash. The news caught Kick short. He borrowed his airfare from Ryan.

"I'll pay you back as soon as Logan moves the harvest."

"Forget it," Ryan said. "That's part of my Christmas gift to you."

Alone in the Victorian, Ryan grew restless. He took to the streets. It was dusk on Christmas Eve. The Castro glowed like a child's dream. Mart Crowley had been right in *The Boys in the Band:* "You know, Mary, it takes a fairy to make something pretty." No place in San Francisco was so well decorated as the Castro. Windows at Gilded Age Antiques and Cliff's Variety and the Rugby Shop were dressed traditionally. Skating bears and bowing elves vied with the Lacoste crocodile splash of designer jock ensembles at the All American Boy store. A drapery of lights outlined the windows and rooftops up and down the four blocks of 18th and Castro. The neighborhood merchants had chipped in to erect a fifty-foot tree on a pedestal outside the Hibernia Bank.

The fir reminded Ryan of the year before, when Mayor Dianne Feinstein, always eager to press electoral flesh, had arrived at the crack of twilight to speak briefly and light the Castro Christmas Tree while the Gay Men's Chorus sang "Adeste Fidelis." Di Fi, as the neighborhood called her, shook hands all around and worked her way through the huge crowd of men. She must have felt like the mayor of the town full of identical twins all fucking each other. A video camera crew walked backward in front of Her Honor. Their bright lights illuminated her fair skin against her dark, conservative suit and her white blouse with its big bow. She hardly deserved the El Lay critique laid on her by the piss-elegant Mr. Blackwell on whose Worst Dressed List she regularly appeared, because, Blackwell said, her sensible shoes and tailored shoulders made her look like a voting booth. Under the bright video lights, she shook hundreds of male hands.

When she arrived at Kick holding Ryan's hand in the huge crowd, she stopped dead in her tracks. Kick smiled. He was not one of the identical clones. The politics fell from Di Fi's face. She reached her hand out to Kick and on impulse, in this whole crowd of men, pulled herself to him. In the stark spotlight in the twilight outside the Midnight Sun Bar, Di Fi leaned in to kiss Kick. He smiled as she moved toward his face. Instinctively, at a range of three inches, eye to eye, the two knew the scenario of their documentary encounter. Their mouths, aimed at each other, both turned at the very last instant. They bumped cheeks and Di Fi kissed air. Kick pulled back. They both smiled. She had for a moment that look in her eyes that women have when they see a man whose classic Look they can only hope to see once in a lifetime. Di Fi was no Judas in her kiss. She meant it, but her miming one on Kick's face earned her votes. A cheer rose up. The Mayor of San Francisco had kissed Mr. San Francisco. She stepped back from him to the roar of applause and catcalls. She had kissed the man most men on Castro wished to kiss.

That was Christmas past. In the year since, AIDS had changed all that. Ryan doubted if even a politician would kiss a gay man anymore.

Christmas Eve made Ryan indulgent. Christmas was the one holiday that seemed to exhibit honorably the childlike innocence of homosexuality. The festive air of the Castro caught him up in its spell. He had no tree at home, but he could not resist the huge Hibernia tree with its six thousand lights and ornaments that came from all around the neighborhood. Some wit had hung a sequined red high heel way up on the tree. Gay Santas set up their chairs under the tree and let gay men and lesbian women sit in their laps for charity. For a buck, fairies and dykes told Santa over a handheld mike what they wanted for Christmas. The proceeds went to the AIDS support fund.

Christmas made the Castro a neighborhood reclaimed from their collective childhoods. Ryan stood on his tiptoes to see the title of a book hanging on a green ribbon from one of the strong lower branches. It was James M. Barrie. Was it innocent irony? Barrie had ventilated his own terribly British thing for young boys in *Peter Pan*. He was the author of the one book common to most gay people's childhood. At Christmas, more than any other time, the recovery and exhibition of the childlike quality that once was the essence of gayness rose flamboyant and decorative across the festooned streets of the Castro. Ryan hated the Peter Pan he had loved as a boy. Peter had never wanted to grow up. "God," Ryan said in the last-minute crush of the evening crowd, "I'm such a Scrooge."

Ryan knew he had to buy at least one gift for the even greater Scrooge, Solly Blue. He spent nearly an hour in the Obelisk boutique as the eager line of frenzied shoppers, bobbing to the disco version of "Scarlet Ribbons," bought pretties on charge cards as fast as the clerks could move them in and out of 489 Castro, wrapping the merchandise in smart gray boxes with smarter gray ribbons and elegant black ostrich feathers tucked under the bows. Straight people crowded up next to gays. They knew where to shop; and, protected by the denial of disease, they even brought their children down to tour the streets, window to window, to see the lights and the animated manikins and the candy houses and, of course, the Big Tree with the two, well, so what, gay Santas: one male and one female and both whiskered. It was all so much Christmas whimsey, and so much more traditional than that offered by the downtown merchants.

Ryan bought Solly the same clean-lined glass-cylinder oil lamp that Kick had bought for his mother. "Everybody in town," the clerk at the Obelisk said, "has at least one size of this family of lamps. It's a sleek design. A Wolfard. Tasteful. The Whitney declared it an American classic. It goes with everything. You can't go wrong buying it. Frankly, I hate them."

The perversity of perversity, Ryan thought. He carried his shopping bag out to the warm dark of the night. To his right the marquee of the Castro Theatre was brilliant with bulbs and neon. The first of the Big MGM Four was playing. Forty-one years after its initial release, the big Christmas flicker at the Castro was *Gone with the Wind*. Customers queued up at the box office. Even on Christmas Eve, maybe especially on Christmas Eve, people sought the brilliant comfort of the light shining in the darkness from the projector, unreeling visions over their heads onto the silver screen.

Ryan turned left and walked past Donuts & Things. He imagined how Kick and Logan had lounged against its windows, the way, once, he and Kick had held court so many afternoons. The Chicana girls, who twenty-four hours a day pushed stale crullers at the gay and gullible, had locked the door. They moved about in the glaring fluorescence of the shop, scrubbing and cleaning. Ryan had never seen their door closed. *Feliz Navidad* was a serious feast.

He walked down to stand at the Corner of It All. A leftover hippie working his Christmas scam was loudly shilling mistletoe to everyone bustling corner to corner.

"A buck a bunch. Mistletoe. A buck a bunch."

No one seemed to be buying in the neighborhood where easy kisses had turned dangerous. He missed Kick. He wanted to hate Christmas. Thom was dead. Sandy and the triplets had moved back to the Midwest. His mother was in the Bahamas. Kweenie was off to El Lay spending the holidays with January. He was alone. All he had was Solly who had invited him to his penthouse to spend Christmas with a young hustler who was to be Ryan's Christmas gift from Solly. He made a note to remember to return Solly's gun.

A vague anxiety hit him. He begrudged everybody everything for a minute, then chided himself again for truly being a Scrooge. He bought a sprig of mistletoe from the hippie and crossed 18th Street, past the cold facade of the Hibernia Bank, and stood alone under the tree shimmering with tiny white lights.

Where had everyone gone? Where was his father? Was he here now? Ryan felt like an invisible child raised by blind parents. He longed to feel Charley-Pop's presence. He longed to feel united this night with Kick. It was no Christmas carol he hummed. It was the love theme from *Casablanca* that constantly swelled up inside him when he least expected it: lyrics about the same-old/same-old story, about love, about glory, about doing, about dying, wondering, "As Time Goes By," about the future. The future. He didn't know what that would forgodsakes be! He didn't know on what he could rely. *Rely.* That was love's operative word. He relied on himself, on his self, what self he had left, and on Kick. He relied on Solly who was maybe the most reliable of them all.

No one else stopped at the late Christmas Eve hour to watch the tree. They rushed past Ryan who stood stock still in close to the tree that Kick with his carpenter's hammer had helped erect. Across the two thousand miles, Ryan sent his Energy toward Kick. He hoped against hope that they both remained manful measure for manful measure what they should be. Or at least that they could get their mutual reliance back again.

Ryan stood amid the final swirl of Christmas. He could not help entrepreneuring strange things the way that he had entrepreneured *Maneuvers*. He knew Solly who entrepreneured his boys into big business would enjoy the fantasy of Bah Humbug, UnLtd. For everyone who loved Christmas, Ryan figured there was someone who hated the franchised feast. Even if someone didn't despise the whole concept, there was always someone to whom they would rather send a Bah Humbug card. He might develop a whole line of merchandise: Bah Humbug wrapping-and-toilet paper; BAH HUMBUG spelled out fancifully in red and green foil letters stylized like the perennial SEASON'S GREETINGS that stretch like unfolded paper dolls across windows. He had visions of Bah Humbug buttons and bumper stickers, and a Bah Humbug nonprofit organization to help people resist and be stronger than Christmas, sort of a Christmas Anonymous Club whose patron saint was Ebenezer Scrooge. Ryan imagined a run on Fuck-Tiny-Tim buttons. He knew deep down he didn't mean any of it. He didn't need to add anything to make life more depressing than it was. The third-level story in the day's *Chronicle,* after all, said everything: in Texas, the day before, someone had shot the March of Dimes poster child in the face with a gun.

Ryan left the tree and walked to a pay phone. He dialed Logan at Bar Nada. "I called to wish you a Merry Christmas," he said.

What he meant was that he had called Logan to check for sure he had not flown back to Birmingham with Kick. That would have been unbearable.

He hung up and dialed again. This time, Solly.

"Christmas Eve," Ryan said, without saying *hello,* "is a last ditch attempt by the world to make us all go back to being the best little boy we all once were . . . and I'm not . . . and I can't . . . and I don't want to. I don't know what I want. I only know what I don't want."

At the ticket booth under the brilliant marquee of the Castro Theatre, he paid $2.50 to see *Gone with the Wind* for the thousandth time. The feature was half over.

Later, as the clock struck midnight, Ryan knelt in front of his image of Kick posing on screen in a slow-motion display of extravagant muscle.

He was crying.

9

Early Christmas morning Ryan drove his VW Rabbit to Solly's penthouse. They distracted each other from the day itself. Solly sat on his couch and reminisced about his long-dead young lover. He was bitter.

"Mickey was really rather clever to jump off the Bridge on New Year's Eve. Clever in the sense that every holiday season since, and for every Christmas to come, how can I help but remember him and the way the afternoon light was that New Year's when the police came to my door. They found his wallet on the Bridge. They asked me if I knew him. I said he'd been missing, which wasn't unusual, for a week. They told me, with all his presents still wrapped under the tree, that he had taken the Final Big Swan Dive and what did they want me to do since they hadn't yet found his body, and I never had to do anything, because they never found him.

"He disappeared. The way everybody disappears. Oscar Wilde said, 'Everyone who disappears is said to be last seen in San Francisco. It must be a delightful city. It has all the attractions of the next world.' But Mickey's never been seen again. San Francisco isn't what it was in Wilde's day. Every Christmas and New Year's, I guess, Mickey's forced me into my own little memorial service. The way things are, the daily funerals, Falwell, Reagan, I'm glad he missed the seventies and will never hear of the ugly eighties. He wouldn't have liked either very much. This may be a good year for California wine, but it will be shit for its whining fornicating."

"I thought I was depressed," Ryan said.

"This whole City is depressed," Solly said. "Do you remember Randy Faragher?"

"Of Randy and Dan Brodie? Sure. We always called them Randy and Dandy."

"They're not so dandy these days."

"What do you mean?"

"Randy's at San Francisco General."

"What?"

"He's a vegetable. He shot himself in the head."

"He'd never do that."

"We'd all do that."

"Why?"

"Because Dan was diagnosed two weeks ago with AIDS."

"But Dan will need him to help him through," Ryan said.

"Dandy won't be needing anything. Randy thought maybe a small sit-down dinner party for two friends would lift Dandy's spirits. But Dandy disappeared before supper. Randy thought he had gone to lie down. But he wasn't in the bedroom. They made the usual jokes about playing hide-and-seek. Dan was always good for a laugh. So they searched for him. They found him dead. He drank an eight-ounce bottle of insecticide and swallowed half a can of Drano. They found him on a pile of garbage bags where he, I think in final comment, had laid himself out to die."

"Omigod!"

"Merry Christmas," Solly said. "Frankly, I don't see why there aren't more AIDS suicides. But there's better ways than swallowing Drano. I've got a checklist from the Hemlock Society. Do you want me to tell you how much of what you have to take to kill yourself peacefully?"

"No!"

"Let me tell you. I, who never join anything, have joined the Hemlock Society and the Neptune Society."

"Are they giving a gay group rate?" Ryan shuddered. "If I must die, take me to their Columbarium."

"We'll make less of a mess that way," Solly said. "Drano, indeed! Come on. Let me fix you some breakfast. I have the neatest little frozen sausage patties. They're the latest in junk food."

"Recommended, are they, by the Hemlock Society?"

"*Au contraire.* They're full of preservatives. Eat them and you'll live forever. A fate worse than Death."

Solly microwaved everything.

Ryan poked at the sausages. Grease oozed out under pressure of his fork. "I usually don't eat things like this. Kick doesn't . . ."

"Spare me," Solly said.

"I miss him. I'm afraid I'm going to lose him. It's more than Logan."

"Give me a break," Solly said. "So there's a little trouble in paradise. How San Francisco! How Bette Davis! How gay! I thought you'd be finished with him in a week, a month, a year. Three years is twice as long as the average gay affair. Drop him. You'll be better off. Believe me, I'm an expert on hustler sex." Solly cocked an eyebrow. "Oh! Did I say *hustler* sex?"

"Don't be cynical."

"Cynical? I'm positively clairvoyant."

"Kick's no hustler."

"And the pope doesn't shit in the woods."

"We love each other."

"You mean you're good sex together . . . when you're on drugs. One good gram of anything can make a hundred and eighty pounds of shit look absolutely divine."

"It's not the drugs. We're onto something. We've broken through to something more than physical."

"You mean if that high-tech monster body got shrunken down with AIDS you'd still be interested?"

"Yes."

"How quaint. I wouldn't be interested in anybody with AIDS."

"You're slime."

"No. I'm the devil's advocate. As a lapsed Catholic, you should remember what that is."

"When will you guys get off my back for being abused by Catholics in my childhood?"

"So if you're so great together, where is he on Christmas day? Where has he been most of the fall?" Solly asked.

"I don't own him," Ryan said. "We both have our freedom. We have our rhythms together and separately. We both need other men for pete's sake."

"For Kick's sake."

"For variety's sake," Ryan said. "And I might add, for my own sake. We both like sport-balling other guys."

"Suck cock and die."

"That's why I don't do it."

"When was the last time you were laid?"

"By Kick?"

"By anyone."

"Three weeks ago by Kick. It's too long to remember when I did it with anyone else."

"He does it with anyone else."

"We believe in homomasculine fraternity," Ryan stated.

"Oh, God! Are you still harping on that?" Solly was more annoyed than amused. "I bet he tells you that he comes back from Logan—how would Kick say it—*Enriched!* That's what he would say, enriched from harvesting—that favorite word of his—the juices from other men."

"We both believe in harvesting other guys."

"So here comes your chance. I have a knockout boy for you to harvest this afternoon."

"Kick tells me no matter who else we occasionally play with, there's nothing like the home team."

"What a line," Solly said. "Eat your sausage. You're such a sucker. If you believe that, how'd you like to buy the Golden Gate Bridge cheap?"

"It's not merely our dicks. Our heads cum together."

"What you're talking about is what goes on in your head. What goes on in his pretty blond bubble head you'll never know."

"Kicks says he feels the same. He thinks the same. We're onto something."

"Something like a collision course," Solly said. "He's having his cake and eating it too. I've heard his line. I've heard thousands of hustlers talk. Hustlers are my business, remember? Good hustlers tell you precisely what you want to hear. Your muscle hustler is no more than an uptown version of my street hustlers. I'm an expert on both kinds. Drop him. Give us all a break."

"It's the epidemic," Ryan said. "That's what's got me more upset than Kick."

"I suppose you think if you agonize over Kick, God will spare you from the agony of AIDS."

"We all have to suffer."

"Catholicism has turned your brain to Brie."

"I know it's ridiculous. I'm embarrassed to say I can't help myself. Sometimes I pray. Sometimes I revert to prayer."

"Truly retrograde."

"I can hardly believe myself. Sometimes when I'm alone I check out my legs for purple lesions. I don't want gay cancer. Without even thinking, I find myself praying."

"That's how all people pray. Without thinking."

"I say stuff like, 'Dear God, deliver me, please. Deliver us all. Protect me. Protect all of us. Make it go away. We don't deserve this punishment.'"

"AIDS is a disease. Not a punishment. Get that straight," Solly said.

"Some people, you know, believe in cause and effect. I don't care if everybody knows I'm homosexual. But I do care if I die of something, for chrissakes, gay!"

"How embarrassing." Solly exaggerated the words. "People will think what they want. They always have. They always will."

"Oh, God! I've got to find some hope in all this disease."

"God?" Solly said. "If he exists, he's keeping his zip code a secret to himself." He threw Ryan a paper napkin. "Get hold of yourself."

"I want to live."

"Thank you, Susan Hayward."

"This plague isn't the end of us," Ryan said. "This will turn out to be only an episode. We've got to think positive. We've got to be unsinkable like Molly Brown." Ryan stopped. "Those gay boys are still going to the bars and the baths," he said. "They deny Death. It's so sad. They don't believe it's really happening."

"Or else they do and they defy Death. Eat, drink, and be merry. Tomorrow we may die. I have no intention of not having sex with my boys."

"We have become Poe's imps of the perverse." Ryan blew his nose. He quoted Poe quoting Corneille: "Weep, weep my eyes, repose in water. Half my life has placed the remaining half in the grave." It was the first time Ryan had ever cried for San Francisco. "I'm sorry," he said. "It's Christmas and all. We've become Poe's desperate revelers continuing to party down, faced with the masque of the red death."

"Stop!" Solly said. "You went to school too long. You went to church too much. You'd have been better off ignorant. Please! Stop the allusions. You are what you are. You're not a metaphor of something else. The *is* of you, can't *is!*"

"I want to stop. I don't want to think about the plague," Ryan said.

"You mean you don't want to think about Kick and Logan."

"I'll go crazy," Ryan said. "I'll think about it tomorrow. Who said that?"

"See? See what I mean! You're not Scarlett O'Hara. You're Ryan O'Hara."

"Nothing but the Death rate has changed in San Francisco."

"I can live with that," Solly said. "Eat some more sausage. You're going to need all your strength when your Christmas present arrives."

They whiled away the morning drinking Irish coffee. By mid-afternoon, Solly was mixing Absolut Vodka and Coca-Cola. They were not drunk, but they were feeling no pain. Ryan was almost having fun. At half past three, the doorbell buzzed. Solly called down the intercom to the street door.

"Party-time," he said to Ryan. "It's your Christmas present."

He buzzed the boy into the lobby. Ryan listened as the elevator groaned and lifted itself up the shaft to the penthouse. Solly waited at the open door of the apartment and welcomed the boy into the room. He was young, husky, tattooed, and blond.

He could have been Kick's delinquent little brother.

Solly had picked the boy for that very reason. He watched the kid's Look register on Ryan's face. "There's more ways than one," Solly said, "to skin a cat. This boy is as beautiful in his own way as any man you know."

The blond hustler ambled on bowlegs toward Ryan on the couch.

"Jake," Solly said, "this is Ryan."

"Yeah, buddy," Jake said. His voice was Oklahoma. "Merry Christmas. I'm your present." He pulled out a joint. "You wanna smoke this or whu-u-a-t?"

Solly shared a toke or two. Then he left for the kitchen. "I've got a roast in the oven," he said. "The bedroom's ready when you are."

An hour later, Ryan and Jake left the bedroom, showered together, dressed, and came into the living room.

Solly looked at his watch. "Safe sex must take longer. You certainly got my money's worth."

Ryan and the hustler both grinned.

"Can he stay for dinner?" Ryan asked.

"They always stay for dinner," Solly said. "Anything Father Flanagan can do for lost boys, I can do better."

The roast came from the oven, tender with overcooking. The gravy came from a package, the potatoes from a box, the cranberries from a can. They sat at a glass table eating and watching the short December sunset.

Jake said very little. He lit another joint and passed it around the table. "It makes the food taste better," he said.

Ryan laughed. Solly made a face.

Suddenly, Jake pushed back from the table. "Can I have a raw egg?" he asked.

Solly pointed him toward the refrigerator.

"And another beer?"

"Now he wants egg in his beer," Solly said.

"Who doesn't?" Ryan said.

Jake juggled the egg and the beer. He walked to the window. He opened it and stuck his head out. "Hey!" he said, "there's a rope hanging from a post on the roof way down below. I think it's a noose."

Solly went to the window. "It's a noose alright. It's been there for years."

"Watch this." The kid held the raw egg out the window. He dropped it, counting and laughing until it splattered on the roof far below.

"Isn't this fun?" Solly said. "Almost as much fun as New Year's. You remember New Year's, don't you, Ry? Before you met Kick. When you had to have a fist up your ass at the stroke of midnight?"

"And you like to get fucked with a knife at your throat."

"There's no aphrodisiac like young meat and cold steel."

Ryan nodded to the hustler. "Show Solly what you have."

Jake pulled open his vest. "You wanna see it?" He pulled a gun from a shoulder holster. "You didn't know I had this, huh?"

"You're full of surprises," Solly said.

"I knew he had it." Ryan walked to the window. "He pulled it out in the bedroom. We played with it. When he rubs it on his cock, he gets hard. By the way, I forgot to bring your gun back."

"I don't need it," Solly said. "They arm themselves these days."

"I showed Ryan how to use it," Jake said.

"Give it to me," Ryan said.

Jake handed him the gun and the bullets. "Hey, man! For sure! It's your day all the way!"

"You load it like this," Ryan said.

"Be careful, Ry," Solly warned. "You don't know anything about guns."

"I know about this gun. Jake showed me. It's exactly like the one you gave me."

It was a .22. He loaded it easily.

"Why not," the hustler said, "shoot it out the window. You know, straight into the air. To celebrate."

Ryan shrugged his shoulders and balanced the gun in his hand. He moved toward the open window. "I can get real crazy," he said. He was bound and determined to be stronger than Christmas.

"Go for it, man." The hustler, rubbing his own crotch, gave Ryan a grope. He was hoping for a big tip from Solly.

Ryan looked at Solly. "You ready?"

"Why not?" Solly said.

Ryan raised the gun, aimed it high up and out the penthouse window. For one moment, everything in the room froze. The three seemed to be a still-life collection of slightly demented Christmas glee. Then Ryan raised his arm higher, took a step back into the room, pointed the gun out at the City, and fired. The bullet took off and the room rocked with the sound and smell. The noise knocked them back. Louder than they had ever believed it would be.

Solly broke up laughing. Ryan blew into the mouth of the barrel. He slipped the gun into his jeans. He rubbed the hard barrel pointing down his leg. Then he pulled it slowly out and handed the gun back to the hustler who slipped it back into his shoulder holster.

Solly went to the kitchen and came back with three brandies. "I propose," he said, "a Christmas toast." He passed the two glasses and raised his own toward the young blond hustler. "We have to thank the fathers and mothers of the United States for continuing to turn out, at so much trouble and expense to themselves, so many beautiful sons for our continued enjoyment. To Jake!"

They drank their toast.

"Merry Christmas, Solly." Ryan hugged his friend.

"Merry Christmas, Ry."

Ryan held Solly out at arms' length. "I know," he said, "somewhere tonight, with someone else, doing what we've always done, the sonuvabitch is all pumped up and has a hard-on."

"Who has a hard-on?" Jake asked.

"No one," Solly said. "At least, no one you know." He stared into Ryan's eyes. "Sometimes," he said, "the inevitable arrives faster than we expect." He shook Ryan's hand. "Congratulations! You've never called him a son-uvabitch before."

"You know what he told me before he left for Birmingham? If he had been anybody else, I would have laughed in his face. He said, 'A man's got to do what a man's got to do.'"

"Then do it," Solly said. "Maybe he was telling you indirectly what he wants you to do."

10

Ryan sang the blues. "Blue Moon." "Blues in the Night." "Blue Velvet." "I'm Mr. Blue." "Blue Bayou." Blue by you. Blue without you. Blue enough to kill you, Baby Blue. But deep down he knew he didn't mean a word he sang. He was only posing. Blue doesn't mean a thing when you're a whiter shade of pale. Besides, he couldn't pose anywhere near as well as Kick who was the best poser in the world.

11

San Francisco was the last-chance sanctuary of men who could live their special lives nowhere else in America. They were immigrants inventing, each in his own way, styles of masculinity that had never been lived so publicly before. The love that once had dared not speak its name suddenly would not shut up. In this way, and in this way only, these men were exactly like the women who at the same time all across the country were asserting the New Femininity. Ironically, while the feminist movement aimed to render women upwardly mobile, gay liberation engineered, with a petulant backhand English I've never really understood, the economic, moral, and physical decline of far too many homosexual men.

For all the noble talk of gay politics and consciousness raising, gay liberation looked to be ending in the intensive care units of San Francisco's jampacked hospitals.

"Never fear," Solly said. "Some dinosaurs always survive the crunch."

AIDS spread its incurable Kaposi's sarcoma cancer and pneumocystis across the City, across the nation, and around the world. It decimated gay men. Even as they became AIDS' chosen victims, their once-proud political victories became academic, pyrrhic. They had gained the City's voting booths and the legal protection of the outrageous baths and bars. But for all their human rights, they died daily. They kissed each other good-bye as the City's doctors switched off the machines supporting life in the bodies with which they had once so prided and preened themselves, and with which they had loved each other so much.

The City's morticians made a fortune shipping the remains of AIDS victims "back to Kansas." Kansas was where Dorothy returned from Oz. Kansas was where you came from if you were gay. It became a cliché of greeting for awestruck newcomers to the gay heart of San Francisco: "You know, Toto. I don't think we're in Kansas anymore." But Kansas comes as Kansas will, as Death will.

Solly found it ironic that the newly founded gay Atlas Savings and Loan at the corner of Market Street and Duboce had previously been a mortuary. When the vast stucco building first went up for lease, Ryan had suggested that it be turned into a gay disco called "Death Takes a Holiday." Upon seeing a *Chronicle* business section article on the affluence of gay males, Solly phoned me.

"Magnus! Have you seen the *Chronicle* this morning? We virtually have wagons trundling through the Castro with the drivers calling, 'Bring out your dead!' What an ironic mistake in bad timing. At the very moment when we need a gay mortuary, the building turns into a Savings and Loan. Give me the days when we were all sexual outlaws. We died quietly in our closets with our high-heel sneakers. The paper says we're now an economic force to be reckoned with: mortgages, IRAs, estate planning. Gone, gone with the wind, are the days and nights of serious sucking and anonymous fucking. What's happened to us? We've become, omigod, bourgeois! A fate worse than Death!"

Ryan always knew the physical joys and medical dangers of casual sex, but he never figured that personal love was more dangerous than AIDS. During wild nights of sex in the City before Kick and before the plague, he was always on his guard. But in-love, first with Teddy, and then with Kick, he let his defenses down. Teddy's first betrayal taught him that not even in-love is everyone a safe person. The first night when he knew he loved Kick, as much as he was in-love with him, Ryan said: "You could hurt me now."

"I won't ever hurt you," Kick said. "I'm fragile myself."

"Then we're safe people," Ryan said. He spoke the declaratory, almost indirect way that he had learned from Kick's nondemanding southern drawl. Until the night Ryan dared to address Kick directly, the night Ryan drove old Dixie down, their dissembling style was to infer their need or preferences to each other.

Ryan perversely found a sexual pleasure in always deferring to Kick. *If Kick wants to top me, I'm his slave.* If Ryan went wrong in love, it was in his deference. It was unnatural to him. He himself had always shone. He had deferred to Monsignor Linotti and the other priests and priestlings at Misericordia until he could defer no more and he had left their cramped little world. He had deferred to his parents but not to his brother and sister. His aggressive strength against them destroyed Thom while it strengthened Kweenie. He had never deferred to Teddy and Teddy had gone down to an alcoholic defeat Ryan had never intended.

"The strength I thought was a virtue," Ryan said, "was no more than selfish pushiness. It is, I think, a fault in my character."

Before Kick, Ryan had always been the sun in any relationship. He had Energy. He burned bright. His style had driven Thom mad. His strength had made Teddy weak. He felt he had two strikes against him. "Three and I'm out," he said. He was determined never to overshadow Kick.

Thom's and Teddy's weakness made him angry. He could not tolerate weak men. He wanted Kick to come to his senses and be more than strong. He wanted to take Kick beyond strength training to achieve real power. *Power is the ability to apply strength.* All his coaching of the bodybuilder to a super physique was his physical way of shoring up the inner strength, the moral fiber, the large soul of the man he wanted to be perfect.

His Catholicism had taught the boy in him lessons the man he became could not forget. In moral theology class at Misericordia, he had learned that grace builds on nature: the more perfect the body, the greater the capacity for sanctifying grace.

"This means," the ancient priest, a professor of moral theology, had taught, "that you must remain healthy in order to receive grace. When the body is sick, the normal channels of God's grace are closed. The sick can receive actual and sanctifying grace from God only by His holy dispensation. Therefore, remember, all your lives: *Mens sana in corpore sano.* Drink no more wine than at mass. Do not smoke, for it is an indulgence and indulgences are not good for the young."

Ryan sported the Look of someone who wanted to forget the mumbo-jumbo of his youth, but could not get over that old black magic. The priests had unknowingly turned him on sexually. "I can't help but think of healthy minds in healthy bodies," he said. At his worst, he was as corny as Kansas in August. "It's Kick Supreme. For once, I'm the moon. He is the sun. Not my usual role, but I think I like it."

"As long," Solly said, "as the sun can keep on shining."

"You don't need Kick's light," I said. I felt like Radio Station Magnus Bishop broadcasting small-craft warnings on the Bay. "You're bright enough to know that." I wanted to tell him that he was dissembling, that dissembling was ultimately dishonest mendacity; but at that early time there was already a madness in him, and I carried no weight against Ryan's joy in Kick's happy acceptance of his total deference.

12

That Christmas night, Ryan drove home alone, without Jake, from Solly's. *Help me make it through the night.* Kweenie had left a message on his machine. "Happy! Happy!" she said. "Catch you tomorrow." He sat alone in his dark Victorian. He gasped for air.

It was Ondine's curse.

"Gemini is an air sign," Tony Tavarossi had told him. "You're forever opening windows wanting more oxygen."

Ryan had all the doubts of a believer. "Maybe," he said, "it's more like the air is too thin on this forbidden planet."

Accidentally, that Christmas night, he made a sad discovery. He opened the refrigerator and found a brown paper sack. He wondered what it was. He thought it might spoil. He pulled open the bag. Inside were four syringes, a dozen hypodermic needles, and four small bottles of Decadurobolin. It had taken his breath away. The difference between the oral steroid he knew Kick had taken and the injectable Decadurobolin was the difference between venial and mortal sin.

All was lost.

Aren't we a pair! They had both lied. In their little night music, they were so Sondheim: one on the ground, one in midair. He had shown to Kick a deferentially false self. Kick had shared with him twenty new pounds of chemically false muscle. Was either one real to the other anymore?

He lay sprawled in the dark on the carpeted floor of his bedroom. Seduced and abandoned. Ground down into the realization that everyone is alone. Lost in their lives. In their deference. In their drugs. In their mendacity. All of them lost. Some more than others. For a while. Maybe forever. The truth weighed heavy on his chest. Squeezing his breath. Lost and alone. "Until the sham of companionship returns," he wrote, "and you can begin again to pretend in your coupling that you're finally making it together through the night."

He missed Kick. He missed the idea and ideal of Kick. For the first time in three years he was admitting to a self of himself that Kick, as much as he, had been lying in his teeth. To get what they each needed for themselves both of them said what the other wanted to hear. And they called it love. Ryan knew he could no longer deny his real self. He had to talk to Kick. He had to save him from himself. They both had to save themselves from themselves. Muscle wasn't worth the consequences of steroids. He had to really communicate with him. Kick had once asked him to move with him to a new plane of muscle. He must now tell Kick that they must move their relationship from the fantasy of muscle to the reality of health.

He had once sold his soul to get Kick. He had sold his own self to keep Kick. He hated himself for selling out what Annie Laurie had cautioned him against. He had bought into the Acquired Identity Deficiency Syndrome.

The needles and the steroids told him more than he wanted to know. Kick was selling his heart and soul for muscle gain. What had happened in his healthy soul to so endanger his healthy body? Solly had read to him in his *Physicians' Desk Reference* about the side effects of oral and injectible steroids.

He was Kick's accomplice. He had swallowed and snorted more drugs with Kick than with anyone else. But they never, never shot themselves up.

Maybe we're bad for each other.

Ryan tried to balance his conscience against his lust. He did not know if he dared ruin everything between them. His hard-on struggled with his heart. Guilt is a strange country. Ryan fell into a habit of his adolescent Catholicism. He examined his conscience. He knew the difference between sins of commission and sins of omission. It was the same old fight for purity against the sexual sins of the world, the flesh, and the devil. If he loved musclesex more than he loved Kick, he would say nothing when Kick flew back from Birmingham.

Christmas was an agony. Something was happening to him.

"Ryan," Kweenie said, "are you alright? You look feverish."

He gave her a present and scooted her down the hall.

"Here's my hat," she said. "Here's your door. Take your hands off me. What's my hurry?"

Ryan envisioned loving Kick with a new love, a higher, purer love. He examined his human heart. He loved Kick more than muscle. He knew the solution. Kick had promised him he could have anything he wanted. Clearly, he knew he wanted one thing only: they must keep on keeping on together, more nobly, more ideally than before. They had to clean up their act. Kick might not like him speaking out, but they were lost anyway if he didn't. Kick was the muscle. He was the talker. He made his living with words. Kick loved his words. He was resolved to the conversation he knew they must have after New Year's.

He feared he did not dare the act. He knew he must. He had been first cause and finally accomplice of Kick's fall. He had offered Kick a pedestal. Kick had climbed eagerly up. Ryan, kneeling in adoration at Kick's early natural splendor, could no longer ignore the poisonous transformation he had steadfastly refused to acknowledge. Kick's feet were turning to clay. He had muddied himself with serious steroids. He was growing too heavy to take high flight. Kick was becoming like everyone else on Castro. He was becoming ordinary against their promise never to become ordinary to each other.

Ryan, in conscience, like Streisand wanting Redford to become even more perfect, resolved, if necessary, to slap Kick awake. That Christmas he reread Flannery O'Connor's "A Good Man Is Hard to Find." He quoted O'Connor often. She was the only Catholic novelist of the American south, and a woman at that. O'Connor had once explained her own grotesques so flat out that Ryan could not forget. She had said that to the deaf you have to shout and to the almost blind you have to write in very large letters. Ryan owed Kick, for all the extraordinary pleasure Kick had given him, at least this warning due his angel, he feared, flying too close to the edge.

Ryan shied away from the A-Group holiday parties. He could not bear to go alone, answering the same question he had been answering for months.

"Where's Kick?"

He was no longer Ryan-Orion.

He was the left-behind half of a Famous Couple.

13

On New Year's Eve, Ryan drove alone to the rocky outcropping of Corona Heights. He pulled his VW Rabbit up to the curb below the gravel path that led to the crest of the mountain. For a long while he sat in the car with the engine running. He wondered how many people in San Francisco had sat in lonely debate behind the wheel of their parked cars wagering whether to drive to the Bridge or not. But it wasn't Death he wanted. It was Death he feared. It wasn't even Logan. Not really. Logan was Kick's bad boy. Logan was Kick's Teddy. Ryan understood all that. What he wanted was Kick himself.

We'll leave the city. We'll move to Wyoming or Colorado. Someplace clean where they've never heard of drugs or disease or dirty sex. Maybe some small town in Texas.

I'll sell Bar Nada and the Victorian. We'll buy a little place—Oh, God, this is sick. I want to take him off to a cottage by the sea. I don't believe I'm even thinking this!

Ryan looked at his eyes in the rearview mirror and laughed at himself. "Oh, God!" he said. "Please, please, please." He laughed again. "Oh, Jesus! I sound like Teddy begging not to be thrown out. Does everybody pleading make the same stupid sounds? Please? Please? Please? Praying is degrading."

This New Year's Eve was very different from the end of the year before. That night Kick had driven them down Valencia Street to the Devil's Herd, a gay country-western bar with a live band. It was one of the few times they ever went out. It was the first and only time they had danced together. They had held back against the wall around the dance floor watching the gay boys in their cowboy drag two-step to "Cotton-Eyed Joe" and line dance to the foot-stomping "Elvira." The band finished its set. The jukebox took over. The crowd of dancers broke up and headed back to their beers.

Kick surprised Ryan. He dragged him onto the empty dance floor. Anne Murray was singing "I'm Happy Just to Dance with You." Kick pulled Ryan close into his crotch.

"Come here," Bama-Alabama drawled. "Let's do a real buckle polisher."

For the first time, they slow danced alone on the floor. Ryan was in heaven. Kick danced as good as he posed. Ryan ignored the jealous remarks.

"What's that guy got that I haven't?"

The record stopped and Ryan stood a beat longer with his arms around Kick's big shoulders. Another record dropped, and again, Murray's sunshine-blue voice soared over the roar of shouted conversations. She was singing "Can I Have This Dance for the Rest of My Life?"

Ryan looked deep into Kick's blue eyes. "Can I?" he asked.

Kick pulled him closer. "Anything you want."

Neither man led the other. The toes of Ryan's cowboy boots met the toes of Kick's construction boots. They stood in place, each looking deep into the other's eyes, swaying to the music. The golden bodybuilder and the tall, dark man were a sight to see. No one dared cut in. They were together, totally into each other, aloof from all else around them. The music rose and ended.

A gay man dragged up in cowboy rodeo gear shouted, "Oh, darlin'!"

The two of them stood stock still with Ryan's arms around Kick's broad shoulders and Kick's around Ryan's waist with his palms on Ryan's butt. They were beyond words.

The band retook the stage. The lead guitarist started the backward count to midnight. The crowd joined in. Ryan felt like a missile on countdown to launch. It was midnight and in the careening bar they stood alone and untouched. They kissed deeply.

"This will be our best year," Kick said.

And it was, until March, when Logan Doyle hit town.

Ryan realized his knuckles were white gripping the steering wheel. He checked his eyes again in the rearview mirror. He hardly recognized himself. He had to save Kick. He felt like a priest whose vocation was to save only one soul whose redemption would be his own.

He looked out the car window at the rocky path leading to the top of the mountain. He feared he could not climb it. He was tired. The agony of waiting so many months for Kick to appear, and then comforting him against Logan's meanness of soul had exhausted him. He knew he must confront Kick, not to compete with him, but to communicate with him. Some things a man does not have to decide. Some things he knows he must do.

In the small heated car, Ryan broke into a Deathsweat. Novels and movies and plays and songs had always been his refuge. He was a part of all that he had bought. He walked through pop culture like a safe dress rehearsal against life's dangerous twists. *Movie dialogue.* "We'll always have Paris." *Song titles.* "Stop Draggin' My Heart Around." Feelings rushed hot through his head in search of a laugh, a smile, a song. Garland singing to Gable: "You Made Me Love You." Judy. Judy. Judy. Chewing up the mike. The road getting rougher. Lonelier. Tougher. All because the man got away.

Ryan adored cheap sentiment. At least in the comedies and tragedies of page and stage and screen he knew how others in similar situations had felt, and survived, or did not survive, the crisis he was facing.

Out in radioland everyone knew the lyrics to "Heartbreak Hotel."

So.

He had promised never to fall in-love with Kick.

So.

He had promised never to say no to Kick.

So.

He had long ago broken the first and was slouching toward bedlam about to break the second.

So what.

Kick had told him he could have anything he wanted; but Kick never expected him to call his hand. Maybe Kick loved his deference more than he loved him; but his deference, given in trust, now that they were in trouble, was no longer virtue. It was sin. If he rose from his knees, if he faced Kick directly, if he made them both persons, ordinary persons, he risked losing the golden, ideal bodybuilder forever.

Cinema montage. Music up. "If You Were the Only Girl in the World and I Were the Only Boy." *Music under.*

Cut to film clip: Crawford and Davis.

Crawford: "You wouldn't treat me like this if I weren't in a wheelchair."

Baby Jane: "But'cha are, Blanche. But'cha are."

Ryan feared running the film backward. He had played the Beatles backward and heard that Paul was dead. He feared retrogression. He feared Kick's descent from the pedestal, from the posing platform, from the bed of their high-wire act. Emerson had feared devolution. Tennessee's Big Daddy raged against mendacity. His Blanche was afraid of falling back into the brutal primitivism of human animals even before we were hairy apes. Ryan's nerves were ragged as a pair of claws scuttling across the floors of silent seas. He wished he had never gone to school because everything he had learned seemed to usurp his own original response to the universe—the same way Hollywood movies caused him to reference not himself but scripts, actors, and directors.

Ryan could no longer deny himself, could no longer defer to Kick, could no longer dissemble to the brute physical power of the bodybuilder, once lighter than air, whose sheer muscle mass, pumped with steroids, no longer reflected who Kick was and insistently defined what Ryan could never be: one of the boys.

Not one of those boys.

Bodybuilding had become a Deathsport of Attitude masquerading as a celebration of life's force.

Death, whatever its face, terrified Ryan.

Ryan: "If you were the only jock in the world and I were the only coach. If you were the only man in the world and I were the only boy. But'cher not, Kick. But'cher not."

But he was.

Ryan was like the man trapped in his car at the beginning of Fellini's *8½*. Ryan had to escape from his overheated car where his breath was fogging the wind against the cooler night air. He climbed free of the tangle of steering wheel and brake and clutch and pushed his way out the door. A downdraft of air from the top of Corona Heights hit him. He breathed deeply fearing he had not been breathing at all. He looked up the long rocky path. He saw the pinnacle of rock crag where he planned to stand at midnight when the known dread of the last year turned into the unknown dread of the next.

Some New Year's.

He began his climb. His rubber-cleated boots hugged the packed gravel. The half-mile climb seemed longer alone. He was not climbing like a lover running in lighthearted slow motion. He was slogging up against gravity like a man struggling to make time, and cover telephoto space, on film un-reeling in motion so slow he seemed he would suffocate in celluloid. He lifted one foot and then the other. He stood gasping for breath at the first level. He looked up at the second and third levels he must reach before he gained the top. The mountain's natural red rock glowed with an eerie violet light reflected from the City humming down below.

He approached the steep climb, hanging onto bushes that overhung the trail. His feet slipped. Loose gravel rolled down the hill into darkness behind him. The sweet smell of wild hemlock took his breath away. He made the second crest and then the third.

The rocky outcropping at the top looked too far away. He was losing out to gravity. He had the weight of the world on his shoulders. Yet inch by inch he made his way up the gravel trail. Every inch he gained glowed brighter and brighter from the lights of the Castro and all of San Francisco surrounding the mountain at its foot. Finally he took the uppermost crest. He stood, catching his breath, turning slowly, fully, to the City, real now only in miniature, spread out far below him. Market Street was a landing strip. The marquee of the Castro Theatre spiked up through the night.

It was a view from Golgotha.

The December night was warm and windless. A wisp of fog lay north over the Bay like a soft blanket thrown out between him and Bar Nada. Christmas trees spaced out on rooftops around the City glowed as brightly as the huge Safeway sign that dominated Market Street. To the west, red lights blinked atop the Erector Set of Sutro Tower. Moonlight bounced off the saucer of rocks where he stood. At night, no one, not even ravenous cocksuckers beating the bushes, climbed this outcropping of ancient moun-tain so wild and primeval in the heart of the City.

He knew what he had come here to do.

He was wearing Kick's clothes.

He unzipped the thick leather SFPD motorcycle jacket with the black fur collar. The jacket had been Kick's gift to him the Christmas before this last one. It was not a new jacket. It had been Kick's before it was Ryan's. It was that much more dear. He hugged the jacket to him like an embrace that would last forever. He shrugged its weight off one shoulder then the other. His motion was slow and deliberate. He intended to savor each station of his stripping himself naked to the night. The jacket slid slowly down his arm till he caught its yoke in his hands behind his butt. He swung it around, kissed the collar that had so recently ridden up against the nape of Kick's strong neck, taking up the scent of his blond hair. He slowly folded the jacket open and stretched it carefully out on the smooth rock of the cliff edge where he stood.

Memories. The autumn before, he had photographed Kick, shirtless, standing perilously close to the edge of the saddleback rim thirty feet below him. Ryan had lain belly-down on the gravel making the rim the horizon. His video camera framed only the cut in the rocks with an immense expanse of blue sky behind it.

Slowly, Kick had made his way up from the other side of the cut. Ryan's angle in the video shows first Kick's blond head, radiating sunlight, rising over the rim. Then, against the blue sky, he rises slowly up, in the flat perspective of the camera, as if he is rising straight up from the rocky mountain itself against the pure blue sky. Beneath his golden head, up rise his wide shoulders and chest and arms, stripped and oiled and thick with body hair. He looks naked, magnificent. He rises farther and the cut of his faded jeans hangs aslant across his slender hips, his cock and balls filling out the basket between his massive blue thighs rising up, until full-body he stands at last, full of golden grace, booted feet planted firmly on the rock rim, resplendent against nothing but the brilliant blue California sky, a man against the horizon.

Ryan knew they could not go back to that. They must go forward. He was warm, too warm. His body was layered in clothes vested him by Kick. He slowly unbuttoned the red-plaid flannel shirt. He moved careful as a priest. He pulled the tails of the shirt from his Levi's and peeled it from his chest and back, holding it over his nose and mouth, breathing Kick's spoor, mixed with his own, for minutes long enough to know that all his breath, and therefore his very life itself, was filtered through the gift of the beautiful shirt. He smiled into the frayed collar. With the smile came a squint that blurred the City lights. He folded the shirt into a tight roll and dropped it down onto the laid-open fur lining of the leather jacket.

His own sweat raised the clean soap smell of Kick's gray tee shirt that fit tight across his shoulders and chest and hung full and jock-baggy down his back and belly. Kick had taught him how to project, if not bulk, then a certain weighty manliness he had never known as a slender young man.

He squatted down on one haunch, boot heel up against his butt, to unlace Kick's boots. His small feet floated in the footpads worn deep where Kick's larger feet had walked so many miles. He pulled his wool-socked feet from the boots. He stood and crossed his wrists over his belly the way Kick had taught him, grasping the bottom line of the gray cotton tee shirt, stripping it up and off his chest and shoulders and neck. The collar rode tight up around his head, tugged at his ears, back-brushed his hair as he pulled the shirt off toward the glowing sky. He tossed the shirt carefully to the pile of clothes that were now his clothes.

The night air touched his skin directly. He was stripping down to receive all the Energy reflected up toward him from the City, out toward him from the American continent itself, down to him from whatever outer space there was behind the light canopy of night sky.

He unbuckled his belt and popped the buttons open on his jeans. Uncinched, the Levi's rode with slow gravity from the small of his back, over the rise of his butt, down his hips, opening the cracks and privacies of his body's biggest arch to the warm damp of the craggy rocks. His jeans fell slowly to denim piles over his socks. He stepped easily out. One sock came off with the left leg. He stood one sock off and one sock on, dinkle-dinkle dumpling, his mother's son, so long as one sock remained; his father's son, so long as he was his mother's. He was Kick's boy. The socks were Kick's socks. The socks were Ryan's socks. The socks were their socks.

Ryan stood naked, above San Francisco, his feet planted on the rough gravel of Corona Heights. The night wrapped around him. Nothing but volition held him to the Earth. He was more sad than he had ever been in his life. He was more happy. He stood in the shimmering City darkness. Fireworks, heralding the New Year, exploded intermittently over the rooftops. Was real darkness in the night? Were ancient spirits in the rocks? Was this the place of close encounters?

Far below, a light breeze swept the City from the Golden Gate, rippling through the lighted flag waving atop the Fairmont Hotel, dividing around the cold black monolith of the Bank of America, threading the needle point of the Transamerica Pyramid, blowing across the Tenderloin, down Market Street, past the white light of the Ferry Building, across China Basin and Potrero, around San Francisco General Hospital, out past Candlestick Park toward San Francisco International and the low strip of the Dumbarton Bridge. Ships off in the East Bay, night ships at anchor, floated quietly on the sheer face of the hidden current. All the noises of the City mixed to a low roar broken only by the syncopated poppings of Chinese fireworks shot off in the night. Across the tight miniature-grid of the dark City, cars, steel units of power and light, cruised the night streets. Closer, below him, cars and bikes edged bumper to bumper down Castro. Revelers, crowding the sidewalks, stood, too far away to be heard, in pools of light outside the open-faced bars. Strangers in the night.

The City's massive Energy rose in updraft around Ryan's naked body. He was stripped and open to it all. How we all end up, he thought, matters less than how we all are now. How we die matters less than how we live. Everything froze beneath him. He recognized the feeling. It was happening. He had to make it happen. This time alone. Without Kick. He had to conjure to save them. He saw a Face in the fog. It was his Face. It was Kick's Face. It was their Face. It was the Face of the Energy they conjured between them. Ryan became the Face, became himself, became the other, became them both, became them all, hanging suspended out of time, spiraling above time and place, flying against all gravity, turning back clocks, speeding forward, zooming, in himself, outside himself, directing his Energy out, collecting his Energy back into himself, fortifying himself for what he must do, taking himself in hand, making love to himself, beating off his hidden rhythms, loathing himself, loving himself, in himself, outside himself, feeling his body, leaving his body, soaring, standing naked on the mountain, erect, pumping, staring hard at Kick's Face in the fog, his Face in the fog, masturbating in wild pulses, saying, saying, over and over, saying, "I want . . . I need . . . I need it . . . I need it," hypno-chanting, "I need . . . I need . . . to know . . . what it is . . . to be . . . fully . . . human!" His body shook at the singsong words wrenched from deep inside him. The Face loomed larger over him. It was himself. It was the boychild he had tried to kill. It was the man he really was. It was the person he would become. It was himself. It was not Kick. It was himself. Gray. Shrouded. The past, and the future-becoming, both mysterious. Seeing Kick kneeling before him. Seeing himself faced with all possibilities, murderously dangerous, visions rising, converging, surreal, mystical, himself naked under his priest's vestments intoning high mass in a dark cathedral, sexy, himself moaning in a sling at the Slot with a fist up his ass, gaudy, himself singing "Muscle Blues" on *The Tonight Show*, flexing his own beautiful body, holding a cordless mike, oiled and pumped, naked but for Kick's brown nylon posing briefs, tight, transparent around his bulging cock and balls, hard-on, bathed in a tight dramatic spot, the Johnny Carson congregation sitting in a church, a silent priest praying for the dead and dying, bumping, grinding slowly through his posing routine, showing them true suffering, exhibiting real pain, the Face of the tortured and crucified, in living color, on network TV, singing "Stars Fell on Alabama," his own man, cuming, shooting, his cock convulsing in his hand, spewing sperm, white, hot, gelatinous across Kick's face, across his blond moustache, into his open mouth, never-ending orgasm, cum shooting up his own belly, down his own legs, across the rock, over the cliff edge, a voice, his voice, Kick's voice, their voice, roaring into the roar of the night, into the roar of the City, below the wild outcropping where he stood, high, alone, naked, afraid of loss, lost, mad with fear, howling into the exploding New Year's night.

14

"What'd you do last night for New Year's?" Solly Blue asked.

"I went crazy," Ryan said.

"Temporary insanity, I hope."

"I don't know yet," Ryan said. "Insanity isn't temporary until it actually goes away."

REEL SIX
Good-Bye, Dear, and A-Men!

1

Kick flew a direct flight from Alabama back to the tangle of San Francisco sexuality and California self-deception. Two weeks in Birmingham had changed him. He glowed with southern heat. He was more muscular. Two weeks shooting Decadurobolin caused more change than two months of hard training on a natural metabolism.

His Look had hardened.

Ryan was almost afraid of him.

His mosey had turned to the exaggerated swagger of professional bodybuilders. His lats rose from his hipless hips up the back of his V-shaped torso spreading like bat wings behind his thick chest. His pecs were massive. His neck thicker. From his broad shoulders, widened with new muscle, his huge arms hung out from his body as if he carried twin basketballs between each inner elbow and his tight waist.

The steroids had made him thicker. Thicker than ideal. He turned more heads than ever in the airport terminal; but this time, Ryan felt the stares more quickly averted—not like before when men with normal bodies had looked pleasantly at him, identifying with his athletic Look, desiring to be like him. Identification seemed to have vanished.

His Universal Appeal was disappearing.

He was beefcake on the cusp of appealing only to hard-core muscle-freaks.

He was meat.

Ryan was embarrassed. His lover looked like a man whose dedication had pushed him over the fanatic edge. The tan was too tan. The blond hair too hard. The blue eyes too brilliant. The muscles from outer space. What had looked dramatic in the hot overhead spot of the posing platform, in the cold fluorescence of the airport terminal was beyond the pale. Ryan suddenly realized why most women don't care for bodybuilders. Something brutal had happened. Something esthetic had died. Kick was no longer a physique artist. Something innocent was gone. That innocence had been his virtue. The well-muscled athlete, turned out like he might have strayed off some college playing field, had disappeared. In his place was a hard-core El Lay bodybuilder. A professional. A mercenary.

"So what do you think?" Kick smiled, anticipating the enthusiasm he expected from Ryan.

"You're too much," Ryan said ambiguously. He had been changing too. He could make one thing mean two things purposely, easily. He dropped back from truth. "You're terrific." He rallied his determination. "You . . . are . . . beyond our wildest dreams."

"I promised you we'd take muscle as far as it could go." Kick worked his seductive grin. "You ain't seen nothin' yet!"

Passengers deplaning from holiday trips streamed around them. Ryan wanted to embrace Kick, hold him, shake him; but he could not. Their feelings were at the public mercy. The straight couples hugging each other, in a way forbidden to them, suddenly made him feel very gay.

"Fuck it," Ryan said. He threw his arms around Kick and hugged him close. "I love you."

Kick hugged him back. "I knew you'd go for it. I did it for us. I'm going to take the Mr. California, the Mr. America, the Mr. Universe." He held Ryan out at arms' length. "I'm taking you along. I'll take the titles and you'll do our book. We're going and we're going together. How's that for a New Year's resolution! You and me!"

You and me. Ryan hated himself. His real face hid behind the face he showed Kick. *You and me.* Reciprocal terms. *You and me.* One can't be understood without the other. Like *father* and *child, love* and *hate, life* and *death, anima* and *animus. Yin* and *yang. Difference* and *deference.* Saying *yes* and saying *no.*

"You and me," Ryan said. "It's reciprocal."

"Me, jock. You, coach! Let's hit it!"

Reciprocity. Ryan had been thinking reciprocity all day. The *Chronicle* that morning had featured a lead story about the isolation of the AIDS virus, a virus turned reverse, a retrovirus that replicated genetic material backward.

Mirrorfucks and real love.

They were all falling through the looking glass.

Kick had changed over the holidays, but not so much that Ryan didn't love him. Kick's bravado was the bravado of steroids. Ryan felt immobilized. He knew what he must do, but he did not know if he could follow his plan. He knew the odds of convincing someone on drugs of anything at all. He would say nothing the first night. He would wait till the next night. In case everything went haywire, he wanted to have at least one last fuck, one last time together. What was it Peggy Ann Garner had said in *A Tree Grows in Brooklyn*? "The last time of anything has the poignancy of Death itself."

In the airport parking deck, Kick was surprised. "Where's the Corvette?"

"I felt like driving my own car," Ryan said. It was an independent act he was already regretting in the face of Kick's disappointment.

"Your car's fine," Kick said.

"A Rabbit hardly compares to a Corvette." Ryan stepped on the rebellion surging in his heart.

"I don't care what we drive as long as it gets us back fast to your bed. I haven't had sex with anybody but myself for two weeks. My balls ache."

"I thought you might be too tired."

"Me tired? I may have a little jet lag tomorrow, but I'm Mr. San Francisco tonight." He waved a small snifter of coke. They blew a couple of lines.

Ryan had readied the bedroom. He had washed the mirrors, turned back the bed, and set the track lights on low. Everything looked as it had always looked.

Kick was pleased. "I love you, madman," he said. "Come sit over here by me." Kick rose and slowly began stripping himself naked under the track light, checking himself out in the mirrors. "How do you like our new Look?"

"I love it." Ryan hated himself. "It's a wonderful Look. How can I help . . . but love you more than ever."

Kick raised his arms in a double-biceps shot. "Come on over," he said. "I want you to feel these arms." He dropped one arm and pulled Ryan's head into his rampant armpit. Ryan breathed the sweat like a man drowning. They moved through familiar paces. Double-bicep pose. Front-lat spread. Heavy-duty Most Muscular. Out of the cold airport fluorescence, under the hot bedroom track light, Ryan felt better about Kick's added size if not about its cause. Maybe the muscle was worth the gamble. *Maybe I'm a schmuck.* They shared a hit of popper. His tongue ran across the thick hair of Kick's pecs. Ryan's tits stood at hard attention under Kick's fingertips. Everything was right. Ryan was determined. If this was possibly their last fuck, it was going to be a fuck to remember. He took his own hard-on in one hand and gently pushed it between Kick's thighs.

"Break, break," Kick said. "Let's take a break." Sweat poured from his face. His dirty-blond hair was streaked with sweat. "Whoa!" Kick said. "I forgot what a workout this can be." He ran his hand down the rippled slab of his belly, palming the sweat toward his hard cock.

Ryan took Kick's sweaty hand and licked it dry. The sweet, sweaty taste he remembered had an almost acrid chemical after-burn.

"Let's lie back for a minute," Kick said. He took Ryan's hand and led him to the bed. "Come here," he said. He lay on his back, both arms pillowed behind his head. His big blond dick flopped hard and wet on his golden thigh.

Ryan knelt up in bed with his knees against Kick's side. "You okay?" Ryan asked.

"Too much popper," he said. "Maybe I have jet lag. The whole trip took a lot out of me."

Ryan smiled at him and shifted gears from heat to affection. He lay down next to Kick. He breathed the beach-fresh smell of Kick's Coppertone. He snuggled in close. The coke rush had been slight. He was content to sleep. Sleep would delay the showdown. Sleep meant one more night together before he sat Kick down to talk. He was happy Kick was home. He laid the flat of his hand on Kick's warm belly and stroked up to the pecs he adored. They were two hard velvet handfuls.

Maybe steroids aren't so bad after all.

Ryan turned chicken. "We can do this tomorrow night," he said. "Maybe we should get some sleep."

"Maybe I should sleep," Kick said. He winked. "You're not tired. Why don't I just lie back and you can carry on."

"I can't do that," Ryan said. More than once, after a scene, Ryan, wanting more, had masturbated on Kick's sleeping body.

"You know how to take care of yourself," Kick said. "Take care of yourself now."

"I can't get enough of you," Ryan said. He was mildly embarrassed. "You weren't always asleep?" he said. "You've known all along?"

"I know everything about you, Ry." Kick paused like a man handing out a belated Christmas gift. "You're my one true love."

Ryan's heart leapt to his throat. Kick had said the words he said so rarely anymore.

Why now? Why after so long? After Logan. After steroids. Why say you love me now? When I'm about to betray you.

Kick took Ryan's dick into his hand. "I want you to feel free to do what you want."

Ryan raised up on his elbow. Astonished.

"I want you to have a wild and wonderful and crazy time." Kick said it like an offhand order. Kick was directing the scene: he wanted to lie back and have his new muscle admired, loved, worshiped.

With ineffable sadness Ryan realized his true place in Kick's world. "I'd like that." It was a lie and not a lie. He pulled himself free from the curve of Kick's rib, feeling not a little bit like Eve pulling up off Adam.

Kick lay still, offering himself as a passive object of love. He was offering Ryan the scene a thousand men lusted for. To Ryan, sex was a sacrament, a Holy Mass, and Kick was sacred. He knelt like a solitary priest before the altar of his God. This was what was. His relationship to Kick had always been a mystery play. Bewildered in the fusion of the sacred and the sensual, he studied in the flesh the Kick he had studied so long on videotape. Kick's flesh looked perfect, but Kick was illusion. He was *maya*. He was appearance not reality. His life was his posing routine.

Ryan could not fault him for it. No one was perfect in an imperfect world. Nothing was what it seemed. That, at least, gave Ryan courage, because nothing, he reasoned, was exactly what you feared it to be. Yet he could not will Kick to change any more than he could change himself. Destiny was a tyrant. They both would be forever the boys they had always been. The way of the past was the way it was and the way it would be ever after.

Ryan was never meant to be one of the boys.

He sat back on his haunches, his knees against Kick's sculpted torso, looking down over the naked length of Kick's glorious body, remembering how he had been, seeing how he was, knowing what he would become.

Kick, his blond head again cradled in the palms of his own hands, closed his eyes. He lay like a beautiful, fallen warrior. He was the lazing soldier-comrade Whitman loved. He was the man Ryan adored.

Ryan touched himself, obediently, ritually, with his hand slick with Kick's sweat, studying for the last time, he knew, Kick incarnate.

This was the last intimacy.

This was the last time of physical company with this man he loved more than life itself.

This was what was. Not because tomorrow Kick might flee from Ryan's announcement; but because in the heart of darkness of this night, this moment, this hard point in a harder time, Ryan himself finally decided, because of the way they were, that, barring Kick's acceptance of the truth, barring his kicking of the drugs, this was the last time he could give more than he received. He had to know if he really could have anything he wanted from Kick. He had to know if he really was the coach.

He hated the peevish righteousness that rose in him like a power play. He didn't want to be right. He didn't want control. He wanted to have Kick. He wanted him alive, balanced, in their high-flying mutual act of love on the high wire, not haywire, not prematurely dead like both their fathers. Kick was the only man since Charley-Pop died who stood between Ryan and Death. He cleansed his heart. He stroked up the Energy, more loving than sexual, in himself. Kick's eyes remained closed; his breathing deepened. Ryan studied his face for a trace of his once soft smile. Ryan was the high priest of the temple of this body. He savored the years of intimacy. He felt the Energy of it all building in himself. Plato had said the soul rides the body the way a man rides a horse. Even if the soul inhabiting this body had faltered, Ryan knew he'd love forever the rider who had fallen so far. No matter the storm. No matter the risk of misunderstood communication.

He stroked himself to still, sad music. Was this always how Famous Couples crashed, burned, and exploded? He was Dido mourning Aeneas. He was Romeo, void, bereft over the unrousible Juliet. They were Daedalus and Icarus cruising too close to the sun. They had come so close to touching something eternal. They had pushed back the barriers of the finite. They had soared and cruised too close to infinity. Perhaps what gods there were had grown jealous or fearful and knocked them both from their high horse.

In his heart, Ryan said, *I'm so sorry. I'm so sorry. For what I must do. Oh, my God, I'm so heartily sorry.* Ryan, rising up into full passion on his knees, ejaculated the hope and sorrow of his seed across Kick's splendid body. He saluted all they had been and all they had tried to invent in a world with no models. He came, not to pleasure, but to sadness for all the joy they'd never know together again.

Kick's face remained expressionless. But he was not asleep. He was more brutally handsome than ever. *Handsome.* Ryan rolled the word like a hard gem in his mouth. *Handsome is as handsome does.* What would Kick do when Ryan asked him to clean up his act?

The thought was blasphemy. *Oh, my God, I am heartily sorry for having to offend thee.* Ryan lay back beside the man who called him *lover,* watching him, until, in the dim, gold light from the spot over the bed, they drifted in each other's arms to sleep together, the way they had the night of their first meeting.

In the morning, in the shower, Ryan washed Kick's body. For the first time, he saw on Kick's back, unmarred by adolescent acne, traces of something more than acne and less than boils. Three small eruptions. One on his shoulder and two in the small of his back. Exactly the blemishes Kick had long ago faulted as signs of heavy steroid use in professional bodybuilders. The angry red bumps signaled a boiling metabolism trying to detoxify poisonous injections. Mortality. Death.

Ryan was more resolved than ever.

Even if no one else spoke straight to Kick, he would; for the first time, he would.

Because he loved him.

All day he tried to find an opening. Some way to broach the subject, but Kick was full of chat about his Birmingham trip, about the Mr. California, about getting back to the gym.

2

That evening, they drove the Corvette to supper at Without Reservation on Castro. They sat at their usual table in the front window. Kick was excited by his return to the crowded street.

"God! Castro gives me face!" He pointed to his grin.

Usually Kick's perpetual optimism made him glow like the blond movie hero who can see the way out for everyone. Not this time. The steroidal changes in his face shook Ryan. He was in a way more handsome than ever, but he looked different from that first night three years before in El Lay. He was changed and he wasn't seeing straight.

He refused to acknowledge AIDS.

He could not see that Castro Street had become the River Styx. The gay parade had slowed to a funeral march. Ryan excused himself and walked a path through the close tables back to the rest room. Maybe he was the one not seeing straight. It was he, not Kick who had made himself the outsider on Castro. He needed a moment alone to catch his breath.

The toilet walls were covered with graffiti. He hated the curse of literacy. Once you can read, you can avoid none of the writing on any wall: "You told your parents you were gay. All they could do was hang their heads in shame. So God in Her infinite understanding sent you AIDS."

Ryan moaned. "Just what I need. Signs and omens are everywhere." He ran from the toilet back to the table. The graffiti resolved his imperative of health. He could not eat the food on his plate. Gay waiters seemed dangerous.

"Let's mosey around before we go back home," Kick said.

"I'd rather go home right now," Ryan said. "I have to talk to you about something."

Kick looked surprised. "You're the coach."

The ride home was strangely silent. Kick sensed something serious was up. He figured he knew what it was. Neither of them had mentioned Logan all day.

Inside the door of the Victorian, Ryan stood square in front of Kick. "Tell me again what you told me last night," he said. "Tell me we're lovers. Tell me I'm your lover. Tell me you're my lover."

Kick looked relieved. All Ryan wanted was stroking.

"Of course we're lovers," he said.

In his own qualified southern way, he meant it.

"I want you to say it. I want to hear you say it. I want you to say, 'Ryan Steven O'Hara, you are my lover.'"

Kick looked him straight in the eye. "Ryan . . . Steven . . . O'Hara." His slight drawl was almost ceremonial. "You are my lover. I am your lover."

Ryan embraced Kick for dear life. "I love you more than you'll ever know," Ryan said. "Don't ever hate me."

"How could I hate you? No one's ever treated me better."

Ryan led him into the living room. "I need to talk to you," he said.

"Okay, Ry. Lighten up. Don't make it sound so serious. You've always talked to me."

"This time I want us to really talk."

"Is this a test?" Kick asked. He sat down on the couch, prepared to right Ryan's delicate balance, even if it meant explaining Logan one more time.

Ryan took the chair opposite him. "Remember the day of the Castro Street Fair when you said you couldn't always be the bodybuilder? And I said you didn't have to be anything but yourself with me? Did you believe me?"

"Yes."

"Everybody knows how beautiful you look. I know how beautiful you are."

Ryan was afraid Kick might speak. He raised the palm of his hand flat against Kick, almost supremely, to stop in the name of love. If Ryan were interrupted, he might never speak his piece.

"You coached me out of my great depression. You aired my blues. You made me happy. You said you weren't responsible for anybody's happiness but your own. You said all of us are responsible for our own happiness. And you're right. But we're also responsible for not making anyone unhappy either."

"I know these past few months with Logan I've . . ."

"Please," Ryan said. "It's not Logan. It's something else. If you stop me, I'll never finish. Once we promised to take muscle as far as it would go. You've done that. Now we have to take our relationship as far as it will go. I'm scared. I admit it. There's a plague in the streets and I don't want either of us to die."

He saw Kick in a worst-case future, bloated with water retention, pockmarked with steroids, stressed out, his liver turning to pudding, his bone marrow rotten with cancer, his immune system depressed by the 'roids.

"Come on, Ry. We're both the picture of health."

"I'm not talking the fantasy of pumping iron. I'm talking bodybuilding as an innocent sport. I'm talking the reality of the muscle business. Not sport. Business. I'm talking steroids, Kick. I'm talking injectible shit. I found the syringes in the refrigerator. I saw the pimples on your back in the shower this morning. You've always told me everything, but you didn't tell me you were a shooter. I love your surprises, but this one scares me. Needles! My God. Intravenous drug users get AIDS. You can't add that risk to the risk of being gay."

Kick raised his arms in his famous double-biceps pose to charm Ryan to quiet. "Does this body look down-home healthy, or whu-u-a-t?" he drawled.

"I don't know anymore whether you're shooting steroids because you want to, or because you think I want you to."

Ryan said the one thing, but he thought something else. *I don't know anymore whether you're putting out to me because you want to, or because you think I want you to.*

"Don't answer that, please. Because if you're shooting up more for me than you, then I can't help but love you more. I like the bodybuilder trip, but I love you. You've got to stop. Think of the side effects. I don't want you to die. I don't want me to die."

"Ry, Ry, Ry," Kick said. "You're not going to die. You shouldn't read so much. You take this AIDS thing too seriously. This is America. Next month there'll be a cure."

"Too seriously? I'm not talking AIDS. I'm talking steroids. I'm talking poppers, coke, Kryptonite, MDA."

Ryan saw Kick did not like the conversation.

"You're talking Logan," he said.

"I'm not."

"You always say one thing and mean another."

"There's no way this can be forced into a triangle. I handled all that from the first. This is between you and me." Ryan looked hard at Kick. "I can't keep up with you. I'll die."

"Don't threaten me with your Death," Kick said. He folded his big arms like a stern father across his chest.

"I'm not talking about our Deaths. I'm talking about our lives. I want you to stay alive for very personal reasons."

"I know what I'm doing," Kick said. "I've always known what we're both doing. In the long and short run."

"We've become, my love, and don't think less of me for saying it, fashionably dysfunctional. Sex, street life, drugs, denial. Our dedication to each other has twisted into addiction."

Kick, engaging his arsenal of southern charm, tried a seductive southern smile. The redneck in him couldn't quite manage the pose. His face locked into a Look of hard, steroid-stubborn grin. He was surprised, the way the exceptionally beautiful, who always get what they want, are surprised when someone finally dares call their game up short.

Ryan was crossing the Mason-Dixon line where Northern values collide with Southern.

Kick, figuring to push Ryan's rebellion back to deference, armored his voice with one of his surefire aphorisms that had always before reassured Ryan. "We're keeping on," he said. "We'll keep on keeping on."

"I said I'd never say *no* to you, and now I am." Ryan started to cry. "Oh, damn!"

"This is hardly your style, Ry."

"I don't want a showdown."

"I love you," Kick said. "You love me. Leave well enough alone. What more is there?"

"I want real communication."

"Please don't cry," Kick said. "I'm not crying."

"I can't help it. I'm real. Look at me, Kick. I'm really real. Remember what Alice said? 'If I wasn't real, I shouldn't be able to cry.' We have to move from our fantasy level. We have to become real to each other."

"I thought we promised never to become ordinary."

"*Real* and *ordinary* aren't the same thing. Something happens between us when we're together. It's real. It's not ordinary. You know what I mean. You feel it, don't you? You feel the Energy we conjure between us?"

"Why do you think I keep coming back for something I told you I can't get anywhere else?"

"I've never said *no* to you. I've given you no bounds, no limits. But we have to have limits or we fall apart."

"The game has changed, Ry. I'm going for the Mr. Cal. I have to take steroids to be competitive. I want to turn professional."

"It's not worth the chance." Ryan sat upright in his chair. "You always said you wanted to be more communicative than competitive." Then he dared. "Do you need the crowds cheering your muscle?"

"No." Kick shrugged his shoulders. "If you want the truth . . ."

"Go ahead. Hurt me with it."

"It was always only you out there. I posed for you."

"Omigod. Don't do this to me. I love you so much."

"As for the other drugs, our use is no more than recreational."

"Don't be angry," Ryan said.

"I'm not angry. I'm hurt."

"I'm dying. I'm scared to Death. I can't go on like this. We'll get sick. We'll die." Ryan grasped. "Everyone's changing their bad habits."

"Fuck everyone," Kick said. "Whenever I do something, I do it the best and see it through to the end."

Ryan's heart raced at his words. *The end.* Just like the movies. *THE END.*

"If there's a problem between us, I never knew till now," Kick said. "We've had three good years."

"You've had three good years. I've had two."

"Don't start, Ry." Kick recognized the darting razor-flick of Ryan's tongue breaking its check. "I remember how you could start on Thom and Teddy, and how you go at Solly. I don't want you to start on me."

"I'm sorry. That was a rotten thing to say."

"I think I'd better leave."

"What?"

"I have to leave."

"Why?"

"If I make anyone unhappy, I have to leave," Kick said.

"You don't want to address our problem?"

"I have no problem. I've chosen quality of life over quantity of life."

"That's a problem."

"It's your problem. If I leave, maybe you can solve it."

"What's with you southern guys? How can one little conversation make you head for the door? What is this? *Gone with the Wind?*" *Southern men! Southern men!* "No working anything out? You just walk out the door and frankly don't give a damn?"

"I give a damn," Kick said. "You can handle this. You can handle anything. You're a writer."

"This is not one of my porn stories. You're not a character I want to manipulate. A long time ago, maybe, I had the conceit to feel I conjured you up in one of my stories. But I didn't. You have a life of your own."

"So do you."

"I don't want a life of my own." Ryan threw his hands up. "What play are we?" he asked. "We're *Six Characters in Search of an Author.*"

Kick read Ryan literally. "What author?"

"God? Maybe God. I don't know."

"You're the only author I know, Ry." Kick hit the pose of his smile.

"Don't look at me that way."

"Why not?" he grinned.

"I won't say what I have to say."

"Sometimes," Kick said, "the best thing to say is don't say anything."

"I sold my soul . . ."

"I told you I bought it back for you."

"You see? You are responsible for my happiness. That makes me responsible for yours."

"So what are we talking about?"

"Muscle and more than muscle," Ryan said. "You have the Gift. I want you to have the knowledge of the Gift. You have strength. I want you to have more than strength. I want you to have power. I want you to be happy with the Gift you have. I don't want you to hurt yourself."

"Hurt myself?"

"By gilding the lily. Taking steroids."

"Do you love me?" Kick asked.

"You know I love you."

"You know," Kick said, "how I depend on your love." He crossed the room and put both his strong hands on Ryan's shoulders.

"I love us," Ryan said. "I love the Energy-Being we create between us."

"So let's keep on," Kick said.

"I don't know if I can."

"We have to." Kick turned droll and his drollness was threatening. "How would we decide who gets custody of the Energy we create?"

Ryan retreated. He could not bear to lose title to that special place outside space and time which he had only found with Kick. "I don't want to cause you pain."

"No pain. No gain," Kick said. "We can grow from this. We can keep on keeping on."

"Maybe we're bad for each other."

"We look good together," Kick said. He kissed Ryan long and hard.

Nothing was going the way Ryan had planned. He wanted to say: *Stop the steroids.* He wanted to say: *Stay away from Castro.* He wanted to say: *Drop Logan and get a job.* He wanted to say: *You woke the man in me; don't kill the child.* Instead, he turned into Mary Tyler Moore, embarrassed at making a fool of herself: "You know me. Dumb old me. Always making mountains out of molehills."

"I do have to leave," Kick stood up.

"Why?"

"I can't stay here tonight."

"Because I opened my big mouth?"

"I hadn't planned to stay anyway. I promised Logan I'd drive to Bar Nada."

"Logan?"

"I want to talk to him," Kick said. "Like you wanted to talk to me."

Ryan could not ask what about. "You mean you weren't going to spend the night anyway?"

"I thought I told you."

"Maybe I forgot." Ryan tested the waters. "You have to leave?"

"I promised."

"You can't stay?"

"No."

"No?" Ryan looked bewildered.

"Don't worry," Kick said. "I'm not saying *no*. I'm saying *not now*."

"To me? To me? You're saying *not now?*"

Not now was the line, *that line,* Kick always used to put off kindly the petulant propositions from strangers on Castro. Ryan had heard him say it a thousand times. He knew on the street it meant *never*. He wasn't sure what it meant in his own house.

His deference smothered his weak defiance.

He conceded. One more time.

Never underestimate the power of sexual attraction.

Kick was no fool. He pulled Ryan's hands to his big pecs. "These are for you," he said. He draped his own arms over Ryan's shoulders. "I know what you're thinking," he said. "Don't worry. I'll only leave you once."

"What's that mean? What's that really mean?"

"I told you before. When I die."

"What do you mean *die?*" He scared Ryan. He sounded like Charley-Pop.

"I think you'll live longer than me," Kick said.

"No," Ryan said, "you can't ever die and leave me. Who would hold me when I lay dying?"

"You don't need anyone like I need you," Kick said.

"How do you need me?" Ryan asked. "I used to know. I need to know now."

"We have my body," Kick said. "We have your words. When my body is gone, all that will remain are your words."

What was is it Kick had said the night of the first muscle contest victory?

I want us to be a story told at night in beds around the world.

"So that's what I'm writing? Your memoirs? *The Gospel according to Saint Kick.*"

Kick grinned. "Who better than you?"

"You are droll," Ryan said. "Do I look," he smirked at Kick's impossible suggestion, "like an apostle?"

Is that what you want? A biographer? A press agent?

Most gay men only want daddies.

Kick silenced Ryan with a kiss good-bye.

"Trust me," Kick said.

Ryan was exhausted. "I'm too far gone not to trust you."

That night Ryan watched no videotapes. He had no lust for Kick's flannel shirts and posing trunks. Instead, he prayed. He actually knelt, for the first time in years, at the side of his bed, feeling more defeated than foolish, praying for Kick, praying against *dee*-struction and depression and disaster, praying for himself, praying for all the boys who had died, who lay dying, and who would die. AIDS was not going away soon.

Kick called from Bar Nada. He had to stay another day. The next day became the next weekend. On Wednesday of the following week, Ryan picked up the phone to call the ranch.

Is it psychic coincidence, or just chance, when two people try to telephone each other at the same time? It's happened to everyone. You reach for the phone. You pick up the receiver. You get set to punch in the numbers. The person you intended to call is already on the line. "It never rang," you both say. Maybe you overhear a bit of conversation you shouldn't hear while the other one waits for your phone to ring. Not a whole conversation, mind you, just a sentence. Not a sentence even, just a phrase: words spoken in the background by someone speaking to the caller on the other end of your line. All you catch through the beeps of your touchtone is an Attitude. Muffled syllables of words you can't quite hear. Then a voice, closer to the receiver, laughing, saying something like, "Shut up." Or maybe *Shut Up! Never let him hear you say that.*

"Kick!" Ryan said. "I was about to call you."

"I called you." Kick was still laughing.

"What's so funny?"

"I was just thinking about you."

"We're psychic."

"How are you doing?" Kick asked.

"Alright. I was concerned about you. How are things at Bar Nada?" He knew Kick understood he meant, "How are things with Logan?"

"The kitchen's coming along fine. It's a great remodel."

"I don't mean the kitchen. How are you? How's he been acting?"

"We've run the new lines for the sink."

"You can't talk. He's standing right there."

"Right. It's really going to be great."

"You sounded worried last Sunday. About him, I mean."

"Everything's okay. Our little plantation is almost ready for harvest."

"I thought it was harvested. I don't understand how growing pot can take so long. Isn't there a normal growing season?"

"We're timing the lights. Logan's been harvesting flower tops for the last month. He's boxed up a nice big bunch just for you," Kick said.

"Oh, really?" *With just a touch of insecticide.*

"He wants me to thank you for letting him stay here."

"Don't put words into his mouth. It's only as a favor to you."

"You make it all possible." Kick's attention was pulled away from the phone, then returned. "Logan says it's a perfect three-way split."

"That's a contradiction in terms."

"Trust me. Let me work with the balance of things," Kick said. "Another month or so and we'll have worked these plants for all they're worth. This little project will make us all a lot of money. Out of season, this crop will have a great going-rate. We'll have more cash to button up some top-notch art direction for *Universal Appeal.* I think it's time to get back on the book, don't you?"

"When are you coming back?"

"Give me a couple more weeks, okay?"

"That long?"

"I need some time to think."

"About what?"

"About what we talked about."

Ryan felt a twinge of hope. Maybe he had broken through. "Are you still working out?"

"You betcha. There's a great gym over in Santa Rosa." Kick paused. He made no reference to steroids. He was testing Ryan's resolve. "Living here at the ranch is great for training. Logan drained your goose pond. The cement bowl makes a great tanning basin. You know how I've always preferred quality of life." The sound of daring to challenge the odds was in his devil-may-care voice.

Ryan ignored the bait. "When will I see you?"

"Give me a couple more weeks. We're hanging pretty close to the ranch right now."

The two weeks dragged into a month. Ryan's Dr. Quack upped his pre-scription of Valium. Ryan said to Solly, "What can I say? Kick needs alone-time to think."

"He's not alone, you fool." Solly looked up from his newspaper. "And the time he's having, at your rancho, I might add, is the time of his life with Loganberry dingleberry. You're now letting two hustlers—count them, two!—live free!"

"When he's with Logan, he's as good as alone," Ryan said. "I trust him."

"Trust is the main mistake you can make in San Francisco. Never trust gay boys." Solly sipped his Coca-Cola. "I hear tell some guys with AIDS are still pulling tricks out of the bars and fucking their brains out at the baths."

"I'm retired from gay sex. I can't even watch gay videotapes."

"Not even mine?" Solly asked.

"Yours are solo jerk off. That's different from gay videos with all the sucking and fucking and rimming that look like sex acts from a lost civiliza-tion."

Solly waxed nostalgic. "Remember what a gay trick used to be? You pick him up. He fucks you and pants and screams and throws you around. He spasms and cums, moaning all over you like you're the greatest lay in his life, and you think he's a liar, and you wonder if he's faking, because you feel so dead, and you wonder if he really came. So when he rolls off you, you run into the toilet and squat it out to check for those few precious clots of proof."

"You're cynical."

"Cynical? You're cynical. You pray to God to stop the epidemic. What kind of God would let an epidemic begin? Your God is cynical. Why pray to a God to protect you from AIDS if he was mean enough to let it start in the first place? If he's so omnipotent, he has all the power. If you believe in that kind of God, you're as hapless as an S&M bottom begging for torture. I re-ally wish you'd stop worshiping at the Church of our Lady of Perpetual Guilt."

"Leave me some consolation," Ryan said.

"There are certain consolations I cannot tolerate," Solly Blue said. "Your Catholic obsessions prime among them."

"I beg your pardon."

"You're obsessive-compulsive. Obsessed with religion. Obsessed with sex. Obsessed with Kick. Now you're obsessed with AIDS. When are you going to realize that these obsessions are killing you? AIDS paranoia is worse than AIDS itself."

"Aha!" Ryan said. "I'm not obsessed. I'm not paranoid. Look at the newspaper you're reading. Even the cops have demanded masks and gloves and plastic resuscitators to deal with guys who might have AIDS."

"Yes, of course. The SFPD is so well known for its logic and compassion." Solly shook the newspaper at Ryan. "Add this to your obsessions. The Los Angeles coroner's office is working on plans to detect murderers who might take advantage of an earthquake. They will inspect all bodies to separate quake victims from murder victims. They figure a big earthquake will provide perfect cover-up for murderers waiting their chance."

"That's so El Lay," Ryan said. "That's your paranoia calling me obsessive."

"Don't protest too much," Solly said. "In an earthquake, you could kill Logan."

"You watch too much television. Besides, Logan's not really the point. He's negligible. He's nothing."

"Oh, yeah?" Solly read from the paper: " 'Coroner Thomas Noguchi revealed his plan last week to a gathering of the county's undertakers, who were told they must carefully inspect the corpses gathered in such a catastrophe for evidence of foul play.' Undertakers know things other people don't know," he said. He stared at Ryan. "I know what you're thinking," he said. "Be very careful of any new obsession."

"I don't know what you mean," Ryan said. "Thinking about what?"

"About shooting guns."

"Out windows?" Ryan was amused.

"At people."

"Come on." Ryan caught his drift. "I might want Logan gone. But dead?"

"Not Logan? Then maybe Kick."

"God! The last thing I want is him dead. I could never shoot him. I could never shoot anyone."

"Not even yourself?"

"You are," Ryan said, "evil . . ."

"And you're too ethereal."

". . . like the Devil tempting Christ!"

"You're not Christ."

"Get behind me, Satan."

"You need to get down to earth. You're overeducated. You need to roll around with my boys. You need to get down off that pedestal where you're kneeling between Kick's legs. You need to forget everything you've ever read or been taught. You need to feel raw and basic and nasty and dirty."

"I did that at the Barracks and the Slot."

"Do it again."

"I did it with Kick."

"Listen to me," Solly said. "I'm a guru of consciousness lowering."

"Consciousness raising."

"Consciousness lowering. For people who got too sensitive in the sixties and seventies."

"How California," Ryan said. "You'll make a fortune."

"We all live our separate fantasies that hardly ever intermesh. When they do, it's comedy. When they don't, it's another story."

"So?" Ryan asked.

"It's time for you to shit or get off the pot."

"Why?"

"Because what honor you have left in this town is on the line."

"My honor? I don't give a fuck about San Francisco."

"If you don't do something to resolve where you stand with Kick, then everything you say is so much a doo-doo about nothing. Stop being a fool. It doesn't become you."

Ryan was miffed. "At least, it's honest 'ado.'"

"Then," Solly said, "prove it."

3

Katharine Hepburn played her part in all this.

Ryan once accused me as well as Solly of a certain coldness. "Nothing ever takes either of you outside your calm, cool, existential selves," he said. He was wrong. About both of us.

The thighs of young hustlers lowered Solly's consciousness.

I, Magnus Bishop, sometimes have what I call *grand moments* when something on screen or on stage truly overwhelms me. In a theater, I sit, up front and center, closer to the action than most of the audience dares to sit. Sometimes I forget who I am. I forget I am a professor of popular culture. Sometimes I am sucked up from my seat into the vortex of drama that art, more intensely than loose reality, tightens down into those old Aristotelian satisfactions of unity: this time, this place, this action, this certain resolution.

Stage and screen in two hours resolve plot and characterization and concepts in a definitive way that real life, suspended open ended, rarely does.

Distractions, unforgivable distractions, in a theater make me want to kill the gum-poppers, the coughers, the whisperers, and those self-important few who wear wristwatches that beep, once, then twice, like electronic crickets calling feebly to one another throughout the dark field of the audience.

Only once for me was the distraction in the audience, perhaps something like the front-row murder committed by the Hell's Angels during the Rolling Stones concert at Altamont, more intense, tighter than the action on stage.

It was a winter-season night at the Curran Theater when Katharine Hepburn, playing her starring role in *The West Side Waltz,* must have felt even her grand self being virtually dragged from the stage to the orchestra where Ryan, glowing more intensely passionate than the Luminous One herself, became larger, immense, explosive, dangerous in the seat next to me. That night in that theater, because of all that was happening, a cast of six and an audience of six hundred sank, in one grand collision, like so many dark ships under the brilliant intensity of Hepburn's face, of Ryan's face, and the third face from which neither Hepburn nor Ryan could keep their eyes.

Kick was where he shouldn't have been. Handsome. Glowing. Radiant. On the arm of Logan Doyle.

It was Saint Valentine's Night. Ryan had bought rear orchestra seats for himself, Solly, Kweenie, and me. With Kick lodged in up at Bar Nada, Ryan was strung out writing what he called "Dear Kick: Letters You'll Never See." They were turgid *Journal* entries.

I feel you receding from me like a sleek white ship moving under heavy sail from the Embarcadero into the windswept Bay and out toward the Golden Gate. Cries of lonely gulls screech over the waves churned up behind the boat. Everything in life seems borne backward on the tide. Time is the only villain. I lie sleepless in the night. My sheets, unwashed, smell of the suntoast sweat of your blond body. I dream of sunlight whipping through your blond hair in the wild wind of your topless Corvette. Once you moved toward me. Now you move away from me.

Ryan's going to bed was a ritual preparation not unlike a little suicide. He straightened up the house. Ran water on the evening's collection of glasses and snack dishes piled in the sink. Washed his face. Brushed his teeth. Carried a glass of water to his bedside. Stripped down to a tee shirt. Opened the pill bottle. Swallowed the Valium Dr. Quack prescribed for him, because, Quack said, the world and he were at odds. He lay in the bed, waiting for pills to slow the rush of consciousness. His *Journal* beside him on the bedcovers.

Signs and omens are everywhere. If my molehill has become a mountain, it is Mt. St. Helens. Why couldn't we have been blown away like that lucky, lucky boy and girl, honeymooners at last alone, sleeping in each others' arms in their small tent on the edge of the volcano. They died the moment when they had said yes to everything about each other. We haven't died. Worse. I sleep alone. He sleeps with someone else. I know I'm losing my grip. My life has never been so star-crossed.

He had pasted a news clipping on the page. "A ground search of the volcano area discovered the bodies of two men who had been riding horseback in the upper reaches of the Green River Valley, about twelve miles north of St. Helens." The script was perfectly Ryan and Kick. "One man apparently was watering the horses at a stream when the mountain exploded. He dived or was knocked into the water, surviving the initial eruption. His companion and the two horses were killed instantly. 'They were burned,' the county chief of detectives said, adding that the hot blast 'burned up the ridge and burned over the ridge. Then it burned down the other side of the ridge. It took everything.' The surviving man picked himself up and stumbled eight miles through the hot ash. But finally, succumbing to his injuries or the fumes from the ash and gases, he lay down, covered himself with a sleeping bag, and died. There were huge blisters on his face."

Ryan's own handwriting picked up after the clipping:

So, like that poor man, I've been knocked from my high horse, my companion irretrievably changed, our horses burned dead, me crawling through ash and gases, but unlike him I cannot die. I can hardly sleep. I want nothing more than to lie back and never wake up again. I can't even take refuge in sex anymore. It is dangerous. There is no joy in it. Other men, because they are not him, would simply remind me of him. There is no one I can turn to. No one can do anything but comfort me with words or with their caring touch, which hurts me worse because their words are not his words, their touch is not his touch. He was the measure of everything in the world. I want to cry. I want to die. But I go on living. The wave of fire has not killed me yet. I've never felt so unloved or so unwanted. I could easily do something crazy. I could easily flip out and never come back again. My brother betrayed my trust. My first lover betrayed my trust. Now this man, I don't know yet, may not have been trustworthy.

Saint Valentine's Day meant something to the romantic in Ryan. With Kick gone this night, all these nights, he needed the feel of company. He had insisted on paying for the four tickets the way he had always paid Kick's way. He was the last of the big spenders. Kweenie and Solly and I were his guests.

If you can't go out with your lover, go out with a crowd.

We arrived at the theater early. Ryan never liked to miss the beginning of anything, and no matter how dreadful the drama, always stayed in his seat through to the end. He was excited by the milling crowd in the ornate lobby. On the sidewalk beyond the brass-and-glass doors of the theater, ticket holders brushed shoulders with street people. The theater was on the edge of the Tenderloin, only four blocks from Solly's penthouse, not far from the Market Street corner where, for years, straight young hustlers, eager for a gay buck, leaned insouciant against the dirty windows of the deserted "Flagg Bros Shoes" waiting for johns cruising by on foot and in cars.

"Ah, yes," Solly said as we walked up the street. "I know this corner well. I want my ashes spread here . . . in the gutter." He pointed to one of his boys working the opposite corner. "You'd like that one," he said to Kweenie. "You're his type of woman."

"Darling!" Kweenie shook her red hair. "Me? Recycle trash?"

Solly loved to find tricks for friends. "You'd like him. He's a good boy. He's nineteen. He's a recovered alcoholic."

"Recovered in what? Chintz? Corduroy? Leather?" She tapped her program on Solly's shoulder. "Behave yourself."

"*West Side Waltz* is a new play." Ryan was acting as tour guide. He was intent we all have a good time. He needed a good time. "The author wrote *On Golden Pond.*"

"That's a credential?" Solly said.

"Who cares if it's good or bad," Ryan said. "Hepburn is the event." He stood taller than usual, putting on a certain Attitude, the kind of air that homosexual men cannot help assuming in a theater lobby.

The incoming theater crowd flowed around us. Small islands of chattering yuppies staked their territory, speaking in clenched-jawed Stanford voices meant to be overheard. We watched faces. We listened in on passing conversations. A cluster of gays in screamer tuxes and full leather camped against the wall nearest us. They were *on.* They *loved* Lansbury whose picture hung in the Coming Attractions poster for *Sweeney Todd.* They *knew* that little Joel Grey was hung bigger than even the superbly hung Roddy McDowall. They called Edward Albee a "gay hypocrite" because he refused, for "commercial reasons," to allow four men to play the two couples in *Virginia Woolf,* "which was his original concept anyway." They loudly dished everything they'd ever read or heard about show biz as if gossip columns and rumor were theater.

"Why is it," Solly said, "just because queens take it up the ass, they think they're critics?"

He stole the line from a German poem written before the turn of the century about decadence among chic Berliners. I didn't call him on it. I let him get away with his bit of borrowed wit. He and Kweenie and I were all on the same mission. Ryan needed any distraction we could offer. He had been hearing new rumors about Kick he did not want to hear. In that well-lit lobby, Ryan's face was carefully masked. The three of us stood with him, minus one, if the subtraction of Ryan's real face, like the subtraction of Kick from his life, counted.

What happened that night happens only in theaters. I've watched the scene in a thousand movies.

Ryan insisted we settle into our seats early. He liked to establish territory by presence, as if being seated first, much like his primogeniture with Thom, gave us some strange squatters' power, showing those arriving after us that they must excuse themselves to us, making them somehow apologetic. After all, they were disturbing us, weren't they, making us stand and press the backs of our calves against the flipped-up seats, so they could crawl and bump, more apologies, through the narrow space between our thighs and the seat backs of the row in front of us.

It's an age-old theater game: well-dressed, overfed bodies trying to make themselves small, crawling, mumbling regrets, toward their assigned places. Specific seats in the universe for three hours. The authority in the usher's flashlight presiding over the ritual, transferring dignity to those of us already so properly, maybe prudently, seated, against the indignity of the crawl of latecomers.

The difficult *pas de orchestra* gave Ryan a vantage from which to command silence, at first warning politely, from those who, after the curtain rose, continued to talk, then whisper, or worse, comment, Look-she's-coming-through-the-door-and-she's-wearing-a-hat, giving a blow-by-blow running commentary as if they'd come to the theater with a party of the blind. By the third warning, Ryan was given to saying things like, "Madam!" They always became "Madam!" by the third warning. "Madam! Quiet! You are not home watching television."

Plays, even movies, were sacred events for Ryan. He did not want to be disturbed, distracted, pulled back from the brilliant light of the stage or screen by noisy wives dragging disinterested husbands out for a night on the town.

A pair of straight couples inched over us and settled down apologetically. Ryan seemed pleased. They would be no trouble. The wives chatted quietly.

The husbands, on opposite ends of the pair of wives, flipped the pages of their programs. They were not so comfortable as their wives. They had been dressed in their three-piece suits since early morning. The wives were fresher. Dressed for the evening. In from the suburbs of Orinda and Milpitas. Wives, not husbands, buy season's tickets.

Suddenly, Ryan leaned across me to Kweenie and Solly. His face was agitated, alarmed, like someone urgently seized by a premonition based on what? A glimpse? A lightning dart of recognizable Energy? Something that distinguishes a special face from the anonymous heads of the dark audience? Ryan started in his seat the way an animal downwind catches the shocking spoor of the hunter, seconds before the glint of rifle flashes once, and disappears through thickets of leaves.

"You're not going to believe," he said, "who in two seconds will come through the side-aisle curtain." He nodded toward the draped arch stage-right of the first three rows.

It was Kick.

Naturally.

Of course.

Why not?

Life has no coincidences. Only collisions.

Twenty rows and three hundred people between them. All of it, the whole theater, dimmed to soft focus. Kick knew instantly what he had walked into. His blond handsome face hardened like a plate. I felt the heat rise in Ryan's body. He sat up in his seat straight as a judge. I felt him growing hotter, growing physically bigger next to me. He was huge. He transmitted to Kick in the same way—now I was witnessing it, actually witnessing—that he had confided to me they communicated in bed and out. Beyond words. Out of time and space. A single laser of light, red-gold at Kick's end, muting to virulent green at Ryan's, cut through the low-lit gloom over the seated audience who were facing the stage waiting for something to happen, and something was happening. Palpable. Real.

"Turn yourself down," Solly said. "You're going to explode."

Ryan said, with no self-pity, and with full salute to the irony, "This could only happen to us." And he knew there was no more *us* for them. Kick was not alone. "Do you see now," he said to me. "I wasn't making it up. This stuff between us keeps happening. Keeps growing. Never stops." He grew big as a blotter that could absorb very little more.

The houselights dimmed. The stage lights came up. The play began. Dorothy Loudon entered the set. Polite applause. The audience, settling into Loudon's opening soliloquy, anticipated the great Hepburn's entrance.

The light from the stage fell, even to my eyes, directly on Kick at the right end of the second row. Kweenie and Solly and I tried to watch the stage, but the lightbeam from Ryan to Kick, and back, was so powerful I was distracted from the stage more than Ryan had ever been by the most unruly audience.

Kick's blondness, objectively and truly, was striking. No matter what drugs he was taking, he was not becoming the mess Ryan projected on him. Kick Sorensen remained a brutally handsome man. Square jawed. Sculpted features. His carefully groomed blond head sat on a thick muscular neck. His broad shoulders spanned the seat back, inadvertently pressuring those seated on either side. The woman on his left did not pull away. Logan seemed to enjoy Kick's hard shoulder pressing against his own. Kick's athletic presence glowed in the stage light. He eclipsed everyone. Even Logan.

I felt sorry for Ryan, really sorry for him, in a way I had never fully realized before from his telling of it. Kick was the stuff of theater. He was dreams and fantasy and ideals and aspirations. He was from Central Casting. He could have played the title role of the drop-dead blond athlete in Albee's *The American Dream*.

The designed curve of the front-row seats turned Kick, at the far corner of the stage, almost full-quarter profile toward us. He kept the impassive plate of his face directly on Hepburn.

He knew. I knew he knew. I knew he knew Ryan knew. I knew he knew we all knew. We were that tight little circle around Ryan that he had never penetrated. He knew he was not one of us. He knew we all knew each other too well, as sure as he knew exactly what was happening to them both. I can't say I saw it exactly, but I feel certain I saw his eyes involuntarily dart fully to Ryan sitting bolt upright next to me. Always, I'm certain, Kick was peripherally aware of Ryan, whose escalating Energy beamed out through the bald screen of his high forehead across the rows of seated heads.

Behind us, a woman leaned forward and whispered, "Will you all please behave!"

Kweenie giggled. "Have a taste of your own medicine," she whispered.

Ryan could not keep his eyes on the stage. Would not. Tried to. Could not. He borrowed Kweenie's opera glasses. He made the set piece complete. He could not *not* do it. He raised the glasses to his eyes, studied the healthy glow of Hepburn's skin, translucent with the dignity of age, of a life she herself lived through an undying love for Spencer Tracy, as part of a Famous Couple; then, slowly, with a great deal of discipline, ever so slowly, he turned his head with the glasses tight against his eyes, and swept them over the dark backs of heads until he was close up on Kick's brightly lit face.

Ryan sat perfectly still, reading the golden face that never moved. Not once. Not during the long instant of the one look Ryan allowed himself.

In that moment, I felt the surge of the long riptide of wild passion. Suddenly I understood.

Passion.

That was the name of the Energy they had so long conjured between them. It was passion. I felt it, felt what it must have been like between them: hot, horny, stoned, roped, muscled, oiled, posing, rapping, stroking, screwing, sucking, sniffing, licking, hugging, lifting off together.

Not that Ryan moved or even shuddered. Quite the opposite. Actresses did not drop their lines. Trains did not roar into tunnels. Waves did not crash on the beach. Trees did not bend and sway under the force of the wind. Lightning did not flash. Thunder did not crack. Dogs did not howl in the night. Crops did not fail.

Nowhere, that is, but in Ryan's heart.

I felt his palpable Energy. I felt Kick's. It was passion and more than passion. Something there was beyond human reason between them. A laser of burning intensity connected them. I felt Ryan rising up, flying up toward the ceiling of the theater, floating over the heads of the audience, as if he had fainted or died or both and he was enduring an out-of-body experience once again. Ryan was on a long leash, but no one, particularly Kick, was holding the other end. Only Ryan, by strength of his own character, held himself, raw, bleeding, and lacerated in the seat next to me.

Sixty seconds it lasted. No more. No less. One minute. And then he lowered the glasses into his lap and turned his eyes back to the stage.

I wonder if Hepburn, herself, up on that brightly lit stage with all those upturned faces adoring her, could not but feel herself, instead of stage-center, triangulated with the two faces burning out in the darkness. I wanted to write to her to ask her if she felt something more fragile than a mirror crack that night when her play became only part of another drama.

Before Hepburn took her final curtain call, Ryan rushed us from the theater. We were escaping.

Jack Woods, the tattooed bodybuilder biker, caught Ryan's arm. "I saw everything," he gloated. He stood 220 pounds in full black leather, chewing the butt of his unlit cigar.

Ryan rushed us out quickly through the Tenderloin night to Solly's penthouse.

"What was Kick doing there anyway?" Kweenie asked. "Some nerve. I thought he was at Bar Nada."

"You could never get him to go anywhere but to bodybuilding contests," I said.

"And to bed," Solly said.

It was true. Because of Kick, Ryan had given up the popular culture that entertains ordinary people as much as he had given up his circle of friends.

"Ryan's not mad because Kick was there," Kweenie said. "He was mad because Kick and Logan were wearing almost identical plaid shirts. He hates couples, straight or gay, who dress like twins."

"Kick lives his own life." Ryan was unconvincing.

"Since when?" Solly asked.

"He always has," Kweenie said.

"Since before I found out about it," Ryan said. "I'm the last to know."

"They say that breaking up is hard to do," Kweenie said.

"Now I know," Ryan said. "I know that it's true."

The jokey song lyrics could not hide his sadness. I looked him straight on.

Face, I've written more than once, is the essence of cinema. RKO once spun movies out of the legs of Fred and Ginger, but the best movies have been built around the memorable faces of the likes of Garbo and Gable, Crawford and Redford, Newman and DeNiro, Streisand and Streep, and Hepburn herself. Television has reduced the mystique of Face to talking heads, but the lure of Face remains.

Ryan's was an open book. I could not hold my eyes on his face. He was at that moment too open, too real, too vulnerable. He had been insomniac for a month. His features were the wreckage of reality.

I never wanted that lovelorn Look in my eyes. For that reason, I've always avoided romantic relationships. I've generally lived alone. I prefer to confront faces only on celluloid in wide-screen color, with the two-dimensional plane of eyes and nose and mouth spread twenty-feet across the silver screen. Face to face in the flesh is almost more that I can tolerate. I fear the fatal lure of Face.

Ryan had fallen through the looking glass of Kick's face.

"So. Ryan." Kweenie took up imperious residence on Solly's sofa. "How do you like it?"

"Like what?" he said.

"The treatment you're getting."

"What treatment?"

"Men," she said. "The way men are treating you. Maybe now you understand why women act the way we do. We're tired of reaching out to men." She had the direct drive of a sister who felt she could say anything. She was angry with the anger of what Kick's seed had planted in her body, but she had too much compassion to tell Ryan the truth of how Kick had betrayed him more than he knew when she herself had caused the betrayal. "Because of a man, I had to have an abortion. I had to do violence to my body."

"To say nothing of the child," Ryan said.

"To say nothing of the father." Kweenie corrected him. "What did that jerk suffer?"

"You never told him?"

"Told him what?"

"That you were pregnant?"

"No."

"That you carried his child?"

"No."

"That you killed his child?"

"His child? His? What's this *his?* What's this *killed?*"

"His. Yes. Yours too. You murdered your own child."

"I murdered nothing but something hateful he left inside me." Kweenie had taken advantage of Charley-Pop's long illness. She had hit Annie Laurie at a weak moment and extricated herself in the sixth grade from Catholic school. She knew little about the moral theology that drove Ryan. She was not a victim of Catholicism. She was an artist.

"Why are we discussing this?" Ryan asked. "I've got other things on my mind. I can't believe this."

Kweenie pulled off her kid gloves. "What can't you believe? That I'd take care of myself? Take a lesson."

"Only a whore would murder a child."

Solly and I could not move from the room without being obvious; but then neither brother nor sister seemed embarrassed. Both of them were busy deflecting their own guilt.

"Only a whore takes care of herself?" Kweenie said. "Let me tell you something, Ryan Steven O'Hara. Let me tell you something you don't know. Let me tell you something only daughters know. Let me tell you what mom told me happened between her and Charley-Pop the first year they were married."

"You can't tell me anything about Annie Laurie and Charley-Pop."

"Our mother had a D and C, Ryan. Do you know what that is? It's dilation-and-curettement surgery. It's a Catholic abortion."

"I don't believe you!"

"Believe me. She told me she had to take care of herself. She told me that baby, who came before you, might have killed her."

Ryan was crying.

"She told me the name of the doctor who took the thing out of her that would have killed her. She told me it was a boy baby, a son she might have had who came before you. Just like you came before Thom."

"No."

"Think of it. An older brother who might have pushed you around the way you pushed Thom around."

"Shut up," Ryan said. "Just shut up!"

They sat staring at each other.

"Why," Ryan finally asked, "are you telling me this?"

"Because I want to get through to you. I want you to take care of yourself. After what I saw tonight, you have to take care of yourself. Kick's certainly not taking care of you. I can't. Magnus and Solly can't. You've got to take care of you."

"It's none of your business."

"You're my brother. I love you. You're so desperate."

"I'm not desperate."

She played her Streisand Jewish shtick: "You want I should sing you 'Desperado' to show you how desperate?" She put out her hand toward Ryan. "Cut Kick out of your heart. He's doing to you what men have been doing for ages to women. Get over it. Get something out of it." She took his hand in hers.

"What am I supposed to get out of it?"

"Abort him. Forget him. Nothing goes on forever."

"Being without him will go on forever."

Kweenie turned to us. "You're wrong," she said to Solly. "Ry's not obsessed. He's possessed."

"Maybe," Solly said, "we should call an exorcist before he says your mother sucks cock in hell."

"Why can't you turn Kick free?" she asked.

"Because," Ryan said, "I'm a carnivore. Because he's a carnivore. Because muscle is a specialty act. An eccentric act. Because muscle is about incarnation, about becoming meat, worshiping meat. Because he wanted me to love his flesh, worship his flesh, become his flesh . . ."

"As always," Solly said, "Catholicism."

". . . because some tribes sacrifice blonds to the sun. Because we promised each other certain things, certain things only buddies can promise each other late at night, certain things that only a man can promise another man . . ."

Kweenie stuck her index finger into her open mouth and made gagging sounds.

". . . certain things I no longer find it tolerable to live without now that I've tasted them."

"Is this love?" Kweenie asked.

"It's addiction," Solly said. "It's harder to get over than love."

"This isn't funny," Ryan said.

Life, John Lennon said, is what happens to you while you're making other plans. Life, Cicero said, is a play with a bad last act. Life, Solly said, is a joke.

Ryan went for the punch line.

4

During the next month, Ryan holed up in his Victorian. He wrote fast and furiously on a new manuscript. He called me on the phone. "It's post-gay. It's post-*Manifesto*." he said. "I call it *Killing Time till Armageddon*."

"Finally, your memoirs?" I asked.

"No way. I hate sensitive little persons earnestly forging their souls in the fire of life and emerging whole as Thomas Merton on the last page. I'm an asshole. How can I confess that to the world? I'm an asshole. If anything, I'm working to get my memoirs into a hundred words or less."

"So what's it about?"

"There is no God in Oz. There is only the phony Wizard. And San Francisco is his City. Castro is a godforsaken place. God may have created the world, but Satan designed it."

Ryan's depression had turned to bitterness since the night at the theater. He was unhappy with life. He understood the Luis Buñuel films with the dog always walking through the plots as if men were only one mad-dog bite away from rabidity.

"Have you talked to Kick?"

"Three times. On the phone."

"And . . ."

"And nothing. He acts like nothing happened that night. We've never mentioned it."

"So you're content to let your affair fade away and die a natural Death?"

"I'm writing him letters."

"Are you mailing them?"

"No."

"Why not?"

"Kick experiences very little of the soul-searching that goes with living. He's too beautiful to be bothered."

"But you're bothered."

"No. I was bewitched, but I'm not bothered. I'm not bothered the way Arthur Jones is not bothered."

"Who's Arthur Jones?" I asked.

"Kick trained with him. He's the guy who invented the Nautilus exercise machines. He's a self-described misanthrope. . . ."

"So now you've replaced misogyny with misanthropy."

"Jones keeps a .45-caliber pistol under the front seat of his car. He knows about human treachery."

"How's that?"

"He deals with bodybuilders."

"How do you know all this?"

"I'm researching him for an article. He likes to quote Twain's line: 'If you pick up a starving a dog and make him prosperous, he will not bite you. This is the principal difference between a dog and a man.'"

"So you're bothered," I said. "What are you going to do?"

"I'm going to wait until he's tired of Logan."

"Solly says you should throw them both out of Bar Nada."

"No. As long as he's living in my place, he's thinking of me. I know he is. I intend to play the gentleman to the very end. If it kills me. It's my only shot."

"I think you're making a mistake."

"I have," he said, "something very important to learn here. I want to milk my feelings for all they're worth. If I don't do that, then all this gay emergence has been for nothing. I want to feel it all. What it felt like at the beginning. What it feels like at the end."

When Ryan's Victorian could no longer contain his exploding despair, he took to the streets, the last refuge of the urban damned, shrouded in a fur parka and gloves against the cold nights. He called me from phone booths. I could imagine him standing masked with dark glasses and a thick four-day growth of beard. He liked to pretend he was down and out, shuffling along the red bricks of Market Street, feeling that his life lay not in his apartment, not in any place or any thing, but only in Kick.

But he did not have Kick.

He forced himself to walk among vagrants and bag ladies, envying them. They survived with nothing. Ryan, despite the gain of his writing, his property, and his past time with Kick, knew that his life lay only in his body, which he indulged in none of the expected vices. He had stopped drugs completely. He neither smoked nor drank nor did any of the things grown men were supposed to do. He purified his body. His body remembered Kick's body. His body was all he had left.

Everything was his body, and his body, as with his father's body, felled at forty-four, dead at fifty-six, was a cache of time bombs ticking toward total explosion. His pancreas, his liver, his lungs, his immune system, were each on a timer counting down; but none counted more than his heart, the ultimate body clock. He had long before thrown the gold Rolex Kick had given him deep into a drawer of old socks. *"It's a fake Rolex," Solly said.* Nightly, the news reminded him he was at the high-risk center of Castro-Folsom roulette. Somewhere the AIDS virus waited for him on the lip of an unwashed glass.

Standing at 7th and Market, dressed like a bum, waiting to cross the street, he was hit hard in the head by a Hostess Berry Pie. At first, he thought he had been shot; but then he realized that someone on a passing Muni bus had thrown the eight-ounce chunk. Unwrapped. Cherries-in-goo ran down his face and onto his jacket.

By the time he called me, he said, "I've been hit in the face with a cosmic pie."

Ryan never let anything be simply what it was. Once I understood his style of portent, I knew where to add the grain of salt.

"I'm an approval junkie," he said. He meant Kick's, Charley-Pop's, God's approval. "I'll do anything to get attention. I'll tell jokes. I'll court danger. I'll let my lover live with his boyfriend in my house. I'll even stoop to taking a pie in the face. I'll do anything to get Kick back and not get AIDS."

In Karel Reisz's film *Isadora,* Vanessa Redgrave sang a nursery song that haunted Ryan. Out of all women, Redgrave was his muse—his *Vanessa-Isadora.* In *Camelot,* her Guenevere, closeted in-love with her Lancelot, sang, "I Loved You Once in Silence." But was the bum-diddly-bummed-out lyrics of La Redgrave swathed up as the dancing, doomed Isadora Duncan that haunted Ryan—all that movie-queen bravado packing up cares and woes 'cause here she goes, swinging low, "Bye-Bye, Blackbird." Fucking A! The voice that sings loops in the back of heads: is it the inner fat-lady singing camp? *So what if no one loves or understands me? What a fucking hard-luck story! I can take it like a man. I made my bed. I lit all the lights. And it's still "Blackbird, bye-bye."*

Isadora, born in San Francisco on the northwest corner of Geary and Taylor, in the Tenderloin, knew it, knew it all, as she tossed her scarf around her neck and settled in next to the young, dark, handsome driver of the red

Bugatti convertible. Ryan felt hurt by so many well-intentioned people trying to adjust what they saw in him to what they thought he should be, that
he turned deeper inside himself. He thought it was a sign and an omen that
Isadora's long scarf, which she tossed so gaily as the car sped off, had caught
in the spokes of the Bugatti's rear wheel and broke her neck instantly. So
much for Quentin Crisp's theory about the tall, dark man. Bitterly he wrote
a poem called "Postmark."

> Dear God: You created me. Then you hated me.
> Dear Folks: You conceived me. Then deceived me.
> Dear Teacher: You told me. Then you sold me.
> Dear Boss: You bought me. Then you fought me.
> Dear Lover: You thrilled me. Then you killed me.
> Dear Death: You embraced me. Then erased me.

"I figured," he said, "that between my adolescent crisis and my midlife
crisis, I'd have at least one day off."

Three years had passed since the Death of his father. He missed Charley-
Pop so desperately that he was jarred to tears in a Market Street cafeteria,
overhearing two homeless street people conversing about a third, also dead,
saying, "He's better off wherever he is."

He felt the grief surge up from his belly. His sorrow was a mix of loss: his
father and Kick; the only difference between them was that Kick was unfinished business. He crushed his napkin, meant for syrup, not tears, to a paper
ball in his hand. He feared any more public sorrow in a City grown so sad
with plague. Three years is too long not to see a father loved so much, especially when those long years are suddenly realized as the beginning of forever.

Not only do people die, you don't know where they go or how they are.
Yet some nights, their presences linger. As much as he could touch Kick in
the dark of his lonely bed, he often felt overlain by his father's remembered
feel, as if neither of them were really gone. More often than he liked, his father hovered over him those dark nights, just as Ryan had hovered for years
over his father's hospital bed, touching the man's forehead, afraid to touch
his own father's hands, grown so soft with sickness, for fear that a loving
touch might be felt by the dying man as a pressure as intense as pain.

He missed his father desperately. He promised: *Wherever you are, as I
promised you so often before, I'll take care of them,* meaning his mother and sister,
apologizing for not having taken better care of Thom for whom he had not
cared enough.

One question chewed at his guts.

Who, if not Kick, will take care of me?

None of this is real. The alarm will ring. Everyone will wake up. The bad dreams will be over. My father will be alive. Kick will return. The plague will go away. We'll sit down to toast and coffee. We'll use our napkins properly, not for tears, but for syrup and cakes.

But the alarm is ringing, can't be shut off, won't be shut off. Everyone's lying alone in their beds staring at their ceilings, missing all the sweetnesses past, fearful of the dead star-vader terrors to come, terrified of traveling alone to some eternal multiple-choice place, better or worse, up or down, wherever it is, or is not.

He was a dedicated moviegoer whom Kick had kept away from films. He made up for lost time. He haunted the sleazy grind houses on Market Street, especially the corroding Strand Theater between 7th and 8th. Blacks smoked. Mexicans sat singly in blue watch caps. Unstoppable cocksuckers roamed the balconies. His feet stuck to the floor. He saw the world in mean montage on the wide screen. The violent intensity of film was for him not an escape. He forked out no admission to escape reality. He paid to intensify reality in images so big and bright even the blind could see.

In that one month, a sudden late-winter revival of art movies and neo-leftist films unreeled before him the repressed terrors of the anti-fascist war of his childhood when he had wakened screaming from his dreams, smothering in his pillow, pissing in terror of the Germans and Japs who were trying to kill him. For that one month of double features at the Strand he watched the comedy of pain and blood and shit that men visit one on the other.

He could not resist his celluloid fix. He understood his relationship to the screen. Dreams, he remembered as his own from childhood, sometimes shocked him in old film revivals and on the late show when those dreams, that he had thought were *his* dreams, appeared as real scenes in real films to which his parents had taken him from birth. They had not been his private dreams at all, but Hollywood dramas drenched in violence and propaganda and chauvinism of all kinds. They soaked into the blotter of his tiny head, were digested like popcorn into his interior self.

To him all images were erotic. During his orgiastic month, masturbating in movie theaters, he was exhausted as much by his unrequited passion for Kick as he was by the cinema bloodlust. The suffering on screen was less than the suffering Kick caused in his heart.

He was a part of all he watched.

Technicolor images hovered over him, huge on screen, like carrion birds over sweet rotting flesh. Catholicism had programmed him into sanctified

sex and violence. Every noon, for ten years, over silent lunch at Misericordia
Seminary, the priests had read *The Roman Martyrology* from the pulpit overlooking the dining tables. Ryan digested his bread and soup to those stories
of mutilated saints tortured to Death for centuries by bearded pagans who
flaunted their own naked bodies, and by barbarian infidels who trampled
the beliefs he held. He swallowed the glamour of martyrdom with his lunch.
But the priests went too far. Ryan had left them, refusing to become a priest
at all, because, once they had admitted him so deep inside Catholicism, he
had decoded the Church's double-talk from inside out. The priests taught
Absolute Truth, but they cautioned the seminarians never to speak the full
truth to the baptized—but unwashed—laity. "They are not really ready,"
Monsignor Linotti had said, "to understand complicated moral theology—
that abortion after rape or incest, for instance, is permitted as a reasonable
self-defense, because the fetus is an unjust aggressor in the woman's body."
It was not sex, but intellect that caused Ryan to exit the Church. He had not
known that he was a born spy.

He had asked the priests about cardinals wearing scarlet and ermine
robes as opposed to their clothing the naked and feeding the hungry. They
shook their fingers at him, accused him of worldliness and pride, and said
the poor needed the vision of hope dramatized in all the pomp of Roman ritual and pageantry. They wanted his obedience, but his intelligence could no
longer let him kneel in blind faith. His first attraction to the Church had
turned to distraction. Faith gave way to reason. His distraction, by dint of
reason, turned to refraction. He saw the world in a different way: bent in
and through and then out of a Catholicism that had shaped then shaken
him.

His soul resounded to Mexican filmmaker Alejandro Jodorowsky's *El
Topo* and *The Holy Mountain.* Jodorowsky's vision of Catholicism, twisted
through mystic myths of Santaria saints and pagan warriors, spit in the face
of Roman theology. Wildly. Magically. Jodorowsky's films, virtually painted
on black velvet, were as ritually crazy as Catholicism's worship of the sweating, naked, crucified, muscular Jesus. Jodorowsky engaged Ryan's Catholic
bloodlust as much as his uncle Les had engaged him sexually for the love of
God in the sacristy. Something sacred and erotic in the dark womb-cavern
of profane movie theaters made him need to cum. The cuming relieved ever
so temporarily his anxiety. If ever Ryan's life was a movie, Jodorowsky was
the director.

Ryan was so fascinated by *The Holy Mountain,* he went back for a second
time to the Ghirardelli Square Cinema, taking, against his loneliness, an ac-
quaintance named Juan-Jose Morales who danced the "Love Act" with a

blonde woman in a North Beach topless club. The "Acton: God of War" sequence had proved too much for Juan-Jose. In the seat next to Ryan, Juan-Jose fainted dead away under the power of the on-screen action.

Ryan watched, in utter surprise, something like Juan-Jose's Catholic soul rise momentarily, sucked up and out of his front-row seat to merge with the screen. With good reason. The young male victim in the film looked physically much like the beautifully built, olive-skinned Juan-Jose himself.

Lithely muscular, he was strapped, on screen, this young Latin boy, to a raised platform, spread-eagled and naked, his cock covered with a black leather sheath, his dark curly hair garlanded with flowers. He was spread for initiation into Acton's army of soldier-lovers. The platform itself stood centered in a hot and dusty military parade ground. A thousand soldiers in green fatigue pants, stripped to the waist, faces covered with gas masks, stood at silent attention, as through the fortress gate rode, on his huge stallion, Acton, the Chief of Police of the Planet Acton.

Kick could have played the part. Acton was as fair as Juan-Jose was dark. Acton's body was fully muscled. His blond hair, unlike the boy's full head of curls, was shaved but for a Mohawk crest of blond from his stern forehead to the nape of his thick neck. His tanned, naked body was harnessed at biceps, chest, waist, and thighs with black-leather bands. The soldiers, as Acton dismounted, jumped up and down in place shouting, "Acton! Acton! Acton!"

Acton himself strode up the platform between the boy's spread legs. He carried a huge shears in his big hands. In close-up, he palmed the young balls, pulled them ever so gently down from the boy's torso, down from the black-sheathed cock. The shears glinted hot around the sweating balls. Then Acton's muscular hand closed to a fist, snapping the shears, severing the balls. *Cut. Quick edit.* Magically, as only movies can do, the young initiate was kneeling in Acton's private, circular chamber, surrounded by row above row of glass jars, each with its own scrotum. The boy's was the thousandth Acton had taken.

In the theater darkness, even this second viewing, Ryan had cum, helpless in his own swoon to revive Juan-Jose in his faint, both of them reviving together, laughing, crying, witnessing in each other the connection of the bright screen to their darkest thoughts.

Kick was slicing off Ryan's balls.

5

At the end of the month of films, Kick, one night, showed up, as expected as ever, as unexpected as ever, on Ryan's doorstep. "I can come in?" he said.

"You remembered," Ryan said. "I have this fatal attraction for men carrying gym bags."

Kick was more massive than ever. He lumbered into the house. He had come back as Ryan knew he would. He had come back and Ryan was determined behind his forced smile to fix it or finish it according to the plan he had made in *Killing Time till Armageddon.* He felt like a gunfighter approaching the Not-So-OK Corral; but as quickly as Kick embraced him, the old rush of feeling pent up for so long inside him broke loose. He could not mention the night with Katherine Hepburn. He wondered if Kick had even noticed him burning in flames in the back rows of the orchestra. "My God," Ryan said, "all this new muscle is unbelievable."

"The Mr. Cal is next month. I came back to buff up. I need to psych up with you. You're my lucky charm." He put his gym bag, nylon jock jacket, and car keys on a table by the door. "Let's go to Castro. I need a six-egg omelet."

"I don't eat on Castro anymore."

"Why not?"

Ryan lied. "Because of AIDS." The plague was his excuse to avoid all the places they had once hung out, places where guys continually asked him, "Where's Kick?"

"You can't catch AIDS eating in a gay restaurant," Kick said. "You're going to live forever." He threw his muscular arm around Ryan's shoulder. "Come on," he said.

"Only if I drive," Ryan said.

"Okay, coach. If you insist."

After supper at Without Reservation, they walked back to Ryan's Rabbit, breaking through the wave of men who turned to gawk at Kick. Ryan had parked on Castro in front of Donuts & Things, three cars up from 18th Street.

He climbed in behind the wheel.

Kick settled his big blond turbo body into the economy passenger seat.

A white van, double-parked, blocked their exit. Ryan did not turn the key in the ignition. *Maybe I'll win. Maybe I'll lose. Maybe I'm cryin' the blues. Ready or not, here comes mama!* He made it short and sweet. "Let's drive up to Bar Nada."

Kick winced.

"I want you to drive up to the country with me."

"No." Kick's face looked pale in the cold light flooding the car from the donut shop. Kick knew, as Ryan was discovering, that his muscular blond power in leading their relationship had been all along a simple gift from Ryan.

"Why not?" Ryan saw in Kick's face that Kick knew the jig was up. The whole film of three years with Kick raced fast-forward through his head. *I shouldn't be doing this.* Ryan was like a man drowning. He could hardly breathe in the humid car.

"I'm tired of impossible demands," Kick said.

"Impossible demands? I've never asked you for anything for myself. You said I could have anything. And now I'm asking for it. I want you to drive up to Bar Nada with me."

"What do you really want?"

"I want . . ."

"Tell me what you want."

"I want us to be the way we were. I want to be loved back."

Kick rubbed the thick blond hair on his forearms. "I don't love you the way you love me. I don't love you that way."

"You don't want anybody that way."

"I don't need anybody that way."

"Not even Logan?"

"No. Not even Logan."

"Good. Then we're clear on that."

"I have a sexual attraction to Logan. I don't love him."

"You said you loved me. You said we were lovers."

"I do love you. But not the way you want me to."

"How do you love me then?"

"You're the dearest man I know. You're a madman. You have madness. You have passion. You have intensity."

"I think too much. I get depressed."

"You feel too much."

"Is that wrong?"

"Not unless it hurts somebody," Kick said.

"Have I ever hurt you?"

"Not unless you're hurting me now."

"Don't double-talk me. I'm the talker."

"You've always got what you wanted."

"I got the fantasy of you. I hoped you were real."

"I am real."

"Prove it. Drive with me to Bar Nada."

"No. I can't. I won't."

"You must have freon for blood," Ryan said.

Kick turned his face away. "This is part of the curse," he said.

"What curse?"

"The curse of looking like this. Of looking the way I look. People make impossible demands. Something you never did. Something—the one thing—that made you different from everybody else. Something that kept you from being ordinary. Something that's making you like everybody else."

"You're no god," Ryan said. Saying it, he felt like a heretic coming out of the closet. "Your Universal Appeal is slipping."

The temperature in the car changed.

"What's that mean?"

"You're becoming a musclefreak, a gym bum."

"I intend to turn professional right after the Mr. California."

"You've always been professional. Now you're going to hustle your muscle." Ryan imagined Kick's picture in the muscle magazines endorsing megavitamins and "natural" steroids, pushing $29.95 mail-order courses screaming ad headlines: "You Can Have Arms Like Mine in Three Days."

"Everything has its going rate."

"You should never have hustled me. Never me." Ryan flashed on Teddy, the original hustler-Judas.

Ryan was too polite, even in his anger, to mention he'd found out on Kick's trips to El Lay to see Dr. Steroid that he'd been invited to that famous swimming pool at that castle in the Hollywood hills where, every Sunday afternoon, the most handsome muscle guys from the gyms stood on one side of the pool and the checkbooks stood on the other.

"I didn't have to hustle you. You gave me everything."

"Exactly. I gave and gave and gave."

"Then I didn't hustle you."

"You hustled my heart. I wish you could have turned my head and left my heart alone."

"I don't believe this," Kick said. "My life is turning into a B movie."

"Just like when you muscle-hustled that poor girl."

"What girl?" Kick's face glowered, afraid that Kweenie had spilt their little secret.

"The Third Runner-Up in the Miss Alabama Contest. The girl who threw herself out of your car and landed on her face when you told her you didn't really love her that way."

"You forget nothing, do you?"

"I take notes. I have a photographic memory. I have tunnel vision around you. I see, hear, think of nothing else. I'm obsessed with you."

"I love you for that."

"Then drive to Bar Nada with me."

"I've had enough," Kick said.

"No, I've had enough. I want more."

"So do I."

"What more do you want?"

"I want you to see me as I really am," Kick said.

"What a hoot. We both want the same thing. Don't double-talk me. I hate reverse psychology. What's all this mean? What has all this meant? What are you trying to do?"

Kick looked Ryan directly in the eye. "Make a man out of you."

The low blow stopped Ryan dead in his tracks.

Outside, late winter rain pelted the sidewalks. Gay men stood huddled in the doorways of stores. The rain brought the street cruising to a cold standstill.

"I've been coaching you, Ry." Kick drawled it softly. "All along I've been the coach."

Ryan sat rocking behind the wheel of the small car. He could not look at Kick and Kick would not look away from him.

"You were the coach?"

"I'm always the coach."

"I want you to drive to Bar Nada." Ryan's voice was low and controlled.

"No," Kick said.

"No?"

"No." Kick's face hardened.

Ryan sucked in all the deep breaths he had been missing.

"Then, this time, Rhett Butler, you get out." With that one simple sentence, Ryan Steven O'Hara avenged every Miss Scarlett ever crossed by a man. He knew it was the end of his life.

Kick slowly moved his hand to the door. He opened it. The cold air sucked body heat from the car. He pulled his big body out the door. For a moment he stood on the curbing. Rain soaked his tee shirt tight against his shoulders and chest. His groomed blond hair curled into steaming wet locks. Then with both his enormous arms he gently shut the car door.

Come back, Shane!

Come back, Little Sheba!

Come back to the Five and Dime, Jimmy Dean!

Oh, Ashley! Ashley dahrrrling, come bayack!
Stell-aaah!
What movie are we?
Without Margaret Mitchell there would be no Tennessee Williams.

The white van double-parked next to Ryan roared into life and pulled away, screeching its tires on the wet street.

Slowly, Ryan turned the key in the ignition.

Kick stepped back from the car.

More slowly, Ryan pulled away from the curb.

He turned once to look, one last time to look, seeing Kick outlined in the glow from Donuts & Things, standing cast out in the cold rain without his jacket, without his gym bag, without his Corvette keys, locked out of the Victorian.

This was the ending against which Ryan had shot the videotapes, written the *Journals* and letters, and saved the gifts of Kick's boots and clothes. They were empty consolation prizes.

He figured it was the last time he would ever see Kick in his life.

He sped north through the City, wildly through the rain, heading toward the Bridge. Through the windshield, his face was lit like a crystal demon speeding through the orange mist of the Golden Gate, heading toward the dark freeway to Bar Nada. A whim to stop and jump crossed his mind, but he was too angry to kill himself. He knew what he must do. He pressed on through the rain. His heart was racing like a bad speed trip. He flew through the night. He felt like a small-town mailbag snatched up by a speeding express train. His car roared up the gravel drive to the ranch house.

Logan was standing in the rain waiting for him. He was big, dark with steroid-rage in his yellow rain slicker. Kick had called ahead and warned him.

"You skinny-necked geek," Logan shouted. "You're not throwing me out of here!"

"You're history!" Ryan shouted. The rain drenched him.

"You're nothing!" Logan walked slowly toward him. "You're not getting any of the grass. We sold it months ago." He pointed to the carport. "See the new truck? It's in my name! It's in Kick's name! We bought it, geek! Together! We took you, you lame wimp! Because you were easy to take."

"You're a liar!"

"No, you dickhead, you're the liar!" He pushed his face close up against Ryan's. "You never even had sex with him. He told me so. Except for that one night when I sat on your face. He said we had to have a three-way with you. Whoa! What a joke! It was a mercy-fuck!"

Ryan threw a punch into Logan's hard gut.

"You fuckin' pussy!" He slapped Ryan across the face "You fuckin' wimp!" He backhanded him again. "You cunt!" He punched Ryan in the stomach.

Ryan doubled over.

Logan wrapped his arm around Ryan's waist, turned him upside down, and shook him. Ryan gasped for air. Logan bear-hugged him and carried him to the barn, dragging Ryan's head through the mud, kicking his face with his boots. "We'll see who's fucking who," he said. He threw Ryan on the floor, straddled his weight across his chest, and beat his face.

"We . . . ," Ryan shouted between the punches, ". . . made . . . love!"

"Pussy!"

"We . . . made . . . love!"

"You geek-cunt pussy!"

"You can kill me . . ."

"Don't tempt me!"

"But we made . . . love!"

Logan tore at Ryan's shirt, ripping it away from his chest. He pulled Ryan around the floor yanking off Ryan's jeans. He kicked him repeatedly on his naked butt.

"You fucking asshole cunt!" He threw Ryan on his back across the leather-covered weight bench over which Thom had committed suicide. He handcuffed Ryan's wrists together below the bench. "I'm gonna show you lu-u-v!"

Logan popped open the fly of his wet jeans. His huge cock stood at full attention. He spread Ryan's legs. He drove his dry cock hard into Ryan's ass. Ryan screamed. It was not pleasure. It was pain. It was not sex. It was violence. Logan slapped him hard in the face, pushed his knees back beside his ears, grabbed his shoulders with both his big hands, and threw the full weight of his muscular body into Ryan. "Take it, you bitch!" He threw a vicious fuck. "That's what you deserve! That's what you need! That's what you get!" Deeper and deeper he plowed into Ryan's ass.

"Get out!" Ryan screamed. "Get out! I'm going to kill you!"

Logan reared back and slapped Ryan's face, riding him like a horse to full lather. "I'm gonna kill *you!*" Logan said. "I'm gonna fuck you to DEATH!"

He pulled his cock from Ryan's ass. He deftly unlocked the handcuffs. He picked Ryan up bodily, turned him over like a wrestler in a ring, and slammed him belly-down across the bench, throwing the full fury of his hate into him, driving his cock home to the hilt. Cuming, he slapped the flat palms of both hands hard on Ryan's back, driving the air from Ryan's lungs. As rough as he entered, he pulled himself from Ryan's bloody ass.

Ryan was nearly unconscious.

Logan pulled him up from the bench and threw him on his back on the floor. Again he straddled Ryan's chest. He thrust his still-hard cock in Ryan's face. He slapped him hard. Once. Then twice. "Clean it up," he said. He shoved the slab of his dirty meat into Ryan's mouth. "Clean it up, you silly pencil-neck geek bitch!"

But Ryan could not. He choked on the slimy head rammed deep down his throat. He vomited the supper he had eaten with Kick.

Logan pulled back in disgust. "No wonder he never had sex with you. You filthy cunt!" Logan stood up over Ryan's face and chest. "You dirty bitch!" He wrapped the long rod of his cock in both his hands. Its big head bulged out angry and purple. "Piss on you," he said. His long stream sprayed across Ryan's body.

Logan left him naked and cold, choking, wet, unable to move on the floor of the barn.

Twenty minutes later, Logan, his new truck, the pink slip in his name only, the duffle with everything he owned, and some of what Ryan owned, roared down and out the drive of Bar Nada.

6

"I want them dead," Ryan said. He had not gone back to the Victorian from Bar Nada. He holed up at Solly's penthouse. "Kick called Logan," he said. "Kick set me up. Kick might as well have raped me himself. I want them both dead. I want them to die in great pain."

Solly was nonchalant. "Is that all there is to a rape?"

"It should happen to you," Ryan said.

"It did," Solly said. "I'll always have Beirut."

"You said they didn't rape you."

"I lied."

"Life's different," Ryan said, "after you've been raped."

"You are sounding," Kweenie said, "very like a feminist." She pulled a copy of the *Manifesto* from Solly's bookshelves. She threw it on the couch. "Eat your words."

"*Touché!*" Ryan said.

"What offended you more?" Solly said. "Getting fucked over or getting called *pussy* and *cunt?*"

The smoulder in Ryan's face turned to fire.

"Just checking!" Solly said.

Ryan sat up slowly on the couch where he lay. His butt was sore. His right eye was black. His face was bruised. "Kick not only lied to me. He lied to Logan too. He told Logan that we never had sex."

"Did you have sex?" Kweenie asked.

Ryan glared at her.

"Just checking," she said.

"What do you mean, did we? Of course, we did. What do you think this is all about?"

"Get over it," Solly said.

Ryan put his hand to the six stitches in his puffed lip. "He shouldn't have hit my face."

"Poor baby," Kweenie said.

"It's not over till it's over," Ryan said.

"It's finished," Kweenie said.

"It's not finished till I finish it."

"Exactly," Solly said. "It's over for Kick. Now you have to let go of it."

"Nothing lasts forever," Kweenie said.

"I'll second that," Solly said.

"I'll tell you what lasts forever," Ryan said. His anger collapsed under the weight of his heart. "His being gone will last forever. Loss lasts forever. Emptiness lasts forever."

"You should be glad he's gone," Kweenie said.

When Ryan returned to the Victorian after a week at Solly's, Kick's clothes had disappeared from the house.

"He broke in and took them," Ryan said. "He even stole the one Most Muscular trophy he said was mine." Ryan had reached into the drawer where he kept mementos Kick had given him. He winced. "He took back the posing trunks he gave me from our first contest."

A week passed before Ryan realized Kick had stolen the typed manuscript of *Universal Appeal* with all its photographs and negatives.

"Call the police," Kweenie said.

"My dear," Solly took her hand. "The San Francisco police do nothing about lovers' domestic quarrels."

"Even about Logan?" she asked.

"Even about Logan," Solly said.

"Then you're treated worse than women," she said.

"The only justice," Ryan said, "is vigilante justice."

"I suggest," Solly said, "you change your locks. That's the one thing I've learned in dealing with my little hustlers. Keys disappear. Once a month I change my locks."

"I already have." Ryan held up a set of bright gold Schlage keys.

Three weeks later, Kick broke into the Victorian again. Ryan was furious.

"What did he take?" Solly asked.

"He didn't take anything. Not this time."

"Then why," Kweenie asked, "are you so mad?"

"This time he made a delivery."

"Flowers and candy?" Solly said.

"He had the nerve to bring back every single gift I ever gave him. He owes me money. But he sneaks into my house and brings back all the special sentimental gifts I ever gave him."

"He's good. He's real good," Solly said. "Signs and omens. Maybe's he trying to tell you something."

"Like good-bye, dear, and a-men," Ryan said. "He really knows how to hurt a guy. He kept all the Pendleton shirts and leather fetish clothes I gave him. Those he can still use with his new tricks." His voice rose. "Don't you understand? He sneaked in and piled on the floor inside the bedroom window all my gifts that were . . . personal!"

"So what are you going to do?" Kweenie asked.

"I'm going to teach Charles Bronson a thing or two about revenge!"

"First you have to find him," Solly said.

"I don't ever want to see him again."

"I've been playing Miss Marple," Kweenie said. "He's been at the gym every day."

"Naturally," Ryan said. "Mr. Schmuck wants to be Mr. California."

"And," Kweenie said, "he's taken a studio apartment in the Castro."

"Location," Solly said, "is everything."

"Some surprise," Ryan said.

"If you want a surprise," Kweenie said, "Logan has left town for good."

"Bad pennies," Solly warned, "always return."

"This one won't," Kweenie said. "Sources close to the couple . . ."

"Out with it," Ryan said.

". . . reveal that Logan split with the truck and the grass."

Ryan felt a rush of pure satisfaction. What he had to do he could now do with full clarity that he was not doing it because Kick had run off to live with Logan. Things were back to square one. What was between the two of them was between them only. He was bent on teaching Kick one final ulti-mate lesson.

I think, and this I have said many times, that when men go against the heterosexual norm and dare to love each other, they love each other some-how more intensely, precisely because the world is against them, and when that intense love ends, its passion becomes enormous rage, at each other, and at themselves, for making the straight world seem right and them seem wrong.

Yet what hurt Ryan most, among all the returned gifts of the un-bonding, was that Kick, a man, a male, one of his own kind, had in fact acted badly, acted in the way women always protest a man in a relationship finally always acts. The seducer becomes the lover becomes the betrayer.

"He woke the man in me," he wrote in *Armageddon,* "but he killed the child."

"Make a man of me, indeed!" Ryan could not forgive Kick for coaching him into a sexual hyper-manhood and then turning him into an abandoned lover worn, like some gay trick, by the wars of the sexual revolution. He had thought Kick's form and face, his manly grace had ushered him into a new state of grace; but finally the best boy on the movie set realized what he had lost in gaining the fast-lane manhood he had come to California to find.

Innocence.

Children live in a state of grace from which adults fall away. Ryan read to me from *The Education of Henry Adams:* "A boy's will is his life, and he dies when it is broken, as the colt dies in harness, taking a new nature in becom-ing tame."

Deep down, this taming of his will to deference, to become what Kick wanted, and not Kick's dalliance with Logan Doyle, was the betrayal. All Ryan's life was a taming: the doctor who, clucking at foreskins, had civilized his penis; the women in the kitchens of his childhood; the priests at Miseri-cordia. Education had fucked him over. Nurture tried to destroy his nature. He had been an innocent who had resisted them all, more or less, for better or worse, until Kick came along and took all his resistance away. He had fought to save his wild innocence for a reason he did not know until Kick walked into that house in El Lay that hot summer night when he surren-dered everything to become the wild man he wanted to be.

When Kick betrayed his innocence and trust, Ryan's wildness turned into a madness. He became bitter, cynical, biting, sarcastic. He did not like himself, so he liked nothing and no one.

He stopped writing his erotic stories. He felt desexed. He could not en-courage serial tricking. Heavy sex was unsafe; tricks were as dangerous as serial murderers. He had dreams, and sometimes dreams are wiser than waking, that his writing grew at the end of his hand like a cancer growing on his fingers.

I've written too much. I've written about the wild, promiscuous, dirty things our mothers warned us against. A bleary life of bars and baths and drugs. We have the bodies of men, the feelings of men, but we are headstrong babies. What if some poor fool gay boy reads my stuff, goes out and does it and dies.

He was afraid his writing encouraged behavior that caused the AIDS that killed the boys who lived in the fantasies Ryan built. He stopped publishing *Maneuvers*. He could no longer glorify sex in its pages.

Solly was appalled. "As a pornographer myself," he said to Ryan, "all I can say is that we're talking major league brain damage. Yours! Maybe you did take too many drugs."

"I'm heavy into *Killing Time till Armageddon*," Ryan said. "I'm into a different trip now."

"So am I," Kweenie said.

"It's about time for you both," Solly said.

"I'm going to Los Angeles," Kweenie said. "January asked me to come stay with her. She knows some people she says I should know. I've never performed in El Lay."

Before Kweenie left, Ryan gave us each a copy of the lead essay in *Armageddon*. It was a confessional titled, "By Blonds Obsessed: Southern Men, Scarlett O'Hara, and Me."

Loss. It stays forever. The only truth that stays forever is Kick couldn't stay forever. It registers in my whole being. Forever I'll feel him in my whole body. I'm filled with him, emptied by him, of him, for him. Somewhere in it all I sinned. I had a false god before me. I made him a god when he was only a man. He couldn't sustain that. Who could? He feared that. He must have seen the way I looked at him, seen adoration in my eyes every time I was behind the cameras shooting him, recording the moments I knew even then couldn't last. I gave him everything you can give a god: myself.

He knew he was no god; but he took the honor I bestowed on him. He shined with divinity. He took my money, my time, my love—everything. Friends said he emptied me like a checkbook; that he was not a god; that he was only a vampire. But I loved him. I loved the ideal I saw incarnate in him. So forever, at least, I have that to remember: that joy of fullness, that pain of subtraction, of emptiness. I hurt. When I die my thoughts will uncontrollably go back, not just to our three years together, but to those ecstatic moments when time stood still and space did not exist, when we were gods together, and my last thoughts will be of him.

I don't think he knows, not really, how I loved—love—him. Maybe he does—did—and that's why, when I told him I was dying, being drained by our relationship, by our way of relating, he said he'd have to go. Period. No discussion. Nothing. He knew. He knew. He knew all along—and that was the greatest betrayal—that he was loved more than he could love, not only me, but anybody.

That was it. That was his betrayal. That was the golden man's deep secret.

He knew he could not love.

That's why he could never be responsible for anyone's happiness. That's what he meant when he said I didn't know what it was like to be inside a body like his.

He knew I could do what he could not.

I never meant love to be a contest.

I didn't mean to win. Not the way he thought I did when he said he hoped to love Logan the way I loved him. At least with Logan he tried. But he failed. Logan left him too.

He said he preferred communicative men to competitive men. In his mind, did he see me as a competitor? Did he feel me outstrip him in love? Did he think he had lost that competition? A competition more important than bodybuilding. Is that what turned him to steroids? Fear of not being big enough for love? Fear of losing? Fear of losing to other bodybuilders the way he feared he had lost to me? I didn't think he was that competitive. I didn't think winning meant so much to him. Has he lost his love of sport? Did he think in love, someone wins . . . and someone surrenders?

Love is not a physique contest.

"You'll never catch on, will you?" Kweenie said.

Ryan drove her to the airport. "Give January my regards," he said. He headed back to the City to call Teddy.

"What do you want?" Teddy was suspicious on the phone.

Ryan had spotted Teddy the day before on Castro. He had looked unhappy. Ryan had heard rumors of fights between Teddy and his leatherman lover. He decided to invite Teddy over for supper to ask him about the possibility of reconciliation; but on the phone he was clever enough not to reveal his motive. Ryan feared sex with strangers; Teddy was not Kick, but he had been, before Kick, the most Ryan had known of love. Ryan knew Teddy inside out. Teddy was safe.

Somewhat reluctantly, Teddy agreed to come. He was a sucker for a free meal.

Ryan carefully prepared the exotic lasagna that had always been Teddy's favorite. The kitchen filled with a warmth it had missed for years. Ryan and Kick had always eaten out. The only kitchen appliances they had ever used were the refrigerator and the blender. Ryan hoped against hope that a reconciliation with Teddy might be the best antidote to the strain of Kick's absence.

"I'll tell you one thing," Solly had said. "When you pushed Kick you made him choose between the drugs and you."

"I'm stronger than drugs," Ryan had said.

"No one," Solly had said, "wins against drugs."

"Ah," Ryan said to himself, checking the oven, "No one, especially Teddy, wins against lasagna." He wondered how Kick and he had survived on only omelets and tuna fish for so long. No wonder the cheeses and sauce smelled so good.

Teddy arrived. Ryan hugged him at the door. "I think I smell lasagna," Teddy said.

"How about some wine?" Ryan poured two glasses.

His tape deck was playing tunes recorded when they had been a couple. Teddy turned nervous when Liza sang "Come Saturday Morning" from her movie *The Sterile Cuckoo*. It had been their song. Both pretended not to notice the lyrics.

"So . . ." Ryan said.

"So . . ." Teddy said.

They sat at opposite ends of the living room. Ryan was careful not to press his game plan. He intended to start the summit somewhere in the middle of the lasagna.

"You surprised me," he said to Teddy.

"Why?"

"I didn't think you'd really come. But I wanted to see you."

"I wanted to see you too," Teddy said. "That's why I came."

Ryan's bruised heart rose up. Teddy maybe felt the same way. Maybe absence had made their hearts grow fonder. A lot of blood had flowed beneath their bridge. Ryan, who could never let go of anyone or anything, knew there were some bridges that never burn.

"I'm sort of horny," Teddy said.

Ryan smiled. Twist Teddy's tits and he'd follow anyone anywhere. This was going to be easier than he thought. He felt a surge of certainty that Teddy, if asked and wooed the right way, might come home to the place he had never wanted to leave, even after Ryan had thrown him out.

"To us." Ryan lifted his wine glass.

"To what once was us," Teddy said. He sipped the wine. "Actually, the reason I came . . ."

Teddy's faced glowed with the happiness Ryan remembered in his face during the best of their times. Ryan felt certainty bloom in the room. Teddy had grown up. He had become independent. He had become, instead of a shadow of Ryan, his own person. That transformation had, before all, been the main reason Ryan had thought Teddy needed a separate peace to get his act together. He sensed in his old lover's face intimations of the joy they had once found in sex.

Teddy rubbed his crotch.

Against the confusion Kick had raised in his head, Ryan felt his confidence return in the dependability of Teddy's presence.

"I thought," Teddy said, "we deserved one more fuck together."

He wants sex. Good. I'll feed him and fuck him and he'll come back home.

"I know the reason you came." Ryan rubbed his own crotch. "It's the same reason I asked you."

"Then you know," Teddy said. "You've heard."

Ryan rose from his chair and sat on Teddy's lap. He turned his voice down to its most seductive. "I've heard what I used to hear," Ryan whispered, "that we were good when we were together."

"We were good," Teddy said, "until we were bad."

Ryan stared at him. *I've always loved him.*

"The reason I've come," Teddy said, "is to tell you myself."

Ryan felt something change in the room.

"I'm leaving San Francisco. Hank and I are moving to Wyoming. We both want to get as far away from AIDS and everything as we can. We want to start over together with each other. I wanted you to be the first to know. I wanted to tell you myself."

"No way," Solly later told me, "did anyone eat that lasagna!"

7

Ryan fled again to the refuge of Solly Blue. At the door, Ryan screamed, "What movie am I?"

"The Towering Inferno?"

"Phaedra. I'm Melina Mercouri in Jules Dassin's *Phaedra.*"

"You've lost me."

"I've lost everyone." He acted like a soldier whose second trench mate had died in his arms. "What's the matter with me? What do I do to people?" He imitated Mercouri's deep voice. "Eagle of the cold north. Falcon of solitude. I give them milk and honey. They give me . . . poison!" He spun around the room like a full balloon with its neck untied. He was pumped up. He was on a mean roll.

"Calm down," Solly said. He couldn't believe the tactic Ryan had tried with Teddy. "You're out of your mind," he said. "Teddy's a jerk."

"You're goddam right I'm out of my mind. I want them dead. I want them all dead."

"Then, my friend, you live in the right City."

"What's that mean?"

"It means we'll all soon be dead."

"I hope so. I sincerely hope so."

"Do you know the Chinese proverb?" Solly asked. " 'May you live in interesting times.' "

"If it gets any more interesting, I think I'll be the one who dies," Ryan said. "And for the first time in my life, I don't fucking care."

"Bite your tongue. Be careful what you say. People usually get what they wish for. Remember, this is California."

"For godsakes!"

"I just thought you might be comforted," Solly watched so much TV he spoke like a news anchor, "that James Curran, chief federal epidemiologist, announced today that AIDS will become evermore the leading cause of Death for gay men through the end of the century."

"I want a freeze-frame ending," Ryan said "Right here! Right now!"

Solly lounged back on his white couch. "What you're saying is like air."

Ryan stood at the window and pressed his hot forehead to the cool glass. The City shimmered in the night below him. He was suddenly afraid of the great height from the street. He was afraid he might jump.

"But air is very valuable," Solly continued. "Breathe deep. Calm down."

Ryan turned from the window. "Paging Dr. Quack!" His humor collapsed. "Sometimes . . ." His need to confess embarrassed him. "I want to mutilate myself. Cuts. Burns. Tattoos."

"Take another breath," Solly said. "I go through this myself about once a month. There's no anxiety like sexual anxiety. If it's any comfort, tomorrow is another day."

"I want him dead."

"Which one?"

"Kick," Ryan said. "Who gives a fuck about Teddy."

"I think I can end all this nonsense about Kick for you."

"Oh, really? Oh, Solly!"

"I can."

"No you can't. No one can. I'll follow him the rest of my life. Wherever he goes, I'll go. I'll worship him from afar. If I can't be his adoring friend, I'll be his adoring fan."

"That's short for fanatic."

"The Mr. California is next Saturday. I'll follow him there. I'll follow him to every contest he enters. When he poses, I'll shout, 'Fag! Fag! Fag!'"

"All bodybuilders are fags," Solly said. "I thought you wanted him dead."

"I'll kill him professionally. I'll . . . Oh, shit! I don't know what I want." Ryan turned ambivalent back to the window. "I want . . . I want . . ."

"What do you want?"

"I want to remember all of this. I'd rather feel what I feel than never to have known I could feel this much . . . passion!" Ryan walked back to the couch where Solly reclined like Madame Recamier. "That's what we had, you know. Passion. More than sex, we had passion." He lifted Solly's feet and scooted in under his legs. "How did we ever get to this point, this time, this place? All my life has been lived and I sit here with my best friend, whom I've never balled, wondering what happened and what I should do next."

"I can end this nonsense for you," Solly said.

"How?"

"Passion costs," Solly said. "Sex pays. Maybe Kick didn't like the going rate of passion. Sex turns a profit. He's opened up a small business, and I think not for the first time."

"I don't understand."

Solly turned the Pink Section of *The Advocate* open to the page where the hustlers, whom *The Advocate* called *models,* listed their personal ads. One of them was circled.

"Read this," Solly said, "and weep."

ARMSTRONG. San Francisco's Biggest Bodybuilder. New in town. First ad. Big Guns. Big Arms. Feel them: thick, big ARMS, muscle-bulked heavily from sweaty workouts, their huge girth sported in a tee shirt, or subtly concealed by shirtsleeves of well-washed flannel stretched across their mass, now stripped to reveal mounds of baseball biceps cabled with vascularity, and thick horseshoe triceps, growing bigger before your eyes, the pump of each successive flex further expressing the disciplined power of the life force that built them. With those Big Guns lifted high in full frontal display of arm muscle, feel them again. Feel the density of each striation as it's gathered down into the depths of muscle armpits rich with the heavy male scent of bodybuilder muscle sweat. After a bit of smoke and a hit of popper; if you find your nose and tongue exploring the depths of those pits, if you can take that big muscular arm in one hand and your dick in the other, and discover that between the stroking of the two that you're cuming, then we're both gonna have fun! I'm on my way to the gym now. If BIG-GUNS rap-n-jackoff make you break into a sweat you can't cool off by yourself, give me a call. Health conscious. No fluid exchange. Universal Appeal. 100% repeat. $300 minimum. I'm expensive, but I'm worth it."

"I don't believe it," Ryan said.

"Didn't I read this once before in *Maneuvers?*"

"The life force. I'll teach him the life force."

"At least he's selling safe sex. He told you he was turning professional."

"He meant professional bodybuilder, not hustler. There's some mistake. Some two-bit model who wanted to be like Kick lifted this ad from *Maneuvers*. Kick's not a hustler."

"Who paid your phone bill?"

"He's not a hustler."

"I always thought you wrote that ad for him."

"He wrote it. This only sounds like him talking like me. Some hustler who read me in *Maneuvers* rewrote that. I'm easy to mimic. It's a sex style."

"Who knows your style best of all?"

"Who would dare to steal this ad?"

"Find out. Call the number in the ad." Solly handed him the phone.

He dialed.

It rang.

A machine answered. The taped voice was unmistakably Kick. "I'm at the gym pumping up right now. After the tone, please leave your number and I'll call you back to verify your message."

The machine beeped and Ryan slammed the receiver into its cradle.

"Easy!" Solly said. "I own my phone now."

Ryan threw *The Advocate* across the room.

"That long ad must have cost him a fortune," Solly said. "But he can afford it. He's charging three hundred dollars an hour."

If only Kick had died like Tony Tavarossi in intensive care, then Ryan could have remembered him the way he was, the way he remembered Charley-Pop, the way he remembered Thom. But Kick had not died. He had gone on living. A walking, talking insult, hustling his muscle.

"Everyone will think I was paying him," Ryan said.

"How many times did you have sex with him?" Solly asked.

"Almost every day for the first two years. Not as often last year."

Solly reached for his pocket calculator. "Say eight hundred times?"

"More than I've ever had sex with anyone else."

"Eight hundred fucks at three hundred bucks." His index finger danced over the keyboard. "That's two hundred and forty thousand dollars," Solly said. "Almost a quarter of a million. You never popped for that much, so I'd say you got more than your money's worth."

"He was my lover."

"He's turned himself into a franchise."

"Love is a stunt," Ryan said.

"And Kick's a stuntman. You know what they say a stuntman is in Hollywood? Two hundred pounds of hamburger in a blond wig." Solly turned off the lamp.

The surround of City lights filled the dark room of the penthouse. They sat for a long moment in silence. Solly cleared his throat. He began to speak hypnotically.

"You told Kick he had the Gift, but not the knowledge of the Gift. You had what Kick wanted. You had the knowledge of the Gift. You had the words. You were his priest. He was your vocation."

"Then I'm a twice-failed priest."

"You had the words." Solly paused. "Let me put this so you'll understand." His voice was soft, insistent. "You had the words of transubstantiation. *Hoc est enim corpus meum.* You did something he could not do. You turned his flesh to godhead."

"He's no god."

"He's your lover," Solly said.

"It's over."

"He's your lover. You're his lover."

"Then we have some unfinished business."

"It's not over till you end it." Solly was intense.

"This hurt will never end."

"Then end it."

"How?"

"Move on. Forget him."

"I can't survive."

"Surviving is your best revenge."

"That's his revenge on me. He walked away from the scene of the accident. He survived without a scratch."

"Then kill him."

Ryan looked startled. "What?"

"Kill him." Solly was deadly serious. "I'm only saying what I know you're thinking. We all think it sometimes. We're all of us murderers in our own hearts."

Something darkly human hidden deep in Solly tried to connect with something unfound deep inside Ryan. "Baudelaire said, 'Life being what it is, one thinks of revenge.'"

"I'm no Baudelaire," Ryan said. "Kick pegged me. With his parting shot, he took my writing away from me. He stole our manuscript. I can't write anything anymore. He gutted me. He knew how to hurt me. He killed me. He said no nine-to-five porn hack was going to ruin his life."

"There you have it."

"Have what? He made sure he left me with nothing."

"All the better," Solly said. "You have your motive."

"What motive?"

"He attacked your very essence. Your way with words. The words he first pursued you for. The words he needed every night. The sex scenarios you created and talked him through. He had read you before he set out to meet you. He was silent as Moses until Michelangelo struck his statue and said, 'Speak!' You gave him words. He spoke and he silenced you. He's your Frankenstein's monster. He made you insane."

"I'm crazy. I'm depressed. I'm not insane."

"Temporary insanity," Solly said. "It worked for Dan White when he shot Harvey Milk." He wove his logic around Ryan's being. "Temporary insanity has nothing to do with the usual insanity defense. Full insanity leads to a judgment of mental incompetence."

"What about erotic incompetence? I know I'll never love this way again."

"Temporary insanity is a euphemism. It's the nearest equivalent a judge and jury can find to a verdict of justifiable homicide." Solly was amazing himself with his mystery writer's logic. "And that's only if you get caught. The fact is most murders go unsolved." He adjusted his butt on the couch. "You set up a situation. You stalk from a distance. You let things happen naturally. When you corner your prey, it's just the obvious conclusion. The murder is simply an action in the order of the hunt. It's just like cruising for sex. You dress yourself up to be appealing. You go where your target hangs out. You pick up on him. You close in. You have sex." Solly paused. "It ends up naturally. Just like you planned. You kill him. You close the door, leave him dead on the floor, and steal away into the night. Think of it."

"I am thinking of it," Ryan said. "Stop scaring me."

"I intend to scare you," Solly said.

"What movie are you?"

"I'm the oldest movie in the world."

"Definitely an Agatha Christie plot . . ." Ryan feebly tried to escape Solly's intense logic. ". . . narrated by Rod Serling's silver-tongued devil."

"You still have the gun I gave you?"

"It's somewhere in the house."

Solly laid flat his snare. "Sometimes it's not wrong to murder."

"I hate reverse psychology." Ryan put both hands to his forehead. "Why does everyone use it on me?"

"He tampered with your affection. He took your money and your hospitality. He got you raped. He broke into your house. He assaulted the very writer in you. He stole your manuscript for *Universal Appeal*. He took your photographs. How can you live with yourself if you don't get even?"

"I love him too much to get even."

"Now he hustles. Publicly. For money."

"You're obsessed with hustlers," Ryan said.

"He hustled you."

"He never hustled me."

"He turned your head and took your heart. That's the ultimate hustle."

"I want . . ."

"What do you want?"

Ryan sat still in the dark "I want him to know my pain."

"Then scare him. Let him know murderers are everywhere."

"I want him to know how far we've both fallen."

"Then kill him."

In the street below, a Muni bus roared up Geary. It was full of light in the dark street. Inside were only the driver and one weary passenger alone in the back of the bus.

"I have to, don't I?"

A man's motives need not coincide with civilization when his style of love has not.

"Cut! Print!" Solly said. "End of scene." He flicked on the lamp, returned them to reality, and offered Ryan his glass of Coca-Cola. "You're not the only one, buster, who can pull off a talk scene."

"Very funny," Ryan said.

"I'm cheaper than a shrink. You've got to let it out."

"I'm so sad I can't even cry."

"Then write."

"Write? I'm a hack, remember?"

"Use your writing," Solly said "Write a revenge story. Title it 'Lords of Leather.' Work it through. Write him off."

"That won't change anything. He loved me. He left me. I'm alone. He betrayed me."

"We all betray each other. It's our nature. Betrayal is what is."

"I love him."

"Stop loving him today," Solly said. "That's truly your best revenge. Stop loving him and start living again. Life goes on."

"Long after the thrill of living is gone."

"Forget Kick. Forget Logan. Forget Teddy. Forget 'em all."

"I don't want to forget," Ryan said. "I want to remember all of this. I meant what I said. I'd rather feel what I'm feeling than never know that I could feel so much at all."

"You must end this."

"I will," Ryan said. "I will."

Solly did not like Ryan's Look. "I think I took my little hypnotic therapy too far."

"No," Ryan said. He pushed Solly's legs from his lap and walked to the fireplace. "I know I must do something."

Ryan missed the excitement of being close to the edge with Kick. He needed the feeling of danger.

He leaned against the mantel and closed his eyes. A nightbird darted by the open windows. A voice that was not his voice came from his face. He was not imitating a movie; he had become a movie. He was Claude Rains, speaking perfectly in that actor's accent, "A vampire can only be laid to rest by one who truly loves him."

"Get out of here," Solly said. "Go home. I was supposed to be the one humoring you. Now you're scaring me."

8

The night of the Mr. California contest Ryan knelt next to his bed. "Listen to us in our darkness, we beseech thee, Oh, Lord." He prayed again the same passage he had prayed before from the *Book of Common Prayer*. "And by thy great mercy defend us from all the perils and dangers of this night." This was the ritual darkness of ending and exorcism.

He had been passive long enough.

The time had come to take his life into his own hands.

In the end he could not deny his human heart.

Always he had known, long before he stood that rainy March night outside California Hall on Polk Street, with the gun in his hand, that his life, scaled down, of course, would be forever like that of the Widow standing, alone in black, with her tiny son, his hand saluting as muffled dreams drummed across a dazed and weeping landscape.

She had been betrayed by a bullet.

Christ had been betrayed by a kiss.

Ryan rocked with images of betrayal: of draft cards burning up in defiant flames; of dogs tearing at black bodies on the Edmund Pettus Bridge in Kick's Alabama; of priests arrested and ministers murdered; of American cities on fire; of frightened Vietnamese fleeing their American saviors on the evening news; of a president refusing to accept another term; of a president resigning; of an ancient movie-star president nuclearizing the twilight's last gleaming; of Contras and mercenaries in El Salvador; of faces, pious with hatred, from Dade County and Lynchburg, Tennessee; of wives beaten and raped by husbands; of countries and continents dying of hunger; of gay young men dying with a thousand diseases in their bodies; of a Golden Man smiling his killer smile, posing, posing for cheering audiences.

Chronology was not his style. Feeling was. Sometimes he forgot to breathe. Sometimes he remembered he had to pay for the good times. Sometimes he had that old high-flying feeling of a man who goes starved to bed. Sometimes nothing mattered. Sometimes everything mattered too much.

Ryan took the Yellow Brick Detour.

He was smaller, more real in size, than the Famous Widow, who like him would mourn her love forever, but who, unlike him, was not approaching the auditorium stage where his victorious lover was posing, handsome, golden, muscular, brilliant, shimmering with sweat, triumphant in the final moments of the Mr. California Contest.

Tidal waves of applause washed him closer and closer to the front bank of the stage. He felt himself moving in slow motion through air as thick as celluloid.

The gun was in his hand.

His hand was pulling the gun from the holster of his pocket.

The man he loved more than life itself was turning, in time with the thunderous music of "Marche Slav," nearly naked, in the cone of a hot overhead spotlight, into a magnificent double-biceps shot.

Death excited him now. He had fused with his lover who had fused with him and together they would fuse—wherefore art thou?—forever with Death.

"I want . . . ," he whispered. This time he knew the answer to what he wanted. The answer was something he could never have again. Something he would have to live without forever. "I want Kick."

The pain was in him now. Thick and thorough and clear. He had to kill the man to save the ideal. He stood stock-still among the photographers jostling each other for room at the apron of the stage. The gun in his pocket was hard in his hand. He hurt from his fingertips to his soul. His body ached for the touch and smell and taste of the man whose body was as familiar to him as his own. He raised his left arm high above the screaming, surging crowd. He cupped his empty left hand in midair, tracing his moves over the imagined, remembered, sweet full curves of Kick's massive shoulders, arms, and chest.

In the hot stage light, Kick powered into his finale, lats spread, shoulders wide, head up, face smiling the confidence of victory, legs planted firm for his final lockdown into the Most Muscular pose, the full presentation of the Universal Appeal of his Command Presence.

He's no longer posing only for me.

This was worse suffering than Death could ever be. Kick had made him fearless. No one could do any worse to him than Kick had done. No courts. No judge. No jury. Not even God.

Kick hit his Most Muscular for the first of the three times he always repeated it. The crowd went wild.

There was no God outside themselves. Even gods could be sacrificed.

Kick powered down into the Most Muscular crunch a second time, extending his arms, revolving his fists one around the other, the rotation displaying the popping intricacies of his massively sculpted arms.

Ryan had once feared Death. Now he wanted it. Murder, not suicide, he had once thought the answer. Now he knew the answer was both. Nothing but Death mattered. Death could freeze them forever together outside space and time.

Kick raised his arms, drawing all the power of the lights and the music and the audience to him, and locked down into his final Most Muscular pose. The audience convulsed, rose, screaming.

Ryan pulled the gun from his pocket. He pointed it through the blinding sea of flash-popping cameras rushing the stage.

Kick rose from his crouch and threw both arms high over his head. His body ran rich and golden with sweat and oil.

In the gun sight, Ryan watched his proud grin.

He pulled the trigger, soundless in the cheering auditorium.

Kick's massive neck bloomed red on blond in the white light. His upraised arms flew back. His whole body rose up from the platform, like a diver, lifting up from his toes, flipping up to a backwards swan dive, through the fine red spray of blood.

He turned the gun to his own temple, but a bodybuilder standing next to him grappled the gun from his hand. The revolver shot off into thin air.

9

None of it worked. He shot Kick alright, but he only wounded him. The brilliant bodybuilder had turned full into the light. The bullet pierced his flesh and lodged in his spine and crippled him from the neck for the rest of his life.

In the instant between Ryan's first shot and his surprise and grief at watching his lover explode in slow-motion Zapruder crumble, something in Ryan flamed hotter than an arc lamp burning through a single celluloid frame caught in a 35-millimeter projector. The dark flicker between frames stopped for the first time in his life. He saw only the frozen single-frame moment with the traveling light burning out the melting Technicolor frame from its center to its edges.

In that pause, muscular hands from the judges' table and from the front row of the audience wrestled him to the floor. A crush of bodybuilders fell across him, smothering him. He felt nothing. He saw nothing. The shots had deafened him. The burning traveling light blinded him.

They took him away. They gave him shock treatments and ice baths and shot him full of Thorazine. For years, he sat, motionless, speechless, staring, wrapped in white sheets, a catatonic patient on the deck of a hospital ship.

He himself had died that night. His soul had left his body, driven by the logic of his passion. So he sat, for weeks, months, years, frozen, immobile, feeling nothing, dependent, as he always imagined he would be, on the blanched kindness of strangers.

10

What is the human heart if not a thing of ambiguity? The truth was Kick was a lover who wouldn't die. Good lovers die young. Bad lovers live forever. That's a fact of life. Kick could not be murdered. Kick could not be shot. At least not by Ryan. Kick had rendered him incapable of even that last act of the incapable: murder.

Ryan had gone to California Hall that night. The gun had been in his pocket. But he could not shoot. He could not kill the winner. He could not murder the new Mr. California. He could not kill his lover in whose magnificent body, he could only hope, lodged, as in his own flesh, the memory of how they had for so long felt one to the other.

He called Kick's muscle-hustle number, prepared to leave at least a threat on his machine.

"You stay out of my way. I love you too much not to warn you. I want to kill you."

But he had not even been able to do that. There is an acceptable level of evil in the human heart, but Ryan, for all his pain, lacked the venom to act.

When he heard that the windshield on Kick's Corvette had been smashed, he wished he had done it himself. When he heard that Kick thought he had done it, he realized that Kick had never known him at all. He was a creator, not a destroyer. He lived only on paper. Kick had nothing to fear. Ryan took small solace from Francis Bacon: "By taking revenge, a man is but even with his enemy; but in passing over it, he is superior."

For months he languished in his Victorian. The place assaulted him. He opened drawers and found sweet old notes:

"I love you, madman!" He decided to reconnect his own answering machine. He tested the tape.

"Hello," the voice said, "you have reached 285-53. . . ."

Ryan's face blanched. It was Kick. It was the message he had recorded when first he had moved in. The drawl in his southern voice was beautiful.

"I was wrong. He didn't fall from grace. I did. He was too good for me."

Small reproaches, sharp as stabbings, creeped out of Ryan's bureau drawers and closets. Small reminders: Kick's brass cock ring, a Baggie of clipped blond hair, forgotten letters, a sweat-stiff pair of weightlifting gloves. He began the slow task of collecting the scattered detritus of their affair. It was like nuclear waste storage and retrieval. Its half-life was eternity.

"I'm tired," he said, "of being mugged by memories every time I open a box I haven't touched in a year. I'm living at the scene of the accident."

For four months Ryan haunted his Victorian. His small appliances danced on the counter tops. His electric meter spun in hungry circles. He could not leave. He could not bear the chance of running into Kick on Castro. Dr. Quack threw up his hands. Ryan's depression required more than Valium. Dr. Quack sent him to Dr. Shrink who smoked his pipe and listened and prescribed Desyrel and lithium to relieve the progress of Ryan's stress, anxiety, and depression. No matter how much medication Ryan took, his pain remained.

He was carrying a torch.

He could not release, any more than he could kill, the ideal he had always known was possible but thought would never happen.

At least not to him.

In the movie *Dirty Harry,* he heard the message he had been waiting for. Clint Eastwood said, "A man's got to know his limitations."

Ryan knew his. He knew he had to let go of what he had promised to hold on to forever. He knew he would never be free of Kick until he himself ended his own heartbreak.

Five months later, on the eve of the following Christmas, Ryan took final matters into his own hand.

Ryan stripped himself naked.

In his room, in his bed, in his video collection of a stupendous lover's performances, in the spread of shirts and posing trunks exchanged in full fetish worship, in all the pictures framed on the walls, in the feel of flannel sheets worn nubby by the many long nights of lovemaking, with the plastic bag full of hair clippings, near the closet full yet with his unclaimed California Highway Patrol uniform, the uniform he had worn the night they first met, under the dim track light spot, Ryan knelt mid-bed, with everything Kick had not stolen back, to commit finally the unspeakable act, the heretical act that would deny all his previous faith.

That morning out on Geary Street, he had Kick's name tattooed across the shaved skin between his balls and his butthole. The needle had felt like a red-hot razor blade. This evening he knelt in what had been their bed, to make it his bed again. Out of all the acreage he owned, ranch and City, the only claim he staked was the forty-two square feet of this bed, this altar of their bonding.

The handgun, the revolver that Solly had given him to hide, was slipped deep into the holster on Kick's CHP utility belt at the foot of the bed. Next to his brass pipe lay a chunk of hash, a marble ashtray, and a beige pack of matches with black ink spelling out Chuck Arnett's stylized logo for the Ambush bar.

Near him, arranged on the wool chessboard of his blanket, like knights and kings and bishops, and maybe queens, lay his tit clamps and a can of Crisco. On the bureau opposite, Ryan had set up both his television sets. A single image was never enough for him. One monitor, a standard nineteen-inch set, was connected to his video camera set to RECORD on its tripod and aimed mid-focus at him on the bed. The other, a new forty-four-inch rear-projection screen, was connected to a recorder set to PLAY. Next to it sat a pile of cassettes. All of them of Kick.

"What is to happen tonight," Ryan announced to the recording video camera, "is an act of freedom. I am untying the knots of our bonding to each other that somehow we both turned into my bondage to him. Enjoy this, Magnus," Ryan said to me on the videotape. "It's the autobiography you always wanted. Look around me in this bed. I have not to remember these things; they have remembered themselves. My memory of the vision, of the man who walked that first El Lay night into that vision and fulfilled it, remains clear and bright. Too clear. Too bright. What movie am I?" He laughed. "Alas, poor Yorick." Sitting naked, up on his knees in his bed, he laughed.

"I guess I'm more narcissistic than Kick. Am I embarrassed? Are you embarrassed, Magnus? I can reveal anything to anyone. People who have been publicly humiliated have that freedom, you know. Stick with me, Magnus, the way you always have. Watch me kill. Watch me die. Watch me fill and smoke the sacred pipe. Watch me break the bonds of gravity and soar into the air with a sky full of angels.

"This is the ceremonial end of ceremony. My childhood and schooling and life choices now seem a strange series of mistakes, arranged first by others, then by myself. It wasn't sex that made me happy. It was Kick who gave me more happiness than I have ever known. You know that, Magnus. You will be my only spokesman—spokesperson. Ah. I have learned that too. Is not Ginger greater than Fred? She did everything he did, Kweenie said, and she did it backward in high heels. It all makes sense, Magnus, and none of it makes sense. Ask the ladies to forgive my joke on them. You have to interpret everything.

"You can become me for a while, Magnus. You are the professor of popular culture. You can write a piece for a professional journal. What will you write? Confession? Apology? Memoir?

"I went to Kick for precisely the same reason Thoreau went to Walden Pond: to front only the essential facts of life.

"Can you give lectures on that to your students? Can you be the genial professor lecturing to young students, handing out mimeographed notes to eager, upturned faces on the pop-culture rise and fall of the Castro, like we were part three of a miniseries that started with the Beats in North Beach and the hippies in the Haight-Ashbury? Was the Castro no more than *Brigadoon*? What will you say about AIDS? Will you trivialize all us gay guys—you see, I can say it; I can admit it—into questions and answers on a pop quiz about our lost homosexual civilization?

"I can't hold that against you, Magnus. Analytical education is what you do best. You remain the teacher I once was, but unlike you I could not remain an observer. I had to go and get involved. I should have known I don't have the strength of character to get involved in anything. I've not been adventurer enough to handle life in California. I should have stayed sitting in my seat in the dark womb-caverns of movie theaters in the Midwest. I'm not cut out to live life. I was born to be a moviegoer, a film fan of dashing, adventurous, romantic men who act out lives larger than my life on brilliant Technicolor screens in Panavision with stereophonic sound.

"Where did I get the idea I could avert fate and change history?

"I smoke my hash pipe and I ramble. The traditional narrative you want from me is impossible in a world of film and videotape that has turned us all into voyeurs of ourselves. I am a man who tried to be gay, and more than gay, because that seemed the way to absolute manhood.

"For one, brief, shining moment . . . Oh, Jack! Oh! Jackie! . . . I thought we all might be onto something; but finally I said *no* when I found no god in man, when I found no angel in him, when I found he was, like me, not perfect, but only a fraction of Adam after the Fall. Welcome, Magnus, to my *Paradise Lost*. What's the line the Eagles sang? "Call some place 'paradise,' kiss it good-bye."

" 'How did you find me?' I asked him that golden afternoon his helicopter landed in my fields at Bar Nada. He never answered that. Not really. He only said, 'I know everything about you.' Did he love me before I didn't even know? I wonder if he did. I wonder if he loved me because of a secret me only he knew. Maybe he was trying to coach me to become that me of the me he loved. If he was, then he was guilty of the same sin as me trying to coach him into becoming the him of the him I loved. I wonder if I drove away the best man I ever met before he had a chance to tell me what to this night, this Christmas Eve, I still think he had to tell me. The last thing he said to me was that he had been trying to make a man out of me. He said it just like Charley-Pop.

"My God! My dad would have loved him for a son.

"What if he were an angel? What if I turned on a truly good man? What if I was too impatient with this young god? What if, as I suspect, it was I, not he, who fell from a state of grace?

"I look at it now. Logan was nothing. The steroids were nothing. I should have put up with anything to keep on keeping on with him. But I couldn't keep up with him. Not physically. Not even sexually. I kept losing part of myself. I thought that was wrong. I feared I would die. But maybe that's the eye of the needle that love must pass through. Loss of yourself, the Death of identity, until the needle is threaded, and you are given back by your lover a new, improved, reborn sense of your self, rewarded, because you trusted him enough to let go of yourself completely.

"I am not a philosopher, nor was I meant to be. I'm so J. Alfred Prufrock. All I know is I wanted something from him. I wanted something I can't have. I wanted something I lost at the baths. Cheap goods, the Wife of Bath said, have little value. I was cheap goods. I wanted him to give me my innocence back. I wanted purity back, his and mine. . . . Dumb old me. Maybe he had never lost his purity. Maybe he was super-pure and I was too sex-crazed, too drug-impaired to recognize it. That's me all over. Call someplace paradise; kiss today good-bye."

Ryan took the remote gun of his video in his hand.

With the video camera still running, he knelt up in the bed, watching himself kneel up on the nineteen-inch live video screen. He was real. He was on video. He was his own Yorick between two mirrors. One thing was instantly, electronically, two things curving off to infinity. He could see his otherness. What was life if not Chinese puzzle boxes filled with cathode ray tubes?

He took the remote-control gun of his video in his hand. He turned from the live screen and knelt before the blank monitor. He pushed the remote PLAY button.

Kick's supernal blondness lit up the empty forty-four-inch screen.

Ryan controlled Kick's onscreen timing. He pulled the trigger of the video gun. Kick posed on stage, in open fields, in the playroom. Ryan's hand controlled the SLOW MOTION, the FAST-FORWARD, the SPEED-SEARCH for the appropriate footage, the FREEZE-FRAME that could hold Kick on screen forever, the SINGLE-FRAME ADVANCE that made Kick move totally under his coaching, clicking off his movements like the inexorable seconds on a clock.

Kick rose majestic as a sun god above the draw atop Corona Heights. He posed on the dais of a spotlighted stage. He strained in classic bondage sculpture against steel chains and black leather. He sat still in close-up as the camera circled again and again around his face. He stood powerful, oiled, pumped, jerking his enormous dirty-blond cock from the screen.

Ryan responded in kind for his live camera.

"This is an intimacy, Magnus, that I want to share with you."

In the background, his stereo played the Doors. Jim Morrison was singing, "This is the end, my only friend."

Ryan smiled into the camera. "At least I have enough self left to be self-consciously theatrical," he said. "That's the song Coppola used to open *Apocalypse Now*. What is this if not *Heart of Darkness*? I ventured out to live on the edge and stayed out too long."

He greased his own hard cock. He set his tit clamps. He watched Kick on screen. He stroked himself with the bittersweet feel of a man who knows he is watching something for the last time in his life.

He reached for the remote-control gun, took careful aim at the golden man muscularly stroking himself on screen, and pressed ever so slowly the button on the gun to ERASE DURING PLAY.

Every image he had so painstakingly recorded of Kick, all the images of Kick he had so carefully saved, he saw play for the last time. He was killing the video image of Kick. He was driving the stake through his vampire heart.

Blood on his hands.

The dying videotapes.

Never to see him again!

The colors breaking up.

Never to hold him again!

The lines per screen dissolving.

Never to be held by him again!

Crying like a comrade bereft.

Stroking like a lover.

Kick dissolving, fading, crumbling on-screen in scene after scene.

He had created this man. He was destroying his own creation. As one video erased Kick, the other recorded, if not Ryan, then the shell of Ryan kneeling in the bed, masturbating his final lust, rocking in tears, crying in his cuming, falling back on the bed, spent, watching the last images disappearing from the screen, lying like a perfect sculpture of late-twentieth-century man, spent, lustless, himself watched by the all-seeing eye of the video camera watching him fall back from his sexual pant to the regular rhythms of drugged sleep, his lean aerobic body adrift on the bed, in the sea of mementos, rolling finally, under the track light, to his side, his knees pulled to his chest, sleeping, dreaming, while the humming video camera looked coldly on, running on AUTOMATIC to the end of its LP cassette early that Christmas morning.

11

Sometime after New Year's, Ryan read in *Iron Man* magazine that Kick had placed fifth in the Mr. America contest. Rumors had confirmed what Ryan figured. After Mr. California, Kick had tossed everything he owned into the Corvette and headed for El Lay. More specifically, he had moved to Venice Beach to work out at the pro-bodybuilder gyms and hang out at Muscle Beach with the big boys.

"He never said *good-bye*," Ryan said. "Did I hurt him that much? I was the one who was raped."

Two months later the "Armstrong" ad was back in *The Advocate* with an El Lay phone number.

"Business as usual," Ryan said. "I wonder what he'd do if I showed up at his door with three hundred bucks in my hand?"

"He'd take it," Solly said, "and give you the time of your life."

He tucked the ad into his wallet. The phone number listed was his last thin connection to Kick.

One thought lingered. He had no idea where Logan Doyle had disappeared. He figured not with Kick. It hardly mattered. Logan had never been the point. Logan finally had been the reality. He had given Ryan the physical beating that Kick had given his soul. Ryan nursed a small fear that their paths might cross and Logan might again hurt him physically. Deep down, he resented Kick's not making sure Logan was safely out of the picture.

"Can we," Solly asked Ryan, "never mention Kick's name again?"

"Kick who?"

"Cool," Solly said.

Ryan finally retracted his animosity to that Dowager Empress, Quentin Crisp, who had said, "There is no tall, dark man."

"There is," Ryan said crisply to Solly, "no short, blond one either."

Solly was acting grand. He was glad Kick was gone. "I can say certain things," Solly said. "I mean I'm one of the original homosexuals. Before me, there was only Oscar Wilde, Allen Ginsberg, and a couple of bishops. I was the first normal homosexual. Once you guys all turned to kinky specialty acts, you turned out thousands of weird homosexuals. That's what got us in trouble. Outrageous dirty sex. You were all trying to be more weird than homosexual. You kept trying to find more and more disgusting things to do. That's what caused AIDS. Since I'm venerable and grand, I can say that."

Ryan gave him the finger. "Twirl on it."

"Did you know," Solly said, "that roofers have more tattoos than any other trade? Murderers have the fewest."

"What is this? *Trivial Pursuit?*"

"It's education. I'm educating you, so when I'm killed you can carry on my business. You may be totally depressed, but you're my only beneficiary."

"Don't be morbid."

"This may seem," Solly said, "to be a moral fable, a story with a point to drive home, an ethical dilemma. Pay attention."

"You mean," Ryan said, "there's more to life than getting fistfucked on the altar of a Catholic Church at midnight on Halloween?"

"See how you are," Solly said. "You're bouncing back nicely for someone clinging to the wreckage."

"Gee, thanks," Ryan said. "What's the difference between a bounce and a rebound?"

"I must tell you that there is more to my business than videotaping young hustlers."

"There's blowing young hustlers."

"As I always say, I don't know if I'm Fagin or Father Flanagan."

"I can answer that."

"Don't."

Solly fingered an antique silver spoon once used by stars in the studio commissary before the MGM auction. He sat on his luxurious new couch. He had been upgrading his penthouse furnishings from Salvation Army to Macy's. Behind his head a Warhol poster of Marilyn hung in a chrome frame on the stark white wall.

"Last night I gave this seventeen-year-old hustler my usual speech. Tiger brought him over. I told him why boys like him exist. I told him what his value was. He already knew his price. I actually tried to give him some direction to what he was doing in life. You thought you had a vocation! That's my calling. I counsel hustlers. He'll remember what I said for about two nights, then I'll have to make my speech to him again. Or to another boy just like him.

"That's the function of a john in a deteriorating society. I'm always giving advice. Me and Auntie Mame. Of course, she had the bucks. If I must be compared, Auntie Mame is my choice. I guess I've always wanted to be Auntie Mame. There was a time in life I would have been offended by that. Shows how times have changed."

"Life in the bizarre lane," Ryan said.

"This Auntie Mame's boys are street trash," Solly said. "My boys are not Colt models. If you're to be my heir and carry on my style and tradition, you've got to learn that thousands of men prefer my boys to the slick Colt Studio glamour-boy El Lay muscle types."

"That's why you never liked Kick. He was too 'Colt.'"

"Colt is too Vargas, too George Petty, too Flo Ziegfeld, too Hefner. He glorifies one type of American gay man, same as you, as if there is no other kind to glorify. I don't like Colt's buffed, fluffed, powdered male 'modelles.'"

I don't buy into the so-called 'Straight Look' impersonated by butch faggots."

"Colt's not selling *straight* so much as he's peddling homomasculine photographs."

"Give me a break. All you homomasculinists, trying to pass as straight, are as much traitors as blacks passing for white, or Jews like me who change their names from 'Katz' to 'Keats.' What you are, you are."

"But what if some gay boy is more 'Keats' than 'Katz'? Colt is what some of us are. Colt glorifies an ideal. If it takes exaggeration of masculinity to teach sissies the alternatives of homomasculinity, I love it."

"That's the trouble with gay porn. *Exaggeration.* It's incorrect, psychologically, and, maybe, as the dykes would say, politically. It idealizes the impossible. Big muscles. Big dicks. Big Looks."

"So you hate Plato? Everybody needs an image to worship and admire. Colt's men should be on Wheaties boxes."

"Ain't you the kid!" Solly said.

"Yeah. I'm the kid who, long before I knew homosexuality existed, wanted to grow up to be like my heroes."

"Spare me your Norman Rockwell idealism. My tapes are jerk-off videos, not training films."

"In porno, a man's reach should exceed his grasp, or what's a camera for?"

"You don't get it, do you?"

"Cut to your point."

"Porn stars aren't meant to be role models."

"But they are, Blanche, but they are!"

"That's the problem."

"I guess I don't get it, do I?" Ryan said.

"Colt puts pressure on ordinary gay men that makes them feel bad about themselves because they don't match the Colt Ideal. Look how that tension got you involved with Kick. You fell in-love with a man on a box of flakes."

"That's a bit cold."

"Frankly, my dear, I don't like pornographers who hire gay men to pretend they're straight. My models actually are straight. Tough. Rough. Crude. Straight trade. I don't like men good-looking enough to sell beer and cigarettes in ads. I like the men who buy alcohol, tobacco, and firearms."

"Handsome men threaten you."

"Wrong. Handsome men don't threaten me enough. Colt shoots gay fantasy for design queens. I shoot straight, abusive reality for nasty queers."

"That makes your stuff scary. No one's scared of Colt models."

"Terror makes my stuff a new style of porn: straight men abusing gay men. Who else has glorified rough trade?"

"Terror is your hard-on."

"Sexual terror is the last closet. I know. My customers love it. I'll gross over fifty thousand this year without ever leaving this penthouse. That's why I can afford to be grand. I owe it all to the boys who ring my bell. You may meet Colt models at a gay cocktail party, but you'll never meet my boys. My boys are boiled eggs and beer, not white wine and quiche."

"How do you say in English," Ryan said. *"Chacún a son goût."*

"You need to know these things," Solly said. "You're my heir apparent."

"I like the fifty-thousand part, but I don't want you dead. You're the only friend I have left in San Francisco."

"Tiger threatened me last night."

"Your one true love. Your adopted son?"

"You haven't seen him in a year. My little boy has been working out. He weighs 190 pounds and both his arms are tattooed."

"So what are you worried about? You said murderers don't have tattoos."

"Usually. Last night he showed up, stoned as usual. He took a look around at all my new stuff and said, 'I should probably rob you, but you know me too well, and you'd probably laugh at me, and then I'd have to hit you.' He has a knack for escalating violence."

"Change your locks."

"I told him it was only a matter of time before he went to prison. He's lucky he's still out. He's a one-man crime wave. He's got a couple of minor bench warrants out. He admitted he used a gun to hold up a trick on Polk Street. Robbing. Shoplifting. It's all gone for drugs. Hustlers and drug addicts are the same thing."

"Get rid of him."

"I can't. I love it when he calls me *Dear Old Dad.*"

"Hustlers always say what you want to hear. You told me that."

"I've known Tiger since he was nineteen. He's twenty-three."

"Has it been that long?"

"You've been somewhat distracted the last few years." Solly paused. "I feel fatherly toward him. He's what keeps me from killing myself."

"So you're waiting for him to kill you?"

"He's my responsibility to go on living. That's what sons are to fathers. If I were detached from everything in the world, it wouldn't make any difference what happened."

"So much for 'What is, is.'"

"What is, still is. You may have ended things with your crypto-Colt model fantasy, but my boy is real. My situation is different from yours. Kick was a puffed and powdered gay man. Tiger is a buffed young straight man. All my boys are straight. He may rent his body, but he's definitely straight. I'm dealing with a straight problem here."

"Whenever you don't answer your phone, I'm always afraid the worst has happened."

"And well you should. My boys are into sex and violence." He hit his palm to his forehead. "Oy! For them sex is violence."

"Like father, like sons."

"Son. Singular. Son. Not sons. But in this respect they are all the same. My friend Boyd, who publishes *Straight to Hell,* warned his readers never to invite boys like these into their lovely homes. I have. I do. It's my living. It's my sex life. In the tradeoff of sex and violence, my survival to this point is that I give them sex. I top off their violence by having sex with them. They've got to have one or the other. After I videotape them, I have sex with them. They slap me around. They pinch my tits. They sit on my face. They strangle me. We both cum. They're not like high-rent Colt-type models who stop when you yell *stop.*"

"They're dangerous."

"They're expensive. When I'm finished with them, all they want is their money, and maybe some clean socks. Hustlers always want clean socks, so they can go out and score some dope and take their old ladies out for the night."

"So how can I help? What do you want me to do?" Ryan asked.

"Nothing. I'm worried, but I'm not sitting here in fear. I've been robbed before. But Tiger is different. He has tracks on his arms. So does Susie Slit."

"Susie Slit?"

"His latest squeeze. They were in a brawl in a shooting gallery. She stabbed Tiger in the thigh. A flesh wound. That's how they met. She's one of those skinny postmodern biker blondes with tattoos on her tits. She wears a buck knife on each hip."

"Ah. A debutante."

"My daughter-in-law. That's what she calls herself when she calls me *Dear Old Dad.* She really pushes it."

"They're both shooting speed?"

"When they can get the money from me."

"Don't give them the money."

"They'd only go out and rob some poor unsuspecting sucker."

"And maybe kill him."

"And maybe kill him."

"And maybe kill you."

"You don't kill your banker."

"Unless you're on speed."

Solly dropped his bombshell. "I'm moving to Los Angeles."

"You're not."

"I am."

"Why?"

"Because I believe one thing you always say: signs and omens are every-where. Tiger is a warning. Maybe I've worn out my welcome in San Francisco. Like Kick wore out his. Besides, I am in the film industry. I'm practically a mogul. I belong in Hollywood."

Ryan was speechless.

"We've all worn out our welcome in San Francisco," Solly said. "It's time you left too. Everybody's giving up sex. That's all the City was good for. It's time everybody moved back where they came from. It's time you moved up to Sonoma County and played Squire Western at Bar Nada."

"Don't leave," Ryan said. "Don't you leave me too."

"Spare me the hysterics," Solly said. "It'll take me a month to get my shit together."

A week later Tiger and Susie Slit climbed the fire escape to Solly's pent-house. He heard the glass break in the kitchen window and climbed over the young hustler sleeping next to him. He found them in his video studio.

Susie Slit stood ready with a buck knife in each hand. Tiger was already unplugging the jacks and cords to all the video equipment: four recorders, two cameras, two 28-inch monitors. No one said anything. They all knew their parts. This was not the first robbery for any of them.

Susie Slit motioned Solly through the bedroom toward the bathroom. She kicked the hustler sleeping in the bed. He woke with her knife in his face. She nodded for him to follow Solly into the bathroom. Tiger crowded in behind her. He was strong. He was loaded. He pushed Solly and the hustler to the floor and tied their hands and feet with electrical cord.

Solly knew better than to struggle. The hustler didn't. Susie Slit dropped to her knees and stuck the point of her blade against his jugular. Solly knew she wanted to slash him.

"Let me do it," she yelled to Tiger rummaging through Solly's goods.

"Do what?"

"Stick 'em!"

"Makes me no difference." Tiger stood in the bathroom doorway.

"Come on," Solly said. He nodded toward the young hustler tied cowering next to him. "You're not scaring me. You're only scaring him. Come on, Tiger. Take anything you want. Just get her out of here."

"Do it!" Tiger said.

Susie Slit slashed her blade across the boy's throat. Blood spurted across Solly's face.

"No!" Solly's eyes widened.

Susie Slit turned to him, her blade aimed across the distance at his naked gut. She looked up at Tiger.

"So long, Dad," Tiger said. He spit down on Solly, dropped to his knees across his bloody chest, and wrapped electrical cord tight around his neck. "Do it!" he said. "It's what he wants anyway."

Choking, with the pressure of Tiger's weight sitting on his chest, Solly felt her drive cold steel into his stomach.

"At least," Solly looked up at Tiger, "you could have done it yourself."

"And give you everything you want?" He stood up. "Fuck you, Dad."

They left the bathroom door open.

Solly, his lifeblood flowing red across the cold tile floor, watched them take load after load of his valuables out to the hall. He heard the ancient elevator rumble up the shaft. They loaded everything they could carry. Then they closed the door to the penthouse. Solly, choking, bleeding, heard the elevator whir and begin its slow descent to the deserted lobby that led out to the streets of the Tenderloin.

Tiger had been smart enough not to take Solly's answering machine. For twenty-four hours, Ryan repeatedly got his recorded promise to get back to the caller. Then he called the police.

12

"GAY PORNOGRAPHER STABBED IN TENDERLOIN SEX DEN," by Maitland Zane.

13

Ryan retreated to his Victorian. He took Solly's Death hard. Not even Solly's work remained. Tiger had stolen the videotape master copies and sold them at a buck a piece on the street to kids eager to tape MTV. Kick was gone. Teddy was gone. Kweenie was living with January in El Lay. Of all the friends and acquaintances he once had in San Francisco, several had moved away from the City, a dozen were dead from disease, the rest were cool, almost unforgiving, for his having dropped them, having dropped everybody, during his affair with Kick. The muscle crowd Kick had drawn to them was no longer interested once Kick had split. When Ryan passed them on Castro, they were unforgiving: they not only ignored him, they gave him Attitude. Readers of *Maneuvers* sent letters complaining he had abandoned the magazine. The few women he had known, mostly Kweenie's friends, remained miffed over the dead issue of the *Manifesto*.

He feared cruising new acquaintances, afraid they'd end up in bed, and he was resolved that could never happen. No one was sure what safe sex was. AIDS was a lottery. The more chances you took, the more your chance of winning, which meant losing. AIDS was like murder. A man's chance of contracting AIDS was one in a hundred; the chance of his being murdered was one in a hundred and thirty-three. He was truly alone. His life became a solitary masturbation. He was a victim of the ass-end of the sexual revolution.

He hated the changing Castro. Old faces gone. New faces eager to find the party they did not know was over. The quaint gay shops that had given the Castro its ambience gave way to chain stores. Asian restaurants opened overnight and competed with the gay restaurants where sometimes, despite his unreasonable fear of disease, for *auld lang syne,* he ventured out to eat alone, still aching with love for Kick, disguised with mirrored CHP shades and a blue SFPD ball cap. He sat alone, insulated from the dapper waiters. He dissolved into the sounds coming from the other tables where he and Kick had once dined.

I could not help but think those gay men and lesbian women had all come, the way we all came, immigrants and refugees from all across the country to become Californians. They—and I mean we, although I am only a scholarly fellow traveler and sympathizer, because I am not exactly one of them—all trekked west for sexual and political freedom, for love, happiness, real estate, and each other. Instead, somehow very much *instead,* they conjured lust and greed and abuse and Death. They all thought they were special. And they were. All of them. Ryan lived and wrote and told them they were chosen, charmed, gifted, exempt. They thought the party would never stop.

Before things turned sour and Ryan turned bitter, he wrote, "Scott Fitzgerald was right. When the best people get together, things go glimmering."

Like the rest of them, he thought the sanctuary of San Francisco was their mecca of Sodom-Oz. They thought, before the drugs and before the breakdowns and before the epidemic Deaths, that they would live forever. I once wrote in *The Journal of Popular Culture* that "homosexuals have always been their own best invention." And also perhaps their worst.

Before Stonewall ignited the seventies when they spun their existence out of media whole cloth, because no one like them had ever before been seen in the streets of America, their history of closets and shame had for years been their prison. I think their newfound freedom, and especially the gay pride that so petulantly for so many became an outrageous vanity, turned into a much more deadly sentence, not of AIDS, but of the heart.

I'm not sitting in judgment. I try to examine what happened and make the best sense possible. Popular culture and cinema, after all, are my specialty. I can tell you more than you probably want to know about *Citizen Kane*. I study movies—forgive me, analytically.

Ryan's memorabilia are my "Rosebud."

"You have too much Attitude," Ryan once told me.

"I'm a critic. I can let nothing obstruct my objectivity."

"That's why you can't get a date," Ryan said. "That's why no one makes love to a critic. Love is not objective." He tried to redeem me. "Maybe you're a critic and more than a critic," he said. "You may be an appreciator, a true appreciator of other people's visions. Most critics are detractors of other people's work. Parasites: that's what critics are. If artists stopped producing, critics would starve. Critics don't act; they react. Most of the criticism I read is no more than Attitude. I'm an expert on Attitude. Kick made me an expert on Attitude. Kick had real Attitude. He taught me everything I know about Attitude."

"Kick was a world-class teacher of Attitude," I said.

We had words, Ryan and I.

Sometimes, I must reveal, I was too close to Ryan Steven O'Hara. Sometimes I thought we were the same person playing Ingmar Bergman's *Persona*. He had that boyishly charming way of pulling people into his center. Teddy had fallen for it. Kick pursued him for it. I felt his undertow, particularly in those last days, pulling me dangerously close to him. My empathy toward him, then and now, worries me.

Objectivity, I believe, even more than passionate love and hate, is the most fragile gift in the human order of things. Passion has to do with the volatile heart. Objectivity is the coolest function of the human mind. I loved Ryan for the Energy of his passion, and I pitied him for what had happened.

I realized early on that it was Kick, and only Kick, who had ever broken through to what Ryan called his soul. It was Kick, and only Kick, whose brilliant golden light was intense enough to pierce the fearful dark night in

Ryan's soul. It was Kick, and only Kick, whose arms, strong as angel's wings, lifted Ryan from his isolation and his terror of Death. At least for a time.

I remember, you see, all too well that morning on Venice Beach when I met a woman who had run into a Golden Man. The startled Look in her eyes has never left me. That Look was the willing suspension of disbelief that lodges in a face when something ecstatic beyond expectation lifts a person once and forever outside the closed circuit of themselves.

It is a profound belief in otherness.

I spent more and more time with Ryan.

He stripped the Victorian. He excavated the mounds of paper and artwork in his study. He boxed everything up for a fast escape.

"Packing boxes are the only way to live," Solly had always said.

Ryan called a mover named Ralph Joy, whose yellow truck, painted with the logo, "The Joy of Moving," appealed to his ironic sense of humor.

"There is," Ryan said, "no joy in this."

The yellow truck, loaded by eager young gay boys, made six trips carting everything he owned into storage in the house and barn at Bar Nada.

Ryan did not move to the ranch. He holed up in the Victorian for six more months, sleeping his prescription-drug sleep like a monk on a pallet on the floor. By night he wrote *Killing Time till Armageddon,* sending photocopied sections to Kweenie and me. By day he painted the large empty rooms of the house. He lived among canvas drop cloths, paintbrushes, and rollers. He pointed to his single wooden stepladder.

"What movie am I?" he asked. He answered the question himself. *"Our Town."* He was suffering, he said, a tenth-rate nervous breakdown, borrowed from Salinger's *Franny and Zooey.* "I've hoped it would be a nervous breakthrough. But it can't be. Not here. Not in these rooms. Solly was right. I have to move."

The fresh paint had not erased his life in those rooms with Kick. The Victorian assaulted him. He put it on the market and sold it in two days to an Asian family. The sale of the house, bought in the early seventies of the great gay invasion into real estate, compounded with Solly's life insurance, brought enough for him to live on the rest of his life. He packed his clothes and his typewriter into his Rabbit and drove north from the City, across the Bridge, to the ranch.

Kweenie wrote to him. "I adore *Armageddon.* It seems you finally understand what men do. January sends her love. We're producing music videos. Come down to see us."

He traveled nowhere. Kick was always out there on the edge of his mind. Warm afternoons he often sat on the exact spot in his field where Kick's helicopter had landed. His fever continued. He wrote a sheaf of unmailed letters to Kick.

Sometimes now, I can go a half-day and you never cross my mind. Then I see a man who looks vaguely like you. Dreams die hard when they don't come true. Loving somebody shouldn't make you suffer pain, but pain seems to be the essence of being in-love. Maybe that's why you warned me from this pain. I was the one who was wrong. For all I loved you, I didn't love you enough. I wanted you to be in-love with me, and all that could have done was cause you the pain it has caused me.

Sitting in the field, Ryan felt something mammoth fly between him and the sun. He didn't see it, but he felt its huge shadow pass over him. He heard the chop-chop of its wings. It was not the multicolored bird that Annie Laurie had hung over his crib. He felt primordial fear. He was a man with a primitive killer beast, a giant hawk, circling over him, waiting for him to drop. It was the first time Ryan ever experienced genetic fear of being eaten alive.

14

For my part, in the next year, I became his frequent houseguest, spending more and longer weekends at Bar Nada. One Saturday he disappeared and I found him sitting in the chicken yard. Rhode Island Reds, Barred Rocks, and Araucanas fought each other for the cracked corn and lay mash he had spread across the ground. Ducks jostled the chickens aside. A peacock and peahen strutted unruffled through the quarreling birds. "This has become my Castro," he said. "A chicken yard is everything you need to remember about pecking order."

I handed him an envelope from Kweenie. A rooster, turned on by the flurry of hens fighting for food, mounted a Barred Rock who squatted bored under his awkward pumping. Inside the envelope was a pink page from *The Advocate*. The "Armstrong" ad was circled. This time it appeared in the Florida *Models* column. It confirmed the rumor Ryan had heard from friends who took no small delight in trampling out the wrath on the gay grapevine. Kick had last been sighted in Miami. The southern gold coast was the perfect place to muscle-hustle rich New Yorkers. They flew down from the dark-skinned island of Manhattan eager to pay for sex with blond beach-boys and blond bodybuilders. Other rumors said he had been sighted in Texas along the Gulf Coast, at an evangelical gym, pumping iron for Jesus.

He was everywhere. He was nowhere.

California, northern and southern, had not worked for Kick. The Florida *Advocate* ad was three months old. The blond bodybuilder, after all his small disappearances, seemed finally to manage his grand disappearance. I once read that nearly two million people in the U.S. disappear every year. Three hundred thousand are never seen again. They take a permanent hike. Many of them are gay men wanting to start over with a clean slate. They are adult runaways. The police call them social suicides.

A horn honked at the entry to the long drive up to the ranch house. Ryan stood up like a man hoping against hope. The rooster crowed.

But it was not Kick.

It was January in her red Mercedes with Kweenie at her side.

"Darlings!" January said. She walked toward us, all high heels and rings and bracelets and dark glasses. "You look so, so rural! I love the peacocks! I love the animals!"

"You sound," Ryan said, "like Saint Francis."

"Saint Frances Farmer, maybe," January said. "This is Maggie O'Hara." She introduced Kweenie as if she were a stranger.

"My God!" Ryan said. "What happened to you?"

"Success," Kweenie said. She walked up to her brother and kissed him.

"Kiss-kiss," January said. "Isn't it wonderful!" She turned to me. "Magnus," she said, "you look drab as ever."

"What are you doing here?" Ryan held Kweenie in his arms. "It's wonderful to see you."

"It's summertime, darling," January said. "Half of Hollywood comes to Sonoma in the summertime. The Sonoma Inn is just divine, don't you agree?"

"I've never been there," Ryan said.

"You should, *mon cher*. You should rub shoulders. I've always told you with your talent you should go to pertinent places to power-lunch with pertinent types."

"So who's pertinent this season?" Ryan asked.

"Everyone on *Falcon Crest*, darling. We're up here to watch the exterior shoot for their third season. When we talk *Falcon Crest*, my love, we're talking major soap-series hit. I just adore shoots on location."

"January means," Kweenie said, "she's fucking one of the crew."

"Maggie, Maggie, Maggie," January said to Kweenie, "must you tell everything you know?"

"Why not?" Kweenie said. "You do."

"Maggie?" Ryan stared at Kweenie.

"A new rad name for a truly radical new Margaret Mary," January said. "You remember her real name. My little protege!" She turned to Ryan. "I keep Maggie around to keep me real!"

"She's not doing her job."

"Actually," Kweenie said, "I'm January's production assistant."

"What's that mean?" Ryan was snide. "You change the sheets?"

"Be tacky, darling," January said. "It shows you're getting your sense of humor back."

"What do you mean *back?*"

"I mean after Kick . . . and your famous nervous breakdown . . . and all. You were so depressed. It was depressing."

Ryan looked at me and threw up his hands. We walked from the Mercedes up the drive, past the barn, to the house. January was bursting with chat.

"Is that the place?" January pointed at the barn. "The place where Thom hanged himself?"

"I love your tact," Ryan said. "What do you care?"

"I care, darling, because I'm scouting locations. I'm here to option *Killing Time till Armageddon* for a made-for-cable movie."

"I don't believe this," Ryan said.

"Believe it," Kweenie said. "Kick told you he wanted the two of you to be a story told around the world."

They reached the house and sat on the deck.

"I own a piece," January said, "of someone who owns a piece of Jon-Erik Hexum. Jack—his friends call him *Jack*—is the hottest unexploited property in Hollywood. He has a face and a body that come along once in twenty years. He's straight. He even has a voice." She motioned for Kweenie to hand Ryan a color publicity still of Hexum stripped to the waist. "Look at those eyes. He's more than a piece of meat."

Ryan was impressed. "So far I like it," he teased. "Hexum's a hunk. He can play me. Who's going to play Kick? Arnold Schwarzembalmer?"

"So droll," January said. "You are so droll. I love it. Don't you love it, Maggie?"

"Hexum has real appeal," Kweenie said. "His muscle isn't overdone."

"He's a natural," Ryan said. "He has the face. He has a body. But he's not blond. He doesn't have a moustache."

"He looks to me," January said, "like he has the hormones to grow one. Besides, he's almost blond. We can help his hair along. With Sly's personal trainer we can even pump his muscle up. He'd be perfect."

"He's already perfect," Ryan said.

January winked. "Keep Hexum's picture, darling," she said. "There's rumors he's gay, but he just laughs at them."

"A man," Ryan said, "after my own heart."

Kweenie leveled with Ryan. "Let me warn you. Hexum is January's bait."

"Why Maggie!" January feigned surprise.

"I told her your manuscript was too personal. That you'd never option it for a TV movie."

"Is this reverse psychology?" Ryan asked. "Or what?"

"Darling!" January said. "Think of it. You can help on the adaptation of the script. You can log your first screen credit. You can be on the set."

"She means you can try for yourself to get into Jon-Erik's pants."

Ryan was chagrined. "Do I seem that venal to you?"

"Everybody," January said, "seems that venal to me. Look at that photo. Look at that hunk." She pulled a sheaf of papers from her hootchy-kootchy Gucci briefcase. "Look at this contract." She waved the folder. "We'll be casting tons of bodybuilders for atmosphere people for the gym locales and the contest scenes. Bodybuilding is so *in* now. Especially with women entering the sport."

Ryan's face flushed. He swallowed his comment about women on male steroids.

January handed him the option contract. "It could be your valedictory valentine to Kick." She paused. "You will, of course, have to tone down the sex."

"I give you permission," Kweenie said, "to write it from my point of view."

Ryan would not touch the folder. "Leave it," he said.

January placed it on the table. "Then you will think about it." She rattled all her bracelets.

"I'll think about it."

January was triumphant. "You're an angel." She looked at her watch. "It's almost four. We're due back at the *Falcon Crest* shoot. Jane is so punctual about tea. She's so lovely. I wonder how she ever married that terrible man!"

Ryan kissed Kweenie good-bye.

"By the way," January said, "where is he?"

He always meant Kick.

"I don't know," Ryan said. "I don't know."

"Fame is so short," January said. "I suppose his Universal Appeal has turned to Universal Ennui." She bussed the air on both sides of Ryan's cheeks. "You were so lucky to have him while he was hot." She settled in behind the wheel of her red Mercedes. "Whoever has him now has less than you had."

Ryan executed his worst Rita Moreno imitation. "I speet on whoever hass heem now."

January raised her hand and made a writing motion in the air. She wanted his signature. "Ryan," she said, "do be an angel." She winked at me. "Later, Magnus."

Ryan waved after them speeding down the drive. "She's such a bitch," he said.

"January?"

"No," he said. "Kweenie." He spit out the secret we'd all kept from him. He proved himself the intuitive mystic. "If only she'd had his child."

"You know?"

"It figures," he said. "Betrayal always figures."

"With all Kweenie's acid and all Kick's steroids, it would have been born a monster."

"Not to me."

"Especially to you."

"I should have killed them both." He kicked at a chicken. "I can't even kill myself. I don't have Thom's courage." He looked at the contract papers and then at me. "Shit," he said, "why not?"

"No," I said. "No. You're not seriously considering January's option!"

"I'll consider anything. It's my story."

"It's his story too."

"It's all *Rashomon,* isn't it? There's my story and his story. Let him tell his. I gave him enough material. Besides, he always said he wanted us to do a project together."

"The secrets of two are secret."

"Unless one of them keeps journals, notes, letters, and videotapes; and the other one wants to be a story told in bed at night around the world."

"But what about your own privacy?"

"He made all our privacy public."

A passion of obsessive love, given the opportunity, can turn to obsessive hate. Passion is one of those things that can birth changeling good-and-evil twins.

"You hate him enough to do it to get even, don't you?"

"No." Ryan's voice was low. "I love him. I'd never hurt him."

"Do you love him enough not to do the movie?"

"I love him enough to make him sit up on the couch, wherever he is, in front of his TV set, and try one last time to make him see what I saw in him. We were the best thing that ever happened to either of us. He knew that. He knows that. I want him always to remember that. I want him to know the hell I've been through these past three years since he went away. I want to know if he thinks of me at all every waking hour of the day. I want to know if he dreams at night about me the way I dream about him."

"You can't want him back."

"I never meant for him to leave."

"You threw him out," I said.

"I didn't mean forever. I meant like I told Teddy to get out. Just for a while. To cool his heels. When I called him 'Rhett Butler,' my mouth got too smart-ass for my own good. When I told him to get out of the car, I meant . . ."

"What did you mean?"

"When I told him to get out, I meant the same thing Charley-Pop meant when he told me to get to my room and stay there until I could come out and behave myself."

"He didn't go to his room. He didn't behave himself. He went to a phone booth . . ."

"Just like Superman. . . ."

". . . and called Logan. You can't forget that. He got you beat up and raped."

"Do you think I care about that?"

"You act like you care. You're still in a rage at Logan."

"Then you don't know me."

"I know you as well as I know myself."

"I've never much had any feeling toward Logan one way or the other. Ever. Not even after his laughable, pathetic version of a rape."

"What's real with you, Ryan?"

"I want something I can't have."

"What movie are you?" I asked. "What movie are you trying to be?"

"This isn't a movie," Ryan said. "This isn't that stupid movie game. This is my life."

"Your life," I trod on eggshells to say it, "is about as calm as a movie theater during the shower scene in *Psycho*."

"Don't trivialize me. Don't take away from me what I feel." Once on the wheel of fortune and men's eyes, there is no escape. "I want to feel everything. I felt the heights. I feel the depths." He stood and made a wide gesture across the valley around Bar Nada. "This is my valley of despair." I hated it when literature made him operatic. "This is my slough of despond. What book am I now, Magnus?" He pulled a pen from his flannel shirt and looked hard at me. "I'm *Pilgrim's Progress*." He reached for January's contract and turned to the last page where Kweenie had put a red X.

"Don't do it," I said. "Don't sign it. You can't."

"Just watch me! I have one purity left: the innocence of my motive here!" He scrawled his name across the line. He thrust the contract at me. "Witness it," he said.

"I can't. I won't."

"Then you're no friend of mine."

"Because I won't do what you want me to?"

"Because you won't do what's right."

"What's right?"

"Signing your witness."

"You shouldn't sign things when you're depressed," I said.

"Don't call me depressed!" He was angry. "I'm not depressed."

"You've been depressed ever since Logan showed up."

"Bull!"

"You were depressed before you met Kick."

"Bullshit!"

"You let everything get at you."

"Nothing gets at me."

"Everything gets at you."

"You're getting at me. And I don't think I like it."

"What I'm saying . . ."

"What the hell are you saying?" Ryan pointed toward a hedge row. "Do you need a larger bush to beat around?"

"I'm saying you blame Kick for missing your father's Death. You blame him for calling you back to pump him up for that contest of sweaty men in colored underwear. You blame him because you weren't holding Charley-Pop's hand when he died."

"Spare me." He picked up the contract.

"What you're looking for is . . . ," I had to say it. "You wanted something from your father."

"Oh, yeah. Sure. I wanted him to fuck me."

"You wanted him to say it was okay you were gay."

"I'm not gay! Gays live on drugs and Castro and die of AIDS!"

"But your father died . . ."

"He left me!"

"He never said what you wanted to hear."

"No one leaves me! No one!"

"You have no control over that," I said.

"Control? Control? Over what? Death? Charley-Pop and Thom and Solly?"

"Such anxiety. Such rage. You're acting very gay."

"What's that supposed to mean?" He folded the contract.

"Anxiety. Anger. At Death. It's the latest rage on Castro."

"And well it should be." He waved the contract. "If you don't sign this, I'll walk down the road and have the neighbors witness it."

"You always saw Kick as the golden reincarnation of your father. He was the jock your father was and you never were. You told me yourself he was the son your father never had. You fucked him hoping to become him, hoping to become the son your father always wanted."

"I don't have to listen to this five-cent analysis. What kind of man doesn't want to become his fantasy?"

"You put impossible demands on him. When Charley-Pop died, you wanted Kick to be your father, but he only wanted to be your lover. Then you tried to discipline him like he was your child. No wonder the man left when you threw him out into the rain with no jacket and no keys. What do you expect of people?"

"Fidelity. Not betrayal." He started for the steps leading down from the deck. "Not betrayal like I'm getting from you."

"God! Sometimes you're nothing more than a bitchy, petulant, old queen! Sometimes you really are Miss Scarlett O'Hara!"

Ryan was furious. "Don't you call me that! You fucking old closet case! You only hang on to all of us because you're afraid to come out! You're no professor of culture, popular or unpopular! Those who can, do! Those who can't, teach! You're worse than a faggot! You're a maggot! You feed on us!"

"I don't want us to fight."

"We're not fighting." Ryan walked toward me. "We're discussing something."

"God spare anyone from a discussion with you."

"I want you to sign this."

"Is this a test of my fidelity?"

"Yes."

"Why?"

"Because everything is a test."

"Like life," I said, "is a test to see if you'll get into heaven?"

"Witness it." He pushed the pen toward me.

"Aren't you going to read it first?"

"It only says one thing. January wants to make a movie out of *Armageddon*. Let her. She shot the special that turned Logan on to Kick. She made something happen. Maybe she can turn Kick back on to me. Maybe lightning can strike twice."

"Certainly you don't think a made-for-TV movie can bring Kick back."

"I'll try anything."

"It's a long shot."

"If I don't have hope, I don't have anything. I want him to hear my voice, my words, one last time."

The movie, telecast out over the airwaves to wherever Kick might be, he saw as his one final chance to communicate with the man who had once been the flavor of the month.

"I'm going to read this contract first, including the small print," I said.

"As long as you sign it."

The next morning we drove into Santa Rosa to mail the option contract with both our signatures. He was depressed. He had always been depressed.

"Why can't people leave love alone?" he asked. "If some intruder, some religion, some politician, some disease doesn't mess it up, then leave it to the lovers. They will. We did."

"It could be," I said, "that love self-destructs. Maybe betrayal is the very nature of love."

"You cynical, atheist bastard! I haven't betrayed Kick. Kick betrayed me. I was raped more ways than one."

"What's that mean?"

"You think this TV-movie deal is a betrayal of our privacy? You suggested revenge."

"The guilty flee. . . ."

"*Armageddon* is fiction. It's not about us. It's about people like us. It's our relationship through a glass darkly."

"How biblical! How Bergman!"

"*Armageddon* is a parallax view." He quoted Osbert Sitwell to me: "When indiscretions become historical, they become discreet." He was more sad than angry. "Kick and I are history. We'll stay that way unless I do something about it. I don't know where he is. I can't call him. I can't write to him." He waved the envelope with the contract. "This is my last and only chance to communicate with him out there wherever he is." He pulled open the mailbox and dropped the envelope. "I feel like a castaway throwing a note in a bottle into the ocean, hoping against hope."

Kweenie kept Ryan posted with monthly updates. The option turned into a contract. The contract turned into a treatment and then a draft screenplay. The draft itself turned into a dozen drafts and then into a final shooting script.

In the end, nothing came of the deal. One afternoon, on the set of his *Cover Up* TV series, Jon-Erik Hexum woke from a nap and was told that the day's shoot was delayed one more time. He did no more than any of us have done when we make a joke about being frustrated once too often: we point our forefinger at our temple, pull it like a trigger, and say *bang!*

Jon-Erik, however, pointed at his head with a prop gun loaded with blanks, smiled to make the joke we all make, and pulled the trigger.

The wadding from the blank imploded a piece of his skull the size of a quarter into his brain. For a week, machines kept his heart alive. The Friday after the Friday of the accident the doctors pronounced him brain-dead. With only two movies and a TV series to his name, Jon-Erik Hexum never became the James Dean of his generation. His healthy body, kept alive on machines, was flown from Hollywood to San Francisco for multiple transplantations.

"I want his face," Ryan said.

For him, another supremely beautiful man was dead and gone.

That was the end of *Armageddon.*

"Hexum was my only connection," January said over the telephone. "Without a star attached, the project is dead."

15

Over the next year, Ryan and I finally became friends. One night, he simply said, "Live with me."

"I am living with you," I said. It was the summer of my sabbatical year and I had moved to Bar Nada to write my doctoral thesis.

Ryan sat at the opposite end of the long picnic table where we both worked under the shade of the ponderosa pines. He had arranged our work places. "You sit here and I'll sit there. Just like Tennessee Williams and Carson McCullers."

"I miss the allusion," I said.

"Williams and McCullers were great friends. One summer they sat at opposite ends of the same picnic table. She was writing *The Heart Is a Lonely Hunter* and he was writing *Suddenly Last Summer.* Or maybe it was *Reflections in a Golden Eye* and *Sweet Bird of Youth.* What difference does it make?"

"Ah," I said.

"I mean I really want you to really live with me. I don't want sex. I need companionship."

That summer he was on even more powerful medication prescribed for him by Dr. Shrink whom he saw weekly in Berkeley. On top of everything that happened, he suffered from total AIDS paranoia. He washed even his own dishes in Clorox.

"Dr. Shrink thinks you're perfect for me."

"Is Dr. Shrink always right?" I said.

"He's righter than I am." Ryan shook the small bottle of Lithobid. Dr. Shrink was an anxiety-depression specialist. "He says I'm starting to remember who I am."

"With an ego like yours, I could have sworn you'd never forgotten."

"I'm a Gemini. Remember? I'm a chameleon. When I wake up in the morning, I have no idea who I'll be that day."

That Acquired Identity Deficiency Syndrome may be the essence of homosexuality. Walt Whitman sang songs of himself, his wonderful multiple self; wandering through the streets of New York and the docks of New Jersey, identifying himself with every appealing male, man and boy, who caught the fancy of his eye. Monsignor Linotti at Misericordia had warned the seminarians that *Leaves of Grass*, despite its so-called literary reputation, was pornography.

The following summer vacation, when he was seventeen, Ryan had checked Whitman's book out of the Peoria Public Library. He wanted to see for himself the truth about a man he suspected was a kindred spirit. He wrapped the hardbound cover in the plain brown paper of a Kroger's grocery bag. He sat under the willow trees in his parents' backyard and read the poems, searching at first for the forbidden parts, and, wondering, when he found nothing dirty, why the good Monsignor had been so stern in wanting to keep something so beautifully written away from him.

Whitman was the first crack in Ryan's vocation.

The priests never wanted Ryan's identity of Ryanness. They coached him to deny his own self, as they had denied theirs, to become "another Christ." A vocation to the priesthood is the supreme act of self-denial, a kind of religious suicide. It murders all the selves a man might become to make him into one other self only. They preached that his self must die to be filled with Christ's self. Souls open to multiple selves were like the New Testament souls possessed by devils whom Jesus exorcised into swine and stampeded over a cliff to their Deaths on the rocks below. The priests forbade Walt's singing because they could not chance Ryan filling himself up with multiple, alternative selves.

But he had.

Against their priestly intent, he had become a student of forbidden romantic poets "half in-love with easeful Death."

"You can't be a priest and have a mind," he said.

He romanced the drowned Byron and gunned-down Shelley and the tubercular Keats. He felt their restless spirits reborn and too soon dead again in obituaries on the evening news. Always there were the ghosts of Jack Kennedy, of Bobby Kennedy, of Martin Luther King.

He kept a pop hagiography of the famous who died before their time: James Byron Dean on a two-lane blacktop; Marilyn in her tangle of sheets; Hemingway sucking off his shotgun; Sharon Tate, Abigail Folger, and Jay Sebring slaughtered by slaves of Charles Manson in a house owned by Doris Day's son; Mama Cass, a nice Jewish girl, choked to Death on a ham sandwich; Janis and Jimi and the pouty Botticelli mystic of the Doors, Jim Morrison, killed by drugs and drink; Tennessee Williams, suffocated by a nasal-spray cap caught in his sinus; Natalie Wood and Dennis Wilson, famously drowned; the original golden boy, William Holden, bleeding to Death in a drunken fall; Richard Brautigan and Jon-Erik Hexum, dead by gunshots; Sal Mineo, murdered by knife; Pier Paolo Pasolini, beaten to Death by a hustler. He held open a blank space for the first big movie star to die of AIDS.

He kept notes for a book he titled *Great Movie Star Deaths*.

He wondered, with Sal and Natalie and Jimmy Dean dead, if there had been a curse on *Rebel without a Cause*; or on *The Misfits*, the last movie for Monroe and Gable and Montgomery Clift; or on *The Conqueror* whose stars Susan Hayward, John Wayne, Agnes Moorehead, and director Dick Powell had all died of cancer, as had most of the supporting cast and a hundred of the crew. They had shot on location in Utah, too near too soon, the site of a nuclear test blast. He saw them as archetype of the AIDS epidemic: innocent people living creative lives while some invisible government Death Ray sneaks in to kill them.

Kick had no feel for Ryan's pop-schlock interests. When John Lennon was shot, Kick shocked Ryan. "Lennon was nothing to me."

Ryan pretended not to notice the difference between them.

Kick was a true southerner, cool to social and emotional issues that he said caused Ryan a world of hurt and depression.

Kick had the gift of sexual alternation of self, but he lacked the knowledge that is the true heart of romantic otherness. He lacked the generosity of love. If he ever, for one moment, had really put his redneck self inside Ryan's creative skin, no matter how *mondo bizarro* Ryan was, things might have turned out differently.

Kick, after his own fashion, loved Ryan. But I doubt if Kick could have identified Ryan's body in an accident. He can't be blamed. Ryan was such a changeling that Kick many nights must have wondered who he was. Ryan was an anticipation of anything he figured Kick wanted him to be. He was a million movies. He had a thousand faces and more expressions than all the Barrymores put together. Kick loved Ryan's sexual madness and creativity more than he loved Ryan himself.

Ryan may have been a Woolworth's Five-and-Dime Wordsworth reincarnate. He understood the poet, who himself had fallen out of space and time. "Our destiny, our being's heart and home/Is with infinitude, and only there." He loved Tennyson's declaration of dependence for imaginative identity: "I am a part of all that I have met."

Ryan's main intensity was an ironic drive, I think, to escape the isolation of solitary confinement in his own skin by becoming anyone and everyone else. He suffered a fatal attraction to otherness, to becoming other than he was, and he had achieved ecstatic otherness beyond his wildest expectations with Kick.

When the golden man of bodybuilding walked into that El Lay room that first summer night, Ryan rose up to shake his hand and was pulled into Kick's otherness. In all their nights together, conjuring on the stolen gym clothes, suiting Kick up in authentic uniforms of quarterbacks, cops, and Green Berets, playing their endless list of construction workers, loggers, cowboys, and musclemen, abstracting Kick's blondness against the tight black bondage of skintight latex, Ryan taught Kick the only trick Kick had not known. It was the trick Ryan knew best. The achievement of otherness. It was both his virtue, and, if not his fatal flaw, then at least also his vice.

His talent for otherness cost him his self.

In their night moments, shooting beyond space and time, powered by drugs and sex and Kick's blond muscle, Ryan spoke, after a fashion, in tongues. His words transmorphed Kick, ritually vested in the fetish clothes of otherness, into any identity they desired. Those identities they called forth in the night from the Energy they conjured and shared between them. Kick became the long parade of Whitman's symbolic males, then returned round-trip to himself, to become the images sometime again.

Ryan did not become them. He had a one-way ticket. He became Kick. He was Kick. He was no longer Ryan. He surpassed Walt Whitman creaming over every man he saw. He saw one man only, even as he turned that man nightly into visions of other men. He knew how to make one thing be two things. He hated the God who had imprisoned his Energy in a body that was neither muscular nor blond. He fixed his identity on Kick. He gave up all his other selves. Monsignor Linotti had been as right as Barbra Streisand and Michael Bennett: it was fitting and proper to deny one's self to become one with one person, one very special person, one singular sensation. And what he felt, he judged, for three years, to be happiness.

"So who does Dr. Shrink think you are?" I asked Ryan.

"He wants me to get to know who the hell you are," Ryan said. "Why have you, Magnus Bishop, out of all the others, hung around? What do you want? Who the fuck are you?"

"I'm just a poor creature," I said, "trying to make my way with intelligence and compassion through the world."

"You are, are you?"

"I am what I am," I said.

"I know what we are," Ryan said. "We are what kills us. We'll all probably be AIDS victims."

"What movie are you now?" I asked.

"How about *The French Lieutenant's Woman?*"

"Try *Magnificent Obsession.*"

"Magnificent am I?"

"No. Obsessed."

"Possessed, maybe."

"Possessed by Catholicism," I said. "Obsessed with sex and Death."

"With life, you mean."

"With lovers. First with Teddy. Then with Kick. Now with this disease."

"It's not a disease. AIDS is a condition."

"Which you don't have. Both Dr. Quack and Dr. Shrink have told you so."

"Not today. But what about tomorrow?"

"Tomorrow is another day."

"Let me tell you something about *tomorrow*. Dr. Shrink said that by the end of the decade, fifty percent of us will be dead from AIDS."

"I thought he was supposed to cure your depression."

"Fifty percent. Between the two of us, you and me, that's one of us."

"If I were gay and if you had AIDS—which I'm not and which you don't."

"But I have this fear. . . ."

"When you're not a hypochondriac," I said, "you're a paranoid."

"Why not combine the two? Have you ever thought that AIDS anxiety may be worse than AIDS itself?"

"Leave it to you to find some complicated way to suffer from something you don't have."

"I'm not guilty." The words bounced off the wall.

"What?"

"I don't want to be punished for all those nights of fun. I don't want someone to say I got sick and died because I was a homosexual." He paused. "Do you understand that I liked being a homosexual? I took pride in it. Even before I was with Kick, I had a positive vanity about it. People can undo every good thing we did by saying we finally got ours. It's all so twisted."

"So let Dr. Shrink untwist you."

"That's easy for you to say with your life record of six sexual contacts." Ryan laid out his diversionary tactic. "You don't even know what's the length of a heartache."

"That's a *non sequitur*."

"I'm a Gemini. Besides, it's very *sequitur* after what I've been through."

"Okay. I'll bite. What's the length of a heartache? Ten inches?"

"Very funny. It's twice as long as the affair was itself."

"So three years with Kick means six years to recover?"

"It's compound interest."

"Then there's something to be said for one-night stands."

"I dreamed last night I was being whipped by a man with muscular, tattooed arms."

"Ryan Steven O'Hara," I said. "You've got to learn to let go."

"Let go? Of the best thing that ever happened to me? No. I can't. I don't know how. I don't want to. If I had been straight and had suddenly seen Kick, I would have turned gay like *that!*" He snapped his fingers.

"You can't go on living like this."

"Don't say that. I have to live like this. Doesn't Jackie keep the Eternal Flame burning? If I find out I'm going to die, I'll find Kick. If tomorrow I find I have AIDS, the first thing I'll do is find Kick. I'll have to. I want to die in his arms."

"Let him be. The man has already given you everything he had."

"Do you remember the Pioneer?" Ryan asked.

"The movie?"

"The rocket. The day they shot the Pioneer rocket out into space. It was the first human-made object to finally break out of the gravitational pull of our solar system."

"This is shtick!" I put up my hand to stop him.

"It was Earth's SOS. I'm sure help is on the way."

"You're nuts."

"Someone out there will come to save us."

"Spare me," I said. "This is not *2001* or *2010*."

"Then what movie are we?"

I wanted to say *Gone with the Wind*.

As God is my witness, Ryan was part of a cast of thousands. On the back lot of the Castro set, they worshiped movie queens who made it, like Vivien Leigh, no matter how bereft, to the last reel. They had been blown, more than they'd known, with the wind.

"Yeah, that's our movie," Ryan said. *"Blown with the Wind."*

Their emancipation politics was their set up for their Civil War. Stonewall was their Fort Sumter. Harvey Milk was their Jeff Davis. They seceded from straight society to create their own. They took to the trenches against Dan White, the worst of the fag-bashing marauders. They danced at fancy balls wearing nothing but the window curtains. They knew nothing about birthing no babies. The burning of the Barracks by a straight workman was their Atlanta. The overcrowded hospital wards of San Francisco were their big scene of countless wounded lying in the rail yard waiting for help. AIDS was their final battle. Their only hope of victory was finding a new sense of themselves in the holocaust that was upon them.

"I asked you a question, Magnus," Ryan said. "I want you to live with me." He had the look in his eyes that must have been the look he used to get whatever he wanted from Charley-Pop. "I'll put your name on the deed to the ranch."

"Don't insult me by trying to buy me."

"I'm offering you something."

"If I stay, I'll stay because I want to."

"Do you want to?"

"I'm already here, aren't I? Do you see anyone else around? There's just you and me, kid."

"I don't want sex," Ryan said.

"I'm not offering sex."

"I want a friend, not fireworks."

"We've always been friends," I said.

"I don't want to sleep alone."

"I think I can manage to sleep with you," I said.

"Sleeping doesn't mean having sex."

"So would a little safe sex hurt?"

Ryan was startled. "You mean affection."

"Call it what you will."

"You'd let me make love to you?" he asked.

"You need to make love to somebody who's real."

"Are you real?"

"What do you think?"

"I don't know if I can handle it," he said.

"Handle what? That I might be someone real saying, 'I love you.'"

"I know," Ryan said, "that you love me. Who else would put up with me? Who else would make such an offer?"

"So?" I said.

"But you're not gay." Ryan hesitated. "Are you?"

"What I am is human. I don't have to be gay to love you."

"You can't just try this stuff on for size, you know."

"What stuff?"

"Homosexuality."

"Who's talking homosexuality? You. That's who. I'm talking about real human love."

"That's easy for you to say."

"Is it?"

"You're an academic. A scholar. You categorize everything. You don't have the feeling for this."

"Is it homosexuality if I love you enough to hold you, just hold you? Charley-Pop held you on his lap."

"Can you hold me?"

"To quote someone I know intimately: 'I may not have eighteen-inch arms, but my arms are big enough to hold you.'"

"Is this what you've always wanted?" He was stymied. "Is this why you've always hung around? Is this why you've stuck by me? Is this a love scene?"

"Are these your questions or my answers?"

"I'm trying to figure you out."

"Stop putting words in my mouth. You can shut up. I want nothing."

"I don't believe this."

"Believe it. You're not running a rap-talk sex scene with Kick."

"I need to reveal myself to you," Ryan said.

"So you can forget?"

"So I can remember. He's slipping away."

"He was always slipping away. Things fall apart."

"Who are you? I've wondered that from the first time I met you."

"I'm a patient man."

"I'm a dangerous man."

"In more ways than one."

"Armies have marched over me."

"Rita Hayworth, *Fire Down Below*. Don't quote movies to me."

"I might be incubating the virus."

"Look at me, Ry."

"I can't chance infecting you."

"Take a good look at me."

"I've ruined everyone I ever touched."

"Don't flatter yourself. You won't ruin me," I said.

"You sound like Teddy. You sound like Kick."

"I'm not Teddy and I'm not Kick."

"That's no problem."

I grabbed his hand. "Can you read lips? I . . . love . . . you."

"That'*sss*," he held the sibilant, ". . . a problem." He held me out at arms' length.

"Only as long as you push me away."

Ryan stared hard into my eyes as if he had not for years looked, really looked, into a straight man's face. "Who the hell are you?"

I stared directly back. He had lived so long, so far too long, in the gay ghetto, inventing gay life, that he had lost touch with the legitimate otherness of heterosexuality. If Ryan liked reciprocal terms—*father* and *son, hot* and *cold*—words whose meaning depends on another word, then, as the last friend he had left—and me with no gay closet door to throw open in blinding straight revelation—I had some, what? Some weird moral responsibility to bring him around full circle: *homosexuality* is reciprocally dependent on *heterosexuality*. Neither is understandable without the other. His gayness needed my straightness as much I needed him in the high-wire act of human life.

"Who the hell are you?" he repeated.

I tried his movie game, toying with his taste for ambiguity, coaxing him into perspective. "Maybe Bergman," I said, "can tell you."

"Ingrid or Ingmar? I've fallen through the silver screen, Magnus. What . . . movie . . . am . . . I?"

16

The TV news called it the eclipse of the century. In Sonoma County, that Fourth of July weekend, Ryan sat in the moon-washed field where Kick's helicopter had landed that long-ago afternoon. Far to the east, over Santa Rosa, fireworks shot up through the early twilight and fell like burning confetti across the full face of the huge moon sitting on the ridge of the far-off hills.

"I'll look at the moon," Charley-Pop had always said to Annie Laurie during their courtship and finally before he died, "and I'll be seeing you."

Ryan had said the same line so often to Kick driving away in the red Corvette that Kick had learned to say it too. He lay in the tall grass wondering if Kick might still remember looking at the moon, especially this night, with the moon's clear face tilted to the right and its mouth in the perpetual pout of *O,* as if in wonderment, especially this night of relativity, when over the land and the sea, and through the sky, the Earth, moon, and sun all were to converge in a straight line of gravity's pull showing who is what to whom and where.

Ryan, less than two weeks before, on the summer solstice, the day of the year's longest light, had turned forty. He had heard nothing from Kick in three years. His head told his heart that the hurt in him must stop. Out there in the stars, extraterrestrials kept their distance from Earth. Its humans seemed so odd, dragging their hearts around, pining, wearing hearts on their sleeves, sending radio waves of Top Ten heartbreak out into the bounce of space.

How can love be explained to creatures of intelligence?

Ryan was in one of his cosmic moods that night, blazing with the last pinwheels and rockets of the Independence Day weekend. The time had come, he knew, to let go—not of the memory of Kick, but of the madness of the last six years. He lay back in the dry grass, feeling sad and ironic, bittersweet, about all that had happened. The night fit his place in the universe. Appropriate, he decided. It was appropriate that, in the dark of the moon, in the slow creeping eclipse of the moon's face, as the huge plate of the Earth passed over the saucer of the moon, he and the sanctuary of Bar Nada would lie in the deepest darkness of his lifetime.

He watched the shadowy curve of the dark Earth eat into the face of the glowing moon. The moon's face was his face. Kick had been the sun, light as the sun, but something sodden as Earth had come between them, had eclipsed them, had brought them down heavy with gravity. His own face for the last three years had hardened around the bewildered *O* of his own mouth, as he in those terrible years realized that the man who once had shown on him, had shined on him, had thrown on him so generously his warming, brilliant light, had fallen, the way Icarus falls forever from Daedalus. But Kick was not Icarus. He had become Armstrong, and it had been an Armstrong, an astronaut named Armstrong, who was the man who first put his bootmarks on the face of the moon, crunching its primal surface with toe and instep and heel, posing for all the world to see.

Millions of faces across the dark interior of North America were turned toward the moon, watching the eclipse like some lunatic video game splayed out on the huge screen of the sky.

In San Francisco, Castro Street was jammed with moon-watchers. This holiday weekend, its nights unusually warm for July, even without the eclipse of the moon and despite the creeping eclipse of AIDS, was enough to trigger the street parties that boiled out from the bars in spontaneous revelry, celebrating any excuse for outrageous merriment, stopping the City's flow of traffic at the intersection of 18th and Castro.

Ryan missed the Castro he had known. He was glad that the Old Castro was gone and a new one on the rise. There was hope in that. Nothing, not disease or prejudice or murders or assassination, could stop their kind. They were an ancient and future race. They had existed before the Druids and they would endure forever. The secret gift that made them different was their strength. The knowledge of that gift was their power.

Since before time, their kind, even though never they themselves, had been immune to *dee*-struction. Their bodies might betray them and die, but their spirit would always be stronger than Death. If and when the last of them should ever lie dying, that last one of them will hear down the hospital corridor the spanking-fresh cry of a boychild newborn with the special gift that was always theirs.

What they were, what they are, and what they will be, faulty and glorious, has always and forever been something with more resistance, more cosmic immunity, than the world will ever understand.

Ryan was exhausted with suffering. He was exhausted by patience. He knew what was and what could never be. It was no longer Kick he wanted back. It was himself. It was his ideal of manhood that he wanted redeemed like a deposit on a bottle. He could not mourn forever Kick's tumble from his pedestal, because when the sailor falls from grace with the sea, the sea remains, turbulent in places, calm in places, rolling under the pull of the shining moon.

What is one sailor on the great sea?

Ryan stripped himself naked and lay back in the bed of grass. The warm night air was soft on his body. His cock filled and rolled untouched up his belly toward his navel. The last sliver of the moon was orange, spectacular, lightly veiled with the dust of young lovers forever drifting through the atmosphere from Mt. St. Helens.

"We were lovers once," he announced to the moon.

He pulled on his dick. He did not close his eyes. He willed to imagine Kick, somewhere back in the deep South, watching the moon at this same instant. He stroked himself, trying to conjure Kick in space and time. He sent Kick his sexual Energy to communicate with him the way they so often had before in the good, golden, gone days.

"I love you," he said, and he said it, sighing, pulling his hand from his cock to keep from cuming. He breathed out a deep breath like a man releasing something he had been holding against all hope for too long. A small pearl formed on the head of his dick. Its clarity caught the last light of the orange underbelly of the moon disappearing into the total dark. He touched his finger to the pearl and raised it to his lips. Then he took his dick in both hands, the way Kick had always done, one above the other, and pressed down the shaft, hard, to the base. The crown of his cock was in direct line between his eyes and the moon. He stroked the shaft with both hands, slowly, inhaling as his hands rose up, remembering the fresh blond smell of Kick's body, exhaling all the air from his lungs as his hands slid down his cock gripping its root hard. The deep breathing made him lightheaded, but it kept him on the cusp of cuming. He raised both arms to the southern sky and shouted the one long sound of Kick's name across the deserted distance.

His body fell back to the grass. His head was lower than his cock standing at full measure against the sky. It seemed larger than he himself was. It pointed to a life beyond him. It was alive, sensate, lonely, calling out more loudly than he ever could to Kick. A teardrop of slick lube juiced from its head and glistened down the shaft.

He hated its carnal betrayal.

He had loved Kick with more than his cock. He spit long white flume at the throbbing traitor. He took it in both hands to strangle it, but the more he hurt it the harder it became. He hated the fact that a masochist can never really punish himself. The pain was his pleasure.

He existed for pain. He mistrusted anything else.

He had always known that his very attraction to Kick was that only someone as perfect as Kick would cause him, sooner or later, the extravagant pain he deserved.

"You pay for heaven either in this life or the next," Monsignor Linotti had said, "and it's far better to suffer here than hereafter."

Heaven's gate had a steep price.

His only insurance against the Death he dreaded was suffering enough pain here and now to enter heaven when he died of whatever killed him. But his body betrayed him. His cock turned his pain to pleasure. He feared there was no way he could suffer enough in this life to be worthy of life beyond Death. There was no way out, no way he could work his way to heaven the way he had tried to work his way into the blessed circle of bodybuilder jocks.

Rejected here, he would be rejected hereafter. He broke into a cold sweat. He put his hands to his face. Naked and alone in the nightfield, he accepted his place in the universe. He was desperate to make any deal he could. He cried out to the darkness. The dark had its own dimension. The dark was not, as Kick had insisted, a void. The dark had stars, and the darkened moon hung, glorious in eclipse, with an imperial Command Presence of its own.

Finally, in his own life-movie, unreeling on the bone screen behind his high forehead, he was fully stuck in the total darkness between the flashing frames of light. He blasphemed and nothing struck him dead. No lightning. No thunder. No God. There was nothing in the dark night of the soul, and if there was nothing, then he ached for what consolation there was.

His asshole flinched for Kick's fist.

He reached out to the dark moon with his left hand and followed its smooth contours with the cup of his palm. It was the moon he saw, but it was the curve of Kick's shoulder and arm and thigh and butt he felt. He had memorized Kick in the palm of his hand. He cupped his hand around the strong nape of Kick's fresh-clipped blond neck. He stroked the massive pecs, the fur on the washboard belly, the hang of the big blond balls and the erect penis. With the left hand we give Energy. With the right, we receive it. Kick was indelible in the palm of his left hand forever. He rubbed his hand into his face, sniffing and licking and biting it. He fingered his butthole and shoved his dick toward the dark sky.

His body convulsed. There was huge pleasure, and enormous ecstasy, in it. White clumps of thick seed spilled back on his belly and chest and face. He curled to his side in the grass and pulled his knees to his chest. He lay still for a long while. He hated himself thoroughly.

He threw himself over on his back. The moon was rolling out from its eclipse.

"God damn it!" he shouted into the night breeze. "God damn it!"

He rubbed his hand through the slaver of cum and sweat and bugs on his body.

"Is this the only goddam thing there is? Is this what it takes? Is this all there is?"

He knew it was time. He had to let go of Kick to release himself. He had waited for a message, an omen. The eclipse was a sign. It was time. It was no coincidence that this once-in-a-century ritual of total shadow should occur at this point in his life. He sank back into the grass waiting, the way primitive tribes wait, waiting for the moon to glide steadily out of Earth's eclipse.

"Come on," he coached the moon. His teeth were gritted. "Come on, you fucker! I'm looking at you!"

The stars shone brighter than he had ever seen them. He rooted for the moon.

"Come on! Come on!"

He reached up with both hands to push away the shadow of the Earth. The dark sky shimmered with the disconnected dots of stars where gazers who watch the sky had sketched the forms of animals and gods and hunters of the Bear, like Orion.

"Come on! God damn you!"

He reached toward the emerging moon and one last time he stroked the naked outline of Kick's golden body.

"I love you!" he shouted. Then, willfully, with the full determination of his heart, as if saying it would make it so, he edited the tension and the tense of the verb, and repeated in a whisper, "I loved you."

He let go of Kick.

The madness that had been in him for so long a time, the lunatic madness of love and loss, receded ever so slightly from him. He had let go of Kick, but something endless, maybe some reciprocal memory still in Kick, wherever he was, was still imprinted in him.

"I'll never leave you but once," Kick had said, "and that will be when I die."

Ryan roamed the rooms of the house at Bar Nada and some nights slept in the barn. Whatever Energy he and Kick had conjured was in his custody. It lingered, passionate, stronger than the spirit of Thom lingered, alive in the barn, adrift among the rafters and beams, asleep in the old iron bedstead, as quiet as the rust on the chrome collars and black plates of barbells strewn among the weight benches.

Ryan was no Sisyphus. He could lift no more.

Exercise depressed him. The very sight in his gym mirrors of his biceps curling a dumbbell toward his chest was pathetic to him. He could no longer address strength physically.

What remained was something better. Something beyond his body. Something beyond Kick's body. Something like a manly spirit, a masculine ghost, that some nights overshadowed him with a dream of manliness from which he hoped he'd never wake.

Charley-Pop.

17

In the pursuit of excellence there is no fault in high expectation. There is only virtue. Then, finally, comes the realization that the quest is of itself the only importance. The quest has no end. The questions have no answers. The questions themselves are the answers, and the quest its own end.

"You've got to dare to put your finger in the fire," Ryan once said, "or there's no passion to fire at all."

There may be embarrassments here, and ambiguities, but there are no lies.

The big house at Bar Nada was quiet. The phone rarely rang. Quiet music came from far-off rooms. I wrote, and Ryan pounded with his hammer on the house and painted the barn and gardened the grounds. Sometimes he stood out in the green field wearing his yellow slicker against the gray rain. He had turned the chickens loose and they gathered expectantly around him and then wandered away. He cooked and cleaned. He spent his evenings watching videotapes or reading magazines in front of the fire built with wood he had split.

He could not sleep.

He took up smoking a late-night cigar. Its sweet aroma drifted dreamily through the house. Some nights he pulled himself quietly in under the covers next to me in my bed. Most nights he bunked alone. He never asked me for sex and I never offered it. He left Bar Nada once a week, always on Friday, when he drove his big red pickup first to the office of Dr. Shrink for his Viennese voodoo, and then to the grocery store. One kitchen cabinet overflowed with vitamins and immunity supplements. He was careful about everything. The way a man is careful when he fears he might not have been careful enough.

Sometimes I caught him staring into the large mirror in the hall. It was the mirror Kick had used to practice his posing. It was the only thing he had rescued from the barn one night when I was off teaching, and he was home alone, and the barn had burned mysteriously to the ground.

He looked at me in the posing mirror standing behind him. "What movie am I, Magnus?" I made no answer.

"You're slipping, professor. I'll give you multiple choice: Olivier and Hepburn in *Love Among the Ruins*; Bogart and Bergman in *Casablanca*; Irons and Streep in *The French Lieutenant's Woman*."

He pushed me to end the game. "Life is not a movie," I said.

"Ashes. Ashes. All fall down."

"It's over," I said. "The party's over." I meant Kick. "It's time to call it a day." I meant Castro. I meant the seventies. I meant the way they all were. "Let it be." I stared at Ryan's face in the mirror.

He stared deeper into the mirror at my reflection.

"We didn't fail, did we?" he said. He meant himself, Kick, and all of gay liberation. "At least we dared."

"What was, was, as Solly would say."

"Touch me." He spoke into the mirror.

I moved my hand forward up his back and over his shoulder.

He reached back and up-caught my wrist and guided my hand to his high forehead, laying my palm horizontally above his eyes the way Liv Ullmann touched Bibi Andersson in *Persona*.

"You're not real, are you?" he said to me in the mirror.

I felt his skin heating my hand. "I'm very real," I said.

"We all came to San Francisco," he said, "to be ourselves. When that didn't work, we tried to become someone else."

"Some maybe," I said. "Not everyone. You can't speak for everyone."

"I can speak for me," he said. "What is sex besides trying to become part of someone until you finally become him?"

"That's not sex," I said.

"Is it love?"

It was the question Ryan had wanted to ask all along.

I made my voice firm. "I can't answer that. No one can answer that."

"I wish I were someone else."

"What you wish for in California, you get."

"Solly said that."

"Be assured," I said. "I am someone else."

"Who the hell are you?"

"Me," I said, soothing his forehead, staring deep into his eyes, pulling him back from the edge. "Like you, I'm just me, Charles Bishop, out of San

Francisco, California, North America, the Earth, the Solar System, the Cosmos. Just me. Just another human."

"Just like Kick." Ryan stared straight into my eyes in the mirror.

"Human. Just like them all."

"Just like me," he said. His face flushed. "What is, is what I am."

"You finally understand," I said.

"I always understood. I . . . just . . . wanted . . . to feel . . . everything."

Fully human was all he had ever wanted to be.

"We are what we are."

"I have no more tears," he said. "I have a sadness."

"Nothing stays forever."

"Sadness stays forever."

Fear, something like Adam must have felt at the first dawn of his first knowledge that he was different from the other animals, caused his high forehead to tighten, relax, tighten, relax, under my hand.

"What can I say?" I said.

"Time wounds all heels?" He managed a sad mood-swinging smile. "How will I feel when today is tomorrow?"

"Old truths," I said. "Better to have loved and lost . . ."

"No, it's not," Ryan said. "No. It's not."

FREEZE FRAME

ABOUT THE AUTHOR

Jack Fritscher has long been a pioneer participant in gay culture, as an analyst and photographer chronicling that history. He is a double-jointed author balancing twin careers in literary fiction and erotic literary fiction. A founding editor in chief of the now legendary *Drummer* magazine from the 1970s, he is also the author of four novels, six fiction anthologies, three nonfiction books, and two produced plays. He is also the director and videographer of 160 feature videos, including gay history documentaries. As an associate professor with tenure, now retired, he had a long career teaching university department of English courses in literature, writing, and film at Loyola University of Chicago, Western Michigan University, and Kalamazoo College. His writing has appeared in more than thirty gay magazines and twenty-five gay anthologies. *Some Dance to Remember* is dedicated to his 1970s bicoastal lover, Robert Mapplethorpe.

Order a copy of this book with this form or online at:
http://www.haworthpress.com/store/product.asp?sku=5430

SOME DANCE TO REMEMBER
A Memoir-Novel of San Francisco 1970-1982

_____in softbound at $27.95 (ISBN-13: 978-1-56023-327-5; ISBN-10: 1-56023-327-3)

Or order online and use special offer code HEC25 in the shopping cart.

COST OF BOOKS_____

☐ **BILL ME LATER:** (Bill-me option is good on US/Canada/Mexico orders only; not good to jobbers, wholesalers, or subscription agencies.)

☐ Check here if billing address is different from shipping address and attach purchase order and billing address information.

POSTAGE & HANDLING_____
(US: $4.00 for first book & $1.50 for each additional book)
(Outside US: $5.00 for first book & $2.00 for each additional book)

Signature_____

SUBTOTAL_____

☐ **PAYMENT ENCLOSED: $**_____

IN CANADA: ADD 7% GST_____

☐ **PLEASE CHARGE TO MY CREDIT CARD.**

STATE TAX_____
(NJ, NY, OH, MN, CA, IL, IN, PA, & SD residents, add appropriate local sales tax)

☐ Visa ☐ MasterCard ☐ AmEx ☐ Discover
☐ Diner's Club ☐ Eurocard ☐ JCB

Account # _____

FINAL TOTAL_____
(If paying in Canadian funds, convert using the current exchange rate, UNESCO coupons welcome)

Exp. Date_____

Signature_____

Prices in US dollars and subject to change without notice.

NAME_____

INSTITUTION_____

ADDRESS_____

CITY_____

STATE/ZIP_____

COUNTRY_____ COUNTY (NY residents only)_____

TEL_____ FAX_____

E-MAIL_____

May we use your e-mail address for confirmations and other types of information? ☐ Yes ☐ No
We appreciate receiving your e-mail address and fax number. Haworth would like to e-mail or fax special discount offers to you, as a preferred customer. **We will never share, rent, or exchange your e-mail address or fax number.** We regard such actions as an invasion of your privacy.

Order From Your Local Bookstore or Directly From
The Haworth Press, Inc.
10 Alice Street, Binghamton, New York 13904-1580 • USA
TELEPHONE: 1-800-HAWORTH (1-800-429-6784) / Outside US/Canada: (607) 722-5857
FAX: 1-800-895-0582 / Outside US/Canada: (607) 771-0012
E-mail to: orders@haworthpress.com

For orders outside US and Canada, you may wish to order through your local sales representative, distributor, or bookseller.
For information, see http://haworthpress.com/distributors

(Discounts are available for individual orders in US and Canada only, not booksellers/distributors.)

PLEASE PHOTOCOPY THIS FORM FOR YOUR PERSONAL USE.
http://www.HaworthPress.com   BOF04